Winner in 1991 of both the Prometheus Award and of the Locus Award for Best First Novel, Michael Flynn's remarkable debut is back, revised and updated, and now with the addition of his fascinating article from *Analog*, "An Introduction to Cliology," explaining the ideas underlying the book.

"What if studying the past allowed you not only to avoid past mistakes but also to create the future of your choice? . . . Most science fiction that tackles this subject is set in the distant future . . . Flynn takes a different tack, one that speaks more directly to today's mood of paranoia. . . . One of the strengths of Flynn's book is his insistence that scientific insight into the forces of history cannot exclude uncertainty."
—*The New York Times*

"This novel of big ideas, now revised and updated by Flynn, explores the consequences of manipulating history. . . . In a thought-provoking, chart-filled appendix . . . Flynn discusses the mathematics and biology of history. Fans of classical SF are in for a treat."
—*Publishers Weekly*

"This page-turner is full of action, intrigue and some historical speculation that may start you wondering how much of it is really fiction . . . Flynn knows how to tell a story, and with this, his first novel, serves notice that he is an author to watch, and read."
—*Mphasis*

"A marvelously intelligent scientific thriller . . . Flynn's great achievement here is the combination of fast action and nail-biting suspense with intense intellectual inquiry into the driving forces of history. . . . this is a book to read, and read again."
—*Locus*

By Michael Flynn

In the Country of the Blind*
The Nanotech Chronicles
Fallen Angels (with Larry Niven and Jerry Pournelle)
Firestar*
The Forest of Time and Other Stories*
Lodestar*
Rogue Star*
Falling Stars*
The Wreck of The River of Stars*

*denotes a Tor book

In the Country of the

Blind

Michael Flynn

TOR®

A TOM DOHERTY ASSOCIATES BOOK
NEW YORK

This is a work of fiction. All the characters and events portrayed in this book are either products of the author's imagination or are used fictitiously.

IN THE COUNTRY OF THE BLIND

This edition edited by David G. Hartwell

A Tor Book
Published by Tom Doherty Associates, LLC
175 Fifth Avenue
New York, NY 10010

www.tor.com

Tor® is a registered trademark of Tom Doherty Associates, LLC.

ISBN: 0-765-34498-X
Library of Congress Catalog Card Number: 2001027199

First edition: August 2001
First mass market edition: March 2003

Printed in the United States of America

0 9 8 7 6 5 4 3 2 1

Preface

Who can resist tampering with history?

Parts of this book appeared originally as a serial and a separate novelette. The redundancies this created have been removed, as have some non-value-added sections of less than immortal prose and the odd adverb or two. Futuristic references to "the national DataNet" have been amended to "the Internet." There are a few other changes of that sort from the first edition. Others, like the now-demolished viaduct in downtown Denver, have been left in place. There are limits to revisionist history.

The essay "An Introduction to Cliology" (originally "An Introduction to Psychohistory") was added at the request of readers at various SF conventions.

My thanks to Stan Schmidt at *Analog* magazine for publishing the earlier serial, novelette, and article; and to Jim Baen, who published the first edition, now long out of print. Thanks also to my agent, Eleanor Wood, who called one day and asked, "Have you ever thought about writing a novel?"

MICHAEL FLYNN
Easton, Pennsylvania
2001

In meditating on the nature of the moral sciences, one cannot help seeing that, as they are based like the physical sciences on observation of fact, they must follow the same method, acquire a language equally exact and precise, attaining the same degree of certainty.

> —ANTOINE DE CARITAT, MARQUIS DE CONDORCET, acceptance speech upon election to the Academy, 1782

In regard to nature, events apparently the most irregular and capricious have been explained, and have been shown to be in accordance with certain fixed and universal laws. This has been done because men of ability and, above all, men of patient, untiring thought have studied natural events with the view of discovering their regularity: and if human events were subjected to a similar treatment, we have every right to expect similar results.

> —HENRY THOMAS BUCKLE, 1856

It would appear, then, that moral phenomena, when observed on a great scale, are found to resemble physical phenomena . . . It belongs only to a few men, gifted with superior genius, to alter sensibly the social state; and even this alteration requires a considerable time to transmit fully its effects.

> —LAMBERT ADOLPHE QUETELET,
> *Treatise on Man*, 1842

I wish I were capable of carrying on a Project [Mr. James Bernoulli] had begun, of applying the Doctrine of Chances to Oeconomical and Political Uses, to which I have been invited, together with Mr. de Montmort, by Mr. Nicholas Bernoulli . . . but I willingly resign my share of that task into better Hands, wishing that either he himself would prosecute that Design or . . . his uncle, Mr. John Bernoulli.

> —ABRAHAM DE MOIVRE,
> Preface to *The Doctrine of Chances*, 1718 (first edition) (All mention of the Bernoulli Project was omitted from later editions.)

Part 1

Horseshoe Nails

Then

The rain fell in torrents, beating a staccato rhythm on the cobblestoned street. It created rivers and oceans on the paving and formed a curtain beyond which only vague shapes could be seen. The man waited beneath the hissing gas lamp in the middle of the block. The water ran off his broad-brimmed hat and down the back of his neck. It was a hot, sticky rain, not a bit of coolness in it. He hitched the waterproof leather briefcase under his arm, changing his grip for the hundredth time. Far off to the south he heard booming; but whether of guns or of thunder, he didn't know.

A drumming of hooves from G Street. The man turned expectantly, but it was only a troop of cavalry that turned the corner: Horses stepping high struck sparks off the paving with their hooves. Leather straps and belts gleamed in the dusk and the metal of sabers and spurs and bits jangled like an Arab belly dancer.

He read their cap badges as they rode by: Third Pennsylvania. He raised his arm and huzzahed and their captain saluted him smartly with his quirt.

He watched them out of sight as they vanished once more behind the curtain of rain, headed for the Potomac bridges and who knew what fate? When he turned his attention back to the street, the landau was there in front of him. The nigh horse, no more than three feet away, blew his breath out and rolled his eyes at him. Startled, the man took a step backward into a puddle, while the driver, a shapeless lump on the lazyboard, pulled on his reins to calm the beast.

The door opened and Isaac poked his head out, smiling sourly. "Well, Brady," he asked in his broad New England accent, "will you climb in, or do you like the rain so much?"

Brady didn't bother to answer. He stepped into the cab and sat beside the older man. The upholstery inside the landau smelled dank and musty, the hint of mold in every breath. Everything in Washington smelled that way. It was an awful town. "All the charm of a Northern city, and all the efficiency of a Southron one." Brady shook the rain off his hat and wiped his face with his neckerchief. The carriage started with a jerk.

He saw Isaac glance covertly at the briefcase. "Impatient, Isaac?" he asked. His Indiana voice twanged like a jaw harp. "My train arrived two hours ago. You could have met me then, at the station."

"Ayuh," Isaac agreed readily. "Could have. Didn't."

Brady grunted and looked out at the passing houses, colorless and gray in the pouring rain. They were headed toward Georgetown. Abruptly the bouncing and rattling gave way to a sticky, sucking sound. The horses' hooves slapped the muddy road. "I see they still haven't finished paving the streets yet."

"Ayuh. Nor finished the Capitol dome, neither." Isaac looked at him, then looked away. "Great many things still unfinished."

Brady let that lie and they rode awhile in silence.

"Town's danged spy-crazy," said Isaac after a while. "Too many comin's and goin's. Draws attention. I was followed last week, I think. Naught to do with the Society, but the Council thought 'twere best we not meet at the station."

Brady looked at him. That was as close to an apology as he was ever going to get from the New Englander. He sighed. " 'Tain't important."

Isaac leaned over and tapped the briefcase with his index finger. "But this is," he said. "This is. Tell me square, Brady, and on the level. Is it what we expected?"

Brady didn't answer him directly. He stroked the leather with his palm. The metal clasps were cold to his touch. "Three weeks of calculations," he said. "Three weeks, even with Babbage engines, and six of us, working in two teams around-the-clock. We used numerical integration and some of that new theory that's come from Galois' papers. When we were done, we switched over and checked the other team's work." He shook his head. "There's no mistake."

"Then he must die."

Brady jerked his head around and looked at Isaac. The New Englander was drawn and pale; age spots were dark against his parchmentlike skin. Brady nodded once, and Isaac shut his eyes.

"Well, that should please some on the Council," he said, gazing on some inner landscape. "Davis and Meechum. Phineas, too. His mill's are idled, with no cotton coming north."

Brady frowned. "Are they allowing their personal interests to . . ."

"No, no. They are guided by the equations, just as we. Slavery had to go. We all agreed, even our Southron members. The equations showed what would come to pass if it didn't." Isaac shivered, remembering. "That was why we . . . took measures." The old man's face closed up tighter. "They will see the need for this action, as well." He opened his eyes and fixed Brady with a stare. "And if they bow to necessity with smiles and we with sorrow, why, what difference?"

"Damnation, Isaac. It should never have come to this!" Brady slapped the briefcase, a sharp sound that made Isaac blink.

"Don't want his blood on your hands? Well, theah's blood enough already. This war—"

"Was an accident! A miscalculation! Douglas should have won. He knew how to make deals. He could have ended slavery and made the South love him for it. Popular sovereignty and the Homestead Act. That would have done for it."

"Maybe," Isaac allowed. "But Buchanan vetoed the Homestead Act out of personal spite for Douglas. The equations are silent when we deal with individuals. After that fiasco at the Charleston convention, the election was thrown wide open; and the Republicans—"

"And that backwoods buffoon!" said Brady angrily. "His victory changed everything! Panicked the South into secession. But how could we have calculated it? The man failed at everything he ever attempted. He failed twice in business; had a nervous breakdown; was defeated for House Speaker, then for re-election; was defeated for *land-officer,* of all things. He ran for the Senate twice and the Vice Presidency once and lost the nomination all three times. Hell's bells, Isaac! He even lost the presidential election!"

"Not in the electoral college," Isaac pointed out. "And he did have a plurality."

"The man is a statistical anomaly!"

Isaac chuckled. "That's what really bothers you, isn't it?"

Brady framed a tart reply, then thought better of it. He slouched in his seat. "Be that as it may be. The war was an accident; *this* is different!" He slapped the briefcase again. "A calculated act, not a calculated risk."

Isaac nodded slowly. "I doubt a corpse cares whether 'twas done in by accident or design. Still, we lift no finger ourselves. A word heah. A word theah. Washington's always been Confederate in her heart. Someone will act."

"Aye. But we will bear the guilt."

"Why, so we will! Was there ever any doubt? Did you doubt it when you took the Oath?"

Brady looked away, out the window. "No."

They were silent again, listening to the carriage wheels rolling through the mud. The rain drummed the roof of the landau.

"And what if he does *not* die?"

Isaac just wouldn't let it be. Brady scowled at him.

"And what if he does not die?" Isaac persisted.

Brady sighed. He hefted his briefcase, then dropped it into Isaac's lap. "Read it yourself. It's all there. The secondary path from the fifteenth yoke. We have clandestine medical reports on him and his whole family. And on Ann Rutledge, as well. His old law partner, Billy Herndon, has been dropping sly hints to whomever will listen. His wife is certifiably insane, save no one has the guts to say so aloud. It's congenital in at least two of his sons. Damn!" He closed his eyes tight. His hands clenched into fists. "I have never liked any task less than the reading of those reports." He relaxed slowly and looked at Isaac. "There's no mistake. He will go mad before his new term expires. Already he has . . . bizarre dreams."

"And his madness, and its disease, will discredit his platform of reconciliation."

"Aye. Leading to victory for the Radicals and his probable impeachment. There will be permanent military occupation of the South, stifling of technological progress there, growing resentment among the whites, sporadic rioting, and racial pogroms, followed by repression and a new Rebellion in 1905 that will be overtly supported by at least two European Powers. That, too, is in the calculations."

Isaac smiled without humor. "Then, 'tain't so much a matter of blood on our hands, but how much, and whose."

Brady chewed on his knuckle. The skin there was frayed, almost raw. Isaac watched him thoughtfully for a moment, then turned his attention to the window. The silence between them lengthened.

"Gloomy night," said Isaac finally, still gazing at the dark outside the landau.

"We haven't built Utopia, have we, Isaac?"

Isaac shook his head. "Give it time, boy. Give it time. Rome weren't built in one day, neither. The Society's too small yet to move the world by much; but it will grow, *if* we persevere." He turned and faced Brady, his eyes sharp and piercing. "Famines, Brady. Worldwide wars. Weapons deadlier nor any Gatling gun and ironclad. It's all theah on the chahts. You've seen 'em. In less than a century there will be explosive shells more powerful than twenty thousand *tons* of guncotton, or of this new stuff, dynamite. God's wounds! The Petersburg mine held only eight thousand *pounds* of black powder! Imagine five thousand such mines exploded at once!" He shook his head. "I faired those curves m'self, Brady. They're exponential. If we've any hope of tempering them in time, we must act, and act *now!*"

For Isaac, that was quite a speech. Brady stared at the older man and, with a sudden rush of compassion, laid his hand upon his arm and squeezed. Isaac looked at the hand, then at Brady. Then the driver called to his horses and the landau pulled up before a modest Georgetown brick house. After a moment, Brady released Isaac's arm and opened the door. He made to step out, but Isaac restrained him.

"Theah's something else, isn't theah, Brady Quinn?"

The wind blew the rain into the cab. Brady would not look at Isaac. "Don't make me tell you, Isaac."

Isaac backed away from him. "What is it?" There was uncertainty in his voice, and the beginnings of fear.

"Isaac, you've been like a father to me for twenty years. Please, don't ask me."

Isaac squared his shoulders. "No. My life is in this work. I built the Society, Brady. Phineas and I and old Jed Crawford. We read between the lines of Babbage's book. Saw what could be done. Saw what *must* be done. We laid out the first ten yokes. If you have found something that—" He shook his head suddenly, violently. "I must know!"

Brady sighed and looked away from him. He had known that this moment would come, had dreaded it. He had known that he would tell Isaac everything. But that did not make it any the less unpleasant. "Young Carson has developed a new algorithm," he said. "Based on a children's game, of all things. It . . . Well, it changes everything after the twenty-ninth yoke."

Isaac scowled, not understanding. "The twenty-ninth . . . ? I don't know what you mean. If everything after the—No! Explain yourself, Brady!"

Brady told him and the old man stared, open-mouthed. Brady closed his eyes briefly; then he left the landau and walked to the front door of the town house. He looked back once, through the rain, and saw the old man weeping.

Now

I

The window was too damned dirty to look through. Sarah Beaumont glanced around the empty room and saw a rag in a corner. It was probably just as filthy as everything else in the old house. There were mouse droppings scattered about, cobwebs, fragments of plaster. In places, the ribs of the walls showed through the broken plaster. With a sigh of disgust, she walked over and picked up the rag and shook it. A spider crawled out, and she watched it go its way.

"How long has this house been vacant?" she asked.

"Five, six years." That was Dennis French, her architect. He was rapping on the walls, looking for the supporting beams. He paused and studied the door frame; ran his fingers over the miter joints and nodded in approval. "Good, solid work, though. They sure knew how to build back then."

"The good old days," said Sarah absently. "When women knew their place."

Dennis looked at her. "They still do," he said. "Just more places, is all."

She laughed. Returning to the window, she ran the rag over it. The grime was stubborn. It had had years in which to settle in. She managed to clear a circle in the middle of the pane and peered out at Emerson Street. "Can we refurbish the place? Bring it up to Code and all. That's what I need to know. This neighborhood's going to be the next to boom, and I want to be here first." She had been late getting in on Larimer and Auraria. She was going to be first here, by God. Let the other developers follow *her* for a change.

She could look straight across the street at the second-floor windows there. Those houses had been built on the same basic plan as this one. Onetime mansions turned rental apartments. A man stood in one of the windows, stripped to the waist, drinking something out of a can. He saw her looking and waved an invitation.

She ignored him and craned her neck to the left, pressing her cheek against the glass. She could just make out the dome of the state capitol, gleaming gold in the afternoon sun. The downtown skyscrapers, though, blocked her view of the mountains. She watched the traffic at the corner, counting cars-per-minute.

When she stood away from the window and clapped the dust from her hands, Dennis had already left the room. She could hear him tapping away down the hall.

"How does it look?" she called. She found her clipboard and jotted a few notes.

"Utilities look good," she heard him answer. "No computer ports, naturally; but we can put those in when we upgrade the rest of the wiring. Sixty-four-kilobyte ISDN channels."

She followed his voice down the hall and found him in one of the other bedrooms. He was poking at a hole in the wall. "There's still piping in the walls for the old gas mantles." He looked at her and shook his head. "This must have been a swank place a hundred years ago, before they messed it up. There's a servants' stairwell down the end of the hall." He pointed vaguely.

"I've got a list of previous owners at home," she told him. "One of the old-time silver barons built the place, but the Panic came along a few years later and he had to sell out."

"Easy come, easy go."

"You're right about the workmanship. If I could find the sonofabitch who painted over the parquet flooring on the main staircase . . ." She loved good workmanship, and that staircase had been the handiwork of a master joiner.

Dennis nodded. "I know what you mean. When they made this place into a boardinghouse and subdivided the rooms, they paneled right over the original walls. Can you imagine that? You should *see* the wainscoting! Here."

He pulled on a section of drywall and it came away. Bits of plaster and gypsum fell to the floor, along with some nails and loose scraps of paper. The original wall behind it was in bad shape. The wainscoting was partially destroyed and there were holes in the plaster, but Sarah could imagine what it must have looked like when it had been new.

The papers on the floor caught her eye. A yellowed newspaper clipping. She picked it up and found a torn sheet of foolscap held to it by a rusty staple.

"What are those?" asked Dennis, brushing his hands and standing up.

"A list of dates. Looks like someone's crib notes for a history test and . . ." She read the headline on the clipping. "An 1892 story from the old *Denver Express*." She handed the foolscap to Dennis and read through the rest of the news story. "A gunfight," she told him. "Two cowboys on Larimer Street. Neither one was scratched, but a bystander was killed. An old man named Brady Quinn."

She frowned. Quinn? She had seen that name recently. But where? It nibbled at the edge of her memory. Well, never mind. It would come back to her eventually.

"Odd sort of crib notes."

"Hmm?" She glanced at Dennis, who was scowling over the foolscap. "What do you mean?"

"Well, the entries here are in two different handwritings, for one thing. The earlier items are in the old Spencerian style."

"Someone started the list," said Sarah. "Then someone else continued it."

"And this, up at the top. What does it say? Biological? Diological?"

She glanced where he pointed. "Cliological. Cliological something. It's smudged. I can't make it out."

"That's a big help. What's 'cliological'?"

She shrugged. "Beats me. I never heard the word before."

"And the mixture of entries is odd, too. Famous events and obscure events all jumbled together. How does the nomination of Franklin Pierce, or the election of Rutherford

Hayes, or Winfield Scott's military appointments belong on the same list as the election of Abraham Lincoln or his assassination, or the sinking of the *Lusitania?* Or . . . Hello!"

"What?" She moved behind him and read over his shoulder. He pointed. " 'Brady Quinn murdered,' " she read.

"Yep, your friend Quinn is right in there with Lincoln and Teddy Roosevelt. And with von Kluck's Turn, whatever that was. Nineteen-fourteen. Must have been World War One."

"No kidding. And 'Frederick W. Taylor, fl. ca. 1900.' Who was he?"

Dennis shook his head. "There are a half dozen entries here that I never heard of."

"Well, that's modern education for you. They don't teach things anymore that our great-great-grandparents took for granted." She tapped Dewey's name on the list with her fingernail. "I think it started with Thomas Dewey's whole-word method of reading. English isn't Chinese and you can't teach it that way. No wonder half the kids in this country grow up functionally illiterate. Some of my own teachers were damn near illiterate themselves."

"I'll bet they all had education degrees, though."

"Which meant they knew all there was to know about teaching, except the subject."

"When I was in graduate school," Dennis remembered, "the education prof across the hall from us told me that that wasn't important." She looked at him and he shrugged. "True story."

"That's the way folks are. 'If'n *I* don't know about it, it ain't important.' Ask any engineer about writing sonnets, or ask any poet about stress and shear."

Dennis chuckled and pointed to the list. "Or ask any architect about factor analysis. There's a note at the bottom, where it's torn. 'Try orthogonal factor analysis . . .' "

"Orthogonal factor analysis? It's a statistical method they use to define socioeconomic groups. Each group is defined by a cluster of mutually correlated traits. I think they use it in physical anthropology, too."

Dennis raised one eyebrow and looked at her. "How'd you get to be so smart?"

She stopped and looked at him. "Because I wouldn't *let* them cheat me!" she snapped. "I've had to fight for everything I've ever had. Because of my sex. Because of my color. I wouldn't *accept* a second-rate education!"

The architect held his hands up. "I didn't mean to sound patronizing," he said. "Christ, you know me, Sarah. I had . . . Well, not the same problems, obviously; but at prep school, they didn't expect the idle rich to want to tackle anything 'hard.' "

"Yeah, I know," she answered. "It ain't yo' fault yo' was bo'n white 'n' rich."

"Hey, I said I was sorry. It's just that you seem to know more things about more things than anybody else I've ever met."

"Jack-of-all-trades, master of none," she grunted. "You're right. I'm sorry I took it the wrong way, but I decided a long time ago I would never apologize for knowing something." She turned away from him. "I guess I just have a bump for curiosity."

But it hadn't always been that way, she remembered as they climbed down the stairs to the entry hall. Once, she had been as content as her playmates to coast through school, and life. Putting in the time, because the Law and her parents said she had to. "It was in the fifth grade, I suppose." She ran a finger along the dirty drywall. "Our class took a field trip to the Museum of Science and Industry. That was . . . oh, more years ago than I care to remember." *Oh Lord, the South Side of Chicago.* She could see herself careening wide-eyed from exhibit to exhibit, a little girl in cornrows who could barely read. There had been an exhibit of calculating machines, ranging from the old key-set mechanisms all they way up to the latest in mini-desktops. There had been a walk-through model of a human heart. There had been a rock that had been brought back from another world!

"It was like being doused with ice water," she told him. That trip had awakened her with a shock; and even now, through the telescope of years, she could feel the shiver of excitement she had felt then. "There was an enormous and fascinating world out there, *and my teachers were not telling me about it!* So . . ." She shrugged self-consciously. ". . . I explored it on my own. I cut classes, snuck off to the public library; later, to the University of Chicago library." She'd had to con her way in there: no one would believe a little black girl had come there to *read.*

And she had devoured everything. African music, physics, law, medicine, Chinese history, statistics, German philosophy, computers. Everything. Some of her friends who knew what she was doing had asked her what she would ever use it for. She had treated the question with the same scorn she felt for the apathy behind it.

Use it? She wasn't looking for training; she was looking for an education.

She had passed all her school classes, of course. She made certain she took all the tests. Most of her teachers, she was convinced, had deeply resented her success, because she had achieved it in spite of them. But there had been some . . . Ah, *those* had been *teachers!*

"Habits are hard to break, I suppose," Dennis' voice broke into her memories.

"Hmm? What do you mean?" They had reached the ground floor and paused at the base of the stairs.

"How many seminars and classes have you taken in the few years we've known each other?"

"Realty law. Wilderness survival. A dozen programming classes. I think the hacking was the most fun. I don't know. I've lost count."

"See what I mean?" he said. "I admire you. You haven't stopped stretching yourself. Sometimes I wish I had your curiosity about things. I must have a score of books at home that I've always meant to read. I bought them all with good intentions; but, I never seem to find the time for them. My journals and technical reading take up all my spare time."

"You can always make the time. It's a matter of setting your priorities."

Dennis ran his hand across his shirt pocket. "Yes. I suppose curiosity is like everything else. It comes with practice. Each entry on that list was marked with a one, two, or three. Maybe those are three 'orthogonal factors.' " He folded the list and tucked it in his shirt pocket. "Well, maybe I'll check some of this out. Find out what it means."

On the sidewalk outside the building Dennis sketched some ideas on his pad. She knew better than to try to peek. He'd throw away a dozen good concepts before he kept a single great one to show her. Over the years she had learned to trust his judgment.

Sarah brushed at the dirt on her clothing. Cars lined the entire block, both sides. She would have to do something about parking when she developed the area.

Dennis tossed the sketchpad into the backseat of his Datsun. "Friday for lunch?"

She nodded absently. She was wondering how much of the block she could buy up before anyone else noticed what was happening and the prices jumped. Maybe she could run it through a couple of dummy corporations.

"Got a name for it."

"Hmm? For what?"

"The project. Brady Quinn Place. We can tie in the historical aspect. The turn of the century with the turn of the century. The eighteen-nineties meet the nineteen-nineties. Solidness and elegance combined with efficiency and technology."

She thought it over. "Not bad," she admitted.

"Not bad? It's a natural. There's a real nostalgia in this town for that era. Cowboys. Baby Doe Tabor. Mattie Silks. Sheriff Dave Cook."

"I'll think about it," she said. "Find out who this Brady Quinn character was. We wouldn't want to use his name if he was only some two-bit tinhorn."

"Why not? Mattie Silks was a madam."

"Ah, but in a woman, sleaze is respectable."

She drove her Volvo through the diagonal streets of downtown Denver, past the steel-and-glass towers of the energy and telecommunications companies. She wondered what would happen to such complexes when telecommuting became common. Her projected renovation included accessing each unit to the Internet as well as to a community satellite dish.

She had planned to take Colfax Avenue home because she liked to watch for commercial property possibilities, but at the last minute she changed her mind and cut down Speer to the Sixth Avenue Expressway. That was a straight run west, nonstop practically to the Hogback, with the Front Range dead ahead the whole way. It was a sight she never tired of.

A few years ago she had taken one of those executive survival courses. Rock climbing. Shooting rapids. Living in the wilderness. How to handle knives and bows. For graduation, they had dropped her off somewhere in the High Country with nothing but the clothes on her back. She had learned a lot about who she was during those two grueling days. And she had grown to love the mountains. They were her refuge when the stress of business grew too great. She promised herself a few days in the High Country after the Emerson Street project was finished.

The afternoon clouds were rolling over the mountains, so close she felt she could touch them. She gauged the sky thoughtfully, estimating the chance of rain; then she opened the sunroof anyway. What the hell. She liked the feel of the breeze and, if it did rain, she could close it up fast enough. She was a risk taker from way back.

Later, in her home, as she sipped a brandy in front of the fire, Quinn's name finally clicked. She set her snifter to the side and pushed herself out of the sofa. A log in the fire snapped, sending a wave of pine scent through the room. Feline P. Cat, her Manx, followed her to the terminal desk and watched intently as she called up the Emerson Street file and scrolled through it. When she finally found the entry she sought, she nodded in self-satisfaction.

Once, a very long time ago, Brady Quinn had owned the house on Emerson Street. He had bought it from the silver baron in 1867 and sold it in 1876 to a man named Randall Carson. From there, through several intermediate owners, it had come to her.

"That makes him some sort of an 'ancestor' of mine," she told the cat. "Maybe Dennis is right and we can use him as a hook for the project. If he was anything more than some poor jerk who got caught in the crossfire of someone else's argument."

Feline blinked his agreement.

"Maybe the files at the *News* or the *Post* can help me. She logged onto the Internet and sent a commercial search engine to look for "Brady Quinn." It came back dry, except for a half-dozen sites dedicated to the *Brady Bunch* television show and another handful to the actor Anthony Quinn. She grimaced. *Syntax,* she scolded herself. *Gotta watch your syntax.*

"What do you think, Fee?"

The cat yawned.

"You're right. We'll have to go downtown and look at old hard copy. The *Express* and the *Times* aren't even around anymore. Maybe the Western History Room at the DPL has something on microfilm. And the tax records at the City and County Building." She jotted some notes to herself. She'd always hated doing research during her reporter days. Now she was actually looking forward to it. It was a break in the routine. *When it's your* job, she thought, *it's never* fun.

When Sarah walked into the city room of the *Rocky Mountain News* the next morning she found Morgan Grimes hunched over his desk. She stepped off the elevator and walked around the pillars past the reception desk, and there he was. The city room was a study in mauve, burgundy, and gray, with the reporters' desks arranged in "pods" of six. There was no one else in the room except the copy editor, who glanced up briefly from her station at the head of the DU of copydesks before bending back to her work.

Morgan was talking on the phone, his face twisted in concentration, holding the earpiece with his left shoulder while he tapped notes into his terminal. When he saw her coming he said something into the phone, then covered the mouthpiece with his hand.

"Yes, young lady, may I help you?"

"Stuff it, Morgan. I came to use the library for a while. Is that all right with you?"

"It's a *morgue*," he groused. "I don't care who says different." He looked her over. "So that's all? Just using our morgue? Not looking for your old job back?"

She laughed. "Not even on a bet. Give up the office suite, the Volvo, the tailored dresses, the condo in Aspen? For what?"

"For the thrill," he answered. "For the glamour. *The Front Page. All the President's Men.* That sort of thing."

"Glamour. Sure, I remember. Obituaries. Press conferences. Media 'opportunities.' Staged demonstrations. Not to mention coolie wages, unpredictable work hours, and last-minute assignments out of town. No, thanks." She tried to peek at his monitor, but he hit a button and it went blank. "What're you working on, Morg'?"

"The Pulitzer, of course."

Morgan Grimes had the straightest face in the business and could fake sincerity with the best of them. During the days when they had teamed up together, she had never been able to tell whether he was putting her on or not—a fact that he used against her mercilessly. She thought about tapping into his files through the Net. Leave him a sarcastic message. Teach him not to play cute. She thought she could hack it, even though the reporters' terminals were not always connected to the Net. There were ways to mouse into any system. *I wonder if he's still using the same access code.* She had cracked it years ago, just for practice; but she had never actually used it.

She looked around the city room. "Everybody out on assignment?"

"Uh-huh. Except Kevin. He's on another book promotion tour. Should be back next week. I suppose you heard about his latest best-seller."

"Yeah. Follow-up to *The Silent Brotherhood,* isn't it? Easy life. Well, tell everyone I stopped by and said hello."

"They will be thrilled beyond words. Actually, it has been good seeing you again. You always were a pretty good—"

"Don't say it, Morgan!"

"—news hen. The morgue's still where it always was, but they scanned everything onto discs. No more microfilm. That shouldn't bother you, though, would it?"

"Nope," she said swingng her body with mock sassiness. "I was born with a microchip on my shoulder."

II

Dennis' appointment was at 1500 hours and he arrived at the offices of the DU history department precisely at 1459. A series of doors opened off of a central reception area. No one was at the reception desk, although an open can of pop hinted at someone's imminent return. Dennis looked around uncertainly until a plump, moon-faced woman stuck her head out of one of the doors.

"Mr. French?" she asked.

"Yes, are you Professor Llewellyn?" He headed in her direction. "Thank you for seeing me. I know how busy you folks are."

"Not at all. The semester is over now and I have some spare time. It's just such a surprise when a nonstudent makes an appointment. Come in and sit down." She guided him into her office. "Gwynneth Llewellyn is my name."

They shook hands. Llewellyn's grip was surprisingly firm.

Dennis sat in a worn high-back chair, pulling up his pants legs so they wouldn't bag. He sat erect, with his hands folded across his middle.

Llewellyn planted herself behind her desk and leaned forward on her beefy arms. Her skin was pale, spotted red with freckles. Her cheeks were plump and round. She reminded Dennis of someone's aunt, and he half-expected cornbread muffins and cocoa; so he was quite surprised when she took up a corncob pipe and lit it.

She blew a smoke ring, gauging his reaction. "So what can I do for you, Mr. French?"

He came right to the point. Neither his time nor the professor's was something to be wasted. "I am trying to discover the rationale behind this list of historical events." He reached into his vest pocket and pulled out the scrap of foolscap that Sarah had found in the Emerson Street house.

He had spent all day Tuesday and Wednesday reading history and talking to some people he knew at Metro and CU. Making time for curiosity, he supposed Sarah would say. He was convinced there was a common theme running through all the items on the list. Some principle that defined what went on the list and what didn't. He was annoyed that he couldn't simply glance at the entries and know what that common factor was, like he could glance at a building and know what principles the architect had used to make his design decisions. Dennis wasn't sure if that represented a problem with his education, with his own abilities, or with the list itself; but the problem niggled at him, like a stone in his shoe.

He unfolded the sheet and handed it over to Professor Llewellyn. She pulled out a pair of old-fashioned bifocals and perched them on her nose. She gave him a quick apologetic smile and focused on the page, her head tilted slightly back and her lips thrust forward in a pout.

When she had finished, she took off her glasses and looked at him. "I take it you're not interested in knowing *what* these events are. You can find most of them referenced in any good history text."

He nodded. "And I have been reading to the extent I have time. I am an architectural consultant and I've simply not the freedom to pursue these things to the depth I suspect may be necessary. The people I've spoken with so far have given me facts. All fascinating. Much of it I hadn't known. Like this Thomas B. Reed character. The 'serenely sarcastic New England Buddha,' they called him."

"He was the most brilliant man in politics in his day," Llewellyn told him. "Like it says here . . ." She tapped the list. ". . . he should have been nominated for President, but McKinley's people pulled the rug from under him."

"But I want more than facts. I am searching—for want of a better word—for insight. Some of those entries concern well-known people or events. Others are obscure. The sinking of the battleship *Maine* and General Twiggs don't exactly pop into one's mind together."

She smiled. "No, they surely do not." She scanned through the list again. "*Insight* is a perfectly good word, Mr. French; and it is exactly what you are looking for. The same thought bothered me as I read this, too. If these are the answers to a quiz or an examination, it would be a very strange unit of study. I'm afraid even I don't know what some of these entries are, let alone what they might mean. I know about Ambrose Bierce disappearing in Mexico, of course; but who was this Brady Quinn fellow, or Davis Belleau, or Agatha Penwether?"

"Murder victims."

She nodded testily. "Yes, I can read; but what are they doing here with Teddy Roosevelt or Lincoln or . . ." Her finger paused as she studied an item. Then she laid the foolscap on her desk and leaned back in the swivel chair. The springs creaked. She puffed on her pipe, staring pensively at the ceiling. "Tell me, Mr. French," she said after a moment. "Who said this? 'Under our system a worker is told just what he is to do and how to do it. Any improvement he makes upon the orders given him is fatal to his success.' "

Dennis did not see the relevance of the question. "I don't know. Lenin? Mao?"

"No, it was Frederick Taylor," she said, nodding at the list. *Frederick W. Taylor,* Dennis remembered, *fl. ca. 1900.* "Taylor was an engineer at the turn of the last century, when American industry was faced with a tide of poorly educated immigrant laborers. Taylor boosted productivity by separating the planning and the execution of work. Engineers and managers made the plans; foremen and workers carried them out. It's been the basis of American business practice ever since."

Dennis laughed. "Oh, no! And I thought it was Lenin or Mao? That's priceless!"

She smiled thinly. "Don't forget that Engels was a factory owner himself, and not necessarily the junior partner of the team. He thought that entire nations could be run rationally, the way factories were."

"I've yet to encounter a business that was run rationally," Dennis interjected.

Llewellyn ignored the interruption. "Socialism is the apotheosis of capitalism—what I like to call the Managed Society. 'Daddy Knows Best.' If you want to see Lenin's state in embryo, study Henry Ford's company. His Sociological Department 'inspectors' could barge in unannounced on employees in their homes and question them on their marriages, their finances, their private lives. And Harry Bennett's 'outside squads' were just minor-league Brownshirts."

"Henry Ford never had anyone executed," Dennis protested.

"Though Bennett's goons *did* beat up and harass dissidents. And other employers during the class war did not shrink from killing union organizers. The difference between Ford and Lenin was more a matter of scale than anything else. Lenin organized his entire country into one vast Company Town, with all that implies. In plain language, the Soviet Union was the largest corporation on the planet. The Party members were the stockholders, and the Politburo was the Board of Directors. Ordinary citizens—employees—had no effective say in running the organization. Corporate headquarters made five-year plans that never worked. Internal criticism was not allowed. Everyone had to be a 'team player,' by which they meant 'follow the boss's orders' rather than genuine teamwork. Troublemakers were exiled to Siberia or to meaningless jobs. Or terminated." Dr. Llewellyn smiled humorlessly. "An interesting choice of words, that."

"Don't forget the hostile takeovers," said Dennis.

Professor Lllewellyn laughed. "That's the spirit!"

"I never thought of it before," Dennis admitted, "but a large corporation *is* run like a socialist state."

"Vice versa, actually. Don't forget which came first."

"Thanks to Frederick W. Taylor."

Llewellyn nodded. "He wasn't the only one involved, but he was the catalyst."

"So your point is . . ." He let the sentence hang.

"Oh, yes, your list. Now this is purely off the cuff, understand, but the items I am familiar with seem to be historical turning points of a rather subtle kind. The events themselves were small—few people were involved—but they had disproportionate consequences. Do you recall the George Herbert poem? 'For want of a nail, the shoe is lost. For want of a shoe, the horse is lost.' And so on. In the end a kingdom is lost. Bosworth Field was a near-run thing. Had Richard the Third not lost his horse, it might easily have gone the other way. And what then? No Tudors, and English history becomes something quite different. Well, these events are like that."

"I see. Like Mr. Taylor's attempts to boost factory productivity led to your Managed Society."

"It's not *my* society," she said a trifle huffily. "I objected to the trend in the sixties and I *still* object to it. The idea that Those in Charge Know Better . . . Those who say that government should be run more like a business should study the Soviet Union or, better yet, some of our own large corporations."

Dennis grinned. "Just between you and me, I've never had too much respect for the way large corporations are run. That's why I'm in business for myself. What about the other items on the list?" He laid the list flat on her desk and they both huddled over it. "How about . . . Oh, Winfield Scott's military appointments? How was that a horseshoe nail?"

She looked at him and took her pipe from her teeth. "A horseshoe nail," she repeated, smiling. "I like that. Perhaps I'll use it in my classes next semester, with your permission."

"My permission?" Dennis was surprised. "Certainly."

"Thank you. I would say that Scott's appointments prolonged the Civil War. Most key posts went to Southerners; so the Confederacy wound up with more experienced officers. Of course, at the time, no one knew there would be a civil war; and Scott was, and remained, a staunch Unionist. So it wasn't as though he planned it that way."

"There seem to be a number of Civil War items on the list. What does this mean? 'Jan/Feb, 1861. The Twiggs Affair: his orders delayed, but not his return.' "

Llewellyn nodded. "That's an especially good example. Twiggs was a Georgian in charge of U.S. forces in Texas. Lincoln called him to Washington because he wondered at his loyalty, but hesitated too long in ordering his removal. So when the Texas secessionists demanded he hand over all military stores in Texas, Twiggs cooperated fully."

"And if the recall *had* reached Texas in time?"

"Well, his designated successor was off in the west fighting Commanches, so command would have fallen to Colonel Robert E. Lee."

Dennis raised his eyebrows. "*The* Robert E. Lee? I thought he was a general."

Llewellyn smiled. "That came later. At the time, Lee was quoted as saying, 'Secession is nothing but treason.' Had the Texas commissioners called on him to violate his oath, he would certainly have refused, and the first shots of the Civil War would have been fired in San Antonio, not Charleston Harbor."

"No way would he have gotten command of a Confederate army after that," Dennis mused. "Yes, I see your point. A very small thing—a military courier taking his good old time—leads to a very big consequence: the army's best tactician leading the Rebel forces. I suppose then that . . ." He scanned the list himself. "Oh, Theodore Roosevelt's nomination for Vice President was a small thing that led to his trust busting and other progressive reforms."

Llewellyn drew on her pipe and sent a cloud toward the ceiling. She looked uncertain. "Perhaps. But then why not list his accession to the presidency instead? Did you know that his nomination for Vice President was actually arranged by his political enemies, who were trying to finish his career by burying him in a dead-end job?"

"Things didn't quite work out the way they expected," Dennis commented.

"No, they didn't." She folded the list and handed it back to Dennis. "Perhaps the Roosevelt nomination was a horseshoe nail that was 'hammered back in,' so to speak."

"By McKinley's assassination. I see." Somehow, he had always thought of history as something solid. Something inevitable. But to hear Llewellyn explain things, history was nothing more than a multiplication of unlikely coincidences that could have turned one way as easily as another. Horseshoe nails. He felt as if he had been viewing a cathedral for a long time, admiring the arches and spires and groined vaulting, when suddenly the angle of the lighting had changed and the appearance of the structure had been transfigured. It was an odd feeling—oddly exhilarating—to see the familiar from a new perspective. He rose. "I'd like to thank you again for your time. You've been considerable help."

"Not at all," she demurred, shaking his hand.

He turned to go and paused. "Oh. One last thing, if you will. The word in the heading. *Cliological.* Do you know what it means?"

"Cliological?" She frowned. "No, I never— Oh!" She laughed.

"What is it?"

"Clio was the Greek muse of history. Apparently, the writer, or someone, coined the term as a parallel to biology or sociology, meaning 'a science of history.' Perhaps the writer was a science student taking a history course."

Dennis thought about his meeting with Llewellyn as he drove homeward down University Avenue. A scientific approach to history. He wondered what Jerry would say when he told him. How could history be a science when one considered the role of random chance? Well, just because some college student a hundred years ago thought it possible didn't mean that it was. College students were notorious for their flights of fancy. Why, when he had been in school, he had . . . Well, that was of no consequence now. He had switched from linguistics to architecture. (Now there was a switch for you!) And his artificial "language" was mummifying in a drawer somewhere.

What was it that had been written at the bottom of the list? "Try orthogonal factor analysis"? The list was in his pocket, but he did not remove his hand from the wheel to take it out. "Try orthogonal factor analysis." Yes, that was it. Now that sounded terribly scientific. Then he remembered that the list was written in two different hands. Two different "cliologists?" And one hand had been much older than the other, he recalled now. He wondered what that might mean.

After three years on the Net Watch, Red Malone still did not know the name of his teammate. They had played countless games of rummy and pinochle. They had swapped lies about the women they had known (and a few that they hadn't). They had monitored intelligence during scores of quiet crises, the kind that *never* appeared in the newspapers. And still Red did not even know which of the Agencies "Charlie" worked for.

And "Charlie," of course, knew as little about Red.

One agent might be turned, but not two paired at random. So, to guard against moles or rogues running unauthorized ops, two agents stood watch at all times. In an age when wars were fought with information, the security of "holes" like the Net Watch was as critical as that of the missile holes.

So each of them was there to keep the other honest, and that made it necessary that they be strangers to each other.

Red picked up the clipboard and scanned the log entries for the last two shifts. Most of them were in codes he was not supposed to know. Other Watchkeepers from other Agencies. Idly he wondered which codes Charlie could read. Red amused himself by trying to crack them. It was better than crosswords. He whistled "East Virginia," off-key, as he read.

Sometimes he wondered what would happen if he were to insert some sort of disinformation program into the Net. Not that he could write such a program, but he knew people who could. It was his business to know People Who Could. It would be great fun, a real knee-slapper; and remembering the prank would help him while away the long hours afterward in Leavenworth.

He sighed. Rules took the fun out of life. He wondered sometimes about those who made the rules their life. Then he remembered what his own job was and he laughed aloud, earning him an odd stare from Charlie.

The air conditioner hissed a cold draft through the gray-painted room. Red always wore his suit jacket in the Watch-Room. He couldn't figure how his companion could sit there in his shirtsleeves. Red shook his head and put down the clipboard. Why couldn't they at least team him with someone who had the same metabolism? He reached into his jacket pocket and pulled out a well-worn deck of cards. He hated Saturday duty. He cut the deck and riffed the two halves together.

The machines hummed in the background. Lights winked on and off. Disk readers buzzed intermittently. Relays clicked. It reminded him of that time he had gone camping. (When had that been? Two years ago. He and—*That* long ago?) The nighttime forest had made noises just like the Watch-Room, except that it had been insects and other animals making them. When he had mentioned the similarity to the other campers, they had looked at him strangely.

Now here he sat. Camped out in the electronic jungle. Listening for the sounds of predators. He riffed the deck of cards once more; tapped them on the console desk.

An alarm rang: a soft, insistent beep, and a winking red light on the console. He sat upright, suddenly alert, the cards forgotten. Charlie reached out and hit the cutoff. "What is it?" he asked.

Red played the keyboard and checked the intelligence he called up on his screen. "It's a trip wire. Someone's accessing files that an agent wanted flagged."

"Yeah? Well, they leave the bait out there and wait to see who nibbles. Who do we notify?"

Red checked his list. "Umm. Someone named Foxhound."

"Must be a code name."

"No shit."

Charlie gave him a sour look. "Don't give me any grief. What's the flag and where'd it go up?" He was already busy entering the notification code. The computer would compare his entry to Red's to see if they matched. Not so much to guard against deliberate disinformation as against inadvertent keystroke errors.

Red scrolled the information on his screen. He read off a Net Access Code and Charlie read it back to him. Active and passive checking, both ways.

"The watchword is . . . uh, *Quinn*," he told Charlie. *Quinn?* he thought. *Well, well.* "Says here that this is the third time this week it's been tripped by the same user. Well, third time's the charm, right? That's what triggers the signal."

"Never mind that crap. What were the CPU codes? All three of them."

Red called off the numbers and Charlie confirmed them. The first one, Red noticed, was a domestic terminal running a commercial search engine. He shook his head. Amateurs.

"That last one is where the user is now?" Charlie asked.

"Yeah. Know where it's located?"

"No, and I don't care. Neither should you."

"The prefix means it's a self-contained system tapping into the Net, but not a regular node. Mmm. This prefix means a public library, I think; so we're talking about the public terminals there, not the library's own on-line deeby. Then the next nine digits is a cipher for the ZIP . . . Denver. The rest of it identifies the port on the system. Not too hard to decrypt once you know what it is."

"Well, listen to Mr. Sherlock Holmes. Look; all we know is the code number. Foxhound or his Handler will have the address where it's located. That's their worry. An agent wants to flag a file, he's got his reasons. All we do is watch the Net and see if anyone accesses it. We don't know who the agent is. We don't know who the user is. We don't know where the terminal is located or what the watchword means."

Red chuckled. "Is there anything we *do* know?"

Charlie swiveled his chair around. "Yeah. I know how to play rummy and you don't. You've shuffled those cards enough to wear the pips off 'em. So, deal."

Red flicked the cards with the ease of long practice. "This has been the most excitement we've had in two weeks. My heart is pounding."

Charlie grunted. "Most folks go on the Net, they don't nose around where they shouldn't. You decided yet what you're doing on your vacation?"

Red set the remainder of the deck down between them. He turned over the top card. It was a queen. "Yeah. Camping."

Charlie picked off the deck. "Camping? Thought you hated that stuff."

"I do. That's why I'm going. Self-discipline. It builds character to do something you hate."

Charlie looked baffled for a moment. Then he shook his head sadly. "Next thing, you'll be roasting rats for lunch. You're weird. I ever tell you that? You're weird."

III

Sarah was in the Western History Room at the Denver Public Library when her beeper went off. It was Monday and she had spent several days at the public terminals. Her eyes felt dry and dusty from staring at computer files and micro-films. Brady Quinn was an elusive man. She had hunted for him through one file after another without success. After sell-ing the Emerson Street house, he had not bought another one, at least not in Denver. In fact, except for a second news article that mentioned him only incidentally, Quinn had left no trace at all in the local records between the sale of his house and his death, sixteen years later.

Well, that was a lot easier to do a hundred years ago than it was today. Back then a citizen could live his entire life without more than a handful of encounters with the govern-ment. Today you couldn't sneeze without leaving a trace in a file somewhere.

However, the second news article had contained a clue that she had followed into the National Archives, where she fi-nally hit pay dirt. She was just reading the printout when her beeper went off. The other patrons turned and looked at her. She smiled an apology and went outside so she could use her phone without bothering them.

The voicemail was from Dennis. If she was downtown and in the mood, give him a buzz and they'd have dinner to-gether. His treat, at the Augusta.

She never could resist a free meal. She called him at his office and confirmed the time. Then she returned to the third floor to pack her things away.

She stopped in the doorway. There was a man standing by her briefcase, reading her notes. For a moment she was too astonished to do anything but gape. "Can I help you?" she asked sarcastically.

The man turned and looked at her. He was tall and rangy, with a thin, prominent nose. There was no embarrassment or surprise in his face. His eyes were dead, without expression. He looked at her with no more interest than if he had looked at the furniture.

"No," he said. "You can't." Only his mouth spoke. The rest of his face remained uninvolved. There was an air of menace about him, an aura of barely restrained violence. It was in his bearing, in the lines of his face. Sarah caught her lower lip between her teeth. Was he a crazy off the street? Maybe she should call the police.

"I'll thank you to leave my things alone," she said, wondering if he would become violent.

The man's smile was cold, a brief contortion of the lips into an unwonted configuration. That smile chilled her more than any threat could have done. No, he wasn't crazy. Not exactly.

He walked straight toward the door and Sarah hastily stepped aside, lest he come too close. He paid her no attention as he walked by. Sarah looked after his departing figure until he had vanished down the stairwell. Then she let out a shaky breath.

"He gone?"

Sarah turned, startled. One of the other library patrons stood there. A small, nut-brown woman of indeterminate age, with a wind-weathered face and wearing a denim jacket.

"I tol' him to leave yore things alone," she said, "but he jest looked at me like I was some kinda bug. A New Yorker, yuh ask me."

"A weirdo."

"Mebbe. Young lady, it mebbe ain't none of my business, but . . . The way he looked at yuh?"

It chilled her just to remember. "What about it?"

"I seen that look once before. Riding fences on my spread out to Buffalo Creek. Saw me a diamondback a-staring down a bird. A lark bunting, it was. That snake stared at that bird the same way that there fella looked at you."

Sarah swallowed. The ranch woman's description was apt, she thought. The man had been very much like a snake. "Thanks for your concern," she said. "I'm meeting a friend for dinner; so, if you don't mind, I'll . . ." She walked to the table where her briefcase lay and gathered up her papers. She fumbled them inside and snapped it shut. When she was leaving, though, the ranch woman stopped her again.

"Missy? That snake . . . Ah didn't stop it. It's nature's way, and even snakes have to eat. But the bird . . ."

"What about the bird?"

"That poor bird jest a-stood there and waited. Never even tried to git away. Jest a-stood there and let that snake strike it."

Sarah thought about the man in the library as she rode the electric bus down the Sixteenth Street Mall. She was still thinking about him when she entered the restaurant. She saw Dennis wave to her from across the room.

Dennis stood while the waiter seated her, then resumed his own seat. "A Bristol cream sherry for Ms. Beaumont," Dennis told the waiter, "and Jameson's, neat, for myself." The waiter left and Dennis turned to her. "What's wrong? You look upset."

"Oh, nothing. Just a little run-in at the library." She told him about the stranger, and he shook his head sympathetically.

"The West is getting more and more like the East," he said. "Here, this will take your mind off it." He reached down and brought up his sketch pad. "I thought you might like to look at a few concepts I've come up with for Brady Quinn Place."

Brady Quinn Place. She had almost forgotten *why* she had been researching Quinn's life—on the Web, in news groups, in archives. *I've spent a whole week doing nothing but research.* It made her feel guilty, having fun like that while Dennis was working his heart out.

She took the sketch pad from him and looked at the drawings he had made. They were good. Dennis' ideas usually were. They batted ideas back and forth for a while over their drinks. Then, after the waiter had taken their dinner orders, the talk returned to Brady Quinn. "It wasn't easy," she told him, "but I finally tracked him down. He was a statistician in the Interior Department for a number of years before and during the Civil War."

"Didn't you tell me Friday that you couldn't find a trace of him anywhere?"

"That's right. Until I came across another news story. It made me think that . . . Well, you tell me. I'll read it to you." She unsnapped her briefcase and pulled out a photocopy. "This was in the *Rocky Mountain News* for Monday, July eighteenth, 1881.

" 'A daring train robbery by masked men occurred on Saturday, July sixteenth, on the Chicago, Rock Island, and Pacific Rail Road, near Cameron, Missouri. The robbers were six in number and were supposed to be under the leadership of Jesse James. The men boarded the train at Cameron. At Winston, when the train stopped, they stood up in the aisle of a car with drawn revolvers. One of the bandits advanced with a revolver in each hand toward William Westfall, the conductor, and ordered him to hold up his hands. The conductor was slow in complying and was shot through the heart. One of the other bandits shot through the head John McCullogh, a stone-cutter of Wilton Junction, who turned in his seat. The same man then shot and wounded Brady Quinn, retired, a government clerk during the late war. The bandits then went to the express car and overpowered the Express Messenger, who was intimidated into opening the safe, from which three thousand dollars was taken.' "

She handed him the facsimile printout. "There's more. The James Gang went after the engineer, too; but he set the brake and crawled out into the pilot and hid."

"Ah, the wild and woolly West," said Dennis. He looked at the photocopy. "Some folks have tried to make the James brothers into heroes. Sure doesn't sound too heroic."

"We only make people into legends after they're dead, so they won't embarrass the legend makers." She pointed. "Well, the story said that Quinn was a government clerk during the war. I figured that must have been the Civil War, so I hacked into the Net from the library and accessed the National Archives in Washington."

Dennis sipped his drink. "They have Civil War files on-line?" he asked. He placed his glass down precisely where he had picked it up, exactly matching the wet ring on the tablecloth.

"Only some things, like indices," Sarah said. "If I want the details, I have to write to Washington." She paused for a moment while the waiter set their food down. London broil for Dennis, lobster for her. "Interior Secretary McClelland appointed Quinn to the post of statistician for special investigations in 1853, on the recommendation of one Isaac Shelton of Massachussetts. His appointment was renewed by each succeeding Secretary down to Usher. After the war, he retired from public life, first to his native Muncie, then to Denver. The Pension Office lost track of him in 1876, when he sold the house on Emerson Street. I couldn't find *any* trace of him at all between 1876 and 1881, when he was shot on that train in Missouri."

Dennis arched his eyebrows. "Yes, and then shot again in, what? Eighteen-ninety-two? Shot *twice* as an innocent bystander? In two separate incidents?"

"Right. That was my own reaction. Someone wanted to kill him, but wanted it to look like an accident. Our Mr. Quinn is becoming quite the mystery man. He evidently went into hiding in 1876. From whom? Why?"

"A statistician in the Interior Department," mused Dennis. "I can see where a man in such a position would make a lot of enemies." He grinned at his own joke. "Well, it was more than a hundred years ago. Whatever it was about is long over."

"Sure, but we want to use his name as a theme, not just a label. We can't call the project Brady Quinn Place without telling people why. It might as well be John Doe Place. No, whatever the mystery is surrounding him, that is what we want to hang the theme on."

"I know it," he said. She watched him cut his steak into careful slices, spear one on his fork, and transfer the fork to his right hand. She had long ago taught herself to use knife and fork the European way and had tried in vain to convince Dennis that his way was inefficient. "If I could discover why his death was included on that list of historical events," he said thoughtfully, "that might give us a lead. It seems so out of place." He looked at her. "Oh, there *was* a common theme that ran through most of the items. They were all horseshoe nails."

"Horseshoe nails? What do you mean?"

He smiled. "A private joke. I was talking to a professor at DU last Thursday. About the list that we found. That was her analysis. She said that these were instances when the actions of a relative handful of people had changed the course of history." Briefly he summarized his meeting with Professor Llewellyn.

Secretly, Sarah was amused to discover that Dennis, too, had been spending his time on "extracurricular" research. "I suppose she knows what she's talking about. It's her specialty, after all. But she credits this Taylor fellow with creating communism? That seems a pretty big accomplishment even for an industrial engineer."

"No, no. She only said that Taylor, Ford, Lenin, and the others were part of a trend toward the Managed Society—with decision-making authority vested in a professional, managerial class of 'experts.' You know what I'm talking about: Just follow procedures. Anything not compulsory is forbidden." He looked at his steak, frowned, and cut it vigorously. "Bureaucrats," he said, bitterly, and looked back at Sarah. "Did I ever tell you? When I was working as a civil engineer, before I took my architecture degree, my firm was swallowed by a conglomerate. The new owners sent in their own people to run things. Not a single one was an engineer."

"Let me guess. MBAs with financial backgrounds."

"Bingo. My own *supervisor* didn't know the first thing about strength of materials or Proctor density. You know what he said? 'A professional manager can manage any business or function, wherever good management is needed.' "

Sarah grunted. "It reminds me of that education prof you told me about. The one who said that teachers only need to know teaching, not the subject matter. So, what happened?"

"What do you think? Efficiency went down; waste went up. The best people bailed out and the firm went belly up. Gutted, just so a corporate staff hundreds of miles away could hold all the reins of power in their hot little fast-track hands." He shook his head. "Funny. I guess I'm still bitter about it, even after all these years."

"If centralization worked that well, Russia would export wheat."

He chuckled. "Well put. Come to think of it, Professor Llewellyn did say Russia was run like a corporation. But tell me. Do you notice the similarities between teachers and managers? They've both dropped their adjectives."

"Come again?"

"When teachers and managers became *professional* teachers and *professional* managers, they forgot how to be *history* teachers or *engineering* managers."

"Judging by the results," Sarah laughed, "someone wants us to be ignorant and unproductive. Maybe Thomas Dewey and Frederick Taylor were part of a conspiracy."

"There are two problems with the list, though, that I still don't have straight in my mind. There are plenty of 'turning points of history' that are not on the list."

"And Brady Quinn is."

"Right. *That's* the puzzle that concerns us and our project. What sort of 'image' will Brady Quinn Place have? How did his death change the course of history?"

"Little events with big consequences," she mused, dipping her lobster into the melted butter. An idea struck her and she pointed her fork at Dennis. "Wait a minute! Nothing important happened because Quinn was killed."

He looked puzzled. "Well, yes. That is the problem."

"No, that's the *answer!* Nothing important happened *because* Quinn was killed. Sure, that must be it. Remember the *Challenger* disaster? They traced the cause and effect all the way back to your friends, the 'professional managers.' I still remember how that one Vice President told his engineering manager to 'take off your engineering hat and put on your management hat!' But suppose the engineers who warned against launching had been listened to instead of fired. Suppose the launch was postponed. Everyone gripes about it. Later, when the weather is warmer, they launch successfully.

Because the warning is heeded, no disaster happens. A small action with a big *un*consequence."

"OK. But that creates a different sort of problem."

"What's that?"

"*How could events like that get on the list?* It's easy to say that because Brady Quinn was killed, or because Ambrose Bierce disappeared, something important failed to happen; but how does anyone know it? How do you trace the fault tree of something that never occurred? Have you ever tried to prove something from the absence of negative evidence?"

"Professional managers do it all the time. That's why they launched *Challenger*, remember? The engineers couldn't *prove* that anything bad would happen." She dabbed at her lips with her napkin and looked at her watch. "Look, Dennis, I hate to eat and run, but I've got a property I want to look at down by Union Station."

"Union Station?" He blinked at the sudden change of subject.

"Yes. I've had it in the back of my head to buy into that area."

Dennis rolled his eyes. "Another project. Oh, good. I don't have enough work as it is."

"Don't worry," she said, laughing. Dennis loved to gripe, but he thrived on work. "I won't be developing it right away. Maybe nothing will come of the convention center talk; but, just in case, I want to have a key property in my purse." She chuckled again. "In an odd way, though, it is a sort of spin-off of this Brady Quinn business."

"How so?"

"The building I'm going to look at was once owned by Randall Carson, the same fellow who bought Quinn's Emerson Street house. I was searching through some old real estate records, looking for Quinn. Handwritten on index cards, if you can imagine. I guess when the County microf-iched their records back in the nineteen-eighties they didn't think these were worth doing. Anyway, I was looking for

Quinn's name, but you know how that goes. Carson's name just caught my eye."

IV

The building sat near the Union Pacific tracks, under the viaduct, on a small side street off of Fifteenth. Sarah parked by the Post Office Annex and walked from there. The street under the viaduct was already dark, even though the sun hadn't set. Fragments of sunlight found their way between the old warehouses and created a spiderweb of shadows out of the abutments and steel girders. Sarah could hear the hum of the tires above her. The old street below was deserted.

Her heels clicked on the pavement and the roadbed overhead echoed the sound back to her half a beat behind. Then—a strange double echo. She stopped and turned. It was an automatic reaction and it was a moment before she even realized she had done so.

There's someone there, she thought, peering into the shadows. A bum. A wino. The railyard was nearby. This was a good place to hop a freight.

She turned and resumed walking. There probably wasn't anyone there. It was just a freak echo caused by the viaduct. No aliens/monsters/mad slashers.

Of course, isn't that what they always said in the movies?

The trend nowadays was to preserve the building's shell, regardless what was done with the interior. Conserving the unique character of the neighborhood or city. Sarah stood on the street outside and examined the exterior of the Widener Building. Solid, redbrick construction. There were three rows of windows, the upper two dark. Widener's Restoration Handicrafts, she recalled from the tax records, occupied only the first floor. The other two were unused.

She entered the building and looked for the second-shift

foreman. Widener's was one of several small employers of the handicapped. The company collected secondhand items and refurbished them for resale to the poor. She paused for a few moments in the broad, open first-floor room and watched while the men and women painted, soldered, sewed, and wired. It wasn't like an assembly line: no two items were alike. It took skill to diagnose and repair the faults of each one.

She found the foreman in his office. Binders and catalogs sat strewn every which way on shelves and atop file cabinets. Papers littered the desk. Dirt and trash had accumulated in the corners of the room. Paul Abbot, the foreman, sat amid this splendor, leaning back in an old wooden desk chair, his feet propped up on the desk, reading a magazine.

"Mr. Abbot? Sarah Beaumont. We spoke on the phone yesterday. About seeing the building?"

Abbot looked at her, waited a beat, then put both his feet on the floor. He laid the magazine faceup on the desk, so Sarah could see that it contained pictures of naked women. The foreman smiled, letting his gaze wander over her appraisingly. He grunted his approval and shifted the toothpick in his mouth from the left side to the right. He stuck his hands behind his neck and linked his fingers together. "Yeah?"

"Yes," she answered. "I'm thinking of buying this building . . ."

"What, ya gonna throw me an' my feebs out on the street?"

Almost, Sarah was amazed that this creature possessed the gift of speech. "Nothing like that, I assure you. I simply wish to inspect the premises."

"Inspect the premises," he mimicked. "Jeez, lady. Ya wanna look the joint over, be my guest; but ya don't hafta go put on airs." He reached out a foot, hooked a drawer handle, and jerked it open. "There's a flashlight in there. You'll need it upstairs. We don't use them floors, so there's no lights up there."

Obviously, he wasn't going to hand her the light, so she

bent over and fished it out herself. It was a large "industrial-size" flashlight. When she stood, he was grinning.

She realized that, in reaching into the desk drawer, she had given him a perfect view down the front of her blouse. Her face burned and she took a deep breath to calm herself. What was it her mother had always said? Some people were no better than they should be. Sarah had never known what that meant before. "Which way are the stairs?" she asked.

He roused himself from his chair. "C'mon; I'll take you." Stepping past her, he held the door open for her. Surprised at this act of chivalry, she walked through, but as she did so, he brushed his hand up against her.

She spun and struck out with the flashlight. It caught him just above the elbow. He howled. "Hey! Watchit, lady, wil-lya!"

"No, sucker. *You* watch it. You try that shit on me again and you're dead meat. Got that?"

"Look. I make a pass, sure. I ask do you wanna do it. You know how it is. Sometimes they say yes. What the hell." He rubbed his elbow.

When they reached the stairway to the second floor, she recalled what Abbot had said about the lighting. The last thing she wanted was to wander around in the dark with this lecher. She stopped and wagged the flashlight at him. "I think I'd rather look around myself."

He shrugged. "Suit yourself."

She climbed the stairs. The air in the stairwell was hot and stale. The runners creaked beneath her feet. At the top, she flicked her light on. The beam was dim but wide. She played it in a circle around the room and saw old manufacturing machinery, sitting in dust-shrouded ranks. The tang of old metal filled the air.

She approached the nearest machine and looked more closely. A metal stamping press, she decided. The drive belt on the flywheel was rotted; the metal, pitted with rust. A patina covered the brass fittings. Some of the machines, she saw, had been partly disassembled.

She toured the room, checking the flooring and rafters. In

one corner, in what had once been a gaging laboratory, she found a musty old bed. It was nothing but a shapeless mattress thrown on the floor. Nearby was a stack of girlie magazines.

She returned to the stairwell and climbed to the top floor. This room was much like the one below, except that the machines were smaller and more varied and, if that was possible, in even worse shape. The smell of rust and of ancient machine oil was heavy. The flashlight cast a circle of light, throwing the nearest machine into sharp relief, a patchwork of lights and shadows, projections and cavities. She wondered why the equipment had been abandoned. It was surely worth money, even today.

On the far side of the room were the lavatories. She stepped in and looked around. Ancient and corroded fixtures greeted her, lined up like the statues on Easter Island. Rusty water seeping from a broken pipe had formed a puddle from which a stalagmite was growing. She had turned and was leaving when an odd shadow in the corner caught her eye.

Inspecting closer, she found a blind dogleg turn with a broken doorway. A shower stall? A closet? There were three boards nailed across it. An old sign with faded lettering was stapled to the boards. Stairway condemned.

A stairway? In the lavatory? She aimed her flashlight through the door. Sure enough, there was a flight of stairs. But they led up, not down. Funny. From the outside, she had seen only three rows of windows; and the main staircase had ended on this floor.

Well, she thought, *nothing ventured* . . . The stairs looked to be in no worse shape than the others she had already climbed. There were no footprints in the thick dust that carpeted them. *To boldly go where no one has gone before* . . . She pulled the boards away and stepped through the broken doorway.

She was wrong about the steps. The sixth one gave way when she put her weight on it. Her right foot plunged through the rotted board and the splintered edges raked her ankle and calf. Pain shot up her leg. She grabbed the banister to keep from falling, but it came loose from the wall. The flashlight dropped from her hand and rolled down two steps, leaving her in semidarkness.

"Damn!" She tried to pull her leg out, but it was caught. She winced in pain and a high-pitched sound escaped her throat. *Calm down,* she told herself.

She forced herself to listen. The silence was palpable. It covered her like a cloak. Within the silence were tiny sounds that served only to accentuate it. The old building murmured and whispered. Drafts sighed and timbers creaked. She could barely discern the muted rumble of the viaduct outside. Somewhere nearby water dripped slowly into a pool.

Call for help? But Abbot was two floors down and unlikely to hear. And even if he did, he would use the opportunity to grope her while freeing her leg. Besides, she had never needed help. She could handle her own rescue.

Bending over, she probed the hole with her fingers. Splinters pointed straight downward like miniature spears. She reached in and broke off the pieces, slowly enlarging the hole. After a few minutes of patient work, it was big enough to pull her foot out.

She turned and sat down on the step, rubbing her ankle. It was scraped raw, and her nylons were ruined. She stood tentatively and tested the ankle. It hurt, but she could stand on it. She gritted her teeth and retrieved the flashlight. It was flickering. She smacked it sharply with the flat of her hand, and the light brightened.

She aimed the light down the stairs, then up the stairs. Then she resumed climbing, testing each step carefully before putting her weight on it.

Without windows, the fourth floor lacked even the promise of light. She played the beam around the room, picking out nondescript wooden furniture. A row of oaken filing cabinets lined one wall; five ancient rolltop desks, another. In the center of the room were heavy oaken tables with ungainly-looking machines atop them. Everything was covered with a thick layer of dust. There were rodent tracks in the dust, but no human footprints.

An eerie feeling stole over her as she made a circuit of the room. She was the first human being to enter this room in who knew how many years. From the looks of things, this floor had been abandoned long before the others. What sort of ghosts haunted manufacturing plants?

She tried to open one of the rolltops, but it was stuck tight. She grunted and pulled and it gave just a fraction of an inch. She played the light over the crack she had opened up but could not bring herself to open it farther. *The darkness is getting to me,* she thought. *How long before I start imagining that someone else is up here with me?*

She walked to the center tables and inspected the machines there more closely. They were all cams and cogs, ratchet wheels and rods. Each machine had a keyboard with lever keys, like an old-style manual typewriter. There were ten rows and ten columns of keys in the center of the board. She rubbed away the dust and saw that each column was numbered from 0 to 9. She reached out curiously to depress a key, but it was frozen in place.

They were obviously primitive calculating machines. As a computer buff, she had always been fascinated by such machines. Dorr's Comptometer had come out in 1885, the Burroughs in 1911. The styling and ornamentation of these machines seemed even older. The cams looked as if they had been machined individually. *Maybe I can check the patent office.* She looked for a nameplate, but she couldn't find one.

She brushed off the other keys and recognized the standard arithmetic symbols. There were also keys marked with the $<$ and $>$ signs. And other symbols that were totally strange to her. What did $\neg$ mean? Or $\notin$? Or $\otimes$ and $\oplus$?

She gave it up and turned her attention to the filing cabinets. Most of the drawers she pulled out were empty, but a few contained loose pages filled with mathematical computations. Her light picked out the title on one torn fragment. "On the Eventual Bifurcation of Highly Connected Dynamic Sets." Must have been a best-seller. . . .

One drawer was locked. She yanked on it hard and heard the metal pins give way, the wood splinter. Another yank and the pins bent. The drawer slid out with a protest of shot bearings and warped and swollen wood. Inside were two thick file folders. She tried to read the tabs in the dim light. The ink was old, faded; the handwriting, ornate.

"Index." She pulled the smaller folder out of the drawer and took it to the table. Holding the flashlight in her left hand, she opened it and tried to read some of the titles in the dim light. "An Optimal Policy for Commodity Purchases Using Integral Simplices." "A Branch-and-Bound Approach to the Job Shop Problem." "On the n-Space Graph Structure of Iroquois Matrilinearity." "Applications of Green's Function to Queues in Semiclosed Networks." "The Dynamical Equations of Ideon Contagion."

What was all this? Mathematical research? No, not entirely. Some of the titles, she saw, dealt with anthropology or economics. Applied mathematics, then. A peculiar mix, and what an odd place for it! The dates written next to the titles of the papers ran through 1892. The earliest one was 1833: a real wowser titled "Some Stochastic Processes with Absorbing Barriers," by someone named Jedediah Crawford. Her light wandered up and down the empty filing cabinets. Sixty years of mathematical papers? A college hidden on the fourth floor of a manufacturing plant?

She pulled the other folder from the drawer and peered at it in the dim light. "Maintenance and Repair of Babbage Analytical Engines."

That stopped her. Charles Babbage had been Lucasian Professor of Mathematics at Cambridge University from 1828 to 1839. He had once described a new kind of calculating machine, far advanced over the simple add/subtract models then available. His Analytical Engine would supposedly carry out an entire sequence of operations without a human being keying each one in. It would also have the capability of running alternative sequences, depending on the results of previous calculations.

The storage was to be purely mechanical, using wheels and punched cards, but Babbage had in effect described the digital computer. Unfortunately, the actual construction of such "engines" had been beyond the state of mid–nineteenth century engineering art. None had ever been built.

A ball of ice formed in the pit of her stomach. She turned and stared at the darkness where the machines sat. None had ever been built. . . .

She carried the folder to the table and flipped through it. There were page after page of mechanical drawings, with detailed specifications and callouts. A Rube Goldberg nightmare. Definitely the machine on the table, though. More pages, of handwritten work instructions in ornate Spencerian script.

It was too much to look at here in the darkness. She decided to take it home with her; but just as she was closing the folder, a note caught her eye. It was written sideways in the margin of one of the drawings:

Discussed possible electrification with Brother Thomas while in Menlo Park. Not presently feasible. B. Quinn. 21 July 1881.

She arched her eyebrows in surprise. B. Quinn. Brady Quinn? Well, well. Had Carson been more than the buyer of Quinn's house? Had he and Quinn been business associates?

And associates of Edison, as well. At least, she knew of no other Thomas in Menlo Park in 1881 with whom one would discuss "electrification."

Now we're onto something, she thought. "Brady Quinn Place" was sounding better and better. Quinn was a local figure. He knew Edison on a first-name basis and was apparently involved somehow with the world's first computers.

This could be *big!* The dust on the floor and tables was thick. No one had been in the room in years. In decades. *No one else knows about these machines,* she thought. *And when I buy the building, the machines will be mine, too.*

Her flashlight dimmed and she smacked it again. This time it did not brighten. Not liking the idea of finding her way back down in the dark, she closed both folders and tucked them under her arm. *I'll come back later, with better light.*

At the door, she paused for one last look and played the light over the black, shadowy mechanisms. The world's first computers. Yet here they sat, long abandoned and forgotten. Odd. With an invention like that, they should have made history.

When she returned the flashlight, Abbot noticed the folders and smirked. "Lootin', hunh? Why'n'cha take some of the copper and brass off'n the stampin' presses? They sell for a good piece of cash down t' the scrap yard."

Sarah reminded herself that Abbot had never been up the hidden stairwell. She hoped he would not wonder where she had found file cabinets. Best if he worried about something else. "Does Widener know you're stealing his property and selling it?"

"Widener? Hell, he ain't never set foot in the place. Me and Babs, that's the daytime forelady, we got a good thing goin'. None of the feebs can climb stairs, so they don't even know what a bonanza is up there. An' you ain't gonna tell, lady, 'cause then I'll say how you walked off with some stuff yourself." He leaned back in his chair and folded his arms smugly.

She smiled tolerantly. "I'm afraid you've got me."

"Damned right." He nodded vigorously. "You ain't no better'n Babs and me. I—" His eyes dropped to her ankle. "Hey! You hurt yourself up there? You OK?"

"Well . . ."

" 'Cause I tolja it was dangerous up there. I offered to come wit' ya, but you insisted to go alone. You ain't gonna sue or nothin', are you?" The toothpick in his mouth danced nervously from side to side.

For one brief moment she had thought his concern had been for her. In a way, it was nice to know his self-absorption was universal. A burst of altruism would have been a flaw in his otherwise seamless character.

"No," she told him. "I ain't gonna sue or nothin'." The last thing she wanted was a troop of lawyers and claims investigators wandering around upstairs.

The sun had set by the time she left the building, and the street outside was black. The street lamps created oases of light at the corner with Wynkoop. Otherwise, it was pitch-dark, not unlike the room on the fourth floor. Suddenly she wished she had parked closer.

She walked briskly toward the corner and the Post Office Annex. Once again she thought she could hear ghost footsteps behind her.

It's only a trick of acoustics, she told herself. *No one's following me.* Years of rational training insisted on that, but millennia of instinct won. She quickened her footsteps.

Just as she turned the corner, one of the big loading dock doors on the Postal Annex rolled up with a metallic clangor that made her jump. A gang of mail handlers began moving large postal bags onto the dock. They were laughing and talking. The footsteps behind her—if they really were footsteps—stopped.

She looked at the mail handlers and recognized their supervisor. She had met him at a party once, during her newspapering days. He was the brother of one of the other reporters. He had taken her for a ride on his Suzuki. What was his name?

"Hey, Pat!" she called, suddenly remembering. "Still riding that bike of yours?"

Pat turned, surprised. "Who . . . ? Oh." He snapped his fingers. "Wait; don't tell me. Sue . . . no. Sarah, right? Yeah, Kevin told me you quit the paper. Went into real estate or something."

"That's right. I was inspecting a property around the corner." She looked back into the darkness of Fifteenth Street. "I may be wrong, but I think someone was following me. Could you hang around and watch until I get into my car? I'm parked right over there."

"Sure. No problem."

It was irrational, she knew; but she felt relieved. Someone who knew her knew she had been there. The other men were waiting, not really interested; but they would remember, too.

The first thing she did when she got in the car was lock

the doors. Then she took a deep breath. *And what if he's already in the car?* She jerked around and looked in the backseat.

It was empty. Sarah let out her breath, feeling monumentally foolish. She laid her head on the backrest, eyes closed. *I'm spooked,* she thought. The desolate air on the top floor of the Widener Building. The emptiness of the street under the viaduct. Too many late-night movies. There probably hadn't been anyone following her at all.

She sat up, started the car, and put it in gear. Unbidden, the thought arose: *I wonder if it was the man from the library.*

V

In the morning, she drank her breakfast of black coffee. The coffee was strong and hot, and by the time she had finished half a cup she had convinced herself that the man in the library was simply a nosy and offensive person and no one had been following her under the viaduct.

She laid the folders she had taken from the file cabinet on the kitchen table and skimmed through them while the caffeine did its work. She spared only a glance or two for the "Index," with its incomprehensible titles, noting only some of the dates and names. It was the manual for the Babbage machines that really interested her.

She didn't know enough about mechanical engineering to decipher the drawings, but the intended function of the machine was clear from the write-ups. It was definitely a mechanical computer, and it looked just like the three that she had seen in the room atop the Widener Building. Brady Quinn had jotted several amendments and marginal notes in the instructions. So had Randall Carson and a man named Dayton Black.

The excitement grew in her. This was a discovery of tremendous historical importance! It was a chance for her to be remembered for something significant, to be more than Sarah Beaumont, upwardly mobile developer and ex-reporter.

She took the folder to her computer terminal and shooed Fee off the desk. There she found a pad of paper and a pen and made a list of the names and key words. Brady Quinn. Randall Carson. Dayton Black. Babbage engines. Isaac Shelton. Thomas Edison. Charles Babbage. Jedediah Crawford. But she paused before logging onto her ISP.

I shouldn't be spending so much time on this. The name of her development was surely its least important feature. There was a development near Indianapolis named Chigger Hollow, so names were not the be-all and end-all. She had already spent an entire week researching Quinn. *I really should be costing the renovations on the Emerson Street house,* she thought, *not meandering through the Net.* There was a kilotonne of work to do. She had to PERT out the schedules. Talk to contractors. Get things moving. The Quinn business had waited a hundred years. It could wait a while longer.

So let the computer do the heavy lifting. She would handcraft an autonomous, semiintelligent search engine—a spyder—that could seine the Internet. Not only indexed Web sites and news groups, but archives and databases. But since she wanted an intelligent search, not simply a dump of every site and archive that mentioned, say, Thomas Edison, the spyder would have to search "in context." She called up a template she had used before, but she disabled its ring of password "skeleton keys." She was hacking, not cracking. She would let the "spyder" run free for a couple of days to find, compile, and sort the information; then she could look over the harvest to see what needed more than a semi-intelligent search.

She flexed her fingers and ran a keyboard arpeggio, like a pianist about to play. Friends sometimes asked her why, with her obvious skills, she hadn't become a programmer. Computers were useful tools, she told them, but she didn't want to be a toolmaker. That response had shocked some of her "propeller-head" friends. They had never thought of themselves in so prosaic a fashion.

For the next few days Sarah sweated over her project, putting in bids on a half-dozen properties in the area, spacing them so that no one else could develop the area without her cooperation. She routed the deals through a complex arrangement of dummies and fronts. There was no way to conceal the volume of activity, but she didn't want anyone to know yet that she was the one behind it all.

She priced the renovations through several contractors she knew, keeping the discussions tentative and basing her estimates on the house she and Dennis had inspected. She was experienced enough to realize that lowest *cost* did not always mean the lowest *price*. She made a note to meet with Dennis and firm up the details on the proposed renovations.

She also put in a bid on the Widener Building. It hadn't been on the market, but every property had its price. If you made the right offer.

It was not until noon on Friday that she came up for air. She closed her real estate files and put a ragtime disk on the CD player. She went to the kitchen and made herself some coffee and, when she returned to the terminal, called in her spyder. Time to see what it had learned about Quinn and the Babbage engines. She had told Dennis about the strange primitive computers and he had been quite pleased with himself. His intuition had been vindicated. Brady Quinn Place, named after a man involved with the world's forgotten first computer, made perfect sense for a project that treated information as a utility and data ports as essential as water taps and electrical outlets.

The disk began playing "Creole Belles" while she scrolled through the spyder's harvest. She hummed along with it. "My Creole belle, I know her well . . ."

Naturally, there was a mass of information on both Edison and Babbage. They were famous historical figures. But there was nothing that connected them with Quinn or Carson or the machines on the hidden fourth floor. She did learn that Thomas Edison used to meet regularly with Henry Ford, Harvey Firestone, and John Burroughs "to discuss the direction of the country." They went on nature hikes in Ford's private preserve in Michigan. Well, businessmen were always grouching how the country was going to hell in a handbasket. Burroughs, she found when she had looked him up, was a naturalist. One of the first ecologists.

"That explains the nature hikes, then," she said aloud. She laughed at the thought of three tycoons of industry slogging through the fields looking at mushrooms and butterflies. The idea that Henry Ford "stopped to smell the roses" bordered on the ludicrous.

As for Babbage, he had popularized the concept of life insurance, a business based on the notion that unpredictable events can form predictable patterns. In 1832 he wrote *On the Economy of Machinery and Manufactures,* anticipating much of what was now called operations research and systems analysis. He actually started work on a "difference engine," a prototype of his proposed mechanical computer. But, after spending £23,000, including £6,000 of his own money, he had abandoned the project incomplete. Sarah smiled a little to herself when she read that.

There was also a note in the 1833 *Proceedings of the New York Academy of Sciences* announcing an open meeting to discuss the importance of Babbage's theories, with a view to forming a Babbage Society to propagate them. The note had been placed by Jedediah Crawford, whom she remembered as the author of the earliest paper listed in the Index she had found. The spyder identified him as Professor of Mathematics at Yale in the 1820s and '30s. Had he actually formed his Society? It fit. Such a society would surely try to build Babbage engines. But how would calculating engines built by a Yale professor wind up in a half-abandoned building under a Denver viaduct?

Her spyder had found no other references in the Net to a "Babbage Society," but many databases were not yet in the Net; a great many older documents had not even been imaged. She ought to dig into some off-line material and see what she could turn up.

She sat for a minute, tapping her fingers on the desktop in time to Botsford's 1908 "Black and White Rag." She really ought to get back on the Emerson Street project, but it was already three o'clock on a Friday afternoon. She did have some business to conduct at the City and County Building and, while she could do it by phone and modem, driving downtown would give her an excuse to drop in at the newspaper and at the library. She fought the temptation, not too doggedly, then gave in. Digging after Quinn and the Babbage Society was just too much fun. She picked up the phone and made an appointment to see the County Assesor that afternoon.

She didn't expect to find anything about the Babbage Society in the *News* morgue and she wasn't disappointed. The *News,* after all, had not started publication until 1859. She told Morgan what she was looking for but not exactly why, just that it was about "early computers." He promised he would ask around for her. He had a friend on the *New York Times.* The *Times* was not much older than the *News* but, being in the East, would more likely have picked up stories about Crawford's Society.

Afterward, she checked deeds and titles on Emerson Street in the Assessor's office. When she left the City and County Building, she decided to cut across Civic Center Park to the library. She jaywalked across Bannock to the park and walked slowly through the afternoon crowds. There were young people lounging around the park. Some were loafing on the steps of the Greek Theater. Frisbees leaped from the crowd like locusts from a meadow.

She remembered the mathematical titles in the Index— some, she now realized, dealing with operations research, another tie to Babbage—and the drawings in the Babbage engine manual. *I'll need advice,* she thought. *A mechanical engineer, at least. And a mathematician. Maybe a historian, as well.* She hated the idea of sharing her discovery. The experts would take over and she would be politely ushered aside. *Thank you, Ms. Beaumont, but we'll take it from here.*

She had gone it alone her whole life, asking help from no one. The thought of being excluded disturbed her. It wasn't just that the publicity over the discovered machines would help sales at Brady Quinn Place. That would happen whether she were personally involved in the investigation or not. But, dammit, that wasn't the point! She *wanted* to be part of it! She wanted to be known as the discoverer.

She was passing the Greek Theater when her right heel caught on a crack in the paving and she stumbled. Something whined and hit the stone column next to her and rock fragments stung her cheek.

"Hey! What the hell do you think you're doing?"

She turned at the sound of the voice. A big, burly man wearing an unbuttoned sport shirt was stalking across the park, hollering. Beyond him, she could see a park policeman reaching for his holster. Some of the kids were turning to look.

What was going on? She turned her head. There was a white man on the other side of the reflecting pool holding a pistol. Two-handed stance. Feet spread wide. The gun was pointed at her. *The gun was pointed at her!*

She didn't stop to think. Reflexes took over. She ducked between two pillars of the Greek Theater and dropped flat to the ground on the other side. *This isn't happening!* There was another spat and whine as a bullet ricocheted off the stone. People were screaming. Heart pounding, she crawled to the end of the templelike colonnade. Dare she peek? He might be waiting for her to poke her head out. But he might already be running toward her position! Hide or run? She had to know. Cautiously she peered around the end of the colonnade.

She saw the man with the gun turn and fire at the big man who was bearing down on him. The bullet took the big man through the open mouth, and the back of his head exploded in a shower of flesh, blood, and bone. The impact flipped the man over backward and he lay sprawled, eyes staring at the sky overhead.

People were screaming and running in all directions. The gunman turned and looked at Sarah. He brought his gun up. Gun drawn and pointed, the park policeman shouted an order. The gunman turned, lightning quick, and fired. The policeman staggered back, squeezing off two fast shots as he did so. The gunman spun and crumpled and the policeman dropped to his knees, holding his stomach with a stunned look on his face.

There were sirens in the distance, growing louder.

Holding to the stone pillar for support, Sarah stood and surveyed the park. There was a confusion of people. Some were still running; others had stopped. A woman was holding the body of the big man, wailing and pressing him to her. He had probably saved her life by distracting the gunman, Sarah thought. What had possessed him to charge an armed man like that?

The gunman himself lay still. A young man walked up to him and stared at the body. A blue-and-white bird flapped down from the sky, cocked its head left, then right, then pecked at the dead man's face.

Sourness rose in her throat. She turned aside and retched. It was a great, heaving, stomach-twisting convulsion. When she had finished, she fished in her briefcase for a handkerchief and wiped her mouth. There was blood on the handkerchief from her cheek, where the stone fragments had struck.

The tableau in the park seemed distant, as if seen through a telescope the wrong way. The sounds were muted. She turned her back on it and began walking numbly down Fourteenth Street. In a walled-off corner of her mind she knew she should stay and wait for the police. *You're in shock,* the voice said. *You're not yourself.*

She'd crossed Cherokee and was passing behind the Mint when a car pulled up and braked sharply next to her. Sarah spun, her whole body tensed, and her heart skipped a beat.

Morgan rolled down his window. "Quick," he said. "Jump in."

She stared at him, then walked obediently around his car and slid into the passenger seat. Morgan drove an old Chevy of indeterminate year and color. She slammed the door closed and hunched over in the seat, hugging herself.

Morgan shook her shoulder. "Take your jacket off. And the big red bow."

"What . . . ?"

"Just do it." He put the car into gear without waiting to see if she was complying. Dumbly she shrugged out of her suit and loosened the bow. The bow was the color of arterial blood. She began shaking.

Morgan shoved a clipboard at her. "Put the sunglasses on and stick the pencil behind your ear. Try not to look like a well-dressed black businesswoman."

She looked at him. "Why . . . ?"

"Because that's what came over the police radio. Some maniac was taking potshots at people in the park, and the description of one of the targets sounded a lot like someone who had just been in to see me."

Fourteenth Street was one-way eastbound. Sarah saw that they were headed back toward the Civic Center. She felt her stomach tighten and she began to shake her head.

"I figured you'd be in no kind of shape, so I came looking."

"Uh, thanks."

"Sure thing."

The police had erected a barricade and were waving all the traffic onto Bannock. Morgan grunted and turned. He rolled down the window and called to one of the officers, "What's going on?" Sarah turned her face away. She could feel the bleeding starting again on her cheek.

"There's been a shooting in the park, sir," the officer answered.

"Anyone hurt?"

"I couldn't say."

"The *News* have anyone there?"

"Yes, sir. A reporter and photographer just arrived."

"OK. Thanks." Morgan rolled the window up and continued down Bannock.

"You didn't tell him who I was."

"He didn't ask."

"They're looking for me."

"Then they'll find you, but tomorrow is soon enough for that."

"Morgan, why did *you* come looking for me?"

He turned his head and smiled at her. "To get the scoop, of course. A firsthand, eyewitness account of the biggest story this year."

"A scoop. Is that all?"

This time he wouldn't look at her. "Sure. What else is there?"

"Morgan, what would you have done if the policeman had said that no one from the *News* was there?"

"Why, I'd've stuck a press card in my hat and you and me'd go cover the story together. Just like old times."

"Morgan, if we'd have gone in there, someone would have recognized me!"

He looked at her, his mouth agape. "Really? I thought all you people looked alike!"

She couldn't help herself. It took her back to their first reporting days together, when they used to ride each other unmercifully. The "Black and White Rag." She started to laugh, but the laughter turned to tears.

Morgan Grimes's apartment on Capitol Hill was in a rambling old apartment building that had gone condo back in the seventies. He took her through a side entrance, three flights up, and down the hall. It was like the inside of a maze. He let her inside his apartment and locked the door behind them.

Sarah stumbled to the sofa and sat down. She stared at the wall. Long, thin Japanese prints hung there. Chrysanthemums and pagodas. Mountains loomed out of misty cloud banks. Faerie waterfalls plunged over steep cliffs. Her tears blurred the pictures, adding realism to the waterfalls.

Suddenly there was a glass in front of her. Morgan was pressing a drink on her. She took it and drank it without tasting anything. She shoved the empty glass back into his hands.

"Another one?" he asked.

"Yes. Please."

"Want to talk about it?" He wandered over to his bar and poured something amber straight out of a bottle.

"Yes. No. Not yet. I'm still shaky. Morgan, that man was trying to kill me."

"I heard on the police radio he shot four people. One dead. One serious. Two slightly wounded. You were just there at the wrong time. You're OK now."

"No, dammit! He was shooting at *me!* The others, they were just bystanders."

"I know it probably seemed that way, but—"

"Morgan, I *know*. He looked straight at me." She thought back, remembering. Every word, every gesture, was etched in her memory. "He looked straight at me. God help me, he smiled."

"A maniac."

She remembered how the first bullet had struck the stone column next to her. Inches away. If she hadn't stumbled, she'd be dead now, her skull blown apart. One moment: the smell of the grass and the trees, the cries of children playing, the shining gold of the Capitol dome at the far end of the Civic Center; the next moment, nothing, not even blackness. She began to shiver. Morgan handed her a refill and she gulped it down.

A time went by when she did not think.

"Here," said Morgan. When she turned, he was holding out a long flannel bathrobe, blue-and-white plaid. "You threw up. Go in my bedroom and get out of those clothes. I'll take them downstairs to the laundry room. Then I'll take care of that cheek. There's iodine in the medicine cabinet."

She did as he said. After she had handed him her soiled

clothing she sat on the edge of the bed, her arms wrapped tightly around herself, and waited. When he returned from the laundry, she stood up and went to him. "Hold me, Morgan," she said.

"Sarah, I don't think . . ."

"Hold me," she repeated. When she spread her arms to him, the robe fell open, but she didn't care. It didn't matter what he saw. Nothing mattered except being alive.

Morgan's ears burned a bright red. "I never thought I'd hear myself say this, but . . ." He reached out and pulled the folds of the robe together. "Look, Sarah; this isn't you talking. Another day, if you're still willing, God knows I'll be more than willing; but not now, not tonight. I've got my standards, low as they might be."

"Morgan." She wrapped her arms around him. "I'm shaking so bad I need to hold onto something solid. Just that. Nothing more."

Awkwardly he returned her embrace, and she felt herself relax at last. Safe. The drinks were catching up with her. She willed sleep to come and, with it, forgetfulness.

VI

In the morning Sarah awoke in a strange bed. There was a moment of disorientation and her eyes searched the walls, finding nothing familiar. She sat up and noticed she was wearing a strange bathrobe and her clothing was hung carefully on the back of the bedroom door. *Where . . . ?*

Then she remembered. The Civic Center. The shootings. But already yesterday's events seemed remote. Something seen on the TV news. Film at ten. A self-defense mechanism, she decided. The mind distanced itself from the horror or went mad.

She rose and dressed mechanically as she remembered. Morgan holding her. She kissing him. He, after a moment, kissing her back. Sarah couldn't decide how she felt about that. She couldn't decide if she had feelings.

Morgan was asleep on the recliner in the living room, twisted into an uncomfortable-looking position and his clothing all wrinkled. Sarah shook her head. He liked to come on like a tough, cynical reporter, but sometimes the real Morgan Grimes showed through. She wondered why the two of them had never clicked as a news team.

In the kitchen, she hunted up some eggs, chilis, and other things and set about making *huevos rancheros*. She was shredding the Monterey Jack when he walked in. He looked at what she was doing, grunted, and walked out again. After a minute, she heard the shower start.

Later, Sarah stood by his apartment window and gazed out at the Rockies, miles away, dimly visible through the haze, aloof and majestic. There were places there, not too far away, where a woman could be alone, with no other humans within miles. With a shiver, she remembered staring out the window of the house on Emerson Street not quite two weeks ago at much the same scene. It had even been the same time of day and not too far from where she stood now. Yet that had been another Sarah, another life; and she thought it was odd to remember something that had happened to someone else. She wondered if everyone who faced death felt the same way: reborn through some terrible baptism of blood.

She turned and faced Morgan, who was sitting in his recliner, a steno pad balanced on his knee. "Do they know who it was yet?"

He shook his head. "I called the paper this morning. No ID on him. They're going through mug shots and showing his face on the tube. Someone will recognize him and call in. *You* don't know who he was, do you?"

"No, of couse not."

"Then, if he wasn't a madman, why was he trying to kill *you?*"

"I don't know!"

"There are only eight reasons for murder. We can go through the list, if you like."

"Only eight? I would have thought there'd be as many reasons as there are victims."

"No, it's the details, not the basic motives, that differ." He held up his fingers and counted off with his pen. "You've already ruled out homicidal mania. What about making a political statement?"

She hesitated. "A terrorist or assassin? What sort of statement would shooting me make?"

"They pick victims at random, don't they? Don't forget he shot four other people and killed one. They think the policeman will live."

"No, that was—I don't know. Window dressing. He didn't shoot at anyone else until I was behind a stone wall."

Morgan looked at her oddly, then shrugged. "All right. He was a pro and it was important that no one know you had been singled out. So, who hired him—?"

"If I knew that—"

"—And why? What about rage or revenge?"

She shook her head. "No. Revenge for what? For bringing off a sharp business deal? That doesn't make sense. Realtors don't hire hit men for things like that."

"Do evicted tenants?"

"Morgan, I've never hurt anyone that badly."

"A grudge doesn't have to be reasonable. And all it takes is one person with a grudge. OK, what about jealousy?"

"Who has time for romance? Abe and I split years ago—"

"Professional jealousy?"

"No, dammit! I get along fine with everyone."

"As far as you know, anyway. It's like revenge. Who knows what might excite someone else to jealousy? You're pretty well off. Some may resent a woman, and an attractive black one at that, being so successful. Or old friends might be jealous of your success."

Chicago's Old Town flashed through her mind. Hyde Park. Faces she had played with in childhood; faces she hadn't even thought of in too many years. Where were they now?

Still in Old Town, probably. Friends left far behind, on another planet. Did they hate her that she had left and never even looked back? "Christ, Morgan, you'll have me paranoid."

"Even paranoids have enemies."

Sudden anger swept over her like a wave on a beach and she let it break on him. "What is this, an interrogation?" She turned her back on him and stared out the window once more. But this time she saw Chicago, not Denver. She leaned her arms against the windowsill and closed her eyes.

"At least you trust me."

She faced him again. "What?"

"We were poor starving reporters together, remember? Now you're rich and I'm still poor and starving. For a while, anyway. I might be insanely jealous, for all you know; but you turned your back on me."

She smiled crookedly. "Thanks, Morgan. You're a pal. I won't do it again."

His face was serious. "I mean it. If you're right. If you're not just imagining things, *don't sit with your back to the room.* That's how they got Hickok."

"All right. I'm sorry I got mad. You're just a reporter doing your job."

He looked at her for a long moment; then his eyes dropped to his notepad. "Yeah." He tapped his notebook rhythmically with his pen. "Well, folks with an emotional reason for murder usually do it themselves; so let's concentrate on the rational reasons. To gain something you possess."

"He didn't try to rob me, Morgan; and . . . And I'm cutting him out of my will as of today." She started laughing. The first time she had laughed since the incident. Morgan frowned and started to rise from his chair, but she waved him back. "No, I'm all right. God! I can joke about it now. I just never realized there were so many goddamn reasons to kill."

Morgan smiled, without humor. "Only eight, remember? Number seven: to cover up for another crime. You're not a witness to anything, are you?"

"You've really made a science out of this, haven't you?" She held her hands up helplessly. "A detective or a reporter or a secret agent might be sniffing around the edges of some dreadful secret and not realize it, but a real estate broker?"

"You might not know that you know it."

"Morg', the only thing I've been researching lately is real estate records. Nothing important. Certainly nothing dangerous."

"Maybe you've stumbled over some high-dollar real estate swindle, but you don't know it yet. What about that Babbage Society thing you wanted me to look up for you?"

"That's just . . ." Sarah hesitated. She didn't want word of her Emerson Street project to leak out yet, least of all on the front page of the *News*. "Look; you've got to keep this under your hat for now, but I'll give you an exclusive when it breaks, OK? Swear?"

Morgan crossed his heart and held his pinkie up. "On my sister's grave." Morgan was an only child, but she told him anyway. The papers in the old house. Brady Quinn. The hundred-year-old Babbage engines. The folders she had found. He listened and made notes.

"Sounds fascinating. Hundred-year-old computers? But you're right. It doesn't sound like a reason to shoot anyone this millennium. Mind if I do a little backgrounding on the QT? You said Paul Abbot was the foreman you talked to? And Dennis French has the paper you found in the wainscoting?" He jotted down the names. "I'll go see them both later, if I have time."

"Abbot doesn't know about the Babbage engines," she warned him, "and I don't want him to know. He'd take them apart and sell them for scrap metal."

Morgan smiled at her. "I will be the soul of discretion. Maybe Abbot is afraid you'll turn him in for looting and hired a killer to silence you. OK. Eighth and final reason: to protect themselves from you."

"Self-defense? Morgan, are you nuts? I'm no threat to anyone. I don't even step on spiders."

"Maybe you should; some are poisonous. But self-defense

is like any other motive; it's in the other person's mind. You may have done something somewhere that someone somehow perceived as a threat."

"Oh, that really pins it down, Morgan! Let's go arrest the son of a bitch!"

"Sarah, I'm trying to help."

"You're trying to get a story!"

"Yeah. Right."

"Besides, why not just warn me off? Why shoot me down in broad daylight?"

"Depends on what they think you know and how they think you plan to use it."

"You've been reading too many spy thrill—" Abruptly she remembered the man in the library and her feeling later that she was being followed to and from the Widener Building. Had they been warnings? And if so, of what?

"What's wrong?" Morgan asked. He nodded when she told him. "This may be something." Then he cocked his head, as if struck by a new thought. "The man in the library," he said. "He wasn't the same one who shot at you?"

"No."

"Hmm. Then if there's a connection, it's an organization, not an individual."

"If there is. I don't know. I've never been shot at, let alone by the Klan."

"An organization." He sat back and tapped his teeth with his pen. "Tell me," he said casually. "What do you know about John Benton or Genevieve Weil?"

She shook her head. "Never heard of them."

"Daniel Kennison?"

"Just what I read in the papers. What has Kennison Demographics got to do with my being shot at?"

"Maybe nothing. Let me check things out and I'll get back to you."

She waited, but he didn't explain further. She had the distinct impression that Morgan saw a possible tie-in with a story he was working on, but he wasn't about to say what it was. He had always played his stories close to his vest, one reason that their team had been so short-lived.

He was going to check things out. She'd have to be satisfied with that.

Much later, after giving Morgan an exclusive interview, after giving the police a less-exclusive deposition, Sarah stood on the balcony of her house, perched high on the side of South Table Mountain, and stared down at the night. She swirled the brandy in her snifter from time to time. Behind her, all the house lights had been extinguished. Only the fire shed a faint red glow—accentuating the shadows, making them dance. She liked to stand alone in the night. Although sometimes the loneliness seeped into her and caused an ache somewhere at the base of her throat.

The black was seamless. Who could say where earth ended and sky began? The lights close below were laid out in geometric precision, like gems on a black velvet cloth; but farther away, urban order gave way to rural disorder, and the lights grew progressively more random, until they blended imperceptibly into the chaos of the night sky. The shopping center at Thirty-second and Youngfield might be a stellar cluster. Some of the lights moved, but were they meteors or automobile headlights? On her left, the looming mass of Lookout Mountain was a dark nebula.

She took a swallow of brandy. The police had been sympathetic. They had even understood why she hadn't come in immediately. Shock, they had said. But they hadn't bought her theory that she had been singled out, that the other victims had been camouflage. The maniac theory was too attractive, too tidy. But they hadn't looked into the man's eyes. They hadn't seen for themselves.

A knowledge had passed between the killer's eyes and her own. It was impossible to describe, but it left no doubt in her mind. It was recognition and satisfaction and anticipation all at once. Thinking back, she could see that he had been a man who enjoyed his work.

Her survival classes had saved her. She had dived behind

shelter automatically, without thinking. But even afterward, she had not resumed thinking; and that bothered her. All her life she had been *making* choices, not *taking* choices. But not yesterday. She remembered walking away in a daze, telling Morgan how she needed to hold him, offering herself to him—and her cheeks burned at the memory. She couldn't remember ever telling anyone else that. She had never needed anyone.

When you stood alone, you never had illusions about responsibility. You could never blame friends, circumstances, bad luck, anything but yourself, as so many others did. But yesterday, she had been moved by circumstances beyond her control, stunned by the surprise, the viciousness, and, most of all, the feeling of utter powerlessness.

Powerlessness. That's what sucked the heart out of anyone. Perhaps all along, other people simply had lower thresholds of psychological pain.

Introspective tonight, aren't we? A faint smile played on her lips while she watched the traffic hurtle along I-70. Folks heading for the mountains. Saturday night at the Old Dillon Inn. She thought about joining them, of jumping into her Blazer and heading for the High Country. She knew places where no one could ever find her. Places where she couldn't even find herself.

Run and hide. But running had never been her style. (*Except running from Old Town, a voice in her head reminded her.*) She wasn't helpless. She knew how to take care of herself. The streets of Chicago had been no safe haven, nor the mountains of Colorado. She was prepared now.

They won't get me the way they got Brady Quinn.

Why, what a peculiar thought that was! That had been over with for a hundred years.

She reentered the house and slid the glass door shut behind her. She had taken four steps across the firelit room when she paused. What was it? A sound? A smell? A shadow among the shifting shadows thrown by the fire? She dropped the brandy snifter and it shattered on the parquet flooring.

There's someone else in the room!

A part of her wanted to roll up into a tight ball and make the world go away. *I can't take any more of this!* But the other part was angry. I *won't* take any more of this!

Two quick strides and she was at the fireplace, with the heavy wrought-iron poker gripped tightly in her hands. She kept her back to the wall.

"It's a bad idea," said a voice in the darkness. "Standing in front of a fire like that silhouettes you." It was a man's voice.

"Who are you?"

"A friend."

"Sure. All my friends are into breaking and entering."

He turned on the table lamp and she blinked at the sudden glare. When her eyes had adjusted, she saw that he held a gun. She felt her stomach drop out of her, but she didn't move.

Then he pointed the gun straight up. The cylinder popped out and the cartridges dropped to the floor. "There," he said. "Now I'm helpless."

She looked him over. "Somehow, I doubt that."

He grinned. "I like that. You've got a sense of humor. But you've got to admit that if I were here to kill you, you'd've been dead an hour ago. So I'm not an enemy and who knows? Maybe I am a friend, after all."

She relaxed a little. He was right. He wasn't here to kill her. But she did not release her grip on the poker, nor did she leave her position by the wall.

He was a stocky man with a brush cut of red hair and short, stubby fingers. He had ruddy cheeks. He sat totally at ease on her sofa, as if he were a long-familiar neighbor. There was a smile on his face. Sarah decided from his laugh lines that he spent a lot of his time smiling.

Which proved nothing. The killer had smiled, too.

"Friends have names."

He looked at her for a long moment; then he nodded. "Call me Red," he said.

"All right, 'Red.' Let's see some identification."

He shrugged and pulled out his wallet. He flipped through the cardholder, extracted a card, and held it out to her.

"Put it on the table; then sit on your hands."

He grinned and did as he was told. Sarah stepped up and snatched the card from the coffee table. It was a photo ID card, issued by Utopian Research Associates. It gave his name as Red Malone and his occupation as Adjustor. The photograph matched. "How many different cards do you carry?" she asked.

He grinned again. "Who counts?"

She was getting tired of standing. She walked to the side of the room opposite the sofa and sat in the stuffed chair facing him. "So, tell me, Red. Old friend. Why have you broken into my home?"

"To warn you that you may be in danger."

"You're too late. I already know that." She tried to sound casual and bitter, but her heart pounded. This was someone who *knew* why she had been shot at. She would not let him leave until he had told her.

He looked sheepish. "Yes, I heard. My fault. I didn't know They had local assets, so I didn't move fast enough. Deep programming is damned hard to uncover. A phone call, a trigger phrase, instructions, and he was running the op before anyone knew it. Good news in one way, though."

"Good news . . ."

"Sure. It means that They're spread thin around here. There are better ways to take out targets than a blatant assassination. They were panicked and used the first disposable asset that was handy. It was really stupid on Their part."

"They were stupid," she repeated. "Oh, good. I feel so much better now."

"You're feeling better than he is," he pointed out.

"That was luck, pure and simple. If I hadn't hurt my ankle—"

"Panic is *always* stupid. But you can't blame Them. They were spooked. They knew you were running an op on them. They saw the signs all around, but never anything that could be traced. Then, you queried the Brady Quinn file with a traceable screen name." He wagged a finger at her. "That was careless."

"I still don't understand," she replied testily. "Who are They? What's so important about Brady Quinn?"

Red's smile faded. "Why were you poking into Brady Quinn's life?"

"Poking into . . . ? What's wrong with that? He once owned a house I just bought. My architect and I found an old newspaper clipping about his being shot, and we thought Brady Quinn Place had a nice ring to it." She almost went on to mention Quinn's connection with the Babbage engines but stopped herself. It was bad enough that Dennis and Morgan knew. She could trust them. She wasn't about to tell a total stranger about her discovery or her project.

He looked worried now. "You weren't investigating the murders of Kenny Robertson or . . . Or Alice McAuliffe?" He frowned as he spoke the last name.

"Who are they?"

He bit his lip. "There may have been a mistake."

"A mistake?" The word outraged her. "A mistake!" she cried. "Someone just tried to kill me, mister! He shot four other people and killed one just to cover it up. And you call it a *mistake?*"

He looked at her. "Mistakes needn't be trivial."

"Now I really feel great! I was almost killed, but it's OK because it was 'stupid' and it was a 'mistake.' Do you have any more good news? Are you going to tell me what's going on, or are we going to sit here and trade banalities?"

"It would be safer if we traded banalities."

"I'm not safe now!"

He pursed his lips and considered. "I can tell you a little bit. Will that satisfy you?"

"Try me."

"You're in no position to bargain. I can walk out right now, and you wouldn't be any the wiser."

"I already know you work for the CIA."

That surprised him. She could see his eyes widen for a

moment. Then they shaded over again and he grinned at her. "What makes you say that?"

"The way you talk. 'Running an op.' The assassin was an 'asset.' That's spook talk. And the guy in the park. Brain-washed and hypnotized, you said. Programmed to kill me and be thrown away. That's straight out of some old spy thriller. Now, tell me what I've gotten mixed up in. Dammit, I *deserve* to know."

Red stood suddenly and began to pace, back and forth across the room. He did not approach her, but instinctively she gripped the poker tighter. Finally, he stopped and faced her. "Look," he said. "If you really don't know what's going on, it's best if we keep it that way. If I can convince Them that you're harmless, They'll leave you alone."

"Why would anyone want to kill me? I've never hurt anyone. And why should Brady Quinn matter? He's been dead a hundred years."

He shook his head. "I shouldn't have said anything, but I thought you already knew. Damn." He resumed pacing. Sarah watched him. Back and forth. Back and forth.

"There's Us and Them," he said after a while. "Never mind who We are or who They are. They have a dirty little secret. So do We, and we both want it kept secret. They'll stop at nothing to keep it that way."

"And you?"

He stopped pacing and looked at her sadly. "We'll stop. At some things." He resumed his pacing. "About three months ago They began getting indications that someone was running . . ." He paused, looked at her, and twisted his lip in a grimace. "Someone was snooping around Their operations," he continued. "Someone very careful. Call him the Intruder. He was asking questions better left unasked. Tying together bits and pieces that should have remained uncon-nected. He was in and out of databases, accessing files that must never see the light of day. They began to get very, very nervous. Life would become very unpleasant for Them—and Us—if it ever got out."

He stood still and faced her. "Then you made a blatant

inquiry into Brady Quinn on the Internet. That was like an announcement, like you were ready to go public. So They panicked."

She was bitter. "Oh, I suppose it's my fault I was shot at. What should I do, apologize?"

He seemed not to notice her sarcasm. "It never occured to Them that you weren't who They thought you were."

"So, if They'd shot the real Intruder, They'd have been justified?"

"Justified? Whose justice? Is a cornered rat justified when it bites? If an organization perceives a threat, it tries to protect itself. It's a natural law of living systems. It doesn't matter one whit if the system is a rat, the Mafia, or the Boy Scouts."

"The Boy Scouts don't shoot their enemies," she retorted.

He jabbed a finger at her. "They would if the alternative was being lynched or getting 'disappeared'! I'm trying to tell you what's natural and you keep talking about what's moral. When I say a response is *natural,* I mean just that. I don't have to like it any better than you do. The response depends on the level of threat; that's all. And for them, the threat is deadly."

"And for you?"

He didn't answer her. When he spoke, it was almost to himself. "You can always run from a threat. Fight or flight. Sometimes that doesn't work, either." Then his eyes focused on her. "Look. None of this helps you. Just lay off Quinn. You don't *need* it for your project, do you? Drop it and what have you lost? A few hours wasted in the libraries and the databases, that's all. I'll talk to Them, tell Them you aren't the one They want."

Red knelt to pick up his bullets. He put them back in his revolver. "Do me a favor," he said. "And yourself, too. Stay far away from Brady Quinn and everything connected with him. All right? Just stick to real estate."

"That was how I started onto Quinn in the first place," she reminded him.

He looked at her bleakly, then walked to the door.

Sarah followed. "When will you tell me?"

He turned at the door. "Tell you what?"

She swallowed. "Whether They agree not to kill me. I deserve that much."

He gave her a long look. "All right," he said slowly, "but only if you promise not to hit me with that poker."

She looked down, surprised, and found she still gripped the iron poker that she had taken from the fireplace. "Fair enough," she replied. "If you agree to ring the doorbell like a civilized human being."

He grinned. "It's a date, then."

VII

After he had gone, Sarah sat at her desk, with her hands clasped in a ball on the desktop, and listened to the silence. The antique grandfather clock was a steady metronome beat in the hallway, but that only emphasized the silence. Her mother's house had always been full of sounds.

Tick. She wondered where Fee was. He was nowhere in sight. Too damned independent. That was the problem with cats. They came and went as they pleased.

Tick. Funny. She had never noticed before how *alone* she was. She could name business associates by the score, but where were her friends, her family? She had always prided herself on her independence, her self-reliance; but when had she slipped over the line from independence to loneliness?

Tick. That damned clock! She stood and strode to the entrance hallway, where she opened the front of the case and pulled the counterweight down. The clock hesitated, skipped a beat, then stopped.

Sarah closed the door and leaned her forehead against the cool glass. After a moment, she stepped back and looked at her reflection. It was her mother's face. A bit younger and more rounded than she remembered her mother, but the resemblance was there, in the eyes and chin.

She could hear the dimly remembered sounds of her mother's house: The hiss of the teakettle on the old gas range, the basso profundo rumble of her father's snores whenever he was home from the road, the gentle drone of her mother as she hummed her beloved ragtime, the screams of her brothers as they chased each other from room to room. *Why did I ever want to escape from that?*

Then the spell faded and it was only her own face in the glass and the only thing she saw in her eyes was fear.

It was past time she took hold of herself. *You're master of your own fate,* she told herself. *No one else.* She felt as if she were in the middle of a minefield. Somehow, by dumb luck, she had gotten as far as she had; but she didn't know which way to go from here. *I know too much,* she thought, *but I don't know enough.*

A little knowledge is a dangerous thing.

The cliché made her laugh, it was so literally true. And what can you do? You can't forget the little you know; you can only try to learn more. Enough to be safe.

She returned to her study and put a CD on the player, setting the volume low, loud enough to hear but not loud enough to distract. The first cut, though, was the "New Orleans Hop Scop Blues," and she almost turned around and rejected it, its melody was so unbearably sad. Then, on second thought, she let it play, because underneath the melody was that unconquerable raggy beat. "You may beat me," she muttered, "but you can't defeat me."

She sat down at her desk and pulled a notepad in front of her. Red had warned her to stay away from anything touching on Quinn, but if she stayed off the Net, how would anyone know?

She looked around the study. Light wood paneling. Cathedral ceiling. Hanging plants. How long had Red been in the house while she stood unaware on the balcony? What if his intentions had been lethal? The thought made her shiver. She would be dead now, without ever knowing why.

And that made her angry. Not the dying—that was only fear—but the not knowing.

The walls were silent; the quiet, ominous. In the background, the ragtime blues wailed. She hunched over her desk, concentrating on the pad in its pool of light from the desk lamp. *Let's take stock,* she told herself. *What is it that I know?*

At the top of the sheet she wrote: "Someone is trying to kill me," and drew a box around it. Staring at the words, she gripped her pen tightly and chewed on her lower lip. Then she took a deep breath and resumed.

Why do They want to kill me? Because They think I'm close to uncovering Their secret. *Why?* Because They think I'm the Intruder. *Why?* Because my research into Brady Quinn tied in with whatever it was the Intruder was doing. From what Red had told her, that involved the deaths of two people named Kenny Robertson and Alice McAuliffe. She drew a double-headed arrow connecting Brady Quinn with the other two names. *Why should those deaths worry Them?* Unless Robertson and McAuliffe had been two others who had been killed for stumbling on the deadly secret . . . The temptation to fire up "Old Charley," log onto the Internet, and search those names was so automatic that she had already reached for the boot-up button when she stopped herself.

Stay off-line. For now. She wrote her thoughts down in schematic fashion, using the fault tree symbols that Abe had taught her years ago. Sarah had found that diagramming her thoughts in an orderly way helped to organize her thinking. Abe had called it a fault tree, but she called it a why-why diagram, which had always annoyed him. He had scoffed at her use of the method for what he called "soft" problem solving.

Funny. She hadn't thought about Abe for a long time. What had stirred up that memory? Where was he now? Mid-level engineer somewhere. He hadn't had the drive to reach the top. Not like she had. They'd had some good times, the two of them; but in the end, he'd left and she'd never been quite sure why.

Never mind that now, she told herself. The point of this

exercise was to get at the root cause of her problem, not to reminisce pointlessly over things that didn't matter anymore.

She made a marginal note: "KR & AMcA. Find out who."

Sarah tapped her teeth with her pen. This branch seemed a dead end. Without further data, she was no closer to the root cause. Except she had a hint—only a supposition on her part, really—that she wasn't the first victim.

What about Quinn? That's what had actually triggered the attack. What had she learned that was so dangerous? A "special project" statistician for the government before and during the Civil War. Resigned abruptly afterward. Maybe Quinn had been killed because of something he knew. What had those special projects been? Something best kept quiet? Something the government wanted kept quiet even a hundred years later? She dismissed the notion. Considering the skeletons that had come jitterbugging out of the closets of recent history, what scandal from the Civil War era could be that threatening?

Besides, from the way Red had talked about Us and Them, she'd had the distinct impression that he had not been talking about the government.

If not his government work, what about Quinn's association with the Babbage Society and its curious machines? Yet that had also been long ago. How could it have anything to do with the attack on her yesterday?

Hold it. She remembered the list of horseshoe nails that Dennis had kept. There had been several murders noted on it, hadn't there? Quinn and two others. She hadn't been interested in the other names before—they'd nothing to do with her project—but now she wondered if they might not also be part of the pattern that had drawn so tightly around her. What had their names been? She wished she had kept a copy of the list. Davis something. Bellows? And Agnes, no, Agatha . . . What? Penwether. That was it, Agatha Penwether. And Ambrose Bierce. He had disappeared, but it seemed to fit in with the murders, somehow.

She wrote the names on her diagram. As she recalled, Bellows had been killed some years before Quinn. Eighteen-seventy-six? Hey! That was the year Quinn disappeared! Perhaps that was why Quinn had gone into hiding in the first place! Excited, she jotted a note on the diagram. She'd have to call Dennis and check the date. Penwether, she thought, was killed later, about 1915 or '16, and a quick check of the encyclopedia told her that Bierce had disappeared in Mexico in 1913. She made another note: "Robertson and McA: when?"

As she scanned her diagram a cold knot of dread stole over her. Jesus! Were the people after her the same ones who had killed Quinn? An organization, Morgan had suggested. Quinn had hidden himself for sixteen years, but they had found him in the end. Would she spend the rest of her life looking over her shoulder? She shivered despite the fire in the fireplace. Bellows, Quinn, Penwether, Bierce, Robertson, McAuliffe.

And how many others? *How many others?*

A new sense of urgency gripped her. What was the connection between the murders and the Babbage Society? Quinn had been a member—maybe. Had the other victims been members as well? Was someone hunting them down?

No. Quinn had gone underground, but his partner, Carson, had not. And Edison. He had been associated with them in some way. Then she remembered something that her search engine had told her. How Edison had met regularly with Ford and the others. *A cell of the Society?* No one had tried to kill them.

So, being a member of the Society was not a *sufficient* condition to become a victim. Was it a *necessary* condition? Did the victims form a subset of the Society?

She opened the center drawer of her desk and pulled out the Index folder that she had taken from the fourth-floor file cabinets. The papers of the Babbage Society? She scanned the names of authors, chewing on her pen. Jedediah Crawford, the founder. Phineas Hammondton. Isaac Shelton. Wasn't it Shelton who had gotten Quinn his job in the Interior Department? Papers written by those three bore dates in the 1830s and '40s. Charter members?

Yes, there was Brady Quinn, too. But his papers bore slightly later dates, so he was not an original member. She went through the names again, more carefully this time. There! Davis Belleau. Not Bellows, after all. His papers were also written in the 1830s and '40s—another founder. Excited now, she looked for the names of the other victims. And . . .

No, Penwether and the others were not listed. So, either they were not members of the Society or else they became members after 1892, the last year in the Index.

And there was another coincidence: Quinn was killed in 1892. Was the Widener Building abandoned at the same time? Was that, in fact, the reason that it had been abandoned?

She remembered how thick the dust in the office had been. How the machines had sat silent and rusting on their heavy, ancient tables for a hundred years. How the stairway to the fourth floor had been concealed; the machine shop below, an apparent front. How, after the brief notice of its foundation, there had been no public record of the Society.

She made another note: "Babbage Society—secret." Their offices, their Analytical Engines, even their very existence. Was that the Secret? The existence of the Babbage Society? But what difference could that make today?

Unless They were the Babbage Society, still secret, still deathly afraid of losing that secrecy.

But that only pushed the question further back. Why had the Society kept itself secret?

She cupped her chin in her hands and stared at the wall. Such a long trail of death. And there was no reason to suppose she had all the names. How many of the other authors in the Index had met untimely ends? Something else to check up on.

Absently she chewed on the end of her pen. But what about Randall Carson, who was Quinn's associate? Carson had *not* gone into hiding.

They didn't know about Carson. Could that be it? She scanned the Index again, looking for Carson's name. She didn't know exactly what she expected to find. Some pattern.

Something *different* about Randall Carson. A special cause, Abe had once told her, always produces a special pattern in the data.

Carefully she went back through the Index and made a list of names and dates. Randall Carson did not appear until after 1867, when Quinn came west. In fact, except for Quinn himself, none of the authors before 1867 appeared after, and vice versa. Two disjoint sets. . . .

Wait a minute. She took the pen from her mouth and stared into space. Us and Them, Red had told her. Two groups with the same secret. Two disjoint sets. What if the Society had split and one faction had gone after the other?

Sure! Quinn had broken with the Society in 1867 when he came west. Started his own rival society. That's why the authors on the postbellum papers were all different.

Great. But when a professional society splits, they usually don't go gunning after each other.

Unless one faction is afraid the other will spill the Secret.

The picture was becoming clearer: Quinn works in the Interior Department as a "mole" for the Babbage Society, Lord knows why. At the end of the Civil War, he quits abruptly, goes west, and starts his own group. Then Belleau is killed—and maybe others, too. Quinn goes underground and becomes a hunted man. The Widener Building offices were Quinn's, hidden for the same reason as the man himself. Carson, a man unknown to the others, is the front man. But then Quinn is killed and they close up shop.

Then she recalled how the file cabinets had been emptied, apparently in haste. The doorway, boarded up. *Maybe they didn't close up. Maybe they just moved elsewhere.*

A thrill ran through her limbs. She was so elated that it took her a moment to realize that she had still not discovered the root cause. She was still looking at symptoms. What had set the whole thing in motion? What was the Secret?

The Society had built mechanical computers. Babbage engines.

Why keep the machines secret? Especially in such a technophillic era as the Victorian Age? Babbage had actually begun construction of one but had given it up as impractical. (Or had he?)

Answer: it wasn't the machines themselves but the way they used them.

To do academic research. Why keep that secret?

It was getting late. Her notepad was filling up with ideas and questions and speculations. Yawning, she flipped the sheet over and started a fresh page. Red had implied a great public outrage, government action; so it wasn't your ordinary, garden-variety secret.

Answer: not the research per se but the purpose of the research demanded secrecy.

Question: what purpose?

Answer: where did the list of trigger events fit in?

That wasn't an answer. That was another question. Was there a connection between the "horseshoe nails" on the list and the researches of the Babbage Society? Quinn appeared on both, but was there a deeper connection? She wrote: "Call Dennis" on her pad and underlined it three times.

She read through the Index once more, this time studying the titles rather than the authors and dates, searching for some sense of their intentions. Most of the titles sounded like gibberish. There were frequent references to "yokes" and "ideons." "On the Effects of the Deletion of 'Stovepipe' from the Fifteenth Yoke." That was one of Quinn's, 1864. "Reinforcement of the Ideon Complex Relative to Incandescent Lighting." Carson, 1871. She looked up *ideon* in the dictionary but found nothing.

On the second page, she found a paper by Phineas Hammondton titled "A Cliological Analysis of Outlandish Settlements." *Cliology* meant a "science of history," according to the professor Dennis had spoken with.

Answer: they were using Babbage's embryonic systems analysis to study history.

That made sense. But still, why the secrecy? Sure, looking for scientific laws at work in history would have been controversial. Look at the fuss people had made over Darwin! But the Victorians had prided themselves on being "scientific."They wouldn't have reacted any worse to the notion of a cultural science than they had to that of a biological science.

Patiently she continued to read. Something would click. The titles couched in mathematical jargon she ignored. There was no chance that she would understand their meaning. But scattered among them were a few titles in plain English. Or masquerading as plain English. "The Impact of Zoöpraxiscopy on Live Theatre," 1879. "Rate of Change of the Powers Accorded the General Gov. vis-à-vis the Sev'ral States & Its Significance Regarding the 15th and 23d Yokes," Meechum Clark, 1836. "Dates of Incorporation for the Various Mexican Territories," Crawford, 1834. "Effect of Wireless Telegraphy on the Propagation of Ideons," Shelton, 1847. "A Geological Appreciation of the Sierra Country and Its Likely Effect on the Peopling of the Californias," J. C. Frèmont, 1841. "Speculations, Stemming from John Hyatt's Artificial Billiard Balls, on the Non-Chemical Nature of the Ultimate Explosive," Carson, 1871. "Ideons Required for the Encouragement of Aerial Flight," 1862. "On the Replacement of Rail Roads by Autonomously Directed Vehicles." "Expected Results of the General European War, ca. 1910–1915." That one, by a man named F. P. Hatch, was written in 1882. "The Desirability of the Third Sub-branch off the 35th Yoke and the Ideons Required for Its Realization," 1853.

An uneasy feeling stole over her as she read. There was something peculiar about some of those titles. Some of them were written long before the events they appeared to describe. *Well, it's a science's business to predict, isn't it?* And if they had been studying history scientifically . . . Yet another tone rang through. Something in the choice of words. Something her literary ear picked out. The anticipation of action, not simply of observation.

They weren't scientists. They were engineers.

The thought rose unbidden in her mind, and it was a moment or two before she realized what it meant. When she did, the implication stunned her. They hadn't been trying to study history at all; they had been trying to control it!

She dropped the Index folder to the desk and stared into space, her mouth slightly parted. *Could that be it?* Had the Babbage Society been trying to manipulate the course of history? That list Dennis had taken. Horseshoe nails . . . Turning points, when the actions of a handful of people had had disproportionate consequences. And some shadowy individuals with great clunking computers had identified those turning points and turned them the way they wanted.

That would certainly explain Their fear of discovery. Slavery, exploitation, wars, recessions. Lincoln's assassination, for God's sake! She remembered that from the list. Today, everyone was a "victim." If people discovered that a specific group was somehow responsible for all their woes . . . Oh, yes. The nearest lamppost would not be near enough.

She remembered all the things she had longed to forget. All the symbols of failure. How hard it had been for her father to find jobs; how the real estate agent had steered them away from certain neighborhoods, forcing them to live among the drug addicts and the gangs that had finally swallowed her baby brother; how her mother had died all too young because she couldn't afford the medicine she needed. Sarah clenched her teeth. So, They feared lynching, did They? Well, she might just give a hand with the rope herself.

But, on the other hand, if They were directing history, why not credit Them with the good as well? The inventions that made life easier; the liberation movements of the last few decades; child labor laws, Social Security, the safety net of laws and regulations that protected the helpless from at least the worst exploitations.

No, it was all too absurd. History was too complex to master.

But was it too complex to *try* to master? And trying, with a secretly suppressed scientific breakthrough, might they not have succeeded *at least a little?* And having succeeded just a little, might they not have killed to protect the secret of that success? Or perhaps, as likely, to cover up colossal blunders. It made awful, terrifying sense.

So, I'm master of my own fate, am I? she thought bitterly.

Not when Crawford, Quinn, and others had scripted things out a hundred and fifty years ago. What a grand illusion! A charade. A Potemkin village. History was folktales, its heroes and heroines capering fools.

Slavery, only with the masters artfully concealed, safe from their slaves' righteous wrath. The past was suddenly askew, and nothing meant what it seemed to mean. It was as if her mother's face had slipped just a bit, showing itself to be a mask, and behind the loved and familiar features was a stranger.

She sat in the dimly lit study, in the pool of light cast by her desk lamp, and shivered while the dying flames in the fireplace cast jeering ghosts upon the walls. In her ears, the cheerful rag "War Clouds" was a mockery. She had never felt more alone.

VIII

Sarah awoke with a start the next morning, slumped over her desk. Her neck and arms were stiff. She had vague recollections of a nightmare, now thankfully forgotten. *I must have fallen asleep at the terminal last night. How late did I work?* She stretched and pushed herself out of the chair. Stumbling to the window, she pulled the curtains open and blinked at the morning sun.

She found her way to the kitchen and turned the coffee on, staring at it numbly until it had started to perk. On her way to the front door, she noticed that the grandfather clock was stopped. *Must've forgotten to wind it.* She yawned and opened the front door and stooped and picked up the morning *News.*

As she did so, she remembered that she had stopped the clock herself and that she had spent hours thinking over what she knew about Quinn and that she had reached a frightening conclusion and that someone was trying to kill her.

The nightmare returned. She stepped back and slammed

the door and leaned against the wall, breathing fast. *Damn! That was careless, Sarah.* There could have been a sniper out there, waiting for her to grab her paper. She remembered opening the curtains. She had stood directly in front of the window, in plain view.

She peered through the peephole in her door and stared at the driveway. Nothing she could see. The ornamental bushes that lined the walk now seemed sinister places of concealment; a squadron of assassins could be hiding among them.

She closed her eyes and let her breath out slowly. Then she sidled back to the window and, back against the wall, drew the curtains, throwing the room into darkness.

Returning to the kitchen, she threw the paper down on the table and tried to pour herself a cup of coffee. Her hand wobbled and the first drops hit the saucer. *Calm yourself, Sarah,* she chided herself. *Panic is always stupid.* She waited a moment, breathing evenly, then filled the cup. Then she sat and deliberately forced herself to review her situation.

Red had warned her to sit tight and he would fix things. But who was Red, that she should put her faith in him? He hadn't killed her and he had certainly had the means and the opportunity. But that was hardly a basis for trust and friendship. *Have you met my good friend Red Malone? He didn't kill me when he had the chance.*

And yet, what else could she do but sit tight? Should she try calling Dennis again? There had been no answer last night. He and Jeremy often went to the theater on Saturday nights. Dennis distrusted gadgets like answering machines and the phone had rung and rung, until she had finally hung up in frustration.

Now, in the morning's light, it seemed less a good idea. As gadget-averse as he was, Dennis would not have gone trolling on the Net. If so, the killers would not know that he knew anything. If she called to warn him and the Babbage people were tapping her phone (and that seemed an elementary conclusion), it would endanger him.

Morgan!

She had gone to see Morgan on Friday, before the incident

in the park, to ask for his help in locating old news items about the Babbage Society and afterward had told him about Quinn and the machines. She hadn't known then, of course, that the knowledge was dangerous or that it had anything to do with the attack in the park. He had promised to check into the Babbage Society for her. He was going to ask questions. He would have no idea what he was walking into. She had to warn him!

She was punching up the city room at the *News* when the incoming line rang. She hesitated, unsure whether to answer. Then she thought it might be Malone or Dennis and clicked the phone hook once to switch lines.

"Yes?"

"Sarah! Thank God!"

"Morgan? I was just going to call you. I—"

"Never mind that. I'll be out there in two shakes. You're in worse danger than I ever thought. Don't go anywhere. Don't open the door for anyone until I get there."

"Morgan, what's the matter with you? I've never heard you sound so—"

The line went dead. A moment later, the dial tone sounded in her ear. She hooked the phone. Then she laughed. She had tried to call Morgan to warn him, and he had called her to warn her! That was priceless.

She returned to the kitchen table and picked up her coffee cup. Her gaze rested on the newspaper. Giant block letters on the front page shrieked her name; a sidebar promised "an exclusive interview" by Morgan Grimes; but she had no desire to relive those events, so she flipped open to the inside pages. She hardly glanced at the stories. How much of the day's news, she wondered, had been engineered by Them?

She felt almost lighthearted. Morgan was coming. It would be good to have him with her. She was still frightened, but the load was not so heavy now. She was not alone.

At first, the headline on page 7 did not register: COUPLE SLAIN IN LOVE TRIANGLE. That sort of thing happened somewhere every day. A man named Joseph Dawson had trailed his wife, Barbara, to a West Colfax motel. There he had shot her and her lover, Paul Abbot, before turning the gun on himself. Sex and violence. The kind of lurid scandal that would grace the front page of a New York tabloid.

But , . . Paul Abbot? The foreman at Widener's? She set her cup down shakily and reread the story. A sordid affair, like hundreds of others. Adultery. Jealousy. Rage. Murder and suicide.

And she didn't believe it for a moment.

Poor Babs, she thought. And her poor husband. She even found a shred of sympathy for Paul Abbot. He had been an odious lecher, but he had been a human being. He hadn't deserved what had happened to him. She wondered if They had manuevered Dawson into doing the deed or whether They had simply killed all three of them and set it up to look like a sex triangle.

But why had They killed Abbot? And Barbara Dawson, the other foreman? She barely knew Abbot; and Dawson, not at all. Yet it must have something to do with the attack on her. It was too much of a coincidence. She took her coffee and ran to the computer desk, where she scrolled the police blotter.

Someone *had* been following her, after all, that day under the viaduct. She had spent a long time in the Widener Building. Had They drawn some wacky conclusion about her and Abbot? Or had They gone there Themselves and found the secret room and the Babbage engines? If so, they could be killing anyone who might know about them.

But the police blotter revealed no assault on Ernst Widener, the owner, or on any of the other employees. Nor were there any reports of burglary or vandalism at the Widener Building. Surely if They had discovered the secret room, They would not leave the machines there for others to find.

Then why kill Abbot?

They must think that she had told Abbott something. Why They would think so God alone knew. But then why the delay? She had gone to the building on Monday, and the attack hadn't been until Friday. Why hadn't They acted immediately against her and her "accomplice"?

Perhaps They hadn't been sure about her at first. After all, any casual researcher might show a passing interest in Quinn for any number of innocuous reasons. Something else must have happened in the meantime to convince Them otherwise. But what?

Her spyder! It was running in the Net, hunting for connections between Quinn, the Babbage Society, Analytical Engines, and a half-dozen other things. Oh Lord! Nosing into Brady Quinn's life wasn't motive enough. By itself, it might have made Them suspicious; but that spyder must have scared Them silly. No wonder there had been no attempt to warn her off. *Given what They thought I already knew, it was long past time for warnings.*

The spyder had been running for several days before They acted, so They hadn't noticed it right away. That meant They weren't omniscient. They made mistakes. Deadly mistakes. They might be just as uncertain of Their next step as she was!

She activated her terminal and recalled the search engine. It was much too late to matter. Red was on a fool's errand. He would never be able to convince Them of her innocence now. In fact, once Red found out about the spyder, he might begin to have doubts himself.

I know what They *do in such matters.* When in doubt, kill. *But what do Red's people do?* He hadn't actually said they wouldn't kill her. With a sudden chill, she wondered what sort of "Adjusting" Red did.

She picked up the paper again and looked at the headline: COUPLE SLAIN IN LOVE TRIANGLE. Now, it seemed, They were backtracking her activities, eliminating anyone else she may have talked to.

She stood up so suddenly that she jarred the desk, spilling the coffee. *Anyone else she might have talked to?!* There was no question now of endangering Dennis. She ran to the phone and punched his number. The phone was preprogrammed, so she only had to hit two buttons. Still, she managed to miss one in her haste. She cursed, cut the connection, and punched again.

The phone rang. "Come on," she muttered through clenched teeth. "Come on. . . ."

Jeremy answered. Dennis' friend.

"Jerry, this is Sarah. Is Dennis there? I need to talk to him right away. It's important." *I might be wrong. I probably am. I hope I am.*

"You mean you haven't heard?" Jerry answered. He sounded distraught, as if he'd been crying. That was likely; Jerry was high-strung and sensitive. "Oh, it's terrible. It's simply awful."

Her heart stopped and her hand tightened on the receiver. "What is? What happened?"

"Dennis was struck by a car last night. A hit-and-run. We were on our way home from the DCPA and . . . They took him to Porter. They were operating all night."

"Oh, no! Will he . . . Is he all right now?"

"I . . . don't know," Jerry admitted. "I've been calling and calling. Making a frightful pest of myself. They won't know until later today. They say his condition is critical. They've got nurses watching him; and he's hooked up to all sorts of equipment, so the doctors will know if there's any change."

They save people routinely now who would have been lost only a few decades ago. She was trying to reassure herself, she knew. Operations weren't miracles, and medicine was not theology. But "critical" wasn't DOA, either. There was still a chance. A good chance.

They must have more assets in place, now, she thought. A hit-and-run late at night was a lot smoother take-out than a mad gunman in the park. The police would ask fewer questions.

"Who did it, Jerry? Do they know?"

"Who? No one knows. Teeners high on mothers' tears or something. The police have a bulletin out, but they'll never catch them."

No, thought Sarah, *they never will. They won't even know to look.* The assaults on her, on Dennis, and on Paul Abbot had played to law enforcement paradigms: kook with a gun, hit-and-run, love triangle. The answers were too obvious to wonder if there was a deeper answer.

"And what damned difference would it make if they do?" Privately, Sarah agreed. But she told Jerry some banal platitudes about having hope and how Dennis would pull through and how everything would turn out for the best. She tried to sound very confident. She wasn't sure she believed it, and she didn't suppose Jerry did, either.

Ah, Dennis, she sobbed softly. If she had called last night, he might not have gone out. He might have stayed home and They would not have gotten him.

Or perhaps They would have gone to his apartment and instead of being in critical condition, Dennis would be dead, and Jeremy as well. It wasn't any use accepting the responsibility for another's act. It wasn't *her* fault that Dennis had been run over. It was Their fault. It was Their vicious, thoughtless paranoia, not her researches, nor her failure to call. And rather than sorrow, what she should feel most of all was anger.

When would Morgan get here? She looked impatiently at the clock. It was a twenty-five-minute drive from downtown to Applewood. There shouldn't be much traffic, not on a Sunday morning.

A new thought struck her with the suddenness of a slap. Morgan had said yesterday that he would call on Paul Abbot and on Dennis. Now, both had been attacked.

A cold, unreasoning fear chilled her. *No, not Morgan! It wasn't in him!*

Yet how did she know that? How close had she ever gotten to him? Never past the surface. Never past the "Hi, how are you, sure is good to see you, have you heard the latest?" She had never known Morgan Grimes, only the face that he kept for her to see. Now Morgan was on his way here. To kill her? That was crazy.

Even paranoids have enemies.

But they could never have friends. Morgan had told her not to turn her back on him. Had he been trying to warn her, despite hypnotic conditioning? In retrospect, his questions seemed more sinister. He had been pumping her to find out what she knew. She'd had the impression even then that he knew more than he was letting on.

The light was blinking on her answering machine. How long had it been like that? How long had it been since she had checked? Since yesterday? Mechanically she played it back.

It was Dennis. He wanted to know how she was. He had heard about the shooting and was concerned. For a sliver of an instant she thought she was listening to him speak in real time and almost started to answer. Then she remembered and she hit the cut off. She stared silently at the machine for a few-moments; then she rewound the tape and played the message again and then again. *Oh, Dennis, what have we stumbled into?*

The garage smelled of oil and gasoline. It was an oversize garage, and rows of bright red storage cabinets lined two walls. The old white mud-splattered Blazer sat on the far side; the Volvo closer to the door. For the next several minutes she busied herself in loading the Blazer. It felt good to be in motion, any kind of motion, even running away. Anything was better than standing still.

Down sleeping bag. It got cold at night in the High Country, even in the summer. Geological Survey maps. Compass. Kerosene lantern. Flashlight, with extra bulbs and batteries. Matches, the kind that struck anywhere. In a pinch, she could start a fire with a bow drill, but why go out of your way to make things hard on yourself? Fishing line and hooks. Wire and wire cutters. Hunting knife and strop.

She pulled the knife from its scabbard. The blade gleamed wickedly in the light of the bare bulb suspended from the garage's ceiling. The knife was perfectly balanced. It would make a complete revolution in thirty feet, a handy thing to know—as several rabbits had discovered to their sorrow.

She turned and jerked her arm and the knife planted itself in the center panel of the garage door. She grunted and recovered the blade, stuffing it into her rucksack.

In the bedroom, she changed into hiking clothes. Bush jacket. Heavy trousers to protect her legs. Sturdy boots. A change of clothing in case she got wet. She was lacing up her boots when the clock on the dresser caught her eye. Nine-fifty. Was that right? She checked her wristwatch. Yes, it was. Morgan was late.

Or was he outside, waiting for her to come out? Had his call been *intended* to panic her into running? She went to the front door and looked through the peephole again.

Still nothing. But then, what could she expect to see? A man with a rifle? They wouldn't be so clumsy this time. A second attempt on the same target in the same way would raise too many questions. Even the police might notice.

Stay put or run for it? A sitting duck or a duck on the wing?

The phone's sudden ring ran through her like an electric shock. She turned and stared at it as if it had suddenly come alive. After three rings the answering machine cut in. "Hello," she heard herself say. "I can't come to the phone right now."

She groped around under the breakfast bar and pulled out a stool. She sat on it and stared at the recorder.

"Sarah? This is Kevin, at the *News*. Call me right away. It's an emergency."

She twisted her fingers together. *Kevin?* A vague sense of foreboding stole over her. She snatched the telephone and punched up the city room.

Kevin was on the line within moments. "Sarah. I'm sorry to have to tell you this, but your old partner, Morgan Grimes, was stabbed to death in the parking lot just half an hour ago."

Morgan? Morgan couldn't possibly be dead. He was a fixture, like Mount Evans. Always there. She remembered how they had traded insults during her cub reporter days. How he had shared bylines with her. How he had taken care of her the day she had been shot at.

When she remembered how she had suspected him, her eyes burned. "God, no!" she said. "Who did it?" They were making a clean sweep of it. Morgan was dead, and it was all her fault. Once fear had seized you, you did stupid, foolish things. Evil had not done half the harm in the world as foolishness.

"A doper," said Kevin. "There was a packet of mothers' tears under his body and a thick wad of bills in his coat pocket. The police think he was scoring some dope and the deal went sour."

"Kevin, you know that isn't true!"

"Hey, I knew Morg' as well as anyone. I know that wasn't his scene. But it looks bad."

What could she tell him? That there were four easily explained assaults in the last two days that were not so easily explained? A mad sniper, a love triangle, a hit-and-run, and a dope deal. The police would make no connection. And if she told Kevin, it would only mark him as another target.

"Sarah. The reason I called . . . His last words . . . He said, 'Tell Sarah the Pulitzer isn't worth this.' " Kevin waited for her to say something. When she didn't reply, he asked, "Does that mean anything to you?"

"I—No. No, it doesn't." She thanked him for calling and hung up quickly.

She couldn't think of anything else to do, so she walked to the kitchen table and sat there. The remnants of her coffee were cold and stale. She didn't bother to clear it away. She shoved it aside and laid her head in her arms. *I never did repay him for how he helped me. Instead, I let him get killed. I could have warned him, but I was afraid. I should have known him better. I should have let myself get closer to him, back when we worked together.*

"Should have" cuts no ice. What happened to the Sarah that was in charge of herself?

She's gotten an awful fright, that's what. She found out she's not in charge, after all.

Bullshit. So the circumstances aren't the best. You can't choose your circumstances. The three billion-odd other people in the world do that for you. But you can choose how you face those circumstances.

*That's easy for you to say. A very dear friend of mine is
lying in a hospital mashed into Jell-O. Another one is in the
morgue. And I don't suppose They'll stop at one try at me,
either.*

No, I don't suppose They will. So what are you going to
do, give up? Giving up is the only solid-gold, guaranteed
way to fail. They won't have to beat you, because you'll
have already beaten yourself.

So what can I do?

Hit back!

At who, sucker? I don't even know who They are.

You don't have to know that.

She straightened. *No, I don't,* she realized. She set her jaw.
She could pay Morgan back now. It wasn't enough. It would
never be enough, but he would need a coin for the ferryman.
She went to her terminal and set to work.

IX

Sarah spent the entire day in front of the screen, compos-
ing a worm. It was rough going, even for her: a bilevel program, with the second program encrypted in the code of the
first. On the surface, it would look like normal e-mail: bill-
board chatter on the hacker network. It could boot from node
to node without arousing suspicion.

Buried deep within the harmless chatter was a cryptogram-
matic algorithm that would create a self-replicating worm.
The cryptogram was self-booting and would trigger a
second-level program embedded as an anagram in the code.
Whenever an off-line database logged on the Net, the worm
would inject a clone into the external system. Once there, it
would hunt for references to Sarah Beaumont, Dennis
French, Paul Abbot, Morgan Grimes, Brady Quinn, Charles
Babbage, and the names from the Babbage Society Index. If
it found a significant fraction of them in the files, the clone
would send word back through a complex relay of nodes,

then scramble the database. Otherwise it would erase itself. She used JUGGERNAUT for the scrambler. An old veteran of the "Core Wars," it was crude but effective; and They wouldn't be expecting it.

It might take a while, but eventually her worm would locate Their databases. An operation of that magnitude had to be on-line these days. Worlddomination.org? Sooner or later, They would log on. When They did, she would know from the bounceback who and where They were, and she would have the satisfaction of destroying Their files. The odds were against any database but Theirs containing that particular collection of names, but at the moment she didn't much care if she scrambled the telephone directory.

She was almost finished when she realized what an idiot she was. There was only one way to be safe when you knew someone's deadly secret, and she had overlooked it. Grimly she set to work adding another subprogram.

When she was done, she stretched and looked at the clock. Two in the morning? She had been at the terminal for almost sixteen hours straight. *Not even time and a half for overtime.* But she felt a satisfaction. She was fighting back. She might lose yet and still get killed, but at least she'd go down like John Henry, with a hammer in her hand. There was even something exhilarating about the thought. Sooner or later, everyone went down. What mattered was how you went: cringing like a slave or defiant like Nat Turner.

God, she was hungry. She hadn't eaten all day. Just a half-cup of coffee in the morning. She yawned and wandered into the kitchen and began to fix herself a sandwich. It was dark in the kitchen. The refrigerator cast a lonely circle of light around her. Everyone around her was being struck down. But she didn't feel helpless anymore.

"Tell Sarah the Pulitzer isn't worth this."

Morgan's last words. Suddenly, she realized what he must have meant. She remembered the day when she had visited the *News* and Morgan had been talking on the phone. (Only twelve days ago? It seemed like twelve lifetimes.) *"What're you working on, Morg'?" "The Pulitzer, of course."*

She leaned on the refrigerator door. Morgan must have meant that the knifing had to do with the story he'd been chasing. He had been trying to get a message through to the one person who would understand. Morgan had wanted her to read his story files.

She closed the refrigerator and ran to the terminal, her sandwich forgotten. She hacked into the *News* system, again using a roundabout method, and keyed in Morgan's secret code, the one she had cracked years ago. A message appeared on the screen:

Hi, Sarah. I know it's you because no one else could break this particular code. I hope you're not reading this, because . . . well, because then I never reached your house. You wouldn't hack into here just for fun. You're honest. A character defect in a reporter, but one I always liked in you.

"I liked it in you, too, Morgan," she whispered. Why was it we never told our friends these things while it mattered?

The file you want is code-named DEATH LIST. It's the story that will win me that Pulitzer, if I ever finish it. Sarah, there are a group of people in this country who make Murder, Inc., look like Mother Teresa. There's no doubt in my mind that they have arranged killings nationwide for many, many years.

Morgan had been preparing a feature story on reporters who had died in the line of duty. A suicide here, a barroom quarrel there. Car accidents. Crazed snipers in towers. The world, it seemed, was populated by innocent bystanders. But he had found odd little connections like two reporters, one in Georgia in 1943, another in Oregon in 1967, who had been working on biographies of William Harrison Hatch, a little-known statistician of the 1920s. Curious, Morgan had begun digging into other obituaries, not just reporters, and gradually unearthed other linked deaths. And there, like a nugget of silver in a vein of lead, he had found a "set of mutually interconnected killings."

Orthogonal factor analysis, Sarah remembered.

At first, Morgan thought of it as a human interest piece: the strange synergies of a small world. His "degrees of Kevin Bacon" story, he had written. Later, he began to wonder if the coincidences were more sinister. For a while, he had thought that he had found the most bizarre serial murderer yet. But the killings went on too long. No one person could have committed them all, unless he had started as a child and continued the grisly work well into old age. It had to be the work of more than one person.

An organization, he had said to her that morning in his apartment following the attack in the park.

He had followed a gossamer web of hints, remarks, half-world gossip. The trail was faint, and sometimes he lost it amid a confusing tangle of pseudonyms and anonymous phone calls. But Morgan was good at what he did. Sarah had always admired his dogged persistence and his native caution. He always found the trail again.

Eventually, it had led him to a small group of people whose sole remarkable feature was that, with few exceptions, they were unremarkable. John Benton, Genevieve Weil, Daniel Kennison, and some others. Except for Kennison, who ran a well-known polling firm, they managed to stay out of newspapers; and they appeared to have nothing to do with one another. They were so wealthy that they were never mentioned in *Forbes* or *Fortune* or *Town and Country*. It was the kind of wealth that *never* advertised itself. As Morgan's note put it: "They bought Xerox before it became a verb."

And there was her own name: Sarah Beaumont. City Park shootings. If the attack in the park had been the work of a group, Morgan had reasoned, it might well have been this shadowy gang. Yet why would these wealthy people take such risks to kill total strangers? Until he knew that, he didn't have a story. No wonder he had been so interested in categorizing the different reasons for murder. . . .

At the very end of the file was a hyperlink that, when she cracked it open, was a self-executing command. AUTOCOPY TO Q FILE. What did that mean? Had Morgan archived the information off-site?

Sarah waited for the hard copy to print. It was clear to her now. Morgan Grimes was the Intruder. In his list of fifty-odd murder victims were the names of Kenneth Robertson and Alice McAullife, the two people Red had mentioned. It was Morgan's snooping into the murders that had spooked Them in the first place. More than fifty killings? No wonder!

Morgan hadn't realized that the Brady Quinn mystery was linked to his own serial murders until he had visited Dennis and read the list of horseshoe nails. They belonged to different centuries. But Agatha Penwether, the latest name on Dennis' list, was also the earliest name on Morgan's. No wonder he had been so agitated on the phone.

So agitated over *her* safety that he had run out of the office and into a knife.

His inquiries into the murders had been quite discreet. If nothing else, the prominence of newspaper reporters among the police detectives, systems analysts, historians, and statisticians ensured that. But he had asked about Quinn and the Babbage Society openly—on the Net and on the phone—and by the time he realized the truth, it was too late. He had exposed himself.

His friendship with Sarah had been the clincher. They were already convinced that *she* was the Intruder. In a tragic irony, They must have figured Morgan for a partner. Immediately after the encounter in the library, Sarah had met with both Dennis and Paul Abbot. Then, after the shooting in the park, she'd spent the night with Morgan and the next day Morgan had visited the same two men. So, rather than take chances, They had gone after all three of her "co-conspirators."

That explained why They had killed Paul Abbot, a man with only the most tenuous connection to her. She could understand now how it must have looked to Them. But she hated Them for the Dawsons and the man in the park, who had been killed only for window dressing.

So much violence. Across so many years. All to protect the one vital secret: that They had been quietly directing the course of history for the last hundred and sixty years.

She wished that she could forget that. She wished that everything could go back to the way it was, where history was something that simply happened.

What you don't know can't hurt you. There was a folk saying for everything. A comforting formula to take the place of thought.

It was wrong. Ignorance always was. What you don't know can *kill* you. Once, she saw a sparrow fly at full speed into the glass towers downtown. It had fallen to the pavement just in front of her. She could see herself quite clearly as that sparrow, rushing full tilt—like how many others before her?—into unseen barriers like a bird flapping against a windowpane. She wondered if the bird would be any happier knowing about glass.

Even if she could somehow forget everything she had learned, it would only be the illusion of freedom. The walls would still be there, even if she never beat her wings against them, all the more powerful, because you can never demolish a wall that you don't know exists.

But knowing that the walls were there, knowing that they had been built by others, that did cause pain. *My whole life I fought so I wouldn't be just another victim. And now I discover we're all victims.* Like a prisoner who finally escapes from his cell only to find himself in a larger cell.

The doorbell woke her up. The insistent chimes repeated themselves like a stuck record. She put her hands over her ears. "Oh, shut up."

She always woke up hard. Abe, her old roommate, had made fun of that. He'd been the sort who jogged in the morning and ate "hearty" breakfasts. Bacon (broiled, not fried) and eggs (soft-boiled, of course). While she struggled with her coffee. Their relationship, she could see now, had been doomed from the start.

She had crashed on the sofa early that morning, after spending all night on the terminal writing her program and reading Morgan's files. Now she looked blearily at the clock on the fireplace mantel, where it sat just under the portrait of Dr. King. Noon. The day half-gone. Dr. King gazed into the distance, looking impossibly noble. "Free at last . . ." Freedom, what an irony. How could there be freedom when an anonymous little group had been quietly setting the limits for everyone else?

The doorbell rang again and she wondered if she was going to answer it. Yesterday she had packed for hiding in the mountains when she had believed, crazily, that Morgan was coming to kill her. Then, last night, she had finally taken steps to fight back. This morning (no, this afternoon) did she still plan to run?

Well, that might depend on who was ringing her doorbell.

Feline leaped up on the back of the sofa and prowled back and forth. He yawned at her. *Yaaaow.*

Sarah held up her hands and Fee jumped into them. "How are you, Fee?" she asked him. "I haven't seen you for a while. Out tomcatting, I'll bet. Where were you when I needed you?" She remembered vividly the feelings of loneliness she'd had . . . What? Two nights ago? Her time sense was all screwed up. Saturday. And today was Monday. Two weeks to the day—almost to the hour—since she had found the papers in the house on Emerson Street.

Fee looked her in the eye.

Miaaou.

"No, you're right. I shouldn't blame you. After all, where was I when you needed me, right?" Being shot at. Going catatonic at Morgan's apartment. She scratched Fee in his special place, just behind the skull. The door chimes rang again. She sighed. "Well, let's see who's so anxious to meet us."

She rolled off of the sofa and got to her feet. Remembering

how carelessly she had gone to the door yesterday morning, she first went to the fireplace and grabbed the poker. Then she went to the door and peered through the peephole.

It was Red Malone. Dressed as a plumber, complete with a plumber's van parked in the road. He held a clipboard stuffed with ragged and official-looking papers. She watched him fidget from foot to foot, then reach out and stab the doorbell again.

Sarah opened the door. Red stood for a moment, then stepped in. "It's about time you opened the damned—" He scowled. "What's so funny?"

Wordlessly she held out the poker. He looked at it, then at her, and grunted. "At least I kept my part of the bargain. I rang your damned bell."

X

Red Malone planted himself on the same sofa he had occupied before. He looked her over and shook his head. "Sarah, you diddled me good. You know that? I really believed you. Can you imagine how stupid I felt when They told me about your spyder? You've been a busy little lady." He didn't smile when he said it. Red had smiled so much on his previous visit that his demeanor now seemed ominous.

Sarah laid the poker on the end table and stood with her arms folded across her chest. "I can explain that."

He nodded gravely. "Oh, good!" He stuck his arms behind his head. "I can hardly wait to hear."

"Don't you get flip with me, Mister 'Adjuster'! Every word I told you was the truth!"

Red leaned forward and stabbed a finger at her. "Sure, but you didn't tell me all the words. You knew a hell of a lot more than you let on. A little spyder told you. Don't play games with me! The stakes are too high."

"Games? My God! A dear friend of mine is dead, and another one may die, and some people I never knew at all are dead—" *Morgan was dead. Every now and then that knowledge intruded on her thoughts and stopped them cold.* "Dead," she repeated more softly. "Don't you tell me how high the stakes are! I didn't tell you everything last time because I didn't want my plans to leak to my competitors. I was researching Brady Quinn because he looked like a good hook for a real estate project. That's all."

"That's not all," he said stonily. "How did you make the connection with Babbage, Edison, and the others?" Sarah hesitated and Red snapped at her, "Come on! This is your life we're talking about, not your damned balance statement."

She pursed her lips and looked him in the eye. Could she trust Red Malone? He acted as if he was trying to help her, but how could she be certain? She stared at him for a time without speaking and he stared back. Then she took a deep breath and retrieved the two folders from her desk. "Here," she said, and dropped them in Red's lap. He looked at her, looked at the folders, and looked back at her.

"Go ahead; read them."

He frowned at her, then at the folder tabs—and his face went white. He paged rapidly through the sheets. "Where did you find these?"

"In an old building down near the train station. Off Fifteenth." She told him about the Babbage engines.

He paused and looked into the distance. "So that's where it was," he said quietly. He dropped the folders to the coffee table. "We knew Carson had been headquartered somewhere in the old downtown, but we didn't know where. There was a lot of confusion at the time. If Carson had been more careful evacuating the place, there wouldn't have been anything up there for you to find. That was bad luck, your stumbling on those machines like that."

"Someone would have found them, sooner or later."

"Sure, and sold them for scrap without ever knowing what they were. That would have been best, I suppose." He riffled through the index of mathematical papers. "Do you know what this stuff means?"

"Sure. You guys are trying to control the course of history."

He nodded slowly, no sign of surprise on his features. "And why do you think that?"

She told him everything she had deduced the night before—about Quinn, about Carson, about the Babbage Society, and what had happened to Dennis, Morgan, and the Widener people. But for some reason—perhaps a residual of mistrust—she did not tell him about the worm she had written in revenge.

Red listened closely. After she was finished, he sat silently for a long moment, rubbing his hands together. The pine logs crackled in the fireplace. Then he shook his head and laughed sadly.

"Well?" she snapped. "Am I right?"

He ignored her question and made a steeple with his fingers. "Where is that worksheet you say you found? The cliological analysis."

"Dennis had it. It's probably in his office at home."

Red reached into his pocket and pulled out a cell phone. "Mind if I make a call?"

"Can I stop you?"

Red punched up a number, shielding the phone with his body so she couldn't see it. He hit more buttons than an ordinary phone call would require. Then he turned his head and spoke into it for a few minutes. He listened awhile, nodding; then he folded the phone and laid it on the table.

"We're bringing some of our assets down to keep an eye on your friend. It'll be a while until they get there, but he should be safe at the hospital. Someone will watch that history professor you mentioned, too, just in case."

"Thanks."

"What? Oh, you're welcome. But it's for damage containment. Maybe we can find that list."

"It's your turn now," she said. "Tell me about this Babbage Society."

"There is no more Babbage Society," he told her. "It died a long time ago." He stared at his hands, turning them this way and that. "I suppose there's no point in concealing things from you anymore. It's too late and it won't change anything." He shrugged and waved her to a seat next to him. "Sit down. I'm going to tell you the damnedest story you ever heard."

She wouldn't sit next to him, which seemed to amuse him. Instead she took the same chair she had taken the last time. She gripped the arms of the chair and waited.

He leaned forward and clasped his hands together, staring at a point halfway across the room. He didn't look at her. "Crawford and the others were interested in mass behavior. Statistics and data collection was all the rage back then. They compiled figures on population, climate, trade, poverty, education, crime—you name it—the way Tycho Brahe compiled figures on the planets.

"Some people thought that, with enough data, they could go beyond Brahe to Kepler, and discover 'laws of mass behavior.' There was a Belgian astronomer, Adolphe Quetelet, who wrote about putting progressive social policies on a scientific basis. Then along came Babbage's book, with its rudimentary system theory. So Crawford and the Founders applied Babbage's techniques to the social data they had been collecting and discovered that, underneath the apparent chaos, the data followed predictable mathematical curves. And, once the underlying equations were teased out—using those Babbage engines you saw—the future could be extrapolated, within statistical bounds." He paused a moment and frowned. "They weren't always right. Sometimes their errors were ludicrous—It was a brand-new technology, and the data wasn't always accurate, and their understanding was still too shallow—but over time their models improved. Still, even today we sometimes get taken by surprise. It's a complex problem."

She shook her head. "Complex? It sounds damned impossible. Like predicting the motion of a mobile with a million parts."

Red glanced at his watch. "We don't need to know the last decimal place or the daily ups and downs, as long as we know the trend." He rubbed one hand with the other. "Crawford and the others, they found a trend that scared them spitless. They found everything converging on a global dark age—complete collapse—in the early 1940s."

Sarah pulled back and stared at him. "Dark age? There was the war, of course, but . . ."

"They saw a confluence of several trends: the unification of the Germanies and their rise as a scientific and industrial power; the compression of her population on her resources after the mid-1800s, leading to a 'breakout' cycle. Meanwhile, explosives were becoming exponentially more powerful. Put them all together and . . . Well, suppose Germany had had atomic bombs in 1939?"

She shook her head. "It never happened. Maybe the equations were wrong. You said yourself that they weren't always right."

"Was the prediction wrong?" Red wondered. "Or was the preventive action successful?" A shrug. "What would you have done? Stood by, because the forecast might be wrong? Or taken action, because the forecast might be right? They did what they had to do. They planted seeds that they hoped to nurture through the generations. The Society was small and it only operated in the U.S. Their activities didn't carry much sociokinetic energy . . ." He smiled as if in apology for the jargon. ". . . so they looked for focal points—fulcra, they called them; 'yokes' were the mathematical operators—times where they could get 'leverage' over large-scale events."

"Horseshoe nails," Sarah said quietly, to herself.

"What? Oh." Red nodded in understanding. "As good a phrase as any. Crawford and his allies wanted to build the U.S. into a counterweight to Germany. Slavery was stifling our technology, so slavery had to go. The South was a feudalistic, agrarian backwater drifting rudderless into a rich, industrial future; but, because of the Constitution, she had an effective veto over anything progressive the Congress considered. *No* to internal improvements. *No* to a transcontinental railroad. They did what they had to do," he repeated.

A strange feeling went through her. The Babbage Society

had ended slavery? But it had been for all the wrong reasons! Not for freedom or human dignity, but for economics and technological progress. She remembered some of the tales her grandfather had told about his grandfather. Economics be damned! "How did they plan to end slavery?" she asked. "Did they start the Civil War?"

Red rose from the sofa and stuffed his hands in his pockets. "Not on purpose. That was one of the mistakes. You see, slavery was already dying for economic reasons. Seward gave the 'peculiar institution' fifty years at most before it expired naturally. No, the Society simply tried to hurry it along the way to its grave."

"Through the abolition movement," she guessed.

"No. Frontal assault would only make the South dig in its heels. The Society used its wealth and influence to push for the Homestead Bill and Popular Sovereignty. Those did more harm to slavery than *Uncle Tom's Cabin* or *The Impending Crisis in the South*. A society of yeoman farmers has no use for slavery or great plantations. Crawford and the others, they never planned on a war."

"But they got one anyway."

Red grimaced and looked away. "The kindling was there and they were playing with matches. We're a lot smarter nowadays."

"Oh, I just bet you are."

He looked away. "We are because we don't meddle so often anymore. That's smarter, isn't it? Not unless we're very, very sure that we know what we're doing. Not until we've studied the proposal from twenty different directions. And then it's just a few minor amplitude adjustments here and there to maximize our earnings. No major surgery. It's much easier to modulate an existing trend than to start or stop one. We don't *control* history," he said. "Might as well try to sweep back the tide." He turned and looked her in the eye. "We gave it up, long ago." He sat back, spread his hands. "That's it. No grand, maniacal plan to rule the world. Disappointed?"

Oddly enough, she *was* disappointed. A secret cabal planning to rule the world had a mad kind of grandeur to it. A secret cabal for personal gain seemed merely sordid. "Getting rich off the misery of others," she snapped.

He grunted. "People will be miserable no matter what we do."

" 'A few minor adjustments,' " she quoted.

He jabbed a finger at her. "Look; we don't start the wars. We don't set the plagues. We don't crash the economy. *All that would have happened anyway!* But eight times out of ten we can calculate what's coming. Is it so wicked to act on that knowledge?"

She stood up from the chair and walked to the window, where she stared down the mountainside at her neighbors' homes. People were going about their normal lives just a few hundred yards away. "No," she said with her back to him. "It doesn't sit right with me. People are killing each other over it and I don't understand how it's possible!" She clenched her hands into fists at her side.

"Ideas are the key," Red said. "Elementary ideas—we call them memes. They're like viruses. People 'catch' them from each other through communication media. It's a process very much like epidemics. I could write the equations for you, if you like."

"Memes." Something went click. Some of the titles she had read in the Index. "You used to call them ideons . . ."

"Yes. Like elementary particles. Protons, electrons . . . and ideons. The analogies were all physical back then. Later, when Darwin's and Mendel's works became better known, biological analogies seemed more appropriate."

"But how can you say that behavior is caused by a set of equations, like a . . . Like a goddamn pendulum?" She turned and faced him and dared him to answer.

He shook his head. "You've got it backward. The equations don't cause the behaviors. The behaviors cause the equations. Get the difference? There's no compulsion. Like life insurance. You can't predict when a person will die, but all those random events pile up into a predictable pattern, and you can predict what percentage of people in various risk groups will die within a given time frame. It's like predicting the weather."

"An eighty percent chance of coups today across South America," she said, waving at an imaginary weather map.

Red smiled. "Something like that."

"Whatever happened to free will?" she said bitterly. She looked again out the window. *I* am *the master of my own fate. I am.*

"It's free will that makes cliology possible," Red told her. "A free choice is predictable more often than not, because it tends to be rational."

"People make irrational choices all the time."

"Sure they do," he replied happily. "But *it works out on the average.* Behavior is an action, and action causes reaction—recognition, money, security, self-esteem. . . . Biopsychological benefits, we call them. People imitate behaviors that seem beneficial. 'Monkey see, monkey do.' We can forecast the frequency distribution of people choosing a behavior by studying the benefits it evokes."

She shook her head. "That's too simplistic. Complex issues don't have simple answers!"

"Really?" He smiled. "That's a prime example of a meme that's flourishing in our culture. People pass it along to each other like a bad cold. But have you ever wondered who planted that particular meme and why? People won't even try to discover laws of history if they think it's impossible from the get-go."

She frowned and turned away from him again, lips pressed together. "So, you figure out what behaviors will lead to the results you want; then you encourage those memes through positive feedback and reinforcement." Sign up for Psychology 101 and rule the world.

"That's right. We reward the people who behave the way we want. We've got the wealth and influence nowadays and enough leverage in the communications industry to—"

She turned and jabbed a finger at him. "God damn it!" she spit out. "People aren't robots. You can't program them!"

"Hell, Sarah. I've known people who weren't half as flexible as robots, and you have, too."

"Well, then, we aren't puppets, either, to be jerked around by your strings."

"You weren't listening. I only said that we publicize and reward the behavior we want. *We don't coerce it!* But people aren't stupid. If they think that a behavior benefits them, a predictable percentage of them will imitate it *voluntarily*. That's why so many of our people are editors, speechwriters, programming directors, people behind the scenes. To make sure the right memes are publicized. Free will does the rest." He smiled ironically. "Besides, what else is a commercial supposed to do? Or a law? Or a sermon? Aren't they all attempts to encourage certain behaviors by holding out the promise of rewards or punishment?"

Sarah swallowed her response. At what point did the power to reward become the power to coerce? Manipulation was more subtle than force, but the results were much the same. And force, at least, had the one benefit of being brutally honest.

Red waited a moment. His eyes flicked to his watch and he grunted. "No answer, right? Because Madison Avenue is doing the same thing we're doing. It's not a matter of right or wrong. Tell me who is better off today, the descendants of the blacks who were sold into slavery? Or the descendants of the ones who were left behind?"

"That's no justification for the slave trade!" she said.

"Who said it was? *Justice has nothing to do with it.* Look; I'm happy I was born in this country, but I'm not happy that a million people starved to death in the potato famine so that could happen. A bad action can have good consequences, and vice versa. *The system doesn't care.* Change one component and the rest of the system reacts, maybe years later and in ways you don't expect. In ways you won't even *like*. That's what we go for: the side effects."

"No. Keep your hands off other people's lives."

"Ah! Laissez-faire. You've got the Humans Should Not Interfere with the System meme."

She did not care for the way he phrased it. He made it sound as if her beliefs were only things that she had "caught" from others, like a disease. "Deliberate interference by humans is unnatural," she said evenly. "It upsets the economic or ecological balance. History should run free—like a wild river!"

He threw back his head and slapped his knee. "Why do people like you think human behavior is unnatural? Just what do you think history *is,* Ms. Beaumont? It's nothing but human intervention! People are constantly trying to change it—or keep it from changing. What was Thomas Jefferson trying to do scribbling away at that Declaration? Or the NAACP? Or the Ku Klux Klan, for that matter? Trying to shape the future a little closer to their hearts' desires. Even you: Buying and selling houses to alter settlement patterns. Changing the course of people's lives, without their knowledge or consent, and for personal profit. Do the residents on Emerson Street *want* your new gentrified neighborhood? Everyone's changing the future, every day. Haphazardly. Blindly. Some tugging one way, some tugging other ways—with their eyes fixed only on their own, immediate, intended goal, giving no consideration to interactions, spin-offs, or the long-term. Maybe a few advertisers, preachers, and the like have a vague grasp of some principles, but that's as far as it goes. Sometimes the Associates don't see things so clearly, either; but 'in the country of the blind, the one-eyed man is king.' Why is it morally superior to tinker ignorantly and haphazardly like the rest of you?"

"It *is* different!" she said, choking the words out.

He folded his arms. "Really? Tell me how."

"The rest of us don't kill people!"

He froze. Then he grimaced and dipped his head in acknowledgment. "I could argue that stumbling blindly through history has killed more people than They ever have, but . . . Yeah, things went wrong for the Society a long time ago." He rubbed his hands together. "Look; when Crawford and the others formed the Babbage Society, they never intended anything like what's happened. Remember, they were trying to save the world."

"Good for them," she said sarcastically.

He looked hurt. "They were," he insisted. "Oh, I'm not saying no one was harmed. People died because of things they did. The Civil War . . . We still don't know why that happened. Something was overlooked in the equations. But people would have died anyway. Only rarely did the Founders ever feel compelled to delete specific individuals."

"Oh, let's tell the Vatican. Maybe they'll be canonized."

He screwed his face up. "I'm not making excuses for them. They weren't saints by any means. They did what they felt was necessary, and the choices often meant personal agony. They never authorized a deletion lightly or simply to protect themselves. It was all for a greater good. To prevent what they saw coming. Weil—"

"Genevieve Weil?"

He looked at her shrewdly. "I see you've heard of her. No, I meant her great-grandfather. He used the Society's own tools to manipulate the Society for his own benefit. A ruthless bastard. I don't know how he ever got past his recruiter. His scheme would have worked, too, if it hadn't been for Quinn. Quinn and Carson had discovered that the Society itself was subject to laws of cultural evolution and had calculated the coup years before Weil was recruited. It broke old Isaac Shelton's heart when Quinn told him—"

The cell phone on the table rang and they both started at the sound. Sarah glanced from the phone to Red. "Go ahead," she told him. "You've been waiting for it to ring."

He cocked an eyebrow at her and she pointed to his wrist. "Because you kept looking at your watch every few minutes, that's how. Go on. Answer it."

Red flipped the phone open. "Talk to me." He listened for a moment without speaking. Then a look of surprise crossed his face. He turned away from her. "Say again," he whispered.

Whatever the message was, Sarah decided, it was not what he had expected. She wondered what her own best move should be. Red was personable and his arguments well reasoned, but she wasn't about to let him decide things for her. She remembered that her Blazer was ready and waiting, packed with survival gear.

Red folded his phone and faced her grimly. "Your architect friend has vanished. He's not in the hospital, and Porter's computer never heard of him. According to their records, he was never even admitted."

His words were like ice water in the face. She had been using his lecture and her anger as Novocain against the pain of reality. Now it was reality's turn. "Dennis? But he was! He was in the critical care unit! Jerry spoke to them!" She had thought Dennis safe from harm in the hospital. Yet, despite Red's assurances, They had gotten him after all.

A hand shook her shoulder and she looked into Red's face. "Come on," she heard him say. "There's been a change in plans. We're supposed to meet Janie at Falcon Castle. She'll take you from there."

Fee rubbed against Sarah's pants leg and she reached down and picked him up. He settled into the crook of her left arm and she stroked him absently—and perhaps a little firmly, because he twisted in her grip. "Suppose I don't want to come with you?"

"You don't have to. We never interfere with free choice. You can come with Us, or stay here and get killed."

Sarah thought that over. "Free choice!" she muttered.

XI

Red laughed when he saw her well-stocked Blazer. "You won't need all that paraphernalia where we're going," he said.

"I haven't decided whether I am going with you," she answered. "Going with you isn't the only alternative to staying here."

He pursed his lips and nodded. "My plumber's van is less conspicuous."

"A four-by-four is hardly conspicuous in Colorado."

"I didn't mean that. I meant that They probably know what cars you drive."

Her patience had worn thin. Red acted as if the whole business was one big game. "Will you quit that Us and Them crap!" she snapped. "They're the Babbage Society and you're . . . What? Utopian Research Associates?"

He nodded. "Yes. But We never call Them the Babbage Society. Men like Crawford and Shelton and Hammondton were men of the highest ideals. Grosvenor Weil perverted those ideals."

Men of the highest ideals, she thought. Trying to save the world. And they had killed people and accidentally set off the Civil War. Maybe that was the trouble with high ideals. Get too high, and ordinary people would look small and unimportant. "Have it your way," she said, "but I plan to keep my options open." She climbed into the cab of the Blazer and slammed the door. Fee settled into his usual place in the center console. She'd removed the lid to it when she bought the car and made a kind of padded cat seat out of it. "See you around," she said and hit the garage door opener. She started the engine and put the Blazer in reverse, but before she could back out, Red yanked open the passenger's door and climbed in beside her.

She braked sharply and looked at him. He was buckling his seat belt. "What do you think you're doing?"

"Well, if you won't come with me," he said reasonably, "I'll have to come with you. Maybe I can answer some more questions for you. Maybe I can still convince you to come to Falcon Castle. Janie'll be sore as hell if we don't show up."

"My heart bleeds for her. Who is Janie, anyway? Your wife?"

He looked startled. "Wife? Me? Are you kidding? I'm the wild and independent sort. No, Jane Addams Hatch runs the local safe house. She was sure you'd opt to join the good guys."

Carefully she backed down the steep dirt driveway to Foothills Road, twisting in her seat to watch. "I know that They're the bad guys," she told him over her shoulder, "but I'm not convinced that you folks are the good guys."

"We're the enemy of your enemy," he said.

"That doesn't make you my friend. You're doing the same thing as the Babbage people. You're just not as ruthless."

Once on Foothill Road, she looked both ways for traffic. There were only a few cars parked alongside the road near the houses. She shifted into drive and headed toward Eldridge Street.

"You know," he said after a few moments' silence, "wild rivers only seem like a good thing if you don't live downstream."

For an instant, she couldn't figure out what he was talking about. Then she recalled her earlier remark, comparing history to a wild river. "But if you dam the river to help the folks downstream," she told him, "you'll flood the folks upstream."

He shrugged. "Sure, but if you *don't* dam the river, then it's the downstream folks who get flooded. No matter what you do, someone suffers. You can't make an omelette without breaking eggs."

"Spoken like a chef. What if you're one of the eggs instead? That whole bit about the good of the group—What about the rights of the individual? Is the group free to trample on them?"

He looked at her. "Would you sacrifice the safety of the group to the whims of individuals? What were Typhoid Mary's rights?"

She glanced at him again, downshifted, and drove through the stop sign. The eastbound traffic on Thirty-second Street was heavy. The day shift at Coors was letting out. She stopped at the intersection, saw an opening in the traffic, and went for it, turning sharp right. The oncoming car braked and honked. In her rearview mirror she saw the driver shake his fist.

"Yeah? Well, you people have been tinkering with history for what? Almost a century and a half? You know what bothers me most?" She made another sharp right at the church and headed up the ramp onto westbound I-70.

"What?"

"The shoddy workmanship."

He turned and gave her a startled look; then he laughed. "I suppose it seems that way. But, hell, we must be doing something right, because we do make money at it."

"Yeah. Good for you," she said.

He didn't answer her and she spared him a covert glance or two as they drove. He was leaning his elbow on the door window, his fist propping his head up, watching the houses go by.

"Here's a puzzle for you," he announced suddenly. "Suppose you saw a young boy about to be run over by a bus. Would you try to save him?"

She glanced at him, then back at the road. "What? Sure, if I could."

"Good. But now suppose you knew that if the boy lived he would grow up into another Hitler. Millions would die because of him. Would you still try to save him?"

She scowled and would not look at him. "How could I know something like that?"

"Grant me the supposition. You know it. ESP. Whatever. What would you do?"

"That's no choice."

"Yes, it is. No one ever promised you that the choices would be pleasant."

She clamped her jaws shut, refusing to answer.

"Of course, *not* deciding is also a decision," he told her. "You will have to save him or not. And if you save him, then are you responsible for the millions he will kill?" Red waited awhile, watching her. "What really makes it agonizing," he said after a moment, "is that you *know* the boy personally. He delivers your morning paper."

She closed her face up tighter and kept her attention firmly on her driving.

"And now take the supposition one step further. This child, who, beyond any hope of doubt, will kill millions of innocent people . . . What if he's *not* standing in front of a bus? Would you *push* him?"

"Jesus Christ!" The words escaped her involuntarily. She looked at him and there wasn't a trace of a smile on his face.

"Yes. Though I don't know if even He could help. Knowing the future is a mixed blessing. Maybe we foresee a disaster. To avoid it requires terrible measures. People will suffer; some will die. But if we do nothing, then the original disaster happens on schedule. Cliology has created new problems for decision makers."

She grunted. "It sounds like an old problem to me. Do the ends justify the means?"

He shook his head. "It's not that simple." He looked away from her, out the window. "Where does responsibility end? No matter what we do or don't do, there will be pain. A different set of people suffer and die, is all. It's knowing about it in advance that changes things. What can we do but try our best, knowing our best isn't good enough?"

They drove in silence after that, only the tires making any comment. She kept the Blazer at the speed limit and cars passed them constantly, their drivers sparing her dirty looks. *This is crazy,* she thought. She couldn't go into hiding with Red tagging along, and she could hardly keep him prisoner. She would have to dump him somewhere soon.

"Do you know how to get to Falcon Castle?" Red asked.

"What? Sure. Out Turkey Creek Canyon to Parmalee Gulch Road. I've hiked most of the Foothills around here. But I'm not going there."

From the corner of her eye she watched him stare through the window at the passing scenery. It was barren country they were passing through, all browns and no greens. Scrub brush and buffalo grass, with a few evergreens spotted here and there. There were a few scattered houses and a trailer park off in the distance on the right. Green Mountain hulked on their left. "Where do you plan to drop me?" he asked abruptly.

Sarah checked the rearview mirror and pulled into the right-hand lane. "There's a foot trail from Morrison up to the castle," she told him. "I'll drop you there. It's a three-mile hike, about two thousand feet up. You up to it?"

He shrugged. "Sure."

They went through the cut in the Hogback, with its odd sign: POINT OF GEOLOGICAL INTEREST. When the interstate had been dug through the high thin ridge that paralleled the Foothills, it had exposed the colorful folds of ancient seabeds, set like diagonal stripes beside the roadbed. A parking area and path had been built so that people could "walk back through time." Red stared curiously at the sightseers.

"Ever been out this way before?" she asked him.

"What? Oh, a couple times. Camping. The Associates have a ranch southwest of here."

They pulled down the exit ramp and Sarah turned left onto Morrison Road. The interstate banked above them, curving up Mount Vernon Canyon toward Georgetown and Silver Plume. The High Country. Sarah longed to be up there, in that wild and beautiful land along the timberline, among the krummholz and tundra flowers. Alone and free. But to be alone, she had to dump Red. To be free . . . Well, that was another issue entirely. To be free, she had to tear down the walls the Society and the Associates had built. Yes, and the walls she had built as well.

The road to Morrison ran south between the Hogback and Mount Morrison. Ahead on the right Sarah could see Red Rocks Park, with its sandstone formations weirdly carved by millennia of winds. She checked her mirror again, made a snap decision, and turned sharply into the park.

Red looked at her. "Someone's following us, right? You keep looking in your mirror."

"Dark blue sedan," she told him. "Only two cars on that interstate were holding the speed limit—and he was the other. He got off at Mount Vernon with us, and . . ." Another glance in the mirror. "Now he's decided to visit Red Rocks.

If you've got another explanation, I'd be glad to hear it."

The blue car was hanging way back. To be less conspicuous, she supposed. That gave her an idea. She kept to the high road through the park. On the lower road, she would be clearly visible to him; but the high road twisted its way in and around the sandstone and the sight distance was limited. Maybe she could lose him.

The park had its usual quota of weekday visitors. Cars were parked along the roadside and people were hiking and rock climbing. One man with a beard was strumming an acoustic guitar to a circle of admirers. *Too many witnesses here,* she thought. Whoever was chasing them wouldn't dare try anything. Then she remembered what had happened in the Civic Center and felt fear. Who knew what They would dare?

No help for it now. Past Ship Rock and the Amphitheater she came to a fork in the road. She checked behind her. The blue car was still out of sight behind the rocks. She made a sharp right at the fork and floored the gas pedal. The Blazer spun on loose gravel; then the tires gripped and they shot through the narrow roadway past Creation Rock. If she could be out of sight before her pursuer reached the fork, he would probably assume that she had continued straight through. The road she was taking now had fewer turns. She could gain some distance on him, maybe throw him off their track.

A few minutes later, they came down from the Rocks past the mouth of Bear Creek Canyon and into the town of Morrison. There was no sign of the blue car. She turned right onto Route 8 and headed south again.

Red twisted in his seat and looked behind them. "Didn't you say you were going to drop me in Morrison?"

"I've changed my mind. It's too risky. I don't know if I shook our friend back there and I'd rather not get caught in the parking lot there. Besides, the first mile or so of the trail is across open meadow. If our friend has a gun, we'd be sitting ducks."

"We?"

Sarah took a deep breath. "We," she admitted. "I guess I do need your help after all."

"It's not disgraceful to need someone's help, you know."

"It is for me."

Mount Falcon rose on their right. Like most of the Foothills, it was a low, broad mountain. The peak was a shade over two miles away, rising just under two thousand feet from the roadbed.

She looked in her mirror and her hopes fell. "Our friend is behind us again and he's coming up fast. Closing the distance."

"Then he knows we're on to him."

"Christ! He's got a gun, Red! He's stuck his arm out the window."

"Don't worry," Red told her. "Shooting a pistol left-handed from a moving car at another moving car at sixty miles an hour at this distance? Hell, he'd be lucky to hit that mountain."

There was a sharp crack and the rear window disintegrated into flashing shards. Something buzzed in the air between them and smashed into the tape deck. Fee howled and ducked into his console.

"Unless," Red continued thoughtfully, "that's Orvid Crayle behind us. He's very good." He zipped open his repairman's coveralls and retrieved his automatic. He checked the action, then unbuckled his seat belt. "Well, Orvid and I were bound to cross swords someday." He looked at her and smiled. "I'm pretty good myself."

"I bet you are."

Red climbed over the seat and made his way to the back of the Blazer. "I think you've met Orvid already," he commented. "Tall, thin fellow. Looks like death warmed over?"

Sarah recalled her encounter in the library. "Yes. I think I have. Pleasant kind of guy? Faultless manners?"

"That's the one. Orvid's Their Station Chief here in Colorado. You know what that means, don't you?"

"Sure. More good news. You don't send management out on a job unless you're shorthanded and there's no one else available. Red, I don't know how much more good news I can take."

He laughed. "That's the spirit." He braced himself against the backseat and, with his feet on the tailgate, drew a bead through the shattered rear window. "Try not to hit any bumps for a while," he said.

"Right," Sarah muttered to herself, and floored the gas pedal. Crayle probably had the edge on them in speed, but there was no point in making it easier for him to close the distance. Unfortunately, Route 8 was relatively straight through this stretch of country, between the Hogback and the Foothills. No twists or turns to confuse the aim. She wished Red would hurry up and get it over with.

Two cars approached from the opposite direction and, glancing in the mirror, she saw that Crayle had pulled his gun in. *He's not going to throw himself away*, she thought, *like he did the man in the Civic Center*. Crayle was at least as interested in getting away as he was in getting the job done. That might give them an edge. "Hey," she said. "What we should do is drive around until we find a police car. Crayle won't dare try anything then."

"Sure he would," Red's voice replied. "He'd gun us down and flash a badge. CIA or something like that. Claim we were fugitives. Local cops would buy it, because, whatever badge it was, it'd be legit."

"Can't you flash a badge, too?"

"Several, but not with a half-dozen bullet holes in me." Red paused, then added thoughtfully, "I'm sure he'd rather not use his cover if he could avoid it. He might get away with killing us in front of the police, but his superiors would know that it wasn't a Company operation. The word would get around the Community that maybe he'd gone rogue."

Bang! The noise was loud inside the Blazer and the car swayed as Sarah jerked convulsively. "Hold the car still," Red demanded. She realized that Red had squeezed off a shot. "Did you get him?" she asked. No answer. He fired twice more and Sarah flinched at the sound. "Did you get him?" she asked again, a slight edge to her voice.

"Yes and no," he told her as he climbed back into the passenger's seat. "I got his radiator and his front tires. Bigger targets than his pointy head. His tires are flat and he's losing water. His engine'll overheat and seize up."

She closed her eyes briefly and breathed a sigh of relief. They were going to get away and Red hadn't had to kill anyone. She didn't like Crayle—she *hated* Crayle—but she was glad Red hadn't killed him. "Then we're going to make it," she said.

There was another loud bang and the Blazer veered sideways. In a panic, she fought the steering as they skidded zigzag down the road.

"Unless," Red said calmly, "he shoots out our tires, too."

Sarah spared him an exasperated glance.

Red shook his head in reluctant admiration. "Damn, he's good."

She managed to bring the Blazer down to a manageable speed without spinning out. Both rear tires were making floppy sounds. She took a shaky breath and was amazed to discover how calm she was. *Uncertainty breeds fear,* she thought. There were no uncertainties now.

Behind them she saw Crayle already stopped by the roadside. Steam poured from under his car's hood. Crayle stepped out, dressed in a long tan overcoat too warm for the weather. His left hand was jammed in his pocket. He looked from his car to them, kicked the car once, then started after them on foot. He didn't run, but he took long, quick strides, the kind that ate miles.

"He's persistent, too," she told Red. Crayle knew that, with their back tires gone, they weren't going far. Certainly there was no chance of making it to the entrance to Falcon Park around the back side of the mountain. And once they were all afoot, Crayle only needed to close to within pistol range. With his aim, he'd have them.

She tried to picture the Geological Survey map in her mind. She'd hiked over this area about a year ago. There was a dirt road that led from Route 8 to the base of the mountain. They could climb from there. It wouldn't be hard. Just hands

and feet. Once they reached the trail on top and the rendezvous point, Janie could drive them to safety. Crayle, on foot,
would be helpless to stop them. If only they could gain
enough of a lead on him.

She came on the turn suddenly and jerked hard to the right.
The Blazer slewed and wobbled and she winced at the abuse
the wheels were taking. She could see hunks of rubber behind them. They'd be riding on the rims shortly.

"If you're thinking about stopping to change the tires,"
Red remarked dryly, "I wouldn't recommend it." He pointed
to where Crayle was cutting diagonally across the meadow.
He was following Strain Gulch, trying to head them off.

"Yeah. Where's the pit crew when you really need them,"
she said. Red snorted. "Besides"—Sarah tapped the gas
gauge—"this needle's dropping faster than usual on this gas
hog. I think one of those shots got the tank or the gas line."
She nibbled on her lower lip. Cars couldn't explode, but a
spark might have turned the Blazer into a giant Molotov
cocktail.

The road came to an end. Sarah braked and turned the
engine off. She reached around behind her and snagged her
backpack. "End of the line," she told Red, kicking the door
open. "We walk from here."

Red hopped out. "Up there?" he asked, staring at the
mountain.

"You got a better idea?" She turned back to the Blazer
and held the pack out with its front flap open. Fee nosed at
it, meowed, and jumped in. It was "his" pocket when they
went on hikes. She sniffed. The mercaptan smell was sharp.
The gas was definitely leaking out.

"You're taking the cat with us?" Red asked.

"Of course! Feline P. Cat isn't just a cat! He's . . . Fee! He
and I have a contract. I give him food, shelter, and affection
and change his kitty litter; and in return he sometimes rubs
himself against my leg. If he feels like it."

Red cocked a speculative eye at her. "Does what he likes,
when he likes, eh? Answers to nobody but himself. Some
people are like that, too."

She had hitched the pack onto her back and was making her way up Strain Gulch. "Are you going to stand here flapping your lips just to feel the breeze? Let's go."

XII

Red spared a look back down the gulch while Sarah began the climb. Crayle was a thin figure in the distance, still coming implacably onward. *Like a force of nature,* Red thought. He gave in to impulse and waved at their pursuer. Crayle paused and raised an arm in reply, but Red didn't think he was waving with all five fingers. He laughed and turned to follow Sarah.

Scrambling up the draw where Strain Gulch came down the mountainside, Red found himself face-to-face with Sarah's cat. Fee's head stuck out of his pocket, surveying the scenery—and Red's struggles—with serene indifference. Red made a face at the cat. Then he slipped on a loose rock the size of his fist and stumbled to his hands and knees. He cursed and brushed himself off, scowling at the cat.

"What good is that stupid cat, anyway?" he asked in annoyance.

"Keep climbing," Sarah answered without turning around, "and stop wasting breath. And if you have to ask what use a cat is, you don't deserve to know the answer."

Red grinned at her back and ran to catch up. The ground became steeper and the sides of the draw closed in upon them. The slopes on either side were lightly forested with evergreen trees and bushes. Looking up, he could see rounded peaks on either side, with a third and higher peak directly ahead. The ascent in that direction seemed more gradual. Sarah zigzagged across the draw, taking advantage of local variations in the terrain. Red followed. He hoped she knew where she was going.

At one particularly steep stretch they crawled on hands and knees to keep their balance, holding onto shrubs and outcroppings to pull themselves along. Red grabbed a plant and it came out of the dry, dusty soil by its roots. He slid three feet down the embankment, scraping the skin on his hands and cheek and striking his knee on a rock. He winced at the pain. Sarah turned and, gripping a sapling with her right hand, reached down to him with her left. He flushed and took it.

He looked into Sarah's calm brown face. *So I'm a city boy and you're a backpacker, but I'll make it. I'm at my best when I'm challenged.*

He pulled himself up by her arm and they resumed climbing. Red threw himself into the effort with renewed energy. He began watching what Sarah did. Where she placed her feet. How she chose the route. He admired the assurance with which she moved, the lithe grace and suppleness. He followed doggedly. His breath came hard and ragged. Once, he looked back and was surprised to see how high they had come. The Blazer was out of sight behind the trees and rocks, but they were easily eight hundred feet higher up. He slipped a couple more times on rocks and loose gravel but managed to grab something each time to keep his balance. Sarah never looked back to check on him again, and he set his jaw grimly.

After a while, he realized that he was pushing himself because she expected it of him. It was such a startling revelation that he stopped climbing for a moment and stared at her back. There were dark stains on her shirt, at the armpits and at the small of her back. He had been sent to bring Sarah in for her own safety and that of the Associates, but it was working out the other way. Somehow, somewhere along the line, he had lost mastery of the situation, and he couldn't quite say where or how. Sarah was the kind of person who, once she had chosen her direction, couldn't help but draw others along with her.

Red had never liked being subordinate. He liked being in charge. *Maybe that's why Sarah and I were so immediately simpatico when we met,* he thought. *Although I was never the kind of loner that Sarah seems to be. I like being part of a team. I like it when everything clicks together.*

He resumed climbing. Sarah's weakness, he decided, was that while she gave help with no questions asked, she had difficulty accepting help. That could be dangerous. At crucial times, it was always better to have someone to watch your back.

So where was the happy medium between the individual and the group? The pendulum kept swinging from side to side but didn't spend much time in the middle. A social pendulum. He could envision the equations. He could even picture the equilibrium manifold. A simple pleat or maybe a swallowtail. Just shift the splitting parameter a bit and it would damp the cycle. All that was necessary was for the Associates to adopt it as a goal, then maintain a constancy of purpose for five generations. But maintaining a commitment that long was impossible, the wreckage of dreams. Like everything else in life, the Associates would change over the years, and one generation's heartfelt goals would become another's hoary fables.

Hell, kids never believed how deep the snow was in their parents' time.

The sound of a crack distracted him. He turned downslope.

"It's Crayle," Sarah told him.

Red could make out the gunman's figure at the bottom of the draw. He was firing uphill at them, but the shots were falling well short, making puffs of dust in the ground below them.

"Even a good marksman has a hard time firing up- or downhill," Sarah commented, "but I'd rather not wait until he gets the range."

"He's only got a pistol," Red pointed out.

"Then I'd rather not wait until he gets lucky."

Red watched the other man reload his gun, holster it, and start up the draw after them. He wasn't giving up, but at least he'd need both hands to climb the rough spots. Still, when it came to Crayle, it was best not to make assumptions.

The rest of the climb was easier than the part they had just gone through, and another half hour brought them out on the relatively flat area atop the mountain. The main peak rose another three hundred feet on their left. The regular trail from Morrison lay to their right.

Red felt light-headed and dizzy. Nauseous. He stopped and squatted beside the trail. Sarah looked at him.

"What's wrong?"

"Don't know. I feel like I'm going to throw up."

"Mountain sickness," she told him. "If you're not used to the thin air, exerting yourself like we've been doing can bring it on."

"Great. What's the cure?"

"Move to Colorado."

He gave her a sour look. She probably made jokes about seasickness, too. "Just give me a minute to catch my breath," he said.

She scanned the slope behind them. "It's a lot worse when you go up one of the really high mountains. You want to give Crayle a minute, too?"

"Hell no. He's probably a mountain goat like you."

"Come on, then. The trail's for the *turistas*. It can't be as bad as coming up the gulch."

"Yeah." He looked around. They were on a high ridge. Several peaks lay to their left and right, separated by draws where the runoff water ran down to the high plains. The ruins of a stone building peeked through the evergreens to their west. The Walker Mansion, he thought. Falcon Castle. Then that peak over there on the right, about a mile away, must be where Walker started building the Summer White House, just before World War One. He shook his head. Walker had been a man of dreams, a sentimentalist at heart.

Sarah dropped back and they walked the trail side by side. She pointed to the wreckage of the mansion. "He was quite a personality," she said. "Newspaperman and realtor, just like me."

Red smiled. "You as rich as he was?"

She laughed. "Not yet."

They reached the ruins. Walker's house had been struck by lightning in 1918. It had burned, and Walker, disillusioned, penniless, and heartbroken by his wife's death two years earlier, had never rebuilt. All that was left now were the stone walls, broken and gaping, with the tall chimney towering above, still improbably intact. A split rail fence surrounded the ruins.

The building was laid out in a U-shape, with the open courtyard facing roughly southwest. The chimney was at the northeast corner. They walked around the south wing to the courtyard. There was a signboard there for the tourists, telling all about Walker and his "Castle" and the Summer White House he had started to build for the nation with pennies pledged by the schoolchildren of Colorado. Red ignored it and walked past into the courtyard. He surveyed the ruins. A fair defensive position. He'd been under worse cover that time in Jacksonville.

"Let's get behind the wall," he told Sarah. "It's too exposed out here." There was no point in going any farther. The parking lot was too open and flat. Crayle would catch them with no cover.

The wall before them had a doorway flanked by two windows. On their left was another wall, its middle section almost entirely tumbled down. They climbed the fence and ducked through the doorway. Red went immediately to the left-hand window and, standing off to one side, studied their past route. He unzipped his coveralls so he could reach his gun quickly, but he didn't take it out, in case ordinary tourists approached.

He scanned the trees to the east. He could see the plains beyond the mountain rim, where they stretched in perfect flatness to meet the sky. There was no sign of Crayle. That worried Red nearly as much as seeing him would have. With Crayle, either way was bad news.

There was no sign of Janie, either; and he checked his watch. They were early. He wished she would hurry. He checked their surroundings. The remnants of walls, about waist-high, showed where the different wings had been. Faded scorch marks discolored some of the stonework. It was all broken up, the original floor plan lost.

Sarah squatted against the wall and shrugged out of her backpack. She took Fee from his special pocket and scratched his head. The cat narrowed his eyes in pleasure. "Now what?"

"Now we wait."

"For Crayle?"

"We've got a good field of fire. Good defensive position. Maybe he'll see that and give up." He didn't think so, but it was a seductive thought, just the sort that could get them both killed.

For a time there was silence, broken only by the wind through the trees. Then Sarah spoke. "Why'd you give it up?"

He kept his eyes fixed on where the trail emerged from the trees. "Give what up?"

"The tinkering. You said the Associates gave it up."

Red grunted. "Quinn laid down the rule. He felt we didn't know enough to risk large-scale changes. Too many unexpected—and unacceptable—side effects. *Observe* and *study* were his watchwords. Over the years, they became *observe* and *study* and *make money*." He grimaced. "Not everyone liked the rule, but Quinn had strong personal reasons; and except for minor revenue-enhancing adjustments the Associates have stuck with it."

"Hunh. Of course, *not* deciding is also a decision."

He was surprised to hear his own words coming back at him. He turned to look at her. "Are you trying to tell me something?"

"You want to start tinkering again."

"Why do you say that?"

"I don't know. The way you talk. Your body language. You want to change things. You don't like sitting back and getting rich off of other folks' miseries."

"The getting rich part is OK, and folks will be miserable anyhow. But you're right. It's past time the Associates stopped being so gun-shy."

She shook her head.

"It's in a good cause."

"Isn't it always?"

"We've got to do something," he said. "Because They're doing something. They're breeding a nation of technopeasants."

"Technopeasants?"

"Yeah. Smart enough to do what we're told and docile enough to accept that. They encourage any meme that downplays thoughtful analysis or encourages docility or self-indulgence or uniformity. A uniform, docile society is more predictable, and Their forecasts would be simpler and more precise."

Red turned his attention back to the trees. He had not looked away long enough for anyone to cover the distance, even at a dead run. "But it can't last, any more than domestic sheep could survive in the wild. It's long-term suicide."

"What I see happening around me is bad enough," Sarah said. "To know that the trend is being encouraged by a secret elite is worse. But to know that They are doing it for no more reason than to simplify their goddamn arithmetic really frosts me."

"Do you want to fight that? Effectively, I mean. Public hearings and debates and 'Full Participation by All Concerned Parties' never accomplishes anything."

"What? Are you offering me a job?"

He turned and grinned at her astonishment. "Yes. Help me get the Associates off their laissez-faire duffs."

"I'm against everything you're for. The whole concept is repulsive."

"Wouldn't you say that makes you the ideal recruit? The last kind of person I'd want in the Associates is one who enjoyed the power."

Sarah opened her mouth to say something, then changed her mind. "I don't get you, Red. One minute you talk like you want to free the puppets; the next minute, like you want to be a puppeteer."

He stifled a spasm of annoyance. Why couldn't she see it? If they didn't do something to blunt the Society's efforts now, their grandchildren would live in poverty and serfdom.

Was she too thick headed? Or his arguments too weak? He turned his back on her and concentrated on his vigil. Damn. He wished he had binoculars. He asked Sarah if she had a pair in her backpack.

"They're back in the Blazer."

"Fat lot of good they'll do us there. What'd you bring along beside a stupid cat?"

"A stupid man."

He grunted. She was right. Who was he to complain? After all, he had brought nothing. Red crouched and crawled to another vantage point. It wasn't good to stay in the same place too long, nor to stick your neck out at predictable intervals.

"Do you see him yet?" she asked.

"No. I wish I did."

"Where's your friend Janie?"

"She'll get here when she gets here." He glanced quickly at his watch. She was already late. And she knew Crayle was loose, too. He wondered if They had intercepted her. . . . No, not likely. If Crayle was coming after them personally, he had no one else to spare. Unless it was simply for the challenge. Mano a mano. He patted the gun under his jacket. Maybe he could pay Crayle back for Jacksonville.

Sara shifted to a more comfortable position and drew patterns in the dirt with her finger. "I'll answer your question for you now," she said.

He glanced her way, puzzled. "What question?"

"About the boy and the bus. The answer is simple. Save the boy. Not for his sake. He may grow into the monster you described. And not for his victims' sakes, either. *But for my own sake! Do you understand that? You don't hurt people for things they haven't yet done.*"

Red nodded. "You would have made a hell of a recruit," he said.

"Yeah. Red, what happened to Dennis?" Red glanced at her and she paused and swallowed. "God, it seems like that was another planet! Do you think he's dead?"

Red searched her face and saw the pain there. He had to

remind himself that she had lost friends in this gambit. That made him more anxious than ever to get Crayle in his sights. There were rules to the game. If you weren't a player, you weren't a target. "It wasn't your fault," he told her. "It was nobody's fault."

"It was Their fault."

"I don't know. The message said that he had vanished completely, even from the hospital records." He scowled. "That makes no sense. Why bother? If They wanted him dead, it would have been easier to short-circuit one of his life support units. Or even start a fire in the hospital."

She shivered. "They're vicious," she said. "Evil."

"That's why we have to stop Them. We have to start spreading antimemes."

"Fight fire with fire?" she said.

"Don't be cynical. Have you ever fought a forest fire? Sometimes a backfire is the only way."

She shook her head violently. "No! You say They've attached puppet strings to us and They're pulling us the wrong way. But your only answer is to attach another set of strings!"

"What would you do?"

"Cut the strings. All of them."

He grinned at her. "Have you ever seen a puppet without strings?"

"Yes. Pinocchio."

He blinked, startled by her answer. Metaphor was always suspect, but frequently it was insightful as well. Almost, he could see where her remark might take them.

"Maybe They didn't want him dead," she said. "Dennis. Maybe They found out about the list he had. Suppose he had figured out what it meant and had hidden it. They would need him alive then, wouldn't They?"

Sometimes people's needs were very basic. "Sure. That's probably it," he told her.

"They'd want to know about the factor analysis that Carson and Quinn did on the entries, wouldn't They?"

"Sure." He looked back out at the forest. Crayle had not

yet made his appearance. That was trouble, because by now he should have. The back of Red's neck prickled. *Where was Crayle?* He took his gun from its holster. He didn't think any tourists were going to show up. A movement at the eastern rim of the plateau? Or was it the wind stirring the tops of the trees? He shifted position and stared intently through the broken window hole.

"Sure," Sarah babbled on. "The entries on the list were numbered one, two, and three, so Dennis and I figured . . ."

He wasn't particularly listening to her, so it was a moment before her words registered. He jerked his head around. "What did you say? *Three?* Are you sure?"

"Yes. Why? Is it important?"

He opened his mouth to answer her, but the words never came out.

XIII

Sarah watched with horror as Red pitched backward against the stone wall. He slammed against it and fell forward on his face. Behind him a red splash decorated the stones. He didn't move. The whisper of the muffled shot echoed in the ruins.

A low partial wall ran at right angles to the wall with the doorway in it, and Sarah hugged the ground behind it. The smell of the dirt was heavy in her nostrils. From the way Red had fallen, the shot must have come from the northwest. Crayle had apparently worked his way through the trees below the crest while they had been watching the east.

Now she was trapped. Red had the only gun and he had fallen on top of it. Besides, his body was almost certainly within Crayle's field of fire. She looked behind her. Could she crawl out without being seen? Not through the door—that was exposed—but through another break in the masonry? Maybe, maybe not. But it was better than lying here and waiting for a bullet. She began to inch backward until her boots touched the wall. She probed back and forth with her feet, searching for a hole.

Yes. There was another way out. It was small, but she thought she could fit. She pushed herself into the hole feet-first, pulling her pack after her. Fee sat curiously atop the pack, like a king being borne on a processional float. Her squirming had pulled her jacket and shirt up, and stones ground into her stomach and ribs. She tried not to think about getting stuck halfway through.

Her hips gave her a bad moment. For a moment, she couldn't move. She bit on her lower lip. Then she pushed as hard as she could and came free. A stone raked her ribs on the left side and she stifled a cry of pain.

Finally, she was through. She gasped, rolled to the side, and sat with her back to the wall. She felt her side where the stone had cut her and her hand came away bloody. No time to relax, she thought. Crayle was coming.

She glanced at the doorway to her right, where Red was partly visible. Was he dead or just unconscious? In art class, she had learned what the body looked like in life and death. A dead man did not lie like a sleeping or unconscious one. All opposing muscle groups should be equally relaxed.

The sphincters relaxed, too; but she couldn't see his pants from where she sat. She took a deep breath, but she couldn't smell anything, either.

She opened her pack and dug inside. She came out with a mirror and her hunting knife. "Come on, Fee," she whispered.

Crouching, she ran to the corner of the ruins, keeping a tall wall between her and where she thought Crayle was. There she lay flat again and cautiously pushed the mirror out beyond the edge. She was careful to keep it in the shadow of the wall so it wouldn't reflect the evening sun. She tilted it this way and that, viewing the "inside" of the ruins.

She could see the low wall that she had lain behind. Red was beyond it, on the other side; but she couldn't see him.

There! She saw the reflection of a man approaching the ruin. She backed away from the corner, keeping the mirror in view. It was Crayle, just as she remembered him from the library. When he reached the wall, he swung his gun over, holding it in two hands. Then, seeing there was no one there, he ducked back, his eyes darting.

She saw him go around the back side of the building and smiled, because that meant Crayle couldn't read the signs. The drag marks in the dirt showed clearly which way she had gone. Sarah edged around the corner. She left her mirror in place but turned it so it now reflected the "outside" wall where she had just been.

She saw Crayle jump out with his gun aimed straight down the wall. Again, there was a moment of hesitation while he took in the empty scene. Then he let the gun drop and looked around.

"I know you're around somewhere, little lady." Pause. "Don't make this hard on yourself. We only want to question you."

Incredibly, Sarah found she had to suppress a giggle. How stupid did he think she was?

She watched him in the mirror as he walked toward her position. *When he reaches the doorway,* she thought' *he'll jump back through to this side.* It was an obvious gambit to try. She readied herself to jump around the end of the wall at the same time. *And what if he doesn't do it?* She swallowed and watched his feet carefully. A man about to jump holds himself a certain way.

Yes. He jumped and Sarah jumped at the same time. Her heart was pounding at this cat-and-mouse game, but she felt strangely exhilarated, as if she were somehow more alive. Every sense seemed stretched to the limit. She could hear Crayle's shoes where they crunched the gravel.

This can't go on forever. I'll have to do something. How long till sundown? She knew these hills. In the dark she might be able to escape. Crayle was not a woodsman.

She kept her eyes glued to the mirror, not daring to glance away even to check the sun. It felt strange knowing that she actually had her back to Crayle. Fee crept up to her and rubbed against her calf. Fee. Maybe he could help. A cat? Yes!

"It's no use, little lady. You're all alone up here and I'll get you sooner or later. Just like I got your friends. You should have heard him beg for his life."

He had to mean Abbot. She couldn't imagine Morgan or Dennis begging.

Her plan had an element of the desperate in it. Crayle was a professional and it wouldn't be easy to trick him. But he thought he was dealing with an amateur—witness his attempts to get her to talk and reveal her position—and that gave her an edge. She pulled the hunting knife from its scabbard and, taking a deep breath, picked Fee up. "Forgive me, Fee," she whispered.

"And once I've taken care of you," said Crayle, "I'll head back to Denver and finish the job on your queer friend."

Turning her back on the mirror, she *tossed* Fee underhanded as far as she could along the outside wall. Fee, terrified and astonished, squealed and landed with a crash and ran into the trees, scattering leaves and twigs.

Sarah jumped to her right with her knife cocked for throwing. She saw Crayle thirty feet away staring through the window hole in the direction of her cat. He was aiming his pistol out the window, but her movement must have caught the corner of his eye, because he turned back to face her just as she threw.

It was a blur of motion. The knife buried itself at the base of his throat. Crayle staggered and arterial blood spurted from the wound. His right hand made an abortive motion toward the handle and his left tightened convulsively on the pistol. The gun went off and sparks ricocheted across the stones. A look of infinite surprise crossed his features. He dropped the gun and collapsed like a deflated balloon, first to his kness, then on his back.

She started to run toward him but hesitated. *Don't take Crayle for granted.* She approached cautiously, ready to bolt for cover.

Crayle lay on the ground next to Red, his legs kicking in

the dirt. He turned his eyes toward her in what looked like disbelief. Then they filmed over and he sagged and was still.

Sarah began shaking and her knees felt weak. She sat on her haunches and covered her face with her hands. It was over. She sobbed and tears ran down her cheeks, leaving muddy trails in the dirt there.

How could you explain someone like Crayle? Once upon a time he had been a child, with a child's innocence; and surely his parents had never thought he would come to this. He had suckled and played with his toes. He had delighted his parents with his hesitant first steps. Now he was dead. Where along his path from toddler to corpse had the soul leaked out of him?

On hands and knees, she crawled past Crayle to where Red lay. She felt his throat for a pulse. Was there one? She thought she could feel something, but that might be only her imagination. "Oh, Red," she sighed sadly.

There was a sharp click behind her and she whipped around. A spare older woman stood there, dressed in denim with a telescopic rifle cradled in her left arm. "Nice work, missy," she said.

There was something familiar about her windburned face. For a moment, Sarah couldn't place her. Then she remembered. "You! You were in the library with Crayle!"

"Yup." She walked over and stared at Crayle's face. "He shore does look surprised. Can't say I blame him. It's always supposed to be the other one. His kind never think it's going to be themselves that git it." She looked at Sarah. " 'Specially not from the likes o' you, missy. I'm a mite surprised myself."

"You're . . ." Sarah stood up and stared at her. "You're Jane Hatch!"

She nodded, still looking at Crayle. "How's Malone? He gonna make it?"

"How long have you been watching?"

She shrugged and spit tobacco. "Long enough. You're one cool lady. Most folks woulda been paralyzed with fear." She put her rifle aside and knelt over Red. Her hands probed expertly. "Shoulder wound," she said. "And concussion. He must've hit his head against the wall. Good thing his skull's so thick."

"How long have you been watching!"

Janie turned and looked at her. In her calm eyes Sarah thought she could see more than a touch of Crayle. A detachment. A distancing from the world around her. "Why d'you want to know, missy?"

Sarah pointed at the rifle with the telescopic sights. "You could have shot him, couldn't you? But you let him stalk me like an animal!"

Janie shook her head. "It's nature's way, missy. We don't interfere. It's always up t' the bird whether the snake strikes or not."

All during her conversations with Red, Sarah had thought that trying to guide the course of history took supreme arrogance. Now, suddenly, she saw that the opposite was also true. There was something equally arrogant in those who stood by and watched and did nothing.

She turned her back on Janie, her arms straight down at her sides, eyes and fists clenched shut. The tears on her cheeks felt hot. It had to end. There had to be a finish to it. The Society and the Associates both. She hated their secrecy, their callousness. Even their good intentions were unfeeling.

Her worm would start it. Scrambling their data banks would throw both of them into confusion. Maybe give her time to think. And the worm had a stinger, too. A codicil that she hoped would shatter their smug little world forever.

When you know someone's deadly secret, there was only one way to be safe. Tell everyone. If it wasn't secret anymore, there'd be no point in singling her out. So she had instructed her worm to copy whatever it found and download it anonymously on the Web—and into every TV network, newspaper, police, and government system it could find. And that included downloading Morgan's files as well.

She knew that both organizations had heavily infiltrated the media and intelligence communities. They were rich, powerful, and they'd do everything they could to ridicule and silence the truth. And maybe they could, this time, but Sarah didn't think so. The facts would be dispersed too widely; too many of them could be verified independently; and, ultimately, the two societies must be too small to block every possible avenue. Otherwise, they could not have kept themselves secret for so long. Perhaps millions would scoff, but millions would believe.

You can never do just one thing. Along with blocking their selfish machinations, she would also be blocking whatever good they could do. The Founders had ended slavery, had possibly forestalled an atomic war. Red had planned to block the Society's attempts to create a Docile Society. Noble goals. Was she right to sabotage those efforts, as well?

She didn't know. Time enough tomorrow to worry about that.

She walked to Crayle's body and stared down at it. Suppressing a feeling of revulsion, she knelt on one knee and pulled her knife from his throat. His unfocused eyes stared at her and she looked away. *The second time will be easier,* said a voice inside her head. Crayle's ghost? There wouldn't be a second time, she vowed. Not if she could help it.

She looked up. It was growing dusk. Janie had picked up her rifle. "I'm goin down t' the pickup to git my first-aid kit. Why don't you come along? You can sit and wait in the cab till I'm ready t' carry him down."

Sarah stabbed the knife into the grass to wipe the blood off the blade. Red would recover. She was glad. She didn't agree with him, at least not entirely, but she was glad he'd be around to argue with. There was more than a touch of Morgan in the man. "No. Thanks," she said. She stood up and tucked the knife through her belt. "I've got something else I've got to do."

She walked through the broken doorway to the outside and climbed back over the fence. She squinted her eyes at the gathering gloom. The trees were tall and black and the wind ran through their needles with the sound of a distant crowd.

I had to do it, she thought. *He'll understand.* She faced the brush and squatted.

"Fee?" she called into the night. "Fee? Come back. I need you."

Part 2

A Rose by Other Name

Then

Davis Belleau's day began slowly, with him lying abed and savoring his morning coffee. Partly that was his temperament. Bred in Louisiana, he was accustomed to taking things at their unhurried, natural pace. Partly it was his age. His bones were brittle and his joints protested at every move.

Sometimes he longed for his lost youth, for the time when he had been strong and fleet. The quickest lad in three parishes, they had said, and meant quick not only in the body. Sometimes the memories rose up so strongly he could almost smell them. Riding to hounds on his father's plantation, the pungent smell of horseflesh in his nostrils; or punting in the bayous, the odor of magnolia or cypress like a mist around him. Creeping through the thickets to spy on the old black witch lady who lived in the swamp. The ferns brushing his face and the black delta mud squishing between his toes. The smell of brackish swamp water. The old woman could see the future, the older boys had told him. She could read it in a ball of mud and chicken bones that smelled of the graveyard, and Belleau had been possessed by an overwhelming desire to read the future himself.

Now, of course, he only wished he could not, because the future *was* mud and bones and graveyards.

At other times he remembered that the world of his youth was gone past all recall. It was not merely that he had grown old, but that the world itself had died. Drowned in blood at Pittsburg Landing and at Gettysburg, and offered as a holocaust in the flames of Atlanta. The new world was better; the equations proved that. This present was better than the future that would have been. Yet Davis Belleau found himself ill at ease in it.

It was not the technology, strange and wonderful though it was. Rails now spanned the continent and iron horses had replaced the keelboats of his youth, but it was the inner life that had changed and left him behind. Of all the passions that had once roused men to action, not one would today stir a flicker of emotion. Men flocked to new banners: silver coinage . . . railroad rates . . . What were such trivia measured against states' rights or nullification, the tariff question or abolition? All the great issues had already been decided. *I have outlived my own life.*

Someone had taken a shears and snipped off the past and it was gone. And the fact that Belleau's hand had helped with the cutting mattered not at all.

The smell of age was in Belleau's room. The curtains, heavy and musty, blocked the sun and shrouded everything in shadows. Belleau set his coffee aside. He closed his eyes and relaxed on the pillows. Behind his eyelids, he could see the equations. The ones that had changed a harmless society of natural philosophers into—what? Saviors? Masters? He heard again forgotten voices. Eli protesting that they knew too little to take any action; 'Diah arguing that delay could lead to catastrophe; Isaac keeping his own counsel but staring fixedly at the chalkmarks on the board as if, by sheer concentration, he could will them into a more congenial solution.

My God, how young we all were!

"No action at all is incumbent upon us," Phineas had protested. His hand had flashed; the chalk scrawled a mathematical curve across the slate. "Those are the figures for the last few decades. I've run them through the engines and fit them to an equation. Here is the projection." The chalk whispered. The curve grew. "Slavery is dying. The border states are already talking of manumission. Virginia had three hundred thousand slaves in 1790; today, she has but four hundred thousand when the natural increase should have produced a million and a half. Only in the Deep South has there been any growth—because of the cotton bubble. All the ambitious young men are seeking their fortunes in cotton, but that bubble shall burst and cotton slavery will go the way of tobacco slavery. If we do nothing at all, the next fifty years will see the end of the whole sorry business. Am I not right, Brother Eli?"

Eli shifted and shrugged. "Do we know even that much? How confident are we in our very data? Our equations may be grotesquely wrong."

Jedediah Crawford's cane had thumped the floor like a judge's gavel. "We know enough that to do nothing would be cowardice of the worst sort. Every year that slavery persists is another year closer to disaster." He pushed himself to his feet and hobbled to the slate board, where he slashed an S-shaped growth curve atop the slavery decay curve. "Slavery may well be dying, but the corpse is still too lively. Delay, and the United States will not have waxed strong enough to stop the United Germanies from exploding the Ultimate Weapon."

"The Ultimate Weapon." Eli's voice was heavy with skepticism. "Extrapolation is chancy at best. What explosive could possibly be so potent?"

Isaac spoke for the first time. "Who can say? It may not even be chemical."

Meechum snorted. "Not chemical, suh? Then what?"

Isaac took a deep breath. "Don't know. Don't want to. I shall be dust long before it is conceived, and I am eternally grateful for that small kindness that God has shown me. Sometimes . . ." And he had gazed once more at the equations, looking for all the world like a Papist before his idols. "Sometimes, theah is comfort of a sort in these calculations."

Davis Belleau, watching with the inner eye of memory, saw his younger self shake his head. Not with the doubt of Eli or Phineas, nor with the dread of Isaac or Jedediah, but with another emotion entirely. Alone of those in that room that day, Davis had had an inkling of what was to come.

"We cannot wait for slavery to expire." That was Brother Jedediah again. A crabby Vermonter, brilliant, incisive, visionary. Hobbled from birth by a clubfoot. Crawford had been the first to see in Babbage's work the potential for a new science, one that treated manufacture, economics, politics, indeed, all of society, as a great, complex scientific riddle. He had built the first crude calculating engine and fashioned the wonderful wooden cards with the holes drilled at strategic loci that enabled the engines to store their statistics and instructions.

And now he was telling them that the world was not a scientific riddle but an engineering problem.

"Suh," responded Meechum. "I do not deny the necessity. You will recollect that the first abolition societies were founded in the South, not the North. Slavery has impoverished my country. Cotton crowds farm products off the land, yet we spin less than two percent of it ourselves. We have less than a quarter of the Federal Union's railroad trackage. Our banks contain less than ten millions of dollars in deposit. Why, New York City alone has twice the liquid capital of the entire South." He gestured toward the tangled curves they had drawn upon the chalkboard. "Our children are rocked in a Northern cradle; our dead, buried with a Northern spade. But," Meecham continued, "we cannot force abolition down the throats of our countrymen. Should we attempt to do so, the South will secede!"

"The South will *talk* of secession," said Phineas. "We have heard that bleat since the Nullification Affair, and naught has ever come of it. Besides, of five million plus Southrons, a mere three hundred and fifty thousand own slaves, and half of those own less than five slaves apiece! Why would four million sharecroppers and yeomen bleed for the privileges of the wealthy planters?"

Isaac had been scribbling on a scratch pad. He glanced up at the faces of the arguing men. "And if'n the South does go?" he said. "Good riddance, ain't it?" He pointed to the technological growth curve. "Without that millstone around our necks—"

Meechum colored and Davis felt himself grow angry. "Be warned, suh," he said pointedly. "You insult our honor."

"If the South secedes," Eli told Isaac quietly, "the North

will fight. And probably the West as well. Not for abolition, but to preserve the Union. No good can come from that."

"Fight?" Meechum laughed. "If the South leaves the Federal Union, the North will dare nothing. Southron gentlemen are trained to combat from birth. How can a nation of shop-keepers and mechanics stand up to them?"

"How?" asked Isaac, amusement in his voice. He rose and walked to the chalkboard. Taking the chalk, he wrote a set of equations on the board and stepped back.

Davis studied the equations and felt his heart grow cold.

Meechum snorted, recovered the chalk, and added another term. The solution changed. Southron victory.

Isaac shook his head. "Neither England nor France will join in the fight."

"They will, suh, for Southron cotton sustains them. They will intervene or go bare-assed." Phineas and he laughed, and Davis marveled at how close Mississippi and Massachussetts stood on some things.

"Gentlemen!" Jedediah struck the floor once more. "We waste time. There can be war only if the South secedes. The South will secede only if she believes abolition will be forced upon her by the National Government. That can occur only if the Electors choose an abolitionist President and the State legislatures appoint a majority of abolitionist Senators. And since neither Whiggery nor the Democracy is in danger of abolitionist control, there is small chance of that. Multiply the probabilities yourselves, if you wish. The product is van-ishingly small."

But not zero. Even now, decades later, Davis Belleau re-membered that thought.

Sir?

Belleau stirred and opened his eyes to the present. "Some-thing went wrong," he told the figure before him. "Something went wrong."

"Sir?" His manservant stood before him, polite puzzlement on his face.

"What is it, Georges?" he asked irritably.

"A message for you, sir. From the banking firm of Gorman

and Stout. The boy has instructions to place the packet only into your hands."

Later, Davis sat alone in the morning room, a plate of breakfast on the sideboard, and held the envelope up to catch the light better. That handwriting . . . It couldn't be, not after all these years! He turned up the gas mantle. The flames hissed and the room brightened. He inspected the handwriting once more.

Yes. It was Brady Quinn's.

How long was it now since Brady had vanished? More years than Belleau wanted to remember. Now, there had been a sharp mind! One of the best in the Society. But Brady had had no stomach for the Society's work. Lincoln. Belleau remembered now. That was the reason that Brady had quit. A regrettable action, but a necessary one. The equations had proven that.

Some of the punched-hole cards had vanished with Brady. Belleau remembered telling Isaac, and Brother Isaac, who never in Davis' memory had shown any emotion but resolution, had hung his head and silently wept. Remarkable how clear such ancient memories were, while those of yesterday were cloudy and indistinct. Isaac had been Brady's mentor, but Belleau had always suspected something more behind the sorrow than his protégé's resignation or the theft of some cards. As if Isaac had nurtured some terrible secret in his heart.

Davis hefted the envelope. And now here was news from beyond the grave.

Or was it? He remembered the cover letter and pulled his bifocals from his vest pocket. "Hon. Davis Belleau, Esq. Salutations," etc., etc.. He skipped the verbal parsley and went for the meat of the message.

Brady had left the enclosure in the safekeeping of Gorman and Stout in 1866 with directions that it be delivered on or about the sixteenth of May 1876 "to whichever of the following gentlemen be hale enough to receive it." Jedediah

Crawford, Ph.D.; the Honorable Mr. Isaac Shelton; Elias Kent, M.D.; Col. Meechum Clark, . . . Belleau's vision blurred with tears. All gone now, save only Brother Isaac, and he senile. A tear fell from his cheek and the ink on the cover letter blurred and ran.

With a sudden jerk, he pulled the letter opener across the envelope. Two pages of closely written foolscap were inside. Belleau hesitated a moment, then pulled them out and read.

My Dearest Comrades,

I do not know whether any of you will be alive when this message is delivered; nor whether I myself shall live. Yet, I know that you deserve an explanation for what I am about to do; and, please God, at least one of you shall read these lines and understand.

Brother Eli was right when he warned that our knowledge was too slight for what we attempted. Too often, our actions have had consequences unforetold by the equations. Yet I have been unable to disssuade you from the path Brother Crawford set us upon. Very well. I understand the urgency and sincerity with which you pursue the Goal.

Yet it is the very sincerity of that pursuit that disturbs me.

My protégé—his name does not matter—has uncovered a dilemma and, between the two of us, we may have devised a solution; but I must be free of the Society to implement it. If our calculations have been free from error, the crisis we foresee is imminent even as you read this.

The warning is this: the Society itself is "an ideonic complex in the sense of Babbage" and thus itself subject to evolutionary change. In the familiar schoolyard game, a young boy whispers a story to his neighbor, who in turn whispers it to his own neighbor, and so on around a circle. When the last boy recites the story aloud, it bears little resemblence to the original. Just so has Jedediah Crawford whispered a set of ideons into the ears of Isaac and Phineas; and they, in turn have whispered them to others, among them myself. By the sixth such itera- tion, the original ideons of the Society will have decayed to the point where they will carry little weight with the then-current membership. They will pursue their own selfish goals, not those of the Founders.

How foolish we were to suppose we could stand outside the forces we studied.

I have taken steps to counteract this, forming in secret a daughter society. We have kept the Oath and the ceremonies but have altered the Rules in a way which, we hope, will be less easily distorted. Our new Society will take no action. Too many mistakes have been made, and too much blood spilled. We will return to the original purpose of scholarly study and hope that in the process we may learn enough to rectify the mistakes of the past.

Some of us were once members of the Society, but I have removed all traces of us from the Cards. Forgive me for that, but it was necessary that we germinate in isolation.

In the event, I remain ever

Y^r Obed^t Svt.
Brady Templeton Quinn

The pages rustled as Belleau set them down. The Society? Abandon the principles set down by Brother 'Diah? No, that was not possible!

And yet . . . Now that the possibility had been pointed out, the mechanism and the equations describing it were clear. And the cusp would come. . . . He did the calculations mentally, cursing the slowness of his mind. Too long a reliance on Babbage engines had impaired the skills drilled into him in youth. He made some simplifications to the numbers. He only wanted an estimate.

The cusp would come . . . soon!

He gripped the arms of his chair until the knuckles stood out large and white. The Council must be warned. Why had Brady said nothing years ago? Why had he waited until now, to speak from the past?

Davis Belleau rose and hobbled to the desk. His fingers ran through the days on the calendar there. Yes. Next Thursday would be a Council meeting. As Councillor emeritus, he was elegible to attend. He would do so. Warned even this late, Grosvenor Weil might yet forestall the coup that Brady foresaw.

Now

I

Easton, PA

The captain gradually became aware of the commotion in the squad room. He laid his pen on his desk and walked to the door of his office and looked out. He was tall and ruggedly built, still slim and hard because he jogged every morning around the South Side. The printer was racing like a machine gun and the officers and civilian staff were clustered around it, talking excitedly.

"What's going on?" he demanded. The paper from the printer was piling up in the basket. "What is this?"

One of his detectives was reading the sheets as they came out. "I don't know, Captain," he said. "A lot of it looks like gibberish to me, but I think . . ." And he pawed backward through the printout, found a page, and tore it off at the perforations. "I think we got a line on that John Doe we found three years ago in Riverside Park."

The captain took the page. Not much happened in this town, and the John Doe had been a nine-day wonder in the *Express*. It had always galled him that the case was still unsolved. There was something not quite right about it, something he could never put his finger on. The papers had referred to the victim as a drifter, but the dead man had not had the appearance of one who lived on the street.

960709.01 T. CRAYLE TO COUNCIL. B. SIMPSON DELETED @ EASTON, PA. CLOSEFILE.

"That's not all, Captain."

He looked up. It was the computer tech who had spoken.

A short, chunky woman who wore "granny glasses" and no makeup. "What?"

"Well . . ." And she held up a handful of sheets. "You need to contact somebody, but I'm not sure if it's the FBI or the *National Enquirer*."

New York City, NY

"OK, OK; but where's it coming from?" Greg Houvanis looked at the other reporters crowded around the terminal in the *New York Times* city room.

"Who knows?" said one with a wave of his hand. "Some hacker playing a prank."

Houvanis was scanning some of the sheets. "What kind of prank is this? It looks like a dump of someone's entire computer files."

"Yeah. Like I was saying—"

"Clear it up! Clear it up!" The managing editor plowed through the sea of reporters like the *Queen Elizabeth* parting the waves. The city editor followed in his wake, wringing his hands and looking uncertain. "What's the party?" asked the M.E. He grabbed one of the pages from a reporter's hands and read it. Then he balled the paper in his fist. "Shut that damn thing off!"

"But—"

"Shut it off, I said. I'm not going to see our office supply budget used up because some crazy hacker wants to tie up our terminal." Someone reached out and the chattering printer fell silent. "Ben!" The M.E. called the office boy over. He shoved the crumpled sheet into the young man's hands. "Take this trash down to the shredder and see that it gets burned. Get someone erasing the junk files from the server. I have to make some phone calls. And the rest of you," he added to the City Room reporters, "don't you all have deadlines you need to meet?"

Greg returned to his desk with the rest of them. He woke his terminal and scrolled until he found the 'graph he had been rewriting. For a few minutes he lost himself in hunting and pecking on the keyboard. Then he sensed a presence by his desk and looked up and saw Ora Harris. She was new to the staff; he barely knew her. "Yes, Ora. What is it?"

She looked left and right, then slipped him a torn page of computer paper. "Don't let the M.E. see this. But didn't you say that Morgan Grimes was a friend of yours?"

He took the page from her and saw that her hand was trembling. "Yes." He hadn't spoken with Morgan in months. Then, two weeks ago, he had gotten a call from Morgan asking him to research some items in the *Times* morgue. Now Morgan was dead. Life was funny. He looked at the sheet Harris had given him.

990620.34 O. CRAYLE TO COUNCIL. M. GRIMES DELETED @ DENVER, CO. CLOSE SUBFILE.

"What is this?"

"Not here," she said. "Take it home and read it. It's not much. Just the one page; but I was reading it when the M.E. came out and I remembered you talking about your friend's death and . . . And Mr. Houvanis? Ask yourself why the M.E. was so anxious to stop the printer."

Montreal, QE

He scowled over the diagnostic readouts. What could have caused the application to stall? Not enough memory? *C'est impossible!* He clicked a few times and activated the catalog. He scrolled through the listing. *Voilà!* An unidentified application. A rogue program. "Merde!" he said under his breath. What was a virus doing in his system? How had it entered? He tapped in a few more commands and studied the result. It took a few moments for the impact of what he was reading to sink in. Then he sat up straight and clicked on the emergency shutdown. "Merde!" he said again, with considerably more feeling.

Langley, VA

The printer suddenly came to life and Jen Samuals jerked in her seat. She put her book aside and swiveled her chair to face the terminal screen. She picked up the phone and read the leader on the first 'graph to see which agency she was to notify.

"Oh, shit!" she said, and quickly cradled the phone. She ran her eyes down the next few pages, speed-reading. "Oh, shit," she said again. She reached out and hit the emergency stop button. The terminal sighed and died. The printer froze in midline.

Working quickly, she pulled the already-printed sheets from the strip and ran them through the shredder. The shredder went silent just as Leslie emerged from the washroom. "What's going on?" she asked as Jen removed a back panel from the machine.

"A short or something," she told her as she pulled a wire loose from its connection.

San Francisco, CA
"Yes, Prudence, what is it?"
"I'm afraid you're not going to like this, Mr. Kennison."

"Hello?"
"There's a better home a-waiting."
"The circle remains unbroken. Report."
"Have you seen it?"
"Seen what?"
"Lord, it's dumping out on every terminal in the country!"
"What is?"
"Summon the Six, Bradford. We've got to take counsel."
"It's that serious?"
"Serious? Everything is changed. My God, everything is changed."

Austin, TX
"In other news this morning, computers nationwide were tied up by an unknown computer hacker. In a prank reminiscent of the famous Captain Midnight incident . . ."

Saint Paul, MN

"Hey, Fred, set up another round for me and my buddies."
He turned to the other men at the bar. "So my boss, she says
to drop the whole thing. That it will only encourage other
pranksters. But I read some of those printouts and I
think . . ."

Seattle, WA

"Station KING has learned, through a confidential source,
the name of the hacker responsible for last week's prank on
the Internet . . ."

Washington, DC

"What do you think it was all about, Vince?"

"Oh, nothing to get excited over, Senator. A hacker, they
said on the TV. Some woman deranged by her boyfriend's
death in a drug deal."

The Senator scowled and jutted his chin forward in his
famous pose. "Is it anything the Senate should consider?"

His aide paused and considered. He was covered with nervous sweat and he hoped the Senator would not notice. There
was no time to call Brother Ullman for instructions. He'd
have to wing it. Later, he would get together with some of
the other congressional aides. Even the ones from the Other
Side. Work out a common strategy. Plugging this leak would
definitely be a "bipartisan" issue.

"These hackers crave publicity," he said judiciously. "If
we make a Federal case of it, by next week there'll be a
dozen incidents." *Perhaps that would be the best strategy,*
he thought. *Flood the system with nonsense printouts and
blatant disinformation. The best place to conceal a murder,
after all, is on a battlefield. Meanwhile, we don't want the
politicos actually* reading *the stuff.* "I think the bill that's
been hanging in the Communications subcommittee should
be reported out. It contains provisions to stiffen the penalties
for computer crime and regulate the Internet."

"Hmm." The Senator nodded. "Harry's been sitting on that

thing for too long. First Amendment issues. But he must realize now that it's better to get the law out, even if it is flawed. Let the courts straighten out any ambiguities later. We've got to do something about the Internet."

Vince nodded in agreement. They would have to do something about "Senator Harry," too.

San Jose, CA, Associated Press

The Center for Computer Disease Control recommended today that universities and research facilities quarantine their computers and purge them of an infectious "virus" that ran rampant through the Internet last Wednesday and Thursday, dumping false and libelous material into terminals across the country. The Federal Bureau of Investigation is launching an inquiry to determine if federal law was violated, calling the incident an "attack" on the integrity of the Net . . .

The man he knew as Bernstein was chuckling as he read the paper. "What is it?" he asked. Bernstein opened to an inside page and shook the paper to straighten it. The paper rustled with the sound of footsteps through dry leaves. "It's your friend," Bernstein replied. "You should see what she's done."

Detroit, MI

"Yeah, I know the Bureau said to put a lid on it, but I been thinking . . ."

Mr. Koppel: But suppose we assume for a moment, Dr. Vane, that the Beaumont Dump is genuine. Wouldn't the fact that individuals have made themselves rich by forecasting the future convince you that such a science is at least possible?

Dr. Vane: Not at all, Ted. Success does not imply method. There is no shortage of people who have made themselves rich by forecasting the future successfully. In the stock market. In real estate. What escapes our notice is that many more people have become poor by forecasting the future . . . *un*successfully. [Laughter among guests.] Random chance dictates that some forecasts will be correct.

Mr. Koppel: Could you elaborate on that?

Dr. Vane: Certainly. Suppose I offer to forecast the sex of unborn babies for a fee of one dollar, with the fee fully refundable in the event I am wrong. All I need do is predict "male" in each case. I would make an average profit of fifty cents per baby, but I would not have a valid science.

Mr. Koppel: I see.

Dr. Vane: Here is another, less obvious example. Enrico Fermi was discussing military history with General Groves when the subject of great generals came up. Fermi asked how many generals qualified as "great." "About three in a hundred," the general replied.

"And how did one qualify?"

"By winning five major battles in a row."

"Well," said Fermi, "considering that in most theaters the opposing forces are roughly equal, the probability of winning one battle would be fifty percent. Of two consecutive battles, twenty-five percent. Of three, twelve percent. Of four, six percent. Of five, three percent. So you are right. About three generals out of a hundred will be called great; but it is probability, not greatness."

Littleton, CO

"I saw her," said Pat, passing the mashed potatoes, "I think it was a week before she disappeared, when I was working the night shift at the bulk handling center down by Union Station. She came from under the viaduct. Not running, but walking real fast. She told us she was looking over a building nearby and thought maybe she was being followed."

"Followed?" Kevin frowned and laid his fork down on his dinner plate. He looked at his brother. "And that was *before* Morgan was killed?"

"Yeah. And before that thing in the park. You know, with the gunman."

Kevin rubbed his mustache thoughtfully. "Everyone down at the *News* is saying that it was Morg' being killed that sent her around the bend."

Pat shrugged. "I don't know. It was just funny seeing someone like that—I couldn't remember her name at first. Then a couple weeks later, she's famous."

"Infamous," Kevin corrected him. He picked up his fork again but didn't eat. He shook his head. "It doesn't jibe," he said. "Granted, I hadn't talked to her since she left the paper; but I knew her. And I knew Morgan. The whole story is out of character, for both of them. And when Morgan was killed, he passed a very mysterious message on to Sarah. You say she was looking at a building? Which one?"

Pat shrugged. "Beats me. She didn't say."

Kevin looked thoughtful.

"What are you thinking about?" his brother asked.

"The Pulitzer," he told him.

■■

Red Malone sat on the fencepost, enjoying the mountain air and watching the horses graze in the corral. His left shoulder was heavily bandaged and his arm was bound up in a sling. He had hooked his feet around the lower rail of the fence to help himself keep his balance. The soft breeze falling down from the High Country rustled his shirt and created waves in the grama grass of the horse pasture. The mares clustered around the fence line on the far side, cropping the grass. Their stallion watched Red suspiciously.

Sarah Beaumont approached him. She was dressed cowgirl fashion, in tight jeans and checkered shirt. The white straw Stetson contrasted sharply with her skin. Red still wore his city clothes.

She threw herself at the fence rail next to him and rested her chin in her arms. She gazed out at the horses, a scowl across her face. "Dammit, Red," she said. "I don't want to become someone else!"

"None of us do," he answered her.

"The rest of you don't have to," she said bitterly.

He returned his attention to the horses. "Sometimes," he said. "From time to time."

"Red, I spent years making myself into what I am. I worked hard at it, and it wasn't easy, and I like the way I turned out!"

"Then you're lucky. Most of us would do major alterations if we could. What are you carping about? Your new persona will be wealthy, secure. We take care of our own. A little plastic surgery, too. Maybe lighten your skin a shade or two. Your own mother wouldn't recognize you."

Sarah's eyes went dead and she looked down at the grass. "She wouldn't know me now," she said quietly.

He wanted to say, "Well, then it won't make any difference," but he sensed it would be the wrong thing. He watched as the stallion came suddenly alert, ears twisting like twin radar antennae. The horse trotted a few paces to the high ground at the rear of the pasture and stared like a statue at the mountains above. After a while, he relaxed and resumed his station by his mares. Red wondered what vagrant scent the mountain air had brought to the stallion's nostrils.

"It's for your own good, Sarah," Red said finally. "Haven't you been watching the news? Ever since you spilled the beans about the Babbage Society, the television newsreaders have been ripping you apart. 'Paranoid' and 'mentally un-balanced' are the kindest things they're saying. Life won't be pleasant for 'Sarah Beaumont,' if she ever surfaces again."

She turned and looked him in the eye. "And what would you have done in my place?"

Red looked at her, looked away, and shrugged. "The same, probably."

"You know what's funny?" she continued, almost to her-self.

"No, what?"

"If They had left me alone, I would never have dug deep enough to find their dirty secret."

Red was not so sure. "Maybe. Maybe not. They had le-gitimate fears."

"So did your people, but *you* didn't try to kill me."

Red grimaced and looked at the ground. Absently he rubbed his wounded arm. "No, we're much crueler than that."

"Yeah, destroy my reputation. Mock the messenger so people won't listen to the message. It's an old tactic."

"It works. How do you think it got to be so old? Dammit, I don't fancy being lynched any more than They do. Why shouldn't we squelch your message?"

"Because it's the truth!"

He shrugged and didn't bother to answer her.

"And because it's futile!" she insisted. "I don't care how many 'moles' you have planted in newsrooms and police agencies. You can't stop it completely. My program will keep on dumping copies of your files—and Their files—until someone figures out how to kill it. Too many people will read them. For every hundred who laugh, there'll be one who wonders. And don't forget the businessmen and politicians."

He looked at her in surprise. "Why them?"

"Think how long they've believed that *they* were pulling the strings. They won't like the thought that they're just var-iables in your cliological equations."

Red smiled thinly. "Less than that, really. Epiphenomena of the midstructure."

Sarah made a sour face and Red laughed.

"You're avoiding my point."

"You have a point?" He kept a cheerful-looking smile on his face and showed it to her.

"Yes. Even if only one person in a hundred decides to follow up, that's still a million people, all around the country. Trying to stomp on me is *useless*. It won't change a damned thing!"

"Maybe not. But if you were bleeding from a fatal wound, wouldn't you try to stanch the blood anyway? Living systems defend themselves. Didn't I tell you that one time? We don't blame you for defending yourself. Sure, We'll discredit your message, destroy your reputation. Sorry. But We'll give you a new identity and a new reputation in compensation."

"Yeah, such a deal."

"It's a better one than most people get. Look; what is it you want most of all, right now?"

"My old life back."

Almost, that stopped him; her voice was filled with such longing. He found he couldn't look her in the eye. "You can't have that. You decided that the moment you ran that worm. Ask for something else."

"All right. I want to destroy Them. I want to find Dennis and I want to make Them hurt for what They did to us."

Red nodded. "OK. That's what I want, too. We've got to get off our keisters and start fighting back. Forget Quinn's Rule."

"The ends justify the means, eh?"

"Don't they? Do you want to see people domesticated?"

"No, dammit! But don't you see, Red? The means have become the end! Why do they want to domesticate us in the first place? To make us more predictable for their equations, to make us more receptive to manipulation. To simplify Their goddamned arithmetic! If you start down the same path, how long before you adopt the same goals?"

"One hundred and twenty years," he told her. "Plus or minus eight years."

She stared at him. "I don't know you," she said.

We don't know ourselves, he thought. *I shouldn't shoot from the lip so much. Not with her, and not about this.* She was right, though, about the means becoming the end. That was why he wanted her so bad. She had insight.

"I'm sorry," he told her. "I didn't mean to sound so flippant. What I meant was that We've got to start fighting Them *now*. The danger you mentioned is real, too; but it's also more remote. We have more time to work on it."

She shook her head once more. "It's more than that. It's the whole notion of manipulating people—"

"Guiding them. . . ." He didn't know if Sarah was just being stubborn or if she really couldn't see it. The future was a branching tree of possibilities, and decisions made today would prune branches years ahead, closing off some possiblilities, opening up others. Often an action that seemed the wisest course at the moment became monumental folly in retrospect. *And those of us who can see further ahead have the duty to guide the rest in the right direction. Don't we?*

Sarah was silent, staring morosely at the horses. Finally she sighed. "If I do decide to join you," she said without looking at him, "will you help me find Dennis?"

Sarah was an impossible woman. Why couldn't she be grateful for coming out of the affair with a whole skin? Which was more than he had. He rubbed his fingers across the bandages and felt the abused flesh and muscles twinge. He remembered the way the shot had thrown him back against the broken wall. *I was lucky.* Memories of that time in Jacksonville . . . Only things had worked out differently then. He didn't want to think about Jacksonville. *She saved my life. I owe her for that.*

"No," he said, and she looked at him in surprise. "No," he repeated. "I'll help you find Dennis whether you join Us or not." He waited for her to say something, grew uncomfortable under her gaze. "I'll not have you join under duress," he explained. "You may choose the new identity or not. You may choose to join us or not. Those are both your choices. But I will help you locate Dennis. That is between you and me."

He turned from her gaze. *I sound like a pompous fool.* He hoped she wouldn't laugh.

She didn't. She shook her head in wonder. "I don't know you at all," she said again.

"Are they treating you all right?" he asked after a while.

Sarah shrugged. "I can't complain." She was silent and Red wondered what was going through her head. Finally, she sighed and touched him gently on the arm. "How's the shoulder?"

"Better, thanks. A little stiff." He moved it experimentally. "The cast will be coming off soon. But I'll never play the violin again." She shot him a look of surprise. "Not that I ever could before," he added with a straight face.

Sarah laughed. She watched the horses with him. One of the mares broke from the herd and galloped across the rolling meadow. Red watched her run, enjoying the beauty of it, the way the legs danced and the muscles worked beneath the tawny skin. The stallion charged after the errant mare, nipping at her flanks, driving her back into the herd. Red glanced down at Sarah and had a sudden impulse to whip her hat off and tousle her hair. *I wonder how she'd react?* He shaded his eyes and looked at the sky. Overhead, an eagle circled. *I'd probably lose my balance and fall, and how would* that *look?*

Sarah pointed at the mares. "Why do you suppose they do that?"

He looked at her, at the mares. "Do what?"

"With this whole wide meadow to choose from, why do they stick their necks out through the fence to nibble the grass on the other side?"

He shrugged. "Maybe it really is greener. How would I know? I don't know anything about farms."

"Ranches," she corrected him. "You don't know anything about ranches. Neither do I, but I think I know the reason."

"Oh? And what is that?"

"Maybe they just don't like fences."

"It's nine o'clock, Brother Malone. Library's about t'close. Don't you think it's time to hang 'em up?"

Red looked up and saw Janie Hatch hovering over him. He marked an entry on the computer printout with a fluorescent marker, folded the sheet once through the middle, then capped the marker and laid it aside. "Nine o'clock already? Time sure flies when you're having fun.

"I just finished the file." He pointed at the printout, wondering what had brought Janie to the library sublevel.

Janie pulled a chair from beneath the neighboring table, turned it backward, and straddled it. "You know it ain't like you're the only one checking through the Dump. We each got assigned a block to check."

"I know that."

"Then why in tarnation are you going through the whole thing yourself?"

Red grinned at her. "Light reading," he said. "Helps me sleep at night."

Janie snorted. "It don't help nobody else. Keeps me awake, wondering what your little buddy spilled to the world."

"She didn't know her worm would endanger us."

"Or she didn't care. Don't get so consarned defensive, Malone. I ain't blaming her. But that ain't the point. The point is to read the Dump careful-like, so we'll know if critical information got released. You try to read too much of it, you git tired. You git too tired, you might miss something."

"I won't miss anything."

"You're a stubborn jackass, Red. How would you know if you missed anything or not?"

"You're right," he said. "I think I will pack it in."

He started to rise from the table, but Janie put a hand on his arm. "It's that Beaumont woman, ain't it? You're doing something for her."

Red looked into the old woman's weathered face. Years of wind and bright sunlight on the open range had narrowed her eyes into a perpetual squint. He could see nothing in them. No hint of emotion. No curiosity. No clue even as to why she had asked the question. "What of it?" he said. "Quinn's Rules allow private projects. Sarah wanted to know if there was anything in the Dump about her architect friend."

"The one that vanished from the hospital?"

"That's the one."

Janie regarded him silently for a moment. "All right. I'll tell Tex to pass the word along to the others to watch for anything in their blocks. What was his name—French?"

Red felt surprise. "Yes. Dennis French. He was at Porter Memorial in Denver." He toyed for a moment with his marker. "Why are you doing this?"

"Doing what?"

"Helping me help Sarah."

The ranch manager shrugged. "Anything we learn about Them is worthwhile. Why'd They bother kidnapping French after They just tried to kill him? Don't make no sense to me. And you shoulda seen the mess his apartment was in, the day I went over there. They fair to tore it apart afore I got there." She gave him a steady gaze. "Like They was looking for something."

He returned her gaze. "I wonder what."

She held him for a moment longer, then released him.

Red figured it was time to leave, so he rose, stuffed the computer printouts into his briefcase, and laid the sheet he had folded carefully on top. Then he closed the briefcase and pushed the snaps shut. He felt Janie's eyes on him the whole time.

"Do you know Mark Lopez?" she said.

Red turned in surprise at the unexpected twist of subject. "Who?"

"Our Station Chief in San Diego. He just sent us that new recruit, Howard."

He shook his head. "I know who you mean. I never met him."

"You may never git the chance. Tex found his name and address in the Dump. In clear. The Council has tried to contact him, to warn him; but no luck so far."

A shiver of fear ran through him. Was it starting already? Government action; mob reaction. What other deadly information was in the Dump? "Anything in the news?" he asked.

"About Brother Lopez disappearing?" She shook her head. "Could be the CIA got him stashed away somewhere. They usually don't issue press releases for that."

He stirred uneasily. Was Janie trying to ask him for a favor? "I could go back to Washington and snoop," he volunteered. "If one of the Agencies has him, I may be able to find out."

"You ain't going nowhere, Red. Not till we know *your* name ain't in the Dump, too."

He knew it was a possibility, of course. He'd been hunting for any mention of his public persona as diligently as he had been for Dennis French or anyone else. He had joked about it with Sarah when he had first gone to see her. "Strung up to the nearest lamppost." A burlesque image, comically grotesque; a parody that insulated one from the reality. Reality was being shot from hiding. Or beaten with fists and baseball bats by an angry mob, delerious with joy that now, at last, they had found a scapegoat for all their troubles. Or simply disappeared, like Lopez, to be questioned with drugs and cattle prods by professionally trained paranoids. Reality was lying a bloody ruin in some back alley.

He shivered. He had just gotten a glimpse of what drove Genevieve Weil.

He looked at Janie Hatch. "What about the ranch? Are we safe here?"

She reached out and gave his briefcase a backhand slap. "That's why we're reading through every line of the Dump. Too many key words and phrases. Search engines can only do so much."

Red looked carefully into her eyes. He wanted to see fear there, the same fear that he felt. He wanted to see something more than academic interest. But Janie returned his scrutiny coldly. "Jest wanted to let you know, Red," she told him. "If'n you're going to git friendly with her, you should know exactly what she done to Us."

III

When Jeremy Collingwood returned to his apartment it took him less than an hour to realize that it had been searched, and only a little bit longer than that to realize that it had been searched twice.

He paused in the foyer to remove his hat and gloves and to place his umbrella in the umbrella stand. As he did so, a nagging feeling stole over him that something was wrong. He frowned and glanced over the apartment and saw nothing amiss, so he put it down to the general malaise he had suffered since Dennis' accident.

Poor Dennis. And he had been there when it happened! In his whole life, he had never seen death or injury. It was appalling how sudden and unexpected it could be. One moment, walking along the sidewalk, discussing the play they had seen; the next, Dennis hurtling through the air and a car disappearing down Arapahoe Street. And the way Dennis had fallen so . . . loosely. Jeremy shivered at the memory.

In the kitchenette, he mixed himself a vodka martini, five parts to one. He stirred the vodka and dry vermouth in a pitcher of ice, humming abstractedly; and before he had quite realized what he was doing, he had poured two highball glasses full.

He stood frozen for a while, contemplating what he had done. It was awful the way habit worked, how the past could turn and slap you across the face. Really, he only needed to pour one drink. Dennis was getting his drinks intravenously, if he was getting them at all.

The ice tinkled as Jeremy set the pitcher down. He stared

at his hand, then gripped the countertop to steady it. Dennis would recover. The doctors all agreed he would recover. There had been a bad time when the hospital records had been mixed up and they told Jeremy that Dennis was no longer there; that he had never been there. At first, Jeremy had thought that the nurse meant that Dennis had died. And the room, when he had run down the corridor, had indeed been empty. But the phone call he had gotten yesterday had assured him that everything was straightened out now and that Dennis was receiving proper care. No visitors yet, however.

Meanwhile, it did no one any good for him to pour two drinks. He carefully poured the second drink back into the pitcher. But then he reflected that by the time he took a second drink, if he did, the ice would have melted and watered it unbearably; so he poured the whole pitcher down the sink. Such a waste, but there was no help for it.

Before he did anything else, he rinsed and dried both the pitcher and the extra glass and set them away. Dennis and he shared the apartment, and Dennis was a meticulous man: in his dress, in his manners. Everything had a place and everything was in it. Jeremy was an accountant, careful by nature, and his habits had meshed quite well with Dennis'.

He walked with his drink to the living room, intending to tune in the all-news cable channel; but in the center of the room the feeling of out-of-placedness returned. He frowned and scanned the room again, more carefully than he had done upon first entering. His eyes searched out everything: buffet, secretary, *bergére* chairs, chesterfield . . .

Why, the pillows on the chesterfield were out of place! He selected a coaster and placed his drink on the sideboard. The ocher pillow went *there* and the rust *there*.

He set them aright, but, once he had noticed one item askew, a dozen others leaped to his eyes. The corner of a paper peeked from the drawer of the secretary. He opened it and saw that the stationery was neatly arranged, but arranged wrongly. The Mondrian on the wall was hanging *upside down*, for Christ's sake! And the chairs were out of place.

He went to hands and knees and explored the nap of the rug with his fingers. Yes, here was where the chair legs had always stood.

A coldness crept through him, starting in his stomach and creeping out to his limbs. *Someone has been in here.* Someone who had searched quite thoroughly and methodically and then tried to put everything back the way it had been.

But why? He made his way to his favorite *bergére* chair and lowered himself into it. A casual thief or burglar would hardly have bothered. Why was it so important, not only to search his quarters but also to conceal the very fact of that search? What had they been looking for? Had anything been taken?

Impulsively he rose and inspected the Mondrian. Yes, it was the genuine article. And if that had not been taken would the thief have left with anything less valuable? Maybe. The painting had been hung upside down, which implied a mis-appreciation for Mondrian's geometric style. Perhaps the thief had simply not recognized its value.

Carefully Jeremy went through the apartment. The silver was all accounted for; so was the jewelry. So was the cash that was hidden none too expertly in a bottom drawer.

When he had satisfied himself that everything of value was still in place, he returned to his chair and sat in it. He steepled his fingers, as if in prayer, and rested his chin on them. The break-in was no robbery.

Should he report it? He caught his lower lip between his teeth and worried it. He couldn't even prove that anyone had been inside the apartment. The pillows were on the wrong side of the sofa? "Really, Mr. Collingwood." They wouldn't understand about Dennis and his fussiness. They really wouldn't. And there would be the knowing smirks and not-so-subtle innuendos.

Yet he had to tell someone. Someone who could help him make sense out of it. He was no good at that sort of thing. Give him columns of figures and ledgers of accounts and he could bring order out of chaos. But when he read mysteries, which was seldom, he could never figure out "whodunit."

Now here was a mystery literally in his own front room. Who could he ask for help? Not Dennis. They still weren't letting him see visitors.

There was that Beaumont woman that Dennis sometimes worked with. She was really quite tolerable for a woman, not constantly playing those teasy, sleazy games that women often did. Dennis had great respect for her.

But Beaumont was gone, vanished; and the TV was saying awful things about her. The television people were rather vague about the details of what she had done, but they were quite certain it was heinous. Unauthorized access to data banks or some such thing.

This is all too complex. Why would someone search his apartment and go to the trouble of straightening it up again, and then botch it by putting things back incorrectly? Anyone careful enough for the former would be too careful for the latter. Unless . . .

There were two of them, of course.

Of course. His head snapped erect and he stared at the wall. Whoever had straightened up the room had misplaced things because they had found the room already disarrayed. No wonder they had gotten some things wrong. Most people would not notice the arrangement of the stationery or the placement of some pillows. The really chilling thing was how much they had gotten *right!*

Somehow, though, that seemed an even deeper mystery. He could imagine that a burglar might try to conceal his tracks. But why would a second burglar try to conceal the tracks of a first burglar? And why was nothing taken?

Could it have something to do with Dennis? That hit-and-run, and now not one but two break-ins. The more Jeremy thought about it, the less it seemed like an accident. He had turned when he first heard the squeal of tires and had gotten the faintest of impressions that the car had veered just a moment before.

Come to think of it, hadn't Beaumont disappeared the same day that Dennis had been struck? That was what? Almost two weeks ago, now. She had called for Dennis, and

Jeremy had told her what had happened, and she hadn't seemed terribly surprised.

Nonsense! He was building elaborate fantasies on very little foundation.

He reached into his inner jacket pocket and retrieved his appointment book. He thumbed through it. He often made notes of Dennis' appointments. He felt vaguely pleased with himself that he was reasoning this out so well. Maybe he did have the makings of a detective. There! There was the day of the accident. Dennis and he had gone to see a revival of *Lady Windemere's Fan* in the Space at the DCPA. The outing had been Jeremy's idea; and so, somehow, the accident had been Jeremy's fault. If only . . .

No! I won't let myself fall into that *trap!* He calmed himself and concentrated.

Ah, yes. Dennis had had a luncheon meeting that same day with a man named Morgan Grimes. Grimes. The name was oddly familiar. On TV? In the newspaper? Newspaper. That was it! Grimes was the newspaperman who had been killed in a drug deal.

A cold hand squeezed Jeremy's heart. Dennis and this Grimes fellow had done lunch, and by the next day one was run over by a car and the other stabbed dead. Later, Beaumont calls, frantic, then disappears. And she had been shot at earlier, he suddenly remembered, by that madman in the Civic Center. Dennis had been very upset when Jeremy had shown him the news story. And hadn't Grimes written that story, too?

He had the sudden notion that he was surrounded by unseen menaces. Menaces who were striking down people around him (some of whom he barely knew), and who, today, had reached in and violated his very home. More anxious now, a flutter in the center of his chest, he searched through the appointment book, looking for other clues to Dennis' activities.

———

Daniel Kennison lounged in his high-backed leather chair and rested his elbows on the arms. He clasped his hands together and watched the others around the long mahogany conference table. *We're a fine crew,* he thought sourly. The other Councillors twittered and chattered and fluttered like birds whose nest had been disturbed. *Fools.* Kennison clenched his teeth and kept his peace. His darting eyes made a circuit of the table and caught Gretchen Paige watching him. She flashed him a wintry smile and he returned one a few degrees colder.

They bicker and plot while everything we've worked for lies on the verge of collapse. The bucket brigade on the *Titanic*. The Founders would be ashamed of them.

There was no doubt in his mind that Genevieve Weil had mismanaged the entire Beaumont affair from beginning to end. She had panicked and had stampeded the rest of the Council with her. Certainly the Intruder had been close to unraveling the Secret, but they should not have assumed so quickly that Beaumont was the Intruder. *He* had argued that she was only a casual researcher. Maybe he had been wrong, too; but hindsight showed him closer to the mark than the Chairman.

Act in haste, Madam Chairman, he thought, *repent in leisure.*

Yet there she sat, plumed and rouged like a Hollywood starlet, calmly assigning portions of the blame to everyone but herself. No sign of repentance on her bony model's face. He wished she would say, "I'm sorry. I screwed up," so they could stop pointing fingers and get on with the business of salvaging the Society. But that, he suspected, was not in the cards.

He had slept with Genevieve once—few were those who dared refuse her demands—and once had been enough. It had been a sobering experience. Lying with her had been like hugging a pile of coat hangers. She had said all the right things and made all the right moves. She had writhed and moaned and clutched in a parody of passion. There was no doubt she was technically proficient, but Kennison had sensed it was all a sham, like an actress giving the two thousandth performance of a dull play. The plot had gone stale and the lines came out flat, but she insisted on performances every night.

At one time or another, Kennison knew, she had slept with every other member of the Council, male and female. And probably, he liked to tell himself, with not a few of their household pets. Kennison kept a boa constrictor in a terrarium just in case it was true.

"We have heard nothing of the Beaumont woman since Brother Crayle was dispatched. That would indicate that Crayle has succeeded in deleting her from the equations."

Kennison cast an eye at Genevieve. "Nor have we heard from Brother Crayle," he commented dryly. And what would *that* indicate? That Beaumont had bested Crayle? Impossible! But there were indications that Betancourt's people were after her, too. Red Malone had made contact that one time and tried to work out a deal.

Had Malone taken her under the Associates' protection? Possible. Possible. Did that mean that Beaumont had been part of an Associate operation? Did they really think they could expose the Society without exposing themselves? No, Betancourt was too shrewd for that. And Malone had seemed genuinely surprised when Kennison had told him about Beaumont's spyder. Besides, that damnable worm had dumped Associate files along with Society files.

He lit a long, thin cigarillo and sent a cloud of acrid smoke toward the ceiling. Madam Chairman had been stupid to call a Council, and doubly stupid, having called it, to make such poor use of it. It was time to throw a few memes into the pot.

"How much longer shall we sit here and discuss spilt milk?" he asked.

The buzz of conversation halted and they all looked at him. Genevieve turned hard, dark eyes on him, like ranging radars for a gun turret, and she swiveled her mouth into position for an answering blast.

"Damn it all, Brother Kennison's right! We've been here

for four hours and we have settled *nothing*. Let the dead bury the dead. Yesterday's gone; tomorrow's what matters." That, somewhat to Kennison's surprise, had been Gretchen Paige. He looked at her and she gave a look back that said, *You owe me one.* He wondered what her game was. The same as his? Possible. Possible.

The wonderful thing about memetic engineering on the micro level was that a few trite proverbs dropped into a discussion acted like seed crystals in a supersaturated solution. The connotations of the proverbs, the cultural baggage they carried, immediately triggered certain thoughts, sometimes below the conscious level. The fact that everyone at the table recognized—and used—the same techniques did not stop them from working. *"Spilt milk." "Bury the dead." "Yesterday's gone." Madam Chairman is wasting our time. Let's get on with it.* Heads around the table were nodding like marionettes.

Genevieve's face was a mask of pure hatred. If looks could kill. The meme sprang quickly to mind and Kennison reminded himself that they were, after all, in Genevieve's mansion, surrounded by Genevieve's retainers. It was time for some salve.

"Gentlemen. Ladies," said Kennison. "Madam Chairman did the best that she could in a confusing and rapidly changing situation. She deserves our thanks for handling it as well as she did. We all supported her actions at the time. If the results have not been entirely to our liking . . ."—he grinned crookedly and shrugged his shoulders—". . . we have only to review our Society's history to gain some perspective. We all know how unexpected linkages can take us by surprise, all the more so when we are dealing with a handful of individuals, too few to comprise a statistical universe. Madam Chairman cannot deserve all the blame."

Since Madam Chairman had not been about to take *any* of the blame, it was left-handed praise at best. But he saw Genevieve smile in satisfaction and sit taller in her chair. The stupid cow! The stupid, scrawny cow. She was like one of those zebu that roamed the streets of India, bones showing through shrunken flesh, not doing anything useful, but too sacred for anyone to touch. Well, Kennison was no Hindu!

He saw that his remarks had not been lost on other Councillors, at least. Ullman had raised an eyebrow, and Lewis was grinning openly. The connotations in his praise were more subtle. They acted subliminally, but they acted nonetheless. "—supported her actions *at the time*—" "—did *the best that she could*—" "—handling it *as well as she did*—" "—*not entirely* to our liking—" It all added up to: "Madam Chairman is an incompetent bungler."

"Yes," said Sister Paige. "Let the minutes reflect a vote of confidence in our Chairman's past decisions." They all rapped their knuckles on the table, some with cynicism but some, Kennison noted, with genuine conviction! He noted who the latter were. They would not be on *his* Council, if and when.

If and when. He counted votes. What if Madame Weil was deleted from the equations? Who could he count on besides Sorenson and Montfort? Not Ullman or Ruiz. And Huang was an enigma, as always. Lewis? Who could tell what went on inside that grinning bullet head? That left Benton, Toohey, and Westfield. No, it was too chancy yet. Too chancy.

"The issue before us now," Paige began, and Kennison decided to let her run the ball. If the discussion *should* trigger any of Madam Chairman's fabled anger, let Paige be the target. "The issue before us now is how best to preserve the Secret. This is the most serious breach of security since Brady Quinn went rogue. That our enemies were able to penetrate our databases and release them to the world indicates the need for twofold action. First: close that particular barn door and keep it from being opened again. Second: contain and redirect the flow of unwanted memes among the general populace."

Too late, Kennison saw his mistake. Paige's not-so-subtle digs at Kennison's handling of the data banks diverted the Councillors' collective subconscious away from Weil's competency and toward his own. That image of the barn door.

It connoted carelessness, inattention. He felt the tips of his ears redden and was glad he wore his hair long. Perhaps Paige was his true enemy, not Weil.

Before he could say anything, there was a knock on the door and Weil's butler entered. He was an old man who walked with a pronounced stoop. He looked like a resurrected corpse, and a not too successful resurrection at that.

Judd, of course, was an Initiate of the Society, but he had been a Weil man since before Genevieve's time. Kennison wondered whether the old man's loyalties lay with the Society or with his mistress. That might depend on whether the old man was lying with his mistress. Kennison suppressed a laugh and kept his face composed. Did Genevieve's escapades include old Judd? Perhaps that was why the man always looked so drained.

Judd bent over and whispered in Genevieve's ear. Madam Chairman's face paled. She looked around the table. "Judd tells me that there are two reporters from the *Sun Times* loitering around the front gate. He has asked them to leave, but they have refused. They claim their car has broken down and they are waiting for help."

"Perhaps they are waiting to see who enters and leaves your mansion, Madam Chairman," said Frederick Ullman acidly.

Good! thought Kennison. *Someone else thought of it.* Under the circumstances, a face-to-face Council meeting had been a stupid idea. Part of the process of discrediting Beaumont was to propagandize the memes that her tales of a secret cabal were the ravings of a disjointed mind. To be discovered, en masse, as it were, in Weil's mansion could destroy that meme set and call into question the entire contra-Beaumont program.

But who could have tipped the reporters? Who? Or did they think of this stakeout on their own and it was just bad luck that the Council was meeting? Kennison did not believe in coincidences.

"Don't be too harsh on Madam Chairman," said Gretchen Paige. "She undoubtedly felt that a Council conducted on our intranet would be even less secure than a meeting *in corpora*." Paige smiled at Kennison. "Brother Kennison is no doubt working around-the-clock to secure the breaches wrought by the Beaumont person, but for now we dare not risk meeting on the Net."

"Oh, yes," said Kennison pleasantly. "I am working to secure all of our weak points." And he smiled most broadly at them all.

IV

Aaron Gewirtz spun his wheelchair around and braked sharply in front of Norris Bosworth, the one Sarah though of privately as SuperNerd. "Can you cite an example of such a spin-off?"

"Ah . . . Automobile production and the Baby Boom?" Bosworth stammered as he answered. Aaron had that effect on most of his pupils. He knew exactly whom he would call on before he turned his chair, but finding those sightless eyes staring straight at you had an unnerving effect.

"Are you asking me or telling me?"

"Ah . . . I'm telling you? The, uh, backseat was a convenient place for, uh, impregnating young women. That led to significant changes in, uh, courtship rituals." Bosworth blushed a deep and sincere red. SuperNerd was a gangly adolescent, recruited into the Associates by his uncle. "That was a spin-off," he finished, "totally unintended by the inventors of the automobile."

"Good. You have the courage of your convictions, however wrong they may be. Would anyone care to . . . Yes, Ms. Howard?"

It was uncanny. Maureen Howard had raised her hand silently. That gizmo Gewirtz wore . . . A motion sensor? Howard was a plump woman from Seattle and dressed in voluminous muumuus and wooden clogs. The Earth Mother.

From time to time Sarah had caught Howard glowering in her direction.

"I can't believe that any significant fraction of the Baby Boomers was conceived that way," the Earth Mother said. "The Boom was simply an adjustment to the Baby Bust of the Great Depression. The pendulum swung from one extreme to the other."

Dr. Gewirtz shook his head sadly. "Am I losing my touch? Are my words like the seed that fell on the hard ground? Perhaps it is time for me to retire. Ms. Howard, no one consults the *Statistical Abstracts* prior to copulation, crying, 'Let us procreate more diligently to compensate for our parents' lackluster performance!' " The class tittered and he favored them with a harsh glare. There were five recruits in the class. Plus Sarah. "Very well. Mr. Bosworth claims that the automobile, by inducing a change in sexual practice, caused the Baby Boom of the fifties. Ms. Howard claims that the 'backseat' effect could not have been so large. Which is right; which is wrong?"

"They're both wrong," Sarah said on impulse.

"Ah, Ms. Beaumont! The Sphinx speaks at last. Enlighten us with your too-infrequent wisdom."

"*Did* the automobile change the sexual habits of teenagers?"

"Very good! You answer me with a question, but—your pardon—a pregnant question. I am an old man. My grandfather once told me how he and his friends would 'spark the gals' in their buckboards—and that many an early marriage or 'late-in-life' baby resulted." He paused and a smile chased itself across his face. "The buckboard, in fact, possessed a singular advantage over the automobile. There was no need actually to 'park' to accomplish one's intentions. The horse knew where she was going, even if her passengers did not. It seems likely, then, that such practices have not so much become more common as more public. (A trend which I deplore, on the grounds of good taste.) However—" He turned his wheelchair and faced the projection screen. "The equations that I've written imply that 'ricochets' in a highly connected network lead to unexpected results, especially when there are significant lags between events—when the system has, as we say, high viscosity. Again: Can anyone cite an example of such a spin-off? Let me make it more challenging—since such examples abound for those with the wit to see them. Can anyone cite an example which includes Mr. Bosworth's Baby Boom?"

Sarah sighed, closed her eyes, and raised her hand.

"Ms. Beaumont?"

She opened her eyes and saw that Dr. Gewirtz had not even bothered to turn around. How *did* he know who to call on? "The Baby Boom," she heard herself say, "was an unexpected spin-off, but of the GI Bill, not the automobile."

Gewirtz turned and the sightless eyes bored into her. "Explain."

She stuck her chin out and answered in a confident voice, "The human breeding strategy is to raise the largest number of affordable children, balancing net resources against the costs of child rearing."

Gewirtz made an exaggerated shiver. "What about love, passion, romance? What is the value of a baby's smile? Many a parent would sacrifice much for such return. Is there no room in your world for human feelings?"

And how had the textbook become "her" world? "No, sir. A statistical relationship is an attribute of the *system,* not of the individuals within the system. They might not do the arithmetic, but Mom and Dad know it when they can't afford another kid."

"That doesn't make sense," said John Starling, another recruit, but one so wrapped up in his own abilities that he questioned everything anyone else said. "Then how come poor people have more get than rich ones?"

Sarah turned and looked at him. *Get?* Human babies were *get?*

But his objection was one she could answer from personal experience. "It's not a matter of gross resources, but *net* resources—whatever the parents don't need to sustain their own status—relative to the costs of child rearing. It simply doesn't cost that much to raise a child in poverty." *No, Sarah,* remembered voices told her, *you can't have a new dress. Mama will let down the hem on your old one; it still has* months *of life in it.* There had been no college funds on the old South Side. No brand-new cars for graduation presents. What did these people, who spoke so offhandedly of "breeding strategies" and "get," know of that reality? "After World War Two," she continued, "the GI Bill made it cheaper and easier to buy a home, to secure a job, to go to school. That reduced the 'cut' the parents needed to sustain themselves, so it increased the residual available for child rearing."

"Very good, Ms. Beaumont." He bowed slightly to her. "However, if you would consult the data, a radical notion, I admit, you will find that while the birthrates had been dropping since 1820—"

"Because the country was urbanizing. Another kid on the farm creates additional income, but in the cities—"

Gewirtz raised his voice. "—since 1820, I say; but it began to increase in the early 1940s, *before* the war and therefore before the GI Bill. So perhaps there are other factors at work. Remember: 'It's a Poor Effect That Has But One Cause.' If you would prepare a complete cliological assessment of the birthrate—using, say, a fault tree—your classmates and myself would be eternally grateful. Be sure to include intangibles in your formulation of costs and benefits. The infant's smile. Show how free will produces a probability distribution around the expected value generated by the equations. We will expect your report in, let us say, two weeks."

Sarah sighed and nodded. "Yes, sir." It didn't matter whether you answered correctly or incorrectly. Dr. Gewirtz handed out assignments with cavalier impartiality.

Red Malone was waiting for her outside the door when Dr. Gewirtz dismissed the group. He was leaning against the wall, his good arm crossed over his sling, whistling a tuneless ditty. "Carry your books for you," he offered.

She handed him one of the thick ring binders that they used for textbooks. He juggled it under his good arm and walked with her down the hall.

"Are you sparking me?" she asked suddenly.

"What?" He stared at her. "Sparking?" He looked puzzled.

"Never mind." Carry her books? How corny could he get?

"How do you like orientation?"

She rolled her eyes at him. "Lord God, Red. I swear I've never studied so much so hard in so short a time as I have for these sessions. Is it always like that?"

"No, I think Aaron is taking it easy on you because you started later than the others."

Red would never die from an overdose of seriousness. Still, the heavy reading schedule she had been given had kept her occupied for the past several weeks and had generally kept her mind off her personal problems. She wondered if that might not be the reason that she was in the classes in the first place. Strictly speaking, she was not yet a "recruit."

Fortunately, she had always had a "bump" for learning. Her classmates had always been "bored" with school, but that was a spiral that led steadily downward into apathy and oblivion. The less you knew, the more boring the world became. Learning was always more fun.

Well, maybe not always. Lately she had learned things that were no fun at all. But not boring. No, certainly not more boring.

They walked along in silence until they reached the elevator. The ranch was a safe house that the Associates kept for training purposes and for hiding people who needed hiding. Above ground it looked like a simple wooden building, but the underground was honeycombed with tunnels and hidden rooms. Sarah had been billeted in a suite on the third sublevel. Along the way to the elevator, she bore the stares of passersby.

"They don't like me, do they?" she asked Red as the elevator door closed on them. "The staff here."

"Should they? You've upset their cozy little world. Not only did your Dump give the professional whiners someone new to blame for their complaints, but it piqued the Official Government's curiosity. 'Whom the gods notice' and all that. Why do you think I haven't gone back to my cover job? Officially, I'm on medical leave. I broke my arm falling from a horse—" He patted his sling. "But until we learn how high you yanked our skirts up, we won't know who is safe from disappearing into custody. My 'colleagues' might be a tad suspicious if they've seen the name of 'Red Malone' in your Dump."

The elevator dinged and opened on the third floor. They stepped out into the hallway and the doors closed behind them. "Do *you* hate me?" Sarah asked suddenly.

Red looked thoughtful. "No. I can't hate a living system for performing a natural function. No, I guess I feel exasperated."

Living system! She would show him a living system performing a natural function! Right upside the head. "Exasperated?"

"The morning news reported that neo-Nazis vandalized several synagogues in the Northwest and South because of your Dump."

The non sequitur stopped her dead in her tracks. Red walked several paces ahead of her before he realized it and turned. "What's that got to do with anything?" she asked him.

"The Law of Unintended Consequences. Wasn't that the subject of Aaron's lecture today? Ever notice how a story changes as it spreads from person to person? Memetic drift, due to random mutations in the words?"

"Get to the point!"

"Your Dump started a story. Thousands of people read the contents. Tens of thousands heard *about* the contents, and millions heard about hearing about it. Understand? There are millions of people out there today who've only heard vague, secondhand rumors about a secret cabal controlling the course of history. Who? Why, the Jews, of course. Or the Masons. Or the Vatican. Or the Trilateral Commission. You can fill in your favorite whipping boy. The World Trade Organization."

"No! That's not right! I never said that!"

"What you said and what people heard are two different things. You spooked the herd. Predicting a stampede wasn't rocket science. That's why Quinn laid down the Law a hundred years ago. Even when you want to do good, you can wind up doing harm."

They had reached the door to her suite and Red handed her book back to her. Then, unexpectedly, he put his good arm around her and hugged her. He brought his lips to her cheek but only whispered, "Eight-thirty tonight, at the horse corral." Then he left her and retreated down the hall.

Sarah looked after him until he disappeared into the elevator. Then she raised her hand and touched her cheek where Red had not yet kissed her.

The western sky had burst into glorious color when Sarah stepped outside. The clouds, drifting in echelon like the battle fleet of an aerial navy, seemed to graze the peaks above the ranch. The cloud tops were dark with the coming night, but the bottoms glowed orange from sunlight beyond the horizon. Sarah found Red leaning on the corral fence. He had finally abandoned Eastern garb in favor of more sensible Western clothing. On him, though, the Stetson looked incongruous, like a bow tie on a gas pump. "Howdy, pardner," she said.

"Pardner," Red grunted. "You really get into this scene, don't you? The West. Cowboys, horses, mountains."

"Don't you? No, of course not. You don't even realize you're sitting with your back to the sunset."

Red twisted his head and looked at the clouds. "Nice."

She shook her head. "Nice, the man says. You'll never see anything like that back East."

Red sighed. "All right, but I still don't get it. You're a city girl."

"Still am, most of the time. Denver isn't such a small

town. Sure, I grew up in Chicago. I knew every alley and hidey-hole on the South Side. But this is home for me, now. I knew it when I first laid eyes on it."

Red glanced at his watch. "We have a few minutes yet. Want to tell me about it?"

She stuffed her hands into her jeans pockets. "Not much to tell, really. One day I just walked into my job at the *Trib* and told 'em I quit. I had no plans, no new jobs waiting for me anywhere. But Chicago was closing in on me. I wanted . . . I didn't know then what I wanted. Something different. Wider horizons, maybe."

"Most young girls would have headed for New York."

"Yeah. But New York is just a bigger Chicago, dirty and run-down and . . ." She shook her head. "I tossed everything I owned in the back of my old Chevy and headed for the interstate. I didn't have any notion of where I was headed. Just out of Chicago. I went south on the Dan Ryan and, when I came to the turnoff for the Skyway, I went west instead of east. Well, then I kept turning west and before I knew it I was on I-80, heading God-knew-where . . ."

She paused and sat on the lower fence rail, bent way over, her knees pressed against her chest. She leaned out and pulled a stem of grass from the ground and began tugging and tearing at the leaves. "I drove through Illinois and Iowa and the flatlands of Nebraska without really seeing them. All along the way I kept asking myself if I was doing the right thing and telling myself that I was being stupid. And then, one day—I think it must have been maybe midafternoon—somewhere between Julesburg and Sterling I first saw that magnificent snowcapped wall of mountains marching across the horizon. 'Purple mountains' majesty.' I never knew what that meant before, but I knew what it meant then. I knew I was *home*."

Red nodded silently. "To each his own," he said after a while. "Me, I couldn't imagine life without the bright lights and action, without the grit and reality."

"Red, between Washington, D.C., and the Sangre de Cristo, which is reality and which is fantasy?"

He hopped down from the fencepost. "I never said I had no fantasies." He gathered himself up. "Well, it looks like a nice evening for a walk." Then, in a whisper, he said, "Behind the barn. The others are waiting."

She looked at him quizzically, but he was already ambling off. Others? What was Red up to? *Why did he ask me to come out here?*

And why did I come?

There were three others behind the barn: SuperNerd and two men she didn't know. They looked at her curiously, indistinct shapes in the dusk. One of the men was middle-aged and somewhat far gone into swivel-chair spread. The other was younger, flat-stomached, and lounged against the barn wall with unself-conscious assurance. He was dressed like a cowhand.

"Well," said Sarah, in a low voice, "who has the cornsilk?"

The older man chuckled, but all she got from the other two were blank looks.

She hunkered down by the wall and pulled a stem of wild grass. She began twisting and knotting it. "You friends of Red?" There was no answer, so she decided the hell with it. She settled in to wait with her own thoughts.

Red reappeared a few minutes later to tell them it was all clear and introduced everyone, speaking low and quickly. The older man was Walter Polovsky; the younger was Tex Bodean, Janie Hatch's *segundo*. Sarah shook her head. Who named their kid Tex these days?

Tex and Walter knew each other. They had never met SuperNerd. They had heard of Sarah, but what they had heard hadn't pleased them too much. "I know what you done," said Bodean. "And I suppose that if'n it'd been me I'da done the same. But I don't expect I gotta like it."

"Never mind that now," said Red. "Listen up. Sarah, tell them what you told me about that list you and French found in Carson's old mansion."

She explained how Dennis and she had come across the

handwritten list of events and how the historian at DU had told him that they were turning points of history. Red interrupted to add, "One of the entries was the assassination of Lincoln."

Walter nodded as if that explained a lot. SuperNerd listened eagerly. Tex simply waited.

"What else was on the list?" Red prompted her.

"I don't remember. A lot has happened. Let's see. . . . Frederick Taylor and his management system. Dewey and his teaching methods. I remember those because Dennis and I talked about them. Oh, and Brady Quinn's death, and a couple of others."

"Davis Belleau? Agatha Penwether?" That was Walter. She told him yes, and he nodded again. He looked a question at Red. "Sounds like some of Quinn's and Carson's early work. What's the point? We already know about it. Hell, Quinn and Shelton helped engineer Lincoln's assassination even before the Schism."

"Tell them what else, Sarah," Red said.

"Well . . ." She wracked her memory, trying to recall fragments of conversation with Dennis. "Teddy Roosevelt being made Vice President. Umm. Winfield Scott's military appointments." She saw Walter's head jerk around, and Tex stood up, away from the wall. "And, oh yes, Lincoln's election, too. And—"

"What is this, Red?" demanded Tex. "They don't belong on that list!"

"And neither did von Kluck's Turn or the sinking of the *Lusitania*," said Red.

"Hell, those happened in Europe, and the Society . . ." Tex's voice petered out and he stared at Red.

"Someone—probably Carson—had done an orthogonal factor analysis," Red told them, "and numbered the entries with ones, twos, and threes."

"Jesus H. Christ on a Harley," said Tex. It sounded like a prayer, not a curse.

"That's right," said Red. "Who the hell is Number Three?"

Sarah laughed and the others looked at her. "All that

sweat," she explained, "and all that anxiety to keep your Secret from leaking out. And all along someone else has had it, too! That's rich; that's really rich!"

Walter scowled. "I don't see how it's funny. As if we didn't have enough on our hands fighting Them and pulling the wool over Cam—"

"And that's not all," Red said. "Can any of you read French?" Sarah told him she could and he reached into his shirt pocket and took out a piece of paper. "Tell me what this says. It's off of a Quebec City node of the Internet."

Sarah looked at him, then unfolded the paper. She saw it was a sheet of machine paper. A copy of a memo. "It says," she told them, "that there is a string of suspicious murders that bear looking into. Then it gives a list of names and dates. Jesus, it looks like Morgan's list!"

Red nodded. "I recognized the names."

Walt reached out and took the sheet from Sarah. He studied it while Tex and SuperNerd hung by his shoulders.

Sarah looked at Red. "Quebec?"

Walt looked up. "We don't have a station in Quebec, but They do."

"In Montreal," Tex reminded him. "Not Quebec City."

Walt shrugged. "Branch office?"

"But why investigate murders that They themselves committed?" Sarah said. "Don't fight it, Walt. It looks like my worm's search list plucked up a file from Number Three."

"I've been going through the whole Dump looking for strays," Red explained. "Anything that I couldn't assign to Us or Them. This"—he flicked the sheet with his fingertips—"is the only one I found. Being in French, it stood out."

Silence fell on them and they looked at one another uneasily. Sarah wondered what they were thinking.

"The question now," said Red, "is: what do we do about it? Do we tell Cam and the others? Or do we nose around on our own before deciding what the best course is?"

"Brother Betancourt'll find out soon enough," Tex decided. "Whoever's reviewing that block will notice it and pass it upstairs."

"Maybe," Red allowed. "But everyone's concentrating on plugging Our own leaks. The checker, whoever it is, may see it, note that it isn't Ours, and not give it any further thought."

"Either way," Walt said, "we should keep quiet. Figure out how this affects our plans. Is Number Three an ally or an enemy?"

"I've got a question," said SuperNerd. They all looked at him. "This third group. We know about them, but do they know about us?"

Walt looked at the printout; then he looked at Sarah. "They sure as hell do now."

SuperNerd rubbed his nose and toyed with a pimple there. "Then time is probably not one of our major resources."

Red walked her back to the complex. He walked with his hands stuffed into his jeans. The others had dispersed on their separate ways.

"Five people?" she asked him. "That's your secret cabal?"

He scowled. "Don't be silly. Not everyone is at the ranch."

"Still, do you have enough 'assets' to locate a group that's stayed hidden at least as long as you have?"

"We should have thought of it ourselves. Nature keeps no secrets. What one person learns anyone can learn. Crawford couldn't have been the only one who read Babbage's book."

Silence closed down as they approached the ranch building. Sarah stopped on the porch and looked up at the stars. Somehow it was always the Big Dipper that caught her eye first. She remembered one time camping out above the tree line and gazing up at this same slowly revolving sky and feeling—really feeling—what an immense distance it was from here to there. She leaned on the wooden railing that ringed the porch, feeling the cool night breeze. There were animal sounds floating in the distance, muffled by the spruce forest around them. Red coughed and she turned and faced him.

"You're going to hear this tomorrow, but I thought you'd rather hear it from me."

"What?"

He shuffled his feet. "Your house in Applewood was vandalized. Vandals smashed everything. Spray-painted the walls. Set fire to the drapes."

She hadn't thought there was anything left in the world that could reach her. Shock after shock had annealed her emotions until they lay numbed and hardened. The brush with death, the loss of friends, the flight from everything she knew and loved . . . She closed her eyes, and tears forced themselves through. "What?" As if repeating the message would change it. "Why?" She opened her eyes and looked at him through a blur. "Everything?" she said. "The piano?"

"That was smashed. But no, they didn't get everything. One of Us went down there a couple times over the holiday weekend to save what we could. It was easy to forecast something like this would happen sooner or later. People always blame the messenger for the message."

"Easy to fore—?" She turned on him and stood with her arms stiff at her sides, her hands curled into fists. "Then why didn't you stop it?"

"How? Post armed guards twenty-four hours a day?"

"Dammit, Red," she said, fighting tears. "I loved that place. It was just right. I picked out each piece for it."

"We've got a piano here. A whole music room."

"That's not the point, Red. It's not *my* piano!"

He scuffed a boot. "I'm sorry. We did what We could. Here." He took her by the arm and led her inside the ranch to the hidden elevator. "I'll show you what we saved." She followed him in a daze, angry with herself for letting the news affect her so. *I thought I was going to be strong from now on.* But there was a limit to the shocks a person could take. When they reached her door, she tried to open it, but somehow she couldn't get the key to go into the lock. Red took it from her and opened the door.

And she stepped into the past. She stopped and looked around, not believing what she saw. The wall hangings and the photographs and the lamps and even the big stuffed chair that she sometimes fell asleep in reading. The painting she had done herself fifteen years ago, when she had thought about taking up art. And her books! Conrad and Trevor and Block and Heinlein. Well worn and dog-eared. Faithful companions, all of them. A chime made her turn around, and there was the grandfather clock behind the door. She gripped it with both hands, like an old friend long lost, and stared at her reflection in the glass. Behind her, on the countertop in the kitchenette, she could see the reflection of Fee's food dish.

And that was one piece she didn't want to see. She had used her precious Fee to distract Crayle during that terror on the mountaintop. It had saved her life and lost her Fee.

"This was the official reason I kept you outside tonight. So Janie's people could get the room set up for you."

Who am I kidding? she thought. *These things don't matter to me. It's not the house and furniture, but the memories and the struggles they represent. Everything that brought me to where I was. Everything that I've lost now, forever.* She didn't think she could stand seeing that food dish.

"They found something else on the last trip," said Red, opening the bedroom door.

And Feline P. Cat strutted out, regal and arrogant. He hopped to the countertop and complained.

"Fee!" Sarah hugged him and the cat endured her patiently. "I looked all over for you. You ran off. Not that I blame you after the way I treated you." She looked at Red. "Where'd you find him?"

"Our people found him at your house. After combing Mount Falcon for three freakin' days. He'd gotten in through the cat door, and boy, was he a mess." He shook his head. "Found his way back, somehow. I've heard of dogs doing that, but never a cat." He edged toward the door. "I'll leave the two of you to get reacquainted."

"Red Malone, hold it right there!" Red froze in the doorway and Sarah stuck a finger at him. "My house must have been under surveillance. Government, neighbors, Them . . .

everyone wondering if I was coming back. Whoever went there to salvage my things was a damn fool, because none of this is worth his idiot neck. Except Fee." She stroked the cat and heard the familiar purr. "For that, I'll forgive him his stupidity." She looked back at Red. "You wouldn't happen to know the name of whoever it was, would you?"

Red blushed. It was the most amazing thing Sarah had ever seen. His entire face turned a deep crimson that ran down his neck and into his shirt. That was the great thing about white folks. You could tell a lot just from their skin.

"Yeah, I thought so. Why'd you do it, Red?"

He looked at the carpet. "Because we owed it to you."

"Nice try. Try again."

"Because it seemed the right thing to do."

"Better. Once more."

"All right! Because I *wanted* to do it! Me! For my own reasons!"

She cradled Fee in her arms. "Now, why would you want to do a fool thing like that?"

"Because I wanted to see you smile, just once before I died."

Her mouth dropped open and she stopped stroking Fee, who twisted in her arms to find out what had happened. "Red, you—"

"And besides, I left my plumber's van at your place."

V

Jeremy watched the pudgy history professor draw on her corncob pipe and send an O of smoke drifting toward the ceiling. Through the office window behind her he could see a few lone students ambling along the paths between buildings, books tucked under their arms. During midsummer, most of the students were studying Tan 101 in California or Florida.

"Yes, Mr. Collingwood. I do remember your friend's visit.

Rather unusual, you know. A nonstudent making an appointment."

Jeremy leaned forward. "I'm convinced he was involved in something . . . Well, something dangerous. I've checked his appointments for the last month and yours is the only one that was out of the ordinary. I thought perhaps there might be a clue in it."

"A clue?" Prof. Gwynneth Llewellyn pursed her lips. "I wouldn't have thought there was much of anything dangerous about the study of history! Your friend wanted background information on a few historical incidents. I answered his questions as best I could and he left."

Jeremy closed his eyes in weariness. Who did he think he was fooling? Jeremy Collingwood, private investigator? Ludicrous! It was worse than ludicrous! Yet he had to know. About Dennis, about the break-in at their apartment. "Well, I'm sorry to have bothered you."

He started to rise, but Llewellyn waved him down. She pointed to her telephone. "Do you know what that is, Mr. Collingwood?" Llewellyn pointed to a device in the phone's mouthpiece.

Jeremy saw that a tape player had been jacked into the opened mouthpiece. He looked from the jury-rigged setup to the professor and back to the setup. The widgets and wires were just widgets and wires. He shook his head. "I'm no good with gadgets. I've never even seen the insides of a telephone."

"I have, Mr. Collingwood; and that doesn't belong there. It's a bug. It picks up and transmits anything that is said in this room, even with the phone hooked. Unless I connect my tape player to its input. Whoever is on the other end is now listening to A Typical Day in a Historian's Office. Sounds of me reading, typing, lighting my pipe, and so forth." She took her pipe from between her teeth and smiled. "Not anything to threaten the Top Forty, but I like it."

Jeremy raised an eyebrow.

"I was a student radical once," she explained, "and I learned a long time ago to recognize tampering with my phones." She looked again at the bug. "I wish I knew who planted this one, and why. I discovered it about a month ago, shortly after I met with your friend, though I didn't make any connection at the time between the meeting and the bug. Not until you called and told me what had happened to your apartment. That is too much coincidence, and I have never liked coincidence." She shrugged and seated herself behind her desk. She leaned forward on her elbows and pointed the stem of her pipe at him. "Now, Mr. Collingwood. Let's you and I have ourselves a little talk."

Two hours later, Jeremy was pacing the room and Llewellyn was jotting notes on a yellow legal pad. "Let me see if I can summarize," she said, picking up the pad. "Your friend showed me a slip of paper with a list of dates and events on it—he didn't tell you where he found it, did he? No? Me, neither. Or I don't remember if he did—I told him that, in my opinion, the list was one of occasions when the actions of a comparative handful had had a disproportionate influence on later events. Horseshoe nails, we called them."

" 'Give me a place to stand,' " Jeremy quoted, " 'and a place to set my lever and I can move the world.' "

"Archimedes. Yes." She tapped her pen against the pad in an irregular rhythm. "I didn't think much of it at the time. I took the notes to be someone's attempt to prove the importance of individuals in the course of history." She pursed her lips before continuing. "But now you tell me that Mr. French was a partner of this Sarah Beaumont who's been in the news lately. I don't pay much attention to the television, I'm afraid. I had heard about her allegations, of course—mostly talk around the department—but the conspiracy business is a growth industry. Every day someone discovers a new one: about Kennedy, about Lincoln, about the pharmaceutical industry. Mostly rubbish, of course; so after a while you learn not to pay attention. Yet put the Dump together with your friend's list of horseshoe nails and . . ."

"Yes. Perhaps it *is* true."

"Hmm. I'd like to read it. It shouldn't be too hard to lay hands on a copy." She frowned and drummed her desk with her fingers. "I have some grant money," she said, as much to herself as to Jeremy. "I was planning to use it for another project, but . . ." She laid her pen down. "I'm going to see the dean about this," she announced. "I think we can put together a study team. Bring top scholars in from around the country. Either confirm what was in Beaumont's download or lay it to rest."

Jeremy tried to look interested. The professor's concern lay not in who had tried to kill Dennis but in the list. She was concerned with history, whatever that was. He wondered if it was possible to be interested in history without being interested in the people who lived it and decided that it was. It seemed a dry and soulless thing to him. Perhaps that was why he had never taken to it.

Llewellyn pointed her pipe stem at him. "Tell you what. I'll make you the project's administrator. You said you were an accountant, didn't you? You can handle the financial end while we academics drift around in the clouds, thinking great thoughts."

"Well, I—"

"Mr. Collingwood, if your roommate's accident was anything more than an accident, it was because of his connection with the Beaumont business. So, the only way we'll set your mind to rest is by resolving the larger issue."

Please, Brer Fox, don't throw me in the brier patch. "Well, I believe I can accommodate you in my schedule. This is a slack time for CPAs. Tax season is over, and we're between quarters. And . . ." He paused, surprised at the depth of his own feelings.

"And?" prompted Llewellyn.

"And none of my current clients are anywhere near as important as discovering what happened to Dennis. If someone tried to kill him once, is he safe now?"

"Hmm. No, I suppose not." Llewellyn's face took on a curious look. "You know, from the sounds of things, it might be somewhat dangerous to dig into these matters." She sounded surprised and perhaps a little pleased.

"Yes," Jeremy replied soberly. "Dennis struck by a car. Beaumont shot at in the middle of downtown—"

"And now disappeared."

Jeremy nodded. "Dead, or hiding. And there was Beaumont's friend, that reporter."

"Grimes. I think his name was mentioned in this conspiracy business, too. Something about his files. You know—" She picked her pen up and fiddled with it. "Now that I think of it, there were several murders on that list your friend had. I didn't see how they fit in then, but—"

Jeremy sucked in his breath. "Other people who got onto this conspiracy."

"Possibly. I don't recall the details. I only saw the list that one time, but it seems to me that the dates of the murders ran well back into the last century." She shuddered. "If it is a conspiracy, it's been around for a god-awful long time." She looked at him. "What's wrong?"

Jeremy had stopped dead in his pacing. "The list! Maybe that's what was stolen from our apartment. I wasn't looking for it, but I don't remember seeing anything like it." He shrugged helplessly. "Dennis would know where he put it."

Llewellyn seemed lost in thought for a while. Then she pushed herself up from her desk and tapped the plug from her pipe. "Well, let's get on with it."

"Get on with it? Get on with what?"

"Let's go visit your friend."

"But—He can't have visitors yet."

"There are ways around that," said the professor. She paused before she disconnected her tape player. "Oh, and one other thing. When you go back to your apartment, check your phones. I think your first burglar may have been looking to take something—the list probably—but your second burglar I think left something behind."

When Kennison reached his offices it was close to noontime and he had to run a gauntlet of reporters. The elevator doors opened and a dozen questions formed a babel of sound; flashcubes erupted like fireworks. Kennison steeled himself and stepped out into the hallway, where the reporters formed a cordon around him. *Like beaters trapping their prey,* he thought. He had a moment's wild fantasy in which they drove him over the edge of the elevator shaft, as their ancestors had driven mammoths over cliffs' edges. Involuntarily he looked behind him, and was reassured by the solidity of the elevator's door.

He turned and straightened his vest and tie. "I'm sorry," he told them, "but I still have nothing to say about that madwoman's accusations. I am surprised that any of you take her seriously." He smiled thinly. "I should think you would be interviewing psychiatrists rather than pollsters." The doorway to Kennison Demographics beckoned to him from the other side of the hall.

"How did the meeting go on Friday?"

He allowed nothing to show on his face as he faced the *Chronicle* reporter. "I beg your pardon? What meeting was that?"

"The *Chicago Sun-Times* staked out the mansion of that Genevieve Weil dame yesterday. You know, the woman who is supposed to head up this secret society. Well, nothing happened for a long time. Then the police came and hustled them away."

"It must have been a slow news day."

"Right. So why'd the cops come and roust them? Somebody high up had to pull some strings, right? So they left, but they circled around and came back again, and whaddaya know? They see about a dozen limos leaving the place. Windows as black as a tax auditor's heart. And the license plates . . ."

Kennison was curious in spite of himself. "What about the license plates?"

"Funny thing. They only managed to copy three of them. They were too far away to read them clearly. But they did manage to trace the three."

"And?"

"One of them was registered to a rental car; but the agency swears the car wasn't rented that day, and anyway, it belonged to a compact, not a limo. And the other two plates, according to the DMV computers, did not even exist."

Kennison grunted contempt. "Obviously your colleagues copied the plates incorrectly."

"Yeah. Well, it was awful funny, all those rich people meeting like that, just like there really was a secret society and all."

"I never heard of this Genevieve Weil until that mentally unbalanced Beaumout woman made these unsupported allegations, but I am sure that if she is as rich as people say, she undoubtedly associates with other rich people and may even invite them over to her house for luncheon. She may even value her privacy enough not to want strangers hanging around her front gate. That hardly provides grounds for a vast conspiracy."

"So, where were you over the weekend?" asked a reporter for the *Bee*.

"At my fishing cabin in Maine, if it is any of your business."

"Can anyone corroborate that?"

Kennison ignored the question.

"Is that your official statement, Mr. Kennison?" asked the West Coast stringer for the *Times*.

He shook his head. "I have no official statement. I am ignoring the entire sordid affair and suggest you do likewise. I am surprised that a medium as respectable as the *Times* is pursuing a story more suitable to the front page of the *National Enquirer*."

They began shouting more questions at him, but he pushed through them, yanked hard on the office door, and twisted through it into the safety of his offices. The door closed, muffling the babel outside. He leaned momentarily against it and fumbled for his handkerchief to mop his brow. This was not going to blow over, he thought. People would keep digging at it. A detective here, a reporter there. Probably government agents as well. And all of the obvious defenses—

like scrambling the national data banks to erase all traces of Brady Quinn—were no more practical now than they were before. There were too many paper records; and even those on the Net were, for the most part, duplicates of paper records stored elsewhere. And the act of scrambling the databases would itself be revealing. Even Vincent Torino's proposal required careful study. Flooding the Net with blatantly incorrect data dumps might appear too obviously an attempt to cover up through confusion. There is nothing more conspicuous than a man ducking for cover.

Whether intentionally or not, Beaumont had created a situation in which the only possible defense was passivity. Any active countermeasure would, in the end, seem to support her allegations.

He became aware that the office staff was looking at him curiously, and he straightened himself up. "Damned reporters," he muttered in explanation. The clerks and operators nodded in mute understanding. Since the scandal had broken, they had all been harassed and questioned. Kennison knew that none of them had revealed anything important for the very simple reason that none of them knew anything important. They were employed by Kennison Demographics, not by the Society. None of them were Initiates except his assistant, Prudence Baker.

And the Night Shift, of course.

The key to analyzing and guiding the course of history was the possession of reliable information on the state of the system. No one could act effectively in ignorance. That was where his firm came in. No one questioned the motives of polling firms as they went about the country asking strange questions. And, in fact, Kennison Demographics did a great deal of "outside" work for corporations, political campaigns, and other advertisers. All data, regardless of auspices, was grist for the Society's information mills.

He liked to think of his operation that way: as a mill. Like the old-time water mills grinding grain into useful flour, the Firm ground data into useful information.

For a century, the Society had struggled along on what

information they could glean from public records and from agents secreted in various government and business offices. Then, fifty years ago, Kennison's father had established the Firm as an adjunct of the Society and data was collected and processed on a more systematic basis. For the first time, it became practical to gather nationwide in-depth statistics on key variables. The Old Man had provided invaluable service to Galbraith and the War Production Board and helped them set up the centrally planned wartime economy and, not incidentally, secured for the Society direct links into the Official Government. Since then, the Society's projections had increased fourfold in their accuracy and precision. That had made Kennison's father—and then himself—a Very Important Person within the Society.

Now everything his father had dreamed of and sweated to build—everything he himself had built upon it—was teetering like a house of cards. And all because of Beaumont and Weil! Sometimes Kennison wished that KD were independent of the Society. His Brothers and Sisters needed him a damn sight more than he did them!

Well, dream on. There was no realistic way to "pull a Quinn" these days. Oh, surely he could drop out of sight— he had created "Fletcher Ochs" for just such an eventuality— but he couldn't take KD with him, and KD was what gave him his power. It occurred to him—and not for the first time—that it also tied him down. Power rewarded, but it also penalized.

He sat at his desk and placed his hands on it, palms down and fingers spread. He held that position, pressing down as hard as he could, for a few moments; then he relaxed and allowed himself a moment or two to enjoy the view from his office window: a panorama that stretched from Coit Tower to the Presidio. An ocean mist was blowing in through the Golden Gate, and Kennison wished momentarily that he were on his yacht fishing for marlin, no cares to distract him. Then, with a sigh, he turned and picked the first of the reports stacked in his in-basket. His secretary brought him his espresso in a small china cup. He thanked her and asked her how her son was doing with his baseball. She said, "Fine," and left, and he scanned the report's summary. He forced his mind to concentrate on the business at hand.

His desk and office were simple and simply furnished. A "butcher block" wood desk and swivel chair. A credenza with papers and bookmarked journals scattered over it. A small round conference table. The computer equipment was plain and functional. Expensive, but not ostentatiously so. The room gave a message to everyone who entered: this was a no-nonsense operation. Subliminal cues could be visual as well as verbal.

The report was a presidential opinion poll. His eyes darted over the essentials. Sample size. Stratification. Standard error. Taken together with previous polls, this was building into quite a nice picture. Not that it mattered who won next year's election, but knowing who would win would enable Society members to position their assets and influence to greatest advantage. He penciled a coded notation in the corner so that Prudence would know to give a copy to the Night Shift. Given reliable estimates of the number of "partisans" for each candidate and of the amount of wealth and media access each enjoyed, the Night Shift could run it through their model and forecast the equilibrium values for the vote fraction for each candidate.

He suddenly became aware that he was being watched. He glanced up, startled, and saw Alan Selkirk standing in the office doorway.

"Yes, Alan?"

"Could I have a few words with you, Mr. Kennison?"

"Surely; come in and sit down."

Selkirk did so, closing the office door behind him. Kennison waited for him to speak.

Alan Selkirk was a brilliant young Scots statistician who had come to the United States for the privilege of studying and applying new statistical theory at Kennison Demographics. After Beaumont's "salami attack" had disrupted the KD system, it had taken several weeks, building on the last off-line save, to restore the system to partial operation; and even so, they had lost data for several current studies and had paid performance bonds to those clients who would now never receive their market surveys. All of the programmers and operators in the office had been angered, but Selkirk had taken it as a personal affront.

Selkirk had announced his intention of tracking down and eliminating the worm that had wrought the damage. Kennison was uneasy about that—he didn't want the regular staff to learn too much about the KD system—but he could find no rational reason to forbid Selkirk from his crusade. It was obvious that whatever slanders had been tacked on by Beaumont, the worm had penetrated the KD database and scrambled it badly.

"Well?" Kennison asked. "What have you found? Don't tell me you've killed the worm."

"No, Mr. Kennison. At least, not yet. But I did find the key to the scrambler." When Selkirk spoke, there was very little trace of his Scots burr. Five years in the United States had Americanized his speech to such an extent that his accent only appeared in moments of stress.

"Oh? And what was that?" Kennison sipped his espresso and felt the caffeine jolt run through him.

Selkirk ran his fingers through his straw-colored beard. "Well, it wore a lot of the usual hacker technology on its head. The worm did. Pretty well put together, considering it was encrypted in another program. I could have done a better job, given the time, but . . ." He shrugged elaborately. "The head only got the worm through the usual security locks. It poked into every system that accessed the Net and may have been loose for days or even weeks before it found our system. By now, it's probably penetrated every database in the country."

"But it didn't scramble all of them." Kennison made it a flat statement.

"No. The Number Three segment of the worm was old Juggernaut. A simple, foot-stomping program that was developed by Core Wars players back in the seventies. It rolls along from address to address, replacing data with random bits. No one ever actually ran it outside the universities, as far as I know; and there are easy countermeasures, like Clone, if you know what to expect. Incidentally, our system is now protected against similar attacks in the future."

"Thank you, Alan. That alone earns you your salary."

"But it was the Number Two segment that was the most interesting. The head let the worm open the door and old Juggernaut stomped whatever was inside, but Number Two was the Go/No-Go for the stomper."

It was coming. Kennison felt it. Selkirk had been leading up to it all along. He had found something he shouldn't have found. The sweat made Kennison's forehead cool, and he forced his voice to remain calm. "And how did it do that?"

"A simple-minded, off-the-shelf search engine, if you can believe it. It searched the database for a list of names. If it found more than a specified fraction, it unleashed Juggernaut."

"Whose names?" he asked, though he already knew what was coming.

"Sarah Beaumont. Morgan Grimes. Dennis French. Someone named Paul Abbot. Quinn. Belleau. Crawford. Penwether. McAuliffe. Should I go on?"

"Hmm, no. I don't think that will be necessary." Behind his calm demeanor, Kennison thought frantically. *If this gets out, Weil and Ullman will have me by the short curlies. My own employee!* Kennison swallowed and looked Selkirk in the eye. The Scotsman was looking back steadily. There was a faint smile on his lips. Smug? Contemptuous? Kennison looked closer and saw the creases at the corners of the eyes, the stiffness of the lips. Selkirk was nervous. Frightened. He had hold of a tiger's tail, and he knew it. Kennison sighed inwardly. He had never ordered the death of anyone he knew personally. He wondered if Tyler Crayle was available. Or had he gone looking for his brother? "Names from one of our surveys, perhaps?" Bluff it out. Play dumb. Gain time.

"No, sir. That was the odd thing. Those names were the key that unleashed Juggernaut, but those names were not in our system. Yet our system was attacked. Curious, I thought."

"Curious indeed. Perhaps the worm malfunctioned?"

"Not a chance, Mr. Kennison. Maybe you don't understand this yet, but that Beaumont lady is *slick*. No, the obvious conclusion was that there was a hidden partition in the system." He grinned broadly. "Do ye know what a priest hole is, Mr. Kennison?"

"A priest hole. No."

"Back in England and Scotland, when the papish church was outlawed, some of the noble families who kept to the Old Religion built hidden panels and secret passageways into their houses for priests to hide in. Well, I found a secret passageway in our system architecture. Whoever wrote it was right canny and I salute him. There is an entire second system in there, piggybacked on KD's system."

Kennison placed a look of outrage on his face. "Do you mean that someone has been parasiting on our system without our knowledge? That is intolerable!"

Selkirk, still smiling, shook his head. "It won't wash, Mr. Kennison. I took a tour around that second system. I turned over a few wee rocks to see what would crawl out. It was an education." He drawled his words out, beginning to enjoy himself. His Scots burr showed through from time to time.

Kennison gave up. He closed his eyes and rubbed his hand over his face. "All right, Alan. Get to the point. Quit the tap dancing."

Selkirk shrugged. "Everything Beaumont said in her Dump is true. There is a secret society trying to direct history. And you're one of the directors." He flashed perfect teeth.

"You understand, Alan," Kennison said wearily, "that I can't let you go to the newspapers or the police with this."

For the first time Selkirk looked surprised. He sat up suddenly straighter in his chair. "Oh, no, Mr. Kennison. You don't understand me at all. I don't want to *expose* you. I want in!"

VI

Sarah was walking along the underground corridor toward
the elevator, on her way to the orientation class, when she
thought she heard her name spoken. She stopped and looked
around, but there was nobody there. Frowning, she started
on her way. Then she heard muffled voices coming from a
small side corridor and, becoming curious, turned into it and
looked around.

There was a door on the right-hand wall. It was closed,
but there was a vertical glass panel that paralleled it, and,
through the panel she could see men and women seated
around a broad mahogany table. She recognized Red (who
was not sitting at the table but was perched on a credenza
that ran along the far wall) and Jane Hatch, the old woman
who ran the safe house. The others were strangers.

Sarah backed away before anyone noticed her. Then she
leaned cautiously forward and put her head close to the door.

". . . make up her damned mind!" (she heard).

"Give her time. It's not an easy decision." (That was Red's
voice.) "We're asking her to erase an entire identity. To become another person. I'm not sure how I would feel about
it myself."

"That from a man who keeps a dozen personae! Brother
Malone—"

"That's different, Brother Betancourt. Sure I maintain several different identities, but one of them is *me!* I may wear
a persona for a particular op; but when the op is terminated,
I can shuck it. We're telling Sarah Beaumont that she can
never be Sarah Beaumont again. Ever."

When Sarah heard that, she closed her eyes and hung her
head. There was an empty feeling in her upper chest, as if
something vital was missing. Red had not been pressing her
for a decision, but the issue had not disappeared.

". . . know what'd happen if folks outside knew who she

was. Not jest Them, but the general public. There's a lot of hoorah going on, and a passel o' folks hold her to blame. This name change, it's for her own good."

"The old argument, Sister Hatch. Do as we say, because we know best."

"We *do* know best!"

"What's that got to do with it? If freedom means anything, it's the freedom to be a damn fool. To do something irrational or even dangerous. To be stubborn and cussed and downright mule-headed. To flip the bird at the inevitable fucking tide of history."

"Like someone else in this room I could name," said Betancourt.

There was a ripple of laughter before Red continued. "Now you know and I know that if she goes on being Sarah Beaumont in public, she will be killed. Maybe by one of Them, for revenge; maybe by some nutcase with a fantasy about what she did or didn't do; maybe by Tyler Crayle, if he finds out she's the one who did his brother. It doesn't matter, except maybe to her. The logical thing for her to do is to take on a new identity. *But who are we to tell her she has to do it?*"

"We're the ones who rescued her. We saved her ass."

"No, Sister Hatch," said a new voice. "Brother Malone is right. We saved her ass, but we don't own it."

"Wish I did," said another voice, a male.

There was another ripple of laughter and Sarah's ears burned.

"Wait your turn, Al. You'll have to stand in line behind Brother Ma—"

"I think you better close your teeth while you still have them, *Brother* Hollister."

"I invoke Rule Nineteen!" That caused more laughter.

Someone banged on the table. "That will be all, gentlemen—if I may employ the term loosely. Brother Malone is a professional. He will guide our ward to the right decision. Isn't that so?"

Red's reply was slow in coming. "Yes, that's so. I'll help her make the right decision."

"Then, if there is no further agenda . . . ?"

Chairs scraped against the floor and Sarah backed hastily away from the door. She returned to the main corridor and scampered to the elevator. She pressed the button and fidgeted, then stabbed it several more times, although she knew rationally that that would not make the cage come any faster.

The overheard meeting preyed on her mind all through Aaron's class. What *should* she do? She had thought that she had severed all her ties to the past years ago, when she had put Chicago in her rearview mirror; but now, when the need came to obliterate them entirely, she found the hand with the scissors shaking. Erasing "Sarah Beaumont" and becoming— who? a stranger—was a little too much like dying. It came to her suddenly that she needed to be in wild country with nothing around her but the sky, alone with her thoughts. Through the window she could see the snowcapped peaks of the Front Range, and she thought about the tundra and the wildflowers and the krummholz and . . .

"We are waiting, Ms. Beaumont."

She jerked her attention back to the class. "I'm sorry. Could you repeat the question?"

"The First Rule of Thumb, if you please."

She sighed and took a deep breath. "The First Rule of Thumb of cliology is: Evaluate the action, not the actors."

"Very well. Can anyone explain the meaning of this rule?" He scanned the class as if he could see them, then stabbed a bony forefinger. "Mr. Bosworth."

SuperNerd had been trying to slump in his chair. He jerked and looked around. "Ah, only that, uh, direct action seldom achieves its objectives. Sometimes it achieves the exact opposite."

"Hmph. Is there another sort of opposite, Mr. Bosworth? Never mind. Can anyone cite an example in which the actual results of an action or policy were the 'exact' opposite of the stated intentions? Ms. Beaumont?"

"The attempts by the Babbage Society to preserve the Secret led directly to the exposure of that Secret."

There was a moment of embarrassed silence in the room. SuperNerd looked surprised and nervous. The Earth Mother bridled openly. The others glowered at Sarah. Slowly a smile spread across Aaron Gewirtz's face. "A truly creative response, Ms. Beaumont; if a trifle provocative, considering the venue. It does have—shall we say?—exceptional poignancy to those of us here in this room. Being engaged in the inspections of the motes in the eyes of others, we did indeed overlook this particular beam in our own. Alas, one needs more than good intentions in order to accomplish a goal. Are there any further examples?"

As the class droned on, Sarah became aware of a new sound. It was faint and squeaking and seemed to be coming from the heat vent. She frowned in puzzlement. The sound bordered just on the edge of familiarity, but on the wrong side of the edge. It swept up and down in pitch several times, then stopped abruptly. After a pause it began again. It repeated this cycle several times while she listened.

All of a sudden, it came into focus. It was the clarinet solo from "High Society." Someone was practicing the racing cadenzas over and over again, tripping up each time on the syncopations in the high register. Yet whoever it was, was patient and determined. Sarah realized that the sound had been going on for some time before she had become fully aware of it.

She tightened the cinch on the saddle while Red looked on unhappily.

"You *are* coming back, aren't you?"

"Of course, I'm coming back. I just need to be alone for a while. Somewhere where I can think things through. My whole life is going to be different from now on. I need to decide how much different, and in what ways."

Red handed her the bedroll and saddlebags. "I could get in big trouble for this, you know."

She tied the baggage down. "No, you won't. We've all taken short rides in the mountains."

"This isn't exactly a short ride you're planning."

"No, it's not. But I'm not going to make this decision under pressure, yours or anyone else's, or on the spur of the moment."

"You know, Quinn did this once himself."

"What?"

"Rode up into the mountains to be alone. It was just after he came west. He had some soul-searching of his own to do. He stayed up there for several months. Wandered up to Central City and down to the San Juans. Story goes that he built a log cabin with his own hands somewhere around here and lived in it for a while." He looked at her searchingly. "You won't be gone as long as he was, will you?"

She laughed shortly. "No, this is the twentieth century, not the nineteenth. We do things faster nowadays. Even soul-searching."

Red scuffed a boot in the dirt and straw of the stable. "You going to be OK up there? I mean, do you have everything you need?"

Sarah patted the horse on the neck, and the mare whuffed in reply. She was a grulla mountain horse, mouse-colored and surefooted. Sarah had fallen in love with her the first time she had walked through the stables. "Don't worry about me. Everything I really need I carry up here." She tapped her head. "The stuff we salvaged from my Blazer is just bonus."

"You don't need food?"

"No, there's plenty of food up there. You just have to know how to 'shop' for it. I'm only packing a little jerky and some coffee."

"Janie said you could have some things from the kitchen."

Sarah shook her head. Red was like a mother hen. "What does Janie think of my little trip?"

"She thinks you're nuts. She says the choice is obvious."

"Easy for her to say. It's not her identity you're talking about erasing."

Red grunted something in reply. She led the grulla from the stable out to the corral. The day was cool. The sun was hiding behind occasional clouds, and a fresh wind was blowing from the west. Sarah paused before mounting, twisting the reins in her hands. She looked at Red. "Well," she said. "Wish me luck."

Red stuck out his hand. "Luck," he replied.

Sarah hesitated a moment, then took the hand. "Thanks." Then she shoved her boot into the stirrup and lifted herself up. Western boots had pointed toes so the foot could enter the stirrup easily and high heels so it couldn't slip all the way through. That way the rider could keep her seat, even under rough conditions.

She kicked the horse in the flanks and pulled on the reins. The grulla's head came around, and she left the corral at a fast walk. At the edge of the property, Sarah twisted around in the saddle and looked back at Red. He waved an arm at her and she waved back.

When Beaumont was out of sight, Jane Addams Hatch came out of the kitchen door of the main house and stood on the back porch watching. Her hair was white and her skin tanned. Red walked over and stood beside her.

"She's gone," he said.

"I kin see that," the small, wizened woman replied. "She gonna see sense?"

"I think so."

Janie grunted. "*You* gonna see sense?"

Red looked her in the eye. "What do you mean?"

Janie snorted. "You shook her hand, Red. If'n I was her, I'da let you have one across the chops. Why didn't you kiss her?"

He turned and looked where the horse and rider had vanished into the trees. "She didn't ask for one."

"Red Malone, you are a fool! Askin's not her style."

"Why, Jane Hatch! Are you trying to interfere with the natural course of history?"

The older woman snorted contemptuously. "I'm jest pulling a few stones blockin' the channel. That's all. Ain't nothin' wrong with that."

VII

Jeremy shifted his feet and glanced around while the nurse behind the admittance desk searched her records. Men and women in white passed by, intent in thought or conversation. One or two glanced curiously at the discussion at the desk. The air was ripe with the half-sensed odors of medicine and antiseptic. Behind him, in the waiting lounge, Gwynneth Llewellyn sat quietly, reading an ancient copy of *National Geographic*. She was listening without appearing to listen. She was even turning the magazine pages at reasonable intervals.

"I don't understand," he told the nurse. "The police brought Mr. French here to Porter the night of his accident."

The nurse set her lips. "Well, we have no record that he's been here, at all. Perhaps the police report was in error. Are you sure he wasn't taken to Swedish or to Denver General or Saint Joseph's?"

He gripped the edge of the admittance desk. "I came here with the ambulance. *I saw him here!*"

"I'm sure there's been a mistake somewhere."

Of course, there's been a mistake, you twit. He stopped the thought before it reached his lips. Besides, he was no longer sure it was a mistake. Dennis' disappearance had to be deliberate, like the searching of his apartment. Like the original hit-and-run. Like the bug Jeremy had found in his telephone after his visit with Professor Llewellyn.

"You people called me just last week and assured me that Dennis was stabilized." But no visitors. His caller had been quite firm about that.

The nurse shook her head. "I have no record of admission or discharge," she insisted.

It suddenly occurred to Jeremy that he might already have seen Dennis for the last time. Something had reached out and whisked him away to vanish down the memory hole, leaving an unfillable void in Jeremy's life. It was an intellectual realization, the knowledge of that void. His mind knew of it, but not yet his body—like an extracted tooth or an amputated limb.

The desolation must have shown on his face, because the duty nurse hesitated. "Perhaps the resident on duty that night remembers something. When did you say? The nineteenth of June?" She punched numbers into her terminal. Dennis glanced around idly while he waited.

Llewellyn was gone!

Panic ran through him. Had someone snatched her while his back was turned? Were they waiting even now to snatch him? He looked around the lobby searching for suspicious faces.

Then he saw her returning to the lobby from the hallway and he closed his eyes briefly in relief. Llewellyn glanced at him without speaking and resumed her scrutiny of the *Geographic*. Jeremy sighed to himself. He was starting to imagine things.

"Here it is," said the nurse. Then, after a pause, "Well."

"What is it?" Jeremy turned and leaned forward on the admittance desk.

"Dr. Venn was on call that night. And Nurse Kilbright." She sniffed.

"How may I get in touch with them?"

"You can't. They ran off together on the twenty-first. They're down in the Bahamas somewhere." Disapproval was plain on her face. "Dr. Venn was always making passes at the nurses; but no one ever suspected those two of being an item. Jane Kilbright was a married woman—" Abruptly she seemed to realize she was telling tales out of school, and her lips closed into a thin line. "I'm afraid there's nothing more I can do for you."

Jeremy thanked her for her help and left the hospital. It was late afternoon and the summer sun was seasonally hot. Heat pouring off automobile hoods created a shimmering curtain of illusion in the air. Puddles of mirage water studded the parking lot. Jeremy pulled his handkerchief from his pocket and mopped his brow.

The inside of his car must be like an oven. He fumbled in his pocket for the keys and opened all four doors to let the hot air roll out. Reaching inside on the driver's side, he started the engine and flipped the air conditioner to maximum.

Llewellyn appeared while Jeremy was recording the gist of his conversation with the nurse in a pocket notebook. When she reached the car he started to tell her what had happened, but the chubby historian stopped him.

"I heard it all," she said. "Or all of it that mattered. While you were chatting I had someone look into the files for us."

"What? How? And why? There's no trace of Dennis in the records. Or . . ."—a new expression crossed his face— ". . . at least that's what they've been telling me."

"And it's true. Dennis French was not listed. So I checked every emergency room admittance for the nineteenth. Then for a few days on either side." She paused and looked at him. "There was a 'John Doe' hit-and-run victim admitted on the eighteenth."

"Oh. The day before. That couldn't be him, then." Somehow, he had expected . . .

Llewellyn smiled. "Suppose you wanted to 'lose' someone, but he was in the hospital and couldn't be moved. How would you do it?"

Why did she always see these things before he did? Was he that dull-witted? Or was it that he had lived so long in such a comfortable rut? He grimaced. "I'd alter the records."

"Right. Those directly involved in the original admittance would know better, but you can bribe them. With a vacation in the Bahamas, maybe? Then you wait a few days and play musical chairs, move a few admittances and releases around, and everyone else figures their memories must be at fault, if they bother to wonder at all."

The excitement knifed through him. "You think that John Doe was Dennis?" He turned and looked up at the hospital building. "He was there, but just erased from the records?"

"Not erased exactly. Just relabeled. Which is encouraging, if you think about it."

"Why is that?"

"They didn't want to hurt him." Jeremy brightened, but the professor added, "At least not until they could learn what he knew and who he had told."

Jeremy started back toward the hospital. "What room is this John Doe in?"

"Was. He was discharged last week. By your Dr. Venn, according to the records."

"But . . . Venn ran off with his lover on the twenty-first! He couldn't have authorized a release last week!"

Llewellyn shrugged. "The records aren't quite in order. But unless someone goes looking for 'John Doe' and thinks about cross-checking dates, who will ever notice? Give them time and they may even straighten that out. This has all the earmarks of being a jury-rigged operation."

Jeremy banged his fist once on the roof of the car. He sighed and walked around to the driver's side, and he sat there for a while, alone with his own thoughts. Llewellyn slid into the passenger seat and waited silently.

Llewellyn said, "There's another thing."

Jeremy looked over his shoulder but couldn't summon the energy to ask what.

"Just after you left, the nurse at the admissions desk punched a phone number, spoke a few words, and then hung up. Then she shook herself and looked mildly bewildered. I don't think anyone else noticed. It was a small thing and I saw it only because I had been watching her."

Jeremy frowned. "Who do you think she called?"

"I doubt she knows herself. I think it was a posthypnotic command. I think whoever altered the hospital records and bribed or coerced the doctor and nurse to run to the Bahamas also left an alarm system behind in case anyone got too nosy." She slammed the car door. "Let's go."

"Where?"

She pulled a slip of paper from her décolletage. "Before I left, I went back to my friend the candy striper and wheedled the addresses of the doctor and the nurse."

Jeremy laid rubber leaving the parking lot.

An empty house has an air about it. A sense of abandonment. Jeremy stood by the fake-leather sofa in the Kilbright living room and felt the emptiness of the house. He ran a hand over the lampshade and his fingertips came away dirty. Nothing had been dusted for at least two weeks. He no longer felt nervous about breaking into the house. No one was coming back.

A creak in the stairwell. He saw Dr. Llewellyn returning downstairs.

"Closets are all empty," she announced.

Jeremy nodded. He had expected as much. A dead end. Perhaps in both senses of the phrase. Behind the romantic triangle and elop-ment he suspected a far bloodier tale. Nothing he had learned so far about the secret cabal suggested that they were in the vacation package business.

"Maybe we can locate them somehow in the Bahamas," Llewellyn suggested.

Jeremy shook his head. No one was ever coming back.

Karin had served the dinner promptly on schedule, a veal timbale in a light béchamel sauce and garnished with mace, and Kennison had just lifted the first forkful to his lips when Bettina, his butler, interrupted. "There is a phone call for you, sir," she said with a small bow. She was slim and graceful and dressed mannishly in a black butler's outfit.

Kennison looked at his meal. Ruth Ann, his chef, was without parallel and he had challenged her to produce a different meal each day for a full year and the year was now half-gone without a single repetition. He sighed. "Can it wait, madam? I've just now sat down to my dinner."

"The caller says it's urgent, sir."

"Very well, Madam Butler. I will take the call in my study. Tell Chef she must keep my meal warm for me. I will only be a moment."

His study was paneled in dark oak, with bookshelves bearing an adequate number of volumes. The matching desk was broad and totally clean, except for a small sign that read in an intricate calligraphy: "A clean desk is the sign of a dirty mind." A touch of understated humor that, coupled with his all-female staff, was meant to give his visitors a certain impression of Daniel Kennison, bon vivant. A man of power, financially and sexually. Of course, he allowed only a fraction of his financial power to show. Enough to be impressive and to open doors that might otherwise be closed, but not enough to make people wonder.

The telephone and the reading lamp were islands of modernity in an otherwise conservatively appointed room. He lifted the receiver. "I have it now," he said. The light indicating the butler's extension winked out. He noticed that the call was coming in on the special line, one that, as far as the phone company's switching system was concerned, did not exist. "Lion, here," he said.

"Eggs, paragraph seven."

Kennison's eyebrows arched. Gretchen Paige, calling him? And she wanted the call scrambled, did she? Which meant she did not trust the land line security, either. He cursed silently. Their best safety for now lay in having no contact at all with each other. His fingers played over the phone buttons, setting up the scrambler for Paige's number seven code.

"Yes?" he said.

"Watch the national news tonight. I caught the story on our local news here, which is an hour early. You still have a chance to see it for yourself. Call back."

The line went dead. There was no dial tone on that line. Instead, there was a silence infinitely deep. An empty universe, vast beyond comprehension. Then, somewhere inside that silence, Kennison thought he heard a tiny click.

He set the phone down shakily. Had someone tapped the private line that he had set up with Paige and a few others? Did Weil suspect his plans? Perhaps it was time to move. Be done with the cautious feelers and double-layered conversations. Bring the others fully into it. Even Paige. *Especially* Paige, before she got the idea of striking on her own.

Or had Cameron Betancourt finally begun to take active measures? Kennison had information that some of Betancourt's advisers were urging him to abandon Quinn's Rule. If the Associates ever awakened from their long sleep, they could be a formidable opponent.

Or maybe no one had been listening at all, he told himself. Maybe he was just edgy after that business with Selkirk.

He looked at his watch and pressed a button on his desk. One of the bookcases swung around, revealing a television set. He pressed another button and the tube lit, showing the face of a well-known television newsreader. He was sitting behind a desk, looking serious and concerned, with a screen and a world map behind him. Kennison wondered how many of the countries on the map the man could name. He crossed his arms and half-sat on the edge of his desk. What was it that Paige had wanted him to see? If it had been on her local news, it would probably have an East Coast dateline.

He waited patiently through half a dozen "stories"—really little more than headlines, with occasional cuts to one-sentence "in-depth" comments by one of a handful of Officially Recognized Comment Makers. About one in twenty of these were Society agents or controlled by Society agents. A like number were no doubt manipulated by the Associates. Did no one ever wonder that the same small group of politicians, celebrities, and scientists were constantly featured, mentioned, and interviewed while others, with perhaps more to say, went unsung—or were bundled quietly offstage through patently set-up scandals?

The "news" stories themselves were portentous announcements by political and business leaders, who really thought they were making decisions of importance. Reports of polls, as if what people *thought* mattered. Trivia about fires and car accidents and wars and movie stars and scientific inventions.

It was the last item or close to the last item.

The newsreader picked up a fresh page of his script and placed a look of concerned sorrow on his face. "A Tragic Death in New Jersey. The country estate of retired businessman John Benton in rural Sussex County was ransacked and burned today by a vigilante group calling themselves Free America. Mr. Benton, who was seventy-five, perished in the blaze along with two members of his staff. One of the vigilantes, an unemployed auto worker who refused to give his name, was captured by other staff members before he could escape the grounds. He had this to say. . . ."

(Cut to disheveled unshaven face. Dirty with soot. Baseball cap on head with name of local hardware store. Police roust him none-too-gently while he shouts at the camera.) "We're gonna get every last one of those [*beep*] who been tryin to run our lives. I ain't had a [*beep*] job in two and a half years. Thank God that Beaumont woman had the courage to blow the whistle on those [*beep*]!"

(Cut to anchorman.) "The man's mention of Sarah Beaumont is a reference to—" Kennison shut off the TV before the impeccably manicured newsreader could offer any inanities about the Meaning of It All.

He took out a cigarillo and fumbled once or twice with the match before he could get it to light. So, they had gotten old Benton. There was an irony in that. Of all the Councillors, Benton had probably deserved it the least. Not that he hadn't blood on his hands, but he had been the most parsimonious at ordering deletions.

Yet the world was full of people who yearned to slough the responsibility for their own lives. Whether they blamed gods or devils didn't matter. The important thing was that Someone Else was responsible. He wished that the Society did have the kind of power the man had implied. The kind of micromanipulation that fine-tuned every detail of life. In the right hands, that would bring an end to the chaos of history. Arrange all the parts of society to mesh smoothly, without the wasteful conflict of wars, strikes, competition, or crime.

Benton's death had been useless, uplifting no one, justifying nothing. There was something unbearably sad about that phrase. A useless death. He plucked the cigarillo from his lips and jammed it into the ashtray on his desk. Perhaps he could make use of it. He picked up his phone and punched a series of buttons. When he heard the click on the other end, he said, "Eggs, Lion three."

When they had reestablished contact, Paige asked him if he had seen the story.

"Yes. Do you suppose there will be mobs coming after all of us now?"

"Monkey see."

"A single swallow."

"How many Councillors can we lose before you would call it a trend?" Her voice was waspish, and Kennison thought he detected a hint of tightly reined fear in it.

"Three," he replied without hesitation. "Three would be statistically significant."

"You're a cold-blooded bastard, aren't you?"

"If we run, it will only prove the allegations to be true. We've got to stand fast."

"And be picked off one by one?"

The idea came to him suddenly. A flash. "Ask for police protection. After today's incident, anyone named in the Beaumont Dump would have ample justification to do so, and the police would ask no questions."

"How can we conduct business with the police following us around? We can't depend on our own agents being assigned to guard us."

"Most of our moles aren't patrolmen anyway. I'd suggest we suspend business for the duration of the emergency—"

"Impossible!"

"Necessary! If we invite the police and the reporters to follow us around and we do *nothing*, how long before they get tired and go home and tell the world it was all a false alarm?"

He could read volumes into the silence at the other end. "A Potemkin village?" She was obviously thinking it over. "No good," she said at last. "We'd all hang separately."

Meaning they'd all have to hang together. Meaning she doubted they would.

Paige sighed. "Madam Chairman would never agree to have the police and the newpapers follow her around. Neither would Ullman or Lewis. Especially Lewis."

"Perhaps they would," Kennison suggested delicately, "if a *trend* were established."

There was another silence, this one longer and more profound. At last Paige spoke. "A trend could be established," she admitted, "if the conditions were right."

"Would you take care of that item for me? Thinking it over, I believe only one more incident would establish statistical significance. And, if it were the *right* incident, take care of any number of other difficulties, as well."

"I'll mention your suggestion about the Potemkin village to certain other Council members." There was a pause on the other end of the line. "Do you think we can carry it off, Brother?"

"I am sure of it, Sister. I have complete faith in you." He cut the connection.

He did have faith in her. She would make an admirable Seward to his Lincoln. The thought pleased him, until he remembered what had happened to Lincoln. Then, brusquely, he dismissed the thought. "And if it doesn't work," he said aloud, "I can always call on Fletcher Ochs."

He returned to the dining room, where Karin was waiting patiently by the sideboard, his dinner plate sitting covered under a portable heat lamp. Karin was solidly built. Smooth muscles under smooth skin, with no trace of fat on her except the delicious padding that rounded all her edges. He allowed himself to admire her carriage for a moment, in her high heels and black mesh stockings and French maid's uniform. He imagined her without the uniform (which required little imagination) and the various activities they might engage in together (which, alas, required much).

He sat down and placed the napkin over his lap, where it lay disappointingly flat. "I'll have my meal now," he said.

Karin brought it to him, bending deep when she turned around to pick it up and bending deep when she set it in front of him. She did that because she knew he liked it and because she knew nothing would come of it.

He remembered that two of Benton's household had perished with him. He didn't want that to happen here. He couldn't bear the thought that lovely Karin or shrewd Bettina or jolly Ruth Ann or wholesome Greta, the parlor maid, would come to any harm. He thought about them, trapped in a burning building with him, like Benton's staff had been, crying and clinging to him, the flames licking close around them. Or chased and beaten by outraged mobs, toyed with by uncouth lower-class workmen.

Something stirred inside him and he looked down at his napkin. *Well* he thought. *Well, well.*

When he finally tasted his timbale some time later, he found it to be somewhat dry.

VIII

Sarah rested with her back to a tall spruce and chewed on a strip of jerky, listening to the silence. The early-morning sun slanted through the canopy overhead, piercing the forest with individual shafts of light. There was a stand of quaking aspen a little bit off to her left. That was how she'd built the fire to brew her coffee. The aspen is a self-pruning tree, and there is always a fall of dead branches underneath one.

Well, it wasn't really silence, she admitted to herself. The trees were always busy from the frequent breezes. Especially the aspen, whose leaves shivered in the slightest breath. The wind soughing through their needles and leaves produced a murmur like a distant crowd. Voices always on the verge of intelligibility. If she listened closely enough (or, perhaps, if she did not try to listen at all) they might tell her something.

Arbormancy, she thought. Divination through the whispers of trees. And what would their advice be? What did the forest say about the Associates and cliology and changing her identity? The breeze freshened and branches swayed in the wind. *Ssssaraaaah,* they called.

A jay cried and flew abruptly from one tree to another, not more than a hundred feet from where she sat. Farther away, something bigger scurried through the brush. A squirrel, maybe, or a porcupine. She took her coffee cup, holding it in both her hands to let the warmth of it work through her, and sipped from it. She glanced at the angle of the sunbeams.

Time to move on.

She poured the rest of the coffee on the fire. Then she carefully stamped all the embers into the ground. She walked to where the grulla had been pinned and retrieved a folding shovel from the saddle pack. Then she dug a hole and buried the fire.

Satisfied that she had left no hazard, she packed up the pot and the jerky, rolled up her bedroll, and strapped them and the saddle to her horse. As she was tightening the cinches, she heard a loud report, like a rifle shot. She started and the horse, sensing her fright, jerked on the reins.

She jumped behind a piñon pine and crouched there. She stroked the grulla's neck, speaking soothingly to her, watching the direction from which the sound had come. She held her breath, waiting.

The sound came again, clearer now, and she almost laughed in relief. Not a rifle shot, but a bursting seed pod. Some flowering plant preparing for the next spring, spreading its seed as widely as possible before it could die.

"I *really* needed this vacation," she told the horse, and the grulla bobbed her head in agreement. Sarah swung herself into the saddle and headed upslope.

Later that day she broke from a stand of Englemann spruce
onto a wide alpine meadow. In the middle distance, the bare
peaks of the Continental Divide shoved the horizon skyward,
like a rocky wave breaking upon the planet. They were
speckled with patches of eternal snow. The Never-Summer
Mountains, the Utes had called them. Closer in, a mule deer
raised his head from a pond and watched her. Sarah reined
in and kept still, waiting to see what the deer would do.

The pond was the creation of a beaver family that had
blocked the flow of the stream with mud and sticks. An
Arapahoe legend taught that beaver had built the world. The
wily Indians had seen with their own eyes how beavers
changed meadows into swamps with their dams.

And what is the difference between a beaver dam and a
human dam? Echoes of the conversation she had had with
Red the day of that terrible drive to Mount Falcon. What
made one "natural" and the other not? Only a matter of
scale? Of intent? Both change the environment and not necessarily for the better. Unless you are a beaver. Or a human.

Perhaps the difference lay only in the ability to foresee the
consequences.

And wasn't that Red's argument? When you know which
way the little roulette ball is going to go, do you sit idly by
and rake in the chips, like the Associates? Or do you try to
make the ball go where you want, like the Society? And what
of the Third Force that they had deduced from Dennis' list
and the Stray? Where did they fit in?

That's a lot of metaphysics to find in a beaver's dam, she
thought.

Red claimed that history was nothing but the cumulative
blunders of millions of bungling amateurs tampering with the
course of history one-by-one. How did you answer that?
Turn professional? She yanked on the grulla's reins and
pulled off to the north. The mule deer, startled by the movement, bolted for the forest.

Valleys lay below her like giants' furrows, turned up by

a great plow. Sharp-sided cuts gouged out by mountain streams as they fell toward the plains far below. Sarah checked her direction against the vegetation. South-facing slopes received more direct sunlight and hence were drier than north slopes. Different plants had adapted to each. At this altitude, Douglas fir marched on the north and ponderosa pine on the south. Farther down, the ponderosas shifted to the north while grasses, brush, and prickly pear cactus took over the south.

When she broached the tree line onto the alpine tundra, the wind nearly knocked her off her horse and she took a moment to yank her poncho out of the saddlebag. It flapped around her like a banner. She pulled it over her head and cinched it tight. The wind blew continuously up here, often reaching a hundred miles an hour. Everything hugged the ground to survive in a world that was never frost-free and where snowstorms could occur any day of the year. The clouds seemed close enough to touch and raced across the sky as if chased by demons.

She was on an old Indian trail, probably Ute this high up. She kept to it, obeying the injunction Leave No Footprints. Tundra plants were incredibly hardy but were so closely balanced between life and death that the slightest stress could tip the balance. This trail might have been untrod for a century, but the vegetation had yet to reclaim it. She blew on her hands to warm them.

The tundra was ablaze with color. The purples and whites of marsh marigolds and Parry primroses. The three-inch golden blooms of the alpine sunflower, which, always facing east, provided a compass to the traveler.

Here and there, limber pine, bent and twisted by the winds, crouched and hid behind rocks and other shelter. This was the krummholz, the twisted wood, sculpted into weird dwarf forms, like some sort of natural bonsai garden. It was no earthly landscape. The cold, thin, high-velocity air. The strange, grotesque vegetation. The rocky, angular horizon.

She imagined herself as a star traveler on an alien planet. Altaflora. It orbited a G-type sun, but one that was hotter than Earth's. On Altaflora, it was possible to freeze and get sunburned at the same time.

A yellow-bellied marmot stood upright amid the flowers and she saluted it, using Spock's hand sign. "Take me to your leader," she requested. The marmot made no attempt to comply. Just as well, she thought. Marmots were anarchists at heart and had no leaders to speak of.

The Altaflorans had a civilization, of course. Underground, away from their harsh climate. There were fabulous cities carved from the permafrost under her feet. Magic caverns of glowing crystal.

Dark clouds had gathered around the peaks to the southwest. The blur underneath them meant rain. Lightning smashed a distant peak and she felt the hairs on her neck rise from the static carried on the moist wind. Time to get back downstairs and into drier climes.

She found a rocky draw that led downslope and turned her back on Altaflora.

The tumble-down cabin had been built of lodgepole pine. The roof was gone and the door, dried and cracked, lay amid the wreckage. Sarah circled the place slowly, checking it from every angle. Old, very old. Was it the one Brady Quinn had built?

But there had been mountain men all over this region in the early 1800s, and some of them probably left cabins behind, too. It reminded her of the ghost towns in Summit and Park counties. Preserved in a precarious state of mummification, the wood dried and bleached into a kind of fossilization.

She dismounted and drove the grazing pin into the ground, so the grulla could wander in a circle and browse. A piñon grew in the center of the cabin, but out the collapsed back wall she saw a magnificent bristlecone! She made her way through the wreckage and stood by the ancient tree. She reached her hand out to it and ran her fingertips over the rough bark. How old was it, she wondered. A century? Half a millennium? Some of those on Mount Evans were two thousand years old.

This was where she would camp and take out her soul and inspect it. The tree was an anchor into the depths of the planet's history. While she sat in its shade she could never lose her bearings.

Turning back to the doorway, she saw slash marks on the inner wall of the cabin. She ran her fingers along them. Someone had once kept track of the passing days. Her fingers encountered something hard partly buried in the wood. She pulled her knife from its sheath at her belt and worried at the object until it fell into her palm.

A stone arrowhead. Ute? Arapaho? She turned it this way and that, imagining what might have happened; and for just an instant, she *felt* the history of the place. The lone trapper in a land he thought of as empty wilderness. The Indians, fearful over an intrusion on hunting grounds that *they* saw as crowded. The attack. The fight. Arrows cutting the air. The answering barks of the rifle. Flintlock? Maybe. How had it ended? With the Indians fled or the white man dead?

And who said it had been a white man! Jim Beckwourth the mountain man had been black—and a founder of Pueblo, Colorado! And later there was Bill Pickett, "the greatest sweat-and-dirt cowhand that ever lived." From the beginning, the West had swarmed with black men and women. So, as long as she was fantasizing, she could fantasize a black man defending this place.

She camped in the ruins of the old cabin, well away from the bristlecone, clearing out the debris and building herself a stone circle to contain the fire. During the day, she wandered the rocks and canyons, exploring. She found a narrow canyon, cut by a cold mountain stream. She found twin sentinels, two spires of rock shaped by millennia of patient sandblasting. She found an overlook above a vast untouched forest and spent many hours on that pinnacle wrestling with herself.

During one of her hikes she crossed paths with a bobcat. The cat backed up and snarled, and Sarah stood very still while the cat looked her over. Then the cat decided that she was too big a bite for dinner, gave her a parting snarl, and disappeared into the brush. Only then did Sarah relax and find that her hand gripped the handle of her knife. It was easy to forget that nature was not a Walt Disney cartoon.

In the evenings she returned to the cabin and sat in the shade of the old pine tree and watched the sun set. The peaks remained lit long after the sun had fallen below the horizon and the slopes and canyons were shrouded in night. The Indians had called these the Shining Mountains, and they were right about that as they had been right about so much else. Hawks floated quietly overhead; and once, a bald eagle.

At night, when the stars lit the sky with a splendor unimaginable in the bright lights of the cities, she sat before a crackling fire and sipped strong coffee from a tin cup. Western coffee, when properly made, should allow the stirring spoon to remain standing upright.

Altogether it was as fine a place as any for soul-searching. She was as alone as she had ever been. The nearest other human was who-knew-how-many miles away. She could sit down beside herself and talk it out. How exactly did she feel about the Associates? About Red and his cabal? About not being Sarah Beaumont ever again?

It was that last question that ate at her more than anything. If a person was anything, she was who she *was*. She couldn't cut away her past without cutting away a part of herself.

One day she returned to her cabin and put some coffee on the fire. She sat tailor-fashion, her legs crossed, with her back to the old bristlecone, watching the front door of the cabin. In a few minutes, the sunset would be framed in the doorway. She cradled the coffee cup between her hands, sipping from it from time to time. It tasted a little sweet, although she had put no sugar in it. She gazed at the dirt floor of the cabin, disturbed by something that she couldn't name. But there were no marks in the dirt, except her own footprints coming in.

She shrugged and looked back at the doorway.

And there was someone standing there!

Her heart gave a leap and she tried to stand up but found that her legs wouldn't support her. A dreamlike lassitude seemed to have enveloped her. The figure in the doorway was a black silhouette, framed by the rays of the evening sun. A glowing shadow. She couldn't make out the features.

Then the figure sat down beside her and she breathed a sigh of relief.

It was herself.

She was dressed in her blue suit, the one with the red bow that she had worn in the Civic Center Park the day of the shooting. She looked successful, independent. She knew who she was and what she wanted. Maybe she was also a trifle smug. She didn't have any friends. At least, she had never let anyone close enough to become her friend. But if she held the entire world at arm's length, at least she was on top of it. Magazines had done feature stories about her.

"Well, you certainly have come down in the world," she told herself.

Herself shrugged. *Not me. I'm what I've always been. You seem a little down on your luck, though.*

"Am I?"

Sure. You don't know what you want anymore. People tried to kill you, and the whole world hates your guts. Tell me that's going up.

"Somehow, I thought . . ."

You thought what?

"After that business on the mountain. With Crayle—" *When you killed a man.* "Somehow, I thought that would be the end of it."

Roll the final credits? Herself was sarcastic.

"And everyone would live happily ever after."

They only roll the final credits once, sister. No one ever lives ever after, and no one ever lives happily.

She didn't bother to answer. "Why are you here?"

You need someone to talk to. Who better? Who else knows you as well as I?

Sarah seemed to hear the hum of another voice underneath the words. As if other words were being spoken and answered. It was barely audible; like the bass note of an organ, it blended in with the other sounds. She tried to turn her head to look for the sound but found she couldn't summon the energy.

She looked at the polished, professional-looking image sitting next to her. "You don't know me at all. You're what I used to be. Even if this blows over, I can never be you again."

Oh, blow me some more tears, sister! I'll need a raincoat before you're through. Who ever said you could? Who in the whole sorry history of the world could ever stay what they were forever? Not you, not me, not anyone. Look at me close and see if you can find Chicago's South Side. There's a little girl back there that I can never be again.

Sarah looked away, at the sunset framed in the doorway of the cabin. "That was a long time ago. It's not real anymore. You're not real. I'm hallucinating."

Does it matter if you are? Tell me that you've never recreated yourself before and I'll call you a liar. When did you last see Lulu or Geraldine? Or Big Martha?

Names from the past. Names without reference. Small childish faces screaming on the playground, the grim Chicago skyline in the backdrop. She couldn't imagine them as adults.

Or Daddy? the vision persisted. *Do you even know if he's still alive?*

Sarah scowled. "He left us. When Mama died. He got in his rig and went on the road and he never came back."

Maybe it was just too damn hard for him to come back, with Mama dead. We were all grown up by then, even little Frankie. He never cut out when it would have been easy; when so many other fathers did, when staying meant scrimping and doing without. Mama stood by him all through that; and then, when they had seen us well and truly started, when they would have had their own time together, she was gone. No, I don't 'spect he could have stayed.

"Maybe that's why I left, too."

Herself sneered. *Looking for him on the road? Have you ever gone back just to put flowers on Mama's grave?*

"No!" She buried her face in her hands. "And if I do what they want me to do, I never can!"

Oho! That's the problem, is it? Not that you ever did, *but that now you never* can. *That lifeline was always there, even if you never tugged on it. Like that ol' bristlecone pine there behind you, with his roots sunk deep into Mama Earth. It's nice to sit in his shade, but it's a comfort just knowing he's there.*

She raised her head and looked at herself. "Tell me what I should do."

No, child. No one can tell you that.

She blinked and it wasn't herself anymore. It was Mama, the way she looked before she took sick, with the square-jawed face and the mischief in her eye.

You always were a headstrong child; but, by God, you never did run wild. You had a compass in your head that always pointed you right. Your daddy told me so. You do what you need to do. You'll do the right thing.

"But I don't want to lose you, Mama."

Oh, don't talk foolishness. There is no way on God's green earth you can lose me, because you carry me here . . . She reached out and touched Sarah's head— *. . . and here.* She touched Sarah's heart.

Sarah leaned over and hugged the figure and cried.

In the morning she awoke lying on the ground, not even on her sleeping bag, and she was chilled to the bone. She pushed herself upright, and her stiffened muscles protested at the abuse. She stretched, trying to loosen up. After a few limbering exercises she felt a little less like an embalmed corpse and a little more like a human being.

She went to pour herself some coffee and stopped. The

fire was burned down, but the coffeepot had been carefully set to one side, along with her cup. She picked up the coffeepot and saw that it had been thoroughly scrubbed. She couldn't remember doing that.

She remembered speaking with her previous self and with her mother. It had seemed so natural at the time, so matter-of-fact; but now the weirdness settled over her. What on earth had happened?

She looked around, at the cabin, at the old pine. Maybe it was the place. *Weird* was the old Anglo-Saxon word for Fate. Maybe there was something fateful about this place.

She began gathering her things together. It was time to leave. Like the old Indians, she had gone to a lonely spot and had a vision that told her who she would be from now on. That was how the Indians learned their adult names. It wouldn't be right to tarry in such a place.

She noticed the dirt. Perhaps she half-expected footprints, some sign of her nightly visitors; but of course there were none.

And now she remembered having noticed the oddness last night. The ground then had only held her own prints coming in, and it should have held her own prints going out as well. In and out several times, in fact. Now even those prints were gone.

Someone had been in the cabin while she had been out walking in the canyon. Someone who carefully brushed out his tracks. Someone who, perhaps, had drugged her coffee. Experimentally she sniffed the coffeepot but she could detect nothing except the sharp smell of the metal itself.

She crouched down and studied the ground. Yes, she could see the signs now. Someone had used a leafy branch to brush the footprints away. She followed the sign out to the old Indian trail. There it vanished, but she found the broken branch that had undoubtedly been the tool. She looked up and down the trail. Which way had her night visitor gone?

Whoever it was must have had a horse and must have stuck to the trails. Going cross-country was a good way to get trapped in canyons or cliffsides or among impassable trees. Better to follow the paths left by the Indians and the forest animals. She cut for sign, walking slowly and carefully in a wide circle around her cabin, studying the lay of the land.

Five hundred feet down the trail she found a small hole in the ground and grass that had been cropped. She found no hoofprints, but she remembered the old trick of bundling a horse's hooves in sheepskin so they would make no definable mark on the ground. He couldn't ride far with his horse hobbled that way!

She scampered back to where she had left the grulla and quickly packed and saddled the mare. Then she set off down the trail in the direction her visitor had taken. Two miles farther on, she found a hoofprint. She studied the print closely, noting the crack in the shoe along the left side so she would recognize it when she saw it again. Then, carefully, she followed the trail.

After several hours, the sun was beginning to get low and she was wondering whether to put off further tracking for the day. She pulled up on the reins and looked around for a campsite.

There was a likely spot off to the right. A grove of aspen and a clearing. She dismounted and walked into it.

It *was* a good campsite—so good it had been used recently. She knelt and felt the ground. Still warm where the fire was buried. The grass was crushed where someone had slept. And there was an oft-used path between the campsite and . . . where?

She tied the grulla to a tree and walked down the footpath. She pulled her knife from her belt and licked her lips, stepping carefully so as to make no noise. No one was in the campsite now, but it was best to take no chances.

The trail led around a knob of rock that looked vaguely familiar. There was a sort of nest in the rock there with a wall-like ledge before it. She stepped into the nest and looked over the rocks.

And she saw the ranch spread out below her. The Associates' safe house.

She could make out two figures on the back porch. With a decent pair of binoculars she knew she could identify them. With a parabolic mike, she could hear every word. One of the figures threw something to the ground and stepped off the porch stretching his arms. The stallion in the pasture below stood still and looked up in her direction. She remembered how he had done the same not too long ago, while she and Red had shot the breeze on the fencepost.

Someone's been spying on us! she thought.

Us?

As simply as that, she had joined the Associates.

IX

Herkimer Vane was easily the most difficult member of Gwynn's study team. He was a short, bald man with a beak of a nose. His clothing was invariably rumpled, and little sheets of notepaper protruded from his jacket pockets. He had the unpleasant habit of wagging his finger in one's face whenever he was making a point.

"But Mr. Collingwood, there is no such thing as a historical fact."

Jeremy resisted a crazy impulse to snap at the offending digit with his teeth. He shifted his vodka martini from his right hand to his left and looked desperately for someone to rescue him. *Help,* he thought. *I am being held prisoner by a historical philosopher.* Aloud, he said, "What do you mean, there is no such thing as a historical fact? What was it that they taught me in school, historical fiction?" He thought he had made a rather fine bon mot and almost sputtered his drink when Vane agreed.

"Yes, exactly."

"I beg your pardon? It was all lies? You can't be serious!"

Vane looked nonplussed. "Lies? Oh, no. I don't believe I said that."

Now Jeremy was totally confused. "Well, then . . ."

"I think you misapprehend the word *fact*," Vane said, finger wagging once more. "You think of it as some sort of category of ultimate truth, but that is not the case. Oscar Wilde once said that the English were always degrading truths into facts. Like so many artistic people, he had intuited something vital."

Jeremy shook his head. "I don't see it. A fact is a fact."

"No, Mr. Collingwood. A 'fact' is not a thing; it is the past tense of a verb. Factum est. A dynamic word. Facto, I make. I create. *Fact* was not used as a noun until the late Middle Ages; and, when it was, it meant 'something done,' like the French *fait* or the Magyar *tény*. Our English word *feat* is cognate. Even in English, *fact* retained that meaning of 'feat' until the early 1800s. When Jane Austen wrote 'gracious in fact, if not in word' what she meant was 'gracious in deeds, if not in word.' "

"That's semantics," Jeremy objected.

"Semantics is the science of the meanings of words, and words are how we communicate. What, then, can be more important than a matter of semantics?"

Jeremy opened his mouth to object, then thought better of it. Vane was right. Jeremy sipped his drink. The little historian was irritating but intriguing. "Still, that's not how we use the word today. Today we mean the 'raw data.' "

"No, no, Mr. Collingwood." The finger wagged back and forth. "There is no such thing as raw data. It is always cooked."

Jeremy laughed involuntarily. "That's a good line, Professor; but what does it mean?"

"It means that there can be no facts without theory. Some notion of what sort of fact to look for in the first place, and some notion of what it might mean afterward. That is why, like Lukacs, I prefer the word *event*. It is neither dry, definite, nor static but suggests life, flow, and movement. 'Event compares to Fact,' Lukacs once wrote, 'as Love does to Sex.' Events are facts in motion. Events have momentum, but facts have only inertia. No fact exists in isolation. We cannot even think of a fact without associating it with others. For example: We cannot state the height of Mount Everest without relating it to other mountains. We cannot measure the body's temperature without some thought as to what that temperature ought to be. Now, *fiction* comes from the Latin *fingere*, which means 'to construct.' A fact cannot be separated from its associations—which are constructions of the mind. Thus, not only is *fictio* of a higher order than *factum*, but every fact is in some sense a fiction. That is what I meant when I said you were taught historical fictions. Every attempt to reconstruct history is exactly that, a re*construction*, and therefore a fiction."

Vane might have a point, Jeremy thought. One found a great deal of truth in fiction.

"Herkimer! Are you pestering poor Jeremy?" Jeremy breathed a sigh of relief as Gwynneth Llewellyn sailed between them like a tugboat separating two ships. She put her arm through Vane's elbow. "Have you met everyone yet, Herkimer?"

"No, wait, Gwynn," Jeremy said. "Professor Vane claims there are no facts in history."

Llewellyn gave Vane an elfish grin. "Herkimer! Have you been teasing him? You've got to realize, Jeremy," she added over her shoulder, "that history isn't all cut-and-dried, like accounting. History is what we make it."

"Historia facta est," said Herkimer Vane solemnly. "Why not do as the scientists do and try an experiment? Let us take a fact. Something as numbingly basic as simple chronology—"

"Now wait. I realize that sometimes the exact date of an event is unknown—"

"Oh, no, Mr. Collingwood. Let us take a fact whose existence is indisputable. Tell me when and where the Second World War began. I don't mean anything as subtle as the roots of the war. They run back into the Middle Ages. I mean the actual hostilities."

Jeremy grinned. Start talking with a professor and, sooner or later, you'd get a pop quiz. "I guess it started in, what? Nineteen-thirty-nine? Germany attacked Poland."

"In September," finished Vane. "So you say. But might it not have started in Belgium in the summer of 1701?"

"What?"

"Certainly," said Vane complacently. "The French and the British fought four world wars between 1689 and 1763. Fighting occurred in India and North America as well as in Europe. Considering their geographical scope, the Great Wars for Empire deserve to be called world wars."

Jeremy sputtered. "That was a trick question!" he protested. He looked to Gwynn for support, but she was chuckling.

"The student mind," she said. "You think that the answers are more important than the questions."

Vane wagged a finger. "I could also argue that *the* Second World War was actually two distinct wars, the European and the Pacific, with a few overlapping combatants. However, leaving such issues aside, we can legitimately ask whether the world war began in Manchuria in September 1931 or in Hawaii in December 1941. Surely those dates are as valid as the Eurocentric one you gave."

Jeremy started to answer, hesitated, then said, "Very well, Professor. I see your point. The European and Pacific wars each had a starting date and place. And you could argue that the *world* war, per se, didn't start until the Japanese attacks brought the Americans and British into the Pacific war. But that doesn't invalidate the idea of historical facts, it only means that we must define our facts more accurately."

Vale shrugged. "The value of facts depends more on their relationships than on their accuracy. Perhaps it is more important to ponder whether there were two wars or one than it is to choose one answer over the other. Perhaps both answers are true in some sense. The more 'accurate' a fact is, the less *truthful* it may be. For example, I might say that the population of Denver on April first, 1999, was—oh, let's say 657,232, to invent a number. That would be accurate. But if I were to say instead that 'Denver's population in early 1999 was between 650,000 and 660,000,' I would be more *truthful,* even though less accurate. Because the latter statement is dynamic and the truth is always dynamical and relational. Who was or was not a resident of Denver at a particular moment is an abstraction, and a static one at that. People constantly move in and out. Does the population include the hoboes down by your train station? The tourists in the hotels? College students and business executives, who are here for a few years and then gone? What of those who have two residences, one in Denver and one elsewhere? When you take *motion* into account, it is impossible to fix with any certainty the absolute size of the city."

"Heisenberg's Uncertainty Principle of History," said Llewellyn.

"Eh?" Vane turned on her. "What do you mean by that?"

"Heisenberg said that the velocity of a particle makes its position indeterminate, and vice versa. If you were as familiar with John Lukacs' *oeuvre* as you claim to be, you would realize that his conscious purpose was to apply Heisenberg's insight to historical thinking."

"Oh, yes." Vane waved a hand in dismissal. "Though it wasn't only Heisenberg, you know. The same *weltanshauung* was emerging everywhere in those decades. In the writings of Pasternak and Ortega, for example; or in Guardini or Hantsch. What was Impressionism but quantum theory applied to painting? Or perhaps vice versa! And remember what Lukacs said. You can always study science historically, but you cannot study history scientifically."

Llewellyn looked at him speculatively. "Isn't that what we are here to decide?"

"My dear woman," Vane said, patting her arm. "The notion of a clockwork history is long discredited. Buckle was wrong. Our task is to discover the flaws in these rather dramatic claims. Meanwhile . . ." He shrugged and put his empty glass on the tray of a passing waiter. "Meanwhile, we may generate a few interesting papers out of our researches." He stretched his arms and glanced at his watch. "It has been stimulating talking with you, Mr. Collingwood. Meanwhile, my jet lag is catching up with me; so, if you don't mind, I'll find my way back to my hotel."

Jeremy watched him leave. "It's been nice talking to me," Jeremy told Gwynn. "He means it's been nice talking *at* me."

"Oh, don't be too harsh on him. Herkimer means well, but he just can't resist lecturing people. Even his colleagues."

"Was he serious? About that fact and fiction business, I mean." Jeremy finished his martini and looked around for a place to discard the glass. He didn't see a tray nearby, so he held onto it.

"Certainly! I know it seems rather esoteric to laymen— Did I say something funny?"

"No. It's just that *layman* means 'a nonaccountant.' "

Llewellyn chuckled briefly. "Yes. Every in-group divides humanity into two sets: Hellenes and Barbarians, Jews and Gentiles, Gaels and Galls. We Professionals and you Laymen. But, as I was saying, Herkimer really is making a valid Heisenbergian point. He means that you cannot observe history without the act of observation affecting what you see. That we 'construct' history by making associations of fact."

"Then how can anyone predict history? Two people may look at the same events and reconstruct them differently. So how do you know if a prediction has come true? Hell's bells! How do you even know what happened in the past?"

"That is precisely Herkimer's point."

"If he doesn't believe it is possible to study history scientifically, why did you invite him to be in your study group?"

"He insisted, actually. When the word got out that I was forming the group, he called me and asked to be on it. But that isn't the issue. None of us really believe that some secret cabal has reduced history to science, let alone that they have been controlling it for the last hundred-odd years. No, that is quite impossible."

"But—"

"Oh, I'm convinced that there is a group that has tried to do so. They might even believe themselves successful. But the existence of such a secret society does not prove that their beliefs are anything more than self-delusions, no matter how ruthlessly they pursue them. It is all too easy to reconstruct events so as to convince yourself that your predictions were borne out. Consider Nostradamus."

Most of the team members were personable enough: Geoff Hambleton. Henry Bandmeister. Penny Quick. Except for a lamentable tendency to throw out casual references to Significant Thinkers whom Jeremy had never heard of, their conversation was interesting. In fact, the talk of historical minutiae was made more interesting by Vane's previous remarks. Whatever the topic, Jeremy would wonder whether it was possible to reconstruct the facts in a totally different way. If it weren't that his thoughts would occasionally return to the central fact that Dennis was missing, he would have said he was having a good time. Sometimes, though, a part of him wanted to *scream!*

But the horror of any situation is that we soon grow used to it. Jeremy didn't recall who had said that. A Significant Thinker, perhaps. But he found it impossible to dwell constantly on his vanished lover. Life goes on, and he was prepared now to take things as they came.

As Jeremy and Gwynn left the reception room, a stranger leaped out of one of the overstuffed chairs that dotted the vestibule of the conference center. A short, thin Oriental man in rolled-up shirtsleeves, he wore dark frame glasses that seemed a little large for his face, and he had a felt-tip pen stuck behind his ear. A notebook and additional pens bulged his shirt pocket. "Dr. Llewellyn?" he asked.

Gwynn looked at him. "Yes, I'm Llewellyn."

"My name is Jim Tranh Doang, from the mathematics department. Could I have a few words with you?"

Llewellyn looked at her watch. "Very well, Mr. Doang. What can I do for you?"

"It's Dr. Doang," suggested the Oriental. "I am a professor of operations research. And it's what I can do for you."

"Operations research."

"You're going about this Beaumont thing all wrong!"

Llewellyn stared at Doang. "I'm not sure it is any business of yours how I go about my research."

The little man seemed taken aback by the hostility and he looked from Llewellyn to Jeremy and back.

"Let him talk, Gwynn," Jeremy said.

"Thank you," Doang said. "Doctor, like Chicago and Stanford, you have assembled a team to study the information contained in the Beaumont Dump. But like them, you have included only historians."

"It's a question of history, Dr. Doang. Of course, I have assembled a team of historians."

"But . . ." Doang glanced briefly at Jeremy. "This secret society claimed to use mathematical models to forecast the course of history. The Dump contained information on the structures of these models—not much, perhaps, I heard that the Dump was terminated in media res—but who on your team is qualified to judge the technical merits?"

Llewellyn cocked her head and looked at the mathematician. Jeremy could see her tongue running around the inside of her cheek, a sure sign, he had learned, that she was thinking things through. "And you think you are competent to do so?" She looked at Jeremy. "What do you think?"

"How can it hurt?"

Doang said, "Many researchers have modeled cultural phenomena. Men like Rashevsky and Hamblin. I can compare their work to that of this alleged society."

"*Alleged* society?" said Jeremy with an edge in his voice. "Alleged? Perhaps, Beaumont was only allegedly shot at; Grimes, allegedly killed. Dennis, allegedly hit by a car. Where there's smoke, Dr. Doang, there's fire."

Doang looked at him. "No, Mr. Collingwood. Where there is smoke, there is smoke. It may be fire, or it may be dry ice sublimating. Or only a cloud. Now we must discover which. That is the scientific method."

"All right, Dr. Doang," said Llewellyn. "I suppose we ought to discover whether the math is valid, at least. Though even if it is *mathematically* valid, it may or may not be *his-*

torically valid. Very well, Dr. Doang—dammit, I hate formality. Should I call you Jim or Tranh?"

"Jim is fine."

"Does anybody ever call you Ding?" asked Jeremy.

Doang looked at him. "Never twice," he said. He swept his hand through the air like a knife and cocked an eyebrow at him.

Jeremy grinned. "No offense, Jim. I'm Jeremy."

"And you may call me Gwynn," said Llewellyn. "The team meets tomorrow morning in the history department conference room—"

"If it is all the same with you," Doang said, "I'd rather not attend your meetings. My work can be pursued independently, and discussions of historical philosophy I would find as tiresome as you would find differential equations. And besides . . ." Doang hesitated.

"Besides?" prompted Llewellyn.

"According to the rumors, people who have gotten too close to this matter have turned up dead or missing. This society may not regard your committee as a threat, but I have a feeling that if they knew *real* scientists were involved, they would become quite upset."

Llewellyn twisted her lips. "You have a pretty high opinion of yourself."

"Doesn't everyone? But that's not the issue. The issue is what strategy to take. Whether I am right or wrong, it minimizes the risks—to all of us—if I work quietly on the side."

Doang bowed slightly, shook their hands, and departed. Jeremy and Gwynn remained in the lobby after he had gone. "Risk," repeated Llewellyn.

Jeremy pursed his lips. The reception had been fun, but Doang had reminded them that they were treading dangerous ground. Whether the so-called Babbage Society had a valid science or not was of academic interest. Whether they were prepared to kill to protect it was rather more personal.

"Brother Ruiz!" Kennison exclaimed, rising from behind the desk. Bettina ushered the older man into the office, then left, closing the door behind her. "What on earth are you doing here? It's too dangerous to meet *in corpora.*" And Ruiz knew that, so why was he here?

Benedict Ruiz planted his wiry body in the visitor's chair. He pulled a handkerchief from his breast pocket and began mopping his brow. With his left hand, he kept a firm grip on his malacca walking stick. Kennison could see Ruiz's knuckles bulging, white and prominent, against the dark wood. "Then you haven't heard?"

"Heard what? Can I offer you anything to drink?" He reached for the buzzer to call Karin, but Ruiz held up a restraining hand.

"No. Nothing, amigo. Gracias. I came—"

"Were you followed?"

Ruiz struck the floor with his stick. "Brother Kennison! I am trying to warn you for your own safety!"

Kennison sank slowly into the chair behind his desk. Something was wrong here. Ruiz was genuinely worried. Kennison leaned his elbows on the desk and clasped his hands into a ball. "Warn me," he repeated. "Why? What's happened?"

"Genevieve. Her car was bombed. She's dead."

Kennison jerked upright. A thrill ran through him. The Great Harpy, dead? He hadn't expected Paige to move so quickly. "Do you know the details?"

"Details?" Ruiz waved an irritated hand. The handkerchief fluttered like a flag of surrender. "Why do we need details? Our enemies have the scent now. They will pick us off, one by one." He resumed his face mopping. "Santa Maria, what have we gotten into?"

Kennison felt contempt for the old man's funk, but he tried to keep that out of his voice when he spoke. "Do you know how it happened?"

Ruiz nodded spastically. "Yes. Yes. Sister Paige had conceived a plan to protect ourselves. She had already contacted me about it. But Madam Chairman—I heard this from Judd himself—Madam Chairman refused to see her. She told Judd she was going to take a drive along the lake. Shortly after, Judd felt the whole mansion shake. He ran to the garage and found Madam's favorite Mercedes in flames. The heat was intense—petrol fires are extremely hot, you know—but he saw his mistress . . ." Ruiz paused, swallowed. He looked at the floor, refusing to meet Kennison's eyes, and his walking stick traced random curves in the carpeting.

Kennison shuddered, and it wasn't altogether theatrics. Sister Paige was far too given to extremes, too ready to let emotions rule her. *A less dramatic end would have served my purposes well enough.* Then he remembered that Sister Paige didn't give two figs for his purposes, that she had purposes of her own. He made a mental note to watch himself more carefully around her in the future. Alliances of convenience lasted only so long as they *were* convenient. One never knew what lay beneath the surface. He wondered if Paige had suborned Judd into setting the bomb.

"Do they know who did it?" he asked Ruiz.

Ruiz responded with an elaborate Latin shrug. "Who? The CIA. The Associates. The Republican Party. *Quién sabe?* The country is filled with people who might want revenge for what we have done. We have been guiding the course of this nation of ours for our own enrichment, and we have treated ruthlessly anyone who stumbled into our way. Can you deny it?"

"That was Grosvenor Weil and his clique—"

"And we were only following orders," Ruiz shot back. "We protested all the way to the bank." He laughed humorlessly. "No, we shall all hang, separately or together. The American government will see us as subversives. Confederate irridentists, the ones who destroyed their society. *Cultural genocide,* isn't that the term they use nowadays? The blacks will see us as those who kept them from their birthright. The greens as the ones who encouraged the Dæmon Technology. Oh, the list of our enemies will be an ungodly long one."

"And no one will blame us for the good things that have happened," said Kennison wryly.

Ruiz shrugged. "Who will take the trouble to think it through? We have enriched ourselves on the misery of others. That is all anyone will need to know."

"I never saw you refuse the fruits of our labor."

Ruiz shrugged again. "And I never said my own hands were clean." He held them up and turned them, as if he could see the blood if he stared hard enough. After a moment he sighed. "What will you do now? Will you follow Sister Paige's plan? That we put on a dumb show before the public?"

And how had his plan become Paige's? But Kennison kept a grip on his emotions. There would be a reckoning someday; but not now, and not with Ruiz. "Paige and I discussed it some weeks ago," he said. "I thought it a good idea."

Ruiz twisted his face. "Better to be slain in public than in private, eh, amigo? But not I." He shook his head. "Not I."

Kennison's eyes narrowed. "And what will you do, *señor?*"

Ruiz pursed his lips and studied the heavy and elaborate ring he wore on his left hand. "Señor," he said after a long moment. "My family has lived in this country for three hundred years. We were rancheros and frontiersmen in Arizona and New Mexico long before the Anglos came. Later, we supported the Americans, because the caudillos in Mexico City gave us nothing and our natural trade was with our fellow frontiersmen from the east. We even managed to hold most of our property during the Land Grant Wars, because our vaqueros were better gunfighters than those the Anglos hired. It is a lovely country. Lonely and barren, pocked with mesas and wild cañons. I have not been back there in far too long. I think maybe I shall leave the business and retire to my rancho."

"You will be no safer on your ranch than Sister Weil was in her mansion."

Ruiz flashed teeth at him. "But I will, Dan." His use of the nickname startled Kennison. "I will. Because my name is not Benedict Ruiz. It never has been. You see, when I was recruited, I was not as sanguine about the security of the

Secret as the rest of you. My true name was never entered into our database, so it has not been revealed by Beaumont's sabotage." He spread his hands wide. "So, I am safe. I can return to my home and live out my days and . . ."—his face darkened— ". . . and study my soul."

Kennison didn't know whether to be angered or delighted. On the one hand, there would be one less Councilor to oppose him. On the other hand, Ruiz would be beyond the discipline of the Society. As Quinn had been.

Had any others the foresight of Brother Ruiz? A secret persona outside the database; and, in Ruiz's case, at least, his true persona. In a way, he would miss the old Chicano. Such foresight was precisely what Kennison wanted on his Council. *If too many of us do disappear suddenly, like Ruiz, will that not appear significant to the suspicious public?*

"Benedict."

Ruiz had risen from his chair, preparatory to leaving. He paused. "Yes?"

"The ship is taking water, but it is not sinking yet. Most of us will stay and do what we can. For the safety of those of us who remain, there must be no question about the disappearance of 'Benedict Ruiz.' Do you understand me? 'Ruiz' must die, in public. You do owe that much to the Brothers and Sisters you are abandoning."

Ruiz pushed out his lower lip. "Yes," he admitted grudgingly. "I suppose I do owe you that much. What would you suggest?"

Kennison thought quickly. The more complex the plan, the more likely it was to go wrong. "When you leave San Diego, go by yacht and fall overboard in the Pacific. Drown. Can you manage that?"

Ruiz nodded slowly. "Yes. I have my loyal retainers. Men whose roots are entwined with my own family. They can arrange things properly and later make their way home. I—" He stopped, took two quick steps to the door, and jerked it open.

There was no one there.

"Who else is in this house?" Ruiz demanded, his voice abrupt.

"Only my staff. Why?"

"I thought I heard a sound outside the door. Do you trust them? Your staff?"

Kennison nodded indignantly. "I trust them with my life."

Ruiz nodded and smiled, and not without a certain savagery. "You may have to, my brother. You may have to."

X

"The Secret Six," said Norris Bosworth.

Red Malone raised an eyebrow and looked from SuperNerd to Walter Polovsky. He marked his place in his book with a forefinger. "Is he making sense?" he asked Walt.

Polovsky shrugged. "Let's take a walk."

Red snapped shut the book he was reading. "All right." He rose from the reading carrel and turned the book in to the librarian. Polovsky glanced at the title.

"Refreshing yourself on the bylaws, Brother Malone?"

Red grunted but said nothing. They left the library, Bosworth tagging along behind, like a lost puppy. In the elevator, Red touched the button for the ground floor. As the elevator rose, Bosworth started to say something, but Red held up a hand to silence him.

Outside, the sun blazed down from just above the peaks. Red judged another hour or so of daylight. When they reached the corral, the three of them leaned on the top rail of the fence and Red pointed to the herd, as if they were discussing the horses. "All right. What have you found?"

"The Secret Six," repeated Bosworth.

Red looked at him, then at Polovsky. "All right, I'll bite. Who or what are the Secret Six?"

"We think they're the Third Force," answered Polovsky.

Red nodded and rubbed the palms of his hands together. "Fast work. How'd you tumble to them?"

Bosworth answered. "It was a question of identifying historical anomalies. Mr. . . . ah, Brother Polovsky set up the equations. The nodes and yokes . . . I'm not up on all the math yet."

"I pulled the history PERT from just before Babbage's day to the present," explained Polovsky. "The kid here ran the programs to flag the low-prob nodes. We cleared all the nodes that we know were generated by Us or Them. Say . . ." Polovsky seemed struck by a new thought. "We can't say Us and Them anymore, can we? There are two Thems."

"Never mind that," said Red. "Tell me about this Secret Six of yours."

"Well, we looked at the low-probs that were left over. We figured some were things They had done that we hadn't known about, and we figured some of them were just random chance. So we did a little digging into the ones that had the greatest leverage."

"Sherlock Holmes and Watson. What'd you find?"

"We found the Reverend Thomas Wentworth Higginson."

"Wonderful. Who is he?"

"An abolitionist. He advocated armed raids into the South for the purpose of rescuing slaves," Bosworth said. "The idea was to set up a guerrilla army in the hills of western Virginia and swoop down on the plantations from time to time."

"He wrote the letters to John Brown," Polovsky added, examining his fingernails.

Red perked up. "Oho."

"Oho, indeed," said Polovsky. "It seems the Good Rev was leader of a group that called itself the Secret Six."

"There were six of them," said Bosworth.

Red looked at him. "No shit."

"The Six," continued Polovsky, "were a group of Northern businessmen and professionals trying to end slavery." He glanced at a slip of paper he held. "Higginson, Gerrit Smith, Theodore Parker, Samuel Gridley Howe, George Stearns, and Franklin Sanborn. At least, those were the names found on some unfortunate documents taken off Brown. We can't pin down the larger membership precisely—but certain names keep cropping up: Jabez Hammond. Lysander Spooner. Like Higginson, they seem to have been connected somehow to the Six."

"Lysander Spooner?"

Polovsky shrugged. "Could I make up a name like that? They tried to get Frederick Douglass in on it. The Brown Raid, I mean. The Six set up a meeting between Brown and Douglass in an old quarry near Chambersburg, PA. But Douglass thought the Raid would backfire and generate sympathy for the slaveholders."

"So, the Six were behind Brown," Red mused.

"Yeah, but here's the kicker. Congress held hearings— they had hard evidence: those letters Brown had—*and they never even subpoenaed Higginson*. The Mason committee lobbed some softball questions at a few witnesses, and no charges were ever filed. Except of course they hanged Brown," he added.

"The lone gunman theory," Red murmured. That sort of clandestine maneuvering had been the Society's forte back then, before mass communications. The equations had not predicted a civil war. No one had ever found an error in those equations, and Quinn had looked God-awfully hard for one. Two groups tinkering, each ignorant of the other's machinations. An interaction effect. A "ricochet" would explain a lot.

"Have you run a simulation yet, incorporating the Six into the equations?"

Polovsky looked at him. "Sure, I got nothing but spare time on my hands. Rewrite the whole Master Program."

"OK, Walt." *I wonder when Sarah will be back. This would be right up her alley.*

"One odd thing," said Bosworth.

Red looked at him. SuperNerd's forehead was creased in a frown. "What is it?"

"Well, based on what we know of their early intentions, I tried to trace the Six up to the present. Factor analysis. Well, they left a pretty clear track of historical anomalies up until about the 1890s. Then, nothing."

"They broke up?"

"There were still anomalies afterward that can't be accounted for. Again, some of it must be just random chance; but there seem to be at least two sets of tracks after that."

"Two sets," said Red.

"Right. If we define a set as a group of anomalies directed toward a common purpose."

"Hard to pin down," commented Polovsky, "even when we knew the players, and had some idea of their motivations. The output of a node might not be what the player intended."

"A couple of nodes dealing with Winfield Scott and Robert E. Lee," Bosworth said, "don't seem to fit in with either the Society's goals or what we figure were the Six's goals. They may have been 'misfires.' And Sarah told us about two nodes in Europe that we haven't decided on. The Six may have tried branching out overseas. But I'm pretty sure there are at least two sets of anomalies that are neither Ours nor Theirs."

"Sounds like the Six broke up, too," Polovsky told Red.

"Except," Bosworth said, "the second track petered out around the turn of the century."

Red nodded. "I'm sure they weren't immune to Carson's Dilemma, either." *And neither are the Associates.* The realization hit him suddenly. *We're acting out the same play ourselves.* The timing was right. The memes inherited from Quinn had weakened over the years. Now he was pushing his own memes.

"Hey!" said SuperNerd. "Who is that?" He pointed up the mountain.

Red shaded his eyes against the setting sun and looked. A figure on the edge of the cliff waved an arm semaphore-fashion and shouted. Red squinted, trying to see more clearly. Then he smiled quietly to himself.

"Sarah's back."

Jeremy was nursing a gin-and-tonic in a booth in the Campus Lounge with a large morocco-bound volume open on the table before him and several manila folders stacked neatly to the side when Gwynn Llewellyn slid into the seat opposite. She had her corncob pipe clenched firmly between her teeth—unlit, for which Jeremy was grateful. Penny Quick sat on the edge of the seat beside Gwynn. She smiled briefly. "Hello, Jerry."

Jeremy looked from one to the other. "Is the meeting over already?"

"Jeremy, it's ten o'clock." Gwynn lifted the book and looked at the spine. "Henry Thomas Buckle? Oh, my." She raised her eyebrows. "I'm afraid he is a little out of fashion these days. That florid, Victorian style."

Jeremy shrugged. "Herkimer said something about him at the get-acquainted reception last month and it made me curious. Buckle was wrong, he said. It obviously touched on the purpose of the study team, or else Vane would never have mentioned it. So . . ." He waved vaguely at the books and notes. He felt oddly diffident, an amateur explaining himself to the pros.

Gwynn eyed the manila folders. "And doing a respectable bit of research, I see." She touched Quick on the elbow. "We'll make a historian out of Jerry yet. You wait and see."

"Oh, don't let her do that to you, Jerry," Quick told him, flapping her hand. "It's a terrible life. Your eyes go bad, and you don't get paid well, and your friends simply can*not* understand how you spend your time." Quick was a thin, fine-featured woman who bubbled when she spoke. Everything she said and did bespoke enthusiasm. Jeremy thought she made a nice contrast to the other academics.

The waiter came and took their orders. Gwynn settled her bulk into the fake-leather seat. "How long have you been here, Jerry? You don't seem the least bit tipsy."

Jeremy pointed to his highball. "That's my first."

"Oh? I'm surprised the waiter hasn't thrown you out."

"Ah! Not if you know the secret. I tip him generously every half hour or so. He leaves me alone, and I can concentrate on my reading. The bustle doesn't distract me—you wouldn't believe some of the places I've conducted audits—and I don't feel as . . . isolated here as I would in my apartment." *Besides,* he added to himself, *I'm careful what I do in my apartment these days.* Gwynn had advised him to leave the telephone bug untouched. Removing it would only alert whoever had planted it.

The waiter brought the women their drinks. "And what has your research told you about Buckle?" asked Quick. She had a pink, frothy concoction with an unlikely amount of fruit. Jeremy couldn't imagine drinking it.

"Well, he was certainly an original," he said. "Sickly. Educated at home by his mother. Then he spent fifteen years of his adult life living with her, escorting her around the Continent. Nowadays, he would have been told to see an analyst."

"He was preparing his book," Gwynn said, tapping the volume on the table. *A History of Civilization in England.* She turned to the title page. "Yes. Eighteen-fifty-seven. Buckle was typical of that age. History was the story of Progress, from primitive beginnings to the very Pinnacle of Civilization—which, of course, meant nineteenth-century England." Gwynn and Quick traded knowing smiles.

No one believes in Progress-with-a-capital-P, Jeremy thought. He wondered if people had grown wiser over the years or only cynical. Literature was like that, too. If the writing wasn't properly "ironic," it wasn't "literature." Realism? *But sometimes,* Jeremy told himself fiercely, *the hero does win.*

"Did you *also* know," he said tartly, "that Buckle was convinced that history could be made into a science?"

All he saw was polite interest. He must have looked crestfallen, because Gwynn squeezed his arm. "Oh, don't be upset, Jeremy. Buckle may be out of fashion, but he is not forgotten."

"Besides," added Quick, "he was wrong. History can't have 'laws' like the physical sciences. History is evolutionary, like biology. Events are dependent on what went before."

"There are laws in biology, too," Jeremy pointed out.

"Oh, yes; but they are different kinds of laws. Certainly

you have the Theory of Evolution, but that isn't like the Theory of Gravitation. Astronomers can take their theory and predict the positions of the planets, but biologists can't calculate what future species will evolve."

Jeremy was an accountant. He tried not to make categorical judgments until he had the figures in hand, and he certainly was not going to get sidetracked by Penny into a discussion in an area where they were both ignorant. But someone had told him once . . . When was it? At a party he and Dennis had gone to last year. Something about making a complete genetic map of each species. The Genome Project? "When we know what each gene does," the young fellow had said, "we'll know what can happen when it's mutated."

"You think I've been wasting my time," he said, looking from Quick to Gwynn and back. "Why bother plowing through this turgid tome"—he picked up the book and let it drop—"when I could have just asked you to explain Herkimer's remark."

Quick reached out and touched his arm. "Oh, no, Jerry. You did splendidly. The whole idea of education is to discover things on your own. What kind of world would we have if everyone simply waited to be told things?"

"The Managed Society," said Gwynn darkly. " 'Don't give me data; just explain it for me. Tell me what it means.' "

Jeremy flushed and yanked his arm away. She was right, of course. Still, it was a letdown to find that what you had discovered was already well known. Like reaching the top of Mount Everest and finding a lemonade stand.

"Look," he said. "I know Herkimer dismissed the whole notion—a clockwork history, he called it. But isn't that the very axiom upon which the Babbage Society was founded? We *should* be interested in it, whether it's correct or not." Jeremy wasn't sure whether he believed history could be reduced to science, either. It didn't concern him a great deal. But the Babbage people did believe it and they had kidnapped Dennis to keep it secret. The easy dismissal by the academics nettled him. He gestured at the book. "Well, Buckle wasn't the only person who believed in the possibility of a social science. There was Adolphe Quetelet, too."

This time he received puzzled stares. "Who?"

Secretly pleased that he had found something new that he could spring on them, he tried to keep his smile from becoming too broad. "A famous Belgian astonomer," he told them. "A contemporary of Buckle's."

"An astronomer," said Gwynn.

"Oh. Well," said Quick.

"Yes. Quetelet and Buckle exchanged an extensive correspondence."

Quick looked at Gwynn. "I never heard that, but Buckle isn't my specialty."

"I was reading a collection of Buckle's letters," Jerry said, "in the university's rare book collection . . ." A musty, tattered volume, half falling apart, with ragged page edges and a sharp, dry odor. He had read it in a special, climate-controlled room, under the stern and suspicious gaze of the rare volumes archivist. Jeremy had felt like a genuine Researcher. "Buckle referred several times in passing to 'my correspondences with M. Quetelet.' "

Gwynn traded glances with Quick. She took the pipe out of her mouth. "Why would Henry Thomas Buckle be writing to an *astronomer?*"

Jeremy shrugged. "Intellectual categories weren't so neatly segregated back then. Perhaps that's something we could relearn from the Victorians."

"Touché," said Quick. "I'll bet Buckle traded letters with Darwin, too. Darwin's theories were all the intellectual rage at the time." She leaned toward him across the table. "This sounds interesting. Tell us more. I never even knew Buckle's letters were ever collected."

It suddenly occurred to Jeremy that Penny Quick was trying to "put the moves" on him. For a moment, he was flustered. That he was a handsome man he knew quite well. Dennis had told him often enough. But he never knew what to do in situations like this. He thought of explaining that there was no point to her efforts, but that would cause embarrassment all the way around. On the other hand, to ignore her amounted to a put-down. She was a nice person and he did not want to hurt or embarrass her.

"Well," he said quickly, "I was intrigued, too. Because none of the Quetelet letters were in the collection. The editor explained in a footnote that none of them had survived."

It occurred to him suddenly that he was doing precisely what Dennis had been doing in the days before his accident: reading history. Now, somehow, by engaging in the same activity, Jeremy felt closer to him.

He could think about Dennis calmly now. The frantic urgency, the kaleidoscopic need to *Do Something,* was gone. Nothing the study team had done so far seemed helpful as far as locating Dennis went, and his current acquiescence to the status quo seemed almost shameful. As if he should be shouting from the rooftops or combing the back alleys of Denver. High-strung, some of his friends used to call him. Well, maybe so. Maybe he had always reacted in that hyper, overwrought way. Perhaps he was only now learning to deal with crises differently. Gwynn, with her careful, plodding approach to life, had had a great calming effect on him. Maybe she could advise him on how to handle Penny.

He sorted through his meticulously labeled folders and found the one marked: QUETELET. He paged through the magazine articles, newspaper stories, and encyclopedia entries that he had downloaded and chose an item from the *New York Times Book Review* to pass to Penny. "I've underlined the relevant passages."

Penny nodded and ran her finger down the page, looking for the promised mention of the astronomer's name:

> ... *it was Quetelet's perception of the wider applicability of the error law that provided the inspiration for the important work in statistics done in the late 19th century. His lasting contribution to science was to establish the concept of a statistical law—the notion that true facts about a mass can be discovered even when*

information about the constituent individuals is unat-
tainable . . .

She looked up. "This is marvelous. I always wondered
who to blame for having to take stats in sociology. But who
are . . ."—she looked again at the article—". . . Maxwell and
Boltzmann?"

"I looked them up, too. They were scientists who applied
Quetelet's concept of statistical laws to physics. But keep
reading." He tried to keep from squirming in his seat from
eagerness.

Penny smiled at him and read another passage:

. . . Beginning in the second quarter of that century, the
collection of data became a wide-ranging enterprise.
The motivation was often reformist; it rested on the be-
lief that statistics would make it possible to erect a sci-
entific basis for a progressive social policy. Adolphe
Quetelet shared the concerns of the reformers but be-
lieved that more than just facts were needed. His aim
was to erect a numerical social science that would bring
order to social chaos . . .

Jeremy spread his hands. "There. You see? Quite a few
people in those days were considering the possibility of a
social science. According to the *Encyclopedia Brittanica,*
Quetelet studied the 'numerical constancy of voluntary acts,'
like crime. Our commonplace phrase, *the Average Man* was
his coinage. Quetelet even wrote a book on the subject, en-
titled *Physique sociale*, in 1835. That led to a lot of work in
what they called moral statistics and to a wide discussion of
free will versus social determinism in human behavior."

Gwynn took the pipe from her mouth. "I should imagine,"
she said dryly.

"So it was natural that he and Buckle corresponded so
avidly. They shared the same vision. Too bad none of their
letters survived. The study team would probably have found
them provocative."

"Provocative," said Gwynn, "is not the word for it." She looked at Quick and smiled wickedly. "Let's do tell Herkimer all about it at tomorrow's meeting."

"You tell him, Gwynn dear. I'll hide under the table."

Not until later that evening, as Jeremy prepared for bed, did he feel a prickling in his scalp.

Was it simply ill luck that lost the Buckle-Quetelet letters, or had it been something more? He paused with his pajamas half-on, seeing in his mind's eye a shadowy figure ripping apart the carefully tied bundles of letters and throwing them into a raging fire. He thought of Buckle dying so unexpectedly in Damascus. The young man had always been of frail health, but could it be . . . ?

He remembered Dennis flying through the air, the gunman who had shot at Beaumont, the dead reporter—what was his name? That Brady Quinn fellow he had read about in the printout. The Babbage Society killed those who drew near their Secret. Buckle had been a somewhat younger contemporary of Quinn, hadn't he? Could Buckle have been poisoned?

Jeremy tossed the pajama top to the bed and strode to the living room, where he fumbled with the clasps on his briefcase and pulled forth a printout that Henry Bandmeister had compiled: an index to all people, places, and things mentioned in the Beaumont Dump. He sat in the chesterfield with the printout in his lap and flipped through the pages, looking for the B's. Then he jumped further back, to the Q's. Finally he sighed and laid the sheets on his lap.

No, it was silly. Neither Buckle nor Quetelet was referenced in the Beaumont Dump. That was hardly surprising. Buckle had traveled extensively, but his travels had been confined to Europe and the Near East. There was nothing to indicate that he had ever been in contact with the Babbage Society, or that the Babbage Society was aware of him or Quetelet. No, the idea of a cultural science was simply "blowing in the wind" during the mid-nineteenth century. It was no surprise that several scholars had speculated about it.

But the prickling in his scalp would not go away.

XI

It was a lot like falling off a cliff. Once the initial choice was made, everything else followed quickly and inevitably. The operation was performed quietly and with a minimum of disturbance. The surgeon flew in and made his suggestions and Sarah made her choices; and she came out of it with her head swathed in bandages, still wondering if she had chosen well.

For several weeks she lay in the clinic bed on the lowest level of the underground warren, and SuperNerd and Tex and even Janie Hatch stopped by from time to time to see how she was doing. She told them she was doing fine and she couldn't wait for the bandages to come off, and she didn't ask them where anyone else might be and why he hadn't stopped in.

When, after an endless wait, the bandages did come off, she studied her new face for a long time after, turning the glass this way and that, trying to see it from all different angles. It was darker than her own had been. The brow seemed higher; the nose, a little broader. Somehow, they had changed the shape of her mouth, so that her smile was wider than it had been. All in all, not a bad face; it would cause more than one head to turn. But, try as she might, she could see no sign of her mother in it.

She suppressed the spasm of regret. It wasn't as if she had gone into it with her eyes closed. She had made her decision, dammit, and there wasn't any point in dwelling on might-have-beens. Yet she couldn't help glancing back a little wistfully at who she had been and wishing that none of this had ever happened.

Sarah leaned her elbows on the library table and rubbed her face. A long day. Too long. She glanced at the booklet she had been studying, a three-ring binder with a yellow cover. *The Life History of Gloria Bennett.*

That's me now, she thought. *Gloria Bennett.* She ran the name across her tongue to see how it tasted. Gloria Bennett.

There was nothing flimsy about the persona the Associates had given her. Gloria had been a real person with a real life, but she wouldn't mind that Sarah would now be living that life because five years ago, in a light-plane crash in the Canadian Rockies, Gloria Bennett had ceased to care about anything at all.

A chance combination of circumstances had enabled the Associates to co-opt the identities of all three people aboard and "bank" them as personae for themselves. The crash had occurred in a remote area of British Columbia, and it had so happened that the area ATC was an Associate. She had deleted all traces of the accident from air traffic control records, and three other Associates had "completed" the ill-fated flight. Then they had "quit" their jobs at home and "moved" to remote areas, where old friends were unlikely ever to look them up.

There was a cruelty in that abrupt and unexplained severing of old ties with family and friends. Kinder by far a spouse's death than such inexplicable abandonment. But Sarah had grown used to—without accepting—the offhand callousness that marked the Associates' activities. When one is accustomed to the abstractions of metahistory, what do the lives of a few individuals matter?

Those who had known the original Gloria well enough to matter had been out of touch with her for many years, and the plastic surgery had made the resemblance as close as was physically possible. Though others had used the Gloria persona for short periods, they had made no close friends.

In one way, that was good news. It meant that she was unlikely to be unmasked by accident. In another way, though, it saddened her. If Gloria had been a person rather than a phantom, she would have been an intensely lonely woman, with no close friends and no ties to her family. The persona was all too close to the life she had been living. Putting on Gloria was like pulling on a worn and familiar dress. It was comfortable and it fit very well. But she noticed now how faded and drab it was.

She wondered momentarily what was happening in the world beyond the walls of the safe house. She was Alice-down-the-rabbit-hole, living in an unreal world full of bizarre events; and every day she spent here was another day further removed from the life she had known. Perhaps that was deliberate—a brainwashing tactic—so that, when she finally did emerge from this underground womb, she would be reborn, almost literally.

She rose from the table and walked idly around the library, stretching back and arm muscles cramped from sitting at the table all day. Sometimes she pulled a book out and leafed through it. She was tired of studying Gloria every day. Tired of sleeping with earphones on.

The library had extensive selections on anthropology, systems engineering, statistics, psychology, economics, topology—all topics that a good cultural engineer needed to master. Most of the "books" were on disc, but there was something comforting about the smell of old paper and ink, about the heft of a morocco-bound volume in the hand. Some chord that had been ingrained into human society since the first Egyptian brushed berry juice on papyrus. Without these rows of books, it just wouldn't have felt like a library.

She paused at a short row of books and ran her fingers across the spines. Science fiction, the shelf label admitted. *Foundation. No Truce with Kings. The Squares of the City. Doomsday's Color Press.* She browsed through a couple of the stories, then chuckled. All of them involved some attempt to direct or control human culture. Psychohistory. Subliminal persuasion. The Great Science. The Kiersten Equations. Evidently, no one else had ever thought to call it cliology.

She continued her slow circuit of the shelves. The librarian, a 250-pound man with a Mongolian scalplock, watched her without interest. He was cataloging files intermittently, not a task that required his full attention. Sarah wondered what role he played on the Outside. Well, it took all kinds.

She came to a set of thin volumes—their spines were too narrow for titles—and pulled one down to look at its cover. *Rules and Bylaws of Utopian Research Associates.*

The typing was crude; the letters, uneven, reminding Sarah of the old manual typewriters. It was signed in faded brown ink by Brady Quinn. She flipped the pages at random. *I suppose I'll have to memorize these sometime.* She read a page.

```
Rule 24.  Associates making use of cliological
   data and projections for their own advantages
   must keep their Brothers and the Council apprised
   of their activities.
```

The entry was followed by the comment that it superseded Rule 4. There was a lengthy "Statement of Intent" and two amendments, one of which had, in 1887, changed "Brothers" to "Brothers and Sisters." Curious, she paged toward the front of the book, looking for Rule 4, but found the first entry to be Rule 21.

"I invoke Rule 19." Whoever had said that at the meeting she had overheard had prompted a great deal of laughter, at her expense and Red's.

"Excuse me," she called across to the librarian. "Where can I find Rule Nineteen?"

The man scratched his double chin and ran his hand through his scalplock. "Aren't you Red Malone's friend? The one they just ran through a makeover?"

Makeover? Well, you could call it that. "Yes, I am."

The man grinned, as if at some secret joke. "I suppose Rule Nineteen's pretty important to you."

"Are you going to tell me where to find it, or not?"

He pointed vaguely toward the shelves where she was standing. "It's in volume one."

Of course. Quinn must have kept most of the Society's

original rules, changing only a few, like Rule Four. The second folio contained only the new ones. She pulled the other thinly bound folios out. *Correspondence of Jedediah Crawford, Ph.D. Proposed Design and Construction of Babbage Analytical Engines. Constitution and Bylaws of the Babbage Analytical Society.*

This booklet, she saw, was handwritten with a flat-nibbed pen in an elegant curlicued script. That had been an era when penmanship was considered an art form and a "good hand" was a mark of social distinction. The ink was brown, almost copper in color; the pages, brittle and cracked around the edges, smelled of more than a century of slow oxidation. The title page bore the signatures of J. Crawford, I. Shelton, and P. Hammondton. The Founders. She wondered what kind of men they had been.

She thumbed a few pages and paused at Rule 4: "Selflessness and the Common Good must be the Motivating Force of all Brothers." The rule forbade members from using their researches for personal gain. Red had told her that this rule had been the original Society's undoing, as it went against human nature.

Red had not come to see her during her convalescence. She had expected him, waited each day to see if he would show, but he hadn't. She hadn't seen him at all since the day she had returned from the mountains and told him of her decision to join.

Brusquely, she turned her attention back to the book.

So, where was Rule 19? She turned the aged pages carefully. Yes, there it was. She read:

> *Rule 19. In order to Assure that Our Brothers have a Vested Interest in the Felicitous Nature of future Social Conditions, it is Imperative that each marry and sire Children, for Whose Well-being and Upkeep he assumes Full Responsibility.*

She snapped the book shut. A sound behind her made her turn in time to see the librarian swallow a smile. Sarah kept a stony look on on her face until the librarian returned self-consciously to his cataloging.

Sarah opened the book again and reread the rule. Son of a bitch. No wonder those bastards had laughed so hard. She and Red? Absurd! She closed the folio carefully and replaced it. Returning to her reading table, she gathered up her things and walked out. The librarian watched her go, still trying to grin without being obvious. "Have a nice day," he said.

She stalked down the hall. Male chauvinists, all of them. Even Janie Hatch and the other women in that meeting. Red must be under some peer pressure to fulfill Rule 19. One of the amendments had specified a time limit, and he might be approaching it. But that gave them no right to discuss her as if she were a breeding cow!

She had turned the wrong way down the hall into a section of the underground warren she did not recognize. The walls were painted a muted pink, with green macrodesigns in abstract geometric shapes. The plants situated here and there were artificial, but they lent an air of spaciousness to the corridor. Doors opened onto offices, some empty, some with people in them doing incomprehensible things. Farther along she saw a canteen with three people sitting around a table drinking coffee from a vending machine. An office complex, no different from thousands of other corporate offices anywhere in the world, except it was underground. But, what the hell, even secret cabals had filing and paperwork.

This facility was one of five spotted around the country. Other offices were in anonymous high-rise towers in major cities, often on secret floors accessible only by means of special elevators. ADMITTANCE TO AUTHORIZED PERSONNEL ONLY. There was a reason that so many office buildings seemed to lack a "thirteenth floor." But the sensitive work was done in hidden safe houses like this one.

The hall ended in a T-intersection, and she flipped a mental coin and turned left. She wandered into a game room with chessboards and go boards, some of them laid out in midgame. One board had a sign: ANYONE CAN PLAY—BLACK'S MOVE. The reverse side announced White's move. She studied the board for a moment or two and saw that Black was engaged in a classic Philidor Defense. Not a very good position. Well, that made it more interesting. She played P to KB5 and turned the sign around. Two women were dozing over a complex gambit at another table. They saw her and the smiling one waved absently. Her opponent scowled at the distraction.

Sarah left the game room and saw an elevator ahead, at the juncture of another T-intersection. As she hurried toward it, she heard the faint, squeaking sound of a a clarinet. It was the same piece she had heard in the orientation class a month ago: the solo part from "High Society." Whoever the secret jazzman was, he had finally mastered the syncopations.

She tracked the sound to a small room thirty feet past the elevator. The door was slightly ajar, and she peeked through it to see a man sitting on a metal folding chair with his back partly toward the door. He was dressed casually, in jeans and T-shirt. The T-shirt was burgundy and read: MY BROTHER'S BAR across the back. He had dark hair and a long nose, but his fingers were short and his build stocky. His face . . .

His face! She stepped into the room.

"Never sit with your back to the door," she said. "That's how they got Hickok."

The man started and turned and faced her. She studied his eyes.

"Red?" she asked haltingly. "You are Red Malone, aren't you?"

"Would it matter much if I told you I was Jimmy Caldero?"

"You *are* Red! What have you done?"

"You of all people should know. Hey! You better sit down before you fall down."

She slumped into a chair like the one Red was sitting in. There were similar chairs and music stands scattered about the room. The metal was hard and cold against her back. Red cocked his head, seemed to see something in her face, and turned away. He toyed with his clarinet. Keys and pads clicked like tiny hailstones.

Sarah couldn't stop staring at his face. It was subtly different from the one she had known—in the shape of the nose and the chin and the ears—but she could see the old Red in there, peering out through the eyes, like a prisoner from behind bars.

"Red. Why?" It was silly, she knew, but she felt as if she had lost an old friend. That was the problem with people. As soon as you really got to know someone, he cut out on you. He died, or he went on the road, or he changed into someone else.

"Why? Why do you think? Same reason as you. Same reason as two dozen others in the organization. You didn't imagine you were the only one who needed a new persona."

"You never mentioned it."

"You had your own problems."

Sarah realized that she hadn't given the matter much thought at all. She had been so wrapped up in her own crisis, she hadn't realized that others might be having one, too. "It's different for you," she said. "You do it all the time."

Red rubbed his hand over his nose and chin. "Not this. Sure, I've changed names and backgrounds before. Who hasn't? But I always managed to keep my own mug. What do you think?" He turned profile. "Am I more handsome than before? I didn't think it was possible to improve on perfection, did you?"

"Red. I'm sorry."

Red shrugged. "Hey. You gotta do what you gotta do. I'm just glad Our system was better protected than Theirs. Nearly all of your Dump was from Society files. Kennison was inexcusably lax. If he worked for me I would have fired him. You didn't even touch my own personal system—" He broke off suddenly. "You know what I mean."

He was talking about the parasite system he and his cabal were running. Red had already told her that it had been off-line while her worm was running. A coincidence, but one that had saved their system. Sarah wondered what Cam Betancourt would have done had he seen Red's secret files among the printouts.

"So, what do you do now?"

"We got word that my old employers—"

"The CIA."

He looked annoyed. "Don't try to be too clever. I was with the Defense Intelligence Agency. Not as 'Red Malone,' but as . . . Well, that persona doesn't matter anymore." He rubbed a hand across his face again. "The fact is, someone in the Agency saw my cover in the infamous Beaumont Dump. We got the word from one of our people still inside. They backtracked my cover identity until they blew it apart." He looked at his clarinet and his fingers worked a few keys. "Do you know how hard it is to get a false persona past those bastards in the first place?" He shrugged. "Well, they knew my old face, so I changed it. But we can't change fingerprints—not enough to fool that crowd. So here I am. . . ." He blew a scale on his instrument.

"You don't sound bitter."

"Bitter? No. I get unemployment. I'm rich, don't forget. Oh, don't get me wrong. The Agency was fun. It was important work. We need pipelines into those restricted databases and I liked what I was doing in that niche. The fact that I would have disappeared into Leavenworth if they'd caught on only added a little Tabasco to the sauce." He put the mouthpiece to his lips and licked the reed. "I think I'll miss the rummy games as much as anything. Still . . ." And he shrugged. "I'm just as happy to be out of it. Try something new. Maybe get back into Adjusting." He began a C-major scale.

"Or raise a family?" asked Sarah.

The clarinet squawked like a duck on high F. He put it down again and inspected the mouthpiece. "Chipped reed." He tightened the ligature. "You know about that, do you." It was a statement, not a question.

"Rule Nineteen," she said.

Red grunted. "Yeah."

"Do you plan, ah . . . compliance?"

"I'm the wild and independent sort. Being tied down isn't my style." He cocked his head and looked at the ceiling.

"Rule Nineteen applies to you, too, you know. You're one of Our Sisters, now."

"Uh-huh. Barefoot and pregnant. That's me. The Utopian Research Baby Machine."

"Don't be cynical." He was silent for a moment. Then he said in a different tone of voice, "Tell me. If you were organizing a group of people to 'design a future,' how would you ensure that they went about it carefully and responsibly?"

She regarded him and his change of subject warily. "Well . . . I'd recruit only people with a sense of responsibility to the community."

Red shook his head. "Won't work. How do you measure it? How do your recruiters screen for it? How do you ensure its continuance, generation after generation? No, it's gotta be something simple, measurable, and automatic, something that makes responsibility self-enforcing."

" 'Every Brother must have someone he loves held hostage to the future,' " she quoted.

Red smiled with half his mouth. "Exactly. The rule isn't about giving birth. It's about accepting responsibility and maintaining constancy of purpose. So Quinn and Carson built self-interest into it. Not altruism. Never trust an altruist. He'll sell you down the river for the sake of a Higher Purpose. It's negative feedback that makes responsibility self-enforcing. Like requiring landlords to live in the buildings they rent, or manufacturers to place their intake pipes downstream from their effluent pipes. See? Compliance is easy to confirm, and that compliance ensures that the businessman or the landlord acts responsibly. Altruism is like building a dam. It doesn't last. Sooner or later, history bursts through. Quinn believed that the best protection against haphazard tampering with the future was to give the tamperers a stake in the outcome. Something that would make them more thoughtful regarding their plans."

"It's a good theory," said Sarah, "but I can think of two flaws."

Red grunted. "Only two?"

"What stops members from just going through the motions? Pop a kid, pay for its rearing, but otherwise ignore it. I've known plenty of parents who never did more. And even if they do care, will they build the best possible future for everyone, or only for their own children?"

"I won't argue with you. It's not a perfect system. Nothing is perfect."

His smugness irritated her. She was talking with a stranger. "Some things are," she said.

"Name one."

"The final section of the 'Maple Leaf Rag.' "

He looked momentarily perplexed; then he laughed. "All right." He nodded at the spinet sitting against the far wall. "Prove it."

"What . . ."

"Want me to twist your arm? Come on." He stood and tugged her off her seat.

Red evidently was willing to discuss any subject but Rule 19 and how it might apply to himself. She allowed him to sit her at the old upright, where she ran up and down a few tentative scales. Her fingers felt huge and clumsy. "It's been a long time," she protested. "I haven't had time for play, lately."

Red shook his head. "You should always leave time for play."

She started the rag, stumbled over a chord, and started over. She was tentative at first, unsure of herself; but she soon found the tempo. Ragtime, Joplin had said, must never be played too fast. Her left hand beat out the steady bass rhythm while her right played with the syncopations. A classical rag followed a set pattern: AABBACCDD; but she played the first two themes without repeating so she could get into the trio sooner. Then she rolled into the dancing strains of the finale, leaping up and down the keyboard. There was a bittersweet triumph about Joplin's music. Something at the same time sad and grand. The "Maple Leaf" had been his crowning achievement. The King of Rags, they had called it. Every note in it was exactly right.

When she had finished, for some odd reason, she felt better than she had felt in a very long time, as if a terrible burden had been lifted from her. Her fingers wandered into another light rag, and she remembered how these tunes had formed the backdrop to her childhood. "Do you want to try it with me?" she asked Red.

He shook his head. "I'm not that good."

"You were doing all right on 'High Society.' I heard you from the hallway. That solo you were playing is a test piece for jazz clarinetists."

"It's not that," he told her. "Not the technical difficulty. It's the . . . The ear, I suppose. I can't play what I hear; I have to read it. Memorize it." Incredibly, he blushed and looked away. "I play notes, not music."

"You say that like you're admitting to a crime."

"Play some more, would you? I kind of like that old-time music."

She let her hands drift into "Panama," then into the "Oklahoma Rag." The "Okie" had been written by a white man, one of the few who had really understood. She was aware of Red watching her the whole time. That should have made her nervous, that concentrated attention of his; but it seemed the most natural thing in the world. She closed her eyes and let the music lift her and carry her along. If she didn't worry about it, her fingers found the right keys without trouble.

But when she opened her eyes at the end and looked at him, she saw that he was not watching her hands at all. She stumbled over a chord, ducked her head, and stared at the keys. "I'm out of practice."

"No, don't apologize. You were very good. They have a little jazz group here, you know. I play with them whenever I'm around. Chicago-style, a little Dixieland. Why don't you join? I think it'd be a good thing."

She searched his face. The strange, new face. She didn't know how to read him anymore. If she ever had.

She shook her head. "I don't play in groups. I just play for myself."

"You should try it. There's something about ensemble playing." He walked back to one of the chairs and sat down. He wet his reed. "I can't describe what it's like. How it feels when everything clicks and harmonizes. I remember one time ... Oh, this was ages ago, in high school. The band was rehearsing one day during lunch period. It was your typical high school piece, a medly of tunes from Tchaikovsky. We were tooting and scraping our way through it when, suddenly, it all came together. The notes, the timbre, the voicing. Everything, just right; like *something* was playing us as a single instrument. It sent shivers down my spine. We played 'March Slav' in big, booming bass notes and segued into the quickstep from the 1812 Overture without missing a beat. Our conductor, Mr. Price, swung his baton like a madman. Kids on their way to class, they stopped in the gym to listen. They crowded in from the hallway. And, when we finally climaxed, they cheered and clapped." He shook his head. "Not polite applause, like you get at a concert. They gave us an ovation. Because they could feel it, too."

Red was an ensemble player, Sarah thought, not a soloist. Yet she had never met a man so much his own individual as Red. Another contradiction in that bundle of contradictions.

"Well," said Red. "I guess I'll be packing it in here."

And Red was not the type for self-revelation. Like a flasher in an alleyway, having exposed himself for a moment, he must button up and vanish. "Yeah. Should I close the piano up?"

"What? Oh, no. Don't bother. People wander in here at all hours, just to relax."

"Sure." She rose and picked up her books. "I guess I'll find my way back to my rooms." She hesitated, wondering if Red would walk with her.

"I'll give you a call tomorrow," he said, fiddling with his instrument case.

"Oh. Sure. See you around." When she left the music room, she did not walk to the elevator but stopped in the hallway just outside the door, leaning against the wall. After a few moments, she heard him play again. This time it wasn't

"High Society," but the first movement of Mozart's Clarinet Concerto. The clarinet sang the throaty notes of the low register and the bright, crystalline notes of the high register with authority and technical precision. He played with grace and clarity. She closed her eyes and let the music take charge. In his own dialect, Mozart had achieved as much perfection as Joplin.

Then the elevator chimed and the doors opened and two people got off; and, rather than have them wonder why she was hanging around outside the music room, she got into the car and let the doors close her into silence.

XII

Kennison often stayed at the office after everyone else had gone home. There were hosts of details to attend to and never enough time to do it. Most of the staff left at five. In fact, some of them started leaving at four-thirty. Kennison never understood working by the clock. You spent as much time as necessary to get the job done right, and that was that. The new breed of worker he found strange and more than a little distasteful.

And knowing that the Society was partly responsible did not satisfy him. Granted, technopeasants were more easily manipulated, but they did not have the inner dedication that Kennison wanted so badly. The whole idea had been to encourage a domesticated public, a simple public, a public that would react in predictable ways.

And a public that left work predictably at five o'clock, if not sooner. Kennison made a face. *Ye have sown the wind,* he thought sourly. The same voices that were taught to whine, "What do we need to learn *that* for?" to ensure their dumb acquiescence to their betters would also whine about quitting time. Yet he wondered if there might not be some way of reaping domestication without the whirlwind of passivity and apathy. Was there such a thing as a dedicated, focused sheep? It was an intriguing research problem, both in fieldwork and in mathematical theory.

He reached for his espresso cup and found it empty. He sighed. With the Night Shift on indefinite leave, there was no one to look to his creature comforts after hours. Wearily he pushed himself from his desk and walked to his office door. The outer office was dim, only a few safety lights glowing. One work cubicle was lit, where the policeman assigned to guard him sat reading a magazine. Kennison wasn't sure what the magazine was. One of those popular do-it-yourself magazines. *Build a Space Shuttle in* Your *Basement!*

In theory, the policeman was young enough that his interests should have been more severely circumscribed. Music, women, cars, and sports. That was the meme complex the Society had been propagandizing to young males. Safe interests, with the music having a superficial veneer of rebellion to act as a bleeder valve for frustration. The technical magazine hinted at an unwonted curiosity. But then, Kennison chided himself, perfect uniformity was a will-o'-the-wisp. There would always be those who ranged above and below the mean. A domesticated public would include domesticated technicians.

"Would you like another cup of coffee, Bill?" It never hurt to show the masses that you had the common touch. Be generous in small things and the great returns would follow.

"No, thank you, sir," the policeman replied.

Kennison nodded an acknowledgment and walked to the coffee station, where he poured himself a cup of decaf. As he sipped it, he glanced at the clock on the wall. He wondered if the policeman was sufficiently bored after all this time with no action. He could sympathize with the man's situation. The local news organs had already given up. Kennison had performed nothing filmable, provided no catchy sound byte; so they had gone back to their audiences with assurances of False Alarm, folks. And on to more important things, like fires and car wrecks.

The deaths of Benton and Weil and the apparent demise of Benedict Ruiz had had the desired effect. The various municipal governments had been more than happy to provide obviously needed protection to their wealthy and important citizens. And it didn't hurt that the mob, once aroused, seldom engaged in fine distinctions and many people with no connection to the Society had also asked for protection. Stories were garbled, and different pressure groups had their own axes to grind. Threats had been made against a great many people, diluting the attention paid to the Society. That had been another of Torino's ideas. The best place to hide a leaf was in a forest. Torino was sharp. A man to watch, in both senses of the word. Kennison decided to keep an eye on him, for all that he was Ullman's man. Especially because he was Ullman's man.

Meanwhile, Kennison thought there was something amusing in having one of the sheep guarding one of the wolves.

"I'm finished now, Mr. Kennison. Will you be closing up?"

He turned with the coffee cup halfway to his lips. Prudence Baker was Vice President of Kennison Demographics and supervisor of the Night Shift. She was short and round-faced and wore her hair in an old-fashioned flip held in place with a plastic barrette.

"Yes, Ms. Baker. You may leave now." In a lower voice, he added, "Will I see you tonight?"

"Downstairs," she whispered. "Fifteen minutes."

"Little Girl Lost?"

She nodded and gave him the wide-eyed look that made her seem so much like a bunny rabbit. She patted her briefcase. "It's all in here."

"Very well, Ms. Baker," he said in a normal voice. "We will take that up on Monday."

He walked her to the door, while the policeman watched with both professional and male interest. That amused Kenninson, because Prudence dressed younger than her years.

He busied himself at his desk for a few minutes, moving papers around. When the fifteen minutes were up, he stuck his head out the office door and told the police guard that he would be in the washroom for a while. The officer nodded briefly and resumed his reading of the magazine.

The executive washroom at Kennison Demographics possessed a number of features, the most useful of which was the small shower. Kennison locked the door behind him and entered the stall. He closed the glass-and-metal door and turned the knobs in a careful sequence. With a click and the hiss of escaping air, the floor of the stall slowly descended. Kennison hummed a tune.

The washroom on the floor below was identical with the one he had just left. This one, however, belonged to the import/export firm of Johnson and Cheng. J and C was modestly successful; did a pedestrian trade in bamboo and rattan furniture and paid a reasonable amount of taxes. It was also the main offices of the Night Shift.

Kennison paused before the washroom mirror and checked his appearance. He straightened his tie and ran a comb through his hair, brushed his jacket sleeves with his hands.

The offices outside were dimly lit by a single desk lamp that had been turned to low. Prudence stood beside the desk, already dressed in her little-girl clothing. The light cast her in curved shadows. He saw the knee-high socks, the matching green jumper.

Prudence was an occasional thing with him. She had distinctly odd notions of what constituted a good time, and Kennison found most of them tiresome. He often wondered whether it was Prudence's conscious intention to degrade herself, and why, and what possible enjoyment she could get out of it. Kennison, however, was only too happy to assist another human being in her pursuit of happiness.

Memories of past failures drew a flush and steeled his resolve to alter the game just a little.

"Oh, mister," she said when she saw him emerge from the washroom. She spoke in a high, squeaky, little-girl's voice. "I'm lost."

"Just a moment, Prudence," he said brusquely. "I'd like to try something a little different today." He reached the desk and turned off the light. The room fell into a dim redness, the only light coming from the emergency exit signs. Prudence was a soft, ruddy shape beside him. Her lips were twisted in a pout. The game pattern had been disturbed.

"You are not simply lost," he told her. "You're being followed." He pointed into the depths of the office: a jungle of file cabinets and partitions. "A bad man is out there, waiting to get you."

Her eyes widened. She looked around at the surrounding office, nodded happily, and scampered off.

Kennison waited impatiently. It wasn't going to work, he scolded himself. It had only been a fluke before, with Karin. Now here he was dragging himself down to Prudence's level. Dammit, it wasn't dignified. He hoped Paige or Weil never found out. Then he remembered that Weil was dead, which cheered him somewhat. The Great Harpy, at least, would no longer gossip about his performances.

He toyed with the penholder on the desk, twisting the pens, pulling them out, and reinserting them. He picked up a hemispherical paperweight and spun it. It wobbled like a top. He checked his watch. He couldn't stay "in the washroom" forever. Where was Prudence?

He listened carefully. The office was hushed. The gentle background susurrus of building noises, fragments of traffic sounds that drifted upward from the street below. "Prudence?" he called in a loud whisper. He waited. There was no answer.

"Prudence?" he called again. This was no time for jokes. He heard a cry, quickly stifled, and a crash, as if something had been knocked over. He stood stiffly, the paperweight in his hand. Something had gone wrong. Was there someone in the office? A burglar, perhaps? Had his innocent suggestion actually put Prudence in danger?

He squinted into the ruddy gloom. Which way had she gone? He took a few tentative steps. If there was a burglar lurking in the dark, it would be foolish to stumble about blindly. He thought about the elevator concealed in the washroom, and looked over his shoulder at the door.

The sound of running feet jerked him around. He heard a chair spin and topple. A choked sob and the tearing of cloth. Kennison discarded the paperweight and pulled a letter opener from the desk organizer. He crept slowly in the direction of the sob, his ears alert for further sounds.

Idiot, he told himself. *Go back to the wall switch and turn on the lights.*

No, that would ruin the game. And if it wasn't a game anymore, turning the lights on would reveal his location, as well as Prudence's. He promised himself that he would look just in the first row of cubicles and that if she was not in any of them, he would turn the lights on.

He could hear a whimper not too far off, but he could not tell its direction. *What if he's . . . doing something . . . to her?* He thought of the man—lower-class, ill-clothed, probably rank of breath and filthy—fondling his little girl, and grew anxious. She needed him. Needed his protection. A soft man would run, seeking only his own safety; but Kennison was hard. He gripped the letter opener tight in his fist.

When he reached the opening for the first work cubicle, he leaped inside, suddenly and quietly, letter opener ready. His eyes searched the space. Nothing.

He crept his way silently down the aisle. The second and third cubicles were also empty.

In the fourth . . .

She was curled up in the knee space under the desk. Her blouse was torn and she was hugging her knees to her. When she saw him, she gave a little cry. "Oh, Mr. Kennison," she said in her little-girl voice. "I was lost, and there was a bad man following me, and he tried to . . ."

Kennison let out his breath. He laid the letter opener aside and crouched down in front of the desk. She crawled into his outstretched arms and snuggled against him. He stroked her hair.

"Mr. Kennison," she said. "Look what he tried to do." And she showed him her torn blouse. Kennison looked and agreed that he had been a very bad man, but he was gone now. He continued stroking her.

"Everything is going to be fine, now," he told her.

Later, back once more behind his desk upstairs, he thought that Prudence was, by any rational measure, a sexual degenerate. He thought of her stumbling and scrambling down the aisles of Johnson and Cheng, casting fearful glances toward her imaginary pursuer. Let's pretend. For a short time, she had managed to make it real for herself.

Kennison, of course, had not been fooled for a moment. Though even the pretense had been sufficient, and he had given her something he had been unable to give for a considerable time. It had been even better than with Karin; and Prudence, of course, had been delighted, too. If only it had . . . endured. But then, he had known the danger was only pretense.

What if it were not *pretense?* he wondered.

Time to close up shop, he decided. He unlocked a drawer in his desk, pulled out a disc, and carried it to the drive. He hummed abstractly to himself while he mounted the disc. The policeman glanced up once, then turned his attention back to his magazine.

The disc was a new virus detector, just delivered that morning from a software security company in New Jersey. Kennison had placed the order himself through a dummy company having no known connection with Kennison Demographics. It was easy to insert a virus into a commercial program, and there were plenty of hackers out there who would love nothing better than to emulate Beaumont's feat by piggybacking their virus into his system.

Computer science students often hacked in for no other reason than intellectual curiosity. There had been a British student, Singh, who had entered 250 sensitive military, commercial, and academic systems around the world in a self-appointed mission to raise security consciousness. The Official Governments had come down hard on him, of course. There was no greater sin than that the Great Unwashed should gain access to official secrets. But then, officialdom had always been more concerned with appearing foolish than with genuine security.

The virus detector Kennison had just purchased compared the sizes of applications against previously recorded sizes and flagged anything that had changed. It was a simple, but effective, screen. It could not prevent system infection—even the best virus detectors could be fooled by a New Kid on the Block—but could detect it quickly afterward. Kennison had personally entered the program sizes recorded in the original Master Logs, not trusting the job to anyone else.

He activated the program with a staccato of keys. Then he leaned back in the operator's chair to watch the screen.

<NOW CHECKING SYSTEM STATUS. THIS COULD TAKE SOME TIME.>

Could it, now? Kennison did not care for programs that pretended to talk to you. User-friendly. He snorted. He felt like typing in: *Hurry up, damn you.*

He spent a couple of minutes watching the screen. Every now and then the screen would blink and the message would repeat itself. *Computers have destroyed our time sense,* he thought. He'd seen operators squirm impatiently in their seats, waiting out delays of a few seconds. *We've grown so used to the Instantaneous that the merely Fast now seems intolerable.* He knew that to compare the system dump against the Master Log would take many man-days and it would be prone to human error. So what did fifteen minutes or a half hour matter?

He left the console and took his cup to the coffee station, where he rinsed it out and set it there for his secretary's attention in the morning. Then he shoved his hands in his pockets and slouched around the room, pausing at various desks and workstations. Napoléon hadn't left this much debris on his retreat from Moscow. He found a personal letter that had been done on the WP application program. He found a confidential folder left atop a desk. He made a mental note to issue stern memos in the morning.

He heard a *<beep>* from his office. Did that mean the program was finished? He glanced again at the clock. Twenty minutes. He would have to plan for that twenty minutes every day from now on. Security meant taking extra pains. They backed up every day now, and Selkirk had designed a buffer system so that their own databanks were never directly plugged into the Internet. Kennison chided himself. He had been inexcusably lax in the past. Despite the stories about other people's systems, one never paid enough attention until it was one's own system that was hit.

He returned to his office and glanced at the screen. Then he froze and looked more carefully. The program was still running. The beep had meant only that a virus had been found. While he watched, it beeped again and a second log entry appeared on the screen.

Two viruses.

Kennison felt as if someone had just stepped on his grave. He reached out for the telephone and saw his hand was shaking. He pulled his hand back convulsively and balled it into a fist. Carefully he lowered himself into his chair.

<Beep>

A third entry crawled across the display. Kennison felt the beginnings of panic seeping upward from his gut. His bladder felt weak. Who was doing this? Beaumont was dead. *Or was she?* Crayle had never failed before. *But where is Crayle now? Why hasn't he reported in?* But it could be anyone who set those viruses. The CIA would not be put off as easily as the local "action" news. He looked again at the screen. Three viruses. *It might be more than one someone.*

He grabbed the phone and punched up a number. "Alan? This is Dan. I'm at the office. You'd better come here right away."

"Problem?" The voice at the other end was instantly alert.

"I need a disinfectant."

There was a moment of silence. Then: "I'm on my way."

Kennison hung up the phone and scrutinized the screen once more. Maybe it wasn't as bad as it seemed. According to the log entries, all three viruses were attached to KD files. None had crossed the buffer into the Society's system. *Fine. Let whoever is tapping in bore themselves with demographic surveys and statistical analyses.*

Were they taps or time bombs? He didn't know. Kennison was computer literate, but he didn't trust himself on such a touchy job as this. If the viruses were bombs, they might blow up in his face if he tried to trash them. His status in the Society would never survive that. If the databanks were scrambled a second time, he might as well pack it in and go join Ruiz in retirement. He hoped Selkirk would hurry.

Kennison called up one of the infected programs and let the code scroll across the screen. He didn't trust himself to do the surgery, but maybe he could palpate the body for lumps. He didn't really expect to find anything. *Dammit, I should have run the virus detector before Selkirk left the office.*

The phone rang and Kennison picked it up absently, thinking it was Selkirk calling back.

"Kennison?" It was a woman's voice, an alto. It had a sly twist to it.

"Who is this?"

"That's not important. I see you found our little bug—"

"Who is this?" Kennison hit the RECORD button and waved frantically to the policeman in the outer office. When the policeman looked up, Kennison stabbed his finger at the telephone earpiece. The policeman nodded and picked up another line to begin the tracing. The KD telephones were equipped with automatic call tracing. It would take only moments to discover the number of the incoming phone and only somewhat longer to find out where that phone was.

"Congratulations," the voice was saying. "I didn't really think you would find it so fast. It was programmed to report back immediately if it was detected, you know."

"Clever."

"Yes, wasn't it? You're finished, you know. You and your whole gang."

Sweat beaded his forehead; his chest felt tight. "What gang are you talking about?"

"Oh, puh-leeze. Save it for the masses. We know better."

"Who are you?" Kennison felt himself close to tears, and a tiny knot of fear twisted itself tighter in his stomach. He felt immeasurably cold.

"You're repeating yourself, Kennison. I didn't answer the first two times you asked me that. Why would you think I'd answer the third time?"

"Then *why* are you doing this?"

"Only to tell you that you *are* finished. We thought you'd like to know."

Anger replaced his fear with the suddenness of a storm. He felt his ears redden and the coldness give way to heat. "Well, that's awfully considerate of you," he snarled.

"Yes. I must go now; but perhaps we shall speak again, you and I."

"Wait!"

But there was nothing but the dial tone in his ear.

Kennison slammed the phone down hard and the bells inside it jingled. He jerked his head up to look at the policeman, just in time to see him slam his phone down, too.

"What went wrong?"

The policeman made a disgusted sound. "We couldn't get the number."

"What do you mean, you couldn't get the number? It's an automatic readout. It overrides call blocking. I pay Pacific Bell plenty each month for the service."

"It's not that, sir. Your caller used an old trick. He cut into the main trunk—*physically,* I mean—down in the underground conduits. Opened up a cable and clipped on with a portable handset. He can dial anyone on the system; but no one can dial him, because the system doesn't recognize him as a legitimate port."

"No way to locate him, at all?"

"Well, there is a trickle power drain that can be traced

electrically. He was calling from somewhere in the Tenderloin, but it doesn't matter. He'll be long gone before we get there."

"Damn!"

"Was it a death threat, sir? We should report this."

Kennison waved to his recorder. "No. Just another kook, accusing me of running the whole damned world. He called to tell me he had planted a virus in my computer system."

"Is that serious?"

"It could be. I've asked my assistant to come in and defuse it." The caller had spoken as if she was a member of an organization. *But who?* The Associates? That would be crazy, with both of them exposed the way they were. But maybe Betancourt had gone off the deep end. Kennison made a mental note to contact Malone and find out what was happening on the Other Side.

He sighed and put his head in his hands and found himself staring at the program code he had called up. Determination took hold of him. *Finished, are we?* He yanked open the vertical file and grabbed the hard copy of the program. Carefully, he went through each line of code, comparing what was in the system to what was supposed to be in the system.

It was a half hour later and Selkirk was just arriving when he found the anomalous line: "Autocopy to Q file."

What the hell did that mean?

XIII

The receptionist in charge of the conference center was sitting at her desk across the room, amid a jungle of hanging and potted plants. She glanced up when Jeremy and Gwynn entered and checked something off in her logbook. "They're waiting inside for you, Dr. Llewellyn," she said, pointing to the room where the study team was meeting.

"Thank you, Brenda. There will be one more coming today. A Dr. Doang from the mathematics department."

"Drs. Hambleton and Quick just went in," Brenda said. "Dr. Vane called and said he would be a few minutes late."

"I'll wait out here and show Jim in when he arrives," Jeremy said.

Llewellyn smiled and pulled the pipe from her mouth. She pointed the stem at him like the barrel of a gun. "When you told them last week that Jim had been studying the math in the Dump, you created quite a stir. Half the team is scared to death that he will make them feel stupid with formulae and jargon; the other half is peeved that a mathematician is even participating."

Jeremy shrugged. "He didn't want to come to this meeting, either. He told me last week that he's personally satisfied with his conclusions and doesn't much care whether your study team agrees with them or not."

Llewellyn chuckled. "He does not have a very high opinion of us, does he?"

"He told me that philosophers have been arguing for more than four thousand years without ever answering a single important question."

"Then he doesn't understand philosophy. It's not the answers that matter, but the questions."

Jeremy chuckled. He liked both Jim and Gwynneth, but they were about as opposite as two people could be. It seemed as if he had spent most of the past month alternately explaining one to the other. "I don't think anything is quite real to Jim unless it can be measured and fitted to an equation."

"Then he's missing half of reality."

"I suppose. As an accountant, though, I can see his point. When one deals with intangibles, nothing is ever settled. An audit can test whether someone followed an accepted accounting procedure, but how can it test for his state of mind when he did it?"

Llewellyn clapped him on the shoulder. "I wouldn't be too sure of the first, either, if I were you. As Herkimer would say, there is nothing so elusive as a fact." They both laughed.

"Bring Dr. Doang in as soon as he arrives, would you, Jeremy? I've got to get this circus started."

She entered the conference room and closed the tall, heavy doors behind her. The receptionist glanced up briefly and returned to her fashion magazine. Jeremy sighed and planted himself on the sofa. He opened the book he had gotten, Quetelet's 1842 *Treatise on Man*. The thick doors and walls, he knew, would allow no sounds from the meeting to distract him.

Jim Tranh Doang arrived shortly after. He stood in the entrance and looked about, blinking his eyes. He was dressed as Jeremy had always seen him: in rolled-up shirtsleeves and open collar. Jeremy doubted whether the man owned so much as a sports jacket. He always looked as if he had been interrupted from his work. And that was probably an accurate assessment.

Jeremy closed his book and waved to Doang, who nodded and walked to the sofa. He lowered himself into the cushions; placed his briefcase on his lap and leaned his head back against the wall. He closed his eyes and sighed.

"They're waiting for you," Jeremy said, snapping the clasps on his own briefcase. "The meeting's already started."

"Let them wait," Doang replied, with his eyes still closed. "Let them jabber to each other in their self-important way. Time enough in a few minutes to tear their playhouse down."

Jeremy's eyes wandered to the briefcase on Doang's lap. He saw how the mathematician's hands stroked the smooth brown surface. The fingers made rapid circular movements, as if they were massaging the padded leather, or as if their owner was nervous and agitated. Jeremy tapped the briefcase. "Give it to me straight, Jim. Is it what we thought?"

Doang opened his eyes and looked at Jeremy. The eyes were dead black coals. Tunnels into sunless depths. "You couldn't follow the math," he said.

"I don't need to follow. Just tell me where it leads."

"Death," he said and closed his eyes again.

Jeremy shuddered at the desolate way Doang had spoken.

He reached out and shook Doang's shoulder. "What do you mean by that?"

Doang stared at the hand until Jeremy slowly removed it. "It's plain enough, isn't it? Do you want me to tell you who will win the next presidential election? When the first city will be built on Luna? The timing of the next stock market crash?"

"You mean the mathematical models in the Dump—"

"Were valid?" He toyed with the handle on his briefcase. "Yes. Yes, they were. Not the fragments that appeared in the Dump. They were incomplete. The system was pulled off the Net before Beaumont's worm finished downloading, but it was elementary to fill in the missing parts. Several of the equations were similar to models that we run in mathematical biology. The excitation of a nerve by a stimulus. The trajectory of a contagious epidemic. Child's work. Kitchen arithmetic." He waved a listless hand in dismissal. "The difficulty lay in discerning what real-world entities the variables stood for."

"What did they—"

Doang lifted his briefcase and dropped it in Jeremy's lap. "Read it yourself. It's all in there."

Jeremy felt his face go red. "Don't patronize me!" he said in a low voice.

Doang shook his head. He ground his fist into his palm. "You're right. I apologize. It is only that . . ." He shook his head again. "I had thought myself objective. Dispassionate. The idea of such elegant and powerful systems excited me." He flashed Jeremy a rueful smile. "But as I studied the models—as I completed them, discovered their meaning—I became . . . I became angry, and afraid. And lost. I ran simulations, using past data. I predicted the past. Post-dicted? And always the equations rang true. The models were simplistic, incomplete, imprecise; but within their limitations they yielded answers consistent with the historical record, with the statistical abstracts and the almanacs. And where they did disagree I began to wonder whether the equations might not be correct and the official values a deception."

"Then those Babbage people really do have something?" He thought again of Buckle and Quetelet, of Condorcet and Bernoulli, and their dream—a science of history—lost for over a century. The viciously guarded secret of a small, elite clique. A secret they had killed to protect. *And now we know the secret.* A thrill ran though him. Not fear, nor exactly eagerness. Perhaps it was only anticipation, the imminence of great events. *Once Jim reports his findings to the study team, the fat will be in the fire.* "You don't seem too happy," he said aloud. No, of course not. Hadn't Jim already said that his conclusions led to death? "At least we know the truth," he offered.

Doang recovered his briefcase. He wouldn't look at Jeremy. " 'Ye shall learn the truth and the truth will set you free,' " he quoted and made a small, angry sound in his throat. "Does it? Or does it enslave you forever?"

Jeremy frowned and studied the morose little mathematician. "What does that mean?"

"I mean that life is a sham." Doang spread his hands out, to the briefcase, to the meeting room, to the world. "I mean that, whatever our hopes and plans, what will happen, will happen. I mean that all we really do is walk through life, speaking the lines, doing bits of business. And for what?" Doang clenched his hands and pressed them against his briefcase.

"It's not as bad as that," Jeremy told him. "Now that we know what they're doing, we can take steps to counter them. We can break this society of theirs—"

Doang threw his head back and let out a laugh, a harsh bark more despair than amusement. "You don't get it, do you?" he said. "The Babbage Society doesn't matter. They are as enslaved as we are. It's the equations themselves. Don't you see? If the Babbage Society never existed, we would be as much prisoners as we are now. As we always have been."

It was not fear of the Babbage Society that was bothering Jim Doang; it was fate. The idea that his life was already woven inextricably into some divine tapestry. Jeremy felt surprise at the depths of the man's reaction. It seemed too abstract a concern to excite passion. Fear of violence, of death. Now, that was real. Real enough that Jeremy could feel it in his own loins. But fear of existential emptiness? "Dammit, Jim, you can't let it affect you this way."

Doang cocked an eye at him. "I can't let it? Are you so in control of your own feelings as that?" He rose to his feet. "Well, shall we go in and shatter their complacency?" He faced the doors. Then he grunted a single laugh. "More likely, they won't understand the math; and, ignorant of the journey, they will deny the destination." He turned his head and looked at Jeremy over his shoulder. His eyes seemed empty and haunted. "There must be value in such ignorance," he said, "if it allows one to keep a sense of dignity. Perhaps our ancestors, with their belief in destiny, were wiser than we."

"A pretty speech, Dr. Doang, but don't you think it is a trifle melodramatic?"

Jeremy turned and saw that Herkimer Vane had arrived. He was standing slouched, with his hands thrust into the pockets of his jacket. With his bald head, his smile, and his stature, he reminded Jeremy of nothing so much as an elf.

"Herkimer," Jeremy said. "I don't believe you've met Jim Doang."

Vane extended a hand. "Our mathematical auxiliary. No, we haven't met; but I deduced who he must be." He smiled at Jeremy. "There, that's scientific, isn't it? Deduction."

"Actually," Doang told him, "science deals with inference more than deduction." Vane looked at him but said nothing.

"I suppose you overheard what Jim told me."

Vane shrugged. "A little."

"Does it change your mind? About scientific history, I mean."

"Oh, my word, no. Dr. Doang has said nothing to change my mind."

"But—"

"Don't you see? Of course not. And neither does the good mathematician. It is just that long-range predictive systems are impossible, even in as simple a system as the Solar System, where there are only a few bodies and a single force—gravity—that must be considered. So how can the trajectories of social systems be predicted, when there are so many more interacting bodies and a multitude of forces?"

Jeremy looked at Doang, who was listening carefully to the little historian. When Doang did not speak, Jeremy answered. "Now, wait a moment, Herkimer. I may not know much science, but I do know that they can predict the positions of the planets. Didn't someone once predict the existence of Neptune just from the equations?"

"Adams or Le Verrier, depending on where you went to school. But they were wrong, you know."

"Eh? But they *found* Neptune, didn't they?"

"But not in its predicted location. Adams and Le Verrier derived two *different* orbits for the unknown planet. It took them years just to perform the calculations. Who would spend a lifetime simply to check the arithmetic? Le Verrier predicted a planet with thirty-two times the mass of the Earth, lying thirty-five to thirty-eight AUs from the sun, and having a period of two hundred and seven to two hundred and thirty-three years. But Neptune is actually only seventeen times as massive, lies only thirty AUs distant, and circles the sun in a mere one hundred and sixty-four years. Had he made his calculations forty years earlier or forty years later, he would have missed Neptune completely! Adams' estimates were even worse."

Doang spoke slowly. "You seem remarkably well informed."

"For a historian? But remember, I am a historian of science and the philosophy of science. And I delight in pricking overinflated balloons." Vane beamed. "No, my friends. The predictive ability of Newton's equations have been vastly overrated. Poincaré saw that quite clearly."

"Yet," said Jeremy, "the equation worked well enough to put men on the moon. They aimed the ship at where the moon would be, and both moon and ship arrived together."

"Ah, but there are two difficulties. The first is the n-body problem."

"The n-body problem?"

"Ask your friend."

Jeremy turned to Doang. "What does he mean?"

Doang paused before answering. "Newton's equation is simple in principle, but it has a solution only in one special case: a single body of negligible mass orbiting another body of great mass. Now the sun contains so much of the mass of the Solar System that, for all practical purposes, we can regard the planets as nearly massless."

"Then what's the problem?"

"*Nearly* massless," said Vane.

"Yes." A long, slow *yes* from Doang. "After accounting for the effect of the sun, astronomers next add the effect of Jupiter. This will perturb the perfect Keplerian orbit in a way that depends on the continually changing positions of the two planets. Next, the effect of Saturn is added; and so on, until a suitable approximation is realized."

"But it doesn't stop there," Vane continued. "Every body in the universe exerts a gravitational attraction on the Earth. The effect may be minute, but it is cumulative. As a result, a planet's orbit cannot be forecast with any reasonable precision for more than a few millennia."

"Long enough," said Jeremy, "to satisfy my own personal needs."

Vane chuckled. "The span of the forecast and its precision also matter. The longer the cast, the less precise it becomes. Projecting a planet's orbit over several millennia, who cares if it is off by a few hours? But in the case of your spacecraft flying to the moon, an error of a few hours is intolerable. Much greater precision is required. But increasing the precision tenfold increases the necessary calculations a thousandfold! One would quickly reach the point where, even with the swiftest computers, the computation would simply take too long. By the time you had pinpointed a spacecraft to a particular small region in space, the spacecraft would no longer be in that region."

Jeremy grew irritated. "The way you've explained things, *any* prediction seems futile."

Vane's finger wagged at him. "My point exactly. Long-range forecasts are impossible. In any system. That is what Complexity Theory is all about. A billiards player setting up a shot need take no account of the positions of the spectators. Their gravitational potential is trivial. Yet what I said about planets holds even here. Effects accumulate. If the player were to attempt a seven-ball cannon, the gravitational influence of the spectators becomes a vital influence on the final trajectory of the ball. Am I not correct, Dr. Doang?"

"Any billiards player who attempts a seven-ball cannon could solve the equations in his head."

Vane threw his head back and laughed. "Yes. Now imagine how many collisions and ricochets there are in a society of millions of people! And, unlike gravity or elasticity, we do not understand what the forces are and how they act. *Even if there were scientific laws in history, they would be useless for making predictions.* With the number of bodies involved, the solutions would become indeterminate much too quickly." He looked at his watch. "Well, we must be getting in there, mustn't we." He turned to go.

Doang seized Jeremy by the elbow. "I know what I saw," he whispered fiercely into Jeremy's ear. "I ran the equations. They worked."

"They were approximate," Jeremy answered him. "You told me yourself. The precision was loose. Give me a wide-enough hoop and even I can score a basket. Make up your mind. A few minutes ago you were upset because you thought the equations were valid. Now you're upset because they might not be."

"What do *you* think?"

"Me? I'm an accountant. I think you're less right than you think you are. And so is Vane."

Doang released his elbow. "Dr. Vane!" Vane turned with his hand on the knob of the meeting room door. Brenda, the receptionist, looked up from her magazine.

"Yes, Dr. Doang?" said the historian.

"I can make one forecast of the future."

"And what is that?"

"That in a few minutes I am going to set your study team into turmoil."

Vane shrugged. "Short-range. Loose precision. You may be right."

Someone struck a bass drum next to Jeremy's ear. The room jumped and his vision blurred. The hanging plants by Brenda's desk swung crazily, and those on her desktop slid off and smashed to the floor. The plaster of the walls cracked and pictures fell off their hangers. The huge, thick conference room doors bulged and splintered and jumped nearly whole off their hinges, as if some giant had kicked them out from the other side.

The left-hand door struck Vane from behind like a monstrous flyswatter, and that was all Jeremy saw, because the room tumbled and he was looking at the ceiling, then at the entryway, then at the floor, which leaped up and smashed him in the face.

Part 3

The Enemy of Mine Enemy

Then

The grass was damp where the bearded man knelt by the grave. It soaked his trouser legs, giving them a pungent, woolen smell. He placed a vase of freshly cut flowers before the headstone, twisting it into the ground so that it would not topple. Then he pushed himself to his feet and made the sign of the cross. A brief gust of wind caught his open mackintosh and it snapped behind him. He pulled his Western-style hat tighter down on his head.

Anyone watching—and he had to assume that someone was watching—would think that it was this grave he had come to visit and that he was unconnected with the funeral now beginning a scant dozen yards away. Though, when the ceremonies started, the bearded man glanced curiously at the cortege, as would be expected of any mortal.

A small crowd, garbed against the imminent resumption of the rain, clustered around an open grave. A few precautionary umbrellas sprouted, mushroomlike, among them. Above, in the moist sky, the sun strove vainly to dispel the damp. A spare wooden casket rested beside the hole. Two men in work clothes flanked a nearby heap of freshly turned earth. They leaned on their shovels, watching the proceedings with professional detachment.

The bearded man turned back to the headstone and clasped his hands and bowed his head as if saying a prayer for his dear departed. His lips moved, and tears tracked the curves of his cheeks as he strained to hear the words the minister nearby spoke to the crowd.

"From the clay we came, and to it we return. Yet what lies beyond the grave, my brothers and sisters? Yea, a better life, amen. We store up merits in our life on this earth against that day of glory and righteousness. Isaac Shelton was a good man and has gone to dwell among the saints of old, for all those who knew him attest that here was a good and righteous man, who walked every day in the fear of the Lord, amen."

"Amen," said Brady Quinn, his eyes fixed on the randomly chosen grave. Rueben Judge had told him he was mad to go near Isaac's funeral. Grosvenor Weil, or his agents, would expect it, and be watching. The beard dyed black, the limp imparted by the pebble in his left boot . . . a flimsy charade, easily pierced. Of what value all the years of hiding if, when They most expected him, he exposed himself?

But Isaac Shelton had nurtured him and trained him and counseled him, had given him all he had to give, and in the end Brady had severed all ties, broken the old man's heart, thrown up in his face the value of his life's work. "How could I," he had asked Randall, "not go?"

Gazing skyward, Brady saw the dark clouds closing in once more. Rain, and not an honest rain, like the epic storms that broke over the western mountains, but a mean rain, half-drizzle. He hated Boston. He hated the miserable weather, the mean-spirited people, the closed-in feeling of the city. He longed for the West, where a man's deeds mattered more than his parents.

Yet Isaac had loved this place: a reminder to Brady that not all men shared the same passions. One man might love family and tradition where another prized freedom and new horizons above all. His roots, Isaac had once told him, were sunk deep in New England's rocky soil. It was not conceivable—it was not even possible—that Isaac Shelton would lie in any other ground.

It was good to remember that this staid, well-mannered, and manicured land had also been a raw frontier, and not very long ago at that. Isaac's sires had tilled its barren hillsides with one hand on their plows and the other on their flintlocks, with a wary eye on the hostile forest before them and their backs to the cold, gray ocean.

Realizing that he had tarried at the grave too long for his masquerade, Brady crossed himself once more, turned abruptly, and walked toward the cemetery entrance, where his horse stood tied to the hitching post, flicking its tail. A miserable nag, thought Brady Quinn. A city horse, rented from a stable. He was accustomed to better.

Good-bye, Isaac. Vaya con Dios, *as we say out West.*

He had expected feelings far more intense; but what he felt now was an aching sense of loss, as of a limb that had been hacked off. Was that what sorrow was? Nothing more than regret and loss, a knowledge of wrongs that could never now be made right?

Isaac had had a long run of it, and had accomplished much good, even while his life's work had drawn him into cold-blooded murder. . . . Ah, to what terrible deeds high-minded ideals drive us. Brady had warned Isaac on that rainy night in Georgetown, so long ago. The ideals would fade, leaving no residue but the terrible deeds themselves. What had he hoped for, telling Isaac after Randall had begged him to keep it secret? That his mentor would forsake his life's work? No, that had been a foolish hope. Does not the captain go down with his ship, fighting to the last to save it? Isaac had sold his soul for the chance of a hopeful future; and even now, these many years later, Brady could not decide if the old man's life had been a tragedy or not.

Two men stepped between him and his horse, large men with the smugness of the bully. They wore checkered jackets and trousers and bowler hats. The one on the left held out a hand as large as a side of beef. "Hold up," he said. "Mr. Weil would like to have a word with you."

Brady looked at them. "Weil? I don't know the man, and I have no business with him." He tried to step around them, but they moved to block his path.

"You don't understand, Quinn," the first man said flatly.

"Mr. Weil wants to talk to you; and what Mr. Weil wants, Mr. Weil gets."

Brady sighed and retreated two steps. "Does he?" Randall had warned him that this would happen. Still, he had owed it to Isaac to come. Now it looked like the problem of attending the funeral would be nothing compared to the problem of leaving it.

Brady had not fastened his mackintosh. The flaps of the long coat hung loosely. "I'll give you one last chance," he told the two ruffians. "Will you stand aside?"

They exchanged amused looks. "You'll give *us* a last chance?" asked the one on the right. "I don't think you're in a position to give chances."

Brady's hands moved like lightning. "How about now?" And the two looked down the barrels of twin Colts. So fast it had been that the mackintosh had barely rustled. They licked their lips and their eyes darted, seeking escape. A moment ago they had confronted a victim; now they confronted death. They hadn't realized they were dealing with an armed man.

Randall Carson and Bill Hatch had taught Brady many things out West. How to draw a pistol quickly and accurately, for one. Always to leave the other man a chance to back down, for another—but not to be a damned fool. When the time comes for action, they had told him, act; and act fast; and don't count the cost. In a fight, such a man has an advantage over those who harbor second thoughts.

"Well, now, this is right convenient, wouldn't you say?" he told the two.

They held their hands carefully in sight, made no sudden moves. They couldn't take their eyes off the guns. The one on the right was sweating. "Convenient?" he asked.

"Why, this being a cemetery and all. You won't have too far to go, afterward."

He motioned with his pistols and they backed away slowly. Brady sidled past them to his horse. He holstered his left gun and used his free hand to unhitch the animal. "I know what you're thinking," he said, keeping the other gun trained on them. "You're wondering if I can get off two shots quickly enough. Well, maybe I can and maybe I can't; but I'll surely get off one, and what I point at I generally hit. Which of you will take that shot for the other?"

He stepped up into the saddle and looked down on them. "I'm leaving now," he announced. "You can tell Mr. Weil that there's no cause for worry on his part. I'm out of it. Meanwhile, my mind will rest a sight easier while I ride if you two lay flat on the ground."

The first man grinned nervously and knelt into the mud. He spread himself out, facedown. The second man looked at his companion, then back at Brady. "I ain't about to crawl in the mud for no man."

Brady shrugged. "Facedown in the mud, or faceup while they throw mud down on you. It's your choice."

The ruffian thought about it a moment longer; then he, too, lowered himself prostrate. "I'll get you for this someday."

"It's a big country. But you are welcome to dream."

"Every man's life should have a goal," the thug said.

Brady gave him a surprised look. He grinned. "Yes, I suppose so. Then you can thank me twice, for I've given you both the goal and the life."

He yanked on the reins and applied the spurs and his horse bolted down the track to the main road. He kept his pistol ready to hand, in case the two men should be so foolish as to pursue him. The two had been young and confident and Brady was no spring chicken. He imagined what Grosvenor Weil would say to them when they reported.

On sudden impulse, he turned the horse off the road, leaping the rail fence of a pasture. Weil could easily have stationed other toughs between the cemetery and the train station. From all that Brady had heard of him, Grosvenor Weil was a meticulous man, not one to tolerate loose ends. He would not rely on this one try to take Brady Quinn, not while Quinn had thrust himself so conveniently into harm's way.

Quinn's mouth drew back in a fierce smile as his horse

cantered across the meadow. His knees gripped the animal's barrel. He had not felt this alive in years. The risks he had run in coming here seemed to have awakened him. The blood coursed in his veins. He was young again, daring great deeds. In a way, he did not care if he escaped this trap or not.

That letter he had left with Gorman and Stout . . . Should he have foreseen that the letter would reach the hands of the very Judas his equations had foretold? That Isaac's mind would have entered the shadows, so that he never saw the letter; and that Davis would so thoughtlessly reveal its contents? Should he have been that wise?

Yet how could he have known? Weil's coup had come early, mocking the calculations; and he had been a far more ruthless man than they had expected. *I was a fool.* And Davis was a fool. Davis' "fall" down the stairs of his Washington mansion had been their first inkling of Weil's ferocity.

Foolish, all of us. Isaac, Davis, myself. Even old Jedediah. Blind. Seeing only what we wanted to see. Weil, too. How could such foolish, fallible men ever believe they had the wisdom to shape the future? Sometimes he thought Elias Kent had been the wisest of the Founders.

He reached the farmstead just as the rain resumed its miserable drizzle. The farmer sat in a canewood rocker on the front porch, an open Bible in his lap, taking his allotted day of rest.

"Excuse me, sir," Brady said to him, reining in, "but which is the road to Providence?" Brady might believe himself a fool, but he was not so foolish that he would ride to the Boston depot with Weil's minions afoot.

The farmer's keen gaze took in Brady, the lathered mount, the Colt pistol—which Brady returned finally to its holster. He rubbed a hand across his stubble. "Well, stranger, the surest road to Providence be this'n." And he held up the Bible.

Brady Quinn laughed.

Now

I

Red came knocking on her door early in the morning. It was a light, staccato rap and Sarah knew without checking that it was he. Smiling to herself, she set her coffee cup in its saucer, straightened her robe, and walked to the door of her underground apartment. When she opened the door, he was leaning on one arm in the doorway. The New, Improved Red Malone. The not-quite-a-stranger with the eyes of a friend. "Hi," he said.

"Hi, yourself. What brings you around at this hour?" Fee circled Red's legs, staring at the boots and jeans, hackles raised and back slightly arched. Fee did not quite approve of Red—either edition. He felt a proprietary interest in Sarah that brooked no competitors.

"Do you feel like going out for pizza?" he asked. "I'm headed for Tony's."

"Pizza for breakfast?"

"No, we won't eat until later; but I'm leaving now."

"Well, I . . . Sure, why not?"

"Good," he said, checking his watch. "You'll just have time to get dressed and pack a bag."

She checked herself in midturn. "Pack a bag?"

He gave her an innocent look. "Not too much. Just overnight."

"Overnight? Red, just where is Tony's?"

"In South Plainfield, New Jersey."

"You're going two thousand miles for pizza?"

He didn't even crack a smile. "It's very good pizza," he assured her.

They threw their bags into the rear of the ranch's battered pickup and crowded into the cab with Janie Hatch. The older woman ground the engine into first and jerked onto the dirt road that connected the ranch to the state highway. Sarah had the shotgun seat. She twisted and looked back through the dust cloud at the receding buildings. The cool mountain wind whipped through her hair. Then she faced forward again but left the window rolled down, resting her arm in the open frame. The rifle barrels in the gun rack felt cold against the back of her head.

"You'll take care of Fee for me while I'm gone?" she asked again.

"Cats take care o' themselves, missy; but I'll keep an eye peeled in his direction."

"Thanks."

Janie didn't reply, but then Janie never wasted a word when a shrug would do; nor a shrug, when silence was enough. She was a puzzle Sarah had not yet solved. Aloof, detached, indifferent, the ultimate bystander. She would not hesitate to do a favor; but, so far as Sarah could determine, neither did she do favors from kindness. Sarah had to believe that there were emotions concealed behind the weathered and stoic exterior, but what those emotions might be remained elusive.

Sarah had mixed feelings about leaving the ranch. On the one hand, she was happy to get out. She had been lost in limbo, like van Winkle among the elves, and half-expected to find that fifty years had passed in the Real World. On the other hand, she was sad, in a curious sort of way. By entering the world at last as Gloria Bennett, she was relegating Sarah Beaumont to the past.

Somehow, despite the drama and the crimes and the conspiracies in which she had found herself entangled, her biggest regret was that now she and Dennis would never complete Brady Quinn Place. The dream would wither and fade, to lie in the attic of her memory, gathering dust and cobwebs; and every now and then, when she would happen upon it, it would remind her of all the things she had never done, and now never would.

And, on the third hand—if there was a third hand—she was apprehensive: Because Sarah Beaumont was a Known Woman and a great many people were hunting for her; and here she was, going out among them. The vengeful, the celebrity-minded, and the merely curious. They were out there. And the government. And the Secret Six that Red had told her of. And the talk shows and the newspapers. And the sheeplike crowd that followed anything famous.

She said as much to Red, and he told her not to worry because no one was looking for Gloria Bennett.

"But still," she said to him while Janie weaved through the morning traffic at the Mousetrap, "I don't *feel* safe. I feel . . . transparent. As if people could look right through me."

"People ain't that smart by half," said Janie.

Sarah turned sideways in her seat and looked across Red to the ranch manager. Absently she ran a finger down the barrel of one of the rifles in the gun rack. She had once watched Janie stand off a good five hundred yards with a telescopic rifle and put four out of five shots into the black. And she also remembered how Janie had stood by with that same rifle and done nothing but watch while Orvid Crayle had stalked Sarah through the ruins atop Mount Falcon. "Janie, why do you have three rifles?"

"I hunt."

"I know that. I was asking why three?"

Janie paused and regarded her a moment. "Well," she allowed, giving her attention once more to the traffic, "the top one is for out'n the prairie. Fires a high-velocity, flat-trajectory round. But, up in the forest, you don't normally git a distance shot, so a fat, slow slug is best."

"Oh." Janie Hatch seemed better armed than some small countries. "What about the third rifle? What's that one for?"

Janie turned her cold, emotionless eyes on Sarah once more.

"Varmints," she said.

A private jet was waiting for them at the general aviation terminal. The captain stood nearby talking with the ground crew, shouting to be heard over the whine of the engines. Red carted their overnight bags to the plane, and the ground man broke off his conversation with the pilot to stuff them into the nose compartment. The pilot saluted Red, then shook his hand. A commercial liner roared down the runway in the distance.

Sarah turned to Janie to say good-bye, but Janie laid a hand on her arm.

"You be careful, missy. Y'hear?"

It was the same warning Janie had given her at the Denver library when Crayle had been nosing through her notes on Brady Quinn. *Be careful, but don't expect me to intervene.* Sarah brushed the hand from her arm.

"I can take care of myself."

"I know that. I wasn't thinking of you."

"Red? Don't be silly. He can take care of himself, too."

Janie gave Sarah a hard look. "He never told you about Jacksonville?"

She shook her head. "No, he's never mentioned it."

Janie shifted her chaw from one cheek to the other and spit a stream at the ground. "Well, I never said anything, understand? And don't you go asking him. If he wants to tell you, he will."

Then Janie climbed back into the truck and closed the door with a slam. The gears shrieked in protest and the truck hopped into the flow of departing traffic.

Tony's Pizza was set in a small, older-style strip mall, flanked by a bakery and a gift shop. Two men behind the counter strewed cheese on their pies with the ease of long practice. Sarah took a deep, delicious breath of onions and peppers and tangy tomato sauce. It was a narrow store, with the pizza ovens against the right-hand wall, behind the counter. Farther back were plastic booths for diners. Two of them were occupied, one with a crew of boisterous teenagers.

"He's waiting for us," Red told her quietly. He nodded toward the farthest booth on the right, where two men sat side by side. The younger man sported a full straw-colored beard. His older companion was well dressed, with a pinched face and gray at the temples.

"Who?"

"Kennison," he said.

"Kennison?" She narrowed her eyes. "Red, if I gave a party for everyone in the world, he wouldn't be on the guest list!"

"It never hurts to talk, even with the enemy. Perhaps especially with the enemy."

"I've got nothing to say to him. Red—I mean Jim. *He killed my friend!* He tried to have me killed!"

"Then it sounds to me like you should have plenty to say to him." He took her lightly by the arm and guided her down the aisle to the booths.

Kennison stood and reached across the table to shake Red's hand. "It's nice to see you again, James. Mind your cuffs." He indicated the pizza in the middle of the table. Red slid into the booth opposite the bearded man. Kennison smiled and looked at Sarah. "And this must be . . ."

"Gloria Bennett," said Red.

"Of course." His smile broadened and he took her hand and raised it. His touch was surprisingly gentle. Sarah thought he meant to kiss the hand and yanked it out of his grip as if she had been burned. Kennison took no offense. "I quite understand how you feel, my dear," he murmured. "Were I you, I should feel the same."

Sarah looked from Kennison to Red and saw no way out of it. She gathered her skirt and sat down at the table. Kennison waited until she was settled; then he sat and placed his napkin carefully on his lap.

The bearded man was staring at her with a frankly appraising gaze. He had already taken a slice from the pan and held it steaming in his hand.

"This is Alan Selkirk," Kennison said. "He joined my personal staff recently. Alan, Miss Gloria Bennett and Mr. James Caldero." Kennison gestured. "Would either of you care for a slice?"

Red studied the pizza. "Anchovies, for crying out loud."

Kennison shrugged. "You can always remove them." He selected a piece for himself and transferred it to a paper plate. He picked up a plastic knife and fork and cut into it.

Fastidious, thought Sarah. *How many people eat pizza with a knife and fork?*

Kennison saw her gaze and paused with the fork nearly to his lips. He smiled across the table at Sarah. "A gentlemen never eats with his hands."

Red handed her a plate with a slice of pizza on it. "Here. Have some." He looked at Kennison. "Shall we get started?"

"My dear fellow," Kennison told him, gesturing with his fork. "Over dinner?"

"Why? Will there be port in the drawing room later?"

Kennison sighed and laid his utensils down. "I understand we have information to trade." He looked for a moment as if he were sucking a lemon. "Since your lady friend appears not to trust me, perhaps I should 'show my cards,' first." He dabbed his lips with his napkin and glanced quickly around. Then he folded his hands on the table. "My information is this: we are under attack. I am not speaking of the random attacks of the ignorant mob, but something far more insidious." In a low voice, he described the viruses that had appeared in his system, the mysterious phone call.

Sarah listened without sympathy. She did not care that Kennison was being persecuted. He had ordered Morgan's death. And Paul Abbot's. And the other couple—she had forgotten their names. And the man in the park, who had been shot in the head. Kennison had tried to have her killed; and Dennis, as well. If Kennison felt threatened, it was no more than he deserved.

And yet it was a different matter to sit across the table from the man and look him in the face. Dammit, villains were supposed to be villainous. They were not supposed to be polite or well mannered. They were not supposed to stare at you through eyes filled with fear.

Red rubbed his hand across his chin. "Three viruses, you say?" He looked at Sarah. "You haven't been doing anything extracurricular, have you?"

Sarah shook her head. She didn't care if Kennison's system was putrescent with bacteria. But it hadn't been she. As to whoever it was . . . Well, it said in the Book: "The enemy of mine enemy is my friend."

"I haven't heard of any such attack against our own system," Red said. "And I would have heard. None of our Council members have reported anything. Have your other Councillors received similar threats?"

Kennison drew a deep breath and let it out. "We've gone incommunicado during this last month, while the media and the police watched us. A ploy to counteract the information in the Dump. I thought of calling Sister Paige, but . . . The phone call may have been to lure me into an act which could have nullified the entire ploy. I did not want to risk it. I am no Judas goat. I thought it best to consult with you, *in corpora* and in camera."

"I think it was the FBI," said Selkirk abruptly, and they all turned and looked at him. "The official government must be disturbed over what they've read in the Dump. I'm sure they've been trying to penetrate your system, as well as ours."

"Perhaps, Alan. Yet, there were *three* bugs."

"FBI, CIA, ATF." Selkirk counted on his fingers. "I'm surprised there weren't more.

"The viruses were taps," he added, "not logic bombs. They didn't hurt anything; they hadn't crossed the barrier I built, into the, ah, main system. There are physical lockouts that only Mr. Kennison controls. All they did was copy some files and download them outside."

"To someplace called the Q file," said Kennison. "One of the taps had that destination. We're not sure yet about the others."

"*Q* for Quinn?" asked Red.

Kennison shrugged. "I assume so."

" 'Twas but routine government surveillance," Selkirk insisted.

Kennison looked at him. "But the call, Alan. What about the phone call? A government agency would not indulge in such foolish bravado. They would quietly gather their intelligence and be done."

Selkirk frowned, looked at his pizza, shook his head. "I don't know."

"The call was to spook you," Red told him.

Kennison didn't smile. "I must congratulate them on their success."

Red leaned back and tapped his teeth with his thumb. He looked into the distance for a few moments; then he turned to Sarah. "I've got to tell him. I gave my word."

Sarah wondered if he was asking for her approval. "Go ahead then."

Red looked at Kennison. "All right. There is another society, an independent group, as old as we are."

Kennison looked puzzled for a moment. Then his eyes widened. "A third society?"

Selkirk leaned forward. "That's not possible!"

Kennison scowled, laid his forefinger aside his nose, and sat that way for a few moments. Then he pulled a pen from his jacket pocket and began scribbling on his napkin. Sarah watched partial differential equations skitter across the tissue. The Greek letters blurred as the fibers soaked up the ink. She recognized condensation equations from Dr. Gewirtz's classes. Ideas that were "in the air" condensed around suitable particles—human minds with high surface areas—and precipitated into the culture. Kennison worked through the solution set and counted the equilibrium points. Sarah's estimation of his abilities climbed a notch.

Kennison studied what he had written. Then he screwed the cap on his pen and put it away. "Yes, Alan. I'm afraid it is possible." He passed the napkin to Selkirk. The young Scot took it with shaking hands.

"Damn it all," Kennison said to no one in particular. "We

should have seen this possibility before." He turned impatiently and jabbed a finger at the blurred figures on the napkin. "There it is, Alan. And there. Yes, the usual solutions are zero and one. Most ideas never do 'catch on' or they have a single 'discoverer.' But, under certain conditions, there can be multiple, independent discoveries." He turned to Red. "Are you sure suitable conditions existed at the time of the Founding?"

"They call themselves the Secret Six," Red told them.

Selkirk took a deep breath and let it out. "The Secret Six?" he said wonderingly.

Red outlined what they had discovered. The list that Dennis and Sarah had found in Quinn's old mansion. The Stray he had found in the Dump. Bosworth's analysis of anomalies. The stranger who had been watching the safe house. Kennison took notes in a small booklet he kept in his jacket pocket.

"And one other thing," Sarah added. She aimed a finger at Kennison. "Tell me straight out. Did your people kidnap Dennis French from the hospital in Denver?"

Kennison steepled his fingers against his lips. "Why do you ask?"

"Because your man, Crayle, didn't seem to know about it."

"Ah. Yes. And where is Brother Crayle?"

"I'm here," she said shortly. "He's not."

Kennison nodded slowly. "You are a remarkable young woman, to have acted so resourcefully under such circumstances." His eyes glittered. "You must have been in considerable danger. Frightened." His tongue darted out quickly, wet his lips.

"You haven't answered my question."

Kennison blinked. "Oh, yes. Your question took me quite by surprise. You see, we had assumed that your people had rescued him."

Sarah closed her eyes and cupped her hands briefly over her face. That was why Red's search of the Dump had yielded no clues to Dennis' whereabouts. The man had vanished without a trace. And maybe her enemy's enemy was only another enemy. She looked at Red. "Jim?"

"If this third group has him," he said grimly, "we'll find him."

"Indeed," said Kennison. "And I shall be pleased to assist you in any way possible." He paused and considered. "It may interest you to know that another intrepid band was searching for Mr. French—at least, at secondhand. His, ah, roommate, I believe."

"Jeremy Collingwood and the DU group. Yes. Jim told me." Jeremy as a man of action hardly seemed possible. He had always struck her as an ineffectual sort of person. Still, who could predict how a crisis would affect somebody? One man may turn brittle and another hard, after his turn in the fire.

"It may also interest you," Kennison continued casually, "to know that he and his team were wiped out this afternoon in an explosion."

Sarah looked up sharply. Her heart gave a thud. Jeremy, too? She struck the table with both fists, and the teenagers on the other side of the room glanced over at the noise. "How dare you sit across from me and—"

"Quietly, young lady!" He drew himself up. "It was not I."

Selkirk spoke. "A reporter for one of the local stations found a two-month-old work order in the building maintenance files requesting the repair of a gas leak. The maintenance super claims he never saw the work order, but he would say that in any case."

"Two months old?"

"Yes. That predates the formation of the study team. So, even though the study group's project was mentioned, the newsreaders concluded that the explosion was a coincidence."

"And you may believe as much of that as you wish," added Kennison.

Red tapped his teeth again. He looked at Sarah. "I believe

him." To Kennison: "Could it have been anyone else in your organization?"

He shook his head. "Not likely. We've had police and media camped on our doorsteps."

"You're here," Red pointed out.

"I see your point. I flew to New York publicly, of course; but my Manhattan penthouse has a secret elevator. As far as the police guard knows, I am in my room, recuperating from my long flight."

"So, one of your Brothers or Sisters *could* have arranged it."

Kennison scowled and folded his hands as if in prayer. *What gods*, Sarah wondered, *could a man like that pray to?*

"Possible," Kennison admitted at length. "Denver is part of Brother Ullman's fief; but . . ." And he shook his head. "It was a monumentally stupid act; and, among Brother Ullman's many faults, stupidity is not numbered." He took a deep breath and looked at Sarah. "So, it appears as though we are to be allies of convenience. I will do whatever I can to assist you in locating your friend."

"Why?" she asked him. "Why should you help me?"

"Why, for the sheer pleasure of aiding another human being in distress." Kennison spread his hands guilessly. "And because the people who kidnapped your friend are threatening me. So, for a little while, our paths converge on the same goal. Later, fortune may cause us to oppose one another once more in the Great Game, but for now . . ." An elaborate shrug. "Who knows? We may find we have more in common than you suppose."

Sarah looked at him and wanted to deny him and his aid both; but if it would help her find Dennis, she would accept aid from the Devil himself. She started to speak, but Kennison held out a hand. "If it is any consolation, I voted against the Action of which you were the object. There was insufficient evidence, I told them. We may be taking aim at the wrong target. But Madam Weil was not to be deflected. A most impossible woman . . . Well, *nil nisi bonum.* I hope you understand that there was no ill will toward you personally. As later events proved—at Mr. Benton's estate, at Ms. Weil's mansion—our fears of exposure were well justified."

He checked his watch briefly. "And now I fear we must take our leave. In the meantime . . ." He turned to Sarah and said seriously, "If you should ever find yourself in danger, you may come to me for protection and you shall have it without reservation."

Sarah searched his face, trying to discern what Kennison was up to. But she saw nothing there but openness and sincerity. Almost an eagerness. Could Kennison be seeking amends for the hell that he had helped put her through? Strange to think of this man as her would-be protector, but either Kennison was a damned good actor or he meant exactly what he had said.

Glancing sidelong at Red, she was surprised to see barely concealed hostility. Red, who never took anything too seriously, did not like Kennison's offer of protection. Was Red jealous? Now, there was a thought!

They lingered for a while after Kennison and Selkirk had gone. Red said that he wanted to finish the pizza, and Sarah sat quietly beside him. She leaned her elbows on the table and clasped her hands. She studied the smooth, dark skin of her arms. When she closed her eyes, she was acutely aware of her body and the position of all her limbs. She could feel her blouse and skirt hugging her figure. She could even sense Red sitting less than a foot away from her. His aura?

Finally, Red spoke. "So, it looks like the Secret Six is gunning for Cousin Daniel. I wonder if the mysterious lookout at the safe house was theirs as well."

She opened her eyes. "Don't forget," she told him, "that the Six split the same way that the Babbage Society did."

"I haven't forgotten that."

"I notice you didn't tell 'Cousin Daniel' that part."

"He's a bright boy. He'll figure it out. Carson's Dilemma is required study."

"Was he serious? About offering me his protection."

Red dropped the last slice on the pan. "I hate anchovies," he said. He wiped his hands on a napkin. "Yes," he told her. "He was serious. Dan is a snake and a slimy son of a bitch, but he's an *honest* son of a bitch. He'll never lie to you—unless he's lying to himself as well."

Outside, night had fallen. They paused a moment in the doorway to the pizzeria. Cars weaved about the parking lot in cavalier disregard for the marked traffic lanes. Sometimes, they roared past the storefronts at what seemed to Sarah dangerous speeds. To the right, at the far end of the lot, a gang of teenagers was clustered around two pickup trucks parked in front of the McDonald's. Sometimes they cheered the drivers of the cars. The high-intensity lamps threw everything into a peculiarly colorless sort of illumination, as if she were watching an old black-and-white movie.

"Well?" asked Red, zipping up his jacket against the September chill. "Was meeting Kennison as bad as you thought it would be?"

She shook her head. "It was worse."

"Worse?"

"Yes, dammit. He was charming."

Red shot her a look. "Sounds pretty wretched—"

"I think I was prepared for anything except that. Jim, he *apologized* for putting out a contract on me and my friends. And he meant it."

"That's Dan. He oozes sincerity the way a slug oozes slime."

She looked at him. "You don't like him, do you?"

He grunted. "I didn't think it showed."

As they stepped off the sidewalk and headed toward their car, another car raced toward them from the direction of the Bradlee's store. The wheels spun and the headlights weaved across the night, pinning her to the spot. Red shoved her hard with both his hands and they dropped behind the nearest automobile. Sarah scraped her knees and palms on the gravel. She hugged the ground, breathing the smell of asphalt and motor oil. Small stones poked into her arms and thighs. *That bastard Kennison...*, she thought. She heard three pops. One ... Two ... Three ... Carefully spaced. The car lurched and a tire hissed like the audience at a bad play.

Tires squealed, followed by a screech of brakes and a long blast from a car horn. Sarah heard a car door slam and ineffectual curses carry in the night air. Looking out, she saw a minivan off the side of the road and a man beside it shaking his fist at a departing sedan. The teenagers at the far end of the parking lot were running toward them.

She became aware of Red's arm wrapped tightly around her, his body sheltering hers. She could feel his heat. Slowly, he relaxed his grip. She didn't move. Then he sat up and brushed at his clothing. "This is getting to be a nuisance," he said.

Sarah was surprised to find she was not shaking. "What do you mean, a nuisance?"

He gave her one of his glances. "Every time you and I go out together, I get shot at." He stood and slapped at the knees of his trousers. Then he looked in the direction their assailant had vanished. "It's almost not worth it."

∎

There was a voice like a distant bell in an endless night. Jeremy Collingwood floated in the darkness, turning slowly end over end while pulsating devil masks in red and orange laughed in a starless sky. A glowing face swelled until it stretched from one unseen horizon to the other. Behind it, another blossomed. And another. They trailed back like a chorus line to the vanishing point. They tried to tell him something in booming bass notes just below the level of intelligibility.

"Jerry? Jerry! Can you hear me?"

His eyelids fluttered and an explosion of light snapped them shut again. He groaned.

"I think he's regained consciousness," he heard a voice say.

He wished the voice would leave him alone. The darkness was peaceful. Floating was pleasant. The devil's mask kept tempo with the hammering in his head. He turned his face into the pillow. "Where am I?"

"You're in Porter Memorial Hospital."

He squinted for the source of the voice and found the face of Jim Doang floating above him. A bandage encircled Jim's head. His eyes were blackened.

Jeremy forced himself to a sitting position. He was lying in a bed, in a room that smelled of antiseptic and fresh linen. The room seemed to be slowly rotating. His head ached and throbbed. He saw Herkimer Vane sitting beside the bed. Vane's ribs were taped and his left hand was bandaged.

In a chair by the wall, her hands curled into a ball on her lap and tears glistening on her cheeks, sat Gwynn Llewellyn. Jeremy pointed at her.

"You're dead."

She shook her head. "The others were all killed."

"All killed," Jeremy repeated. All of them. Torn apart like rag dolls. He tried to conjure up a feeling for Geoff and Penny and Henry and the other team members, but all he could feel was a vast relief that he himself had not been in there. He looked again at Gwynn. "All except you," he said.

The historian looked uncomfortable. "I had gone out the other door to wash my hands."

"We all should have been in that room," Jeremy said.

Their faces told him that they knew that fact very well. Vane slowly rubbed his palms together. Llewellyn was looking at Doang, who left his post at Jeremy's bedside and found a chair against the wall. He leaned his head back and closed his eyes.

"Do any of you really believe," Jeremy asked, "that it was an accident?"

Llewellyn shook her head slowly. Vane gave her a bleak stare. "It was a stupid thing to do," he said. "The bombing. It can only inflame suspicions." He shook his head. "How could a society behave so foolishly and survive so long?"

"*Foolish* is not the word I would use to describe them," Jeremy told him.

Vane turned to him. "*Foolish* and *vicious* are not mutually exclusive."

"Still the academic, eh, Dr. Vane?" Doang's voice was heavy with sarcasm.

"Has it occurred to any of you yet," said Llewellyn, "that, having survived the original attack, the four of us are now prime targets for another attempt? And that this is, in fact, the very hospital from which Dennis French disappeared?" She clenched and unclenched her hands.

"Since regaining consciousness," said Doang, "I have thought of little else."

Jeremy felt his heart thud. They would come for him here. He knew it. He had only to wait and they would come and he would be taken to wherever it was that Dennis had been taken. Vane rose from his seat and paced. The little man's brow was beaded with sweat, and he glanced nervously around. His right hand massaged the fingers of his left, where they protruded from the bandages.

"We've got to do something," Llewellyn said.

Vane stopped his pacing. He stood by the door and ran his good hand up and down the metal frame. "They won't find you," he said at last.

Doang watched dispassionately. Llewellyn pursed her lips. "How can you say that, Herkimer? We are sitting ducks here."

He turned and faced them. "The hospital records show that we died."

There was a pause while they digested his words. "Clever," Jeremy said into the silence. "But aren't you afraid of going to that particular well too often?"

Vane flashed a weak smile. "Bear with us. We aren't accustomed to this sort of thing."

Llewellyn looked from one to the other. "What are you two talking about?"

Jeremy nodded toward Herkimer Vane. "Your friend is an agent of the Babbage Society."

Vane raised his eyebrows. "Oh, good heavens, no!" He seemed shocked.

"Jeremy! What are you suggesting?"

Doang spoke. His voice was harsh. "He is suggesting that it was too damned convenient, the way Dr. Vane delayed entering that room."

Vane's brow darkened. "And I might point out with equal conviction that Mr. Collingwood and yourself *also* delayed entering that same room. And that Dr. Llewellyn *conveniently* left it barely in time. A more suspicious mind than my own—"

Gwynn rose suddenly from her chair. "Stop it, Herkimer!" There was an edge to her voice. "You're being offensive. We are all friends here." She hunched her back away from them and studied the instruments bolted to the wall. "When the explosion shook the building," Jeremy heard her say, "I hurried back and found . . . and found a shambles. Do you know the original meaning of a shambles? It meant the floor of a slaughterhouse." She turned and Jeremy saw her face was red and moist. "Herkimer, you were struck by the door. Do you want me to tell you what was on the other side of that door? What was *spread* across it like jelly on toast? I say 'what' because there was no hope of identifying 'who.' "

Vane blanched and turned his face away, covering mouth. "No."

Jeremy struggled to sit erect. "We know the Babbage Society kills those who learn their secret. Last week, I announced that Dr. Doang would present his analysis; and the room exploded shortly after we should have entered it. It seems clear that someone did not want us to hear Dr. Doang's report."

"Someone in the room?"

Vane looked at her. "Yes, Gwynn. Someone in the room. Who else would know the agenda?"

"Do you know what you're saying, Herkimer? You're saying that one of us is a member of the Babbage Society. That one of *us* set that bomb and killed our friends."

"They were your friends and mine, Gwynn. Longtime associates. Colleagues. But Jeremy barely knew them; and Dr. Doang, not at all."

Doang stood abruptly, knocking his chair over. "If I had wanted to conceal the validity of those mathematical models, I had only to present a false report. Or no report at all. Had I not come to Gwynn with my proposal, none of this would have happened."

There was a silence, and Doang listened to his own words. "None of this would have happened," he whispered. He righted his chair and sank back into it.

"No, Jim. It could have been you," Vane persisted. "To discover what we knew or suspected you had to attach yourself to the team. As a mathematician, there was only one plausible way."

Doang glared at him but said nothing.

Jeremy laughed. They turned and looked at him.

"What about me, Herkimer? The Babbage people assaulted and kidnapped my dearest friend. Make me the centerpiece of your scenario. I dare you!"

Vane spread his hands. "Very well. This Dennis French was never your lover, only convenient camouflage. Once you learned what he and Beaumont were up to, you eliminated them and others they may have spoken to. You went to Gwynn because you wanted to know what Mr. French had told her."

Jeremy felt cold. It was plausible. It could have happened that way. He saw Gwynn eyeing him warily. How easily the facts could be twisted! "And the study team?" he asked. "Why would I let her go ahead and form the study team?"

Vane shrugged. "Why, to unearth any other historians who took the Dump seriously. Why do you suppose I went to such pains to show that I did not? I am sure you had agents on the Chicago and Stanford teams as well."

"Herkimer," said Llewellyn. "Do you believe what you're saying?"

"Do you want to hear the scenario featuring yourself?"

Llewellyn looked at him for a long moment. "No," she said.

"Ah. So, you see? Each of us can suspect the others. Each of us can lie awake in the dark wondering which of the others is a murderer." He shook his head.

"But you did conceal our presence here in the hospital," Jeremy reminded everyone.

"The administrator feared an attack on the hospital if it came out that we were here." A fatalistic shrug. "Sooner or later, someone will talk, but, in the meantime, no one searches for dead men." Vane stuck his right hand in his jacket pocket. "It is a temporary expedient, a ruse to get us out of the hospital safely. We must move quickly, now that Jeremy is conscious. Everything has been arranged."

"Where are we to go?" Jeremy asked. "Obviously, none of us can return to our homes." He thought briefly of his possessions. Of the books, the Mondrian, the crystal. What would happen to them? Who would get them? He had never bothered to make a will and had no relatives who would own him. Well, it was all behind him now. If, under these conditions, a man wasn't prepared to abandon his baggage without a second thought, then he wasn't prepared to go on living. Life could always bring new possessions, but possessions could never restore life. Curiously, the thought of walking away from his past life brought him a feeling of exhilaration, a sensation almost of liberation.

"You said you weren't the Babbage people," Jeremy asked Herkimer, "but who are you with? There was another society mentioned in the Dump," Jeremy said. "A splinter group."

Vane walked slowly around the ward, picking things up and putting them down. He rubbed his good hand along the smooth metal of the bed rails. Finally, he faced Jeremy. "I am a junior partner with Detweiler, Barron, and Stone."

"The investment firm?" asked Jeremy, surprised.

"Who are Detweiler, Barron, and Stone?" asked Llewellyn.

"An old-money Boston investment firm," Jeremy told her. "Founded in . . ."

"Eighteen-forty-eight by Adrian Detweiler the First," supplied Vane.

"Thank you. They have an uncanny ability to identify hot new growth industries. I've steered several of my clients in their direction."

Llewellyn spoke from the other bed. "But, Herkimer, why should an investment firm care about hiding us from the Babbage people?"

Jeremy saw it an instant before the others did. He began to laugh. That resurrected his headache, and he leaned back upon his pillows. "You're another," he said, pointing a finger at Vane. "Aren't you? Another of these cliological groups." It made perfect sense. Hadn't Gwynn told him that Vane had invited himself onto the team? Hadn't Vane spent most of his efforts belittling the very idea of historical science?

Vane faced them. "We have a few minutes before the van comes," he announced. "So I will fill you in on what you need to know." He paused, rubbed his hands together, thrust them into his jacket pockets. "It's true. The Firm's investments have been successful largely because we have made use of certain natural laws that occur in human affairs."

"Bastard," said Doang, and Jeremy looked at the mathematician's angry face with some surprise.

"I beg your pardon?" asked Vane.

"If our lives are to be imprisoned by these laws of yours, at least we should be allowed to see the bars."

Vane shrugged. "I had hoped for deeper understanding from a man of your abilities. Is your spirit restricted by the law of gravity? Your soul enchained by thermodynamics?"

"Then your group has no connection with this Babbage Society?" Llewellyn asked.

Vane turned to her. "Good heavens, Gwynn! We were unaware of their very existence until lately. And, I daresay, they of ours. I begged onto your study team to learn what I could about a potential danger." He paused and appeared to gather his thoughts. "You see, we have always believed that the anomalies in our data were due to the complexity of cultural processes and to our own imperfect understanding.

The Firm's work was purely empirical. We lacked the computing machines and the theoretical framework that the Babbage Society seems to have had. We were content to ride the financial trends and cycles." He smiled thinly. "The forces of history are as unmalleable as the forces of the ocean. We could study them, analyze them, even forecast them within the constraints of precision and time span; but we could not change them."

"Yet the Babbage Society believed otherwise," Jeremy pointed out. "Are you saying that they can't?" Jeremy could not say why that prospect disturbed him so. Unless killing to protect an error was somehow worse than killing to protect a truth.

Another shrug. "There are undeniably anomalies in the data, but might they not have occurred regardless? Perhaps this Babbage Society is simply deluding themselves with their own self-importance. Considering how elusive cultural 'facts' are, self-deception comes easy."

"Facts are constructions, you told me once," Jeremy said slowly.

Vane's smile was faint. "I see that my impromptu lecture made an impression. Yes, the same facts can be reconstructed differently. Did Wellington win the battle of Waterloo? Or did Blücher? Or did Napoléon lose it—which is not quite the same thing? The poet Simon once sang, 'A man hears what he wants to hear and disregards the rest.' How easy it would be for any group to construct the meaning they prefer."

"Between 'powerless' and 'omnipotent,' " Llewellyn said, "lies a wide range of possibilities."

"Indeed. Which makes it all the more important for us to learn what the Babbage Society knows. It may be that, never having acted on the 'social state,' the Firm has created no anomalies, and, therefore, left no 'footprints' that might be assigned to it. This is a point on which we would very much like to assure ourselves."

Vane was telling them too much, Jeremy thought, and that must mean that he did not expect them ever to be in a position to reveal what he had said. What ought he do? Running was out. He was weak, dizzy. And to where would he run? His apartment? No, D, B, and S would take them where it would. And that meant, if he was ever to be free again, he would have to keep his eyes and ears open, ready to seize every advantage.

All this he considered and decided in an instant. A part of his mind, even as he listened to Vane, marveled with self-satisfaction. He was making decisions, taking charge of his own life. The helpless funk he had experienced in the days following Dennis' injury seemed to have happened to another person, a man of whom he was now vaguely contemptuous.

The van was parked in front of the hospital's main entrance with its side doors open. Jim Doang was already inside, and Jeremy took a seat beside him on the rearmost bench. A few minutes later, Llewellyn was wheeled out and assisted aboard. She sat on the middle bench while Anderson, the driver, returned to fetch Vane.

"Shall we hijack the van?" asked Jeremy. He was only half-kidding. He leaned over Gwynn's shoulder and looked at the dashboard. No keys. "Does anyone know how to hot-wire an ignition?"

"Jeremy, don't be ridiculous. I've known Herkimer for a long time. I can't believe he means us any harm. Besides, we have a more immediate concern."

Jeremy sat back on the bench. "What's that?"

"Our nurse friend at the desk? After you passed by, she made another of her zombie phone calls. And that means it would be a good idea to keep a watch out the rear window."

Jeremy glanced at the hospital entrance, where Herkimer Vane was being helped from his wheelchair. "Should we tell Vane?"

"It's your decision, Jeremy."

"Mine? Why?"

"Because whomever the nurse called, they are no doubt

the same ones who kidnapped Dennis. If they do follow us, they could well intend to capture us. In which case, they would take you to wherever your friend is."

Anderson made a face in the rearview mirror. "You can't be sure they're following us."

Jeremy looked again out the back window. The blue sedan was still there. "They're following us," Jeremy assured him. "They're very clever about it. They don't ride our bumper, like in the movies; they leave two or three cars between us."

"Well, don't worry," Anderson told them. "Even if the men in that car are Babbage Society agents, they wouldn't dare try anything. It's too public." The traffic light changed to green and he turned right onto Colfax. "What can they do?"

The gunman who had shot at Sarah Beaumont had done so in the midst of a crowd. He had opened fire in the sure knowledge that he, too, would die. Jeremy shuddered. Gwynneth had suggested that the man might have been "programmed" in the same way as the nurse. In some ways that was worse. It was one thing to sacrifice yourself for your own fanatic beliefs. It was something else entirely to be sacrificed for another's.

Herkimer Vane turned around in his seat and looked at the three in the back. "What do you suggest we do? The Firm is unpracticed at such desperate games."

Jeremy waved an irritated hand. "Am I more practiced than you?"

"Jeremy?" Gwynneth Llewellyn spoke. "We've got to do something." Her voice was tight, controlled. Jeremy could hear the edge of hysteria in it.

"I know." Jeremy fell silent. *I'm only an accountant. I don't do this sort of thing.* Yet leadership seemed his by default. The others had thrust it upon him. Was that how it always happened? Were leaders only those who were slow in stepping back? "How well armed are we?"

Anderson laughed. "There's a jack handle by the wheel well in the back."

Good Lord, but Vane's people were babes in the woods! You would think that, after what had happened, they would have brought Uzis along on the rescue mission—not one man and a minivan. He looked at Jim Doang. "What about you?"

"Me?" Doang looked at him. "Do you have a plan?"

"How good are you?"

"Black belt. But if the men behind us have guns—"

"Never mind that, yet. I'm an accountant. I'm taking inventory." He clasped his hands together and frowned at the floor of the van. He could see a way. It was a desperate chance and a lot depended on what their pursuers intended. If they were only waiting for a clear shot with a Stinger missile, it didn't matter what plan he came up with. He decided not to worry about contingencies like that. Start with the basics. Fight or flight. Pick one. Details to follow.

"All right," he said after a while. "Here's what we'll do."

"This isn't going to work," Jim Doang told him.

Jeremy glanced back down the dusty Douglas County road. "They can't hang back there forever. They trailed us out here to the sticks hoping we might lead them to a safe house or hideaway. But the longer they sit back there, the more obvious they become." He pointed to the culvert that ran under the road. Dank drainage water stood in the bottom of the corrugated metal tube. The odor of mold and decay.

Doang sniffed. "I promised to follow your directions, but—"

"Then do it!" Jeremy said harshly. Doang looked at him in surprise, and Jeremy did his best not to look surprised also. Since when had he become a forceful person? He clapped Doang on the back again. "Don't worry. I had Anderson park the van so they couldn't see us get out or crawl through the culvert. When they finally drive up and get out, they'll be facing the van and have their backs to us. With your karate, my jack handle, and the element of surprise, we should be able to take them."

Doang hunched over and crawled into the culvert. Jeremy grasped the handle on the van's sliding door to close it, but Gwynn stopped him. "Leave it open, Jeremy. If they get out of their car with guns in their hands, I want to be able to jump before they open fire."

"Maybe you should get out now. Hide in the ditch."

"No, Jeremy. You're our leader. Stick to your decisions. The worst thing a leader can do is change his mind after setting things in motion. If they don't see anyone in the van, they will suspect a trick."

"Well . . . If there is trouble, don't linger inside."

"I don't intend to. Good luck." She extended her hand and Jeremy grasped it. Vane stood before the opened hood of the van, ready to slide into the ditch at the first sign. With his arm in a sling and his ribs cracked from the explosion, he hadn't wanted to leap from the cab into the ditch. He licked his lips and nodded to Jeremy. Anderson looked down from the driver's seat.

"I hope you know what you're doing," he said.

"Yeah. Me, too." Jeremy followed Doang through the culvert. It was smaller than he had thought it would be. A tight fit. A good thing Anderson hadn't been the one to try it. Jeremy shoved the jack handle through his belt and squirmed through. His trousers became soaked in the fetid water. Stones in the water poked him. So did the jack handle, and he paused to adjust it as best he could.

Then he was through and found himself in the drainage ditch on the other side of the county road. He slid into it, rolled onto his back, and took a few deep breaths.

"Claustrophobic, wasn't it?" Doang was lying prone on the bank of the ditch, peering through a stand of weeds that allowed him to watch the sedan without showing his head. He spared a grin at Jeremy, and Jeremy grinned back. It wasn't bravado. It was sheer nervousness.

"Have they moved yet?"

"No."

Jeremy crawled beside Doang.

"I suppose," Doang said, "now is the time to ask what if they toss a bomb?"

"Then we never did have a chance, and we're no worse off than we were."

"You are a bright-eyed optimist, aren't you?"

"I think if they meant to do something like that, they would have done it already."

"Wait!" Doang said. "Here they come."

They fell silent as they heard the motor of the approaching car. It stopped almost on top of them, and Jeremy realized that if the driver looked down when he stepped out, he would see him and Doang lying there. Jeremy laid a hand on Doang to keep him still, but Doang was a rock.

Vane evidently noticed the same thing, because as the driver's door opened, they heard him call, "Hey! We've got a little trouble here. Do you fellows know anything about engines?"

Feet scraped on dirt. "Put your hands up."

Jeremy tapped Doang. Now! They crept from the ditch and took cover behind their pursuer's own car. Through the windows they could see two men in jeans and cowboy hats. They had revolvers in their hands. Vane stood by the opened hood of the car with his hands in the air. Jeremy cursed under his breath. The little man hadn't had time to jump into the ditch. Should he change the plan?

No. Everyone knew what to expect. Even Vane. If he changed the plan, no one would know. They would begin to wonder. Start looking around, which would warn the men with the guns. That must be what Gwynn had meant.

"You can tell your friends," said one of the gunmen, "to get out of the ditch." Jeremy's heart skidded, but the speaker had meant the other ditch, where Gwynn and Anderson had jumped.

"We aren't going to hurt you," said the other.

"Then you don't need those guns," said Vane, and one of the gunmen laughed.

Jeremy slapped Doang on the shoulder again. A prearranged signal. They ran around opposite sides of the car. Doang to the left, Jeremy to the right.

The gunman on the left must have seen something out of the corner of his eye. He started to turn just as Doang let loose with the most bloodcurdling cry Jeremy had ever heard. Doang had warned him of the cry. It was supposed to make the opponent freeze for a fraction of a second, and Jeremy could well believe that it would. Doang spun like a dervish and one foot kicked the gun from the man's hand; then the other came around and connected with his temple.

Jeremy was swinging the jack handle in an arc as he ran and connected with the other gunman's wrist. The gunman howled and the revolver dropped from his numbed fingers. He snatched at Jeremy with his left hand, but Jeremy danced out of the way, kicking the fallen gun before him like a soccer ball.

Then Doang landed with both feet on the man's back and it was over.

Anderson had recovered the gun from Doang's man. Jeremy picked up the other. Their two assailants lay still.

"They're not dead, are they?" Jeremy asked. He began shaking from the adrenaline rush. The revolver was heavy; the barrel, long. The handle felt rough in his palm.

Doang sat on the van's running board. He mopped his brow with a tissue. "My man is stunned from the blow to his head. Yours has had the wind knocked out of him. And he probably has a broken wrist as well. Otherwise . . ." A shrug.

Jeremy said, "You did a good job, Jim."

"Thank you. I have never attacked an armed man before, or any man, except in sparring."

Jeremy looked at him. "I'm glad you didn't say so earlier. Dammit, where is the safety on this thing?"

Anderson stepped up to him and took the gun from him. "If you don't know that, you shouldn't have it in your hand. Let me see." A pause. "Well, I'll be damned."

"What?"

"The safety is already on." Another quick inspection. "So's the other one."

Jeremy looked from the guns to the men on the ground. The man he had attacked was beginning to stir. "They didn't mean to kill us, then."

"At least, not immediately."

"That doesn't fit with what we know about the Babbage Society. They shoot first and ask questions later, don't they?"

"That's because," said the man lying at their feet, "we ain't the fucking Babbage Society." He hugged his broken wrist to himself.

Jeremy leaned against the van and began to laugh.

III

Kennison looked up from his work as Alan Selkirk entered his office and dropped a sheaf of computer paper on his desk. Kennison flipped through the printout and watched the numbers dance, as if in an animated cartoon. "Thank you, Alan. I will take this home and review it." He retrieved his pen and returned to his interrupted work. He checked the items one at a time, reviewing each one methodically. Slow and steady wins the race, after all. After a moment, he looked up again and saw Selkirk lingering by the desk.

"Was there something else, Alan? The virus hunt is proceeding smoothly, is it not?"

"Yes, no problems. Ms. Baker is an extremely capable programmer—although I told you I could have handled the job myself. We've gotten all the viruses out of the system. But . . ." He tapped the printout he had just delivered. "Aren't you going to tell me what *this* is all about?"

Kennison raised an eyebrow. "Simply another job, Alan. Another job. Kennison Demographics has many clients, who sometimes have odd requests."

Selkirk leaned over the desk, bracing himself with his

hands. "Come off it! The 'client' for this job is *you!* What are you up to?"

Kennison stared at Selkirk's hands until the the young Scot backed away and straightened up. That was better. Alan sometimes seemed to forget who was in charge. He behaved disrespectfully, and respect for one's betters was the sine qua non of civilization. A place for everything, and everything in its place. He would have to teach this young man his place.

And yet there was also something about Alan that appealed to him. Perhaps a wispy memory of his own youth. The young man was certainly not one of the docile sheep. Well, sheep needed sheepdogs, did they not? And kings, crown princes. Would Alan make a suitable crown prince? Perhaps. Perhaps.

"Yes," he told his protégé, "but this project of mine is very important to, let us say, our future security and peace of mind."

Selkirk shook his head. "What have the Spanish Land Grants in the Old Southwest to do with our peace of mind?"

"Loose ends," he told him. "Loose ends. Have you identified those Grants which came through the fighting intact and which remained thereafter in the possession of the same family?"

"Aye. But shouldn't we be running a check on the Secret S—"

Kennison cut him off with a raised hand. He nodded toward the main room where the policeman sat drinking coffee and chatting with the secretarial pool. "Tomorrow things will be back to normal, Alan. Ask me tomorrow about our plans. Prudence has been doing some investigations for me. She has not been idle."

Indeed, Kennison mused, he and Prudence had held "consultations" nearly every evening since his return from the meeting with Malone. It was, he admitted to himself, growing to be rather tedious. Perhaps the pretense of Little Girl Lost had become a shade too transparent and had lost its ability to entice him. He sighed and checked his watch. She would be calling any moment now, with her insatiable demands.

"So, all in good time, Alan. All in good time. Meanwhile, it is seventeen hundred hours. Time for the Daily Bug Hunt and Backup—" The intercom buzzed and Kennison picked it up. "Yes?"

"Danny?" he heard a frightened voice say. "I'm in trouble. Hurry down here, please!"

Kennison covered the mouthpiece. "That will be all, Alan," he said, stressing the words. It was important that the help know who was in charge. "And close the door when you leave."

When he was alone, Kennison uncovered the phone. "Now, see here—!"

"Please, Danny! I'll never ask you again. There's someone else down here. I need you." He could hear tears in her voice.

"My dear," he murmured. "What you need is more of the spice of life." Kennison wondered. Perhaps a new game? Prudence needed her shabby little charades the way an addict needed his mothers' tears. Each time he left her, Kennison felt unclean. He would scrub himself down with a hard brush in the executive shower until his skin tingled.

So, why did he always go to her? Perhaps he was overly considerate of her feelings. She would beg and wheedle until he was induced once more into her grotesque pretenses. Yet it would be callous to deprive her of her needs, the more so as she was one of his own people. Besides, "all work and no play . . . ," after all.

"Very well. I shall be there presently." He hung up before she could prattle her thanks. He stood and straightened his pants and headed for the washroom elevator. Noblesse oblige. He sighed. No one ever said being the boss would be easy.

The offices of Johnson and Cheng were dark. *Tomorrow,* he thought, *things can return to normal.* The police protection would be withdrawn. The Night Shift would return to

work and these offices would resume their wonted bustle—
and these nightly encounters would come to an end. He
walked out to the middle of the main office, wending his
way among the red-lit shadows. *Let us get the squalid business over with.* He stood still, listening.

Nothing.

There was a slight whispering sound that was either someone's breathing or the air conditioner. "Pru?"

No answer.

Perhaps there had been a burglar, after all? Perhaps Prudence had tried valiantly to stop him and had been struck
down. Perhaps, even now, she was lying battered and bleeding, precious moments ticking away.

Kennison stode up and down the aisles, glancing into each
cubicle. He remembered how she had cowered earlier in the
knee hole of one of the desks. Perhaps the burglar had been
real then, too, and now, frustrated, he had returned to the
scene of his earlier, thwarted crime. Kennison found a pair
of scissors on one of the desks and took it with him. He crept
slowly, carefully. If the burglar was still in the offices, Kennison's own safety lay in silence.

He finished the last row of cubicles without finding Prudence. His pulse raced faster. Had the burglar raped her?
Burglars came from the lower classes, and rape was always
on the minds of that ilk. Prudence would have resisted, naturally, fought back gallantly as he ripped her clothes from
her. Kennison pictured her lying, bruised and naked, while
the ill-bred brute had his will.

He entered Cheng's office and there she was. She was
sitting in Cheng's high-backed leather swivel chair, grinning
at him, fully clothed.

It was a trick, after all.

Kennison felt a wave of anger like the heat from an open
furnace. He walked around to the chair in a few quick strides.
"Damn you, Prudence!" He spun the chair so she would face
him and her head flopped loosely onto her shoulder.

Kennison noticed several things at once. The smile on her
face never wavered. There was an awful smell, as of an ill-

kept rest room. And there was a large stain that covered the front of her dress from breasts to lap. The stain was black satin in the ruddy light that infused the room. He reached out and touched it and his hand came away wet.

He felt a grave sadness. "Oh, Prudence . . ."

"How touching."

He spun and faced the doorway to the office. A ghostly figure in shades of red and black. A .38-caliber pistol with silencer pointed directly at him. Kennison squinted into the gloom. "You!"

Genevieve Weil stepped inside. "Come around where I can see you, Danny Boy." She waved with her gun barrel. Kennison carefully stepped around the desk. Weil looked him up and down. Her eyes fixed on his trousers. "Well, well, you impotent piece of slime. I see you were finally able to get it up. Unbelievable. What has that fat slut got that I haven't?"

"More dead," Kennison said, "than you alive."

Weil's face tightened and the gun came up and Kennison regretted the haste of his words. *Control*, he thought. *You must act with control.* Prudence Baker had not been the great love of his life. And yet, were the scene to replay, he knew he would speak the same words. Curious.

Weil grinned and lowered the gun a fraction of an inch. "No," she said. "Not quite yet."

Not quite yet! Then there was hope. Kennison's mind switched into high gear. "You survived the assassination attempt! We were all so worried—"

Weil laughed. Kennison could feel the sweat on his forehead, in his armpits. His knees felt weak. He knew he must smell of fear.

"You son of a bitch," she said. "I never did like you. You should never have gotten your father's Council seat."

"But—"

"Shut up and listen, you pompous, flaccid piece of shit. You want to know how I survived the car bomb? That's easy. I wasn't in the car. I knew that one or more of my devoted followers would try to take advantage of the confusion. I had you and Ullmann and Paige on my list; so when Paige showed up on my doorstep with that asinine idea of hers, I knew she was up to something. It didn't take long to find out what. Judd is very good at what he does."

"She and I—"

The gun came up again. "I thought I told you to be quiet. I know exactly what you said to her. I've got my own ears in your mansion."

Desperation made him speak. "Then you know I never said—"

"Of course, you 'never said.' You never say anything. You're the only man I've ever known who could speak entirely in innuendo." She smiled coldly. "Do you want me to tell you how she screamed while Judd questioned her? It was pathetic. The sight of blood completely unnerved her. She bawled. She whimpered. She offered to betray you. It did her no good. I needed her information; I didn't need *her.*"

Slowly Kennison's fear and desperation gave way to anger. Sister Paige had been his rival, his "Seward." But she had been acting for him when she had gone to Weil's mansion. He was responsible for her. "What did you do with her?"

"Don't be dense. There was a body in the car, you know."

"Was she—"

"Oh, certainly, she was conscious." Weil was matter-of-fact. Simple deletion was not enough for her. There had to be cruelty as well. Silently Kennison cursed her and spared a curse for her mother, too. *Concentrate on the present, Daniel. On the Now. There might not be too much of the Now left you.* Thank the gods she had wanted to taunt him. It gave him time.

"She watched us wire the device in place," Weil told him. "Judd even explained the circuitry to her and what it would do. Oh, how she squirmed and twisted; but the seat belt was welded shut. I can still see her eyes as I waved good-bye to her."

Kennison wanted to tell her she was an evil woman, but he clenched his jaw tight and wouldn't let the words out. He tried to imagine how Paige had felt, strapped into that car, knowing her fate but helpless, helpless.

Weil saw something in his face, though. "What? Is it different when it's done at a distance? Are you somehow better than me because you've always hired those who hired those who did it?" She laughed. Her eyes went past his shoulder to the body in the chair. "Your porcine playmate didn't whine. I'll give her that. She knew it was no use. I could have used her."

"Then why—"

"Why? You silly ass. Because she actually liked you. I won't use so bourgeois a word as *love*. That's hard enough to imagine where something like you is involved. She actually thought you would save her, like some knight in a goddamned fairy tale. She threw it in my face, the bitch, and I had to prove her wrong."

He had failed her. She had waited for him to come and save her and instead she had gotten a bullet through her heart. Kennison was shamed. A man protects his own, and he had failed. Brave, brave little Prudence. His stalwart, gutsy aide, who went down heroically into the darkness. Somehow, Kennison knew, he would avenge her, even if it meant his own life.

"I'll be damned," said Weil. "So that's what does it for you. Danger." She aimed the gun at his crotch and Kennison stiffened.

She uncocked the gun. "It seems a shame to waste it, don't you think? I mean, as long as we've got it, why not use it? I tell you what, Danny Boy. If that thing lasts long enough for me to get something out of it, I may not kill you at all. How does that grab you, Danny Boy?"

Kennison had no illusions of what was in store for him. What she wanted from him was not something she would want twice. This was one rooster she'd always been unable to have, but there were, after all, plenty of others in the barnyard. Yet her offer meant a few moments more of life, and Kennison had discovered how precious those moments could be. Supply and demand . . . . "Yes," he said in a husky and cracked voice. "Yes."

"That was good, Danny Boy. You always did know how to crawl. Now come here and—don't forget; I've still got the gun. If danger is what does it for you, then as long as I've got my gun, you'll have yours." She laughed again, as if she had said something funny.

Kennison moved toward her, his mind working furiously. It was a desperate ploy, but this was a time for desperation. What was it Montrose had written?

> *He either fears his fate too much,*
> *Or his deserts are small,*
> *That puts it not unto the touch*
> *To win or lose it all.*

He slid into her embrace and tried to repress a shudder of revulsion. He could feel the cold metal of the gun barrel against the back of his head. She turned her mouth up to be kissed, and he pressed against her as hard as he could. She liked it hard and brutal, he remembered.

Her body remained skeptical, stiff in his arms. So he blanked his mind and imagined it was Prudence he was holding. He turned her around so he could press her against the desk. Over her shoulder, he stared into Prudence Baker's sightless eyes.

She finally relaxed into him. Her arms snaked around his neck and shoulders. He could still feel the cold metal of the gun; but it was the butt, not the barrel.

Now!

He grabbed the scissors off the desk and, with both hands joined in a fist, he rammed it into her back with all his strength. At the same time, he clamped down hard with his left arm, pinning her gun arm to his side.

Weil jerked as if electrocuted, arching her back around the fulcrum of the scissors. Her breath shrieked out in a hiss. The blades scraped on bone and he pushed harder. His hands grew warm and wet, but he kept her tight in his grip. She couldn't bend her arm far enough to bring the gun to bear on him. She twisted and squirmed. *Like Sister Paige must have done.* Her muscles contracted spasmodically and he heard the gun spit behind him. The muzzle flash singed his hair; the bullet grazed his back and buried itself in the far wall.

His grip on Weil grew slippery as her struggles became more frenzied. Another silenced bullet shattered the elegantly framed diploma by the bookcase. He could feel her gun arm sliding, wriggling free. If she ever got the gun loose . . .

He released her, seized the gun in both his hands, and twisted, hard. The third shot ran up his arm like a streak of fire and passed though the fleshy part of his shoulder. The pain was blinding, but to lose his grip now would be death. *Pain means nothing to men like me.* She beat on him with her left fist, but he ignored it, twisting the right arm more and more until something snapped and the gun fell from limp fingers.

"My God!" she cried. "Oh, my God!"

He pulled away from her, kicking the gun into the corner. Madame Weil, he thought, should be the last person on Earth to call on God. She staggered away from him. Cheng's desk was covered with a black, glistening pool. The scissors were set in the back of her dress like a pair of eyebolts. Her arms twisted and flailed, trying to reach it. "Pull it out, God damn you!"

He stepped forward and grabbed the scissors, hesitated briefly, so she would cry again for his help; then he yanked them free. He tossed the scissors into the corner with the gun and turned her roughly around to face him. Her face was pale in the red light.

When he released her, she crumpled to the carpet. He had done it! He, Kennison, had been to the brink of the Great Abyss and had escaped! He had looked Death itself in the eye, put it all to the touch. He had bested Genevieve Weil.

He stood over her and looked down. She stared back at him with hopeless eyes. She knew he would never call an ambulance for her. She had given no mercy to others and could expect none in return. She knew she would bleed to death in the dark.

He had it all now. With Weil and Paige both gone, the Society was his for the asking. No, not for the asking. For the taking. He would never again ask for anything.

And yet Prudence Baker's eyes on the other side of the desk seemed infinitely sad. He did not have it all, he knew. There were some things now he could never have again. And so he went to her and held her to him for a very long time, until his need had passed and the light had gone out forever from the eyes of the woman on the floor.

Later, he used the phone in Johnson's office.

"Alan? Would you come downstairs, please? We've got a small problem to clean up."

IV

Sarah was playing a quiet blues number on the piano in the music room when Tex Bodean entered. Her eyes were closed; her head, held back. She let her fingers mourn: for her friends, for herself. Morgan, Dennis, Jeremy. *I'm a-goin' down that long lonesome road, yes I am.*

"Did you find it?" she asked without stopping the music. *I'm goin' where the water tastes like wine.*

"Yup." She heard him rustle inside a sack. There were dull, metallic sounds. "In the barn with the others. Woulda maybe found it sooner, 'cept it was in the discard pile. Horse musta threw it a while back." *Goin' down that road feelin bad, Lord, Lord.*

From the corner of her eye, she saw him place a horseshoe on the ledge of the piano. "Bad luck," she told him. "You should set it with the open end up. Otherwise the luck runs out of it." *I'm goin' where I've never gone before.*

She let the blues fade away on a minor chord. She held

her hands poised for a lingering moment over the keyboard. Then, she sighed and reached out and took the horseshoe.

"Jimmy told me you played the ivories," Tex said.

She ran her finger down the left side of the shoe. There was a hairline fracture there. Just like the tracks she had found that day on the mountain. *Someone here,* she thought sadly. *It was someone here.*

"I play the 'bone, myself," Tex said.

"Do you." Someone had watched and spied. And drugged her.

"Yup." He pushed his cowboy hat back and leaned against the piano. He stuck his thumbs in his belt loops. "Hear tell your new persona had a field test."

"News travels."

"Held up all right?"

"I'm here, ain't I?"

Tex nodded. "Told you not to worry."

She wasn't sure how to take Tex Bodean. He was friendlier than Walt and most of the others at the safe house. Tex smiled easily and, like Red, seemed perpetually amused by life; but he made her uneasy. It wasn't simply his cool assurance, bordering on arrogance. It was the feeling that she was always on exhibit around him and he was only waiting to see what she would do next. Red was a player, ad-libbing his way through the script, while Tex was the audience, chuckling over the gaffes. As Janie's *segundo,* he had soaked up some of her awful detachment.

"Red doesn't think Kennison was behind the hit," she told him.

Tex considered that. "Hunh. What do you think?"

She paused. "I don't know." If not Kennison, one of his colleagues? From what she and Red had deduced, the Babbage Society was unraveling under the crisis.

Sarah shook her head. "Whoever it was, they wanted to kill us." My God, how could she discuss it so calmly? Was she getting *used* to it? "They tried to run us down, so the cops would think it was an accident. The kids race their cars in the parking lot at night. When that didn't work, they tried a few shots; but they took off because they didn't want to get caught."

Tex smiled wolfishly. "Ah, but who were they? Kennison's playmates? The Secret Six? Or . . . Who knows? Jimmy's briefing the Council right now. The Atlanta Office found the Stray, so he figured to bring Cam up-to-date on everything."

She handed him the horseshoe. "Do you know which horse wore it?"

Tex studied the shoe, turning it end for end. "This is the one, then?" he asked.

"Which horse?"

"I figure the sorrel. That's the only one threw a shoe last month."

"And who rode it?"

"The stablemaster gave me a list. Names and dates." He reached into his shirt pocket with his left hand and pulled out a sheet of paper that had been folded several times. He handed it to Sarah and she unfolded it and read, looking for the one date that mattered.

She found it and chuckled sadly. "For want of a nail . . . ," she said.

"What's that?" asked Tex, frowning.

She took the shoe back from him and hefted it, open end up. "Good luck," she told him.

"How do you rotate the world?" asked SuperNerd.

Walter Polovsky sighed. "Move over, kid; and watch how I do it." He rolled his chair in front of the terminal keyboard. Sarah sipped from a can of diet soda as she watched over their shoulders. The screen showed a complex tree diagram— they called it a weighted digraph—filled with tiny bubbles, arrows, and logic gates.

"It makes me nervous," SuperNerd said, "people watching me like this."

Polovsky played for a moment on the keyboard. "See? You gotta increment the gamma and kappa parameters at the right ratio." Polovsky hit the return key authoritatively and sat back with his arms folded to watch. "You gettin' this, Bosworth?"

SuperNerd nodded. "What about her?" He pointed to Sarah.

Polovsky looked at her. "She don't need my help."

Sarah smiled at him, but he didn't smile back. *The hell with him,* Sarah thought. She turned her attention back to the screen. Bosworth clicked on one of the bubbles and a window opened, showing the details. *15.05.07. Sinking of the LUSITANIA.*

"That's the one," she said. "It was on Dennis' list."

Bosworth moused the cursor to an adjunct bubble and opened that one, too. The second window read: *"German Embassy telephones LUSITANIA passengers, advising them to cancel passage; places advertisement in NY papers, announcing intention to sink ship.*

He scrolled into the menu bar and pulled down COUNTER-FACTUAL. Then he clicked on the Lusitania and selected the logic gate for negation. The digraph flickered as bubbles burst, shifted, or were replaced by new bubbles. An automatic window opened with the heading: SELECTED EVENTS ALTERED BY COUNTERFACTUAL.

Sarah set her can down and studied the list. Dates and events in two parallel columns. Everything seemed to track about the same, but the analogue events in the Counterfactual ran later than they had in actual fact. U.S. troops did not arrive to stiffen the Allied line until May of 1918, nearly a year late, and after the Hindenburg Offensive was in full swing. The March 1919 armistice declared the war a "draw."

Polovsky looked back over his shoulder at her. "Is this what you wanted?"

"I'm just rolling over rocks. Why did the Germans sink a passenger liner, even if it was carrying war supplies? It was stupid. It brought us into the war sooner."

"They didn't care," Polovsky told her. "The Germans rated our army about equal to the Rumanians, and Hindenburg thought he'd have it all wrapped up before any Americans arrived."

Sarah pointed to the screen. "They'd've gotten their wish if they hadn't sunk the *Lusitania*."

Polovsky waved a hand in irritation. "Sure, *we* know that; but they didn't have any cliologists to tell them so."

Sarah did not reply and there was a long moment of silence. Finally Polovsky turned and scowled at the screen. "Shit," he said.

SuperNerd jerked his head from one to the other. "What?"

Polovsky looked at him. "Wake up, kid."

SuperNerd's mouth opened into an O.

"Sure," said Sarah. "European scientists were no duller than American scientists."

Polovsky took a deep breath and let it out. "Yeah. Yeah, I know. But the kid here, he found actual documents on the Six." He scowled again at the screen. "This is just inference. Just because an event was a high-leverage turning point doesn't mean it was *planned* that way. There are *always* residual anomalies in the data." He poked a finger at the bubbles and logic gates. "With millions of unit events in the digraph, some of them *have* to be improbable. It's like throwing a dart at a dartboard. There's an infinite number of points it could hit, right? So the probability of hitting a particular point is one over infinity. Zero. But"—he stabbed a finger at her for emphasis—"the dart has to hit *somewhere*. Afterward, we look where it hit and say how damned improbable it was. So we figure it must have hit there on purpose."

Was Polovsky being deliberately obtuse? *It's only when we like the answer,* she thought, *that we accept the reasoning. If we don't, we'll pick every nit there is.*

"Let's say some group wants Germany defeated," she said. "Maybe the same gang that convinced von Kluck to wheel his army short of Paris in 1914. But they need American troops to do it. So somehow they convince the High Command to sink a passenger liner with over a thousand civilian men, women, and children. Meanwhile"—she tapped the adjunct bubble—"another group is working for German *victory* by keeping Americans off the *Lusitania* and thus the U.S. out of the war."

Polovsky looked at her. "How many groups do you want to find?"

"As many as there are," she answered.

"Here's another swing point," said Bosworth, reading the detail window for another bubble. "Wilson wanted to use the regular Army as cadre to train the National Guard and the newly authorized National Army and didn't plan on sending troops until spring of 1918. But the French talked him into sending an expeditionary force right away."

Polovsky twisted his face. "I suppose you think Joffre and Viviani were part of a secret cliological society."

She shook her head. "Purposeful behavior creates patterns in the data, and factor analysis helps us identify those patterns. But everything anybody does has a purpose behind it. If we analyzed events at a fine-enough level of detail, we'd find that every person who's ever lived has been a cliological factor." She flashed, suddenly, on her living room, in a home she would never see again. Red sitting on the sofa, that big, stupid grin on his face, telling her how she and everyone else were tampering with history. She hadn't believed him then. Now she saw that he had been right. "What marks the footprints of the Babbage Society and the Secret Six is that the patterns are in the *indirect* consequences."

Polovsky shook his head. "Three billion cliological societies," he said. "Jimmy's gonna love this." He ran a hand across his face and glanced at SuperNerd. "What do you think?"

"Why are you asking me? I'm just the dumb kid."

"I'm asking."

The teenager shrugged. "OK. Then I think she's right."

"You think she's right. Great." Polovsky shook his head again.

The door to the computer lab opened and, thinking it was Red, Sarah spun around. But it was only Tex Bodean. He stopped just inside the door and looked around with lazy eyes. He pushed his cowboy hat back on his head and slouched against the wall. He stuck his thumbs in his belt loops. "Here you are," he said.

"Yeah, here we are," Polovsky replied. "We been here all day. What is it?"

"Meeting. After Red finishes up with Cam."

"What meeting is this?" asked Polovsky. "Why wasn't I told?"

Tex looked at him. "Because I'm telling you now."

She looked from Walt to Tex. What a mixed bag Red had collected. He wanted to repeal Quinn's Prohibition, yet how did he expect to do it? Tex and Walt and the others she had yet to meet who had joined him in this . . . Had they really made common cause? Even she could see that Walt and Tex rubbed each other the wrong way, that Walt thought Norris an adolescent freak, that SuperNerd thought the whole business was a computer game. They had agreed that it was time to stop drifting with the current, but had they agreed in which direction to lay the course?

She herself felt as close to Red as anyone reasonably could. They had saved each other's lives, and that bound them closer than most lovers. Yet even she could not agree with his goal. The answer to manipulation was not counter-manipulation; it was no manipulation at all.

And if she felt that way, what of the others? What personal ambitions did each one harbor? After the Revolution comes the Coup. Red had a vision; but visionaries were always discarded afterward, and the merely ambitious took over. Ask Trotsky. Ask Robespierre or Commandante Zero. Ask Sun Yat-sen and Bismark.

Ask Brady Quinn.

Tex nodded to Sarah. "Did you find what you expected?"

Sarah glanced at the screen with its altered digraph. "I'm afraid so. There are at least five European horseshoe nails that we *know* weren't engineered by the Babbage Society; and they don't seem to fit in with what we know about the Six, either."

Tex grunted. "We didn't have enough troubles." He shook his head.

No manipulation. She had vowed that while she searched for Fee in the long forest shadows that awful sunset at Falcon Castle. No more manipulation. An end to the Society and to the Associates. And now: to the Six and its offshoot, and to who knew how many others?

A noble resolution. Yet Pandora's box was already open. How can you assure that no one will use a tool when that tool has already been in use for generations? How could you even know it was being used? Cliology could be applied subtly, over the course of decades. *We're too accustomed to rapid change,* she thought. *We celebrate every ephemeral swing of fashion, while generational trends go unnoticed.* Cliologists were patient; their machinations could creep up on you like the tide. And there were too many cliologists.

She straightened slightly in her seat. Or were there? She remembered, suddenly, that Hope had lingered there in Pandora's open chest.

"Ah, Ms. Beaumont," said Aaron Gewirtz. "We are so pleased to have you back amongst us. I trust that you were able to complete your project during your vacation."

Sarah took her seat while the Earth Mother, SuperNerd, and the others watched. Personally, she did not regard either surgery or target practice as "vacation." Especially when she was on the wrong end of the target practice. She settled in and opened her notebook without responding.

"Perhaps, Ms. Beaumont, you would care to enlighten us on the status of your project."

She looked up and into the old man's whitened eyes and wished that the sight would not unnerve her so. "Actually," she admitted, "I've changed my topic."

"Indeed? Without my approval? I discern a commendable penchant for independent thought. I hope your new topic is as penetrating as the one originally assigned."

"I think," she told him, "that you will find it worthwhile."

"Would you be so good, then, as to enlighten the class?" Gewirtz motioned toward the board at the front of the room.

He pulled on his wheels and backed himself away from the center of the room.

Sarah picked up a stylus and rolled it between her fingers. She had never cheated in school before, but what she planned required more than a simple assertion. So Red and Tex and the others had spent the entire night helping her develop her thesis.

"Very well," she said. She turned and began writing equations on the board, explaining them aloud for Gewirtz's benefit. She did not get far before he interrupted her.

"Just a moment," he said. "The condensation of memes is a well-understood phenomenon. Surely someone of your caliber intends more than a rehash of such a familiar topic."

"I believe you will find my conclusions stimulating. I intend to explore the conditions required for multiple and simultaneous centers of condensation."

Gewirtz pursed his lips. "I do not see the benefit, but . . . Go on."

Sarah continued. She pointed out the population density needed to supply a sufficient number of susceptible minds. The need for high connectivity of the communications network. The cultural momentum, as described by the speed and volume of transport. The fraction of the population engaged in travel. She cited numerous examples of simultaneous discovery: Newton and Leibniz; Wallace and Darwin; Edison and Bell; and so on. She noted that, in prehistory, agriculture had been "discovered" simultaneously by widely separated cultures, that fascism reared its head in several different countries at once, that the "population explosion" that began during the sixteenth century occurred in India and China as well as Europe. She began to generalize from these examples.

"One moment," said Gewirtz. "You mentioned connectivity of communications yet cited the near-simultaneous invention of agriculture in Mexico and Mesopotamia. Surely there were no communications between the two."

"No, sir," she replied. "But both cultures were communicating with the common, global environment. Similarly, the global warming that began in the sixteenth century affected all societies. It opened more land to farming; and that opened more mouths, to consume the increased harvest."

Gewirtz chuckled. "Nicely put. You may continue."

"We come now," she told the class, "to a specific application. Namely, the condensation of the memes required for the formation of a Babbage-like society during the early nineteenth century."

There was a stir among the class. She kept her back to them and continued to write. "As you see from the equations, the conditions during the 1830s were such that the formation of more than one such Society is a virtual certainty." She listed the relevant parameters quickly. "Researches into the database have revealed several anomaly tracks. One is a group calling itself the Secret Six. The Six, of course, has since bifurcated, as predicted by Carson's Dilemma, but one branch's tracks have disappeared. Either it has ceased to tamper with the 'social state,' thus leaving no 'horseshoe nails,' or it has dissolved."

The murmuring in the class grew louder. Aaron Gewirtz's voice overrode them. "Young woman, are you quite sure of what you are saying?"

She faced him. "Yes, Dr. Gewirtz. Quite sure. May I go on?"

The old man's face appeared troubled. "This is disturbing news."

"The Council has already been briefed."

His eyebrows arched. "Indeed? Then . . . Yes, yes. Please continue."

The stylus skittered across the board. She could feel the eyes of her classmates on her back. "However, we must not neglect Europe. Conditions there virtually guarantee the precipitation of at least one and possibly three additional societies. Given Carson's Dilemma, we may expect upward to five or nine societies currently active, barring collapse, dissolution, or merger."

The class was silent now. She turned and faced them. Except for SuperNerd, who was smiling nervously, they were stone-faced. "Merger," she said, "is unlikely, however, since secrecy is a necessary condition for a Babbage-like society to operate."

"I see," said Gewirtz. "Then these putative societies are as mutually ignorant of one another as we have been of them?"

"There is no way to be sure. Certainly, they are now aware of Us. One society seems to have been searching for evidence of others. One of their electronic fishing expeditions stumbled on the notes of a reporter named Morgan Grimes and downloaded them into something called the Q file. Since that took place *before* I wrote my worm—"

"Absurd," said the Earth Mother. "Beaumont is trying to avoid responsibility." Others in the class murmured their agreement. Gewirtz remained silent and immobile.

"It is clear," Sarah said, "that someone is nosing around both ourselves and the Babbage Society. Jimmy Caldero,"— she always felt a pang when she referred to his new persona; he was Red Malone, dammit; he always would be—"who has experience in intelligence matters, has assessed a number of these indications."

"Can you tell us what they are?" asked SuperNerd. Sarah thought he was hamming his part a little too much, but no one else seemed to notice.

"Dr. Gewirtz? I don't want to occupy too much of your class time on my project."

The blind man chuckled. "No, my dear. I am sorely tempted to accept your bluff, but I fear your classmates would rend me limb from limb were I to terminate the discussion now. By all means, finish." He waved a courtly hand toward her.

"Very well. Mr. Bosworth's researches into low-probability, high-leverage nodes have already identified the Secret Six." SuperNerd beamed at the compliment. "But there are other indications as well. I've already mentioned the Q-file tap on Morgan Grimes. In addition, the Q tapped into Kennison Demographics, and someone placed a threatening phone call to him. Third, the Stray, a lone file found by Dump searchers in the Atlanta Office. It was written in French at a Quebec node, urging an investigation of the murders in Grimes' files. I'm sure I don't need to point out that we have no Quebec station and that the Babbage Society would hardly need to launch such an investigation. Fourth, there is the bombing of the Denver University study team. That was not a Society operation. They lost a valuable agent in the explosion, and it couldn't help but inflame public suspicions. Finally, there is the fact that I was followed and drugged during my mountain sabbatical. All these events lead to what Jimmy called 'an assessment of capabilities.' He believes it would be imprudent to assume that all these activities were the product of a single organization."

She paused and looked over the class. They couldn't take their eyes off her. SuperNerd was grinning wide enough to crack his face. The Earth Mother was twisting her hands together. Reynold was staring with narrowed eyes. Gewirtz was unreadable.

"Now, let's put ourselves in the place of one of these other societies. What is the first thing we would do once we knew about the Dump?"

That was SuperNerd's cue. He raised his hand. "Check for doors."

"Explain."

"A 'door' is information that can be used to gain entry into the Associates or the Society, either physically or through the Internet, using taps, bugs, moles, or personal surveillance."

"A door. Exactly. And they found one."

Dr. Gewirtz spoke. "And what was that, if I may inquire?"

"Very little of Our data was leaked, which made our research easier. We tested each item in the Dump to determine whether it allowed access. For example: the location of this ranch was not revealed, but Councillor Louise Vosteen was compromised. So, her home may have been bugged, or she herself put under surveillance."

"Sister Vosteen is safely under cover now," Reynold said. "If she was being watched, she eluded them."

"And fortunately—or unfortunately," Sarah added, "her

home was burned by vandals, so it doesn't matter if it was bugged. Nobody learned anything."

"The point, Ms. Beaumont," said Gewirtz. "Get to the point."

"There was one open door. Mark Lopez was also compromised by the Dump. If the Six—or anyone else—acted quickly enough, he might have provided access, inadvertently or through coercion. Brother Lopez has not been located since then, but before he disappeared he did send us a new recruit. Or *was* it before he disappeared?"

In the sudden silence, the eyes of the class turned to Maureen Howard. She looked from one to the other. "This is ridiculous. Mark did a thorough background check before he sent me here."

"Did he?" asked Sarah. "Too bad we can't find him to ask him."

The silence in the room had grown deeper. "You don't have to. The Associates verified everything after I arrived."

"Oh, there's more," Sarah said with a smile. "If the ranch's location was not revealed in the Dump . . . who drugged me?"

Reynold's head jerked up. "You mean it's—"

"Someone at the ranch. Yes." She walked to her desk, opened her briefcase, and removed the horseshoe. She held it up. "This shoe was worn by the horse ridden by that spy. You can tell from the hairline crack that runs along it here." She pointed to the shoe. Maureen Howard reached out and took it. She studied the crack for some time, then passed the horseshoe to Reynold.

"According to Tex Bodean, it was worn by the sorrel gelding," Sarah continued. "The stablemaster checked the log sheet to see who was riding the horse that day. That person was Ms. Howard."

The Earth Mother jerked her head around. "That's not true!"

"The stablemaster says different."

"I rode out on the horse; that part's true. But I tied him up and went hiking on foot. When I came back to where I left the horse, he was gone. I hunted around for hours and finally found him just before sundown. I didn't say anything to the stablemaster because I didn't want her to think I wasn't taking good care of my horse."

Sarah shrugged. "It's a good story, Sister. But what false identity is perfect? Especially one prepared hastily. Suppose others pick away at it? What overlooked flaw might they find? What chink in the paper trail of altered records? Believe me, no one has had more reason in the past few weeks to ponder that issue. So, when Brother Malone and Brother Polovsky began investigating your past, they found—"

She got no further. Howard leaped from her desk and ran for the door. SuperNerd rose on cue to stop her, but she toppled the last desk into his path and he fell in a howl and a tangle.

When Howard threw open the door, however, she found Red Malone and Walt Polovsky barring her way. She spun and glared at Sarah, a look of such hatred as Sarah had never seen before, not even in the white neighborhoods of Chicago. Then Howard clenched her jaws together.

"Watch it!" said Red.

Howard stiffened and her eyes rolled up in her head. She arched backward stiffly, sighed, and fell. Polovsky caught her. She sagged limply in his arms. "Shit," he said and let go. Howard slid to the floor in a shapeless heap.

There was a moment of uneasy silence. Then Aaron Gewirtz said, "You were perfectly correct, Ms. Beaumont." Sarah turned and looked at him. The old man nodded somberly. "As you promised, a most stimulating proof of your thesis."

"She . . . She wasn't supposed to do that," Sarah stammered. She could hear how foolish the remark was. "Her cover looked flimsy when we checked it closely, but we couldn't break it. We were sure she was a mole, but we had no real proof. We hoped we could panic her into running."

Gewirtz turned his wheelchair to face the body. "Indeed. She ran as far as anyone could."

V

Seven phosphor-dot faces gazed back from the computer monitors mounted on the hidden wall of Kennison's study. They wore a variety of expressions: impatience, doubt, barely concealed hostility. Four other screens were blank. Benton. Paige. Ruiz. Weil. Kennison wished more of the screens were blank. It would be better to start his new regime with a tabula rasa.

But a man must work with the materials he has to hand. Kennison took a long swallow of the espresso that Karin had brought to his study. He had always prided himself on being a realist. He composed himself, joined his hands together on the desktop, and stared earnestly at the bank of screens.

"The Queen is dead," he announced. *And they could not help but finish the phrase in their own minds: Long live the King! Even as they looked into Kennison's face. Plant the seed. Plant the seed.* He did not update them on the timing of the Queen's death. Only three people knew of that: he and Alan and Judd; and that was two too many. Judd was safely stashed away in a cabin in rural Wisconsin, under strict guard, until Kennison could decide what to do with him. And as for Alan . . . Well, Alan would keep quiet, for his own good. He was an accessory after the fact.

"The Society has been without a chairman for too long," Frederick Ullman said acidly, "while we play-acted that foolish game of Paige's." Ullman's eyes flicked to his left. He was looking at his own screens, wondering why Paige's was blank. Let him wonder.

"It worked, didn't it?" said Montfort. "It convinced the public that we were not what the Beaumont Dump claimed we were."

"I went along with it," Ullman admitted. "But I doubt it was necessary. The public will believe what they are told to believe. What they want to believe."

A gaggle of geese, thought Kennison. *Quack. Quack.* "Our first order of business," he pointed out, "is to elect a new chairman. A center to hold us together." ("Things fly apart; the center cannot hold; Mere/ anarchy is loosed upon the world.") He smiled and spread his hands. "The Net is open to nominations."

"I nominate Brother Ullman," said Brigit Toohey.

"Second," said Westfield.

"Move the nominations be closed," said Toohey.

"Second."

"Call the question."

It happened so fast that it was over before Kennison knew it had started. Reynold Sorenson, who had been poised to nominate Kennison, looked back helplessly from his screen.

"Well, Brother Kennison? The question has been called," Ullman's thin, wrinkled face cackled at him from his screen.

Kennison reached forward and fiddled with the knobs on his transmitter. "I'm sorry," he said. "I lost the audio for a few seconds. What did you say, Brother Sorenson?"

Sorenson took the cue. "I said that I nominated Brother Kennison."

"What are you trying to pull?" asked Ullman. "Sister Toohey called the question."

Kennison shrugged for the camera. "A tree falling in the forest."

"I didn't hear her, either," said Sorenson. "There was static on the line."

"Nor I," said Peter Lewis. He was a big, broad-shouldered man with close-cropped blond hair and a face ruddy from high-mountain skiing. The window behind Lewis' shoulder opened on the snowcapped vista of the Bitterroot Mountains. Lewis' hidden retreat lay somewhere in Idaho or Montana; no one knew where. Kennison's staff had been comparing that vista against the Geological Survey maps for several years without success. Someday, perhaps . . . Although Kennison had lately wondered whether the backdrop was nothing more than a hologram, a virtual landscape.

Lewis smiled. "I no more doubt Brother Kennison's honesty, Brother Ullman, than I doubt yours." Lewis showed teeth that were white, even, and plentiful.

Kennison admired Lewis' dental work. He wondered if this meant that Lewis would support him in the balloting. Possible. Possible. It would be a close thing, he realized, if Toohey was in Ullman's pocket. He hadn't known that. Could he postpone a vote? Not given the urgency of the situation. See it through, then. Hope for the best and damn the torpedoes.

"No one has seconded Brother Kennison's nomination," Ullman pointed out.

Lewis shrugged. "Oh, I'll second it. Fair's fair, after all. There should be a contest."

"Are there any further nominations?" asked Kennison. He saw the eyes flit from screen to screen. The pygmies wondering who might challenge the giants. None. They lacked the guts. They would never dare what he had dared, nor what Ullman had dared. Never risk it all on one toss. He and Ullman were cut from the same cloth. He looked at Ullman's screen. *I salute you. It will be an honor to destroy you.*

"I move the nominations be closed," said Toohey with a contemptuous look in Kennison's direction. "Did you hear it that time, Brother?"

"Loud and clear, Sister."

"Second the motion."

"Call the question."

"Then shall we vote?" Kennison reached forward and entered his own name into the Net. He pressed the button and settled back to await the results.

It took only a moment. "Ullman: 3; Kennison: 2; Not Voting: 4."

The look on Ullman's face would have been far more enjoyable had Kennison not known that his own face bore the same look. "Gee whiz," said Lewis. "Look at that. No one received a plurality." He smiled his smile again. Perfect white teeth against sun-reddened, nordic face. Kennison thought what a pleasure it would be to smash those teeth.

He glanced at the special display that Alan had wired into

the computer circuits. "For Ullman: Brigit Toohey, Frederick Ullman, Carl Westfield. For Kennison: Daniel Kennison, Reynold Sorenson. Not Voting: Roman Huang, Peter Lewis, Dana Montfort, Gretchen Paige."

Damn Montfort! She had betrayed him. Who had bought her? Not Ullman; she hated that shriveled old geezer and had promised her vote to Kennison to forestall the older man's election. *Now I know what her promises are worth.* Kennison ground his teeth and smiled.

Ullman's eyes narrowed to slits. He worked his lips. "Give me a moment," he said and blanked his audio. Kennison watched him pick up a telephone. Kennison punched up another of Brother Alan's electronic gifts. TRACING . . . , his screen told him. TRACING. . . . Ullman spoke a few words into his phone, then listened nodding. He spoke some more. TRACE COMPLETED. PORT INDETERMINATE. A paper emerged from Ullman's fax machine. The old man pulled it, scanned it quickly, and fed it back in. LOCATION . . . LOCATION . . . AREA CODE 505. Kennison's own fax machine rang and began printing. The other Councilors also looked to their sides, wondering what rabbit Ullman had produced to break the deadlock.

Area Code 505? Where was that? Even as the thought formed, his terminal screen blinked: LOCATION: NORTHERN NEW MEXICO. FURTHER FOCUS NOT POSSIBLE.

New Mexico? Ruiz! It had to be. Damn that greasy Chicano bastard! How did Ullman know that Ruiz was alive? And how did he know how to contact him? It must have been planned from the beginning. While Kennison had laid his plans with Paige and Sorenson and (he had thought) with Montfort, Ullman had been conspiring with Ruiz, Toohey, and Westfield.

The fax was Benedict Ruiz's proxy. Kennison gave it barely a glance. "Brother Ruiz is dead," Kennison told Ullman. "This proxy is worthless." Ullman knew better, of course. The comment was meant for the other Councillors.

"Not so," Ullman announced with a satisfied smile. "Brother Ruiz knew quite well that he was in grave danger as a result of the laxity exercised on our database. *[Zap!]* So he took himself into hiding; much as Brother Lewis has done, only in a much more thorough manner. Brother Lewis wishes only to keep his location a secret. . . ." A pause, and a smile that asked just how well kept that secret could be from a man as wise and knowing as Ullman. Kennison enjoyed the discomfited look on the big man's ruddy face. "Brother Ruiz wished to keep even his very existence secret. He has agreed to reveal himself now only to forestall, as he puts it, the further degradation of the Society."

Kennison hated the way their eyes all sought him out. He saw Montfort and the others counting votes in their heads. It was 4 to 2 to 4, now. Ullman had a plurality under the Rules. It was bandwagon time. "Just a moment," Kennison said. He blanked his own audio and picked up his private line. "Alan," he said, "can you make it appear as if I am talking to an unidentifiable port in the New York area?"

"Sure. 'Tis as easy as—"

Kennison didn't want to hear what it was as easy as. He cut Selkirk off. "You may send me that fax now."

The machine rang three times and a sheet emerged. Kennison checked it, to be sure of its contents; then he fed it back into the system so the others would receive copies. It was Paige's proxy, authorizing a vote for Kennison. There was an artistic symmetry to the ploy. Ullman had voted a live man whom everyone thought dead. Kennison was voting a dead woman whom everyone thought alive. He was quite proud of the authorizing signature.

Ullman read the proxy, then gave Kennison a long, hard look. "And where is Sister Paige?"

"Need I repeat the tale you gave us concerning Brother Ruiz? These have been hard and frightening times. Sister Paige felt the same need for concealment as Brother Ruiz and Brother Lewis. I am sure none of us blame them for their behavior. Prudence, after all, is not cowardice." But juxtaposing the two words would plant that equation in their minds, especially with respect to Lewis, who had gone into hiding long before there had been any public outcry. And the phrase *the tale you gave us* might cause the others wonder about Ullman's veracity. Kennison was beginning to enjoy the election.

"In hiding, is she?" said Ullman. "I suppose we can accept that contention." Two can play at the game of innuendo. Ullman's calmness made Kennison wonder. *What does he know? Judd had sworn—bragged—that no one else knew.* Weil would never have brought the Ancient One into her confidence. She had hated him at least as much as she had hated Kennison and Paige. If she had only chosen Ullman as her second target, it would have solved so many problems. Ah, well. Spilt milk. Spilt milk.

The vote was 4 to 3 to 3 now. A plurality for Ullman, but barely so. Kennison watched Montfort's screen, daring her to continue her abstinence. *If you sit on the sidelines, you little bitch, you'll guarantee that old fart's election.*

Montfort's head turned. She was looking at someone's monitor, but whose? *Damn it. She should take her cues from me.* Kennison's eyes darted from screen to screen, but if a signal was passed, he did not catch it.

Montfort reached out and pressed a key. Kennison watched the tally. *For me!* A great sense of relief washed over him and he unclenched his hands. He hadn't realized how tense he had been, and it was another moment or two before he remembered that he had achieved a tie and not a victory. Lewis and Huang had not yet voted.

Lewis studied the returns on his own screen. Then he shrugged. "Let's end this," he said, "or I'll miss the best skiing." He dug into his pants pocket and pulled forth a coin. He flipped the coin spinning into the air, slapped it onto the back of his hand, and studied the result. Then he entered his own vote into his terminal. Kennison was astonished. It was the most contemptuous act Kennison had ever seen. A slap in the face to both Ullman and himself.

The vote was for Ullman. Which made the slap more tolerable for the geezer.

That made it 5 to 4 to 1. A plurality for Ullman. Kennison

looked at Lewis' image and saw nothing there but the bland smile he always showed.

Huang could still tie the vote. Kennison turned to his lower right-hand monitor. Roman Huang lived on a private island somewhere in the Hawaiian chain. He lounged on a chaise, framed by bright sand and surf and a smoldering background volcano. Ultraviolet sunglasses concealed his expression. The Hawaiian could still save things for Kennison. A tie would buy time. There were ways to change people's votes. Persuasion. Or something.

He could not read Huang's face. *I will not beg,* he told himself. *I will not crawl. Prudence did not beg, and I cannot be less than she.*

Kennison was amused to see that the others were also watching one of their monitors—presumably Huang. So much for the secret ballot.

Huang made no move, and the moment lingered. Finally he said, "Will there be any further business at this Council or have we concluded?"

And that was that. For whatever reason of his own, Roman Huang remained in abstention. Kennison saw that Ullman was also irritated. Once the decision is inevitable, why hold out?

Kennison, as temporary Chairman of the meeting, passed the virtual gavel to Ullman as the newly elected permanent Chairman. Ullman spread a few unctuous phrases around, thanking his supporters, praising his opponent, and telling everyone that it was now time to close ranks "in this, the direst hour of the Society's history." Kennison smiled and congratulated him on his victory and pledged his support on his behalf. Everyone pretended to believe everyone else. *Enjoy yourself, Ancient One* he thought at the monitor. *You're old. You won't last.*

"There are two items of business that we must conclude today," Ullman croaked. "The first is to propose nominees to fill the two Council vacancies of which we are aware."

Cleverly phrased, thought Kennison.

"I myself propose Vincent Torino, whom many of you

know and who, as you are all aware, has done excellent work for us in countering the Beaumont revelations."

I must get one of my own in those slots. But who could he trust to be his man? Prudence. Yes, Little Pru would have been the perfect nominee. But she was gone. And that left . . . "Alan Selkirk," Kennison announced. *Now why did I say that?* Whatever Alan might be on the Council, he was not likely to be Kennison's tool. An ally, perhaps. And perhaps an ally was better than a tool. Paige, after all, had given greater service than Sorenson. "I propose Alan Selkirk. He was the Brother who finally tracked down and destroyed the Beaumont Worm."

Ullman nodded. "He is rather new to our ranks, but he comes highly recommended. You will forward his dossier to the other Councillors?"

"Certainly."

"Very well. Anyone with further nominations will please supply the appropriate dossiers to the Council by Close of Business tomorrow and we will consider the candidates at our next regular meeting. As our final line of business, I propose to revive the office of Vice Chairman, which my late predecessor regrettably left dormant. I believe the events of the last several months have shown us how crucial it is that a vacancy in the chairmanship be filled quickly and automatically during an emergency."

The Vice Chairmanship, thought Kennison. *A meaningless post, but mine by right.* The Vice Chairmanship would give him a beachhead. It was only a matter of time before Ullman died—a very short time, if Kennison had any say in the matter—and then . . . Yes, he could humble himself in the Vice Chair for a while.

"Because of the close working relationship needed between a Chairman and his Vice," Ullman told the Council, "I feel it is appropriate that the Chairman nominate a suitable candidate for your advice and consent to ensure uniformity of policy. While it would be appropriate for me to name Brother Kennison as my Vice, I feel that the data collection and analysis performed for us by Kennison Demographics is a full-time job, one too valuable to entrust to anyone else. Furthermore, Brother Kennison is in too exposed a position, being the only one among us who is publicly prominent. Therefore, I propose Benedict Ruiz for Vice Chairman. If some unexpected catastrophe should catch the rest of us unawares, Brother Ruiz would be well positioned to catch hold of the reins."

Kennison felt the blood drain from his face. Ullman had castrated him! The sly geriatric bastard! He had given the Council a rationale that would block Kennison forever from the top position.

Kennison kept his face perfectly still while the others registered their approval. Even Sorenson, the traitor. The relief on Sorenson's face was as disgusting as the triumph on Ullman's. Kennison voted affirmative along with everyone else. No sour grapes, he; and the time for safe dissent had obviously passed.

Afterward, Kennison called a meeting of his own council and filled them in. They met in the boardroom of Johnson and Cheng, where they sat in new high-backed chairs around a broad mahogany table. The afternoon sun streamed through the window, bathing the dark wood paneling in rich, natural hues. A staffer wheeled in a beverage cart. The flash of cut glass; the light and subtle colors of the drinks, the tinkling of the crystal decanters against each other. There were too many pleasures in the world—sights, colors, tastes, sounds, sensual experiences of all sorts—to waste much time in bemoaning defeat. Water under the bridge. It's what comes next that matters. Revenge.

"Bourbon and branch for me," Kennison told the staffer, "and whatever the others will have." Nathaniel Johnson took his usual microbrew; Cheng Tsu-shih, a white wine.

"Scotch, neat, please." Selkirk favored Kennison with a smile. "I don't really like the stuff, but I feel it's my duty as a Scot."

Kennison chuckled with him. The staffer served the drinks

and was dismissed. Selkirk tasted his. "My, but this has a bonny nose." He looked at his glass, then at the anonymous crystal decanter on the serving cart.

"It's a private distillery I own in the Orkneys," Kennison told him.

"Ah." Selkirk nodded. After a moment more of silence, he said, "It didna go verra well, did it?"

Kennison frowned into his glass. "To see everything I've lived for vanish in the blink of an eye. Well—" He tossed the drink back into his throat. It burned going down.

"Was it?" Selkirk asked.

"Was it what?"

Selkirk played with his glass. He ran his finger around the rim. The crystal sang. "Was it everything you've lived for?"

Kennison frowned at him. "I'm not sure what you mean." Johnson shifted in his seat and turned a puzzled look on the Scotsman. Cheng sipped his wine.

Selkirk shrugged. "You have Kennison Demographics, do ye not?"

"And?"

"And is not KD the tail that wags the dog? I'm not one for speaking up when it's not my place, but it seems to me that the Council needs you more than you need them."

Kennison rose from his chair. He walked to the beverage cart and poured himself another drink. He drank half of it. Then he turned and faced Selkirk. "What do you propose, then?"

Selkirk smiled at him. "They trust the data you give them, do they not?"

Kennison regarded him silently for a moment. "Alan. I made you supervisor of the Night Shift, not Chairman of KD. Don't get above yourself."

"Above myself? After what I did for you?"

Kennison stiffened. Bad form, really. One did not remind others of favors owed or given. He glanced at Johnson and at Cheng, and they carefully avoided his eyes. They didn't know what had happened in their offices last week, and they didn't want to know. Furniture and carpeting had been mysteriously replaced. Prudence was gone and in her place sat this dour straw-haired Scot. Long-schooled by Genevieve Weil's management methods, they knew better than to ask questions.

"The corruption of the data will not be too blatant," Selkirk insisted. "Just enough to suboptimize their projections."

"Ullman's no fool," Kennison said. "How long before he suspects?"

"That's why we need to keep two sets of books," said Selkirk, leaning back in his chair and looking around the table. "If your former colleagues suspect that they are receiving suboptimized data, they'll mouse into our banks to check things out. We canna allow them to discover aught amiss. So I propose we back up our entire system to a remote location. We'll keep a false front here, and hide the corrrect information elsewhere, for our own use."

Cheng scowled. "Too hasty. Much too hasty. We are in no danger from Ullman. What matter who sits at head of table, when *we* set table? Better to be power behind throne."

Johnson rubbed his chin. "Hmmm. Uneasy lies the head, and all that?" He looked at Selkirk. "They both have a point, but perhaps we shouldn't go through with this plan." He shook his head. "To go against the Society . . . I don't know if that's wise."

Cheng nodded again. "Act from plan, not from pique. Where is cliological analysis? What are consequences? We never make decisions without such."

"Damn it all!" Selkirk struck the table. "Our situation requires boldness, not equivocation."

Kennison pressed his palms against the table as hard as he could, and held them there until his arm muscles began to tremble. True, he had often thought of striking out on his own. His heart was with KD, the fruit of his own loins, and not with the Society. Yet, it would be difficult, in several ways. Ullman would never let him leave, not with KD in his pocket.

What else was there? Stay, and kiss Ullman's shrunken

butt. Leave, and lose the fruits of his and his father's labors. Or . . .

What if KD were to swallow the Society whole; eliminate the other Councillors; make KD into a New Society, shaped in his own image? Possible. But how to swallow such a lump without getting indigestion? It might be possible. Old Grosvenor Weil had done it. Yet Kennison had waited patiently far too long. He yearned for action, for the reward that he had so justly earned. *Aut Caesar, aut nullus.*

There was another possibility. A risky one, but he could cut himself loose *and* keep KD. Selkirk had shown the way. He would need Selkirk to bring it off, damn the man; he would need his computer expertise. He glanced covertly at the Scot. He could not afford to keep Selkirk around afterward. That would be too risky. Too bad, but cookies *did* crumble.

He made a decision.

"If we take this step, we are committed. The Red Flag. Are you each prepared to stay the course?" he asked.

Johnson hesitated, then nodded. Cheng shrugged fatalistically. Alan stared back unwaveringly. "It was my idea."

Yes, thought Kennison. Your *idea.* "Very well. Brother Alan: Prepare a suitable plan for securing our database elsewhere; but take no action until all four of us have reviewed it. Brother Tzu-shih: Conduct a cliological analysis of the effects of our actions. Use the Night Shift. Brother Alan: See that he receives whatever manpower he needs. Oh!" He held up a hand.

"And Brother Tzu, be sure to factor in the information Jimmy Caldero gave us regarding the other Society, this 'Secret Six.' And keep that information from the regular information pool. Our most significant edge over Ullman may be that our analyses allow for their existence, while his do not. Consult Brother Alan for the details. He has discovered a number of things about them—most diligent work, Alan; thank you. Brother Nate: You will be in sole charge of Johnson and Cheng while this operation runs. We will depend on you for the usual cover and for the security of whatever channels we need to access during daytime hours. Any questions?" He scanned the table. "Very well. Make it happen."

He remained in the conference room after the others had left. There was no turning back now. *Jacta alea est.* Was this how Caesar had felt? Perhaps. Even the great ones must have felt uncertainty when the moment of truth arrived. Elation, yes, at the chance of success, and perhaps even at the chance of failure. The rush of adrenaline when the mind realized that one stood at a cusp and the future could fall either way.

That was what had been lacking before. Reckless daring. He had relied too much on caution; on weak reeds, like Montfort and Sorenson. Only Paige had proved her mettle, to her own misfortune. He vowed to enshrine her bones properly, once Judd yielded the secret of their disposal.

He doodled on the notepad before him. Weil. Ullman. Selkirk. The Secret Six. The three viruses. The phone call. He thought for a moment, then added: Bennett and Caldero.

The Great Harpy had said that she had an ear inside Kennison's organization. He drew an arrow from Weil to the viruses. As Chairman, Weil had access to the Johnson and Cheng offices. And she was surely capable of having a virus planted in the system.

And Ullman had hinted at knowing more than he should have. Kennison drew another arrow, from Ullman to the viruses; and then another, from Ullman to the phone call. He added several ornate question marks. That would account neatly for the three viruses. Weil. Ullman. The Secret Six. And the phone call would have been one of them, too. Probably not Ullman, though. Bravado was not his style. He sketched in the remaining arrows, studied the results, and sighed.

He tore the top two pages off the pad and ran them through the shredder. It was standard practice at the end of any meeting to shred any used pages off the fixed notepads at each seat, but only Kennison had the imagination to shred the blank sheet beneath that. Then he leaned back in his chair and stretched. He rose and walked around the table, tearing the top sheets off the notepads at the other places. Then he returned to his seat and rubbed each one carefully with the side of his pencil point.

Brother Nathaniel Johnson had, as usual, taken no notes. There were advantages to having a subordinate as stolid and unimaginative as Johnson, but there were difficulties as well. It was hard to discern what such a man was thinking; or if, indeed, he was thinking at all.

Cheng's pad revealed several Chinese characters. Ah, the Inscrutable Oriental! Kennison had once taken the step of seeking the translation for the characters he had found on Cheng's pad and discovered that, loosely translated, they read: "Nosy, aren't we?" He smiled to himself. There were advantages and disadvantages also to having clever subordinates.

Selkirk's pad yielded a series of ornate and interlocked Qs surrounded by vines and flowers. Kennison loved expressive doodles and kept a practicing psychiatrist on retainer in case there were hidden meanings in them. One never knew when such information might prove useful.

Mentally, he added "Q file" to his own, now-shredded doodle. That was another fragment of information on the viruses. The Secret Six's "Quinn" file? Possible. Possible.

As he left the conference room, he nodded to Cheng, who was in his office working at his terminal. Johnson, by the mainframe, was going down a checklist with the head programmer. Kennison knocked on the window of the computer room and waved to them both. He stopped at a few workstations on his way through and exchanged pleasantries with the staff, asking after spouses or children or hobbies. The common touch was a good thing to cultivate. People might not follow a leader with a vision, but they would follow one who remembered their birthdays and anniversaries.

The washroom elevator lifted him silently to the upper washroom. He walked to the door but froze with it only partly open. Alan was using the terminal in Kennison's office, talking in a very animated fashion. Kennison closed the washroom door carefully and leaned his ear against it.

"We'll need an entire mainframe core, I tell you," said the muffled voice. Kennison had to strain to make out the words. "Yes. That's confirmed. They were headquartered in Oberlin, Ohio." Pause. "No, I *don't* know where they are now." Pause. "Awareness is too widespread, but I think we can salvage something. . . . No, don't worry. I can take care of myself." Pause. "*You* did that? Was that wise?" A long pause. "I see. Och, aye. You were quite right. You didna ha'e a choice, not if they were going to discuss *him.* What about Bernstein? Does he know . . . ? Good. Let's keep it that way. And French . . . ? Very well. Adieu."

Kennison waited a decent interval, then went to the stall and flushed the toilet. At the sink, he splashed icy cold water in his face. He leaned his hands on both sides of the basin and gasped. Then he yanked a paper towel off the dispenser and covered his face. When he pulled it away, he looked at the dark designs the water had made, as if he could see in them his own visage. Then he wadded the towel into a ball and slammed it into the trash can, yanked open the office door, and walked into an empty office.

He lowered himself into the chair—*his* chair, dammit. And *his* desk. Then he punched up a number on the terminal. *Carefully, Daniel.* To whom had Alan been talking?

"Yes. Bertie? . . . Kennison here. Could you have my limo brought around? I'll be coming down in a few minutes. . . . Thank you." He depressed the cutoff, punched in another number.

"Madam Butler? . . . I will be leaving the offices shortly. Could you please inform Cook? . . . Yes, thank you." This time, when he cut off he continued talking. "Do you know what Cook is preparing?" he said into the silent handset. He quickly tapped in the code that displayed the most recent numbers called. A glance at the screen confirmed what he had feared. There was no record of the call that Alan had just completed.

"I see," he said aloud. "Well, it sounds delicious. I shall

look forward to it. Good-bye, Madam Butler." He replaced
the handset. On his shredded doodle pad, he placed a mental
question mark beside Selkirk's name. A very large question
mark.

"I can take care of myself," Selkirk had said.

Can you now? Kennison wondered.

VI

"Miss Bennett!" said the concierge. "We're so glad to
see you back."

Sarah looked at the slim, elegantly dressed white woman.
She had never seen her before in her life. "Thank you, Helen," she said. "I do love San Francisco. I wish I could come
more often, but—" A wave of the hand. "The press of business, you know." She turned to the bellman and handed him
her key. "Take my trunks to the suite, would you please?
The gray one goes in the sitting room, the black in the bedroom. Have I had any messages, Helen?"

The concierge pulled an envelope from a pigeonhole. "A
Mr. Caldero phoned. He wants you to phone him as soon as
it would be convenient." The bellman was out of earshot,
and the concierge added sotto voce, "Your suite is clean. The
boy's name is José. He's not one of us, but you met him
when 'you' were here two years ago. And Brother Caldero
checked in three hours ago. He has the suite just below
yours."

Sarah did not break character. "Thank you, Helen." She
took the envelope. "Could you phone Mr. Caldero and ask
him if he would lunch with me in . . ." She checked her
watch. "Oh, say forty-five minutes, in my suite. Have a light
meal put together. Sandwiches and cold cuts. Mineral water.
You know what to do."

"Certainly, Miss Bennett."

"Thank you." She walked quickly to her suite, where she
removed her gloves and hat. The bellman was waiting.

"That's fine, José. It's nice to see you again." She tipped him twenty.

He touched his pillbox cap with two fingers. "It's nice to have you back with us, ma'am."

When he was gone she went to one of the plush chairs and sagged into it. She took several deep breaths to still the thumping of her heart. This was method acting with a vengeance. She wasn't just acting a part; or even living a part. She *was* the part. She *was* Gloria Bennett.

Only a handful of people in San Francisco knew otherwise. Helen was one; so was a man named Frank Chu on the building maintenance staff, who took care of the private suites. But she did not dare fall out of character with them. She would have to be careful to maintain the persona at all times, even among friends. She did not think she could switch the role on and off without becoming careless.

Sarah rose from the chair and wandered to the window. The bellman had opened the curtains and Sarah gazed out over the city. In the foreground stood Telegraph Hill and Russian Hill, the former crowned with the graceful fluted concrete pillar of Coit Tower. A cluster of trees formed a bush of greenery at the base of the tower. In the distance, the blue waters of San Francisco Bay lay tranquil and flat, and beyond them, in the morning mist, the hazy wilds of the Marin headlands. The panorama was framed on the right by the Bay Bridge and on the left by the Golden Gate Bridge. It was a vista she knew she could never tire of. Most of the houses were light-colored, and the whole town seemed to shine in the sun.

A knock on the door announced the arrival of room service, followed closely by "Jimmy Caldero." Red set his bulky briefcase on the floor and threw his arms wide. "Gloria! It has been too long." Sarah stepped into his arms and he hugged her.

"Jimmy," she said. "You old scoundrel. What have you been up to?" Over his shoulder, she saw SuperNerd. "And who is this?" She disengaged from Red's embrace. *A pimple-*

faced chaperon, that's who. Red, you're a . . . But she couldn't think of a word to describe Red.

"Do you remember that computer project we discussed over the phone? This is one of my star programmers. Norris Bosworth; Gloria Bennett."

SuperNerd extended a hesitant hand. "Glad to meet you," he said.

"That's fine," Red told the room service girl. "Leave it like that. We'll serve ourselves." He waved Sarah away. "No, Gloria, I insist." He tipped the girl generously and she left.

When the door had closed, Red threw himself onto the sofa and laid his arms out along its back. "I'll have roast beef, mustard, cheese, and a slice of tomato, on rye."

Sarah handed a plate to Bosworth. "Make your own sandwich, Jimmy," she said over her shoulder. "I'm not your maid."

Red grinned and looked around the suite. "Be that way. How do you like your digs?"

"Plush. I saw them so often on the training videos that it's like I've already been here."

"You have," Red reminded her. "Several times. Helen will cue you in on any of the little details that didn't make it into the training material." He roused himself and ambled to the lunch cart. He picked at the cold cuts on the platter. "Is this the best they could do? Maybe we should send out for pizza."

Bosworth sat in the plush chair and balanced his sandwich plate on his knees. Sarah found a chair by the writing desk and set her plate there. She watched Red pile things into his sandwich. "When do we meet with Kennison?" she asked.

"In a little while," he replied.

"Is he coming here?"

"In a way." He turned and bit into his sandwich. Juice from the tomato ran down his chin and he wiped it with his napkin. "Meanwhile, don't you want to hear what the kid found out?" He gestured to Bosworth. "Go ahead. Tell her." To Sarah: "You'll love this."

SuperNerd glanced from Sarah to Red and back. "Brother Polovsky and I finished the factor analysis on the European anomalies. We had a pretty good base to start from, using the items you remembered from the French list. But it turned out Carson was wrong after all. He thought he had identified a third factor, but it was really a confounding of two others: the Six's domestic efforts plus some European spin-off that impacted over here. You know how tricky factor analysis can be. There are miscalcu—" He caught the look on Red's face. "Anyway, we think we've identified four sets of 'tracks' in the European digraph."

"Four?" Then she laughed. "Four? Oh, that's priceless!"

"Yeah," said Red sourly. "Might as well ask who *wasn't* inventing cliology back then."

"As nearly as we can tell," Bosworth continued, "one of them aborted almost immediately. Probably broke up from internal dissension. Two of the others fissioned sometime during the last quarter of the century. Carson's Dilemma."

"Hmm," said Sarah. "About the same time as the Six and the Babbage Society."

"That's right." SuperNerd nodded eagerly. "The distribution of times to failure is shaping up into a nice PDF. An extreme value distribution. I think—"

"Stick to the point, kid. Gloria can get the details later, if she wants to."

Bosworth turned to Sarah. "There were five tracks left going into the war era. I lost one during the first war, and two more petered out during the second. And guess what? The Nazis actually uncovered one of those and destroyed it."

"What?" Sarah saw that Red was surprised, too.

"You didn't tell me that," he said.

"My search engine reported in just before we left," the teenager replied. "I thought I'd save it as a surprise."

"Yeah?" Red thought about it for a while. "I don't like surprises."

"You guys have no sense of drama. Anyway, I moused into the old Nazi files just to see if I could turn up a cross reference, and I found a thick dossier on a group called the Gemeinschaft für der historische Wissenschaft, or GHW. They were headquartered in Vienna, and somehow Röhm and his SA goons got onto them. The GHW were wealthy and several key members were Jews. I mean, the Nazis were always anti-Semites, but this really set them off. Jews and bankers running the world. Himmler rounded them all up, even the 'Aryan' members. I think Röhm tried to make a deal with them, because Himmler grabbed the whole SA organization, too."

"The Night of the Long Knives," said Red. "Then there was more to it than intramural rivalry between the SA and the SS."

"It seems that way."

"And you found this file in the German archives?" Sarah asked.

"Ganz bestimmt, gnädige Frau," Bosworth replied. "Auf Generalstaatsarchiv Berlin."

She looked at Red. "Then the German government must know something."

Red frowned and looked uncertain. "Maybe," he allowed. "But those old records were scanned in using automatic character recognition algorithms. Could be that nobody actually looked at them. A lot of Germans go three sides around the barn to avoid noticing anything from those days. There was some fuss about putting Nazi-era records into the Net at all. It was only pressure from France and Poland and Israel that forced them to do it." He shook his head. "You sure have managed to shake things up, lady."

"Things were always this way, Jim. You just never knew it."

"Yeah, I suppose you're right. I guess it's better, knowing about them." Red turned back to Bosworth. "All right, finish up. Tell her about the last two societies."

Bosworth shrugged. "Nothing left to tell. One of the two survivors vanished in the sixties."

"And then there was one," Red announced with a flourish.

"It's hard to discover 'horseshoe nails' more recent than that," Bosworth reminded them. "It can take decades for the spin-offs to appear."

"Mmmm," Red nodded thoughtfully. He looked at Sarah. "Speculate."

"One of the survivors stumbled onto the other and wiped it out."

"Or vice versa. Yeah, that's what Norris and I thought." It was the first time Red hadn't called Bosworth 'kid,' and Sarah noticed how the teenager sat up straighter.

"And then the winner began wondering if there were any other rivals around," Bosworth said. "Like in North America."

Red pursed his lips. "Makes sense. So they fish around for a couple decades until the Internet starts up."

"They must have planted a parasite inside the Net," said Sarah. "Something that randomly sampled police files, reporters' notes, things like that, and tested for the sorts of patterns that a secret society would make. Like the trail of bodies the Weils left behind."

"Yeah. Then you turned on the lights, and they saw us, too. Well, at least we know how many others we're dealing with. The Secret Six, their daughter, and this European gang."

"Call them the Q," Sarah suggested.

Red was tapping his teeth with his thumbnail, looking thoughtful. He glanced at Sarah and nodded. "What? Oh. OK. The Q. It's as good a name as any." He paused, looked down, and rubbed his hands together. "Norris, I want you to go all out on locating the Q when you get back to Buffalo Creek. If they do have a parasite in the Net like Gloria thinks, it must be pretty well camouflaged. I don't think the regulars will pick it out, so give them a hand."

"Sure thing, Brother Caldero. I think I'll start with a survey of the scientists who were around in the early eighteen-hundreds. Find out who was capable of putting a show together. Those old records aren't camouflaged as well."

"OK, but be discreet. Don't let 'em trace the worms back to the ranch. They sound as dangerous as Weil was. Christ, the way that Howard woman killed herself . . ." He shivered.

"Howard must have reported in," said Sarah, "don't you think?"

Red glanced at her. "Maybe not. We watch recruits pretty closely."

"You let her go riding up in the mountains," she pointed out.

"Sure, but there aren't any phones up there." He grinned and looked back at Bosworth. "Be discreet anyway, would you, kid? I don't like taking chances."

The device Red attached to the windowpane looked like a giant suction cup. Sarah watched him plug the wires into their sockets and run them to a speaker and cassette recorder.

"I don't believe it," she said.

"Believe it. Here, help me aim this thing." He stepped aside and Sarah came closer. "There. Look through that and tell me where the crosshairs are." Red bent over the dials on the cassette recorder.

Sarah closed one eye and squinted through the eyepiece with the other. Telegraph Hill swam into view. "I can see Coit Tower," she said.

"Too far east. Turn that knob. No, no, not that one. The third one in."

"You've got enough knobs on this thing."

"We're on Nob Hill, ain't we?"

She heard SuperNerd stifle a laugh behind her. "That's really funny, Jimbo," she told him. "You should be on the Leno show." She turned the vernier and her view shifted slowly. "What am I looking for?"

"That tall building on Greenwich. Thirteenth floor—except they call it the fourteenth. Second window in from the right."

Sarah looked out the window and spotted the building. Then she put her eye back to the vernier. "That's Kennison Demographics?"

"No," said Red. "It's an apartment he's rented under an assumed name."

Sarah shook her head. "I know I'm new to this game, but wouldn't it be easier if we just drove over there?" She got the crosshairs lined up on the window. "Got it!"

"OK, lock it in." Red did something to the speaker and it began to hiss. "No, it wouldn't be easier. Because we don't know who's watching. He doesn't want to be seen with us because Ullman might wonder; and, frankly, I don't want to be seen with him, either."

"Because of Ullman?"

"No, because I'm particular about who I'm seen with."

"Oh, come on, Jim. I only met him the one time, but he wasn't so bad."

"For a multiple murderer, you mean?"

"I didn't say I approved of him."

"Hell, Sarah. You've never said you approved of me."

She looked at him in surprise. He was hunched over his equipment. "You just broke character, Red."

Red scowled at his knobs. He made an adjustment. "So, Danny Boy is paranoid. He called me from a public phone booth. Says he doesn't have anyone else he can trust, and can I come out here with a computer expert? How could I refuse such a touching plea?"

"I understand that, but why the parabolic mikes?" She gestured at the elaborate equipment Red had pulled from his briefcase.

"Kennison's mopped his apartment and it's clear, but autonomous search engines in the phone system—government, the Society, who knows who else—sift the traffic for key words. This way, Danny can sit in his apartment and talk to thin air. Our mike reads the vibrations of his window and translates them into sound. We talk to him the same way. No one can listen in unless they've got parabolics and know which windows to aim them at."

He flipped a switch and a voice issued from the speakers. ". . . know you're there. I can hear you talking. Can you hear me? Answer, God damn it."

The speakers squealed and Red jumped to a knob and twisted it. "Feedback," he explained. "He's picking up his own voice from our speakers. And we're picking it up from him." He faced the window. "Cut in your filter, dammit!"

The squealing cut to a low hiss. "Is that better?"

Red found a seat on the sofa. He leaned back and put his arms behind his head. "Copacetic, Danny. No, Gloria," he added, "don't bother with the recorder. It's voice-activated. Kicks in automatically."

"You're recording this?" Kennison's voice trembled ever so slightly.

"Sure. Aren't you?"

"I wish you would not."

"OK." Red waited a beat. "There. It's off. Now, what did you want?" He ignored Sarah's accusing look but scribbled something on a notepad he had placed on the arm of the sofa. He handed the pad to her and she read it:

All's fair in love and war.

And which was this? Sarah wondered.

Kennison told them about the Council election—of which they had heard only rumors. About Selkirk's plan, and his apparent treachery. Red scribbled another note: *Carson's Dilemma: The Society is fracturing again.* He looked positively gleeful. So Sarah took the pad from him and wrote back: *So are the Associates. Red's cabal.* And Red didn't think that was nearly as funny.

"So why do you need the Associates, Cousin? You thinking of joining us?" Red made gagging gestures, pointing down his throat with two fingers.

"I don't need the Associates, only you and your friend."

"You'll get by with a little help from your friends, is that it?"

"Exactly."

"Gee, Danny. It would help if you had some friends."

"I know where Dennis French is."

Sarah jerked as if an electric shock had run through her.

She turned and faced the window. She could see Kennison's apartment on Telegraph Hill. The morning sun sparkled in the windows. She squinted her eyes against the brightness. "Where is he?" she asked. She felt silly talking to the empty air. Kennison was a ghost in the room.

"Ah, Miss Bennett. How are you? Are you the computer expert James brought?"

"Never mind that! Where is Dennis?"

"Will you help me?" Red was making warning motions with his hands.

"Yes. Now talk." Red gave an exasperated shrug, but Sarah ignored him.

"Very well. But first things first." There was a long moment of hesitation before Kennison spoke again. "I have decided to leave the Society and strike out on my own. And I plan to take my company with me."

Sarah looked at Red, who raised his eyebrows. "That would be a neat trick, Danny. Especially if you also plan to survive." Red was scribbling furiously on his notepad.

"I plan to proceed in four steps. Firstly, under a secret persona that I maintain, I will purchase an established firm dealing in, say, securities or market consulting. A company that might plausibly establish a public opinion subsidiary. Secondly, I will copy the KD data banks to that new base. Thirdly, I will corrupt the original database so that it will be useless to Ullman and his ilk. Fourthly, I shall die and be resurrected in my new persona."

"After three days?" said Red.

"As long as it takes," said Kennison.

"And where do we come in?"

"I had originally planned to use my protegé, Alan Selkirk, for the computer work. His original plan, as I told you, was simply to feed corrupted data to the Council, while hiding a 'clean' database in a secret location. He does not know that I plan to take it a step further, and I have no intention of telling him. I no longer trust him. I suspect he is in collusion with either Ullman or your Secret Six. That's why I need your people: to verify the integrity of my system and to help me copy it into the host system that I select."

"The job sounds simple enough," Red told the window-pane.

"I would also like your help," the windowpane replied, "to set up the deal with the target company. To avoid attracting undue attention to myself, it would be best to create an ar-bitrage consortium with several partners."

"Hmmm." Red glanced at Sarah and Bosworth. "We could call it Caldero, Bennett, and . . . ?" He let the sentence hang, and there was a moment of tentative silence.

"Caldero, Bennett, and Ochs," said Kennison after a while. "Fletcher Ochs will be the name of your junior partner."

"I look forward to meeting him," Red commented dryly. "Have you selected a target yet?"

"As a matter of fact, I have several in mind; but there is one that looks especially promising, an investment firm with an already-impressive record of successes. It will not look unduly suspicious if we take it over and begin using cliol-ogical analysis to increase its earnings. No one is surprised when the rich grow richer. Nor would it be unreasonable for them to establish a market research arm. It would mesh quite nicely with their profile."

"Uh-huh. Does this firm have a name?"

"Yes. Detweiler, Barron, and Stone."

"Never heard of them."

"They are an old Boston firm, but they trade on the New York and Chicago exchanges as well." A long pause and a sigh. "Boston, alas, is not San Francisco, but it is as close as the East Coast can come to it."

Sarah drifted to the window. She looked out and across to Kennison's apartment. The hills, the sparkling white city, the Golden Gate. Genuine sentiment from a monster she had not expected. "You'll miss San Francisco, won't you?"

"Who would not? There is not another city like her, Miss Bennett. Not in all the world. Rudyard Kipling once said that her chief drawback was the difficulty of leaving."

Red was humming the old Tony Bennett tune. "I left my heart . . ." Sarah turned and scowled at him and he grinned and shut up. Red shouldn't make fun of anyone's private loves, not even Kennison's.

"All right," Red announced. "I'll set up a lunch with the Detweiler people. How do you know they want to sell?"

"I don't, but everyone has a price. We need only find it out and offer it to them."

"Yeah? No horse heads in the bed, though. OK? That's not our style. How do we get in touch with Fletcher Ochs to let him know about the meeting?"

"I'll contact you when it is safe."

"Look; it's your neck we're trying to save. There's nothing in it for us."

"There is Dennis French."

"Yeah. If you really know where he is."

"By the time we close the deal, I'll know."

They left the monitoring gear in place. Just in case, Red told them. However, he attached several small devices resembling mechanical spiders to the window. When he turned them on, their legs began tapping. Red explained that by setting up a large number of unsynchronized vibrations in the windowpane, he could frustrate any attempt to "read" conversations in the room. The net result of so many random patterns was that they canceled one another out.

He asked Bosworth to stand watch while he took Sarah to dinner. If he got bored, he could work on the computer problem Kennison had outlined. Bosworth gave them a look but didn't object. "You kids have fun," he said. "But be sure to bring her back before midnight."

For some reason, Red thought that was funny.

When they entered the elevator Red pressed the button for his own floor.

Sarah looked at him. "Did you forget something?" she asked.

"No," he said.

The door opened and he led her to his suite, where there was a dinner table set up for two in his sitting room. A single red rose in a bud vase adorned the white tablecloth. The meals, under cover, sat under portable heat lamps. The drapes were drawn, the room lit by twin candles in golden holders.

Sarah looked at the arrangement. "I thought you were taking me out to dinner."

"I couldn't get a reservation."

"Isn't this a little intimate?"

"No, it's a lot intimate. Does that bother you? I could have the hotel staff serve us." He held a chair out for her.

She sighed and sat down. "Just don't get any ideas."

"Hell, I haven't had an idea like that since June of 1990."

Sarah noticed how he wouldn't meet her eyes. She watched him load a CD into the player. There was a lot about himself that Red kept hidden. There was a wall of glass between them. She could see him, hear him. She could get as close to him as she wanted; but somehow, she couldn't touch him.

Red pressed the play button and a lone harp filled the air. Not a concert harp, with its thrumming resonances; but a curious, metallic-sounding harp that made her think of castles and kings.

"It's a clairseach," Red explained when she asked. "An Irish harp, strung in brass and played with the nails. The music is Ó Carolan. He lived in the late seventeen-hundreds. The last of the old Gaelic harpers. This particular piece is called 'Ó Flainn.' "

They ate in silence, enjoying the food and enjoying the music. Red broke the silence only occasionally, to announce a song title. Ancient half-remembered melodies passed along by country fiddle players, resurrected by mountain cloggers and Delta bluesmen. She glanced at Red across the table and he smiled and nodded to her. Somehow, there was nothing uncomfortable in their lack of conversation.

She thought about Kennison's appeal for help. He was a strange bird. Repulsive, but at the same time attractive. Half devil, and half gentleman. But of course wasn't the Devil always portrayed as a gentleman? Kennison was a kingpin of the Society, yet now he wanted out. Not from moral revulsion, but simply because his ambitions had been thwarted. And Red would help him, not because he approved of Kennison's ambitions, but because he would do anything to thwart the Society's program. And so, for the moment, the three of them were curiously wary allies. She wondered if Kennison really did have a line on Dennis' whereabouts. He had asked her to bug his own telephone at Kennison Demographics, but how would that help locate Dennis?

The music paused and Red cocked his head to the speakers. "This next one's called 'Fanny Power.' Fanny was the daughter of Ó Carolan's patron and he wrote this piece for her wedding. I wanted you to hear it because I didn't want you to think that there was only one perfect melody in the world." He laid his silverware aside and leaned his arms on the table. He stared into infinity.

The music began simply, with a melody of unaffected grace that floated through the upper registers. It was followed by a lower-pitched countermelody that complemented it. Then the harpist began alternating the phrases, ornamenting them with grace notes and arpeggios of crystalline elegance. Gradually the music became fuller and grander, swelling to a great climax from which the original, simple melody emerged. Then the harp fell silent, the overtones shimmering in the air.

Red was still for a few moments; then, as the CD began another cut, he shook himself. "Well?" he asked. "What did you think?"

Sarah was surprised to see that his eyes were moist. "She must have been very beautiful."

He looked at her. "Who?" And his voice was suddenly wary.

"Why, Fanny." Sarah sighed. "There is magic in that old man's music, if it can move us to tears for the beauty of a woman two centuries dead."

"Ah, yes. Fanny." There was a distant look in Red's eyes and she sensed the sadness in his voice. "I suppose she was. Beautiful, that is. But beauty is in the eye of the beholder, you know; and Ó Carolan was blind."

VII

"Saudi Arabia?" Adrian Detweiler the Fifth worked his
lips and looked from face to face around the conference table. "Saudi Arabia," the old man repeated.

Red kept his face composed and let Kennison handle the
discussion. Not that it mattered. It was already obvious that
the old man was not going to sell, that he never would sell,
that he had never had any intention of selling. Not when you
were the fifth consecutive Adrian Detweiler and the Firm had
been in your family for a century and a half.

Red glanced at Sarah, who was sitting on Kennison's far
side, and shrugged with his eyebrows; and she gave him a
"who knows?" look in return. So. Sarah had drawn the same
conclusion as he. The negotiations were a charade. A waste
of time. Only Kennison seemed oblivious to that fact. But
then, of course, to Fletcher Ochs this was a life-or-death affair.

"Saudi Arabia," said Detweiler, "is considered to be quite
a safe investment."

Now why, Red wondered, were they so taken up with this
one projection? Kennison had argued—and Sarah had
agreed—that they must prove themselves more astute than
the normal corporate suitor. A firm as successful as D, B,
and S was not going to sell out to amateurs. So, they had
prepared a number of projections dramatic enough to impress
Detweiler with their insight.

Kennison smiled. "Sir, we do not wish to divulge our
methods. Suffice it to say that we rely on unusually keen
intelligence of conditions there. A fundamentalist revolution
is imminent, say within the next five years. We have been
divesting ourselves quietly from our own interests."

"Have you?" Detweiler smacked his lips. He frowned and
turned to the man beside him. "Mr. Stone, what have you to
say?"

"Snake oil, sir," answered the younger partner in a high, nasal "Ha'va'd" accent. "And were Mrs. Barron heah, she would say the same, I am sure." He faced Kennison. "This is Boston, Mr. Ochs. We don't care for your slick Manhattan ways, with your fast money and your faster bankruptcies. D, B, and S has gotten along quite nicely for over a hundred and fifty yeahs doing business the old-fashioned way." The gallery of portraits that lined the D, B, and S boardroom frowned their agreement. Stolid, dour New England paintings hung on stolid, dour New England walls. Adrian Detweilers, I through IV, scowled importantly from the dark oak panels. Red wondered what it was like to have numbered ancestors.

Sarah leaned forward. "Is it part of the old-fashioned Boston way to gratuitously insult one's guests?"

Detweiler looked at her. "I beg your pardon, Miss Bennett?"

"What Miss Bennett means—," said Kennison, with a nervous glance at Sarah.

"I am quite capable of saying what I mean, Fletcher." She fixed her eye on Stone. "I agreed to buy in on this deal," she said, "because it looked like a good investment and a way of attaining certain objectives I have set in my personal life. We believe that, among the three of us, we have valuable resources that can enhance this firm's position. I cut short a vacation trip to San Francisco to be at this meeting. It was a long flight and a tiring one, and I do not appreciate being called a 'snake-oil salesman.' And, Mr. Stone, I, too, made my money the old-fashioned way. But I started from ground zero. Did you?"

Detweiler did not take his eyes off Sarah. He rubbed his hand through his white Commodore Vanderbilt beard. Then he nodded and smiled in a grandfatherly way. "Apologize to the lady, if you please, Mr. Stone. There's a good fellow."

Stone shot his partner a quick glance, then bowed his head. "I am sorry. I spoke unkindly. But it is our Firm's position that takeover mania has been the bane of American business. It squanders capital better spent in research and maintenance of equipment, and works to the benefit of no one but the

Japanese and the Europeans. We refuse to be a part of it."

As an apology, thought Red, it had shortcomings; but he knew that Sarah had made the insult an issue to put Detweiler on the defensive. *It's a good thing we have her.* She had spent more time in the rough-and-tumble of business than either he or Kennison. *We should have made her the chief negotiator.* Detweiler, he was sure, had recognized her ploy and had disposed of the issue quickly rather than wrangle over it. In fact, Red wondered if Stone's insult had been just as calculated.

Detweiler continued to watch Sarah, to Red's growing annoyance. Just what did the old man find so fascinating about her? He hadn't taken his eyes off her since she had first spoken. Was he a Dirty Old Man? That Detweiler might find Sarah attractive was vaguely unsettling.

Forget it, he told himself. These old-family Boston Brahmins never crossed the color line, except to diddle the occasional maid. And besides, what business was it of his?

He decided that there was only one reason to meet with a prospective buyer when you had no intention of selling. And that was an intense interest in the buyers themselves. *They didn't want this meeting to sell us their company. They just wanted to meet us. Perhaps to do some polite sniffing. "Not interested just now, thank you; not in this deal. But maybe we can do other business together."*

If we can't buy D, B, and S outright, we might be able to form a joint venture, say in demographic polling. A joint venture would suit Red, but he wasn't sure what Kennison would say. The symbols of power meant as much to him as the power itself. Red didn't mind if Kennison owned his own hidey-hole or just "rented" it from D, B, and S, so long as he sabotaged the Society in the process; but Kennison probably minded a great deal.

Normally, Red wouldn't care what Kennison minded; but Kennison had some sort of lead on Dennis French's whereabouts, and that meant Sarah cared. He hated depending on Kennison for anything. There was something unclean about the man. And he was most repellent when he acted the most charming.

Detweiler was polite but firm. Stone was equally firm and considerably less polite. Barron had not even attended the meeting. When Detweiler, at last, formally declined the proposal, Kennison started to raise the ante, but Red and Sarah both kicked him under the table. Never show your opponent how eager you are. Even Red knew that much about buying and selling.

Furthermore, he suspected that old Detweiler would be offended by an offer of more money. The suggested price had been a fair one. Both parties recognized that. But Detweiler's refusal had been predicated on principles, and people didn't sell those for cash. For other considerations, maybe; but never for cash.

The meeting ended amicably at precisely two o'clock. Even Kennison managed to project affable good loser-ship. Detweiler served highballs. They toasted one another's good fortune and parted in a flurry of handshakes. Detweiler—the old goat!—even gave Sarah a kiss on the cheek.

They walked down the hallway and through the accounting department. Sarah had taken Red by the arm, as if he were her escort; and Red felt an odd tingle at the light touch of her glove on his sleeve. He glanced back once and saw Stone and Detweiler in animated conversation, partly framed in the doorway of the boardroom.

Sarah's grip tightened on his arm. He glanced at her, but she said nothing. Yet he could see that she was alarmed. He scanned the office looking for the source; but there were only the staff accountants and analysts, displaying various degrees of disinterest in the departing guests.

He turned to her again and looked a question. "Later," she whispered.

They picked a small coffee shop on a side street just off State in Boston's downtown. Red ordered three cups, cream, no sugar. When the waitress was gone, he spread his hands out. "Well, it was a nice try. What's next, Fletch? You had some alternate choices, didn't you?"

Kennison didn't touch his coffee. "Several," he admitted, "but none as suitable as this one. Detweiler's record of success would have been admirable camouflage. With the other firms on my list, it would draw unwelcome attention if we became too wealthy too fast. Raise questions better unasked."

"Well, patience is all," Red told him. "The important thing is to get you set up on your own. Someplace where They won't think to look for you."

"No," said Sarah, "the important thing is to find out what D, B, and S is up to."

It was an unexpected remark. He looked at her and saw that she was staring into her cup like a tea reader. "What did you see back there?" he asked.

"Jeremy Collingwood."

"Who?"

Kennison's head jerked up. "Collingwood? From Denver? But he was killed, wasn't he? What was he doing there?"

Because D, B, and S has a really good retirement program. . . . Red fought the impulse to say that aloud. There was a moment of silence. The cash register at the lunch counter rang and the cashier made some remark to a departing customer. The men at the counter laughed. The bells on the entrance door jingled. Kennison frowned and took a sip of his coffee. "Are you certain?"

Sarah shook her head. "I didn't know him all that well, but I couldn't be mistaken."

"This Collingwood fellow may have survived the explosion," Kennison said, "and come out here simply to make a break with the past."

Sarah shook her head. "No, he wouldn't have given up looking for Dennis."

"At Detweiler, Barron, and Stone?" asked Kennison.

Sarah reached across the table and grasped Red's wrist. "Jimmy. What if they're players?"

"Who? Detweiler?" That smiling grandfather in the three-piece suit? He couldn't imagine the old man as a player. He didn't have the demeanor for it. Stone. Now, Stone was a different matter. The younger partner had had a coldness about him.

"Yes. What if they rescued Jeremy from the bombing?"

"Why would they do that?" asked Kennison.

"Maybe because they don't like people being killed," she shot back at him.

"Then why," Kennison replied reasonably, "would they not rescue everyone?"

"OK, maybe Jeremy survived the explosion on his own. The DU study team discovered something and were killed for it, but Jeremy has tracked Dennis to D, B, and S."

"Never mind that now," Red said. Christ, they could yack about this till the cows came home. They could create and demolish a thousand scenarios and none of them would be right. They needed some hard facts. "OK," he decided. "We need to talk to Collingwood, and we need to know more about D, B, and S. Our people here in Boston can find out where Collingwood is living and plant a bug there, and I'll have Bosworth mouse into D, B, and S's background."

"How soon?" asked Sarah.

"Let us not be hasty," said Kennison. "If they are players, we do not want to alarm them. And if Collingwood is with them incognito, we would not want to blow his cover."

Red smiled. Kennison was worried that they would get another line on French's whereabouts, and that if they did he would lose his leverage with Sarah.

Don't worry, Danny Boy. I would never pass up the chance to corrupt your database. But he couldn't resist a chance to make Kennison sweat, either. He downed the rest of his coffee in a gulp and stood. "How soon?" He flipped open his cell phone. "How about right now?"

He entered a private encryption key and dialed an 800 number. The voice that answered wasted no time in pleasantries but asked him curtly for his number. Red turned away from Kennison and entered his own code and Bosworth's code at the ranch.

He waited impatiently for the connection. Kennison was right about one thing. Haste did make waste. If D, B, and S was the Secret Six—or an outpost of the European gang— it would not do to flail around at random. This called for some very discreet mousing.

Bosworth came on the line. "Brother Caldero. I just left a message for you at your hotel—"

"Never mind the small talk, kid. We've got a job for you. Priority One."

"This is an emergency, Jimmy."

Jimmy? Red held the phone away from his face and looked into the speaker. Whatever Bosworth was about to say, he wasn't going to like it. "All right, kid. You got my attention."

"The trip wires on 'Caldero' and 'Bennett' went off this afternoon. Someone tried to mouse into your confidential files. You know. Social Security. Birth records."

"What about 'Ochs'?" Kennison jerked his head up and looked alarmed.

"Was I supposed to watch that file, too?"

"Yeah. Politics makes strange bedfellows." And they didn't get much stranger than Dan Kennison. "Where'd the balloon go up, and when?"

"Give me half a sec. I'll call it up." There was a pause. "An Internet node in Boston at, uh, two-thirty-five this afternoon. They didn't access anything sensitive."

Two-thirty-five. Right after they had left Detweiler's office. Well, well. They didn't waste any time. He had to give them that.

"Here it comes," said Bosworth. "Let me check this." A pause. "You were right. The same terminal tried to access the 'Ochs' files, too. Any idea who it was?"

"Yeah, I think so. But I'm not sure why." He briefed Bosworth on their visit to D, B, and S and the mysterious presence there of Jeremy Collingwood. "Can you worm your way into their system and mouse around for us? Without them knowing it?"

"Does the Pope wear a funny hat?"

"All right. Find out whatever you can. On the QT. Then meet us in the suite in San Francisco, say . . . Thursday."

"Can do, chief."

Red hooked the phone and stood quietly for a few moments, trying to get his thoughts straight. So, D, B, and S was checking up on them, were they? A legitimate firm might dig into the backgrounds of people they dealt with. But if that was the case, why do it after turning down their offer? There had to be more to it.

It was useless to speculate. Never go beyond the data on hand. Don't guess until the guess is reasonable. He had forgotten that precept only once, and look what it had gotten him. No, the only things to go on were the facts: A. Someone in Boston was poking into things. B. They had done so immediately after he and his companions had left D, B, and S. And C. Jeremy Collingwood was sitting in the accounting department there. And A plus B plus C equaled . . .

Who knew? He never was any damn good at algebra.

Jeremy was not precisely sure how he felt about being accepted into Detweiler, Barron, and Stone. It had not been exactly a free choice on either part. Not only that, but by an odd travesty of reason, he had been accepted as a leader of some sort—which only confirmed his previous judgement that D, B, and S were tyros. Still, it did put him one step closer to finding Dennis. He had resources now. He had powerful help. People whose own uncertainties made them want to find out as much as he did.

But why had Detweiler asked him to sit in the bull pen with the accountants? Accounting was the last thing on his mind these days.

Like the others, he glanced curiously at the departing trio of arbitrageurs. A rumor had been going around the office about a takeover bid, but Jeremy didn't see how that was possible. D, B, and S was privately held; and, considering the true nature of their business, it was inconceivable that the old man would sell.

The three visitors made an interesting impression. A tall, distinguished-looking gentleman. A short, stocky man, who would have looked more at home on a construction site than in a boardroom. A lithe black woman with braided hair. "Caldero, Bennett, and Ochs," the woman at the next desk whispered to him. Jeremy nodded. He wondered which was which. The black woman saw him watching her and stiffened. *Don't worry,* he thought. *You're not my type.*

When they were gone, Peter Stone appeared in the hallway. He crooked a finger at Jeremy. "Collingwood, step in here a moment, please."

Jeremy stood, shot his cuffs, and straightened his tie. He didn't much care for Peter Stone and, he suspected, the feeling was mutual. The man looked as if he used a lemon for Chap Stick. Stone stepped aside carefully as Jeremy entered the boardroom. Jeremy smiled to himself. *Don't worry; you're not my type, either,* he thought. Too dark and intense.

Old man Detweiler shook his hand briskly. No reserve there. No buried hostility. What was it about the old rich? Was it noblesse oblige, or was it just that they didn't have the insecurities of the nouveau? Detweiler was as obviously unafraid of a rabid homosexual attack as Stone obviously was.

He smiled and took a seat at the table next to Jennie Barron, Detweiler's daughter, who had also been summoned. Stone took the seat on her other side. Barron glanced sideways at Stone and shifted a little, and Jeremy suppressed a chuckle. Did Stone know that Barron reacted to him the same way that that he reacted to Jeremy? Probably not.

"Jeremy," said Detweiler. "Did you notice the tall black woman who just left? The one who calls herself Gloria Bennett?"

Jeremy turned to face the head of the table. He nodded cautiously. "Not particularly. But I did see her. Why?"

"Because my father is having paranoid fantasies," said Barron.

Jeremy looked over his shoulder at her.

"I tell you she is Sarah Beaumont," the old man insisted. "Before she left, I gave her a peck on the cheek, just so I could get a closer look. She has a scar right here. . . ." He ran his finger behind his left ear. "Typical of plastic surgery."

"Dad, millions of people have had plastic surgery! She didn't look at all like her pictures."

"Jeremy," said Detweiler, "did she look at all familiar? Normal plastic surgery, as my daughter knows so well, simply removes wrinkles or bobs noses. There are limits to what it can do. The nose. The cheeks. The skin around the eyes. But the underlying bony structure cannot be altered, short of a disfiguring accident. Think, Jeremy."

Sarah Beaumont? Dennis' partner? His pulse hammered and he began to feel light-headed. Was Detweiler right? He closed his eyes and conjured up Beaumont's face. Finally, he shook his head. "How can I tell? I didn't know why you wanted me out there or I would have—"

"I did not want to bias you. Ah . . ." He faced the door. "Did you get the photographs?"

Herkimer Vane and Gwynneth Llewellyn entered the boardroom. Vane was dressed in a doorman's uniform. He looked like a fleet admiral, splendid in ribbons and fourragère. Gwynn placed the glossies on the table. "We had a good look at them as they left the building. The other two are strangers, but there's no question that the tall gent was Daniel Kennison."

"Kennison?" said Stone. "Of Kennison Demographics? Why would he . . . Oh."

"Yes. Also Kennison allegedly of the Babbage Society."

"Then the black woman wasn't Beaumont," said Jeremy. "She blew the whistle on the Society. They killed her friend and tried to kill her and Dennis. She wouldn't be with them."

Detweiler shrugged. "I can imagine off the top of my head at least five scenarios in which she and Kennison would appear together. What I don't understand is why they appeared *here.* Our cliometricians have assured us that there is no hint in the historical record of our existence and none of our records touching on cliology are accessible from the Internet. So what is the Babbage Society doing at our door?"

"If the Babbage Society were at your door," said Gwynn, "your door would have been blown off its hinges."

A sudden knock made them all jump, and Jennie Barron giggled in embarrassment. Jim Doang entered with another man whom Jeremy did not know. The latter was dressed in the chasuble of the scientific priesthood. He said, "The public dossiers on the three people you asked about are clean. They all have a paper trail straight from birth to today. Nothing looks funny."

"Of course nothing 'looks funny,' " said Detweiler. "Except that Fletcher Ochs looks very much like Daniel Kennison."

The boardroom telephone warbled. Doang, who was closest, walked over and picked it up. He listened for a moment, then handed it to his companion. "It's for you." He took a seat at the board table next to Vane. "Hello, Herkimer. Gwynn."

Jeremy sensed a change in the atmosphere of the room. Barron and Stone seemed more reserved. They had greeted Vane politely but barely acknowledged Doang and Llewellyn. The new kids on the block. D, B, and S had been very comfortable for a very long time, and they didn't like the way their world had been turned topsy-turvy. And they especially did not like the prospect of direct, physical action represented by Jeremy and his friends. Even Vane, because of his association with them, was tainted. Only old Detweiler himself seemed unfazed, even exhilarated by the new uncertainty.

The computer man hung up the phone. "Bad news, chief. There's a mouse in our system."

Stone jerked around. "What? When? What is it doing?"

"What is it doing? It's mousing."

Stone pushed himself up from his chair. "Trace it, then!"

"We're on it. Don't worry."

"Don't worry? And how long was it in there before your people stumbled on it?"

The computer man looked at Stone carefully and addressed his answer to Detweiler. "It couldn't have been in there too long, chief. There are safeguards. The mouser, whoever he is, is pretty damned good; but our cat should catch him."

While they argued over computer security, Jeremy reached across the table and took the still of Gloria Bennett that Gwynn had taken as they left. He studied the jaws, the skull. He shook his head. He had met Sarah Beaumont only a few times. How could he hope to pick her out of a stranger's face? "Can we get a photograph of Beaumont for comparison?" he asked Gwynn.

She looked thoughtful. "We had a complete rogues' gallery on the study team. Every name in the printout for whom we could secure a photograph. That's how Herkimer and I recognized Kennison. I know Beaumont's was among them. But that's all gone now." Her face clouded at the memory. "It shouldn't be too hard to find her picture, though, all things considered."

He looked again at the photograph. *Beaumont, is that you in there? Do you know where Dennis is?* He laid the picture aside and wondered if he was finally nearing the end of his quest.

VIII

Kennison's life had been turned upside down. At one time he had been certain of everything, and his destiny had seemed assured. Now he was certain of nothing. He had been in control of affairs, but now affairs somehow controlled him. He cut and chewed his food without tasting it. *Baked chicken breasts à la Russe*. Marinated overnight in a sour-cream-and-cayenne paste, then carefully breaded and baked. Ordinarily he would have praised the meal, sent his compliments to Cook. He would have enjoyed Karin's presentation of the dishes. He would have smiled and joked. Now it all seemed a pointless sham. Daniel Kennison bon vivant? Daniel Kennison japing fool!

They had outmaneuvered him. All of them. Beaumont with her worm. Ullman. Ruiz. Selkirk, damn his insolent blackmailing hide! Even Weil had fooled him for a time, until her foolish lust for revenge had driven her to reveal herself.

He had, at least, that one victory to savor; and the savor was sweet, even though it had cost him his beloved Prudence. He saw now that Weil had gone utterly mad. Beaumont's exposures, Benton's murder, Ullman's and Ruiz's treachery had driven her over an edge that had never been any too distant. Even his own valiant attempts to salvage and protect the Society had been misconstrued in her savage and twisted mind.

And now, the ultimate comedy. After 160 years of carefully guarding the Secret, he found cliological societies crawling out from under every rock he turned over. The Secret Six. The Europeans, the ones that Beaumont had called the Q. The now-defunct GHW that Caldero had told him of. Even that Boston investment firm!

He shook his head. Who would have believed it? The dikes were leaking and the fingers of a thousand valiant Dutch boys would not suffice. Protecting the Secret now would require such massive deletions that even Genevieve Weil might have blanched. Perhaps if all the societies cooperated . . . A Cliological League. Difficult. Each had an interest in the continued ignorance of the masses, but each had also a deeply ingrained fear of exposure, even to one another. Cooperation would be as awkward and delicate as porcupines making love. It would require a man of exceptional talents to weld them into a single force. A man such as himself? Perhaps. Perhaps. He allowed himself to toy momentarily with the scenario. Let Ullman chair the Babbage Society. He would represent but one member society in the Cliological League.

Yet Jimmy Caldero seemed convinced that one society, the Q, had deliberately hunted down and exterminated its only surviving European rival. And perhaps it had also "blown the whistle" on the GHW, the one that the Nazis had destroyed. Were the Secret Six any less dangerous?

Of one thing Kennison was certain: The Babbage Society was wide open. Not only to the assaults of the Q but also to the Six, the CIA, even the Boy Scouts. The public furor had died down, at least on the surface. But then, the ignorant masses had always been the least of his worries. There was little to fear from a public that thought Charles Lindbergh was a blimp and could not locate Mexico on a map. It was the knowledgeable elites that worried him. Government agents. Scholars. The nosy and inquisitive.

The Associates had sustained some minor damage in the affair. One mole unmasked and deleted. A few public embarrassments. But they seemed to have contained things. Not so the Society. Weil's panic and Ullman's plotting had paralyzed any effective response. The Society sat dead in the water. Did he really want to become the captain of a target hulk?

No, of course not. It was better for Ullman to play that role. To sit happily oblivious in the bull's-eye, while Kennison himself faded safely out of sight. Forgoing the chairmanship had actually been a stroke of genius on his part.

The more he considered it, the more attractive his new plan seemed. When you are in the bull's-eye, the first order of business is to *move*. Time to become Fletcher Ochs. Time to move his database into a secret location, until it would be safe to reemerge.

He noticed that his palms were moist and wiped them on his napkin. Ochs Demographics? No, his new base of operations must have a markedly different name. Kennison Demographics must be buried forever. Too bad, but there was no help for it. What would Father have said? He glanced momentarily at the severe portrait that graced the fireplace. Then he took his crystal wineglass in his hand and sipped. A mediocre vintage. He must speak to Bettina about it.

He sighed. No, for his own safety, Ochs must live a life-style utterly different from that of Daniel Kennison. Rough-hewn, rather than refined. Perhaps a touch less witty. There must not be even the whisper of a connection. Too bad. He would miss Bettina and Karin, Ruth Ann and Greta.

He watched Karin carry the now-empty plates from the dining room. The high heels forced her calf and thigh muscles into delicious shapes. Karin must have sensed him watching, because she stiffened ever so slightly. Just a hint of fear. Kennison was pleased. She would never be as adept at playing the lost, frightened girl as Prudence had been. But Kennison was teaching her. He was teaching her.

He reached inside his jacket and pulled forth a cigarillo. He struck a match and lit it. *Very well,* he decided. *The Babbage Society is finished.* It was dead and lacked only the formality of a funeral. *Too bad. Had I been her leader, this contretemps would have been avoided.* But now, her enemies had her ranged and bracketed.

He laughed. He was in the bull's-eye, surrounded by enemies. Surrounded. But if he ducked, they could would wind up shooting one another!

Bettina opened the double door and stood inside. "Master Selkirk to see you, sir," she said.

Kennison grimaced. The young man was growing more and more a nuisance. He pulled his pocket watch from his pants and studied it. Beaumont should be installing the physical tap on Kennison's terminal about now. Normally, Selkirk would be managing the Night Shift on the floor below. That he sometimes came upstairs alone to contact his superiors was the reason for the tap, but also the reason for inviting him over to the mansion. If Selkirk were here, he could not walk in on Beaumont unexpectedly.

"Send him in, Madam Butler; but instruct Karin to serve no port until after he leaves."

"Yes, sir."

She left; and a moment later, Selkirk entered. He strode to the dining table, pulled a chair out, reversed it, and straddled it, leaning his arms on the back. Kennison watched him steadily. *Who are you, young man? Who do you work for? Ullman? The Six? The Q?* Or was Selkirk playing his own solitary game? Kennison wondered if Beaumont—Bennett—had made any progress investigating Selkirk's background.

"What is it, Alan?"

"You were gone yesterday and the day before." A flat statement, but gravid with accusation. Kennison studied the cold eyes, the insolent twist to the lip, and bristled. Who did this pup think he was, demanding an accounting from him?

"Why do you ask, Alan?" he asked blandly. "Did you encounter a problem you could not handle? I expect you to deal with any difficulties that occur during the Night Shift."

Selkirk seemed disconcerted and he stammered something in his own defense. Kennison kept a smile from showing. The best defense is a good offense. Pride in his own abilities was Selkirk's weak point. Prick him there and it would throw him off balance. It was best, in any confrontation, to keep one's opponents off balance.

". . . but I still don't think it's a good idea," Selkirk finished, "for you to go off that way without informing me."

"Indeed. And why is that?" Kennison stared closely at Selkirk and saw the other's eyes narrowed in suspicion. Curious, edgy, nervous. It reminded Kennison of the day Selkirk had first entered his office with the damning evidence. *"I don't want to* expose *you. I want in!"*

"Because we're partners, you and I," Selkirk said, with overweening arrogance. Partners, indeed! "I helped you when you needed it, so I deserve a little consideration. I kept the business with Weil quiet. I've kept word of your plan to corrupt the Society's database from leaking back to your friends on the Council."

Meaning he could let it leak, if he wanted to. *Try to be a little more subtle, Alan.* "That was your plan, Alan," he said aloud, "not mine."

"You agreed. It's too late to back out now."

Kennison shrugged. "I have not backed out. But only fools rush in."

Selkirk's smile was condescending. "Yes," he replied. "But he who hesitates is lost."

"And so, *festina lente*. Let's be done bandying clichs, Alan. Have you finished your search for a safe repository?"

"Aye. I've found one. Not only can you be secure from your former associates, but you can also be an important and honored man."

Kennison took the cigarillo from his lips and knocked the ash into the tray. "Yes, what about it?" *It will be a cold day in Hell, my friend, before I follow any scheme that you have engineered.* Then he remembered that, in Dante's *Inferno,* the center of Hell was a vast frozen lake, imprisoning those who had betrayed their benefactors; and he nearly laughed.

Selkirk gave him an uncertain look, took a deep breath, and let it out. "I have run across evidence of another cliological society," he said. "Not the Six, but a European one."

"Ah." Kennison raised one brow.

"You don't sound surprised."

"Should I be? It was mathematically obvious, once the possibility was pointed out. In fact, there may be more than one." He dangled the bait.

"That could verra well be," Selkirk admitted. "I hadna thought o' that."

Was there a tightening of his eyes? A hesitancy in his speech? Kennison leaned back casually in his chair. "Go on," he said.

Selkirk nodded. "You see, I was puzzled by some residual anomalies. Even after I allowed for our own activities and those we've attributed to the Six, there were still more anomalous nodes than could be accounted for by chance."

"Horseshoe nails," said Kennison absently. "Gloria Bennett calls them horseshoe nails." He gathered himself. "No one ever noticed these extra anomalies before . . . ?"

"No. As long as the Six's activities were pooled with the residual anomalies, the value of P was inflated with assignable causes and thus—"

"And thus the value of σ_p and the limits of random variation. Spare me the details, Alan."

"Shrinking the error estimate made the other anomalies stand out like rocks at low tide. So I did a wee bit o' poking around trying to discover which were directed and which were really chance, and whether there were any second-order commonalities in their sequelae."

"Very diligently, I'm sure. And you found that a significant fraction were . . . ?"

"Eurocentric," Selkirk responded. "The anomalous nodes were the outgrowth of European events. If I had to guess, the Europeans have been active as long as we or the Six."

If he had to guess . . . "I see. But what has this European group to do with our plans for the database?" *And how does it make me honored and important?*

Selkirk stood and paced the room. Kennison kept his gaze locked forward but followed him with his peripheral vision. "There are indications that these Europeans are moving into North America. Do you remember what Caldero told us that day in the pizza parlor? That one of the documents in the Dump was written in French? Well, we know it wasn't us and it wasn't Caldero's people. And the Six are strictly homegrown, so why communicate in French?"

"In Quebec, it is the law. But I take your meaning. Go on."

Selkirk rubbed a hand across his mouth. He toyed with the decanters on the sideboard. "I thought that if this group wanted to expand into North America, they might give the franchise to someone with a ready-made infrastructure."

Kennison stiffened. "The franchise?"

Selkirk turned and faced him. "Aye," he said eagerly. "Put yourself in their place. Suppose you were planning to open branch offices across an entire continent and someone came to you with not only a ready-made infrastructure but a massively detailed database. It would cut years off your start-up time. How would you feel if the alternative were to start from scratch?"

Kennison took a final drag on his cigarillo, then snubbed it in the ashtray. "Gratitude?" he suggested. Kennison was a great believer in gratitude. Encouraged in others, it was the most useful of emotions. "You believe that, were I to approach this . . . What do they call themselves?"

"I don't know that yet."

"Ah. Yes. That were I to approach them, they might offer me a job? As branch manager," he added dryly.

Selkirk approached and leaned on the table across from him. "Yes. And think. Would that job not be the equal of the post Ullman stole from you?"

The notion gave him pause. He hadn't thought of it in quite that way. He would be as powerful as Ullman. Wouldn't that be a delicious revenge? Deprived unjustly of the top job in one organization, to return with the backing of an even greater one. Oh, the look on Ullman's face when he found out!

Kennison allowed himself to look directly at Selkirk. "Very well, Alan. Take whatever steps you think necessary to locate this European association. But be careful that you do not alarm them, and take no steps to contact them until we have reviewed your findings with the others."

Selkirk nodded. "I'll do that." He turned to go.

"Oh, and one other thing."

Selkirk paused. What's that?"

Kennison rubbed a finger by the side of his nose. He toyed with his wineglass. "Bennett's friend, the architect? It seems that she has a very good lead on his whereabouts."

He thought that Selkirk's eyes narrowed and his voice became wary. "Oh? What lead?"

"I am not sure, but she believes that he is held by another group and not by the Secret Six." Kennison cocked his head. "Do you suppose it could be the Europeans you've uncovered?"

"It could be," Selkirk said slowly.

Kennison nodded and pursed his lips. "We did promise to help her find him, after all."

Kennison smiled thinly after the Scotsman left and savored the port Bettina had brought. At least he knew now who

Selkirk's employer was. Alan had probably come to America as part of an advance guard, searching out likely companies to acquire as fronts and hidey-holes.

Much as Kennison himself had attempted to do with D, B, and S. Now that was a disturbing thought! Cartoons of bigger fish swallowing smaller fish swallowing tiny fish. Kennison tossed off the dregs of the port. He was accustomed to playing the predator, not the prey. Now he was a tiger suddenly finding itself stalked. A new and unpleasant sensation, in many ways more frightening to a tiger than to a gazelle. Gazelles, at least, were accustomed to it.

But the Europeans hadn't known they were "stalking tigers," Kennison told himself. Not at first. Selkirk had been planted on him because a demographic firm was an invaluable resource. That was all. They had no doubt planted agents with Harris and Gallup and the others as well. The Beaumont Dump must have taken him by surprise. Suddenly he had found himself with his head halfway in the tiger's mouth. No wonder he had been so shaken that day, when he had come into the office and asked for admission!

One danger in finding a good hidey-hole was that something could already be hiding there.

He rose from the table and straightened his tie. Had Selkirk actually offered him the post of North American Coordinator for the Q? There were possibilities there. As much power as he had sought in the Society. A subordinate position, true; but in a larger organization. An ambitious man might make much of such an offer.

If the offer were sincere. Selkirk could not download the database without the encryption keys that Prudence had fashioned. Only Kennison possessed those. *Once they have my database,* he thought, *they won't need me.* Would the offer still hold? It would depend on their sense of honor, and Kennison had not achieved his current position by overestimating the honor of others.

Still, the bait that Selkirk had dangled was tempting. The Q would undoubtedly offer more scope for his genius than a two-bit investment firm like D, B, and S. If only he could be more sure of the dangers. He glanced at his watch. Beaumont had had quite enough time to install the tap on the terminal. She would be long gone by the time Selkirk returned to the offices. And Selkirk, Kennison knew, would try to contact his superiors as soon as possible.

And what of his "partners"? How would they react if he took Selkirk's offer? Caldero would never agree. Kennison was not fooled by his old nemesis' protestations of friendly assistance. Caldero would not help Kennison exit the Society only to help him enter a larger, more powerful society. Caldero would become an obstacle. Obstacles could be removed.

And what of Gloria Bennett? Selkirk and his organization was his lead to her friend—via the man called Bernstein. It was hardly likely that the Q would release French. Not after holding him for so long. But Bennet would not give up looking until she found him; and finding French meant finding the Q, a prospect the Q would not find entertaining. So, the Q must either capture Bennett or delete her.

Which meant that she was in very great danger.

Very great danger. Kennison's tongue darted out and he wetted his lips.

"Weren't you spooked?" asked SuperNerd. His face was wide and gaping, eager for stories of danger and suspense. As long as they were vicarious.

"Of course, I was nervous," Sarah told him. "But it wasn't any more dangerous than that night on Mount Falcon." Sarah Beaumont, hardened veteran, spinning tales of past adventures. "If anyone had tried to come upstairs from Johnson and Cheng and found the secret elevator shut off . . ."

Bosworth hugged himself. "I don't know if I could've done it. I'd be too nervous."

"Well, it's done now; and I'm back. That's it. No excitement, just another boring assignment." Sarah heard her own words and smiled to herself. She was coming across like an old pro. She broke in and installed phone taps every day.

She turned on the receiver and twisted one of the knobs.

The suite was starting to look like a Crazy Eddie store. The PC terminal. The window tappers. The parabolic and its tape recorder. The receiver for the phone tap and *its* recorder. It was a good thing that Helen and Chu were taking care of things. Lord knew what the regular hotel staff would think if they could see all this.

"Nothing? No close calls or anything?" SuperNerd looked so distraught that Sarah felt obligated to supply him with some secondhand adrenaline.

"Well? Has he used the phone yet?"

Sarah jumped and she heard Bosworth suck in his breath. Kennison's ghost, speaking from the windowpane. Sarah hunched her shoulders over the equipment. "Go turn off our tappers," she told Bosworth. She fiddled with the knobs until she heard the tiny hailstone sound cease. Then she turned and faced the window.

"Hello, there, Cousin Dan," she said. "What are you doing in the city at this hour?" She knew she did not need to be facing the window to be heard; but it was bad manners to talk with your back turned.

"I expect our friend will want to make a call tonight, as soon as he returns to the office. I was curious to hear what he has to say."

"Aren't we all," Sarah replied.

"Has Cousin James returned yet?"

"No," she admitted. "He's still in Boston, conducting surveilance on D, B, and S." She wished Red were here. Playing the old pro was a lot easier for Red than it was for her. But they had two leads to follow up, and it made sense for her to work this end because of her computer skills. Still, she felt oddly vulnerable when he wasn't around. That wasn't a logical feeling. After all, she could take care of herself—and had for most of her life. There was no reason for her to feel dependent. And she had saved Red's life, too; so he had as much reason to feel dependent as she did.

"Have you heard from him?" asked Kennison.

"Not since yesterday. He thinks he'll be here tomorrow. They're on to you, you know. D, B, and S is."

"Yes. Regrettable. One of the drawbacks of being a public person, I suppose. But there was no time for plastic surgery; and makeup, close up and in person, looks like makeup."

"They are even wondering about me." *All those assurances, and old man Detweiler sees right through me.* That was another reason Red was working the Boston end. She didn't think she could deal with exposure. She would be too distraught to function effectively. "What has them really concerned is that they don't know why we approached them."

"Why, we told them! We wanted to buy their company."

"They didn't believe you. They think there's some hidden purpose behind it all."

Kennison sniffed. "They are too subtle by half. Sometimes things are exactly as they seem."

"Detweiler is afraid that the Babbage Society has found them out. Jimmy wondered if we shouldn't lay our cards on the table. Explain what we want and see if they will give you shelter."

"No!" The answer was immediate. "D, B, and S may not be the best repository. And we don't know how far we can trust them yet. Let us not be panicked into a hasty move."

Now who was being too subtle? Sarah wondered if Kennison could ever be made to move except by panic. Somehow—though his schemes seemed endless—his accomplishments were few. "What other repository do you have in mind?"

A series of flat, well-spaced tones interrupted Kennison's reply. Someone was punching numbers on the Touch-Tone pad of Kennison's office phone. "Is that him? Is that Selkirk?" asked Kennison. But Sarah ignored him. The second tape recorder started automatically and she made a note on the log sheet. She had never realized before how much clerical work spying involved.

"Two-one-two," said Bosworth, cocking an ear to the pitch of the tones. "Manhattan." He scribbled down the rest of the numbers and slid into the chair by the computer terminal. "Let's see who he's calling."

The speakers warbled. A phone was ringing. Once. Twice. Dial tone. . . .

"What?"

"He hung up."

"I know that."

"Do you think he noticed the bug you planted?" Kennison's voice was tight. "Perhaps you left some sign of your work."

Sarah shook her head. Then she remembered that Kennison was not in the room at all and said, "No. I double-checked everything." It was weird, holding a normal conversation with a man who was a mile away.

"Haste makes waste," Kennison told her.

Sarah suppressed a spasm of irritation. "I told you I double-checked everything."

"Maybe you—"

The Touch Tones sounded again. This time the phone at the other end was picked up on the first ring. "Yes?" said a voice in Manhattan.

"The first call must have been a signal of some sort," Kennison said.

"No kidding? Shut up and listen."

"This is the West Coast office," said Selkirk.

"Did you make the offer?" The voice was suave, assured. Underneath it, Sarah could hear muted background sounds. The rush of tires on pavement. The honking of horns. Fragments of talk; some old-fashioned rap music played on a passing "boom box." She could close her eyes and picture the setting. Bosworth looked up from his terminal.

"I've got it pegged," he said. "It's a public phone booth."

"I know," said Sarah.

"Upper East Side."

Sarah shot him a look. She knew that she could replay the tape at leisure, but she wanted to listen to what Selkirk was saying. He had made an offer. Of what? To whom?

". . . very cautious," Selkirk said. "Naturally, I was careful in what I said."

"Naturally. You are certain you cannot secure the data yourself?"

"No, I told you. There are certain access codes that only he—"

"Yes, yes." The voice from Manhattan was waspish. "Still, with your abilities—"

"Oh, I could do it." The assurance was serenely confident. "It wouldn't be easy, but I could do it. But 'tis so much simpler this way."

"Yes, I suppose so."

"Look here. The reason I called you instead of Control. Has there been any unusual activity around you?"

"Ah, and I had thought you yearned for the sound of my voice."

There was a short pause. Then Selkirk spoke in a low, tight voice. "We may not like each other, Bernstein; but we're in this together. So learn to live with it. Beaumont's still looking for her partner."

"I am not concerned with Beaumont. That has been taken care of."

"And Kennison is helping her."

"Nor am I concerned with Mr. Kennison. He is your responsibility." Sarah could almost hear the smile in his voice. "A summit meeting in a pizza parlor? Americans."

"Well, Kennison dropped out of sight for a few days last week, and when I talked to him earlier tonight he said something that made me wonder if . . . But you say there's been nothing happening at your place?"

"What exactly did Kennison say to you?"

"Only that Beaumont had a new lead on French's whereabouts." Sarah jerked a look at the window. Why had Kennison told Selkirk that?

"I see. And how did the subject come up?"

"Kennison brought it up. We'd been talking about the other matter and he mentioned it just as I was leaving."

"He did." There was a silence at the other end. Then Bernstein hissed, "You bloody fool," and cut the connection.

Selkirk gasped, "Oh shit." Sarah heard fumbling sounds.

Then there was a crackle of static; then nothing.

Sarah pulled the earphones off. She spun and faced the window. "Kennison! I spent an hour putting that damn thing in! What did you tell him?"

"My dear lady, I told him nothing at all. I told him you had a lead on your friend's location. That is all. I said nothing of D, B, and S, or where we had been last week. I had no desire to wait until happenstance moved him to contact his superiors and I thought that by dropping such a hint—I never thought that he would catch on."

"He didn't. Bernstein did." That had actually been clever of Kennison, to trick Selkirk into making contact with Bernstein. Dennis' jailor? It seemed that way. And he was somewhere in Manhattan. Possibly on the Upper East Side, although the pay phone needn't be too close by. Her pulse raced a little faster. Yes, it did! If the first call was a signal, Bernstein would have had to be nearby to reach the pay phone in time for the second call. She *was* getting closer.

She closed her eyes and tried to picture Dennis, but she couldn't. His face seemed faded, indistinct. She frowned and concentrated, but he still wouldn't come into focus. She couldn't have forgotten! She couldn't have. She fought an urge to look at his photograph and had actually fumbled with her purse for a moment or two before she remembered that Gloria Bennett carried no pictures of Dennis French.

She turned her face to the wall so Bosworth could not see her.

Later that night, after Bosworth had gone to his own room and Kennison's ghost had been exorcised, Sarah sat in the large wing chair watching the lights of San Francisco. Coit Tower was awash with spotlights. There had once been a telegraph station on that hill, Helen had told her, to send news of incoming ships to the wharves. Beyond the hill, the sky was lit garishly by the neon flash of Fisherman's Wharf and the Barbary Coast. The Golden Gate Bridge was a fairy web in the distance. Beneath it the running lights of some large vessel drifted out toward the open ocean. Bound for the China trade, she thought. San Francisco always made her think of Hawaii and China and the Pacific trade. The city seemed oddly closer to Honolulu and Shanghai than it did to Los Angeles.

When the lights wreathing Coit Tower abruptly snapped off, she realized how late it was and smothered a yawn. Things were happening, or about to start. Selkirk had made an offer to Kennison. She was sure of it. But what sort of offer? To join the Q? Perhaps that was why Kennison was not so wild to use D, B, and S anymore. Yet if that was so, why had Kennison tricked Selkirk into using the tapped phone? She shook her head to clear the cobwebs. What was Kennison's game? Both ends against the middle? Or dithering, like the donkey standing halfway between two bales of hay?

"I am not concerned with Beaumont. That has been taken care of."

She shivered to remember that smooth, confident voice. The comment seemed more menacing for its casualness. She wished again that Red were here.

She paused at the PC terminal on her way to bed. Idly she ran her fingers along its smooth plastic frame. Then she reached around back and powered it up. She pulled out the chair and sat down and, a few moments later, she was linked to the Associates' database. The database was well defended—after the Dump, every deeby in the country was; but, as a member, she had her own key. Getting in was easy. As for the rest . . .

She had the system run a cross-correlation between Red Malone and Jacksonville, Florida.

A few moments later a folder appeared in the directory. A cue box asked for the entry code. Sarah leaned back in her chair and stared at the screen thoughtfully. She tapped her teeth with her thumbnail. Then she hunched forward again and typed in: FANNY POWER.

FOLDER UNLOCKED, the screen told her, and she smiled to herself.

A list of subfiles appeared in the directory window. They bore anonymous alphanumeric codes. Except for one. That one was named SARAH, READ THIS.

She grunted in surprise. "I'll be damned." She moused over and clicked on it and a bulletin board opened up. There was a single note on it.

SARAH, THE OTHER FILES IN THIS FOLDER ARE UN-LOCKED. YOU CAN READ THEM IF YOU WANT, BUT I AM ASKING YOU PLEASE NOT TO. RED.

She sat regarding the screen and its message for a while longer, drumming her forefingers arhythmically on the table-top. Then she gave a hard, final rap with her knuckles; took a deep breath and blew it out through her nose. "You're a son of a bitch," she told the absent Red. She closed up the folder and quit the application. It was late and she was tired anyway.

IX

"They still haven't talked," said Herkimer Vane.

Jeremy inserted the key into the apartment door. "I don't expect they will." He opened the door and the others followed him inside.

It was a plain apartment, simply furnished; a hideaway until D, B, and S could decide what to do about them. For the moment, the four of them were supposed to be dead, but that jury-rigged deception would not last much longer. Meanwhile, Detweiler had secured apartments for them in Charleston. Jeremy surveyed the worn, anonymous furniture and thought regretfully of his possessions in Denver. He could never regard this place as home.

Jeremy closed the door behind them. "Then we still don't know who they were working for," he said. Aside from the comment that they were not from the Babbage Society—

which Jeremy was inclined to believe, if only for the spontaneity of the remark—the two men they had captured in Douglas County had given out no information, not even name, rank, and serial number. They were being held on Detweiler's estate, which was as close as D, B, and S could come to a jail. As Vane constantly reminded them, D, B, and S had never needed safe houses and false identities.

Jennie Barron was urging "more rigorous" questioning of the two; but Detweiler had vetoed that on the grounds that nothing, not even survival, was worth the price of uncivilized behavior. So, unless the luxurious surroundings and steady diet of caviar broke their captives' spirits soon, they would get no leads from that direction.

Vane dropped a manila envelope to the coffee table. He wandered into Jeremy's kitchen, where he pured himself a glass of milk. Gwynn picked up the envelope and pulled out the photographs of Gloria Bennett and Sarah Beaumont. She held them side-by-side and studied them carefully, working her lips. Then she overlaid them and held them up to the light. "How far would that surgeon commit himself?" she asked.

"He would only say," Vane replied, "that it was possible that the one face could be altered into the other."

"Cautious."

"Wouldn't you be?"

"Do you think there was any connection between the mouse and Kennison's visit?" *Of course, there was a connection—but what?* It was all a tangle, Jeremy thought. There were a thousand loose strands around them. Yet they couldn't seem to grab onto anything. They would yank on this strand or that only to pull out a frayed end, leading nowhere.

Doang shrugged. "I think that when we probed those identities—Bennett and Ochs and Caldero—it triggered an alarm of some sort. Apparently, that is standard practice on sensitive files that must be left in the Net. Tim told me that the next time he goes fishing, he'll masquerade his query as official government business. They can get in just about any-where."

"Does anyone want pizza?" Gwynn asked from the phone. "I'm about to call one in."

"Make it two," said Jeremy. "Is pepperoni OK with every-one?" He looked around the little group. Vane shook his head and rubbed his stomach. "Make it one pepperoni and one plain. Gwynn, what's wrong?"

Llewellyn was frozen in place, staring at the telephone.

Jeremy saw the look on her face. Gwynn had told him once—and, Lord, that seemed like an eternity ago!—that she had learned how to recognize tampering with her phones.

And his mind skidded back suddenly to the day he had discovered the break-in of his apartment, just after Dennis had disappeared from the hospital. He remembered how helpless he had felt, how frightened and impotent. He never wanted to feel that icy knot in his stomach again. Now here it was, reaching into his dwelling once more. Like a haunt-ing, a ghost.

A ghost. With a shiver, he realized that he had not thought about Dennis in days. Yet, at one time, he had been unable to think of anything else.

Doang started to speak, but Gwynn put a finger to her lips. She looked at Vane and asked a question with her eyes, but Vane only stared at the phone and shook his head.

For an instant, Jeremy was tempted to find four police whistles so they could all blast the ears off whoever was listening. Then anger seized him with a surprising force: a red heat that surged up his neck and out his limbs. He grabbed the telephone from Gwynn and held it like a micro-phone.

"Look, whoever you are!" he shouted. "I'm sick of these games! Do you hear me? If you've got Dennis French, let him go! Or come and get me and take me to him! Beaumont? Kennison? Do you hear me? What gives you people the right to put me through hell!" He slammed the phone down so hard the bells jangled.

A moment of awkward silence; then he turned and faced

his companions. "Sorry," he muttered. The heat changed from anger to embarrassment. What if the phone was not bugged after all? He felt like an idiot.

Gwynn patted him on the back. "It's all right, Jeremy. We understand." The others would not meet his eyes. "It's all right," she repeated.

She led him to a chair and he sat. He wiped his cheeks with his coat sleeve. "It was so easy," he explained to them. "So easy to get lost in the intrigue and the danger. To forget why I started all this. Even to take pride in forgetting. Telling myself that I didn't need—Didn't need—" He found he couldn't finish and covered his face with his hands.

He was not surprised when, a few minutes later, the telephone rang.

"Oh, I don't know," said Red Malone with a grin. He removed the paper-and-net delivery boy's hat and tossed it aside. "I thought it was a nice touch." He laid the two pizza boxes on the table. "You *were* calling out for pizza, weren't you?" He found the most comfortable chair in the room and sank into it with a sigh.

The others huddled around the dining table in a tight knot. Taking strength and comfort from one another's closeness, Red thought. The Four Musketeers. Well, facing danger creates bonds. Who should know that better than himself?

Collingwood was watching him with his fists clenched. Sarah had told him about Collingwood, yet the man returning his stare did not strike him as ineffectual. And he could tell from the way the others stood that they looked to him for their lead.

Gwynneth Llewellyn lifted the lids on each box in turn and inspected the contents. "You got the order right, too." She closed the lids carefully and faced him. "I suppose that was to demonstrate that you were listening in."

Collingwood read the logo on the lids of the boxes. "Where did you get these pizzas?"

Red grinned again. "You'd never believe me. I ordered out."

Collingwood crossed his arms. "Is this some big joke to you? Because I'm not laughing."

Vane snorted and strode to the phone. "I think I had better inform my partners."

"I wouldn't try that if I were you."

Vane paused with his hand on the receiver. "Why?"

"Because we disconnected your phone."

Vane made an impatient sound in his throat and picked up the phone. He punched a few buttons, paused, and jiggled the receiver hook. He scowled and faced the room. "The phone's dead," he announced.

Red twisted his face up. "Of course it is. Didn't I just tell you that?" Actually, he thought Vane had showed good sense. After all, why should he have taken Red's word for it?

Vane sucked in his breath. He strode to the door and yanked it open. Two large men dressed in workmen's coveralls stood on an oil-stained tarpaulin stretched out on the floor before the open elevator door. Tools hung from their belts. A bright trouble light dangled in the dark, empty shaft. One of the workmen turned and faced the apartment. "I'm sorry, sir," he said, "but the elevator is out of service."

Vane chewed his lip. He looked at Red. "I suppose the stairs are out of order, too."

"We're working on them," Red told him. "They should be back in operation soon."

"Calm yourself, Herkimer," said Llewellyn. She closed the door softly and took Vane by the elbow, leading him back into the room. "Mr. Caldero means us no harm, I'm sure." She looked at Red. "I assume that you are with that other group, Utopian Research Associates?"

"Loose lips sink ships." Christ. He was beginning to sound like Kennison, the Cliché That Walked Like A Man. But, by assuming Sarah had already known, he had let too much slip the first time he had met with her and had almost gotten them both killed. He wouldn't make the same mistake twice.

The less anyone knew, the better off they were.

"I see," said Llewellyn after a moment of silence. "And the woman with you yesterday. Was she Sarah Beaumont?"

He had heard them speculating on the tape, so the question came as no surprise. He remembered telling Sarah not to worry about being identified, and he wished he could be detached enough to chuckle over the irony. "Her name is Gloria Bennett," he said flatly. The Associates had gone to a lot of trouble to make that persona airtight. He wasn't about to poke holes in it just to satisfy their curiosity. If Sarah wanted to tell them . . . Well, he'd advise her not to. The best-kept secret is one that no one knows. "You can read all about her in *Who's Who*."

"She's a black woman," Llewellyn pointed out.

"That doesn't make her unique. There are more than one."

"She has a scar typical of plastic surgery," put in Collingwood.

Red shrugged. "So do I."

Llewellyn gave him a sober appraisal. "So might we all before this is over. But I'm sure you did not come here simply to refuse to answer all our questions. You could have done that at home."

Red decided that he liked her manner. He reminded himself that these people were not his enemies, even if they were not precisely his friends. People had their own drives and goals, their own circles of friends and enemies. Sometimes the circles intersected, a little. "I came to do a little horse trading," he said. "I want to know more about D, B, and S—"

"And why should we tell you anything?" demanded Vane.

Red kept a rein on his patience. He supposed that it was natural for Vane to be reticent about his own organization, but he was wasting time in ritual. They both knew that they would be trading information in the end. Red smiled at the historian but addressed his reply to Collingwood. "Because we have a lead on Dennis French." There was an irony there. Red remembered how Kennison had used the same bait to secure help from Sarah and him.

Collingwood uncrossed his arms and leaned forward. "Where is he?"

Red spread his hands. "I don't know exactly yet."

Collingwood flapped his arms out and turned away. "Great." He stared at the wall.

"But I know someone who knows someone who might know."

Collingwood looked back over his shoulder and gave him a long stare.

Red twisted uncomfortably under his gaze. He hadn't meant to sound flippant. It had just come out that way. Sarah was always telling him that. That he never took things seriously enough. Maybe she was right. Collingwood was hurting, and there was no point in aggravating the hurt. "Sorry," he muttered. "It's not much of a lead, but it's the only one we've got."

"If you want our help, ask for it," Doang said abruptly. "Don't try to buy it."

The mathematician had been silent up until now and his sudden comment surprised Red. He said nothing for the moment. People who spouted altruism annoyed him. In a pinch, he wanted the people covering him to be people who had a stake in his success, not people doing a favor. That was an ironclad rule. Once—just once—he had neglected it.

Llewellyn stuck her jaw out and looked from one to the other. "Jeremy and I started this together. We will finish it together." She and Collingwood locked gazes for a moment, and Collingwood smiled at her. Llewellyn flushed and looked at the carpet.

"And I," Doang admitted. "Jeremy and I have fought together. And how else may I find my way back to my family?" He walked away from the table and stood before the window. The lights of Boston twinkled across the Charles. A helicopter made its way like a firefly across the estuary from Logan Airport. "I have no desire to disappear," he whispered. "I have no desire to have my life turned upside down. Never to see my brothers and sisters again." He turned and faced them. "I will not cower and hide my name or my face." He looked at Red as he said that.

Vane sighed. "And if I say I will not help, it will make me a false-hearted poltroon." He crossed his arms. "I will help Jeremy if I can, but not if it means going against my partners."

Red put his elbow on the arm of his chair and rested his chin on his fist. "That's the ticket," he said. "You want to know what's in it for you. How about this: We'd like to know who it was that blew your friends and colleagues to kingdom come. Wouldn't you?"

Vane jerked his head up. "Who? We already know who. The damned Babbage Society."

Red smiled thinly. "I won't argue whether they are damned, or why. But the Babbage Society is paralyzed. Their Council is in disarray. A third of them are afraid that the other third is out to bump them off."

"And the third third?" asked Llewellyn.

"Already bumped off. They aren't the ones you need to fear." It seemed strange to him to think of his long-standing enemies as virtually powerless. If not exactly harmless, at least for the time harming only one another. "Besides, they had an agent on your team. Someone named Bandmeister—"

That shook them. "Henry?" "I don't believe—" "You mean—"

Red held up a hand to quiet them. "And he was far too valuable an asset for them to sacrifice."

"Assets," said Llewellyn. "I've always detested those who regard people as 'assets.' " She heaved a sigh. "Christ, I miss my pipe."

"Besides," said Jeremy carefully, "they've sacrificed . . . assets . . . before."

Red shook his head. "Pawns, not bishops."

Vane protested. "I can't believe that a man like Henry Bandmeister was a spy for a secret society."

Jeremy leered at him. "How can *you*, of all people, say that?" And Vane had the grace to blush.

"If the Babbage Society didn't do it," said Llewellyn cutting them off, "then who did?"

He favored her with an approving glance. "You stick to the heart of the matter, don't you?"

"It saves wasting time," she said.

"All right. I'll take a chance. Here's some free information. There are at least two other societies beside the ones you know of from the Dump. We suspect one of them destroyed your team."

"Why?" asked Llewellyn.

He shrugged. "If we knew why, we'd know who."

"We thought," said Doang hesitantly, "that because I had evaluated their mathematics—"

Red laughed. "And you think no one else has? Every mathematician in the country has been poring over those fragments like a rabbinical student going over the Talmud." He pointed to the boxes on the table. "Pizza's getting cold. I'll have some, if you aren't." Wordlessly, Collingwood pulled some paper plates from a cabinet. He put a slice on one and handed it to Red. No one else made a move.

"Thanks . . . No," he continued to Doang. "The validity of the mathematics in the Dump is no secret. Only a fool would think so; and, with Weil gone, we're not dealing with fools." He took a bite—and flashed on the time he and Sarah had met Kennison at Tony's. The smell of the cheese and the tomato sauce, the voices of the men behind the counter. Kennison's rat-sharp face across the table. Sarah sitting beside him, close enough to sense, but not quite touching. He wondered briefly how she was managing out on the West Coast, and experienced a brief pang of anxiety that he could not quite pin down. "No, there had to be some other reason why someone wanted you out of the way," he continued, waving the pizza in the air as he spoke. "From what I know," he added, nodding toward the telephone, "we can do business together. What do you say? Do we trade information?"

Collingwood looked across to Vane. "I say we take Caldero to Detweiler's estate."

Vane looked like he was sucking a lemon. "Do you think it might do any good?"

Llewellyn shrugged. "It can't hurt."

"What are you people talking about?" Red asked in irritation. Take him to Detweiler's estate? Did they mean to take him prisoner, with his own people standing guard in the hallway?

Vane smiled thinly. "Trading information. Do you play poker, Mr. Caldero?"

"A little. Why?"

"Well, our Mr. Detweiler is holding a pair that we'd like to beat."

Red Malone studied the two men in Detweiler's library through the one-way mirror. One man wore a cast on his right wrist. He was walking around the room, picking out books and flipping through them in a desultory fashion. The other sat in an overstuffed Queen Anne chair playing a game of Canfield on the card table.

"They don't look like they're having a very good time, do they?"

Adrian Detweiler the Fifth cackled. "Boredom can be the cruelest torture of all. They don't even talk to each other for fear we are listening in." The bray of old New England came through in the old man's clipped, nasal voice. Not for him the flavorless, pear-shaped tones of television English.

Red refrained from pointing out that they *were* listening in. The two prisoners were playing it right, though. *Professionals,* he thought. *But whose?*

"Seen enough?" Detweiler reached out to close the shutters on the mirror, but Red laid a hand on his arm.

"Give me another minute." He studied the two prisoners. After a while the one playing solitaire squirmed in his seat. He squared the cards in his stock, tapping all four sides in turn against the table, looking slowly around the room. When his gaze reached the mirror, he scowled and tapped the stock again nervously. Red grinned.

"Let me talk to the cardsharp for a few minutes," he said.

The cardplayer looked up suspiciously when Red entered the library. Red smiled at him and walked over, hand extended. "Well, I see they got you, too. Who are these clowns anyway?"

The cardplayer pulled three cards from his stock and exposed the first. It was the eight of clubs. "Isn't that ploy just a little bit too transparent?" he asked.

"Hey, it was worth a try, wasn't it?" Red pulled one of the other chairs over and sat so that he faced the other over the card table. "Try playing it on the nine." He pointed to the tableau.

"Up yours." He played it on the nine anyway. "What'd you do with my buddy?"

"You mean the big guy with the bad case of tennis elbow? Does your buddy have a name?"

The man looked at him. "Yeah. Bud. Where is he?"

"Taking a potty break. Play the queen there."

"Who's playing this, you or me?" He threw his cards down and shoved the tableau across the table. "Here, you play." He slouched in his chair and stared at Red with narrowed eyes. "I've seen you somewhere before."

Red gathered the cards together. "Possible. It's a small world." He righted the cards and squared the deck. Then he shuffled the cards. "I was thinking the same thing myself." He cut the deck in two and riffled the halves together. He began dealing cards. "So what do you say, Charlie? A game of rummy?"

Charlie jerked suddenly. He stared intently into Red's eyes; then he screwed his face up. "Oh, Christ," he said. "Oh, Christ."

X

Red watched Charlie pick up the brandy snifter and swirl it around. Charlie scowled into the glass; then he looked around the table until he spotted Detweiler. "You don't have any beer, do you?"

Stone rolled his eyes up in his head, but Detweiler smiled and crooked a finger to his manservant. "A beer for 'Charles,' " he said. "And 'Bud'? Yes, two beers. Will Sam Adams lager do?"

"Make it three," said Red.

"They came around and questioned me about you," Charlie told him. "The DIA stiffs. Thanks." The servant placed three tall pilsner glasses in front of them. Charlie lifted his. "They wanted to know everything I knew about you."

Red took a sip. "What'd you tell them?" he asked.

"Does it matter? You can't go back." Charlie took a long pull and set his glass down. "I told them I didn't know nothing, except you never cheated at rummy."

"I did," said Red. "You just weren't quick enough to catch me."

Charlie snorted and turned to his partner. "Five years him and me sat in that room, close enough to kiss, and I never once caught on."

"Watch what you say," said Bud. "We aren't among friends." He cast a dark look at Collingwood and rubbed his wrist.

Red smiled. He had never suspected Charlie to be anything but a government spook, either. Looked at from a distance, it was almost comical.

Stone rapped the table with his knuckles. "Can we get down to business?" he demanded. "We want a full accounting from each of you. Who the hell are you and who do you represent?"

Red looked around the table. Detweiler and his daughter. Stone. The Four Musketeers. Charlie and Bud. A summitt meeting. "My name is Jimmy Caldero," he continued, "and I represent Utopian Research Associates. . . ." Jennie Barron looked at him with a coldly appraising gaze. *That's one hard bitch*, Red thought. He contrasted the grandfatherly geniality of old Detweiler with the offhand callousness he sensed in the two younger partners.

Sarah was right, he decided. Cliology dehumanized its practitioners. When people were your subjects, how easily they became objects. And from cold detachment and study grew the itch to make people behave the way you knew they *ought* to, to make them "subjects" in quite another sense of the word. How often had caseworkers lorded over the very people they were supposed to help? D, B, and S had a century and a half of profitable passivity behind them; yet he could sense that Stone—and probably Barron as well— itched to intervene. How was it different from what he intended with the Associates? *Because my goals are worthy?*

The same old story, Sarah had said during that wild flight to the Walker Mansion. The end justifies the means. But it should count for something, he thought, that he took hold of the reins reluctantly.

"My old stablemate here . . ."—and he gestured toward Charlie, who was finishing his beer—"represents the Secret Six."

Bud set his glass hard on the table. "How did you know that?"

Charlie let out a gust of satisfaction, set his glass down more gently, and wiped his lips with a napkin. "That's great beer," he told Detweiler. Then he folded his arms across his chest and smiled at Red. "He didn't know. He guessed. It was your people who moused into the Lysander Spooner file, wasn't it?"

Red saw the narrowing of the eyes. The wary look. *He doesn't know how far he can trust the Associates.* "Our real enemies," he told the others, "are not Charlie's people but a European gang that we call the Q."

Charlie pursed his lips. "So, you know about them."

Bud spoke to Charlie. "You got a big mouth, you know."

Charlie jerked a thumb at Red. "He already knew."

"Yeah, but none of them others did."

Charlie shook his head. "No, Jimmy here's right. This 'Q' of his is our real enemy. Look what they did to our Oberlin office. Don't worry, Bud. I'll settle up with the Circle later, but I think they'll back me on this." He faced the group and put his hands flat on the table. "Let me start at the beginning. The download came as a shock to us. We always thought we were unique. We decided to investigate." He looked at Red. "One of the taps your friend Kennison found was ours. So was the phone call. Unauthorized, but Ora . . . The Babbage people had killed a friend of hers—a reporter on the *Times*."

Red cocked an eyebrow. "Houvanis?"

Charlie looked at him. "You keep a scorecard?" He twisted and motioned to the servant. "Set up another round, would you, please?" He made circles with his finger. "So, we were sniffing around inside Kennison's data banks and what do you suppose we found? Three other taps. Isn't that a scream? Remember that scene in *Take the Money and Run* when Woody Allen tries to rob a bank and there's another gang in there robbing the same bank?" He shook his head. The servant set the tall pilsner glass in front of him.

"Kennison only found two other bugs," Red commented.

"Yeah? Well, we're smarter than he is." He took a long drink of beer and Red began to feel irritated at the way the man was stringing his story out. He knew Charlie was trying to organize his thoughts; trying to decide what he could safely say and what he couldn't.

"We traced another bug to an investment firm in Saint Louis," Charlie continued.

"Global Investment Strategies," said Red.

"You know them?"

"It's a front for Frederick Ullman."

"I know them," Stone smirked. "If they are who you claim they are, they should be a great deal more successful than they are."

Red looked at him and smiled. "Oh, they are, Stone. They are." Stone flushed and Red turned back to Charlie. "I'll bet Ullman's bug was built into the original system architecture, so Kennison's virus detector never saw it."

Charlie shrugged. "Who's telling this story?" He elbowed his partner. "You see? The Babbage clowns are spying on each other. That's something we didn't know before.

"We thought Saint Louis was another independent group," he told the others. "Well, the third virus had been planted by the FBI, of course; so ... What's so funny?"

Red wiped a tear from his eye. "The official government finally rears its head. I was beginning to wonder if there were anyone involved in this affair that *wasn't* a cliological society."

"Cliology," said Charlie. "I like that word. We called it political metaeconomy." He drank some more beer. "But what makes you think they aren't?"

"Eh?"

"Do you know of any group engaged in cultural engineering on as massive a scale as the government? Or do you think the tax code is for raising revenue?"

"Teddy Roosevelt," said Llewellyn suddenly, and they all looked at her. "Teddy Roosevelt and the Progressives," she said. "That's when this whole idea of government-as-manager first took hold. The Progressives' avowed purpose was—and I quote—'to apply rational, scientific techniques to the management of business, labor, and the government itself.' Funny, isn't it, that no one took them at their word."

Red rubbed the side of his nose. *Teddy Roosevelt's nomination as Vice President.* That had been on the French list, hadn't it? And Walt had pegged it tentatively as a Six operation. Had they killed McKinley just to get their man out of a dead-end office? But the Six had broken into two factions, just like the Babbage Society. Over the assassination? So ...

"One of your factions wanted to infiltrate the government," he said to Charlie, "and the other didn't." No wonder they had lost track of the Six's daughter! It was too big to be seen. Like the old cartoon of the hunter in the forest who can't see any game ... but the reader notices that some of the tree trunks look an awful lot like legs.

"That's not important now," Charlie said, waving a hand. "It's the Europeans we have to deal with, and quick." He turned his pilsner glass in quarter-turns. "The fourth bug in Kennison's system was theirs, the one that dumped into the

Q file. We started tracing it back. . . ." He shook his head. "Sleeping dogs . . . They must have had a trip wire on their virus. We were running the op out of Oberlin. When we realized security was compromised, we skedaddled." He turned the glass another quarter-turn. "Two hours later, the building was in flames."

Red stirred uncomfortably. "They didn't even try to find out who you were? Did you have the place under surveillance? Put a tail on whoever came by?"

Charlie looked at him. "Are we amateurs? We did that. They never reported back." He frowned at his glass. "About the only intelligence we managed to uncover—which we got through their tap—was that they call themselves the SQPS."

"And what does that stand for?" asked Barron.

Charlie did not look away from his glass and Red wondered if the lost tails had been friends of his. It was a hard life that they led. Friendships were as unwise as they were unavoidable. Best to keep people at arm's length; so that, when the time came to go to Jacksonville—

"The Societé," Charlie said at last. "The Societé de Quetelet pour le Physique Sociale."

"Quetelet?" said Collingwood. Red looked at him, and his face seemed drained of color. "Quetelet? Oh, my God!" He hung his head and shook it slowly. "My fault, my fault." He looked up. "I was going to give a little report on Quetelet and Buckle after Jim was through."

"But it was simply background," Llewellyn protested. "Nothing that revealed this Q's crimes."

"The guilty flee," Red told them, "where no man pursueth."

Collingwood raised haunted eyes. "They didn't exactly 'flee,' did they."

"It wasn't your fault," Llewellyn told him. "How could you have known?"

"That's why we staked out the meeting," said Charlie. "Penny told us about the agenda—"

"Penelope?" said Llewellyn. "Penny Quick?"

Charlie nodded. "Our plan was to nab Collingwood after

the meeting and find out what he knew about the SQPS. Afterward, we followed him to the the hospital and hung around until he and his friends slipped out. The rest—" He glanced at his partner's wrist. "The rest, you know."

"Wait a minute," said Collingwood. "The nurse didn't alert you?"

"What nurse? No. We were out in the parking lot the whole time."

Collingwood and Llewellyn explained about the nurse at Porter and Red saw how that made the others uneasy. If people could be hypnotically programmed, who could be trusted?

The nurse had called the Q, Red decided. That was the only thing that made sense. Except it didn't quite make sense. If the Q had bombed the building at Denver University, they surely had local assets. So why hadn't the Q been waiting when Collingwood and his friends left the hospital? They had set that bomb at the first sign that the study team was even thinking about discussing Quetelet. It wasn't like them to let the Four Musketeers elude their grasp.

Red stood on the veranda of Detweiler's mansion, enjoying the cool night breezes. A little ways off, a stone staircase gleamed in the moonlight where it led through an embankment down into a landscaped garden. Red could not see the end of the property. He took a deep breath and rubbed the palms of his hands together. The nights were colder in the Northeast. He could see his breath.

The moon was setting, fat and tawny, shrouded by streamers of umber clouds. He wondered if Sarah was watching the same moon out there in San Francisco. A mystic link between them.

He turned suddenly and saw Jeremy Collingwood with his hands stuffed into his pants pockets. "Chilly night," he said to Red.

Red faced the night once more. "Autumn. Happens every year, but it always takes us by surprise. The heavy clothes are still packed away and we have to go rummage for them. How's the computer search going?"

"Not too badly. On the day of the Dump, there were two dozen phone calls from San Diego to Brussels and Paris and Quebec from public phones in San Diego. On the map, they make a nice little cluster around the home address of that Howard woman you told us about."

Red nodded. He had expected as much. The Q had found Mark Lopez's code in the Dump and seized the opportunity, forcing him (through torture?) to vouch for Maureen Howard, then disposing of him after she'd had time to reach the ranch house. They'd been smart enough not to put a tracer on her, anticipating the Associates' thorough screening of recruits, and patient enough to wait for her to emerge from the training center with word of its location. That had been a clever idea of Charlie's, doing a cluster analysis on phone calls to French-speaking regions against the time frame of the Dump. "What about San Francisco?"

"You mean the mole that infected Kennison's system."

Red grunted. "Who *didn't* infect Kennison's system?" He turned and faced Collingwood, who was sitting on the porch swing, his arms spread out across the backrest. Red leaned back and half-sat on the railing. "You can infect a system from anywhere in the country. You just piggyback the worm or the virus on a commercial program, or on shareware or a bulletin board."

Collingwood shook his head. "I wouldn't know about that. I'm a simple man with simple needs. Oh, I use spreadsheets, of course; but not, I am sure, to their maximum potential. And Dennis . . . Well, he had—has—a positive horror of computers."

"They're tools. As well be afraid of T squares or vacuum cleaners. Or quill pens."

Collingwood grinned crookedly. "The Decline of the West can be traced to the invention of quill pens. When people had to pound their writings into stone blocks they gave more thought to their words, I think."

Red smiled. "You could be right."

Collingwood kicked with his feet and the porch swing began to rock. "My grandmother had one of these on her porch. I feel like a kid again." He swung slowly, like a pendulum. "Are you going to tell me what you know about Dennis French?"

Red crossed his arms. "That's all this affair means to you, isn't it? Finding your friend. You don't care about the bigger issues at all."

"Don't I? I'd always thought friendship was one of the bigger issues."

"I didn't mean it that way. I meant . . . Well, *beyond* your concern for your friend. Don't the philosophical issues concern you at all? Do you want your life controlled by some secret elite?"

Collingwood snorted. "Do you mean that it hasn't been?" The porch swing glided quietly. "Has there ever been a time since the pharaohs when some small clique of would-be managers hasn't insisted on running the show? As long as they do so in a reasonably competent fashion and leave me to my own devices, I have no quarrel with them. I don't see how applying a little science to the task can be worse than the trial and error we've always endured."

"You really don't care." Red could not keep the surprise out of his voice. He had expected anything but indifference. "You're deeper in the middle than just about anyone, and the fundamental issues mean nothing to you."

"Is that an accusation? Most of those who bleat about removing the yoke of the oppressor are only upset that the yoke isn't theirs." He stopped the swinging of the glider, his feet sliding against the wooden flooring of the veranda. "But I did add that one proviso. I said it makes no difference to me, provided you leave me to my own devices. And that you have not done."

Collingwood had not raised his voice, yet Red found himself flinching from it. He turned away from the man's accusing gaze and wrapped his left arm against one of the pillars. The paint was smooth and cool against his cheek. "No, we haven't, have we." And never mind that it had not been the Associates who triggered the whole affair. It could have happened in any of a dozen ways. The whole structure had been rife with fractures, too many fractures to blame the one that had finally sheared.

"You aren't going to tell me, are you?"

Red looked away again. "I'm sorry," he said. "It's second nature." He ran his hand up and down the post. There was a crack in the paint, and he picked at it with his fingernail. "You don't know what it's like," he told Collingwood, still keeping his back to the man. "To be sworn to a secret like ours. You daren't let anyone know about it. Not even that there *is* a secret. Not your parents. Not your closest friends. So, you learn to conceal, to hold things back, sometimes even to lie. To spout glib stories about your new 'summer job,' but never the truth. Soon—" A long, thin sliver of paint came loose and he turned it around in his fingers. "Soon, circumspection becomes second nature. To be safe, never say everything. To be safer, never say anything. But cliological distance is defined by the inverse frequency of communications between two points." He smiled bitterly. "We learn that in training. So the distance grows between you and everyone you've ever known. And the worst of it is you know why it's happening. You can even work out the equations. Soon, your only friends are others like yourself, locked away in a secret world, secure in the knowledge that, after all, you are the world's true masters, and it is the round pegs who, in truth, don't fit." He flicked the sliver of paint into the night air; leaned forward on his elbows and clasped his hands. "Why am I telling you all this?"

"I don't know," said Collingwood. "Who should you be telling?"

Red glanced over his shoulder. "Are you sure you're only an accountant?"

"Tell me, Caldero," he heard Collingwood say. "How do you get into your line of work? You don't advertise in the employment sections, do you?"

Red ran his hand up and down the post, remembering Emmett Blaine. How long since he had thought about the crusty old man, with his polka-dot bow ties and his hair parted in the middle? The very antithesis of cool, but a teacher who had made ideas come alive. "We're always on the lookout for people who show an interest. And a talent." *Like high school students,* he thought, *who don't quite fit in.* Shy square pegs, awkward in a universe of round holes. The sort who might fall under the spell of a charismatic teacher. Independent enough to resist rounding off their own corners, and visionary enough to imagine squaring off the holes. Those long discussions about how one person could make a difference, if he could do just the right thing at just the right time. He was startled to realize how much of his own thinking echoed with Emmett Blaine's voice. The propagation of memes . . .

"That makes twice," he heard Collingwood say.

"Twice what?"

"That you've avoided telling me about Dennis."

Red slapped his hands together. The night was getting colder. Autumn, he decided, was the saddest time of year. "The Q must have him," Red said. "I wasn't sure if it was the Six or the Q until tonight. Someone in Kennison's organization knows. Kennison overheard him once on the phone. He hasn't told us who the mole is, but I have a guess. Bennett is back there now, tapping the phone so we can get a trace." He stood, turned, and faced Collingwood. "There. Was that open enough for you?"

Collingwood nodded. "It will do. Why is Bennett so anxious to help locate Dennis?"

Red shrugged. "It's her assignment," he temporized.

Collingwood seemed amused. "Circumspection, again? Never mind. I won't press you. As long as you promise that, when you do learn where Dennis is, you will tell me immediately."

He hesitated only a fraction of a moment. "Of course."

Llewellyn pushed the door open and light flooded the veranda. She squinted into the darkness. "Jeremy? Are you . . . Oh, there you are. And Mr. Caldero, too, I see."

Red sighed. "What the hell, call me Jimmy."

"Charlie has finished the correlation and found a cluster of public phones in San Francisco called by your Howard woman, or vice versa. The gentleman working at the other end checked through the data banks at Kennison Demographics and found that an Alan Selkirk lives in the center of the distribution."

Selkirk. Red nodded, unsurprised. Kennison had said that he didn't trust Selkirk any longer. The shooting in the parking lot made sense, too. No one but Kennison and Selkirk had known that they would be there. He remembered how shocked the Scot had been when they had told him that there was a third society. (Only three? Lord, how simple that seemed in retrospect!) And he remembered how relieved Selkirk had seemed when told of the Secret Six. Of course. He had probably been afraid that they had uncovered the Q.

"And Jeremy," Llewellyn continued, "Mr. SuperNerd had a personal message for you from Gloria Bennett."

Collingwood blinked slowly. "Oh?" He kept his face neutral. "What did she say?"

"Only that Dennis French was being held by a man named Bernstein somewhere on Manhattan's Upper East Side."

Collingwood nodded. He looked at Red. "Fast service."

Red could not help grinning. "I keep my promises."

XI

Kennison opened the door to Johnson and Cheng, and Sarah stepped into the darkened offices. The man beside her was only a black shape. Sarah tried to tell herself that her uneasiness was illogical, but it *was* dark and Kennison *was* a bogeyman. At least that Night Shift of his had gone home. She yawned suddenly and stifled it behind her palm. "We couldn't do this by remote?" she asked again.

"There are hardware safeguards we must deal with."

If it was hardware, SuperNerd would have been a better

choice to go with Kennison. But he had insisted on her. He wouldn't trust anyone else.

The computer room in the back was dimly lit; but the machine itself was powered up, a hydra restless in her not-quite-sleep. "Some programs run during the graveyard shift," Kennison explained, "but we don't keep people here just to watch blinking lights."

"Turn the overhead lights on," she said. "So I can see what I'm doing."

"No. Someone might see from outside and wonder what was going on."

"There are no windows in this room," she pointed out. "And we can close the door."

"If we close the door, we might not hear it when someone enters the main offices." He sounded petulant.

"Oh, for Christ's sake! Who'd be coming at this hour?"

"A burglar?" Half-question, half-suggestion.

"Don't be absurd."

He answered sulkily, "Oh, all right." And he touched the panel next to the door. The fluorescents twinkled and came on, bathing the room in a pearly glow. Kennison's lower lip was thrust out in a pout. His whole face had the puffy, pinched appearance of a disappointed child. *What is his problem?* she wondered.

They worked together for an hour. Kennison unhooked panels in the backs of the drives and disabled switches. Sarah followed him on the terminal screen. <FILE UNLOCKED>. <FILE UNLOCKED>. *He could have done all this himself,* she thought. *Once these physical locks were disabled, I could have worked from my own apartment.* So why had he insisted that she accompany him? To hold his hand?

Kennison emerged from the rear of the left-most cabinet. He had taken his jacket off, and his tie. He had rolled up his shirtsleeves. His top shirt button had been unhooked. "That's the last of them," he announced. "Anyone can get in now and highjack the files." He frowned slightly, bit his lower lip, and turned to stare at the drives. "Jacta alea est," he said sadly.

"And this is your Rubicon?" she suggested.

He turned his head and smiled. "Alas, so few are grounded in the classics these days."

"Yes? And whose fault is that?"

Kennison shook his head. "We can encourage and nurture a trend, Ms. Bennett, as you well know by now. We cannot force it." He looked again at the drives he had unlocked. "I am determined upon this course of mine. Yet who can resist a glance backward? Who can abandon his past without some pang of regret?"

"Tell me all about it," she said, her voice heavy with irony.

Kennison turned to face her. "Yes. You would know about that, wouldn't you? You and I, we cannot slough off everything we have been and might have been for the convenience of the moment. That is a bond between us. Brother and sister." His face brightened, as if struck by a new thought. "Yes, brother and sister."

That'll be the day, she thought. She had to remind herself that this sad creature had ordered the deaths of people—of Morgan and Dennis. That he was interested in finding Dennis only because of his need to know who had taken him. Why couldn't he be a hard and arrogant psychopath, like the killers in the movies? Why did he have to be so wretched and pathetic?

She turned her face to the terminal screen. She had to study the system architecture so she could duplicate it quickly and dump it into Detweiler's system before anyone became aware of it. Only Selkirk, Johnson, and Cheng knew of the plan to secure a pristine copy of the files. If anyone else on the Night Shift detected the activity, the fat would be in the fire.

"You're sure that Detweiler has agreed to hide your system?"

"Jimmy Caldero called this evening and confirmed it."

She wouldn't look at him. Why had Red called Kennison and not her? Too busy, maybe? According to Bosworth, there was quite a lot brewing out there in Boston, with D, B, and S and the Secret Six. He could have forgotten. He might have been distracted.

She did not have to make excuses for him.

Kennison caught her attention. He held his hands up. "I'll go wash up while you get started, Sis." His hands were not dirty. She watched him leave the computer room. He turned the light off before he opened the door. When he had closed it behind him, she strode to the light panel and slapped the switch.

Sis.

It was an hour before she realized he had not returned.

She cocked her head and listened, but all she heard was the subdued pings and murmurs of a building late at night. The hum of the terminal and the overhead lights.

She finished the shutdown, reactivated the lockouts, then gathered her things and walked to the door, where she hesitated, remembering Kennison's paranoia about showing a light. She sighed and turned the lights out.

In the darkness, her hand froze on the knob. There would be something horrible in the doorway, waiting for her. *Don't be absurd.* She was paying the price now for all those horror movies she had seen as a teenager. *You aren't in some schlock TV movie here.*

No. The horrors were real. Drugged and hypnotized killers. Anonymous automobiles with screeching tires. A knife in the ribs in a parking lot. Bombs that turned meeting rooms into charnel houses. An implacable killer with dead eyes. And where was Tyler Crayle? He had dropped from sight, according to Kennison. Was he hunting for his brother's killer? Was he hunting for her? *Was he waiting on the other side of the door, with his knife red with Kennison's blood?*

No, dammit, she chastised herself. *Real-life killers didn't do that.* If Crayle were out there, he would not be waiting for her to open the door. He would have come in after her. To prove it, she yanked the door open.

There was nothing there.

She leaned against the door frame. *Go ahead; work yourself up into a state. A little hysteria is good for you. Helps purge the mind of an excess of rationality.*

She stepped out into the main room dimly lit by a few EXIT signs. The partitions for the cubicles seemed like the walls of a maze. She could see over the tops of the cubicles. A large, open room broken up into nooks and crannies. The room creaked as the building swayed in the wind. *Enough of this shit,* she thought, and reached around to hit the light switch inside the computer room.

A pool of light spilled out into the room and threw the partitions into pale relief.

Kennison shot up from behind the nearest partition. "What are you doing?" he hissed.

This time she did scream.

In a moment, Kennison was by her and had his arms around her. "Don't worry, Sis," he said. "I'll take care of you." He pressed against her a little too hard for a "brother." She shoved him away.

"Don't you touch me!" she warned. "What do you think you're doing frightening me like that? Is that how you get your kicks or something?"

He looked confused. "I . . . No . . . Of course not."

"Then what were you doing, hiding in that cubicle?"

He looked around and leaned toward her. "Selkirk is coming," he said in a confidential whisper.

"Then we'd better blow this joint before he sees us together."

"No. No," Kennison protested. "He's looking for *you*. He knows that you know about him and about the Q and about Bernstein and French. He knows that you won't give up looking for your partner. And finding him means finding the Q."

She grabbed him by the shirtfront. "Then why is he coming *here?*" she said into his face.

Kennison pulled her hands from his shirt. His grip was remarkably strong. "Because I called him and told him."

"You what!"

"Don't worry. I'll protect you."

"You're crazy!"

"No. Selkirk trusts me. He offered me a job with the Q. He wants me to download the Society's business into the Q's computers. In return, I get to be North American Coordinator for their organization."

She tried to pull her wrists from his grip and couldn't. "I told Red we couldn't trust you."

"I—Hush!" There was a noise at the main door. A shadow against the frosted glass. Kennison pushed her into the nearest cubicle. "Hide there. Under the desk." He slipped off down the aisle.

It had all been a ruse, that business about Red calling and Detweiler offering sanctuary. Why had she come here with him? How could she have let a vicious killer lull her into feeling safe? What was Kennison up to? Had he offered her to Selkirk as a token of good faith? Then why had he told her to hide? Did he think he could give her up to the Q and still protect her because they might give him an important office?

There was one thing she did know. Never hide anyplace where there is only one way out. Red had told her that. One of his secret-agent aphorisms. And Red, even three thousand miles away, was a more reliable guide than Kennison.

She crept from the cul-de-sac of the cubicle and made her way silently down the aisle. If she could position herself close enough to the door, she might be able to escape when Kennison led Selkirk to her "hiding place."

The door opened and closed quietly. Sarah heard the rustling of clothes and a shoe moving on the carpet. Then there was a sudden cry and a thud. Something crashed into a partition and shoved it a few inches across the carpet.

Now! She darted for the door.

But Kennison was there, at the light switch, and she brought herself up short. A single fluorescent panel glowed over the entry foyer. Selkirk lay like a flour sack against the skewed partition. Kennison saw her and smiled.

"Hi, Sis. I figured you would try to sneak around in back of him." He pointed to the motionless figure on the floor. "But I didn't really need your help. I told you I could handle it."

Sarah looked into his eyes. She had always wondered what a madman looked like. Now she knew. Completely and utterly sincere. She was suddenly afraid of Kennison. More afraid than she had ever been of Orvid Crayle.

She looked to Selkirk. For what? Help? Did one ask the scorpion for help against the rattler? Yes. Sometimes. But Selkirk lay loose, his arms and legs askew, a smear of blood across his face. Kennison held out a bloody paperweight. "I hit him with this," he said, as if expecting a compliment. "He was going to hurt you."

Kennison stepped toward her and she backed away. A potted plant blocked her retreat and he reached out and seized her wrist. "Don't worry. It's all over now. You're safe with me." He tried to pull her into his embrace and Sarah felt with icy certainty what he meant to do.

"Wait! No!" *Think, Sarah. Think!* "Not here. What if Selkirk comes to?"

Without loosening his grip on her wrist, Kennison twisted and kicked Selkirk hard in the rib cage. The unconscious man slid from his half-sitting position into a heap on the floor. "He won't. Not for a while. And besides . . ." He smiled weirdly. "Won't that add a little spice?"

Oh, God. "No. I can't. Not with him here." She rubbed her hand up his arm. "Take me back to my apartment, Brother. We'll be safe there." Safe with Helen and Chu. And Bosworth. And Polovsky, who had flown in that morning from Colorado.

Kennison might be crazy, but he wasn't stupid. He shook his head. "No, Sis. Too many people would see us. And what we have is . . . forbidden. No, we'll go home." He put an arm around her shoulder and guided her into the corridor toward the elevator. His grip was like steel. "We'll go home."

Kennison's car was in the building's parking garage, and there was no one in the elevator or in the garage, or even at the automatic toll gate. Kennison inserted his card in the slot and the garage door rolled up out of their way. He pulled up the ramp onto Stockton and turned left toward Telegraph Hill.

He laid his hand on her thigh and squeezed. "Don't worry," he kept saying. "You're safe now."

Polovsky and Bosworth were asleep when Red checked back into his suite in San Francisco. Bosworth was curled up on the sofa, but Polovsky had commandeered the king-size bed. Red rousted them both awake.

"I'm beat," he told them. "Weather in Boston delayed our takeoff." He yawned and stretched and looked straight at Polovsky. "I was looking forward to a nice warm bed."

"So sue me," said Walt. "You never showed. If I sleep on a daybed, I get a crick in my back."

Red didn't answer him. He wandered into the sitting room and the other two followed him like puppy dogs. The sitting room had been converted into a command center with drives and monitors. Printouts hung from the walls. Red tossed his flight bag onto the sofa and walked to the nearest wall to inspect their work.

"Don't you know what tape does to the wallpaper?"

"Listen to him," Walt said to Bosworth, jerking a thumb. "Go ahead; read it. The worm that Kennison let Gloria insert into his computer system gave us complete transcriptions of everything that's gone in or out. Files. E-mail. You name it."

Red ran his finger down the transcripts of the messages. "You send copies to the Council?"

"Oh, they're delirious with joy. By knowing what They're up do, Brother Betancourt thinks we can increase the values of our portfolios by a good fifteen percent."

Red looked at him. "It'll also help us counteract Them. Don't forget our Objective."

Polovsky returned the look. "Sure." Bosworth hunched his shoulders and concentrated on the terminal screen.

Red stuck his hands in his pants pockets and fiddled with

his key ring. The thumpers attached to the window made a
tiny hailstone rattle. He walked over and pushed the curtain
aside with his finger. Streetlights hung like strings of pearls
on Telegraph Hill. Here and there a window glowed. "I
thought Tex was coming."

"Yeah? Well you're stuck with me," Walt said. "Janie
went off somewhere and left him in charge of the ranch."
Red grunted but made no reply. "How was Boston?" Walt
asked.

Red turned away from the window. "Wet. I met some of
our competitors."

"Yeah, I heard." Polovsky found a chair and eased into it.
"So what do we do about them?"

"Nothing, for now. We're allies in the search for the
SQPS. First things first." Red stretched again. "And first
thing . . . I'm for sacking out. If I can find a bed," he added
pointedly.

Polovsky jerked upward with his thumb. "Try upstairs,
why don't you. There's a nice warm bed up there."

Red gave him a sharp look. "Watch your mouth, Walt.
Your parents spent too much money on the orthodontia to
have it go to waste now."

Polovsky shook his head. "Naw. She's not up there. She
went over to Kennison Demographics about one-thirty or so.
He wanted her to go over the architecture for the megaworm
she's designing to corrupt Their database."

Red scowled and looked at the blind-shaded window. "She
went? This late?"

"They had to wait for the Night Shift to go off."

"I wish she hadn't gone."

"Why? Kennison's with us on this one, ain't he?"

"I just don't like the idea."

"Jealous?"

Red scowled at him. He drifted to the window and pushed
the curtain aside again. "Maybe I should go over there."

Kennison's apartment glowed in flickering lights and shadows, as if from a fire. A cold fire: she could feel no heat; but there was a smell as of cinders. Sarah stood on the threshold, not wishing to enter, resisting the persistent pressure of his hand against her back. She sensed a strangeness about the place. Kennison was the Devil and this was Hell. She would not see, not feel, the flames until she entered.

Kennison pushed against the small of her back and she staggered into the flickering twilight.

Her eyes darted about the room. The apartment did not seem lived in, but that made sense because Kennison did not actually live there. Still, it seemed to her that there should be something personal in it. A photograph. A book. Anything. Instead it was bare, anonymous, and devoid of personality. All she could see was the electronic gadgetry set up by the window and the busy little window tappers "jamming" the vibrations of the glass.

He locked the door behind them and leaned against it. "Now, we're safe."

Not until he closed the door could she see what was behind it. A bank of votive candles in red and blue glass cups set in a brass stand of curled metal. The flames danced within their containers, casting halos on the wall and ceiling. Above the votive candles hung a framed photograph of a round-faced white woman. Some of the candles cast halo shapes above her head. Her eyes smiled at Sarah. The photograph was surrounded by vases bursting with sprays of colored blossoms. A small, blackened cup in the center held the remains of incense cones.

Oh, Sweet Jesus, she thought. *What have I walked into?*

She jerked her head around to stare at Kennison. There were tears in the corners of his eyes. He looked like a small child. Sarah backed slowly away from him until her heel caught the leg of the coffee table and the sound brought Kennison's head up.

"It's gone," he complained. He closed his eyes tight and clenched his fists. "But we'll get it back," he added in what sounded almost like a normal voice. "It will be . . . hard on you, but worthwhile. You'll see. You'll understand." His voice was the calm, reasonable voice of a madman. He began to advance toward her.

Sarah darted suddenly around the coffee table, intending to outflank him and reach the door. But he vaulted the table with surprising agility and cut her off. "Now, Sis, that's no way to act. If you cooperate, it won't hurt so much."

"I'm not your sister!" she cried. He reached for her and she danced toward the sofa. "What's wrong with you?" She had to stay out of his grasp.

"Are you afraid?" he asked with a peculiar smile. "That's good. I'll protect you."

"Afraid?" She reached the end of the sofa and pulled it out into his path. "You bet your ass I'm afraid." She threw one of the pillows at his face and he batted it aside. Her eyes cast about the room for something to throw at him.

She faked left and cut right toward the window. She ran both hands across the glass pane and brushed aside the little mechanical spiders. They fell in a cascade to the floor, where they clattered and danced in the nap of the carpet. She grabbed a double handful of the tiny devices and dashed around the other end of the sofa just as Kennison reached the window.

She turned and threw one of the spiders as hard as she could at his face. He ducked, but it struck him in the cheek and he howled. He cupped his cheek with his hand and brought it away bloody. Sarah hurled another tapper at him and ran for the door.

"Walt!" she yelled over her shoulder. "Norris! Someone help!"

Helen shook her head. "She hasn't come back, Brother Caldero. I've been here since she left, so I would know."

Red was in no mood to be reasonable. He leaned far over the concierge desk, so that Helen backed up deeper in her chair. "Maybe she came back while you were in the john. I just want to see." He held the pose for a moment, staring into Helen's face. Then he straightened and looked away. "Please?"

Helen snatched her key ring from the desk drawer. She stood and straightened her skirt. "Follow me," she said.

Red trod on her heels. "I know where her suite is," he said. *She's probably there, fast asleep, dreaming the dreams of the innocent.* Sure, that was it. She had come back late. Helen had been away from her desk, so she had tiptoed off to bed. If she was there, he would wake her up and give her a good tongue-lashing on proper procedure.

And if she wasn't . . .

Well, she was a big girl, wasn't she? She could take care of herself. Just ask Orvid Crayle.

But no. None of us can really take care of ourselves. The French hadn't stopped at liberty and equality; they had added fraternity to make it work. We need each other. Or maybe, what is more important, we need to need each other. It's not that one's back must be guarded; but that, when it was, life was a hell of a lot less lonely.

She wasn't in the suite.

Red prowled from room to room, calling her name. Helen waited patiently by the door. When he returned to the front room, he looked at her helplessly.

"I told you she wasn't back yet."

"But where is she?" He threw his arms out.

"With Cousin Kennison." Helen's pinched lips showed what she thought of Cousin Dan. "At the Demographics offices." She pointed to the phone. "You could just call over there, you know. If it would make you feel better."

"I—" Red wondered if he looked as stupid as he felt. "Well, sure. Jet lag and late nights, right?" He grinned and picked up the phone. He punched three numbers. "Frank? . . . What? . . . Yes, I know what time it is. This is important. Do this one thing for me; then you can go home. Put me through to Johnson and Cheng. . . . Right. So nothing shows up on the suite's regular phone usage." He put a hand over the mouthpiece. "I suppose by tomorrow night every Associate in the country will know about this."

Helen shrugged. "You won't be the first one of us who's been flustered by Rule Nineteen."

The phone was ringing. Ringing. "Dammit. No one answers." Sarah could glance at the readout and recognize her own number. Why didn't she answer? He pushed the phone into its cradle.

Had they gone to Kennison's apartment? Why he couldn't imagine, but it was a possibility. He squinted through the eyepiece on the eavesdropper. Kennison's apartment window swam into view, but it was too far away for him to see anything.

He turned off the randomizers and checked the speakers, but all he heard were the randomizers on Kennison's window. He hunched his shoulders. "I still don't like it." Helen said nothing. He ran his finger up and down the phone handle. "Tell me. Was Brother Walt checked in before Sister Sarah left?" He looked up at Helen.

Now the concierge looked worried, too. "Why . . . Yes, he was. He arrived about midafternoon."

Red swatted the telephone and it flew from the table with a crash of bells. "Dammit! He knew better! He should have set himself up as handler. Made sure she knew to check in and when. He should have arranged for backup with Frank Chu. And he should have kept watch! He let her go out by herself!"

Helen didn't say anything. She seemed to close in on herself and wouldn't meet his eye. "He . . . He didn't like her. Because of the Dump."

"Because of . . . My God, what has that got to do with anything? This was Associate Business. You don't have to 'like' someone to do a job with her!" Brother Polovsky would have a lot to answer for. But to Betancourt, not to himself. If he called Polovsky to task everyone would think it was a personal thing. No, this had to go by the book. Later, he could invite Walt outside and make it personal.

An insistent beeping from the floor reminded him that the telephone was off the hook. He bent down and gathered it up. "Jeez," he said, fumbling it into place. "They sure do build these things rugged."

"I suppose a lot of people throw theirs across the room."

He glanced at Helen and smiled crookedly. "Yeah." He let out a deep breath. Then he turned and sat against the back of the sofa. Outside the window, San Francisco slept.

"Should I leave you here?" Helen asked.

"What?" He looked over his shoulder. "Oh. Yeah. I'll wait here. Maybe I'll toss out on the sofa. Buzz me when you see her get off the elevator."

Helen shut the door gently and the room darkened. Red thought about turning a light on, but that would mean getting up and he didn't feel up to it. He was tired. If he just held tight, she would show up. Tomorrow, they'd both have a good laugh over it.

How long he sat there he didn't know. The hailstone sounds from Kennison's apartment faded in and out. He dozed.

The sudden change in the sound jerked him awake. The speakers rushed liked a wave crashing on a pebble-strewn beach. The autorecorder clicked on and he heard sounds: feet running, a howl of pain. Then a voice: "Walt! Norris! Someone help!"

The world seemed to freeze for an instant, and an icy hand seized his heart and squeezed. Jacksonville. It was Jacksonville all over again.

Kennison beat her to the door. Sarah threw another spider at him, but she missed and its tiny legs struck in the door like miniature daggers. "No," he pleaded. "This isn't right. You've got to be afraid. You don't know how to play the game at all."

"You're crazy, Kennison. Walt! He's trying to rape me!" The recorder in her apartment would kick in automatically, but what if no one was there to monitor it? They thought she was at the Demographics office, not here. They were probably asleep.

Well, at least she could leave a message with them. Tell them what had happened. She threw the spiders at Kennison's eyes, keeping him at bay, and gasped the story out in short bursts.

"He lured Selkirk over. Ambushed him. Without warning."

Kennison seemed oblivious to the fact that she was talking for the eavesdropper. He paused in his pursuit and gave her a puzzled look. "But he was Q, Sis. He was coming to hurt you. I protected you. Aren't you grateful?"

Grateful! She was running low on weapons. She ran back toward the window to grab some more from the carpet, but Kennison was too close behind her and she couldn't stop. The tappers crunched and popped under her shoes.

Kennison's fingers closed on her shoulder. She spun on her heel and slapped him hard, boxing his ear. She pulled away and her blouse ripped at the right shoulder.

"This isn't right," Kennison complained, holding his ear.

"You're sick, Kennison. You're very sick." This wasn't the dapper, well-mannered foe she had known. This was a sad and pathetic wretch. She could, and did, fear him. If once he got his hands on her . . . But she couldn't hate him, not for being ill.

Kennison paused and a tiny crease appeared between his brows. "Sick?"

She threw words now, instead of metal spiders. She could actually see the wounds each one opened. "Yes, sick. You are vile and disgusting." She turned with sudden inspiration and pointed to the votive shrine by the door. "What would *she* have said?"

Kennison howled and covered his face with both his hands. "No! But I had to . . . Everything was out of control." He dropped his hands. Tears lined his cheeks. "Prudence understands. She helped me. You can help me, too."

"How can I help you . . . ?"

His eyes pleaded with her. "Stop me."

She kicked forward with all her strength and caught him

squarely in the groin. He doubled over, clutching himself, and made retching sounds in his throat.

"Always glad to oblige a friend," she said. She jumped for the door and threw it open.

And screamed.

It was Selkirk, and he was very, very angry.

XII

What's black and blue and red all over? The old joke shot through Sarah's mind. Answer: Selkirk's face. The bruise where Kennison had struck him covered most of the right side of his head. Sticky, half-dried blood created rivers and tributaries down his cheek and chin, staining his shirt collar. Hard, angry eyes squinted through puffed and blackened flesh.

He held a pistol in his hand.

"Out o' my way, lassie," he snarled. "Where is that snakin', crowlin' ferlie?" He shoved her aside and stepped into the apartment. "Ah, there ye be." He grinned, but the smile broke open a half-healed cut in the lip and blood dripped onto his chin. He raised the gun.

"No!" Sarah grabbed him by the gun arm and tried to hold on.

"First things first. I'll treat wi' ye next, lassie. Ken wha ye've learned o' the Societé." Sarah could barely understand him. Selkirk pushed her away and pointed his pistol at Kennison.

Her hand felt something sharp in the carpet. One of the spiders she had thrown at Kennison. She seized it and threw it hard at Selkirk's face. He cried out, half-turned toward her.

And—incredibly—the elevator chimed.

The apartment door was still open from Selkirk's entry. Sarah made a flying leap out into the hall, slamming the door closed as she did. "Hold that elevator!" she said and ran for it.

A young man had just stepped off the elevator, a dozen paces down the hall. He stood unsteadily and favored her with a bleary-eyed stare. He grinned. "Hey, baby," he said. "You wanna—"

Kennison's door opened and Selkirk stepped into the hall. He saw Sarah and the young man and raised his pistol. The man stared at him, bug-eyed. Sarah almost rolled into the elevator car. She seized the man as she went in and pulled him after her. He staggered and fell against the back wall. Sarah hit the button that said: LOBBY.

The doors slid shut just as something like an angry hornet ripped through the air and shattered the plastic panel by the young man's head. "He's got a gun," he said.

"No shit," said Sarah.

"Why's a white man shooting at a sister?" He sounded angry, defiant. His use of the word *sister* reminded her of Kennison and his sick game.

"I think he was shooting at you," she said.

"Oh." The elevator hummed and they rode down together in silence.

When they reached the lobby, Sarah pulled the red switch that shut off power to the car. A ringing like that of a small alarm clock issued from the panel. Sarah wondered how long it would take before anyone ventured forth to investigate. There was a staircase, of course, and Kennison's apartment was only five flights up. But this would give her a lead.

The apartment house had no night doorman. Sarah saw the splintered wood and bent metal where Selkirk had forced his way in past the locks. She ran out to the sidewalk.

The cold night air struck her like a knife, sucking her breath from her. The sea breeze worked its way through the tear in her blouse, freezing her arm. She looked around, disoriented, at the dark and empty streets. Her breath was cotton in the air.

"You a'right? Who was that honky?" It was the man from the elevator. "Wuzzit drugs?" He eyed her warily, sobered by the night, suddenly aware of his vulnerability.

"No," she said, casting about for a short, plausible answer. "Espionage." She couldn't wait here. Selkirk would be coming after her.

"I'll come with you," the man declared, and the offer was so sincere and so patently suicidal that she paused just a moment to touch him on the arm.

"No, thank you. Wait here. Hide. Someone will come."

So saying, she sprinted up the street without looking back. *He's probably killed Kennison by now,* she thought. The idea depressed her. There had been a time when she had wanted nothing less than for Kennison to die horribly. But between the rage and the reality, she had softened. In her memory she could see Orvid Crayle's glassy and unbelieving eyes, staring at the clouds, the darkening skies, the stars, and beyond. *The second time will be easier,* his ghost had whispered. But self-defense was one thing; execution, another.

The fog rising off the Golden Gate was a ghostly lover caressing the city. The foghorn in the straits moaned like a lost soul. The false dawn suffused the air with the color of pearl.

Thank God she had kept herself in shape. Those weekends in the mountains. The survival training. Who would have thought? Her breath came in short, rapid gulps as she ran; but she sped rapidly and smoothly up the street. The staccato clicking of her shoes striking the pavement echoed in the foggy night air and deserted streets. Between one stride and the next she kicked her shoes off—first one, then the other—and ran barefoot in the dark. It seemed she ran faster that way, at one with her warrior ancestors in the steaming jungles of Africa. Hard-soled, enduring. They shored her up and carried her along. The steam was the mist of a Pacific morning; the jungle was concrete. The pavement was damp from the fog and cold, chilling her feet.

She heard the slap of shoe leather on cement. Away from her; and she closed her eyes and allowed herself a moment of relief. She broke stride and halted, bending way over, hands on her knees, breathing in great gusts.

Then she heard the footsteps change direction and follow her up the street, and she resumed running without even thinking about how tired she was.

She thought about shouting, awakening some of the people in the sleeping houses, calling for help. But Selkirk would reach her more quickly than any befuddled householder. Confused and half-asleep, no one she awoke would be help against her pursuer.

She crossed the street and darted into a park. The wet grass whipped at her calves and ankles, soaking her feet, numbing them with the cold dew. She stepped on a rock, and the sudden, unexpected pain caused her to let out a high squeak, quickly stifled.

But it had been loud enough in the silent night air to cause her pursuer to change direction. She cursed silently and forced herself to push on, hobbling slightly now because the rock had cut her foot.

Then, unexpectedly, she came out into a parking lot and found herself staring up into the noble and farsighted gaze of Christopher Columbus. Past the twelve-foot bronze and saw the tall, fluted pillar of Coit Tower. She was at the dead end of Telegraph Hill.

Red paused at the door to Kennison's apartment and put his ear to it. Nothing. No sounds of a struggle. Someone had left the building, afraid of pursuit. The elevator grounded on the first floor proved that much. *Let it be Sarah,* he thought. *Let it be Sarah who escaped.*

He reached inside his jacket and his hand closed on nothing. I really am tired, he thought. He knew exactly where his gun was. In the sealed and bonded suitcase the porter had left in his suite. All he had were the lock picks he carried on his key ring. The lock on Kennison's apartment door was a Rabson, but it took Red only a moment to open it.

Two legs protruded from behind the door. A quick stride and he was beside the body on one knee. Kennison. He lay staring at the ceiling. The front of his shirt was stained red and the carpet beneath him was wet and sticky. Red had come over intending to thrash Kennison within an inch of his life, but to find this. He wondered if Sarah had shot him. *She never needs my help.*

He rose and brushed his knee and turned on the speakers for the eavesdropper. "Bosworth, what happened?"

"We're playing back the tape now, boss—"

Polovsky's voice cut in. "Hey, Jimmy. I'm sorry this happened. It's all my fault. I was senior man on station and I shoulda taken charge, but—"

"Save it. Just tell me what happened." Red quickly inspected the rest of the apartment. When he came to the shower stall, he hesitated before drawing the curtain, afraid of what he might find behind it. But there was no body. No Sarah. He closed his eyes briefly and gave thanks.

"We played back the tape," Polovsky told him when he returned to the living room. "As near as we can figure, Selkirk barged in while Sarah was fighting off Kennison." Walt's voice plunged. "Jesus, Jimmy, you should hear the kind of crap Kennison was spouting at her. He's a real piece of work, he is. But this Selkirk had some private grudge against Kennison, and Sarah gave him the slip while he was plugging our boy. He took off after her. Fired a shot down the hall, we figure. Anyway, the acoustics sound different."

"There was a bullet hole in the elevator. No blood. He must have missed. She must have gone east, up Lombard. I would have seen her if she'd gone the other way. Where's Chu?"

"He already left for home. We called him on his car phone and he's on his way back. Make it half an hour."

"Shit. I can't wait. But I need backup."

"Let the kid man home plate, Jimmy. I'll get a car and be over."

"All right, but I'm not waiting. Seconds may count." He started toward the door, but Kennison's hand reached up and grabbed his pants leg. Red cried out in a moment's terror and looked down into Kennison's eyes.

"James." It was a hoarse, breathy whisper. "James. I'm so sorry."

"Shit! The sunuvabitch is still alive!"

"Who?" asked Polovsky. "Kennison?"

"How many dead sons of bitches do we have over here? Of course, Kennison. Tell Helen. Get some medics over here right away." He shook loose from the iron grip. "Take care of the scene, Walt. You and Helen. You know what to do. Don't let the regular cops find anything." And what was the use? Ever since the Dump they had been bailing water frantically. But there were people like Doang and Llewellyn all over the country. Probing. Wondering. Historians and mathematicians finding themselves together as odd bedfellows. Why bother concealing what had happened here?

Because, by God, you finish the course.

"I didn't hurt her, James." Red stared at the man, wondering if he was dying. "I wanted to. I tried. But I didn't."

"Yeah, I'll give you a medal." He turned to leave.

"No." The hand reached out again, faltered, dropped. "Jacksonville."

Red froze. He would not turn and look at Kennison. "What about Jacksonville?"

"I'm sorry for that, too."

"I'm no damn priest. If you want absolution, apologize to Alice. I'd say you'd be seeing her soon; but you're probably not going to the same place."

"I am sorry."

He turned and lashed out at him. "Dammit, we play by rules! She was under my protection. She wasn't a target anymore. But you forgot to call off your man. She trusted me and, because of you, *I failed her!*"

Bubbles formed at the corners of Kennison's lips. "I once . . . I once left an enemy to die," he confessed. "Alone. In the dark."

What does he want from me? Red turned to the door. *Sarah needs me more than he does.* He paused with his hand on the knob. "Help is coming. I don't hate you that much."

The head turned to follow him. "Then . . . stay with . . . me."

Red opened the door. "I don't like you that much."

When Red emerged from the apartment building, a young black man leaped from the bushes and blocked his way. The man had a knife, which he held up so Red could see it. He had also been drinking heavily, and his breath was sour. "Your cab's gone, mister. They don't wait around, you know."

Red was in no mood for petty delays. He took a step back and fell into a fighting stance.

"You the one she was expecting?"

It was an unexpected question for a mugger to ask. Red hesitated.

"The lady that ran out of here. She told me someone would be along. Is that you?"

Red slowly relaxed. "Tall black lady?" A nod. "That's me. I'm her friend."

A suspicious glare. "You're white."

"So?"

"Man chasing her was white, too."

"Short and young? Shaggy yellow hair and beard?"

"Yeah, that's the one. He come running out a minute or two after her. The mother had a gun. Shot at me in the elevator. Shit. I never got sober so fast." He hefted the knife. "Tell me, whitey. This have anything to do with drugs? With mothers' tears?"

"With . . . No. We're, ah, spies. Want to see my badge? Genuine U.S. Government."

"That's what she told me. Spy shit. No, I don't need to see your badge." He put the knife away. "I believe you. Know why? She pulled me into the elevator. She was running for her life and she pulled me into the elevator. She could have left me to die."

Red thought of Kennison upstairs. "Listen. Go up to five-ten. I left the door open. There's a man up there, gunshot.

He might be dying. He ... He shouldn't be alone. I have some people coming. Big white guy. Tell him Jimmy posted you. His name's Walt. He'll handle things." He turned to go.

"Hey, wait. I followed them. The bearded guy and the sister. They went across Pioneer Park toward the tower."

Red paused. "You followed them?"

"Yeah, just far enough to see which way they went. Then I came back here and waited. I figured, shit, why not? It wasn't much to do; but I figured, shit, she saved my ass."

"Yeah," said Red. "She does that a lot."

Sarah was cold and wet and the sole of her foot was bleeding. Her breath came in gasping heaves and she knew she could run no farther. She needed a place to hide. Coit Tower loomed above her, massive and graceful. The fluted concrete soared; the lines drew her eyes upward and she stared into the concrete statue of a bird, wings outspread, taking triumphant flight. Phoenix, rising from her bed of ashes. Death and Resurrection. She staggered up the stairs. Death and Resurrection.

The entrance was a revolving door. She grabbed the handle and shook. It was locked. She sobbed in frustration and drew back and threw herself at the doors. They rattled but did not budge. Pain shot up her shoulder and she staggered back. She hunched over, holding her arm, and looked over her shoulder for Selkirk. But he was not yet in sight.

When she looked back at the doors there was a man standing there watching her through the glass, and she gave a little cry and shoved her fist in her mouth. He was an old man, dressed in a Park Guard uniform. He had a thermos in one hand. "What the hell do you think you're doing, lady?" His voice sounded distant, muffled by the glass.

She pressed her face to the door. "Let me in, please. He's got a gun."

"What?" The old man frowned. He looked past her shoulder; then he studied her again. "What's the matter?" She turned her face up in mute appeal. The guard made a deci-

sion. He pulled out a key ring and unlatched the main entrance door.

Sarah pushed her way in. The air rushed; the rubber stiles
slapped against the housing. She staggered out and fell to
her hands and knees. "Lock the door, quick."

"What's wrong, miss? Where are your shoes?"

"There's a man chasing me. He's got a gun. Is there a
telephone?"

The guard straightened and blinked rapidly. He pointed
with his thermos. "In there. To the right. Hey."

Sarah paused. "What?"

"Here." The guard dug into his pocket and pulled out some
change, which he pressed into her hand. "It's a pay phone."

"Thanks. Look. If he bangs on the door, don't answer. If
he thinks there was no one to let me in, he'll go somewhere
else."

"Miss, you said he had a gun. Parks and Recreation put
me here so's kids don't break in and damage the frescoes. I
ain't getting in no firefight. If this guy comes along, I'll lie
low." He grinned a gap-tooth smile. "Learned that in 'Nam
a long time ago."

She clenched his quarter in her fist and stepped inside the
tower.

And paused. The inside walls were covered with murals.
Men larger than life toiled sweatily. They guided plows,
swung hammers, packed oranges. The colors were somber;
the faces, brooding and angry. To her right, a weed-grown
shipyard, with sullen out-of-work stevedores. Directly ahead,
two farming scenes flanked a doorway. On the left, an idyllic
landscape of nineteenth-century farmers. On the right, in
sharp contrast, modern, mechanized farming, with a steam
shovel devouring a hillside. A pair of all-seeing eyes, surrounded by sun, moon, rain, lightning, stared back at her
from the center panel above the doorway.

She had never seen anything like it in her life. The murals
encircled the tower, covering both the inner and the outer
walls of the hallway.

Socialist realism, she thought. The glorification of work

by those who did no manual labor themselves. Would the painter have depicted preindustrial farming in so idyllic a fashion if he had ever had to sweat on such a farm?

"The phone's to the right." The guard had come up behind her. He guided her to a small alcove in the inner wall of the corridor. "I'll be in the gift shop if you need me," he said.

Sarah inserted the coins and dialed her room at the hotel. Bosworth answered on the second ring. "Norris? Norris!" She held the phone in both her hands. It was so good to hear a friendly voice. "This is Gloria. I'm—"

"Sister Bennett! We've been worried. Is Brother Caldero there yet?"

"Red? He's back?" Why did that thought make her feel so irrationally relieved? It wasn't as if he were there with her. "What do you mean is he here yet? How does he know—"

There was a loud banging on the doors of the tower. Someone rattled the locks. Sarah backed deeper into the telephone alcove. She dropped her voice to a whisper. "Listen, Norris. I'm in Coit Tower. Alan Selkirk is after me. I think he killed Kennison—"

"No, Brother Cal—"

"Listen!" Her whisper was harsh, urgent. "He may not have seen the guard let me in—"

Two muffled shots. Whining, spitting sounds. The glass in the doors sang. "Or maybe he did. He just shot out the doors."

Sarah dropped the phone and ran from the alcove, cutting right, away from the door. A giant steelworker watched her impassively; a surveyor ignored her. She ran past joyless foundry workers.

"Hsst! This way." The guard beckoned from the gift shop entrance. She ducked inside with him. There was a counter directly ahead of her. To the right was a token booth: RIDE THE ELEVATOR TO THE TOP. To the left, the turnstile to the elevator. Past that, a metal grate blocking the stairwell. She and the guard crouched together in a nook where they could not be seen from the entrance

"Where's the back door?" she asked in a whisper.

"There isn't any."

Then they were trapped. "I'm sorry I got you into this."

He shrugged. "I didn't have to let you in."

Or were they trapped? The corridor was circular. If they could avoid Selkirk until he was on the north side . . . She remembered how she had played the game with Crayle on Mount Falcon, ducking back and forth to keep the assassin always on the other side of the brick wall. Would it work again? She remembered how terrified she had been at the time, and cold sweat sprang again on her face and arms. Her foot throbbed where she had cut it.

The inner doors rattled. Selkirk was trying them. But they were exit doors for people returning from the top of the tower. The entrance was where she and the guard were hiding.

The old man crouched beside her, his eyes white and wide against his dark face. His breath was shaky and irregular. Sarah touched him on the arm. She pointed to where Selkirk was and made a circling motion. Then she pointed to the two of them and arched her arm toward the turnstile. The man swallowed, licked his lips, and nodded.

She listened carefully to the quiet footsteps, trying to follow his route in her mind. A pause. A sound. He had found the telephone dangling and hung it up. *Now he knows for sure.*

A door opened. Which door? She closed her eyes and thought. The men's room was directly across from the phone alcove. *Methodical,* she thought. *He's checking all the hiding places closest to the main entrance.* Would he actually step inside the men's room? No. He would leave the door open and look inside. He wouldn't give anyone a chance to slip past him.

Sit tight, Sarah. Sit tight. Women's room next. On the other side of the entrance. And then . . . Around the corridor, clockwise. Which would bring him to the gift shop entrance last. She exhaled carefully. Had he gone widdershins, he would have found them before they had a chance to make their move.

She waited until his footsteps faded. Then she scampered barefoot across to the turnstile and hopped over it, landing on the balls of her feet. The jar of landing reopened the cut and sent a lance of pain through her left leg. The guard followed her, squeezing through the turnstile arms.

Now, a straight shot through the exit doors to the revolving door and down the stairs. Barefoot across broken glass. Could they do it before Selkirk heard them and raced around from the antipodes of the corridor? They would never have a better chance.

Softly, but quickly. She tiptoed to the doors and pushed them gently open. Then she dashed for the front entrance.

And Selkirk had her in his grasp before she had taken three steps.

The revolving doors had been shot out. Small saw like teeth of broken glass rimmed the empty frames. Red studied the door, trying to guess the caliber of pistol Selkirk might have, and wondering what the hell difference it would make anyway. You were just as dead from a .22 slug as from a .38. The smart move would be to wait for Walt to catch up. Walt would come heeled and that would help even the odds.

It would certainly be a lot smarter than storming Coit Tower barehanded.

"Hell, I never was very smart," he growled aloud. Before he could think twice about it, he bounded through the two shot-out panels, hit the floor inside the tower, and rolled. He came to his feet, looked in both directions, and took cover in the phone alcove.

No shot. Good news or bad news? It might mean that Selkirk had come and gone already. And if that was the case . . .

A shudder ran through him. He had to believe that Sarah was still alive; and that meant he had to believe that Selkirk was inside the tower, armed and waiting for him.

He didn't know I'd be unarmed. Had he stayed to cover the door, he'd have been exposed to my return fire. Some people just didn't have the sand to stand there and take it. So if he hadn't been covering the front door, where was he? Think, Malone! Three possibilities: around the back, up the top, not here. Which was the more dangerous? Around the back, because he could come at you from either direction.

He glanced down and saw blood on the floor and his heart skipped a beat. Someone had stood by the telephone and dripped blood on the floor. He knelt and examined the spot. It was a bare partial footprint. Sarah's, by the size of it. He played his light along the floor and saw two others.

She had come in the door; her foot was already bleeding. She had come to the phone. Of course, she would have called in at the first opportunity. *That means that Bosworth knows she's here and he would have called Walt and Chu on their cell phones. They would head straight here as soon as Chu gets in.*

Meanwhile, though, I am the man on the scene.

He lay on his stomach and peeked around the corner. Nothing. Another glance behind him was equally reassuring. He wished he knew Selkirk better, so he would know what to anticipate. He stepped around the corner and flattened himself against the inside wall. *You are crazy, Malone. You know that? Wait for Walt. How can it help Sarah if you get your fool head blown off?*

He inched his way along the corridor until he came to the gift shop entrance. Then he leaped inside, rolling to his right.

He rolled into a body.

XIII

Sarah had made no attempt to scream when she saw Red enter the base of the tower, but Selkirk kept a hand clapped over her mouth anyway. They were on the observation gallery, and the night wind whipped through the open arches, grabbing at their clothes and hair. Sarah felt chilled and hugged herself. Her teeth chattered. Selkirk had picked the arch that faced the front side of the tower and kept looking over the balustrade toward the parking lot, a hundred feet below. "Don't worry," he kept saying. "He'll leave as soon as he sees no one is here."

That was exactly what she was worried about, but she didn't see what she could do about it. Selkirk had used the guard's keys to shut off the elevator, and the steel grate still blocked the stairs. So, Red would figure that no one could have gone upstairs.

Selkirk took his hand from her mouth. "I'm sorry, lassie. What did you say? Softly, now."

"I said you didn't have to kill the old man." Selkirk had known that the tower had no rear exit; so he had waited by the side of the exit doors, knowing that Sarah would have to come out that way. He had grabbed her and threatened the guard with his pistol while he forced her toward the door. Then, spotting Red crossing the parking lot, he had turned and very coolly shot the old man through the heart.

Selkirk looked surprised. "Of course I did. Be reasonable. I couldn't bring him up here with us. If Caldero didn't find the guard somewhere on the first floor, he would conclude that we had come up here. But I couldn't leave him behind, either, or he would simply have told Caldero where we had gone. Even if I left him unconscious, I couldn't take the chance of him reviving. This way . . ." And Selkirk paused and glanced once more over the balustrade. "This way, Caldero will conclude that I came here, shot the guard, and took you away before he showed up. There was no other logical course of action for me. We're not monsters, you know. We don't kill people for no reason."

The most horrifying thing about Selkirk's speech, Sarah decided, was the utter sincerity with which he uttered it. Of course, he didn't kill without reason—but his reasoning was monstrous. She looked into Selkirk's eyes and saw the child-like innocence of the sociopath. Kennison, but without the jaded cynicism. Human beings might be no more than variables in a set of equations, but he was still young enough to feel the need for justification.

"Then why not kill me, too?" Danger had made her reckless. But if he had wanted Red to think he had gone . . .

Selkirk looked at her. "There's no need for that, lass. You're going to help us."

"Never."

"Ah, but we'll help you rescue your friend."

"What?"

"Hush, lassie." He clapped a hand over her mouth and looked around. "Your friend, French? Bernstein has him in Manhattan, but we can't get near him. His penthouse is like a fortress. But *you* he might allow inside."

"I don't get it. Why should you care about rescuing Dennis?"

He shrugged. "I don't. I care about getting to Bernstein. He's dangerous. He's been defying the *Cabinet Cachette*. You'll help us get to him, and we'll free your friend as a reward."

It was an easy choice. Bernstein was Selkirk's opponent in some sort of power struggle within the Q. That didn't make him one of the good guys, but it made him the enemy of someone who had shot an old man through the heart because it was "logical."

"What makes you think I would want to help you, for any reward?"

"It's easier if you want to," he responded cryptically, "but it isn't necessary."

The body was that of an aged black man in the gray-and-black uniform of a security guard. One glance at the wound was enough to tell Red that the man was gone. A heart shot. The floor and the wall behind him was a scarlet backdrop. Red pushed himself upright, feeling sick. The guard was unarmed, dammit; but Selkirk had shot him anyway. Why? And where was Sarah?

He quickly checked through the rest of the alcove: the gift

shop and the token booth. He was afraid of what he might see when he looked behind the counters. His arms shook and would barely support him when he leaned over.

When he saw that she was not there, he slumped against the token booth, half-relieved, half-distressed. *Get ahold of yourself, Malone. You'll be in no shape to help her, the state you're in.*

He walked past the body of the guard and ducked through the turnstile into the elevator vestibule. Selkirk wasn't a homocidal maniac. He'd had a reason for killing the guard. Not self-defense; not against a sixty-year-old unarmed man. Then why? Because the guard had seen something that Selkirk didn't want revealed.

Back to basics. Downstairs, upstairs, or outside. Downstairs was out. What about upstairs? Two means of access. He shook the gate. It was locked shut. He pressed the elevator button. Nothing. No lights at all; so the elevator was turned off. The Parks people must do that at the end of the day.

That left outside. *Selkirk must have left before I got here.* Either with Sarah or chasing her. He had reached the exit doors before he froze, one hand on the handle. He looked back over his shoulder. Then he returned softly to the elevator and went to his hands and knees.

Yes. Another partial footprint in blood. Several of them. In front of the elevator. And some of them had been overstepped by a shod foot. He returned to the guard's body and searched it. No key ring on his belt or in his pockets. He sat on his haunches with his arms resting across his knees. Then he looked toward the ceiling; wiped his palms on his pants legs, the back of his hand across his mouth. She was up there. He knew it. And Selkirk. Lying doggo. Trying to avoid a fight. *Not so brave, are you, if you think your opponent is armed?*

If only he were. *All right. Think it through. Liabilities. I'm unarmed. Selkirk is armed and has no compunctions about killing. He's got the high ground and both means of access are blocked. He's got Sarah as a potential hostage.*

Assets.

He stifled an involuntary chuckle. *My good looks. And a lock pick.* He glanced at the metal grate that blocked the stairs. If he could open the grate without making a noise, he might have the benefit of surprise. Selkirk wouldn't be expecting that.

He dug his jimmy out of his pants pocket and went to work. It was a large lock and not meant to resist a clever assault. The pins clicked easily into place.

Selkirk shifted rapidly from one foot to the other. He checked his watch. "Why doesn't he leave?" He didn't really expect an answer, and Sarah didn't supply him one. She didn't know what she wanted more: Red to come upstairs to rescue her or Red to leave so he would not be hurt.

A motion at the head of the stairs, barely sensed out of the corner of her eye. A figure creeping silently toward them. *Oh God, it's Red.* Sarah turned suddenly away, lest she betray his presence. She pointed over the balustrade. "Damn," she said in a voice heavy with disappointment. "He's leaving."

And Selkirk, of course, looked.

It was all the advantage Red needed and he ran and leaped suddenly at Selkirk. Seizing the gun arm with both hands, Red pushed it down and away. A shot whined and sprayed stone off the balusters. He ignored Selkirk's pummeling with his left hand and slammed the right repeatedly against the rail until the gun fell from his fingers. Red kicked it. It spun, bounced off a baluster, and skidded down the walkway. Sarah ran and picked it up. She trained it on them, holding it in both hands.

Red and Selkirk were a tangle of limbs. Selkirk was pushing Red out over the railing, but she daren't risk a shot. Red wrapped a leg around Selkirk's legs and they both fell to the floor, grunting. Selkirk worked an arm loose and tried to gouge Red's eye, but Red twisted away and gave him a head butt that bounced Selkirk's skull against the paving.

Then Selkirk glanced at Sarah, saw she had them covered, and went unexpectedly limp. He relaxed and held both his hands up, grinning broadly.

Red disentangled himself and backed away, keeping his eye on Selkirk.

"It's about time you showed up," Sarah told him.

He shot her a glance. "Yeah? Well, we've got to stop meeting like this."

She barked a laugh and Red frowned at her. "You all right?"

"Aside from assorted bruises and contusions? I've nearly been raped by one sick maniac. I've been chased, kidnapped, and terrorized by another. I've seen a gentle old man murdered in cold blood because he did me a favor. Aside from that, I'm fine."

Red grunted. He studied Selkirk, who still stood grinning with his hands clasped atop his head. The grin bothered Sarah. What did Selkirk have to be so cheerful about? "Where's your gun?" she asked Red.

Red grinned and shrugged. "I was in a hurry and I forgot it."

She glanced at him. "You came up here unarmed?"

"I thought you might need some help."

Her thoughts were confused. There was an aching in her chest. What if Selkirk had been quicker? What if he had been watching the stairs instead of the main entrance? "He expected you to give up and leave."

"I almost did, but he killed the guard. Why would he do that except to keep him from telling me where you'd gone? And if you'd left the tower and vanished into the night, why bother silencing him?" He shrugged again. "It was a logical deduction. He might as well have left a note."

Sarah saw how that jarred Selkirk. The grin wavered slightly. "I never thought you'd be unarmed," he said. "I wanted to avoid a shoot-out."

"Yeah," said Red. "Gunning down bystanders is more your speed." He shook his head and turned to Sarah. "Now that we've got him, what do we do with him?"

"Turn him over to the cops. Murder One. I'm an eyewitness."

"A public trial? Too much might get said. Besides, what's a trial for? To establish guilt. Do you have any doubt he's guilty? The only possible thing that could happen in a trial is that the twelve couch potatoes they pick for a jury could let him go free."

Was Red trying to tell her they should execute him right here? Take justice into their own hands? "I won't shoot him down like he did the guard."

"It's more convenient that way," he said. "Tidier."

She narrowed her eyes, watching Selkirk across the gun sights. "It would be the *logical* thing to do," she said bitterly, and she saw Selkirk's lips twist into a smile. "But if I did, then I would be like him; and I don't want that. I made a promise once that I wouldn't kill anyone again, if I have the choice."

"A promise? To whom?"

"Crayle's ghost."

Red grunted. "You're right. You don't break promises to dead folks. I don't know what I would've said if you had shot him. Tried to understand, I guess. Shit. If anyone has a reason to be quick on the trigger, it's you, after what you've been through."

"Touching," said Selkirk.

Red turned on him. "You shut up. We've got a place for you. It's very far away and you don't get much sunshine. The food is adequate but plain; and the accommodations, somewhat spartan. But it sure as hell beats twitching and kicking on the ground." He looked at Sarah over his shoulder and backed toward her. "We'll march him downstairs. Walt should be here shortly. We'll fly him out to North House and throw away the key. Suits?"

"Suits."

"If he tries anything—"

"Red, I'm not stupid. I'll kill him if there's no other option, but I think losing a kneecap would be just as effective."

She wasn't sure she could make a knee shot on a running man, but Selkirk wouldn't know that.

So why was he so cheerful?

When Red was about halfway between them, Selkirk spoke, clearly and distinctly. "Sarah Beaumont. Quetelet requires your service."

His voice seemed to echo in her skull. The words resonated. Her mind receded far, far away from the scene on the balcony. The two figures remained the same size, but they seemed tiny to her. She was encased in cotton. Her last independent thought was the realization that Maureen Howard had done more than interrogate her, that night in the mountains.

"Kill him," the voice rang. "Kill Jimmy Caldero."

Red saw Sarah stiffen at the command and knew instantly what had happened. She turned and shifted her aim to him. The pistol's muzzle was a cannon. Blank eyes stared at him over the sights, the first, golden rays of dawn reflected in them.

He had a chance. A leaping kick would send the gun sailing in an arc up and over the balustrade.

And Sarah, too.

That was the trouble. The move had a follow-through and he didn't know if he could perform the first part fast enough and still check himself in time.

A heartbeat went by. It took a long time.

Then Selkirk gave a cry of rage and said, "Throw me the gun, you bitch!"

Sarah turned like a zombie and tossed it to him underhand. Selkirk caught it deftly and pointed it at Red.

The sweat on his back was freezing cold in the wind. Over Selkirk's shoulder, he could see the Golden Gate. "Wait," he said, both hands held out. "Don't shoot. Release her first."

"Why?"

"So . . . So we can say good-bye."

Selkirk stopped smiling and backed away from them until

he came up against the balustrade. The gun never wavered. "Aye," he said sadly. "I'm no monster for a' that. I do what I must do, but I've no liking for it. *You* understand."

Wretchedly, Red Malone *did* understand. "I've never killed anyone simply from duty," he protested.

"Aye, but you would have."

Red flinched. Was Selkirk right? Was he looking at himself only a little ways further down the road? Was this what it ultimately meant if he reactivated the Associates?

Selkirk nodded to Sarah. "Don't try any tricks. You'd never cover the distance." He coughed and looked at Sarah. "Sarah Beaumont. Quetelet releases you."

She started, looked at Selkirk, then turned and looked at Red. Then she burst into tears and covered her face with her hands. Red stepped toward her and gathered her up. She buried herself in his shoulder. "Oh, Red. I should have shot him after all."

"No, no. You were right. It's one thing to die for your principles; it's another thing to kill for them." He stroked her hair and the back of her neck.

She turned her face up. "Red, kiss me. I've . . . Morgan wanted . . . But I never—"

He saved her from her confusion.

The kiss was not like he had imagined it would be. Farewell kisses never are. Alice's lips had already been cold when he . . . But Sarah's were warm, yielding. The contact was overwhelming and his head seemed to whirl, yet there was nothing erotic about it. He held her for a long moment, and noticed that their heartbeats were synchronized. An odd, trivial, last detail to notice.

"I've always hated long good-byes," said Selkirk.

Red held her tighter. "Don't look."

"No." She turned in his arms and faced the Scot. "No, you should always look."

He didn't want his last sight to be Selkirk. He kept his eyes fixed on Sarah. When the shot came, he jerked and squeezed her tight, but she gasped, "No," and spun him to face Selkirk.

A scarlet flower had blossomed on the Scot's shirt. His eyes were white and wide and his mouth had opened into a silent O. He put his hand to his chest and brought it away wet. He held it out to them in amazement, as if seeking some explanation. His lips moved soundlessly. The color had drained from his face.

The second shot took him under the chin. His back arched and he flipped over the balustrade as if tossed by a careless giant. The sound of the shot came a moment later, followed by the sound of Selkirk striking the ground.

Red dashed to the rail and looked over. Selkirk was a rag doll twisted over the steps. Chu and Walt stood there staring up at him in astonishment. Chu's station wagon sat in the center of the parking lot, its doors wide open. They had pistols in their hands. Walt saw Red looking and put his gun back in his holster.

Red turned and faced Sarah, who was staring at the anonymous apartment buildings that lined the hillside behind them. "Our ride's here," he said.

She didn't reply. Red came over to her and put his arm around her shoulder. "I don't get it," he said. "Those weren't pistol shots. And Walt didn't have the angle. What was it?"

Sarah hugged herself. "Varmint rifle," she said.

XIV

Jeremy looked toward the top of the building. How many stories was it? Manhattan depressed him. It was too cold. Too large. He checked the address on the slip in his palm and compared it to the building number. Four-thirty-two. There was a bar-restaurant on the ground floor. He looked at Gwynn.

"Well, here goes."

She placed her hand on his shoulder. "Good luck."

He shrugged. "That Bosworth kid managed to contact this Bernstein fellow, using the same routine that Selkirk used. I understand he was surprised—but not too surprised—to hear from us. He admitted having had Dennis with him the whole time. Something about a difference of opinion with the Cabinet Cachette. I don't pretend to understand any of that stuff. That—What was it Caldero called it?"

"Carson's Dilemma," said Gwynn.

"Right. Apparently, this crowd never went through it before. Just random chance, but they've never had a split-up until now. And why am I babbling like this?"

"This is where the message said to meet him?"

He checked the slip again. A hell of a thing if he got the number wrong. "Yes. This is the place. In the bar. Third stool from the right. Dash it all, Gwynn. I feel like a kid going on his first date."

"You haven't seen him for a long time."

"Not since the accident. We've . . . never been apart this long."

Gwynn gave him a push. "Then don't put it off any longer. I'll wait in that coffee shop there on the corner."

He pulled his handkerchief from his breast welt pocket and patted his brow. "You don't think it's a trap, do you?"

She shook her head. "No, there'd be no purpose to it. If Bernstein wanted to stay hidden, he'd have simply moved his headquarters. Either taken Dennis with him or . . . not." She gazed toward the penthouse. "I think maybe he's looking for allies."

The barroom was dimly lit; the clientele, a typical weekday-afternoon midtown crowd. Businessmen stretching their lunch hours to quitting time. Salesmen pitching to jaded buyers more interested in the free drinks than in the product, talking a little too loudly and with a little too much enthusiasm. Jeremy paused in the doorway and looked around carefully. A few men here and there returned his gaze calmly. He had no idea what Bernstein looked like but had been told about his tight defenses. The entire building was supposed to be a fortress. Some of the men in this room, Jeremy was sure, were bodyguards. Probably the ones who sat well back from their cocktail tables, with their jackets loose and unbuttoned and their right hands unencumbered with drinks.

One man was looking at him with sexual interest. Jeremy smiled at him and shook his head in the briefest of gestures, and the man shrugged and looked away. Jeremy tugged his gloves off and walked to the bar. The stools were small director's chairs on very tall legs. Most were empty, but the third from the right was . . . occupied.

From the back the man . . . No. He was much too broad-shouldered to be Dennis. Could it be Bernstein? Jeremy walked up behind him and touched him on the sleeve. "Excuse me, but—"

The man's icy stare cut him off. He looked down at him across a huge, cavernous nose, impaling Jeremy to the spot. He held the silence just long enough for Jeremy to feel fear; then he nodded. "I'm sorry. Was this your stool?" Without waiting for an answer, he gathered his drink and moved off. Jeremy had a glimpse of something black and shiny under his suit coat. Jeremy watched him join another man at a cocktail table near the entrance, where they watched Jeremy and the doorway with equal interest. Jeremy took a shaky breath and perched himself on the vacated stool. The bar was clean and dry and Jeremy laid his gloves and fedora there. He clasped his hands on the bartop and waited.

The bartender was a slight dark man with a scar over one eye. He saw Jeremy and limped over. "Can I get you something?"

Jeremy glanced over his shoulder toward the entrance. "Yes. Anything. I'm waiting for someone."

"Aren't we all?" said the bartender, but it was a rhetorical question. He moved off and reached for a bottle and a glass. Jeremy watched him pour, measuring each ingredient with punctilious exactness.

A motion at the entrance caught Jeremy's eye and he turned. But it was only two young women, loaded down with bright bracelets and long, elaborate "Jersey" hair. They were whispering to each other and laughing. A few of the other men watched them settle into a booth, and one of the sales-men straightened his tie and walked over to them. It was all so normal, it was frightening.

When Jeremy turned back to the bar his drink was in front of him. He swirled the toothpick and its impaled victim, a pearl onion, in idle circles, watching the ripples in the icy clear liquid. He checked his watch and glanced again at the entrance, feeling uncomfortable and conspicuous. He had to twist in his seat to watch the door. The canvas cut into his thighs and back.

How would he know Bernstein when he walked in? Per-haps by the reaction of the others in the room. But no. Most of them were legitimate citizens going about their legitimate business, padding expense accounts or cheating on their wives. Jeremy didn't know them anymore. He had lived the past few months in a secret world, hidden behind the wain-scoting of reality. A world that existed in anonymous board-rooms and secret hideaways. Where decisions were made on the future and politicians, the public, and large corporations were taught to carry them out. He had lived, for a little while, among the stagehands; and he didn't know if he could ever sit happily in the audience again.

He took a sip of his drink. It was a vodka martini, and very good. He pursued the play analogy in his mind. He had told Caldero that he didn't care if the world was contrived or not, that the play was scripted. But now he felt an odd passion for improvisational theater.

A footstep at the doorway. He turned and saw a slim middle-aged man, gray at the temples, dressed in a Brooks Brothers suit of dark worsted wool. He wore kid gloves of contrasting silver and carried a walking stick with a knob of chased gold. He tucked the walking stick under his arm like an officer's crop and locked gazes with Jeremy.

Jeremy swallowed. He felt the other's detached interest, his mild sexual appraisal. Cold and aloof. Not at all a friendly gaze; but not unfriendly, either. The man—was it Bern-stein?—nodded coolly and took a seat at an empty table.

Jeremy saw that the table was surrounded by large men nursing their drinks left-handed.

He turned back to the bar and took a hasty swallow. Was that Bernstein? Was the nod an invitation? What should he do?

He stared at the remains of his cocktail, rotating the glass slowly back and forth between his palms, like a Boy Scout with a hand drill. Suddenly he froze. A vodka martini? He had told the bartender to give him anything and he had given him this?

He raised his head and stared at the bartender, who, he saw, was staring back at him. He studied the scar, the dark complexion, the limp; and the man walked over and stood before him. He wiped the counter with a bar towel. "Another one, sir?" he asked.

"Dennis?" Jeremy whispered it, half-afraid he had guessed wrong, half-afraid he had guessed right.

The bartender nodded. "Hello, Jerry. It's been a long time."

"You've . . . changed."

"Jerry. Clichés? Of course, I've changed. We all change. We only notice it when we've gone away and come back. Or . . . when we remember." His eyes seemed to turn inward as he spoke. "You've changed, too. Paul told me you had."

"Paul?"

Dennis nodded to the man who had come in moments before. "Paul Bernstein." The man had his hands clasped on the table watching them. He bowed his head, once.

Jeremy faced Dennis again. "Maybe I have changed, but not like you. You've . . ."

"Had surgery? Yes. It was quite dreadful; but you realize that, after my accident, they were working almost from scratch as far as my features went. You haven't asked me how I've gotten on."

Jeremy choked on the words. "How . . . have you gotten on?"

Dennis wiped his hands on the bar towel. "It was awful at first. I woke up and I wasn't in the hospital. I was in some private clinic, and I hurt all over. After a while the pain died away and people came and questioned me. What did I know, how did I know it, who had I told. That sort of thing. I thought it was the Babbage Society that had got hold of me." He shook his head slowly. "They had that list I had gotten from the Quinn Mansion on Emerson Street. They were very interested in it, and very worried. They thought it meant that their existence was already known, that they might be walking into a trap. Here." He took the martini glass. "Let me freshen that." He walked off a short distance and refilled the glass from a pitcher. He brought it back and set it down. Jeremy watched him silently.

"Well, I suppose you know some of this, maybe even most of it. Paul's organization is expanding into the United States. One faction wanted to—" He bit his lip and dropped his eyes. "They wanted to dispose of me after they were done questioning. They tried to kill you, as well, with a bomb. But Paul managed to slip me out and stash me here where they couldn't—Well . . ." He rubbed his hands brusquely on the bar towel. "That's the main reason for the new face."

Jeremy toyed with his onion. "Why should Bernstein protect you?"

Dennis' eyes flicked over Jeremy's shoulder. "Why? A lot of reasons, I suppose. He has a grudge of some sort against the Cachette. Something about his grandfather and the Holocaust and some group called the GHW. I don't know all the details. He hasn't told me, but I have the impression that he has been nurturing his plan for a long time."

"And why would that lead him to defy his confrères over you?" Jeremy shook his head. "He didn't have to help you at all."

Dennis looked away. He shrugged.

Jeremy grunted. He glanced at Bernstein, who smiled thinly. So, it was like that. He supposed he should feel jealousy, but it was difficult to harbor resentment against the man for saving Dennis' life. He turned back to his drink and glowered into it. He didn't like the idea of people behind him watching his every move. "This isn't working out at all the way I'd supposed."

"What did you think would happen? That I would run into your arms?" Dennis shrugged again. "People change. I had to survive, Jerry. And to do that, I had to cut loose from everything in my past."

"Everything."

"Yes."

"Do you . . . ever miss it?"

"What? The past?" Dennis twisted the bar towel into a knot. "Every day. You. Our apartment. My practice. Sarah. All gone. Everything I ever knew, or owned, or loved. Do I ever miss it?" He looked down at the towel, unknotted it. Smoothed it out. "Well, that's all done."

"I see."

"Don't think I don't know what you've gone through. And why. I'm grateful, and touched. It's just that—"

"Never mind." Jeremy slid off the bar stool. He took his hat and gloves. "I'll be going now. I won't bother you anymore."

"Wait." Dennis laid a hand on his forearm. "You will come back. Paul wants it."

He looked at Bernstein. "Well, if 'Paul' wants it . . ."

"Don't be bitchy. He wants a liaison. Paul does. Someone who can act as a contact between his faction and . . . well, the group you've been associating with."

Jeremy twisted his lips. "Which is that? There have been so many."

"That's part of it. We need to find some concert of interests."

"Do we? And why me, particularly?"

Dennis looked him in the eye. "Paul feels that you and he have certain interests in common."

"Why should I not stay out of it entirely?"

"Because there are those who would run down harmless architects or blow up history professors, and there are those who want to stop them."

Jeremy tugged his gloves on. He picked up his hat. "I'll

discuss it with . . . my friends. Good-bye, Dennis. I'll take your regards to Sarah." He turned to go.

"Jerry."

"What?"

"You've changed, too, you know. If we had broken up last June, you would be a complete wreck. You're different, now. More confident. Less dependent."

Jeremy paused and looked back. Dennis was twisting and untwisting the bar towel. "Yes, I suppose I am. You're right. People do change. Sometimes they become less dependent." He settled his hat upon his head. "We'll be in touch."

In the coffee shop on the corner, Gwynn asked him how it went.

Jeremy gazed wistfully at the building down the block. "I met a man who once was Dennis French."

XV

The piano wept. It was slightly out of tune, and the blue notes ripped at her heart. She let her hands slide easily over the keys, wringing out the melancholy chords. She hummed along with it, shaking her head slowly from side to side. Fee sat atop the piano listening with half-closed eyes. The rest of the underground safe house seemed far away.

"I sing because I'm happy," she sang, but not too loud, because she was only singing for herself and that did not require volume. "I sing because I'm free." And she stretched out the last word, holding the note and letting it tremble just a little at the end. "Oh, His eye is on, is on the sparrow, 'cause I know He watches me."

"Oh, He sure does that. Either He or Janie Hatch."

Sarah struck a dissonant chord. "Red, how long have you been listening?" She twisted around and saw he was assembling his clarinet. "It's embarrassing," she said. "I don't sing well."

"Oh, you'll never play the Met, that's for sure, but sometimes heart counts as much as art." He stuck the reed in his mouth to moisten it. "Like me." He took the reed out and gestured with it. "Like that song you were singing. You hit it dead right. By all rights we should be dead." He replaced the reed in his mouth. "You explain it."

"Janie won't admit to being in San Francisco. She claims she was out hunting."

"Hunting." Red grunted. "And you can take that any way you want it."

"Red, can you explain Janie Hatch? Because I can't."

"No one can. She does what she wants and then she thinks up reasons for it. Maybe she's taken a shine to you."

"It's ironic, don't you think? Selkirk didn't have to grant your last request. It was probably the first genuinely kind act of his life, and it killed him."

"The good die young," said Red philosophically. "What are you trying to say? If he had been a kinder man he would have died a lot earlier?"

"If he'd been a kinder man, he would never have been on top of that tower." Her hands wandered through the rest of "His Eye Is on the Sparrow." "I think he needed to prove that he wasn't a monster, after all."

"Why bother to prove anything to us? He was going to kill us, wasn't he?"

"No. Prove it to himself."

"Oh." He took the reed from his mouth and strapped it to the ligature. "Well." He blew a few experimental scales, removed his instrument, studied its keys. "Why didn't *you* shoot me?"

"Now that's a hell of a question."

"On the tower. When Selkirk triggered your program. You didn't shoot. Don't misunderstand me; I'm glad you didn't. But I don't understand it. I *know* how deep conditioning works."

She played a few bars of "Good Blues," then stopped with

her hands elevated. "It's funny, you know. I can remember everything that happened. Every detail. The cold breezes. The salt smell of the ocean. How the dawn made everything seem to shine. But it's like a dream. Unreal, as if I wasn't there at all, but watching from a long distance." She turned on the bench and looked at him. "He ordered me to kill Jimmy Caldero, and I remember looking and looking. But all I could see was Red Malone."

Red jerked slightly. "That shouldn't have subverted a ductifacient drug."

"It wasn't semantics, Red. I never could see 'Jimmy Caldero,' not deep down. Selkirk ordered me to kill a man who did not exist."

"Ah." He toyed idly with his keys. "Well."

"What's wrong?"

"I was hoping that it was the power of love overcoming the power of the drug."

"Are you serious?"

"No. Not really. It would have made a hell of a story, though, wouldn't it?"

She turned her back on him and played a chromatic scale, slowly and softly. "Have you ever been in love?"

"Yes. Once."

She paused a moment, then resumed the scale. "I see. Jacksonville, wasn't it?"

"Someone told you."

She shook her head so he would see it. "No. But 'when the wind is nor'-nor'east, I can tell a hawk from a handsaw.' And I can recognize the scab of an old wound when I see one. What was her name? Not Fanny Power."

"No," Red told her, "Alice McAuliffe. Her name was Alice McAuliffe."

Alice McAuliffe. A faceless name from a forgotten list. "What happened?"

"Oh, she was someone like you. Someone who learned more than was good for her. A systems analyst with an interest in history. She did a little of this and a little of that, and before she knew it, she knew too much. Weil had hysterics and ordered her dead, and Cam sent me to warn her. The two of us holed up for a few weeks in a cabin in the Smokies while Cam negotiated with Them to bring her Inside. Those were . . . long weeks, and we came to know each other pretty well. The negotiations went well. Everything seemed copacetic, but Kennison forgot to call off the dogs. Or he didn't bother to. They caught up with us in Jacksonville."

He was silent and she looked back over her shoulder. "And?"

"And what? It didn't work out so well as it did with you and me. She didn't have your training. I trusted some people I shouldn't have had to trust, and we . . . Things just didn't work out. Leave it at that. Why do you have to know all this, anyway?"

"Because I need to know why an otherwise intelligent man would climb Coit Tower unarmed, knowing that there was an armed, ruthless killer at the top."

"It seemed like a good idea at the time."

"Nothing is too serious for you to make a joke, is it?"

He looked at her and smiled sadly. "Some things are too serious for anything else."

"Who did you think was on top of the tower, Alice or me?"

"That's a fool question. Why do you care? You're the one who never needs any help. The solo player."

She looked at Fee, reached up, and scratched him between the ears. A flicker of faces flashed before her eyes. Mama. Daddy. Abe. Morgan. Dennis. "Sometimes I do. Sometimes I even know it. You aren't the only one with scabs."

"Maybe . . ." He hesitated and she turned again and looked at him.

"Why didn't you ever try to kiss me?" she asked.

He looked surprised. "I . . . Janie asked me that once. About you, I mean. I don't know. What if you had pushed me away?"

"What if I hadn't?" Sarah wondered suddenly, irrationally, whether Janie had set up the whole scenario atop the tower just to get them to kiss. *And if we hadn't, would she still have shot Selkirk?* No, that was crazy. "Red, if it had been Walt Polovsky held hostage at the top of the tower, would you still have come charging up, unarmed, the way you did?"

He grinned. "Well, maybe not quite so fast."

She laughed. "But you would still have done it. Good. Doing the right thing should never depend on who you're doing it for. Come and see me tonight, about seven, and we'll see about that other unfinished business. Fair's fair. I owe you a dinner. Janie promised me the run of the kitchen. Meanwhile . . ." And she nodded toward his clarinet. "Is that licorice stick for showin' or for blowin'?"

Red stopped and looked at his instrument. "Give me an A." She tapped the key and Red played a note, frowned, and cocked his head.

"You're sharp," she suggested.

"I know that, but the note wasn't quite right." He twisted the ligature. "Try it now."

"Sounds better. What did you want to play? 'High Society'?"

"I thought we might do your favorite. 'The Maple Leaf Rag.' "

"I didn't know you'd learned it."

"I've studied the score, but I want to try it your way. By ear."

She smiled at him. "That's quite a departure for you."

"Yeah. Do me a favor, though. Play it through once on the piano, so I can hear it."

She started into the first theme. Red leaned forward in his chair, frowning intently. After a minute or two, she said matter-of-factly, "I'm going to see Dennis next Tuesday." Red grunted an acknowledgment. "According to Jeremy, he's changed a lot since I last saw him. Captivity, I suppose. The hostage learns to love his captor. I don't know. Pay attention to this transistion." She played it twice so he could learn it. She saw him fingering the clarinet.

"I don't know," she repeated. "Maybe it was his free choice. Maybe his gratitude became something else, and maybe this Bernstein had more in mind than a gambit against his colleagues. Or maybe Dennis was programmed like I was." She shook her head. "I think that was the most horrible experience I'll ever have."

"Selkirk's faction was planning to use you to assassinate Bernstein, but once you'd been triggered and knew . . ." He shrugged.

"The whole idea of slavery has overtones for me that it can't possibly have for you. And chaining the mind is the ultimate slavery."

"It's a wicked practice. I don't approve of it."

She stopped playing. "And how is it different from what They do, and the Six, and what you want the Associates to do? It's control and manipulation. Is there some moral difference between wholesale and retail?"

He looked away from her. "I don't know. I used to know, but I'm smarter now."

"The smarter we get, the less we know. Or the less certain we are that we know it. That's why fanatics are so successful. They sell certainties. Are you ready? OK, follow me." She started the rag, played the first phrase, and Red joined in on the repeat. He hit a few wrong notes and Sarah tried not to wince too obviously, but he managed to stay in the right key.

"At one point," she continued over the music, "I thought that there were too many cliological societies around. The Society; the Associates; the Q; the Six; D, B, and S; even the U.S. Government—or a faction within it, if we can believe your friend Charlie. But lately I've been wondering if maybe there aren't enough."

He stopped playing. "Not enough?"

"Not enough. What if *everyone* knew how to do it? What if cliology were taught at MIT and Cal Tech? You told me once that everyone tried to alter the future by trial and error. What if we all had the tools to do it better?"

"It would be chaos. People have different ideas about what the future should be. You'd have everybody pulling in different directions."

"So what? At least everyone will play with the same

equipment. And whichever direction society did move, it would mean that a lot of people were pulling in that direction. When there are millions of players, the variations cancel each other out. That's basic probability theory, isn't it? Quetelet's normal distribution."

He stood and walked closer. He put a hand on her shoulder and leaned over. "Play that rag again. I hit too many clinkers the first time. Play it loud," he added in a whisper.

She looked at him and he put a finger to his lips. She hit the keys hard and he leaned close and whispered in her ear, "Let's not talk about it here. Tomorrow, we'll go horseback riding. You can show me that Altaflora of yours."

"Don't be ridiculous. It must be under a ton of snow by now."

"Then show me something else." He leaned closer and kissed her on the cheek.

"I'll come back later," said Tex Bodean from the doorway, "if this isn't convenient."

Sarah waved at him without losing the beat. Red held up his clarinet. "What the hell, Tex, why don't you join us?" he said. Sarah kept up the melody but softened the sound.

"Sure. Just let me make a phone call." He went to the wall phone by the door and spoke into it briefly. Then he went to the closet and pulled out a trombone case. He assembled it with a few quick moves and worked the slide a few times experimentally. "What are we playing?"

"Ragtime," said Sarah. "Maybe some Dixieland."

"Do you play Chicago-style?"

"Maybe later, if you're a good boy." She closed out the "Maple Leaf" and played the intro to "High Society." Red looked at her and grinned. "Thanks," he said.

"Always put your best foot forward," she replied.

The three of them played for a few minutes, Tex laying a decent bass line with his 'bone even though Sarah thought he was hearing the tune for the first time. He had a good ear for improvisation, she thought. While they were playing, a bald-headed man with a curly chest-length beard scampered into the room, carrying a trumpet in his right hand. He slapped Tex on the back and settled into the chair next to him. He listened for a while, tapping his foot; then he put his horn to his lips and the bright trumpet sound blended into the music.

Red got through his complex solo without a single error, which caused Tex to whoop a cowboy yell and brought a scatter of claps from the doorway. Sarah looked back that way and saw that a small crowd had gathered there.

As they concluded the piece, she heard someone say, "Excuse me. Coming through." And she saw Walt Polovsky pushing his way in with SuperNerd in tow. Polovsky pointed him toward the drums in the corner. "There, I told you we had a set. Now, put your money where your mouth is. You come in after Jimmy there." Bosworth looked around, blushed, and took a seat behind the drums. He picked up the sticks and waited, testing the reach to the various drums in the trap set. He rapped out a paradiddle.

"Thanks for the call, Tex. Hi, Stosh, Jimmy, Glo—Sarah." Polovsky hoisted a battered old tuba to his lap. " 'Joe Avery,' " he announced. "Any objections?"

"Better do as he says, Sarah," Red told her. "It's his big chance to shine. Come on, Cam. You want to sit in, too?"

A man Sarah hadn't met yet seated himself against the wall. He was thin-faced and sharp-featured, and his hair must have been white for a long, long time. He plucked a chord progression on his banjo. "Depends. You folks posing or playing?"

"Joe Avery" began with a strong, jaunty bass line and Polovsky played it with clear authority. The notes boomed and danced with an agility not normally given to the tuba. When the trumpet player took over, Polovsky dropped back and kept up a steady background rhythm.

They traded the melody around, each instrument giving it a twist all its own. The trumpet, bright and brassy, suggested the melody as much by the notes it omitted as by those it played. Tex's trombone was sweet and mellow, and no riverboat ever heard as fine a banjo as the one Cam Betancourt played. When it was her turn, Sarah closed her eyes and pretended she was playing solo. Her hands danced back and forth across the keyboard. She soared with the music.

Red went by the book, improvising very little; but that was all right because he had two registers to play in. When he played the low register, he carried the main theme; but he switched over to a counterpoint in the high register. The long, sweet notes above the treble clef hung in the air, contrasting with the bouncing, persistent rhythm that Walt kept up.

When Red finished, it was Norris' turn, and the teenager hit the skins just as if there were not an easy two dozen onlookers and his face were not the color of choice Grade A beets. His riffs were more rock than jazz, but he went through them without a fluff.

While he played, Sarah saw Janie Hatch standing in the crowd, watching them with her usual stony look. She turned up her mouth and shook her head slowly. Sarah caught her eye and mouthed the word, *Thanks,* but Janie only shrugged in reply. Then she rubbed her hands against her pants legs and stepped into the room.

There was a big double bass lying on its side along the back wall. Janie set it upright and ran her hand up and down the fingerboard. Then, when Norris finished his drum solo, she leaned into it and slapped out a reprise of the tuba part with stoic precision. It was almost comical, the contrast between the rollicking melody and the calm, inexpressive look on her face.

Sarah watched with her fingers poised over the keyboard. When Janie gave the nod, they all jumped in, playing tutti. Walt's bass, Red's counterpoint, all the parts blended into the joyous cacophony of Dixieland. The crowd in the doorway and the hall beyond burst into spontaneous applause while they played, and Sarah felt a thrill shiver up her spine.

When they had finally finished, they sat there looking at one another while the onlookers clapped and whistled. Sarah had lost herself in the music. She sat staring at the keyboard for a few moments longer, still hearing the ringing chords in her mind. Then she closed her eyes and relaxed. She let out a deep breath.

She heard Tex say, "Wow," and the trumpet player, Stosh, pounded him on the back. Walt shook Norris' hand and waved an arm at him, inviting the crowd's applause. Bosworth couldn't stop grinning. He stood up and gave a short, jerky bow and quickly sat down again.

Janie Hatch was leaning across her "dogbox." She caught Sarah's eye and looked at her. Then Janie looked at Red, and back to her. She raised an eyebrow. Sarah nodded once, and Janie Hatch, for a fraction of an instant, smiled.

Afterword: An Introduction to Cliology

Part I: The Mathematics of History

We have to be prepared to be surprised by the future, but we don't have to be dumbfounded.
    —KENNETH BOULDING

How many race riots will the United States experience during the outbreak of A.D. 2010? How many orbital factories will go bankrupt during the Recession of 2033? Is the breakup of India inherent in her topological connectedness? What does the location of Babylon or the administration of Ancient Egypt have to do with the success of L5 colonies?

Years ago, Isaac Asimov imagined a mathematical science of history that might answer such questions. His fictional psychohistory hasn't happened yet—no Hari Seldon has emerged to tie everything together—but researchers in fields ranging from ecology to differential topology have already laid the "Foundations."

But the curves, if they meant anything at all, included free will
. . . Every morning three million "free wills" flowed toward the center of the New York megapolis; every evening they flowed out again—all by "free will," and on a smooth and predictable curve.
    —ROBERT A. HEINLEIN,
    "The Year of the Jackpot"

Cliology* attempts to understand the forces shaping human history and to express them in useful mathematical

---

*Because the term *psychohistory* has been used for works psychoanalyzing historical personages, we will use the term *cliology,* instead.

terms—in short, to replace anecdote with analysis. There are obvious objections to such an endeavor, emotional and structural. The emotional objection is that science is dehumanizing. But this objection misses the point. Science is de*mystifying* rather than de*humanizing*. It seeks the material causes of measurable phenomena. If conditions like war and poverty have material causes, they can only be corrected by attacking those causes, not by wishing the symptoms away. Besides, as anthropologist Marvin Harris has commented, the study of culture is not currently suffering from an *overdose* of the scientific method.

The structural objection is more serious. It holds that human societies are too complex for scientific analysis and that "laws of history" are impossible in any event because human beings have free will. Yet complexity means only that laws can be hard to discern, not that they don't exist. Many of the examples cited in this essay are simplistic, but *simplistic* needn't mean "wrong." Physicists cannot solve the general three-body problem, but our space probes manage to rendezvous with planets and asteroids tolerably well. Why demand more of cliology?

Nuclear physics does not predict the fate of every neutron; nor organic chemistry, that of every molecule. Similarly, a scientific study of history need not predict individual events or behaviors. However, in large groups these individual variations can cancel out, producing regularities or patterns. Thus the *average* behavior of a group may be predictable. That's what keeps casinos and insurance companies solvent.

The free will objection is similarly based on a misunderstanding of scientific laws. Freedom is the opposite of compulsion, not of causality. A scientific law is a description, not a cause, and could no more compel us to behave a particular way than an actuarial table compels us to die.

The first question we ought to ask is whether cliological laws are plausible.

Common Causes A system is a set of causes that combine to produce a result. Even the simplest system consists

Figure 1

Outbreaks of Wars

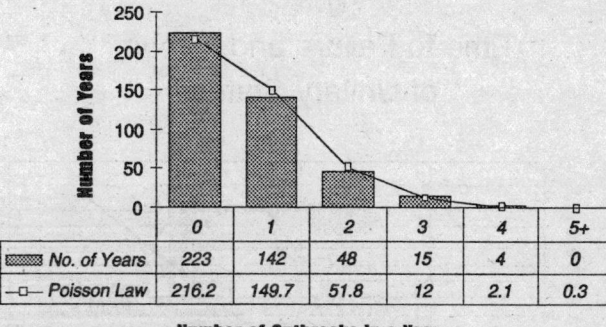

	0	1	2	3	4	5+
No. of Years	223	142	48	15	4	0
Poisson Law	216.2	149.7	51.8	12	2.1	0.3

Number of Outbreaks in a Year

Figure 1: A Constant Cause System. The number of wars that break out each year follows a Poisson distribution almost perfectly, consistent with a small, constant probability coupled with a very large opportunity. For example, there were 223 years when no wars broke out, while the Poisson law predicts 216.2 such years. The difference from theory is insignificant under the chi-square test. The implication is that the probability of a war breaking out is constant. *Data after Quincy Wright, reported by L. F. Richardson.*

of a great many causes, and these are not all constant all the time. By random chance, some will be causing an increase in the measured result; and some, a decrease. The net result is a statistical distribution around a central tendency. Variation within the distribution is not due to any one particular cause but to chance combinations of many small causes. These randomly acting causes are called *common causes*.

Example 1: Outbreaks of Warfare. The number of

wars that break out each year fits a statistical Poisson distribution nearly perfectly. This distribution models events of

Figure 2
Time to Failure and Repair
of Unitary States

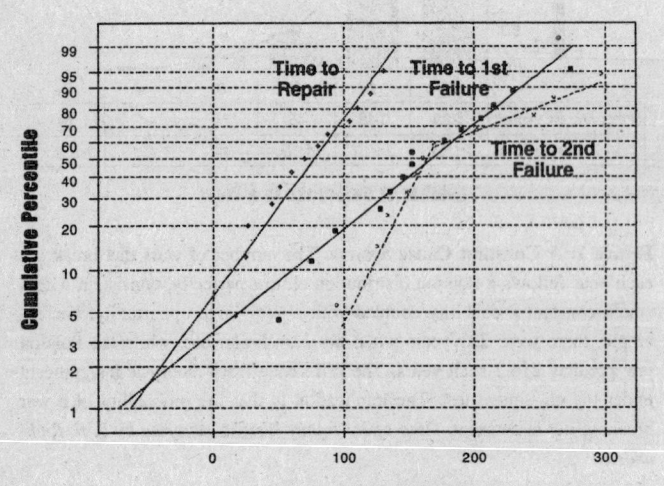

Years to Failure/Repair

Figure 2: Lifetime Distributions. The times to failure and times to repair of unitary states follow an Extreme Value distribution. A straight line on such a scale indicates a fit to the distribution. Random variation means that not all points will be exactly on the line, especially the largest and smallest values; but they are all within the 95 percent confidence bounds. Note that the second breakdown of a revived imperial state falls into two linear segments: there is a distinct elbow in the plotted points. This means there are two distinct failure modes. *Data after A. J. Toynbee and other history texts.*

low probability but great opportunity, such as the number of industrial accidents or of calls received at a switchboard. The chilling implication is that wars break out at random—or at least as randomly as industrial accidents.*

Example 2: Lifetimes of Unitary States are plotted against an Extreme Value probability scale in Figure 2. Reliability engineers use Extreme Value distributions to model complex systems that fail due to a "weakest link" or "peak overload" failure mode. It doesn't matter mathematically if the complex system is electrical, mechanical, or cultural. Empires have a Mean Time Before Failure (MTBF) of 160 years for the first failure. The Mean Time To Repair (MTTR) is 70 years, after which the repaired state survives for an additional MTBF of 185 years. Do they come with warranties, one wonders?

Of course, knowing an average and a distribution does not enable anyone to forecast the outbreak of a particular war or the demise of a particular empire any more than knowing the actuarial tables enables an underwriter to predict the death of a particular policyholder. But even though variation within a distribution is unpredictable, people often try to "explain" the fluctuations.

Special Causes Sometimes a process is disturbed by a cause that is not normally part of the system. These *special causes* often appear as outliers, or Extreme Values. This sort of variation *outside* the distribution can be assigned to particular causes.

Example 3: U.S. Slave Revolts/Race Riots have been plotted in five-year increments on a Shewhart chart (Figure 3).* Except for a few spikes, the series is consistent

---

*To put it another way: each war may have causes, but war itself does not.
*A Shewhart chart distinguishes between random fluctuations, inherent in the system, and nonrandom fluctuations, caused by disturbances to the system. The limit is set customarily at three standard deviations from the mean.

Figure 3

Slave Revolts and Race Riots

(In Five-Year Increments)

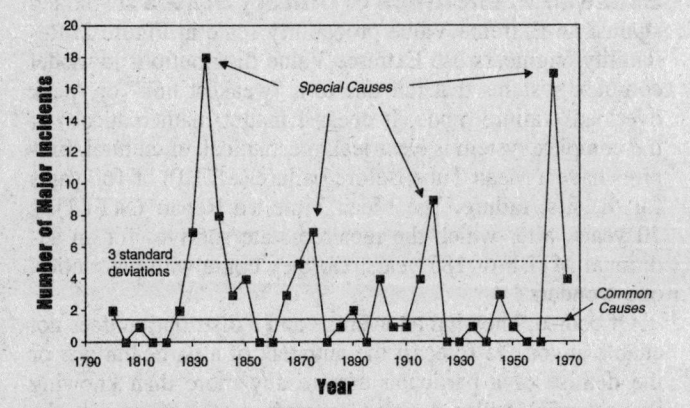

Figure 3: Common Causes and Special Causes. The number of slave revolts and race riots in the United States shows special causes (indicated by the spikes) overlaid on a constant, chronic level of roughly three such outbreaks per decade. (The data are plotted in five-year increments.) The regularity of the spikes may indicate a process within the system similar to the buildup and release of pressure in a geyser. *Data from various texts.*

with a stationary Poisson process "emitting" $\lambda = 0.29$ riots or slave revolts per year for the last 170 years. This mean value is inherent in the U.S. cultural system. Peaks occur every other generation. Since regularity does not occur by chance, there is probably a systemic cause for the spikes as well. Note that Emancipation did not change the underlying

---

Points falling beyond these limits are so unlikely to be due to chance (on the order of a quarter of a percentage point) that the hypothesis of random chance must be discarded.

cause system and, unless the Civil Rights Movement *did*, the next peak will come around A.D. 2010.

Time Series Patterns However, if the underlying cause system does change, the data will exhibit patterns, such as shifts, trends, cycles, or more chaotic behavior. That a process has run at a certain average, even for a very long time, does not imply that it must run at that average forever. There are many examples of changing means.

Example 4: U.S. Business Bankruptcies have been plotted annually in Figure 4. The limits of random variation have been calculated from the moving two-year range. While some special causes are evident (the great depressions of the 1870s and 1930s, especially), the main feature is the sudden shift in the process mean. A **shift** indicates an abrupt change in some major systemic factor(s).*

Example 5: U.S. Median Household Income in constant dollars has been plotted in Figure 5. The main feature in this chart is a **trend.** A trend means that some factor is operating on the system continually in the same direction. Note that the great inflation stopped the trend flat. When tax rates were indexed and the number of brackets severely reduced, income growth resumed in the eighties. In fact, the rate of growth was the same as it had been in earlier decades.

Example 6: U.S. Birthrates, plotted in Figures 6a and 6b, have declined linearly since at least 1820, with boom and bust cycles snaking their way around the trend line. An interesting note is that the "postwar" Baby Boom started *before* the war, so any explanation of the Boom that relies on the GI Bill or postwar prosperity is automatically wrong. The

---

*Oddly enough, there is no similar effect on the unemployment rate. The median unemployment has fluctuated around 5 percent (with some spikes) since 1890, the first year of the series.

Figure 4
U.S. Bankruptcy Rates

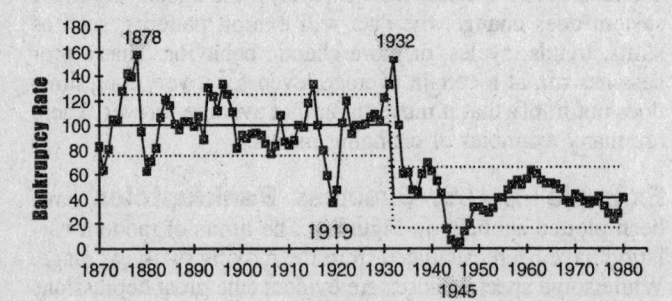

Figure 4: Shift in Process Mean. U.S. business bankruptcy rates show a distinct change in the expected value in the early 1930s. Such patterns indicate a sudden change in the underlying cause system. This could be any factor ranging from a restructuring of U.S. business practices to the definition of "firm" or "bankruptcy." A companion chart, not reproduced, shows no such change in the unemployment rate. *Data from Historical Statistics of the U.S. plus annual supplements.*

main feature of this chart is a **cycle.** Cycles indicate a cause that comes and goes or changes direction regularly.

Notice that the birthrates spiked due to World Wars One and Two but returned to the trend line once the disturbance was removed. The same thing happened to income growth rates when the disturbance of "stagflation" was removed. The tendency of a process to "seek its natural level" is called *homeostasis.* We will take up this topic later.

Perspective You cannot evaluate a datum in isolation. Remember, *fact* comes from a verb—*factum est.* Too often, we see facts one at a time. But it is hard to enjoy a motion picture looking at one frame at a time. Examining a

Figure 5

Median Household Income
In 1994 Dollars

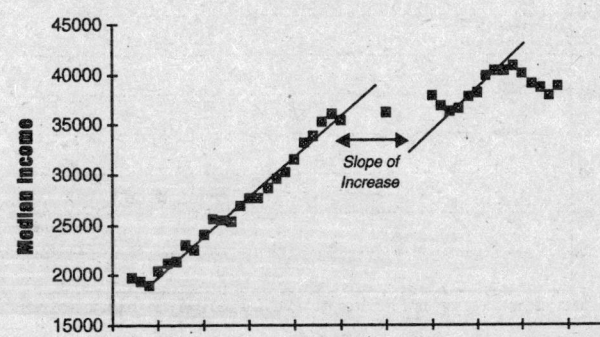

Figure 5. Trend in Process Mean. U.S. median household income, measured in constant dollars, grew at a linear rate from the end of the Second World War until about 1970. During the great inflation through the 1980 recession that ended it, income stagnated. (Data points are missing because the annual *Statistical Abstracts* available to the author skipped some years.) Starting after 1982, income growth resumed *at the same rate as before* until the early nineties, which saw the first sustained *decrease* in median income in recent history. *Data from Historical Statistics of the U.S. plus annual supplements.*

long-term trend lends perspective. It is often the case that the "reasons" given for some phenomenon cannot possibly account for the pattern in the data. Birthrates in the 1960s fell—but not because of the Pill. Women's participation in the labor force doubled between the 1950s and 1980s—but not because of women's liberation movements. The import share of the domestic automobile market has increased—

Figure 6a
U.S. Birthrates, 1820–1990

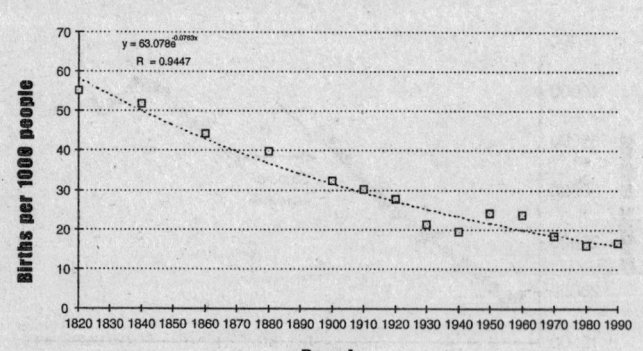

Figure 6a: Trend in Process Mean. Birthrates in the United States have dropped exponentially since 1820, despite the lack of a centrally planned government program to discourage births. The trend long predates the Pill, women's liberation, or any of the other conventional explanations. One suggestion is that birthrates dropped because the country became more urbanized. Farm families tend to be larger because more children on the family farm means more hands for the farm work. Source: *U.S. Statistical Abstracts,* Ser. B5 & 1996 Suppl. No 90

but not because of the Arab oil embargo of the mid-seventies.*

Example 7: U.S. Homicide Rates (Figure 7) seem immune to both gun control laws and executions. The high rates of the 1980s were blamed on the abolition of the death

---

*Charting second and third examples is left as an exercise to the reader. Your library carries the *Statistical Abstracts,* too, and why should I have all the fun?

Figure 6b
U.S. Birthrates, 1909–1994

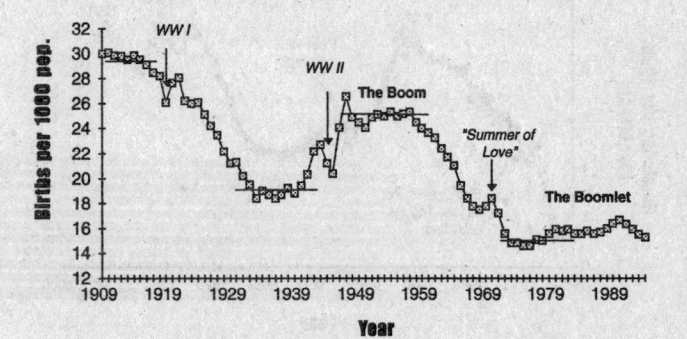

Figure 6b: A Cycle in Process Mean. Records of annual birthrates have been kept since 1909. There is a wave in the trend, with the decline of the 1960s matching almost perfectly the decline of the 1920s. Regularity argues for a recurrent cause. One possibility lies in a rhythm of generational attitudes based on child-rearing practices. Each generation tends to raise its children the opposite of how they themselves were raised. Young people of the sixties and the twenties shared many of the same attitudes. Note the special causes associated with the First and Second World Wars. The birthrate dropped when large numbers of men went overseas and spiked above the curve when they returned before settling to the level that the trend line would have taken them. Note, too, that the postwar Baby Boom started up before the war.

penalty, but the rates were just as high in the 1930s, when executions were common. Do executions (or the lack of them) cause the homicide rate to change? Or do changes in the homicide rate cause people to demand executions? The key to understanding may be the realization that *homicide* is a word that covers a variety of different acts, from gangland

Figure 7
U.S. Homicide Rates

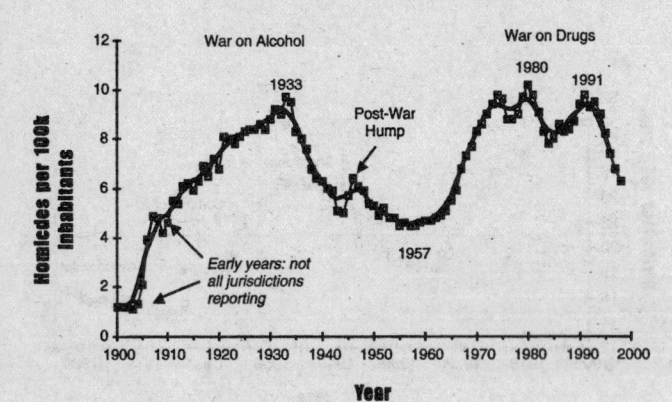

Figure 7: The Long-Term Perspective. Most of us focus too closely on recent data and do not know the long-term trend. The cause of a phenomenon must explain what happened and what did not happen. If the high murder rates, climbing in the mid-to-late sixties and only recently dropping, were due to the lack of executions, how are we to explain the high rates during Prohibition? More likely, similar behavior means similar causes. *Data from Historical Statistics of the U.S. plus annual supplements.*

killings to drunken brawls. Which sort is cycling up and down? It may be that there is a constant "background radiation" of random loss-of-temper killings on which premeditated murders are superimposed.

Regularities in History History does not "repeat" itself, but that does not mean there are no underlying regularities. The planets never come around to precisely the same configuration, yet they each go in predictable orbits. Some examples of regularities include:

Figure 8
Approximate Timing of Four Major Rhythms in the American Economy

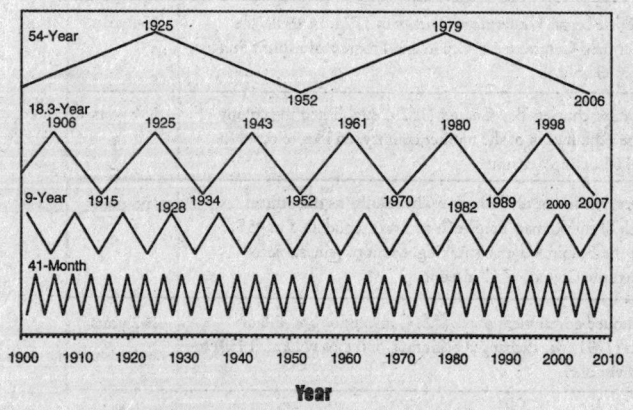

Extension of a chart in Dewey and Dakin, 1948

Figure 8: Cycles upon Cycles. Apparently chaotic behavior can often be decomposed into the sum of several simpler patterns. A cycle may piggy-back on a trend, for example. Some researchers profess to see multiple cycles in the U.S. economy. These cycles are particular to the specific series, but they are shown here as generic "sawtooth" patterns for simplicity. The Long Wave (50+ years) seems to be due to public infrastructure and power generation, with each wave being the buildup and maturity of major trans-portation technology and every other wave seeing the advent of a new source of energy. Note that the 9-year cycle starts down in 2000, putting the three major cycles on the downswing. The 41-month business cycle will swing down in 2001, indicating a major slowdown in a "rising" economy or a "recession" in a flat economy.

Table 1 Half-Lives of Ideas	
Idea	Reaction
The Russian intelligentsia created by Peter the Great beginning in 1689 rose up against the Tsar in the 1825 Decembrist revolt.	136 years
The Porte began Westernizing Turkey in 1774. In 1908, the Westernized Committee of Union and Progress overthrew Sultan 'Abd-al-Hamid II.	134 years
The Massachussets Bay Charter (1629) established the colony for the exploitation of the mother country, an idea rejected in the 1765 Stamp Act riots.	136 years
The establishment of Orthodox Christianity as the official church of the Roman Empire in 313 was repudiated in 451, when the Empire's Syriac speaking, Monophysite subjects rejected the Council of Chalcedon.	138 years
The limited government of the U.S. Constitution and Bill of Rights (1791) was exchanged beginning in the New Deal (1933) for an activist one.	142 years

Example 8: U.S. Business Cycles (Figure 8), plotted by Dewey and Dakin in 1945, accurately forecast the 1980 recession, "recovery," and "slowdown in the recovery." Economic activities, such as building starts or steel production, follow a composite of these four cycles. Seemingly chaotic patterns can often be decomposed into several of these simpler ones, each being the reflection of a basic cause. Projected forward, the next contraction of the 50+-year wave should come around 2033.*

---

*The Kondratieff cycle appears to stem from the capital sector of the economy. Each wave represents some transport infrastructure (canals, railroads, airports and interstates, and SSTO spacecraft) or some energy source (steam, electricity, and solar power satellites). The success of the boom years encourages other investors and soon enough there are (e.g.) five rail-

Example 9: Half-life of Ideas. There is often a lag of five generations between the establishment of an idea in a society and the reaction against it, as illustrated in Table 1. Perhaps ideas have half-lives . . . ?

Example 10: Nomad Eruptions. Nomads seem to come off the steppes or desert on a somewhat regular basis (Table 2). The desert nomads may have missed an appointment around 100 C.E.† The periodicity may be in response to a long-term weather cycle. Populations expand during the good centuries but find themselves pressed for resources when the climate goes bad.

Example 11: Growth and Decay of Civilizations. As long as we are on the grand time scale, consider the three timelines shown in Figure 9. The Chinese and Classical civilizations have been aligned on the establishment of their societywide unitary states (Prior Han and the Principate, respectively). Remarkably, analogous events occurred in each society at roughly corresponding times! When the equivalent timeline for the West is also matched to them, certain "low-granularity" patterns in its future course may be roughly anticipated. Of course, as Flaubert noted, "God is in the details." The European Union is not quite like the bloody accomplishments of Augustus and Han Wu-ti—unless there is some awful War of European Unity waiting in the wings. . . . But that's rough granularity for you.

---

roads between Chicago and Detroit. This excess capacity leads to a downturn in the marginal return on investment. If you build it, they don't come. We have all the canals (railroads, airports, interstates) we need so we stop—and the cycle heads down.

†Arab populations established themselves in Syria/Palestine and in Iraq during Seleucid times, but this was probably the tail end of the Nabataean movement.

		Table 2			
		Nomad Eruptions			
Century	The Steppe	Interv		Century	The Desert
				-1900	Amorites
-1200	Dorians, Iranians, et alia.		6	-1300	Aramaeans, Chaldeans
-700	Scythians	5	5	-800	Arabs (repulsed by Assyrians)
-200	Sarmatians	5		-400	Nabateans
+400	Huns	6	5	+100	????
+900	Turks	5	5	+600	Muslims
+1300	Mongols	4	5	+1100	Qarmatians
+17(50)	Calmuks and Dzungars (destroyed by Manchus)	4	6	+1700	Wahhabis
+2200		5	5	+2200	

However, these examples have served their purpose. Cultural processes do exhibit "lawful" behaviors. The problem, of course, is to discover the law!

> History being a branch of the biological sciences its ultimate expression must be mathematical.
> —COLIN MCEVEDY

Mathematical Models One approach is to devise mathematical equations linking various factors in the system and validate the model by "postdicting" past events. If the model simulates Real World behavior, that is strong evidence

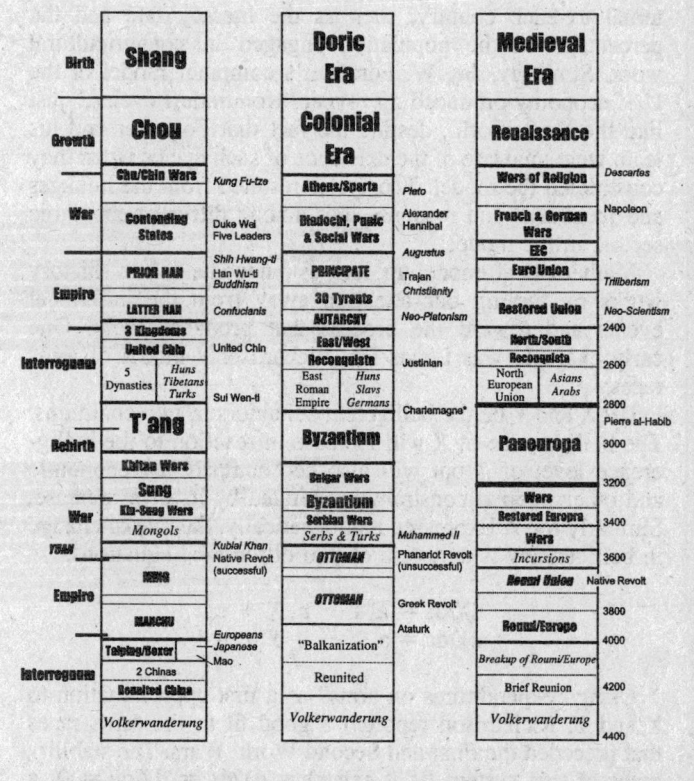

Figure 9: Large-scale Patterns. If we pull back to the very long view, the irregularities of years or even of centuries begin to smooth out, perhaps leaving a consistent pattern of growth and decline. Both the similarities and differences are interesting. The former argues for common underlying causes; the latter, for special and local causes. To what extent do other societies, less well documented, conform to this pattern? (A warped sense of humor led to the "completion" of the Western Europe column.

in its favor. For example, political scientist Robert W. Jackman developed a model for coups d'état that correlated 92 percent with the actual coup frequencies among Black African states. The model was based on structural factors internal to each country, such as the literacy rate and the percentage of the population engaged in nonagricultural work. Similarly, Jay W. Forrester's computer model of the U.S. economy produced 50+-year "Kondratieff cycles," just like the Real World, despite the fact that Forrester and his team were unaware of the existence of such cycles when they constructed the model. The cycles resulted from the linkages and feedbacks and response lags among different economic sectors in the model.

Mathematical modeling lets us understand how history works by turning our attention away from the individual events and toward the process that produces them. One early example was Lewis Fry Richardson's model of arms races:

Let X and Y be the belligerent behaviors of two coalitions. The belligerence of X will increase in reaction to the belligerence level of Y but will also be "damped" by economic and other internal constraints generated by its own increase. Similarly for Y. Expressed mathematically, the rate of change in belligerency is a system of two differential equations:

$$dX/dt = a_x Y - b_x X + c_x$$
$$dY/dt = a_y X - b_y Y + c_y$$

Using "expenditures on arms" as a first approximation to X and Y, Richardson reported a good fit to the arms races that preceded the First and Second World Wars. The stability point of this system (if it exists) is $dX/dt = dY/dt = 0$, a bilateral freeze. But such a freeze cannot be *imposed* on the system at an arbitrarily chosen point (X, Y). Rather, it occurs naturally at a particular point determined by the values of the a, b, and c parameters.*

---

*Unfortunately, there is no guarantee that war will not break out before the stability point is achieved.

In his book *Looking at History through Mathematics*, pioneer cliologist Nicholas Rashevsky showed how the mathematical techniques of the hard sciences could be applied (at least in principle) to such historical processes as village and class formation or the "kinematics of social behavior." *Transformations: Mathematical Approaches to Cultural Change*, edited by archaeologist Colin Renfrew and mathematician Kenneth Cooke, gives many further examples, including the uses of topological catastrophe theory.

Let's look at some further examples of modeling:

1. Ecozones.

Historian Colin McEvedy described a graphical technique for identifying *ecozones*, regions that are "attractive" to certain ways of life. He defined the "littoral ecozone" in the Mediterranean as follows: First lay a fine grid over the map and define *coastal* squares as those that contain a segment of coastline. Then define a *littoral* square as one a majority of whose neighbors are coastal. The coastal connections of such sites outweigh their inland connections, making them "attractive" to seagoing societies, such as the Greeks, Carthaginians, Venetians, or Byzantines. The ecozone concept may explain the geographical distribution of cultures and customs, even when no obvious geographical barrier stands in their way. For example, the Bantu culture spread southward across Africa beginning in the first century C.E., inundating Pygmies and Bushmen, but stopped short at the Great Fish River, not because the river was impassable— their ancestors had crossed the Congo—but because the agricultural suite that had served them so well in the tropics did not function in the Mediterranean-style ecozone farther south. The distribution of continental monasteries founded by Irish monks during the Dark Ages almost exactly matches that of the ancient Celtic Hallstatt culture. Compare the boundaries of the Arab Caliphate to those of the Achaemenid Persian Empire and Carthaginian sphere of influence. Coincidence or ecozone?

2. Settlement Formation.

Is there a *general* process that explains how settlements arise? If there is, it may tell us something about the success of projected lunar or orbital colonies. Robert Rosen has studied this problem. Starting with an abstract landscape and a function, α, defining the population density at each coordinate, he postulated two "forces" at work: a preference for sites of lower population density and an affinity (ρ) for sites providing positive reinforcement (such as access to fertile soil, Broadway theaters, or interstellar wormholes.) McEvedy's ecozones are examples of affinity functions. The two forces define gradients on the landscape: one trying to clump the population around "attractive" sites, the other trying to disperse the population uniformly in a kind of cultural "heat death." When combined with the birth–death process, these assumptions produce the same formula that describes a chemical diffusion-reaction process, namely:

$$\alpha/t = [\alpha\, f(\rho) - \alpha^2\, g\,(\rho)] + D_1\sigma^2\,\alpha - D_2\sigma^2\rho^*$$

It's intriguing how often the same—or similar—equations appear in such widely different contexts.

3. Topological Networks.
The settlements generated by the preceding processes form the nodes of a topological network. The nodes with the highest connectivity are likely candidates for capital cities. Geographer Forrest R. Pitts studied the connectivity of medieval Russian towns (which lie, of course, in the riparian ecozone). Moscow ranked second; nearby Kolumna, first. The older capital, Vladimir, was also in this region. Topologically, Petrograd was an unnatural, "un-Russian" aberration. Similarly, all the historic capitals of Mesopotamia (Kish, Agade, Babylon, Ctesiphon, Seleucia, and Baghdad) are clustered in the same small region. Only briefly was Iraq ruled from outside this small region. A topological analysis of internal commodity movements reveals the startling fact that there are four (or

---

*Sorry! I promise not to do that again.

possibly five) Indias (cf. *Ekistics*, by C. A. Doxiadis). These are regions of relatively high population density and industrialization separated by areas of subsistence agriculture and may represent the future political boundaries of the subcontinent.

4. Cultural Zones of Influence. Geographers

have found through empirical studies that the amount of traffic (and other forms of communication) flowing between two sites is best described by:

$$I = C[m_1 \, m_2] \, / \, d^k,$$

which they call (with straight faces) a gravity model. *Mass* is here a function of population and wealth, while *distance* is the time and energy needed to travel between the two sites.* Using "nearest neighbor" analysis of Aztec-era settlements in the Valley of Mexico and their known political boundaries, archaeologist John R. Alden derived an empirical value of $k = 1.9$.† He then used the model to "postdict" the unknown political boundaries of Toltec-era states.

We can use gravity models to determine cultural "potential fields," including "natural" political and economic boundaries. Applied to New York City, for example, we find that the "cultural boundaries" with Boston and Philadelphia lie just short of Providence and Trenton, respectively. In fact, this is just about where Red Sox and Phillies fans begin displacing Yankee fans.

In "Exploring Dominance: Predicting Polities from Centers," Colin Renfrew and Eric V. Level described a computer program, XTENT, that would draw boundaries based on the

---

*This concept of "cultural distance" explains why High Earth Orbit is "halfway to anywhere" in the Solar System. Half the ΔV is needed just to get that far!

†John Alden may speak for himself, but that looks like an inverse square law to me. This makes sense because the area influenced will increase with the square of the distance from the center.

size and locations of settlements. In addition to Stone Age Malta and Late Uruk Mesopotamia, they applied the model to 117 cities in modern Europe. Although their model was an inverse linear model (not an inverse square) and distance over open water was treated as distance over land, the results were interesting, as the following comment (made in 1979) makes clear:

"A second apparent distortion is the tendency toward autonomy of a number of areas within the USSR. For instance, when the slope parameter is 0.006, Tbilisi, Baku, and Yerevan emerge as the capitals of autonomous provinces . . . The computer is mischievously predicting the autonomy of the Transcaucasian People's Republics of Georgia, Azerbaijan, and Armenia. This need not give comfort to separatist movements. . . . [When the slope parameter is 0.014] an alarming number of localities in the southern USSR emerge as independent." Renfrew and Level were unwilling to predict a breakup of the USSR (or, elsewhere on their map, the partition of Italy), but the zones are those of *cultural* influence, which may or may not coincide with political rule. An interesting question is to what extent air travel and Internet redefine "distance" between sites.*

5. Central Place Theory.

Villages cannot supply every possible service. Goods offered for sale have minimum and maximum ranges, based on the distances people are willing to travel to buy (or sell) them. This gives rise to a hierarchy of central places (market towns) that, on an idealized landscape, forms a lattice of interpenetrating hexagons called Christaller grids (Figure 10). Central Place Theory, first proposed by the German geographer Walter Christaller in the 1930s and further elaborated by August Lösch, predicts the geographic distribution of central places and the hierarchical relationships among them. It may also explain the placement

---

*Based on the number of scheduled flights connecting them, Los Angeles may be "closer" to New York than to Omaha.

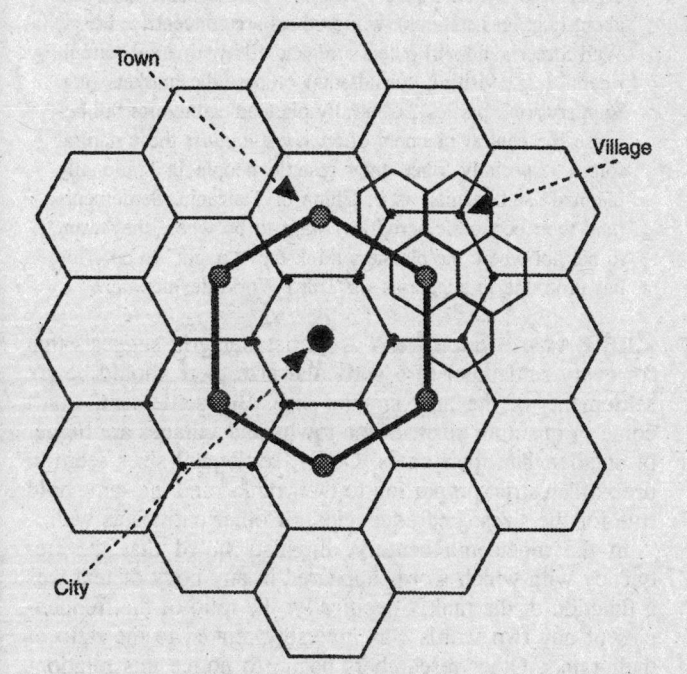

Figure 10: Geographical Patterns. A village's hinterland is set by the maximum distance a villager can walk to and from his plot and still put in a good day's work. (This also sets a limit on village size.) The location of market towns is set similarly by the time required to carry goods to the market. On a plane, this would result in a Christaller K = 3 grid, as shown. The reality of mountains and deserts distorts the grid, so we must use the time and energy needed to travel between the two points to measure the "cultural" distance. Smith's study of settlements in western Guatemala (reported in Plattner) revealed two interpenetrating grids: one of Ladino villages centered on Quetzaltenango and another of Indio villages centered on San Francisco el Alto. Like parallel universes, they existed side by side without touching.

of services within modern cities: Why are some scattered about (e.g., gas stations), while others are concentrated (e.g., Wall Street), and still others are handled by itinerant "circuit riders" (e.g., visiting consultants) or periodic markets (e.g. Tupperware® parties)? Centrally planned economies fail because the central planners often work *against* these natural forces, especially when they resettle people in "rationally planned" settlements, as in China or Tanzania. Settlements (and their economic activities) want to be where they want to be, not where the planners think they "ought" to be. This has profound implications for Third World development.*

Zipf's Rank-Size Law A Christaller grid suggests that for every settlement of a particular size there should be six settlements of the next smaller size. But settlements don't come in quantum sizes. Some towns and villages are bigger or smaller than their peers. Oddly, settlement sizes seem to drop off in strict proportion to their ranks; and the same hold true for the sizes (or frequencies) of other entities as well.

In the nineteenth century, linguists noted that the frequency with which words appeared in any body of text was a function of the rank. Specifically, the ratio of the frequencies of any two words was inversely related to the ratio of their ranks. Other researchers began to notice this relationship in other fields, such as the distribution of wealth (Pareto) and the distribution of manufacturing defects (Juran) and wars (Singer and Small). See Figure 11. The general form is called the *Pareto Distribution*:

$$S_m/S_n = (n/m)^k,$$

where m and n are the ranks and S_∞ is the size of the ith entity. On log-log paper, this gives a straight line of slope k, which is a measure of "concentration."

The law is a consequence of two assumptions:

---

*Since 1988, when this essay was originally written, many Third World governments have reached the same conclusions.

Figure 11
Zipf's Rank-Size Law
Bank Holding Companies
and Metropolitan Areas

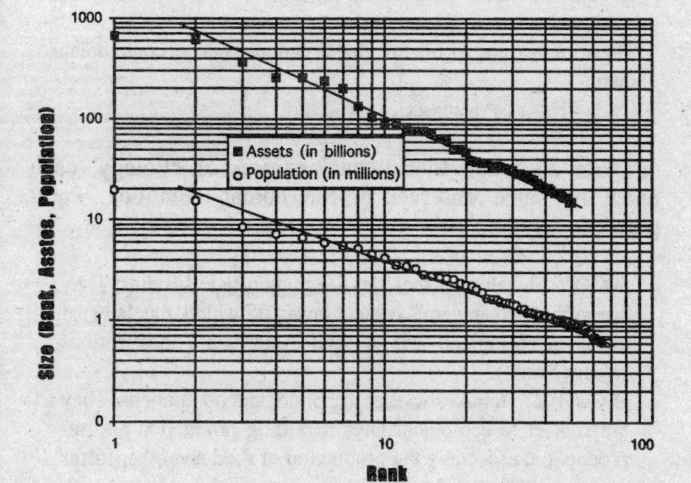

Figure 11: Zipf's Law. "The bigger, the fewer." Plotted on log-log paper, a Pareto distribution produces a straight line as size (or frequency) drops off with rank. Shown here are U.S. bank holding companies and U.S. metropolitan areas listed in the *World Almanac.* The slope is a measure of concentration in the largest entities. Note that both series have about the same slope and that the very largest entities are smaller than they "ought" to be. Furthermore, the same slopes would be found if we ranked cities and banks (or other firms) fifty years ago or at the turn of the century. That is, there has been no change in the concentration, despite mergers and acquisitions (or urbanization and population growth).

1. The birth–death spread is independent of settlement size.
2. The immigration–emigration spread is proportional to settlement size already attained.

For business entities, these assumptions are:

1. Likelihood of death by merger or acquisition is independent of entity size.
2. Average assets acquired by merger and acquisition are proportional to size already attained.

These things are so bizarre that I cannot bear to contemplate them.
— HENRI POINCARE

There are three fundamental axioms of cliology, each noted by some observer of the human condition. Paraphrased, they are:

Axiom 1. Human societies are homeostatic systems. They are subject to general system laws, of which the laws of physical, biological, and cultural systems are localizations (Adam Smith).
Axion 2. Human societies are biological populations. They are subject to ecological laws regarding production and reproduction, especially the production of food and other forms of energy (Thomas Malthus).
Axiom 3. The causes of cultural institutions are material, not mystical (Karl Marx).

It may seem odd to list Adam Smith, Thomas Malthus, and Karl Marx as *co*-founders of anything. Marx, for example, called Malthus a "baboon in parson's clothing," and the level of debate in the social sciences has changed very little since then. Neither has the mutual animosity among capitalists, environmentalists, and socialists.* But, despite

---

*Since this essay first appeared in *Analog* April/May 1988, socialists no

their respective shortcomings, all three did try to use the scientific method. In fact, Marx's pronouncement that cultural phenomena have material causes amounts to a simple statement that cultures *can* be analyzed scientifically! A scientist cannot explain a custom like Hindu cow love by calling it a religious duty. He must discover natural, material reasons *why it became a religious duty in the first place.*

Homeostatic Systems
A homeostatic system is one that "seeks" an equilibrium. Mathematically, the system is governed by a potential function. A society is attracted so strongly toward its equilibrium that even when it is disturbed, it will return to its former trajectory once the disturbance is removed. (See Figure 12, as well as some earlier trend charts.) The set of equilibrium points is called the *attractor* of the system. Some attractors are fixed points, like an average around which the system fluctuates; others are simple orbits, like the business cycle. However, in complex systems, we must deal with so-called strange attractors, such as René Thom's "catastrophe" surfaces, whose topology is not so simple. The climate, for example, is the strange attractor of the weather.

Rashevsky developed a mathematical model for the "kinematics of social behavior," based upon psychological stimulus–response theory (making him truly a *psycho*historian). The model predicts the number, location, and stability of the equilibrium levels—that is, the fraction of the population that will ultimately "exhibit the behavior."

When we see (hear, read about) a new behavior we are stimulated to imitate it. The strength of the stimulus depends upon three factors: X, the number of doers ("Mom! *Everyone* is doing it!"), Am the persuasive (or coercive) resources of the doers ("C'mon! What are ya, chicken?"), and A, the population's innate willingness to imitate ("There's one born every minute").

---

longer claim that environmentalism is just an excuse for denying a better standard of living to the poor masses of proletarians.

Figure 12
U.S. Beer Produced

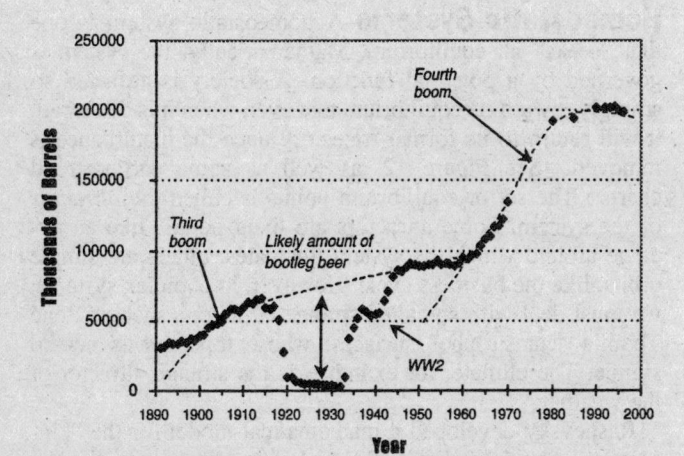

Figure 12: Homeostasis. Systems governed by a potential function are "attracted" to an equilibrium value. If a stable equilibrium is disturbed by a special cause, the system will return to it once the disturbance is removed. For U.S. beer production, the attractor is the carrying capacity of the beer-drinking niche. Beer production has gone through four logistic growth periods, of which only the last two are shown. The first reached carrying capacity in 1878; the second, in 1900. The third wave was just topping off when Prohibition upset the system. But notice that if the curve is extrapolated, it predicts the level to which production "snapped back" when Prohibition ended. Even more intriguing is the trend from 1900 to 1914, which, if extrapolated linearly, will hit the level of the 1990s. *Data from Historical Statistics of the U.S. plus annual supplements.*

Imagine a behavior B advocated by X_0, a group of "partisans." Another group, Y_0, advocates the opposite, not-B. The remainder of the populace choose either B or not-B as the spirit moves them. According to Rashevsky's model, the equilibrium level is determined by the "coercion/imitation" ratio $(A_x X_0 - A_y Y_0)/A$. When this ratio exceeds a critical value, C^*, a majority of the society will eventually adopt B. If it is less than $-C^*$, a majority will adopt not-B. If it falls in between $\pm C^*$, then B and not-B are *both* potential equilibria. That is, the society would be attracted toward both levels; and *identical* initial conditions could lead to *different* behavior in different societies!*

Given the number of partisans for each candidate, plus some measure of their ability to reach and persuade voters, Rashevsky's model could forecast the outcomes of elections. Provided, that is, that the elections were *free* and were always held *after* the equilibrium was reached! Unfortunately, the latter isn't always the case. Furthermore, the equilibrium level itself can change before the system reaches it! The equilibrium is determined by the parameters of the system, and *the parameters themselves are variables*.

Complexity Theory Usually, small parametric changes result in small changes in the equilibrium, but not always. Sometimes a small parametric change can cause a large, sudden change in behavior. For example, as a rubber band is stretched, it grows incrementally longer—until it passes through a singularity and snaps, a behavior utterly unpredictable by extrapolating its past growth. Societies can snap, too. Revolutions, coups, fads, economic booms and busts, technological breakthroughs. Sudden change often interrupts the path toward equilibrium.

Consider, for example, the winning speeds at the Indian-

---

*Central planners, take note. Also: advertisers, movie producers, and all sorts of other folks.

Figure 13

Winning Speeds at Indianapolis 500

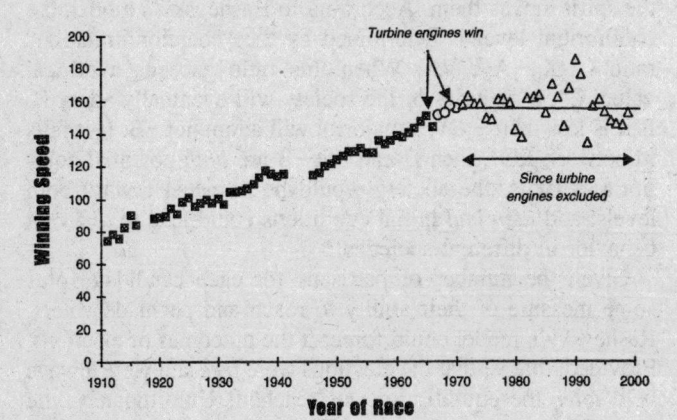

Figure 13: Punctuated Equilibrium. Systems evolve to become more fit for their environment. But if the environment changes, this evolution stops. There is a new equilibrium on a new attractor. Notice how the steadily evolving speeds of Indy cars reached a ceiling when the rules of the race were changed. We hope nothing similar is done to stop microchips from getting smaller, although there may be a limit set by Mother Nature. *Data from World Almanac.*

apolis 500 race (Figure 13). The steady, linear increase, although interrupted by war years, is an example of the intensification of a particular technology (somewhat as microchips have become steadily smaller over the years). But at a certain point a new mutant species (turbine engines) threatened to take over the niche. The rules were changed to exclude the new technology, and since that time winning speeds have not increased at all.

Complexity theory (sometimes misnamed chaos theory) does not eliminate all possibiltiy of prediction. Remember that Newtonian mechanics is "chaotic."

Perhaps the most dramatic such changes have been the collapse of certain state-level societies, whose complex structures simplified rapidly into chiefdoms or even tribes. The collapses of the Mayan and Aegean societies were the most complete such collapses, but the Egyptian society after the Sixth Dynasty and the Graeco-Roman society in Western Europe are also well-known examples.

There are also cases of equally sudden complexification: e.g., the formation of the Saxon and Zulu kingdoms and of the Iroquois Confederacy. A smaller scale example is the collapse of passenger railroads in the United States. Passenger miles increased and decreased in sudden "exponential epochs." What are the causes of sudden change?

Strange Attractors We usually blame sudden change on *exogenous* factors: barbarian invaders, communist subversives, outside agitators, the CIA, and the like. However, **topological catastrophe theory,** developed by René Thom, has shown that sudden change can result from *endogenous* factors, internal to the society.

The roots of sudden change lie in the existence of two (or more!) equilibrium levels at the same parameter values. We can visualize this situation by means of a "catastrophe surface."

For simplicity, imagine that there are two parameters (the "control variables"). These define a plane called the parameter space. (Even in very complex situations, a relatively few control variables determine the bulk of the actual behavior.) Also suppose that there is one state variable, represented by a potential function, and express this as vertical distance above the parameter plane. For each point in parameter space there is one (or more) equilibrium state(s). The set of all equilibrium points forms a manifold that sits over the parameter space. This is the "catastrophe surface," the strange attractor of the system. Thom's theorem shows that all catastrophe surfaces can be decomposed into some combination of seven elementary surfaces. For two control variables and one state variable, that elementary surface is called the cusp, a "sheet with a pleat." Let's look at two simple examples.

1. Collapse of State-level Societies.

Archae-ologist Colin Renfrew developed a cusp surface to describe the sudden collapse of early agricultural societies. The two control variables were E, the energy assigned to cultural devices used to promote adherence to the central authority, and M, the margin between productivity and taxes. The state variable is C, the "degree of centrality," which is some measure of the information-carrying capacity of the society. Archaeologically, C is indicated by a Christaller grid of central places, the maintenance of bureaucratic records, flags and insignia, and so on. How do E, M, and C combine?* Let's follow the trajectory of a typical society in Figure 14.

An egalitarian, tribal society (1) intensifies production through the urgings of so-called big men, and invests its surplus in the trappings of central authority (2). "Big men" become "chiefs," then "kings," then "monarchs." Complexity increases until the state appears (3). However, population growth eventually compresses production. It is no longer so easy to increase the per capita yield enough to support the central authority. The society is under stress (4). As E decreases slightly, the society enters a region of the parameter space called the bifurcation set (5). In this region, there are *two* equilibrium levels for which social efficiency is maximized. However inertia (caused by the time lags or "viscosity" of the system) keeps the society on the upper fold of the pleat (6a). Then, as the society leaves the bifurcation set, the local maximum vanishes, and the society is now attracted only by the lower sheet (6b). The society "falls" off the edge of the pleat.

(Renfrew went on to add two more control variables [kinship and external threat], producing the multidimensional

---

*No, the model is *not* E = mc². That would have been too cute for words, though. Wouldn't it?

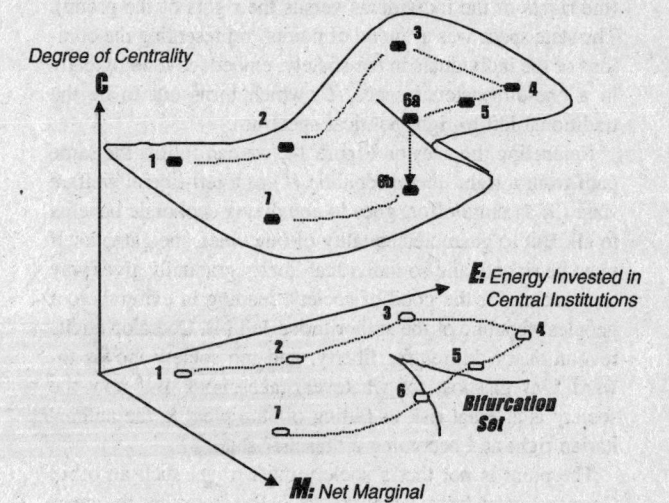

Figure 14: Equilibrium Manifolds. In a system governed by a single potential function over a parameter space of two variables, the equilibrium points will form a surface shaped like a sheet with a pleat in it. These are the "central tendencies." Actual measures will vary randomly around these values; so the sheet is more like a cloud. A system following the smooth path on the parameter space will exhibit "discontinuous" sudden change at 6. If the path is a closed ellipse (say, connecting points 6 and 5) the system will run at the lower level, then suddenly spike to the higher level, then drop back down. (See Figure 3.)

Butterfly Catastrophe, whose hypersurface contains a pocket. The pocket in this example corresponds to stable chiefdoms, a level of social complexity partway between tribal and state organizations.)

2. Political Ideologies. E. C. Zeeman developed a cusp model of political ideologies. The two parameters were E (economic opportunity versus economic equality) and M

(the rights of the individuals versus the rights of the group). The state space was a "cloud of points" representing the opinions of the individuals in the society, embedded topologically in a one-dimensional space, C, which turns out to be the traditional left-to-right political spectrum.

Relabeling the axes on Figure 14, we can follow the same path from a right-liberal republic (1) to a left-liberal welfare state (3) as more effort goes to equalizing economic benefits to all. But to guarantee equality of outcomes, the game itself must be rigged; and so individual liberty gradually gives way to coercion for the good of society, leading in extremis to a peoples' republic of the authoritarian-left (4). Coercion elicits revolutionary desires for liberty, and the society moves toward 5 as glasnost (or whatever) takes hold. But now the society is at great risk of falling off the pleat to the authoritarian right and becoming a "fascist" state.

The point is not that a society must travel such an orbit. Germany went from 1 straight to 7. But note that the more authoritarian a society is, the greater the dislocation if it tries to liberalize its economy. The Czechs and the Poles managed because they were not as far out the M axis, but the Romanians and the Serbs did not. Russia may not. China is currently liberalizing its economy without liberalizing politically. It is moving from 4 to 5. Danger may lie ahead.

Zeeman's catastrophe surface shows why the left-right axis (vertical in the figure) actually has a complex structure. Projecting the surface onto the EC and MC planes reveals why dictatorships of the left and the right resemble each other so closely and why right-wing populists often sound like left-wingers.*

So cultural processes are, in principle, susceptible to mathematical analysis and modeling. Far from being inappropriate, the tools of the hard sciences can have great utility in

---

*In the 2000 presidential campaign, there we are eerie overlaps in the statements of right-wing populist Pat Buchanan and left-winger Ralph Nader, especially on economic matters, like free trade.

clarifying structural relationships and large-scale dynamic processes. Not the least benefit would be the translation of cultural theories into *testable* formats.

However, even the most sophisticated mathematics is sterile. We must also have a theory to support it. That brings us to the other two basic axioms.

Part II: The Biology of History

It is not enough to note a regularity. We also need insight into why it holds and into the conditions in which it will or will not continue to hold,
—COLIN RENFREW

Biology and culture are closely related. If nothing else, a human society is a biological population, subject to various ecological laws. But there are also structural parallels, or analogies. Adam Smith and Karl Marx relied heavily on biological analogies in developing their economic theories, and Charles Darwin explicitly borrowed the notion of evolution through natural selection from Adam Smith.†

History itself is analogous to biological morphogenesis. Both deal with the evolution of structure within a system. Genetically identical cells differentiate into nerve cells, muscle cells, etc., becoming complex organisms with many specialized organs. Similarly, hunter/gatherers differentiated into priests, kings, metalworkers, etcetra, developing complex states with many specialized institutions. Are the mechanisms in the two cases analogous?

In his book *Living Systems,* biologist James Miller com-

---

†Which is why the left resists Darwinism so bitterly (putting them in bed with right-wing religious fundamentalists!). A reviewer in *The New York Times Book Review* once wrote that "evolutionism [sic] was the ideological reflection of economic exploitation and class conflict in an age of rapid capitalist economic development and imperial expansion."

pared cells, organs, organisms, organizations, and nations and concluded that all "living systems" share a common structure consisting of nineteen subsystems that process information and/or matter-energy. For example, a cell's membrane and a nation's border/custom guards are *boundary* subsystems and function in analogous ways by regulating the flow of both information and matter-energy between the system and its environment. If any of the nineteen subsystems fail, the system "dies."

Dr. Miller's model provides a framework for applying knowledge about one type of living system to other types. But analogy is not equivalence, and societies are no more "superorganisms" than organisms are "supercells." They are distinctly different sorts of systems that, nonetheless, possess significant structural parallels.

All living systems process information as well as matter/energy. Biological systems use DNA, while cultural systems use language. Both forms of information processing are called intercourse. The information content of a system is called its *complexity*. Nonliving systems become progressively less complex (entropy), but living systems can absorb information and matter/energy from their environment and become *more* complex.*

We can estimate the complexity of a society by the number of its functional specializations. In a chiefdom, for example, everyone is a farmer, even the chief and the smith; but in a city-state, these roles become full-time administrators and artisans. A century ago, Derid Wersh observed, "a 'specialist' meant a cavalry officer or an organic chemist." Today we have astronauts, media advisers, arbitrageurs, test engineers, science-fiction writers, and a host of other specialists. Warsh makes a persuasive case that general rises in price levels are the result of social complexification, as the costs of innovations "cascade" throughout an economic "price

---

*The dividing line is fuzzy. There are "self-organizing" systems that bridge the transition between the living and nonliving: viruses, for example.

web" analogous to the food web in ecology. A stay in the hospital, he wrote in 1984, costs more because it is no longer the same thing as a stay in a 1930s hospital. Thus general price rises usually follow periods of intense technological innovation.

Systems become more complex through the dual processes of *specialization of function* and *centralization of controls*. Archaeologist Kent Flannery explored these processes and studied the mechanisms by which they come about. As societies become more complex, they become larger and more durable. The sage advice of the Old Man of a hunting band might influence a score of people around the campfire. But the Code of Hammurabi—written, promulgated, and backed by a civilized State's monopoly on force—influenced hundreds of thousands of people for centuries throughout the ancient Near East. Parts of the Code survive in the Bible (e.g., in Exodus) and continue to influence millions to this day!

However, complexification can lead to *hypertrophy*. By centralizing and specializing, a biological trait becomes progressively better suited to its habitat. Then, once the species has reached equilibrium, evolution "stops." But if the physical environment changes, the species may be unable to re-adapt in time. Organs and behaviors cannot be instantly abandoned! The result is often collapse: mass extinctions.

Hypertrophy can also afflict societies. By centralizing and specializing, a culture trait becomes progressively better suited to its habitat. But if the cultural environment changes, the society may be unable to re-adapt in time. Institutions and customs cannot be instantly abandoned! The result is often collapse: Dark Ages.

History contains examples of both convergent and divergent evolution. Sometimes different societies behave the same way—often at the same time. Two large-scale examples are:

1. the near-simultaneous invention of agriculture in habitats containing very different plants and animals; and

2. the worldwide population explosion, beginning in the sixteenth century, in regions very different in their sanitation,
medicine, and religious beliefs.

The causes in such instances must be global or "common
causes." In other cases, societies take divergent paths. The
first states to emerge in regions like Egypt, Mesopotamia,
and North India were centralized despotisms. In Europe,
West Africa, and South India, the first states were "feudal
republics." Rulers like Louis XIV or Othman dan Fodio
never wielded a fraction of the power of a Cheops or a Hammurabi. Does this tell us anything about the kind of state that
would evolve in orbital colonies?*

Sometimes, societies converge *and* diverge. China and the
Mediterranean had remarkably parallel histories, with the
analogous events running about two centuries "late" in
Greece and Rome; but their later histories diverged just as
remarkably. The Sinicized Turk, Sui Wen-ti, reunited Chinese society; but his analoucg, the Romanized Frank, Char-
lemagne, did not reunite Classical society. Consequently, the
Classical East and West spun into separate tracks while the
Chinese North and South did not.

Complete divergence can be easily explained by Random
Chance. Complete convergence can be easily explained by
Instinctive Behavior. Explaining both is a tougher proposi-
tion.

A proper theory must be predictive and at least potentially
quantitative.
— AUGUSTE COMTE

Some theories of culture, like Sociobiology, try to explain
social behavior genetically. However, societies can change

---

*Hint: Despotism was possible in irrigation-dependent societies because the
controls were centralized. The ruler could "turn off the tap" on his enemies.
But in rain-watered lands, the rain fell alike on the King's enemies and
friends.

radically, even within a single biological generation: witness the modernization of Japan by the Meiji reformers or the adoption of horse nomadry by the Plains Indians.* Cultural traits like the lightbulb, Marxism, or the theory of relativity spread through society regardless of whether their inventors and their close kin produced offspring. This does not mean that genetics plays *no* role in culture. Genetic theories describe the human "design envelope" within which change is possible, but they cannot explain variation *within* that envelope. For that, we must look elsewhere.

History happens when people alter their behavior. People settle down and farm. Or abandon their cities. Or adopt a new religion. Physicians begin to prescribe a new drug; farmers, to plant a new hybrid rice. People learn to use postage stamps or to hijack airplanes. Sometimes these behaviors "catch on" and sometimes they don't.

Richard Dawkin's concept of the **meme** may clarify the process. Memes are the cultural analogue of genes. They are "elementary ideas that replicate in human minds." Facts, proverbs, slogans, etc., are examples of memes. So is the idea of a meme! This essay is a meme complex. Memes "prosper and die in brain tissue in accordance with their usefulness and appeal . . ." They "propagate from brain to brain by word of mouth, by demonstration, or by radio-waves" and are acquired by imitation (mimesis). They induce learned behavior just as genes induce instinctive behavior.

Sociologist Robert Hamblin and his associates have studied hundreds of cases of cultural change, ranging from the amount of U.S. railroad traffic to Latin American revolutions. Plotting the behaviors over time, they discovered that the adoption and usage of innovations follow mathematical laws analogous to those of epidemics.

Let p be the proportion of a society "infected" with a particular meme, and suppose that members of the society are

---

*Surely you didn't think that rapid change occurred only in advanced, industrialized societies!

in continual interaction through shared communication channels. "Members" can be people, organizations (such as industrial firms), or nation-states. Examples are: the diffusion of the "paid vacation meme" through industry; of the "compulsory education meme" through the states of the Union; of the "postage stamp meme" through Western nations. When a "nondoer" encounters a "doer," there is a probability, k, that the nondoer will "catch" the behavior. In other words, that:

$$dp/dt = kp(1-p),$$

which integrates to a logistic curve similar to those describing contagious diseases, like measles. Available data on cultural diffusion indicate that the logistic curve provides a good fit to the data in many cases.

Behaviors can also spread through contact with a central information source (e.g., TV, professional journals, government news releases, etc.). This is analogous to an environmental disease, like cholera. A decaying exponential curve provides a better fit to this sort of data.

The notion that behaviors are like epidemics (and ideas like viruses) is an intriguing one but not a new one. Lewis Richardson, in his "Mathematics of War and Foreign Politics," wrote in 1946 that "eagerness for war can be regarded . . . as a mental disease infected into those in a susceptible mood by those who already have the disease . . ." He even developed an equation similar to Hamblin's. We might say that while memes are "like" genes as far as a society is concerned, they are "like" viruses from the individual's viewpoint. In light of Dr. Miller's Living Systems Theory, much of the mathematics of genetics and epidemiology may find application in the study of social change.

There is also a geographical, or spatial, element to the spread of memes. We've assumed that the members of the society "are in continual interaction through shared communication channels." Prior to the invention of telegraphy, that meant face-to-face contact. Memes circulated with the traveling people, especially with those engaged in trade. Rashevsky expressed the number of travelers in a society as a function of (among other factors) w^2, where w is the product of the speed and carrying capacity of transport technology—that is, of how much can be moved how fast. Since ships could carry more goods faster than carts, regions with significant connectivity to rivers and coastlines would have a higher w^2 than other regions.

One way to measure this effect is through the *specific shoreline*. This is the ratio of the total length of coastline and river to the total land area. Regions with high specific shoreline, like Western Europe and the Mediterranean, should experience higher rates of cultural development, once they reach a sufficient population density.

Most communication consists of people repeating familiar memes to one another and teaching them to children and new hires. This is how a society perpetuates its "pattern of culture." Sometimes old memes are strung together in a novel way. This is called "originality." On rare occasions, a genuinely new meme appears: either a spontaneous mutation or an alien meme from another society. When it does, the society resists vigorously. Previously existing memes may confer immunization against invading memes.

What determines whether a meme will be adopted or rejected by the society's "immune system"?

> Why should we plant when there are so many *mongongo* nuts in the world?
> —KALAHARI BUSHMAN
> to a Western anthropologist

Individuals learn through trial and error, but in social groups we also learn through observing and imitating the successful behavior of others. Monkey see, monkey do. (This may be part of our sociobiological envelope.) The more "successful" the behavior appears to us, the more likely we are to imitate it.

Every behavior has a cost: the time and energy needed to

perform it. Every behavior also provokes responses from the physical and social environment that reinforce the behavior. Farming, for example, produces food, which positively reinforces the act of farming. Gravity, however, negatively reinforces the act of jumping off tall buildings. *The probability of imitating a behavior is directly proportional to the margin between effort and reinforcement.* More people imitate farmers than jumpers.*

Some reinforcers are natural, part of our sociobiological design envelope. We are born wanting them. Marvin Harris proposed a minimal list of four natural reinforcers, namely:

1. People need to eat and will generally opt for diets that provide more rather than fewer nutrients.
2. People are highly sexed and find reinforcing pleasure in heterosexual intercourse.
3. People need love and affection and will act to increase the love and affection that others give them.
4. Law of Least Effort: People cannot be totally inactive, but when confronted with a given task, they prefer to carry it out by expending less rather than more energy.

Harris calls these reinforcers biopsychological benefits. (The fourth "benefit" actually affects the "cost" of the behavior.) Cultural institutions grow out of people's attempts to meet them. Others reinforcers, like money, are conditioned—we must *learn* to want them—and use them as substitutes for the natural sort.

Systems being complex, the pursuit of more benefits sometimes results in less, especially when the immediate results of a behavior appear beneficial, but the long-term and spin-off results are not. Like happiness, it is the pursuit, not the success, that is guaranteed. Hunting provides calories for primitive societies; but the continued intensification of hunt-

---

*Although starting a farm and jumping off a tall building may have something in common these days.

ing will drive the game away, resulting in fewer calories. That is why hunters cannot build large settlements.

Spin-off behavior can be quite unexpected. Effects may lag many years behind the cause. No cause has a single effect; no effect, a single cause. "You can never do just one thing." System behavior is independent of anyone's intentions. For example, environmentalism has strengthened the large oligopolies—surely not what the small-is-beautiful people intended! *

It may plausibly be argued that the shape of a culture—its mores, evaluations, family organization, eating habits, living patterns, pedagogical methods, forms of government, and so forth—arise from the economic necessities of its technology.
   —ROBERT A. HEINLEIN,
   "Waldo"

The mode of production in material life determines the general character of the social, political, and spiritual processes of life.
   —KARL MARX,
   "A Contribution to the Critique of Political Economy"

The **behavioral infrastructure** of a society consists of the modes of production and the modes of reproduction. The modes of production, according to Harris, are "the technology and practices employed for expanding or limiting basic subsistence production, especially the production of food and other forms of energy, given the restrictions and opportunities provided by a specific technology interacting with a specific habitat." The modes of reproduction are "the technology and practices employed for expanding, limiting, and maintaining population size." These include such things as rites

---

*Because the large corporations can afford the administrative overhead to comply, while the Mom-and-Pop shop cannot. See Figure 14, where the demands of the central authority close in on the productivity of the society at 3 and 4. When the margin is too compressed, it is easier (Harris' Fourth Biopsychological Benefit) to close the shutters and walk away.

of passage, marriage rules, contraception, abortion, and infanticide.

> *Principle of Infrastructural Determinism: The behavioral modes of production and reproduction statistically determine the behavioral domestic and political economy, which in turn statistically determine the mythology and mental superstructure of the society.*

This principle is the basis of Harris' theory of Cultural Materialism. It is the result of our inability to change two ecological laws: 1) we must use energy to obtain energy and 2) our ability to produce children exceeds our ability to obtain energy for them.

The infrastructure is "the interface between culture and nature." It is where the material restraints of physics and biology interact with the cultural practices aimed at overcoming them. The origins of culture lie here, not in the myths and beliefs of the society. As Harris puts it: "Nature is indifferent to whether God is a loving father or a bloodthirsty cannibal. But nature is not indifferent to whether the fallow period in a swidden field is one year or ten." Put another way, a society that farms with hoes cannot have the same institutions as a society that farms with plows.

Consider, for example, the Middle Eastern pig taboo. The pig converts 35 percent of its energy into meat, making it a premier food animal and, indeed, plentiful pig bones have been found at early sites, like Jericho and Ur. Yet after Hammurabi's time pigs nearly disappear, and Herodotus reports that an Egyptian of the New Kingdom would throw himself in the Nile fully clothed if he so much as accidentally touched a pig. The taboos laid down by the Hebrews (Leviticus. 11: 7–8) and the Arabs (Koran 2, 168) are well known.

The reason lies not in mysticism but thermodynamics. Unlike other domesticates, pigs cannot be ridden, milked, or hitched to a plow. They are useless save as meat animals and scavengers. Furthermore, they fatten best on foods that humans can eat directly: nuts and tubers. As agriculture spread, the Near East became deforested. Pigs can't sweat, and to cool off in arid, treeless lands they must wallow in precious water holes and oases. So, in arid, deforested regions, swineherding societies would be at a selective disadvantage. Ruminants are altogether a better idea—they can digest cellulose and so provide a net increase in calories. A meme such as "God forbids pork" would be positively reinforced by its biopsychological benefits. However, it was the infrastructural conditions that led to the divine injunction, not the other way around.

When infrastructural conditions aren't right, a meme won't spread, no matter how useful it appears to outsiders. Some Amerind tribes knew about the wheel. They used them on toys. But without traction animals, building carts provided too little reinforcement.* The Kalahari Bushman quoted earlier knew *how* to farm; he just saw no reason, under the Law of Least Effort, that he should bother. Hiero's steam turbine, da Vinci's helicopter, Coanda's jet airplane, Lillienfield's transistor—all failed to "catch on." Why should we transistorize, people reasoned, when there are so many vacuum tubes in the world?

But memes can—in Margaret Silbar's phrase—be "born again." Newton, Leibniz, and the calculus. Darwin, Wallace, and natural selection. Henry, Edison, Bell, Gray, and the telephone. When conditions are right, the right thoughts will be thought—often by several people simultaneously. "Great ideas are in the air," says Stephen Jay Gould, "and several scholars simultaneously wave their nets." That's why God, in His infinite wisdom, created patent attorneys. (Alexander Bell and Elisha Gray applied for telephone patents on the same day!) When it's time to railroad, people start railroading.

These considerations lead us to:

---

*In effect, you *can't* put the cart before the horse.

Basic Axiom of Cultural Evolution: Cultures evolve through natural selection acting on memes to maximize individuals' biopsychological benefits.

You knew your place if you belonged to a caste. Perhaps more importantly, if you belonged to a caste you knew there was a place for you.
—PAUL COLINVAUX

Cultural Species Now let's turn to the energy-processing side of society. A human society is a biological population. As with any such population, our ability to produce children exceeds our ability to obtain energy for them. The resulting compression of reproduction on resources is the driving force of cultural evolution, just as it is of biological evolution. However, there are a few twists to this analogy.

A society is more like a mosaic of species than a single species. Ecologist Paul Colinvaux equates social class with species. A species is defined by its role in the ecosystem—that is, by its "lifestyle": what to eat (and be eaten by); what sort of nests to build and where; how to find mates; etc. We call this its *niche*. A broad niche (e.g., that of bears) requires many resources; a narrow niche (e.g., that of squirrels) requires fewer.*

Similarly, a social class is characterized by particular jobs, clothing styles, housing, and neighborhoods, and usually marries within its class. In caste societies, like Hindu India, Victorian England, or the late Roman Empire, the marriage, residency, sumptuary, and occupational rules may be spelled out explicitly; but they are implicit in all human societies. We can even extend the ecological analogy to predator–prey

---

*Behavioral barriers are as important as fertility barriers. The two interfertile populations of Atlantic bluefin tuna are considered different species because they, quite literally, swim in different circles, reaching the mid-Atlantic spawning grounds at different times.

relationships, if we substitute a "price web" of exchanges for a "food web" of calories. Thus barbers are predators and men with hair their natural prey.

The fundamental law of animal ecology is that **niche sets numbers**. It is the niche size relative to the resource base that determines the population size, not the reproductive effort. Thus the number of lawyers (to take one example) is set by the size of the lawyer niche, not by the reproductive efforts of the law schools. The same resource base will support more narrow niches than broad ones, which is why squirrels outnumber bears and salesclerks outnumber lawyers.

There is one crucial distinction between biological and cultural species. A cultural species is a "fuzzy" set. Surplus squirrels must die, but surplus lawyers can drum up class action suits or change niches and find honest work. *The ability to change niches (and to create additional niche space through technology) is why humans have histories and squirrels don't.*

Population Pressure

Because each socioeconomic class is a "species," with its own lifestyle and resource needs, each, consequently, has its own intrinsic growth rate. The concept of reproductive pressure only makes sense in this context. The pressure is experienced independently by each class, not by the society as a whole.

Each class tries to maximize reproductive success by raising the largest affordable number of children. Not the largest absolute number, but the largest number that can be raised *in the niche*. Given a *biopsychological* resource base, R, the parents need a share, P, to maintain themselves in the niche and a share, C, to raise each child. Conceptually,

$$N \propto (R - P)/C$$

Poor families tend to be larger than wealthy families because the cost of raising a child in a narrow niche is less than that in a broad one. No one *expects* to go to Harvard!

Furthermore, children in narrow niches often begin contributing to family resources at an early age by doing chores around the farm, by begging in the streets, or (before child labor laws) by working in mines or factories. In contrast, broad-niche children are expensive to raise and rarely, if ever, repay their parents' investments. In many so-called yuppie niches, children are so costly relative to the parents' own lifestyle needs that the parents opt out of child rearing altogether.

In short, the poor have larger families because they can "afford" them.* R may be low; but so is P, leaving a larger "piece of pie" to split among children and, because C is also small, a lot more slices can be cut. Contrary to popular belief, it is the well-to-do, not the poor, who feel the reproductive pressure most keenly. As Colinvaux remarks, there is always room for another poor devil, but not for another successful merchant, professor, priest, or senior official. That's why Zero Population Growth was discovered in the white suburbs rather than the black ghettos and why the Limits to Growth were first noticed by the wealthy Club of Rome.

Controlling Growth Population growth has been regulated in two ways:

1. **Restriction of Breeding Privileges.** This includes such customs as dowries, rites of passage, arranged marriages, homosexuality, celibate priesthoods, state-required licenses, high status for virgins, monogamy, the Pill, etc. An example: Chaka Zulu forbade his warriors from marrying until they were thirty years old.

2. **Culling the Surplus** through abortion and infanticide, especially of young girls.† The ancient Greeks left

---

*And *not* because they are more highly sexed.

†Abortion and infanticide are only effective population controls when females are the preferred victims. Males are largely irrelevant to population growth and do not figure in the mathematical models. A village of a hundred

their surplus babies on the polis midden heap; modern Americans, in the clinic dumpster. During the Victorian Age, East End slum babies were frequently found in trash cans. Hansel and Gretel's father took them into the woods and abandoned them. *Foundling* sounds better, but it's part of the same behavior complex. Figures from seventeenth-century Milan, for instance, show that 10 percent of the babies were being abandoned on the steps of churches and orphanages. (And the orphanages weren't called "angel makers" for nothing.)

Technology These painful measures produce a strong drive to avoid them by producing more resources, *R*. Rulers work hard to raise the wealth of their subjects, to bring more and more people out of poverty.

1) The easiest way is to *intensify the technology of resource production.* Send out more hunters; sow more acres; drill more oil wells. For a short while, resource production may even surge ahead of population growth. But intensification eventually flattens out. Habitat damage reduces the biopsychological benefits of the technology at the same time that the marginal biopsychological costs are increasing. Intensified hunting drives the game away, so hunters have to hunt longer and wander farther to bring home fewer calories.

2) Eventually, the reduced margin demotivates the old technological behavior and a *breakthrough to a new technology* occurs. The new technology allows greater numbers to live comfortably in a habitat that previously felt crowded. Swidden farming will support ten to a hundred times the population as hunting/gathering. Even if they *tried* to coexist, farmers would eventually swamp hunters in a sea of progeny. That's how iron-using Bantu farmers seized southern Africa from stone-using Pygmy and Khoisan hunters between the first and fifth centuries A.D.*

---

women can have no more than a hundred births in a year (roughly), whether there are a hundred men or only one very tired, but happy one.

*You didn't think only Europeans took over continents, did you?

This relieves the pressure on resources. But the relief is only temporary and a new cycle of compression will begin. The human breeding strategy assures that numbers will continue to grow, and the increase in resources due to new technology will be consumed within a few short generations. The net result of more resources has always been more mouths to consume them. "The poor," said Jesus of Nazareth, "you will always have with you." According to Colinvaux, ecology's first social law is, "All poverty is caused by the continual growth of population."

To summarize, Colinvaux's theory predicts that:

- The middle and upper classes will feel the crowding first.
- Rulers initially sympathetic to the poor will become selfish and oppressive.
- Social troubles will be episodic (as new niche space is first created, then filled) and will originate in the middle classes.*
- Methods of allocating people to narrow niches will evolve: e.g., caste systems, market forces, government regulation.

They shall beat their swords into plowshares and their spears into pruning hooks; Nation shall not raise the sword against another, neither shall they study war anymore.
—Isaiah 2:4; Micah 4:3

Let all the soldiers report and march! Beat your plowshares into swords, and your pruning hooks into spears; Let the weak man say, "I am a warrior!"
—Joel 4:10

To everything there is a season; and a time for every purpose under heaven . . . A time of war and a time of peace.
—Ecclesiastes 3:1–8

---

*Revolutionaries like Robespierre, John Adams, Lenin, Sun Yat-sen, Ho Chih Minh, et al., were all members of the upper or upper-middle classes.

Warfare is probably the most compelling aspect of history. It hangs over our lives like a threatening cloud. No one knows when the storm will strike, when some would-be Napoléon will spring forth. Like lightning, it is unpredictable.

Or is it? What does the record say?

Eurasian nomads have erupted off the steppes regularly every five centuries (± 1 century). Coincidence? Quincy Wright's list of wars, plotted on a Shewhart chart (Figure 15), hints at a 200-year cycle. A statistical analysis of wars conducted by Singer and Small also discovered a 25-year cycle in "nation-months of war underway per year." Perhaps the most startling such analysis was one that J. S. Lee made of the wars among Chinese states recorded in dynastic annals. His chart reveals two and a half repetitions of a pattern *800 years long!*

Such regularity argues against the "conqueror" theory of war. Even if wars are instigated by ambitious captains, we must still explain why the captains pop up on schedule. Colinvaux's ecological theory offers some plausible explanations.

Expanding Niche Space "When you run out of niche space for the good life," writes Colinvaux, "you can always look for more elsewhere—through trade, colonies, and aggressive war."

Culturally speaking, you occupy more space than your immediate surroundings. Your "space" includes pro rata shares of all the farmland, mines, parks, theaters, etc., that are required to maintain you in your accustomed niche. That is why people can feel crowded even when there seems to be plenty of open country.

1 *Trade* lets you live partly in someone else's country. The ancient Hellenes imported wheat from Sicily and the Ukraine; so we might say that their stomachs "emigrated" to those places, just as our gas tanks have "emigrated" to the Middle East. Most important, trade creates many broad new niches for traders. And for the workers who produce the trade goods. And for the soldiers who guard the caravans and

Figure 15
Frequency of Wars (1480–1940)
Five Year Periods

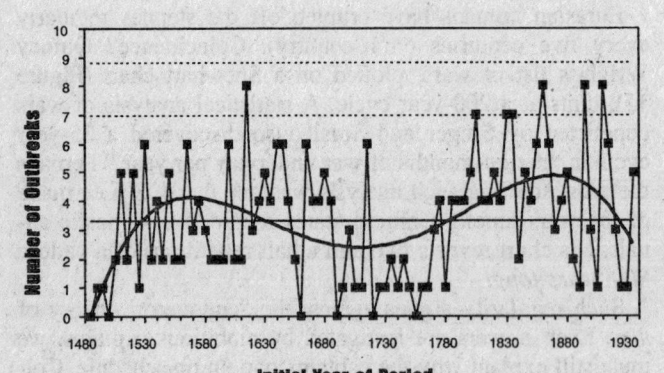

Figure 15: A Shewhart Chart. Walter Shewhart of Bell Labs developed a simple graphical method for identifying nonrandom changes in a system. Probability limits (dotted lines) can be calculated from the short-term variation or from a model distribution that is assumed to be constant. Data series that go beyond those limits or have unusually long runs should be investigated for special causes of variation. The Quincy Wright data on wars, plotted in a histogram in Figure 1, is shown here in a Shewhart chart with limits based on a constant Poisson distribution. The trendline highlights a long cycle in the data that was invisible in the original histogram.

ships. Eventually, as numbers increase to fill the additional niche space, the country becomes dependent on the trade. Notice that the dense population is a consequence of trade dependence, not a cause of it.

2 *Colonies* come next. The relatively small numbers of colonists will not reduce the masses at home. The home country remains densely populated. This will remain true even when the colonies are in space. However, the colonies

do relieve the pressure on the crowded middle and upper classes!

(Notice the confluence of theories: The high specific shoreline suggests that the Atlantic states of Europe will experience high rates of cultural evolution. Their broader niches will therefore feel "crowded" first, with "island" countries like England and Holland being the most severely compressed. A potential field centered on the Atlantic seaboard, and with distance based on sailing times [given the prevailing winds and ocean currents], defines the ecozone of European colonization. The connectivity of the network indicates the importance of the Iberia-to-Carribbean route. The higher complexity of early mechanic societies vis-à-vis swidden farmers and hunter-gatherers foreshadows the outcome. Thus the outlines of early European colonialism can be sketched in quite easily from geography and basic cliological principles. Chances are that crowded, well-to-do island countries will also be ultimately more successful in planting space colonies. Any candidates?)

3 *Aggressive War.* Finally, the trading state will realize that it can more easily obtain the resources it needs by direct theft. This leads to aggressive war. There is nothing of the "naked ape" or "territorial imperative" involved here. Culture, not biology, is the cause. "The state is calculating," writes Colinvaux. "The soldiers are armored and cautious. The enemy is weak and a victim. The object is loot."

Colinvaux gives the ecological requisites for aggressive war. The aggressor is a rich, dense, and growing country with rising expectations. In operational terms, we can say that the country has: 1) a high population density, 2) high per capita income, and 3) high growth rates in both of these. The standard of living is rising, and people expect their children to live better than they.

Intriguingly, the aggressor always believes he is fighting for liberty—his own, of course. "A higher standard of living always includes more chance to choose a path in life and is, therefore, seen as a form of freedom." This is true even if the state is a totalitarian one. Colinvaux predicted in 1970 that Russia would eventually have more freedom in the Jeffersonian sense. She is too rich in resources. "All that is wrong," Colinvaux wrote, "is an excess of policemen . . . And policemen come and go."

When rising population threatens the standard of living of the upper classes, aggressive war results.

There must, of course, be a suitable victim. The victim is technologically backward by the standards of the aggressor but has resources that the aggressor needs to maintain its broader niche spaces. In short: wealthy countries attack poor ones. Examples include: Austria-Hungary's attack on Serbia; Germany's attack on Poland; the Japanese attack on Manchuria; the British attacks on India, the Gold Coast, and other colonial areas; the United States' attacks on Mexico, the Spanish Empire, and the various Amerindian tribes; the Russian and Soviet attacks on Afghanistan, Finland, the Siberian tribes; etc., etc.

Military expansion continues until the aggressor state encounters ecozone or communication boundaries—or the armies of another state. Successful aggression requires a superior military technique. (At least, superior to the victim or the victim's friends!) The Greek phalanx went through the Persian army like . . . Well, like bronze through cotton. The armored citizen-phalanx, drilled since boyhood to fight as a unit, was a superior military technique—a walking tank—which the Persians could not hope to imitate in time. But the Greeks made little headway against one another or against other phalangist states, like Rome and Carthage; and they eventually fell after Rome perfected a better technique, the legion. Similarly, the legion gave way to heavy armored cavalry; the latter, to the pike square and longbow; and so on.

However, among literate, technological states, most military techniques can be imitated quickly. The victim or his friends can learn the new methods and use them against the aggressor. The Third Reich, for example, fell to an Allied air-and-armor blitzkrieg. Modern, non-nuclear wars are, therefore, likely to be inconclusive or unsuccessful. Only a nuclear attack holds out the possibility of a successful aggression—provided no retaliation by the victim or his friends is likely!

The good news is that a nuclear war between the United States and the Russian Federation (formerly the Soviet Union) does not meet the ecological requirements. Both states are continental, with biopsychological space for many broad niches. Populations in both countries are low compared to the niche space available, and numbers are rising slowly. Neither country is "resource-compressed" badly enough to trigger an attack on the other. And neither side believes it has a "winning" military technique.

To find a potential nuclear aggressor, we need an "island" country (one circumscribed by water, desert, or other unsuitable terrain) that is "rich, free, ambitious, literate, skilled in trade and commerce, but dependent on the living space of other lands for the wealth and freedom of a large population." Ecological history suggests that countries like Athens, Carthage, Venice, England, Japan, or Singapore will feel resource compression first and most severely. We like to think of England as "peace-loving." Just ask the Irish, French, Bengalis, Kenyans, and others. England leveraged the biggest real estate deal in history on the point of a bayonet.

None of today's "island" countries is severely compressed, although Japan waged a rather aggressive trade policy in the eighties. However, the future may tell a different story. Year 2100 will differ from Year 2000 as today differs from Year 1900. Populations continue to grow and, slow or fast, it's the *growth itself* that matters. Colinvaux suspects that the twenty-first century may see a small-scale atomic attack by a rich "island" nation on a weak "victim" nation, with the aggressor banking on the fact that the super powers (whichever they are by then) will accept the fait accompli rather than risk worldwide conflagration.

The stars at night are no less beautiful now that we can measure their distance and magnitude and calculate their size and age.

   —Colin Renfrew
   (paraphrased)

This essay is too short to do justice to the broad scope of cliology. We have not even addressed such crucial issues as operational definitions of terms or the reliability of measurements. (Just what is the population of the Soviet Union? How do you know?) These issues are important. Catastrophe Theory (and the newly emerging Complexity Theory) demonstrates that tiny differences in the input variables can cause a big difference in system behavior. Yet, many terms in the cultural sciences are poorly defined. Singer and Small compared lists of wars compiled by different researchers. No two lists were alike!

But we must stop somewhere.

We have seen that a scientific history may be possible. "Empiricists" like Hamblin have discovered the underlying lawfulness of social behavior. "Model builders" like Rashevsky and Renfrew have constructed mathematical facsimiles of cultural processes. "Ecologists" like Harris and Colinvaux have sketched plausible theories of material causality. Cliology is possible, but is it desirable? What are the implications for human dignity? Could some "Babbage Society" be meeting at this very moment?

The meme that science is somehow dehumanizing is strongly entrenched in our society. "There is a growing sense," one critic once wrote, "that the time-honored methods of history, based largely on those of the natural sciences, are conceptually and morally bankrupt." The statement that scientific methods are "time-honored" in any of the social disciplines will no doubt surprise many, but the attitude behind the comment will not.

Science has been turning the humanities upside down for quite a while. The physicists' first venture into archaeology—radiocarbon dating—resulted in a complete revolution of prehistoric chronology, one that some archaeologists *still* refuse to accept. Similarly, the biologists' mapping of gene frequencies has uncovered intriguing facts—like the Attack of the Milk-Drinking Mutants, whose peculiar ability to digest milk as adults led to the Cow-and-Plow revolution.

However, a detailed timetable of the future may not be possible. History is contingent. Each moment is a consequence of the previous moment. Changes are cumulative. Random fluctuations can be amplified by sequential dependence. "For want of a nail, a shoe was lost...." Given dinosaurs and Darwin's theory, could a biologist forecast a giraffe? Look at our trouble forecasting the weather—and that's only physics!

But just as meteorologists can reasonably forecast the climate, if not the weather, and biologists might forecast "long-necked treetop browsers," if not the diplodocus or giraffe, psychohistorians may be able to forecast the broad outlines of the future. Certainly they may be able to shed light on what has happened in the past or what is happening now.

There is no doubt of one thing. If there are such things as historical forces, *they are operating whether we are aware of them or not!* Is there more human dignity in being the victim of circumstances than there is in trying to study and change those circumstances? As Marvin Harris has written, subjectivity and self-deception are hardly the measures of being human.

By better understanding the processes of history we can take greater charge of our own lives. It's past time we stopped blaming the gods or bad luck or the Rosicrucians—or the Babbage Society—for everything that happens.

Does science have a rôle in culture? Let Marvin Harris answer:

> [T]here are many ways of knowing, but ... it is not mere ethnocentric puffery to assert that science is a way of knowing that has a uniquely transcendent value for all human beings. In the entire course of prehistory and history only one way of knowing has encouraged its practitioners to doubt their own premises and to systematically expose their own conclusions to the hostile scrutiny of nonbelievers ... Unless [critics] can show how some other universalistic system of knowing leads

to more acceptable criteria of truth, their attempt to subvert the universal credibility of science in the name of cultural relativism ... is a crime against humanity. It is a crime against humanity because the real alternative to science is not anarchy, but ideology; not peaceful artists, philosophers, and anthropologists, but aggressive fanatics and messiahs eager to annihilate each other and the whole world if need be in order to prove their point.

Memeology

Alden, John R. "A Reconstruction of Toltec Period Political Units in the Valley of Mexico." In Colin Renfrew and Kenneth Cooke, (eds.), *Transformations: Mathematical Approaches to Cultural Change*. Academic Press, 1979.

Bellman, Richard. "Mathematics in the Field of History." In Colin Renfrew and Kenneth Cooke, (eds.) *Transformations: Mathematical Approaches to Cultural Change*. Academic Press, 1979.

Colinvaux, Paul. *The Fates of Nations: A Biological Theory of History*. Simon & Schuster, 1980.

Dewey, Edward, and Edwin Dakin. *Cycles*. Henry Holt, 1950.

Doxiadis, Constantinos A. *Ekistics: An Introduction to the Science of Human Settlements*. Oxford University Press, 1968.

Flannery, Kent. "The Cultural Evolution of Civilizations." 1972.

Forrester, Jay W. "A Great Depression Ahead?" *Futurist* (December 1978).

Hamblin, Robert, R. Brooke Jacobsen, and Jerry L. L. Miller. *A Mathematical Theory of Social Change*. Wiley, 1973.

Hammond, R., and P. S. McCullagh. *Quantitative Techniques in Geography*. Clarendon Press, 1978.

Harris, Marvin. *Cultural Materialism*. Vintage, 1980.

Isaak, Alan C. *Scope and Methods of Political Science*. Dorsey, 1975.

Jackman, Robert W. "The Predictability of *Coups d'Etat,*" *America Political Science Review*, 72, no.4 (December. 1978).

Klausner, Samuel Z. (ed.). *The Study of Total Societies*. Praeger, 1967.

Lee, J. S. "The Periodic Recurrence of Internecine Wars in China." *China Journal* 14, no.3 (March 1931), pp. 111–115 and 159–162.

Malthus, Thomas R., "Mathematics of Population and Food." In James R. Newman (ed.), *The World of Mathematics*, vol.3. Simon & Schuster, 1956.

Miller, James. *Living Systems*. McGraw-Hill, 1978.

Pitts, Forrest R. "A Graph-theoretic Approach to Historical Geography." *Professional Geographer* 17, no. 5 (September 1965), pp. 15–20.

Plattner, Stuart. "Rural Market Networks." *Scientific American* (May 1975).

Rashevsky, Nicholas. *Looking at History through Mathematics*. MIT Press, 1968.

Renfrew, Colin, and Kenneth Cooke (eds.). *Transformations: Mathematical Approaches to Cultural Change*. Academic Press, 1979.

Renfrew, Colin and Eric V. Level, "Exploring Dominance: Predicting Polities from Centers." In Colin Renfrew and Kenneth Cooke (eds.), *Transformations: Mathematical Approaches*.

Richardson, Lewis Fry. "The Distribution of Wars in Time." *Journal of the Royal Statistics Society* 107, parts 3–4, series B (1944), pp. 242–250.

Richardson, Lewis Fry. "Mathematics of War and Foreign Politics" and "Statistics of Deadly Quarrels," both in James R. Newman (ed.). *The World of Mathematics*, vol. 3. Simon & Schuster, 1956.

Shewhart, Walter F. *The Economic Control of Quality of Manufactured Product*. Van Nostrand, 1931.

Singer, J. David (ed.). *Quantitative International Politics*. Free Press, 1968.

Singer, J. David, and Melvin Small. *The Wages of War*. Wiley, 1972.

Von Bertalanffy, Ludwig. *General System Theory*. Geo. Braziller, 1968.

Warsh, David. *The Idea of Economic Complexity*. Viking, 1984.

Wheeler, Raymond H. *War, 599 B.C.–1950 A.D.* Foundation for the Study of Cycles, 1951.

Woodcock, Alexander, and Monte Davis. *Catastrophe Theory*. Avon, 1978.

Zeeman, E. C. "A Geometrical Model of Ideologies." In Colin Renfrew and Kenneth Cooke, (eds.), *Transformations: Mathematical Approaches to Cultural Change*. Academic Press, 1979.

prelude: the ship

They called her *The River of Stars* and she spread her
superconducting sails to the solar wind in 2051. She must
have made a glorious sight then: her fuselage new and
gleaming, her sails shimmering in a rainbow aurora, her
white-gloved crew sharply creased in black and silver uni-
forms, her passengers rich and deliciously decadent. There
were morphy stars and jeweled matriarchs, sports heroes and
prostitutes, gangsters and geeks and *soi-disant* royalty. Those
were the glamour years, when magsails ruled the skies, and
The River of Stars was the grandest and most glorious of that
beautiful fleet.

But the glory years faded fast. Coltraine was still her captain when the luxury trade dried up and the throngs of the
rich and famous slowed from a torrent to a trickle and even
those who still craved the experience could see that it was
no longer the fashionable thing to do. But as he told Toledo
when he handed her the command, the luxury trade had been
doomed from the start. Sex and vice and decadence were
more safely found earthside. There were yet honorable—if
more quotidian—pursuits for a ship with such wings to her.

Mars was the happening place back then. Adventurers,
sand-kings, ne'er-do-wells, terraformers, second sons, bawdy
girls, and zeppelin pilots—Mars sucked them in, broke some
and spat others out. Even crewmembers would sometimes
cash out on reaching Mars and head for the gaudy entice-
ments of Port Rosario. "Some of them struck it rich," the old
song had it,

"And some of them Mars struck dead
And some showed up in the hiring hall,
Begging their old berths back."

Toledo and, later, Johnson and Fu-hsi carried hopes out-
bound and the shattered fragments back. There was a raw
energy to the age that tired old Earth hadn't seen since the

taming of LEO during the Terrible Teens, and *The River* took greater pride in pushing the frontier out than she ever had in stroking the rich and famous.

It was the Farnsworth engine that finally brought her low. Fu-hsi saw it coming and resigned, the only one of her captains ever to do so; and so it fell to Terranova to see the once proud vessel humiliated. Magnetic sails had ruled space for forty years, and *The River of Stars* for almost twenty of them, but Farnsworth engines made the Jovian moons the new frontier. The Luna-Ganymede Race went down in history, and the magnetic sail went down to the fusion thruster. Terranova should never have taken the bet; but it was a matter of pride—and pride prefers loss to surrender.

For a while, hovering in Jupiter's magnetosphere, *The River* maintained a precarious trade harvesting hydrogen from the gas giant's outer atmosphere. Passing the long hours under the maddening whine of the compressors, the *Rivers* told each other how important they still were.

> "The Farnsworths can't fly
> Without the 'H' we supply."

But in their hearts they knew they were no more than water-boys for the nukes.

In 2083, Centaurus Corporation bought *MSS The River of Stars* and fit her with a quartet of Farnsworth cages in the Deimos Yards. To the crew it was the final humiliation. Sacrilege, some of the old-timers shouted as they resigned their berths; and the engineer and his mate received a less than heartfelt welcome from the remnant. She kept her sails and rigging—for flexibility, management claimed—and her precious MS designation. Officially, she was a "hybrid ship," unofficially, a bastard. The sailing master brooded over the situation and, four days out of Deimos, cycled through the 'lock for the Long Walk, leaving the engineer behind with a knife in his heart.

It was the scandal of the day. The Board of Inquiry was a sensation, the disposition, foregone. Centaurus put *The*

River of Stars on the block without ever flying her.

Save The Riv'! the cry went up; and sailing enthusiasts, brimming with nostalgia for the days of grace and romance, pledged their ounces and grains—though there was little of grace or romance to save by then. The crew threw their bonuses and hazard pay into the pot. Coltraine himself, on his deathbed, added a generous codicil to his will. The consortium bought her up, stripped her down, and rigged her for cargo. Long gone were the luxury modules, the Three Dolphin Club, the Black Sky Casino. Now she was reduced to the single, broad disk of the old primary decks—and large portions of its interior spaces had been abandoned in place. Only the long, faerie, aerogel main mast recalled sailing days gone by—but the mast was purely ornamental, in more than one sense a thing of little matter. The bottom line ruled and, after one last and all-too-brief flight under sail, the superconducting hoops were coiled into stowage.

And so it was that in 2084 of the Common Era, *MSS The River of Stars* cast loose as a tramp freighter, hustling after cargoes across the Middle System.

After that, her luck turned bad.

the engineer

The openness, the abandon, the sheer forever of space both terrified and seduced Ramakrishnan Bhatterji. While he contemplated the upcoming EVAsion; while he suited up; while Miko, like a knight's squire, tested his valves and fittings; while he waited patiently in the afterlock for the pressure to drop to the ambient of space, Bhatterji trembled—in his limbs, in his guts, in his heart—but whether they were temblors of eagerness or of fear he did not know, and perhaps the edge between them is a thin one.

For, when he stepped outside and planted his boots on the ship's skin, an exhilaration ran through him like an electric current and he became more heightened in all his senses—

as if he could hear the grinding of the crystal spheres or smell the sharp tang of the aether. It always puzzled him afterwards that this euphoria faded so rapidly while the fear remained to haunt his dreams; as if joy were a tide, which, at its ebb, leaves exposed the jagged rocks.

The engine cages, along with most other equipments, were mounted around the rim, one engine in each quadrant. They loomed above their surroundings like the sacred monuments of a lost race. Around each, a bare space had been left out of reverence, if not for their monumental nature, then for the fusion plasma that pulsed from them when they spoke God's name. When he reached Number Three, Bhatterji did not bother to inspect the projectors that knelt like acolytes around it, nor even the focusing rings that directed the plasma in the desired direction. He examined first where he thought the trouble would lie and gave a small grunt of dismal satisfaction on finding his intuition vindicated.

The inner spherical grid, the anode, had melted. In place of gracile, superconducting geodesics, he found a ragged and warped tangle. In melting, the hoops had begun to sublime but had quickly frozen in the ambient of space, and they looked now as if they had been drawn in India ink and smudged by God's careless thumb. Filigrees of meta-loceramic curled where the radiating vapors had cooled. They were beautiful, like iron ferns. Bhatterji broke off a lacey branch with the thumb of his gauntlet. Brittle. The entire anode grid was a useless, blackened tangle.

"That looks bad," Miko's voice told him. Everyone on the ship was watching through Bhatterji's suit's cameras, but that did not inhibit the engineer as it might another. His life demanded an audience.

"The hobartium hoops have been thermally stressed," he told his apprentice in a stroke of understatement worthy of the Japanese paintings he favored.

"Can we salvage the mass and re-draw it to wire?"

Musing on the failure mode, Bhatterji shook his head, then remembered he was on radio. "No. An overstress of this magnitude ruins the molecular alignment. The surface will have been hardened by the vacuum quench and will not draw without severe cracking. Describe the failure mode to me." Miko must learn the craft, and the unexpected has always provided opportunities for learning.

("Describe the failure mode?" said Ratline aside to Satterwaithe. "Did he go blind?" But Satterwaithe did not laugh.)

"Ah ... The anode draws electrons into the convergence zone, which ..." Miko spoke hesitantly, as if reciting. The mate, too, was aware of the audience that watched and listened, but was less welcoming of its attention than the engineer. ". . . which creates a virtual cathode. And that, in turn, draws the ions so they can compactify and fuse . . ."

"I asked not how it worked, but how it failed."

"Well, thermal stress is usually due to ionic or electronic impact. I would guess that the magnetic insulation failed."

"You would guess," said Bhatterji.

Miko hesitated. "I'm certain. Almost."

"Very good," said Bhatterji. "Certainty must never be absolute."

("Go to the head of the class," sneered Ratline. Satterwaithe sought to hush him with a hand to his wrist, but the cargo master yanked his arm away and glared at the Third Officer. "You know better than that," he whispered harshly.)

"And so," said Bhatterji, "we inspect the magnetic projectors."

Corrigan, from the bridge, interrupted. "Did you examine the fiber optic controls?"

"They're fried. The Florence struts are buckled, too. Secondary failures caused by the anode slagging." He touched a helmet control and his vision went to infrared and he was engulfed in a starless haze. The slagged anode was a dull ember. Far off to his left, he could just see Number Four still cooling down after the automatic cut-off. To his right, the comm tower obstructed his view of Number Two.

Bhatterji examined the CoRE magnets and could see the residual heat in swirls of yellow and orange. The scale on his visor gave him the temperature and a whispered query to

Ship told him how hot the coils must have gotten to be so warm yet. He did not like the answer, not at all.

"The magnet overheated," he said.

"The safeties tripped," Miko told him. But they had known that from the diagnostics soon after the shutdown.

Bhatterji restored his sight to the visible bands. "So they did," he said, "but perhaps a little too slowly. Two of the breakers I see are visibly worn. In any event, the CoRE superconductors have also been quenched."

Gorgas broke into the channel. "Can it be fixed?"

Bhatterji snorted. "Of course. I expect it will be fun."

"Fun! This is a serious matter."

Bhatterji made no response. Gorgas did not know the pleasures of engineering. Indeed, Bhatterji did not think Gorgas knew any pleasures. Already, Bhatterji had thought of three possible repair designs and a workaround for the Florence struts, though which design he would use would depend on what parts and materials he could scrounge.

"I am going to check Number Two now," he told Miko.

"But—That was the automatic shutdown, wasn't it?" his mate said.

"Think it through. The ship can boost on any three Farnsworths. The AI knows that."

"But, then—"

"It can even fly on two," Bhatterji went on. "Pay attention. It can even fly on two, *provided* they are antipodal on the rim. But if two *adjacent* engines go down, the ship will twirl around its diameter, which makes navigation problematical. So the AI performs a complete shutdown."

("Damned cages," Satterwaithe said off-circuit to Ratline, "you'd never get a failure mode like that with a magsail." Ratline cackled.)

"For two engines to fail at the same time—," Miko began to say, but Bhatterji interrupted again.

"Ponder why the CoRE magnets failed. Don't distract me." He stood still for a moment, eyes closed, nerving himself for flight; then he loosened his boots from the rim and rose slowly on his suit jets. The conviction welled within him that he was falling away from the ship into a vast and endless pit. The hull was no longer a surface, but a precipice. Breathing hard, sweating, he brought himself to a stop at ten feet, paused to orient, then jetted toward the Number Two Farnsworth. A dangerous maneuver. Motion wants always a straight line, and that means tangent to the ship's rim and her considerable forward velocity. But fear wants danger to vindicate itself, and that means tangent to one's desires.

Following the curvature of the rim, Bhatterji coasted above moribund shroud motors for the old magnetic sails; above empty connector cradles for long-gone luxury modules; around the antennae for the comm system; above a junkyard of sensors and couplings and equipments that resembled a great coral reef. His pulse rattled like a snare and his groin tightened into a hard ball. He tickled the jets himself, not trusting the suit's AI to judge the complex topography below. If he miscalculated he would fly into the Void. But that was as it should be. A man's fate ought to be in a man's own two hands. Enver Koch had made a fatal error, but he had died a man.

That one as terrified of the Void as Ramakrishnan Bhatterji would work in space affronted reason; but reason wasn't in it. Some men find their fears more addicting than their loves and so come to love their fears. They take pride in defying them. Bhatterji could have swum through that reef, or even gone back inside the ship and across the quadrant, but he was more afraid of showing his fear than he was of the fear itself. History has named such men heroes, and at other times fools, and called their behavior brave or self-destructive as intellectual fashion decreed; but whatever she called them, history has always taken note. People write songs about the likes of Ram Bhatterji and whether the song is ballad or dirge or satire matters less than that it is sung at all.

(Men like Gorgas inspire no music: a gray man with a gray mind; aloof and abrupt because he lived much inside his head; single-minded and unyielding when once he had grasped the pattern of events; but quick to see those patterns, as well. Such men do not inspire. At best, they merely convince.)

Coming at last to Number Two, Bhatterji saw immediately that its anode had also melted. It was a curious thing to be so astonished at something so expected. "Both engines have slagged," he announced. Something struck his outstretched arm and, turning, he saw the loose ends of the Hyne cables writhing Medusa-like in the airless void.

Bhatterji peered closer at the torn cables just as two bare ends chanced to close with each other and a white spark jumped the gap. He had not actually grasped hold of anything and so was not grounded and the charge dissipated harmlessly; but his mind by reflex worked out the voltages. Miko, who was monitoring Bhatterji's life support from within the ship, saw how the heartbeat spiked.

"Miko," the engineer's voice said ever-so-calmly over the link, "I've found the source of that transient that concerned you. Please shut down all subsystem power to the Number Two pylon."

Miko threw the switches and locked them out, one by one. The engineer was terrified of outside work. He tried to keep it secret, but Miko could tell. A cold start would require recalibration of the flicker. Someone must physically adjust the focusing rings after each test burst. It was dangerous work, normally done in the Yards. Get the rhythm wrong—miss a beat—and a nanopulse of fusion would be more than flesh and bone could bear. The situation must be serious indeed if Ram was willing to accept that risk while under way and with a high velocity.

Aboard *The River* only since Amalthea Harbor, Miko still found pleasure in contemplating duty, in being *useful* to a ship that had provided refuge from an intolerable life. And so she had studied the manuals with great diligence, memorizing assembly and disassembly procedures, creating mental pictures from the views and sections. "I could do it." The words escaped on a breath and Bhatterji, not quite making them out, asked for a repeat. Miko flushed and said, "Nothing."

Or did something else move the engineer beside a reluctance to entrust great work to a green apprentice? Miko sometimes sensed an edge to the older man, a fascination with death and risk. He might seek the Void as another might grasp a serpent—as an act of defiance. And yet, the Universe could be pushed only so far before it pushed back.

Simultaneous failure argued a common cause. A whispered command to the AI brought the schematics up on Miko's screen. What systems did Two and Three have in common?

While his mate searched deebies, Bhatterji turned away from the damaged cage. He noticed that he was casting a shadow and, turning to look, saw the smoky opal gleam of Jupiter off the fore starside quarter. It was a minute disc, not even a tenth the size of the Moon over the Bay of Bengal, and for just a moment, Bhatterji wondered what he was doing here, so far from the temples and the forests and the jangly cities. He remembered that Miko came from Amalthea and one of the wranglers from Callisto. They had signed the articles within a day of each other on the previous transit. Yet Circumjovia was the new frontier. Odd, how people fled from heavens that others scrambled to reach.

Turning back to the rim, he squinted his eyes at the forest of pylons back the way he had come, then he lifted off the hull once more. This time, he stayed closer to the surface and toed down a moment later at the Ayesaki valve, halfway between the two damaged cages.

"Mr. Bhatterji," Miko said, "I think you should check the north exterior coolant diverter valve."

"The Ayesaki. Yes, I'm already there." Bhatterji's satisfaction at having reasoned so well was tempered by what he saw. The valve had cracked and molten lithium had sprayed, coated, and ruined every piece of equipment around it before the cut-offs could shut down the flow.

"How did you—"

"Because I have the ship up here," Bhatterji told his mate, tapping his helmet—a wasted gesture, though Miko understood. "The anodes failed. Why? Because they both lost their magnetic insulation. Why did the insulation fail? Because the CoRE magnets failed. Why did the CoRE magnets fail? Because resistive heating in their coils quenched the superconductor. Why did the coils grow hot? An interruption in their coolant supply. And why *two* cages at the same time? A coolant failure at the diverter valve that served them both. You must always ask 'Why' five times when diagnosing a failure. It's really quite pretty, the way everything falls into place."

("Pretty!" said Gorgas, who was watching and listening from the bridge.)

("It's more than pretty," Fife told Wong and the others in the common room. "It's beautiful." He had itched to track the root cause himself, but had lacked sufficient knowledge of the system to leap ahead of Bhatterji. Yet following another on the scent was pleasure still.)

"The only thing left," Bhatterji said, "is to discover why the valve failed."

(Corrigan, who was on the bridge with Gorgas, shook his head. "No! What's left is to fix the forsaken thing." But Gorgas silenced him with a gesture and Bhatterji never heard.)

The engineer studied the equipment closely. Frozen lithium coated everything with a grim yellowed frost. The Lotus Jewel's comm antennae were badly damaged. As for the valve itself, what Bhatterji saw was so simple that at first he could not comprehend it. His mind tried and discarded a dozen templates while he struggled to understand the bent and mangled casing. Curiously, of the others watching through his suit camera, only The Lotus Jewel, who did not know what was reasonable, saw plainly what must have happened.

"We have been struck," Bhatterji concluded at last, something like awe in his voice; as if he had won a cosmic lottery or, more accurately, lost one in which winning had been ensured. "By a small object, the size of my fist." Yes, there were the broken ends protruding on the far side of the shell.

Bhatterji wondered at the trajectory and squatted to sight through the holes.

Gorgas had watched Bhatterji's EV Asion on the ship's monitors, watched the man's progress from one piece of equipment to the next, saw through the suit camera what Bhatterji saw; and if Bhatterji saw puzzle and The Lotus Jewel fear, and Satterwaithe vindication, it was Gorgas who saw beyond the immediate phenomena to a glimmer of what lay ahead.